OXFORD WORLD'S CLASSICS

THE AWAKENING
AND OTHER STORIES

KATE CHOPIN, one of the most innovative, subtle and open-minded of nineteenth-century American writers, was born Catherine O'Flaherty, to a prosperous Irish/French family in St Louis, Missouri, on 8 February 1850. After the death of her father in a rail disaster in 1855, she was brought up by her widowed mother, grandmother, and great-grandmother, speaking French and English, a keen and perceptive reader, and a gifted pianist. Growing up in a vibrant city, at the crosscurrents of change in the United States, she developed broad cultural perspectives, which were further enriched when she moved to Louisiana after her marriage to Oscar Chopin in 1870. After Oscar's sudden death in 1882, left with five young sons and an infant daughter, she eventually returned to St Louis where in the late 1880s she began to publish fiction and poetry. After completing two novels in 1889–90, *At Fault* (1890), privately printed, and *Young Dr. Gosse* which she destroyed, she came to feel that her strength lay in the short story. Drawing largely on her observations of the varied cultural groups of New Orleans and rural Louisiana, her writing began to appear in a range of journals from *Youth's Companion* to the newly founded *Vogue*. Two collections, *Bayou Folk* (1894) and *A Night in Acadie* (1897), consolidated her reputation, but *The Awakening* (1899) caused a sensation. While most readers acknowledged her superb art, there was widespread disgust at her sympathetic treatment of adulterous passion, and her radical criticisms of nineteenth-century ideals of marriage and motherhood. The book sold well in St Louis, where she remained a celebrity, but her work gradually sank into years of critical neglect. She died on 22 August 1904.

PAMELA KNIGHTS lectures in English and American Literature at the University of Durham, England. She has published on American writers, including Edith Wharton, Louisa May Alcott, and William Faulkner, and has a particular interest in women writers for children.

OXFORD WORLD'S CLASSICS

*For over 100 years Oxford World's Classics have brought
readers closer to the world's great literature. Now with over 700
titles—from the 4,000-year-old myths of Mesopotamia to the
twentieth century's greatest novels—the series makes available
lesser-known as well as celebrated writing.*

*The pocket-sized hardbacks of the early years contained
introductions by Virginia Woolf, T. S. Eliot, Graham Greene,
and other literary figures which enriched the experience of reading.
Today the series is recognized for its fine scholarship and
reliability in texts that span world literature, drama and poetry,
religion, philosophy and politics. Each edition includes perceptive
commentary and essential background information to meet the
changing needs of readers.*

OXFORD WORLD'S CLASSICS

KATE CHOPIN

The Awakening
and Other Stories

Edited with an Introduction and Notes by
PAMELA KNIGHTS

OXFORD
UNIVERSITY PRESS

OXFORD
UNIVERSITY PRESS

Great Clarendon Street, Oxford OX2 6DP

Oxford University Press is a department of the University of Oxford.
It furthers the University's objective of excellence in research, scholarship,
and education by publishing worldwide in

Oxford New York

Athens Auckland Bangkok Bogotá Buenos Aires Cape Town
Chennai Dar es Salaam Delhi Florence Hong Kong Istanbul Karachi
Kolkata Kuala Lumpur Madrid Melbourne Mexico City Mumbai Nairobi
Paris São Paulo Shanghai Singapore Taipei Tokyo Toronto Warsaw

and associated companies in Berlin Ibadan

Oxford is a registered trade mark of Oxford University Press
in the UK and in certain other countries

Published in the United States
by Oxford University Press Inc., New York

Editorial matter © Pamela Knights 2000
'The Storm' reprinted by permission of Louisiana State University Press
from *The Complete Works of Kate Chopin*, edited by Per Seyersted
Copyright © 1969 by Louisiana State University Press

Database right Oxford University Press (maker)

First published as an Oxford World's Classics paperback 2000

British Library Cataloguing in Publication
Data available

Library of Congress Cataloguing in Publication Data
Data available

ISBN 0-19-282300 0

5 7 9 10 8 6 4

Typeset by RefineCatch Limited, Bungay, Suffolk
Printed in Great Britain by
Cox & Wyman Ltd., Reading, Berkshire

CONTENTS

modestly humorous persona Chopin often adopted in public: an amateur, who spontaneously penned her tales between struggling with a dress-pattern and trying 'a new furniture polish on an old table leg'.[10] In this role, she could express her divided obligations as mother and writer, but also conceal serious professional and artistic ambitions behind a mask of womanly self-deprecation. Although she did not depend upon her writing to support her children, she undertook her new career with the same formidable energy with which, on being widowed, she had settled Oscar's debts. She had her first novel, *At Fault*, privately published (1890), circulated review copies, and argued in print with critical commentary. In 1891 alone, she completed 'The Christ Light', 'The Maid of Saint Phillippe', 'Doctor Chevalier's Lie', 'Beyond the Bayou', and a further dozen stories, including 'Mrs. Mobry's Reason', a much-rejected Ibsenesque tale of hereditary syphilis, as well as writing a one-act comedy, and printing translations from French in a local newspaper. In 1893, over a few similarly packed months between June and November, she wrote eight of her most powerful stories, including all those in this selection, from 'A Matter of Prejudice' to 'In Sabine'; following *Bayou Folk*, she brought out a second collection, *A Night in Acadie* (1897), and prepared a third; and over her whole career, she published about a hundred short works of fiction. However, there is considerable evidence that, although Chopin wrote quickly, she took trouble to revise and polish her work, and that many stories and poems were long in contemplation (tantalizingly, she destroyed an unfinished novella, a story of 'Grand Isle', begun almost ten years before *The Awakening*). She also produced translations, reviews, and often controversial articles, all of which mark her as a dedicated literary practitioner.

From the outset, she aimed to place her work with the leading literary magazines, where much now-classic nineteenth-century writing was first printed. 'Athénaïse', for example, appeared in the *Atlantic Monthly* (Aug.–Sept. 1896) along with Booker T. Washington's 'The Awakening of the Negro', and the journal's current serials: Henry James's *The Old Things* (*The Spoils of Poynton*), and Sarah Orne Jewett's *The Country of the Pointed Firs*. Time and again, '*Century*', '*Atlantic*', '*Harper's*', '*Scribner's*' head her carefully dated

---

[10] Untitled essay, *St. Louis Post-Dispatch* (26 Nov. 1899).

records of submissions, rejections, acceptances, and earnings. But, although she often yielded to the compromises required for publication, she would also defend her artistry, and was prepared to resist editorial suggestion ('I hope I have succeeded in making the girl's character clearer . . . but I made no attempt to condense the story', she wrote to *Century*'s influential Richard Watson Gilder[11]). In her essays, she spoke out against censorship, even of young people's reading.

She also specifically targeted other markets. She sent certain editors stories almost as soon as she had finished them, and often received an acceptance within the shortest possible time after submission. Among her first choices for many of her children's tales was the *Youth's Companion*, which paid well and had a vast circulation. A *mélange* of travelogues, topical features, puzzles, and advice, and popular for its fiction (Louisa May Alcott had been a regular contributor), the magazine was America's most venerable family journal, and maintained a strong tone of propriety. Chopin had a sure sense of what would suit it, and it accepted her work throughout her career: her final printed story, 'Polly's Opportunity', appeared here in July 1892. The newly founded *Vogue*, in contrast, became Chopin's preference (or in Emily Toth's words, her 'show-case'[12]), for much of her most openly adventurous writing: *Vogue* addressed an audience of both sexes (the advice column warns one correspondent against perfuming his beard), showing refreshingly little desire to protect its readers, and here Chopin could direct her writing to adults. Its chief editor was the dynamic Josephine Redding, on whose eccentricities, Toth suggests, Chopin may have drawn for Mademoiselle Reisz, Edna's artistic mentor. Redding, too, urged artists to 'soar above the level plain of tradition and prejudice' (p. 92), and challenged readers throughout the period with a sequence of splendid editorials, on topics ranging from the abuse of carriage horses to the need for easy-care clothing. Their frank language and vigorous tone often sound extraordinarily like Chopin's, as they announce a woman's right to defend her time from the tyranny of 'callers', or to take up with a younger (decorative) man: 'However it terminates, the woman will have chosen what pleased her fancy and

[11] Letter (12 July 1891), *KCPP*, 203.
[12] Emily Toth, in an illuminating discussion of Chopin and *Vogue*, *Kate Chopin: A Life of the Author of 'The Awakening'* (1990; London: Century, 1991), 279–81.

ACKNOWLEDGEMENTS

During the preparation of this edition, I have called upon the help and advice of many individuals and institutions. I wish to thank the following for their kind assistance both during my visits to their libraries, and at long distance subsequently: Carrie Bickner (New York Public Library), Linda Sweeney (Condé Nast, New York; with thanks to the library for generous assistance with resources), Joan G. Caldwell and Wilbur E. Meneray (The Louisiana Collection, Howard-Tilton Memorial Library, Tulane University); librarians and staff at the British Library, London; and, in particular, for their local knowledge, and their tireless responses to my questions while preparing the notes: Dennis Northcott and Jason D. Stratman (Missouri Historical Society), and Mark Cave (The Williams Research Center, The Historic New Orleans Collection). My thanks also for help with resources and inquiries to Arnold A. Markley (Penn State University), Sylvia Verdun Metzinger (Rare Books and Special Collections, Public Library of Cincinnati and Hamilton Co.), Jim Woodman (Boston Atheneum); and staff in the Interlibrary Loans division at the University of Durham. I am grateful to the Department of English Studies, University of Durham, for a term of research leave during this project, and, along with the Central Staff Travel Fund, University of Durham, for assistance with travel to libraries. For their warm interest, generous hospitality, and practical help, my deepest thanks to Felicia Kahn, Felicia Michelson, and Dick Troy (New Orleans), and Grace Caporal and William Stephan (St Louis). Judith Luna, Pamela Clemit, Fiona Robertson, Diana Collecott, David Fuller, and Ben and Sol Knights have all offered patient advice and support throughout. I owe especial thanks to Michael Watts for help with Louisiana patois. Any errors that persist are my own.

I am grateful for permission to publish writings from the Kate Chopin Papers, Missouri Historical Society, St Louis, Mo.; and to the Louisiana University Press, Baton Rouge, for permission to publish 'The Storm' (see Note on the Texts). My debts to the insight and enthusiasm of other Kate Chopin scholars will be very evident throughout.

P.K.

INTRODUCTION

"I have got into a habit of expressing myself. It doesn't matter to me, and you may think me unwomanly if you like," insists Edna Pontellier towards the end of *The Awakening* (p. 117). In 1899 Edna, and Kate Chopin, startled readers. For some, Chopin had betrayed her calling. This was 'gilded dirt'. Her material could 'hardly be described in language fit for publication'; her tone was unhealthy and morbid; her influence potentially dire: 'The worst of such stories is that they will come into the hands of youth, leading them to dwell on things that only matured persons can understand, and promoting unholy imaginations and unclean desires.' Just as Edna should have 'flirted less and looked after her children more', her creator, in refraining from pointing a moral, was 'one more clever author gone wrong'. As *The Nation*'s reviewer summed up: ' "*The Awakening*" is the sad story of a Southern lady who wanted to do what she wanted to. From wanting to, she did, with disastrous consequences.'[1] Both author and heroine, in short, had wilfully pursued unwomanly ends. But for others, the work was an extraordinary achievement, something entirely new: 'Your book is *great*! I have just finished it and am wild to talk to you about it—' wrote one excited friend.[2] Friends and reviewers alike, even some of the most disapproving, exclaimed over Chopin's 'consummate art'. Many were struck by the force of her subject matter, praising it in surprisingly modern terms: 'it is a psychological study—the development of a soul—an awakening to the possibilities of life—an emancipation of the whole being from the trammels of conventionalism.'[3] Others, conceding that *The Awakening* was indeed 'not for the young person', welcomed her respect for the powers of her readers: Chopin wrote for 'seasoned souls'.

Such comments make clear that contemporary reactions were by

[1] Unless otherwise indicated, all cited reviews may be found in the useful selection reprinted in Alice Hall Petry (ed.), *Critical Essays on Kate Chopin* (New York: G. K. Hall, 1996), 37–58.

[2] Letter from Sue V. Moore (?1899), rpt. in *A Kate Chopin Miscellany*, ed. Per Seyersted and Emily Toth (Oslo: Universitetsforlaget and Natchitoches: Northwestern State Univ. of Louisiana, 1979), 133 (subsequently, *KCM*).

[3] Letter from [Lizzie] L. (16 May 1899), in *KCM*, 135.

no means entirely negative. Chopin's major modern biographer, Emily Toth, has now also decisively dismissed the well-entrenched legends that the book was banned, and that, after its publication, its author, like Elizabeth Stock, 'relapsed into a silence that remained unbroken till the end' (p. 336). Faced with the immediate fuss, Kate Chopin printed an ironic apology for her heroine's behaviour, but she did not apologize for writing the novel. On the contrary, she was publicly honoured in her home city, St Louis, and was featured in the first edition of *Who's Who in America* (1901); she continued to see her work accepted by national magazines, and she embarked on various projects, including a long, much revised story, 'Charlie', and others left unfinished at her death five years later. But, remembered as she was as a regional rather than a radical writer, her name became associated with a faded genre. Her work lapsed largely out of view until, rediscovered in the energies of the women's movements of the 1960s, her stories re-emerged to startle and challenge new generations of readers.

Chopin is now acclaimed as a cosmopolitan writer. Her work has been compared with Greek myth or classical tragedy, and with the nineteenth-century contemporaries whose interests and techniques she shared: Flaubert, whose *Madame Bovary* the young Willa Cather saw echoed in the story of Edna Pontellier; Daudet and the Goncourt brothers, whose sophisticated books circulate among the Grand Isle vacationers in *The Awakening*; Guy de Maupassant whose work Chopin claimed as a revelation in her own artistic development, or Whitman and Swinburne, whose passionate verse her enigmatic character, Gouvernail, murmurs at two of the most significant moments in her fiction. She longed to see 'something— anything'[4] over her name in *The Chap Book*, the short-lived, but highly significant, avant-garde magazine which helped introduce European *fin-de-siècle* art to America. (It published, among others, Yeats, Beardsley, and, in translation, Mallarmé.) As important, however, are her affinities with other (then more famous) American regional writers: among them, Louisiana's Ruth McEnery Stuart and George Washington Cable, or, from New England, Sarah Orne Jewett and Mary E. Wilkins Freeman to whom she paid generous tribute ('I know of no one better than Miss Jewett to study for

⁴ Letter (2 Jan. 1896), Emily Toth *et al.* (eds.), *Kate Chopin's Private Papers* (Bloomington, Ind.: Indiana UP, 1998), 209 (subsequently *KCPP*).

technique and nicety of construction. I don't mention Mary E. Wilkins for she is a great genius and genius is not to be studied').[5] With new approaches to the more locally specific elements of such writers, readers are now becoming far more interested in reading the broader range of Chopin's fiction: the stories for children, sentimental narratives, and touches of 'local colour', long dismissed as dated or narrowly insular. Here, working within the popular and highly marketable genres of her day, she expressed her vision obliquely, to explore dimensions of experience outside the conventional limits preferred by editors, in stories often as impressive in their nuance and subtlety as others are in their forthright openness.

Chopin's Beginnings

When Chopin finished *The Awakening*, she had been a published author for almost a decade. But her habit of expressing herself went back considerably further. Her Commonplace Book, begun as a 16-year-old schoolgirl, reveals a highly individual eye, a quick humour, and a keen sense of irony—qualities that were to distinguish her adult writing, and which contrast strikingly with the weighty extracts she earnestly copied out from elevating authors. Like her fiction later, the journal hints, too, at some of the frustrations of conventional feminine roles. As a young débutante in St Louis, she was admired as a beauty, wit, and mimic, but in private wrote cynically about the art of flirting and about dancing with men 'whose only talent lies in their feet'. She lamented the time taken up by the visits and amusements that kept her from her 'dear reading and writing'. At 20, however, she records that she is to marry 'the right man' (Oscar Chopin); and a description of her wedding day, followed by a lively account of the Chopins' honeymoon travels in Europe, closes the diary.[6] After this, the arrival of six children within nine years, her support in Oscar's various business ventures, and the demands of maintaining both new relationships in Louisiana, and, across a distance, connections with her mother in St Louis, presumably left little time for writing.

[5] Diary *Impressions* (1894): (Kate Chopin Papers: Missouri Historical Society, St Louis, Mo.), 11: transcribed in *KCM*, 89–99, and *KCPP*, 179–94.

[6] Commonplace Book (1867–70): (Kate Chopin Papers: Missouri Historical Society), 126, 94, 160: now fully transcribed in *KCPP*, 12–122.

But it was during these years, for which no first-hand records survive, that she accumulated much of the material she would use in her fiction. The Chopins settled first in the politically turbulent, visually exciting, and ethnically diverse city of New Orleans. Then, after nearly ten years, they moved to the tiny, gossip-filled, French-speaking, rural community of Cloutierville in Natchitoches Parish, in northwest Louisiana. As Emily Toth's biographies make clear, Kate Chopin, from St Louis, like her heroine Edna Pontellier from Kentucky, would, in Louisiana, have been regarded as an outsider, almost an 'American'. (Tales of her smoking, elegance, love of riding, and dashing behaviour are still recalled today for visitors to her Cloutierville house, now the 'Bayou Folk Museum'.) Unlike Edna, however, her French side had not been 'lost in dilution' (p. 6) and, although her accent would have differed from that of her Louisiana Creole relations, she was at home in the various forms of French used in the state and which play such a significant role in her stories. Able to communicate with, as well as to observe the people around her, she absorbed the details of the lives, speech, manners, and social rivalries of the varied cultural and linguistic groups of post-Civil War Louisiana, who were then so fascinating to Northern, Protestant, American readers.

Louisiana as a whole had suffered economic devastation in the War, which affected the entire population. Nevertheless, the Chopins must have felt relatively privileged. In New Orleans, they lived in the modern, progressive, 'American' section of the city; and in spite of Oscar's declining fortunes, they occupied a large house in Cloutierville where Oscar owned land and property. But in her fiction, Chopin's vision goes far beyond the concerns of her immediate social circle. She knew that, for many in the defeated state, Reconstruction (1865–77) and the period that followed were as troubled and difficult as the war years had been. New Orleans was burdened by debt and disease, and the former plantations were now worked, often by the freed former slaves, on the iniquitous 'share' system which locked many workers into poverty. (Many of Chopin's strongest characters emerge from backgrounds of gripping agricultural hardship.) In addition, the complex political divisions—between the former white ruling classes, the American Federal occupying forces, the potential new black voters, and the groups of poorer, lower-class, whites—all contributed to increasing social and racial tension, erupting in riots, demonstrations, and acts of lawless violence.

While critics are divided about how far, if at all, Chopin's writing reveals any specific political or racial attitudes, she had grown up in a slave-holding household, and her family supported the Confederate cause during the war. Oscar's father—from whom, Emily Toth argues, Oscar tried to dissociate himself—had been a planter notorious in Natchitoches Parish for his cruelty both to his wife and to his slaves. Oscar had not fought in the war (having been removed with the family to France, for safety), but, in 1874, he became involved with one of Louisiana's most powerful white supremacist groups, joining Company B of the First Louisiana Regiment, a New Orleans branch of the Crescent City White League. This was a state-wide organization newly formed (under the guise of a volunteer police-corps) to campaign, with armed force, against Republicans and black citizens. Described by the Select Committee on the Condition of the South as a 'menace of terrible import',[7] it rapidly grew in strength to some fourteen thousand members by the end of the summer. On 14 September its activities came to a climax in the bloody clash on Canal Street between over eight thousand White Leaguers (Oscar among them), several hundred police, and about three thousand Government-controlled black militia. Leaving over thirty dead, the conflict (later known as the Battle of Liberty Place), though mixed in its immediate effects, was locally celebrated as a white victory. In retrospect, it is seen as one of the major incidents of Reconstruction, and it led eventually to the restoration of white Democrat power, and the removal of black rights. During this entire summer, Kate Chopin, awaiting the birth of her third son, lived with her mother in St Louis, far from the action. There is no evidence that she ever took any particular interest in issues of government, and for many critics, she seems far more aware of gender issues than she is of race or racism. In her first novel, *At Fault*, however, a murder across the racial divide occupies a crucial place in the narrative, and though rarely directly depicting such extreme incidents, many of her stories concern themselves with cultural difference: the tense interactions between different groups, and the dynamics of power, force, and violence in the widest terms.

[7] *Condition of the South ... Report No. 101 to House of Representatives*, 43rd Congress, Second Session (1875), 19.

Apart from letters home, which, it is believed, later led a friend to suggest that she turn to fiction, she wrote of Louisiana only once she had left it. In the aftermath of her sudden widowhood and the consequent settling of Oscar's monumental debts, she returned to her family home in St Louis, only to suffer the further shock of her mother's death the following year. Yet, for Chopin looking back later, these emotionally devastating years were the start of the 'years of my growth—my real growth',[8] a statement which echoes the opening chapter of *At Fault*, where widowhood, for all its sorrow, 'awakened unsuspected powers of doing' in her heroine. By the late 1880s she had settled in her own house, she had found herself part of a stimulating cultural circle, remembered by her son Felix as a 'liberal, almost pink-red group of intellectuals';[9] and, at 38, had begun to turn herself into a professional writer.

Chopin's Reputation, Markets, and Subject Matter

Within five years of seeing her first work in print (a polka for piano, and a poem), Chopin had established a reputation as a story-writer. For general readers, she was known as the charming purveyor of delightful sketches of Louisiana life, the more complex notes of many stories being lost under the folksy titles of the two collections that made her fame. *Bayou Folk*, the first of these, appeared in March 1894, to enthusiastic reviews. Keen to promote her book, Chopin (who commented on her own 'commercial instinct') accepted invitations to read her work aloud and to meet admirers. She was paid tribute in several author-profiles, and was given pride of place in an anniversary issue of American *Vogue* (6 Dec. 1894). There, in a column alongside 'Seen in the Shops', wedding announcements, and tips on etiquette, dress, and dental flossing, she was hailed as 'an honored contributor', and as a nationally recognized author. Chopin's diary for this period is that of a professional writer: sharp literary observations, interwoven with caustic remarks on 'society' people and reviewers, personal meditations, and her own short stories, poetry, and translations. She even gave her journal a title: 'Impressions'.

These 'impressions' could hardly be more different from the

[8] *Impressions*, 11. All subsequent references to Chopin's diary are to this book.
[9] Felix Chopin, Interview (19 Jan. 1949), in *KCM*, 167.

touched her heart. And to be independent and powerful is well worth the price of a tragedy or two' (22 Dec. 1894). Chopin clearly found these notes encouraging. She sent the magazine some of her most radical fiction, and continued to see *Vogue* print her work even after *The Awakening* (including, in 1900, the decadent 'An Egyptian Cigarette').

Some stories, however, were harder to place. Chopin strove for years to find a publisher for her second novel, *Young Dr Gosse* (according to a friend, her very strongest work), but she finally destroyed it. Even *Vogue* had turned down 'Miss McEnders', no doubt concluding that its upmarket clientele would hardly welcome the story's open attack on fashionable philanthropy and its direct questions about the origins of a (true-life) millionaire's wealth. (Chopin eventually published the story, but under a pseudonym.) In the very week of the complimentary profile, *Vogue's* editors returned 'Lilacs', a story which sympathetically presents a disruptive model of a divided self, allowing unacceptable and exiled energies to share narrative space with the virtuous and legitimate. The following year both *Vogue* and *The Chap Book* rejected a similar subject in 'Vagabonds'. Like 'An Egyptian Cigarette'—unusually for Chopin, narrated in the first person by an unnamed woman—the story hints at forbidden knowledge, ventured through contact with a male wanderer, darkness, vision, and dream; and Chopin never saw it in print. Many other stories in this selection appear in her records with a string of submissions and rejections, which witness to her persistence in pursuing interests many editors found unacceptable. 'The Storm', which she must have recognized was too advanced for any nineteenth-century magazine audience, remained among her papers until the 1960s. As *Vogue* had summed up in its tribute: 'Mrs. Chopin is daring in her choice of themes, but exquisitely refined in the treatment of them, and her literary style is a model of terse and finished diction.'

Chopin was, indeed, daring: 'I am so proud to know "the artist with the courageous soul that dares and defies," '[13] wrote one friend, quoting *The Awakening*, acclaiming Chopin as the artist Edna Pontellier never quite becomes. From the beginning, Chopin filled her stories with courageous souls, men and women. Her very first

[13] Sue V. Moore (?1899); *KCM*, 133.

published heroines demand larger destinies in a world where matrimony 'marks too often the closing period of a woman's intellectual existence' (p. 141). '[D]on't speak like a mad woman', rejoins Paula's suitor, as she declares that her music is 'something dearer than life, than riches, even than love' ('Wiser Than a God', p. 137). Recoiling from her marriage announcement in the newspaper, Eleanor Gail resists being written into the 'proprieties' even in 'the palest and smallest of type' ('A Point at Issue!', p. 139). Both seek a different kind of male/female relation, richer forms of expression. Chopin's themes were particularly bold for a woman writer in a culture where, as Willa Cather wrote in 1895, 'All we demand of a national literature is that it shall not injure our "sweet young girls".'[14] *At Fault* tackled female alcoholism and (ahead of its time) divorce. The brief list of stories in *Vogue's* profile alone included topics seldom risked in other magazines: a prostitute's suicide, contented wives who contemplate adultery, a slave woman's pregnancy, interracial sex. Even in the more decorous journals, Chopin had begun to enter territory beyond the typical limits of wholesome family fare: the crises of psychological trauma in 'Beyond the Bayou', of disturbing sexual force in 'Azélie', or of rigid cultural division in 'A Matter of Prejudice'. Still more unusually, she approached these materials, it seemed, with an eye on other matters altogether. Long before *The Awakening*, readers found themselves left on teasing, haunting, or hesitant notes. Where was the guiding moral voice or reforming call to action? where the tidy resolution, and final self-righteous compact between upright narrator and virtuous audience?

Many of these stories turn on moments of awakening, as characters become aware that they are caught up in larger histories. In 'The Maid of Saint Phillippe', Marianne chooses her destiny as vast imperial deals close over the heads of the villagers, to create the modern United States. Elizabeth Stock writes her story in a narrowing gap, as superior forces converge to dismiss her work and her writing, and consign her to silence. From the poorest to the most privileged, Chopin presents individuals trapped in limiting personal relationships, entangled within the codes and conventions of their culture. 'Tite Reine's illiteracy ('In Sabine') keeps her tied to a violent white drunkard; La Belle Zoraïde, within the slave-owning

---

[14] Willa Cather, *Lincoln Courier* (28 Sept. 1895).

South, is robbed of love, child, and reason. Désirée is caught in the snares of patrilineal ambition, the racial classifications of a culture, and in a world of mysterious and terrifying doubles and reversals: black and white, fire and ice, passion and hate. Edna struggles (as critics point out) within whiteness, ladyhood, patriarchy, Presbyterianism, sexual repression, Creole respectability, capitalism, and the ideology of romantic love. The power of many stories lies for readers in those moments when characters painfully begin to awaken to their limits, often incomprehensible, faintly expressed. Georgie McEnders feels 'an indefinable uneasiness' (p. 181); Edna is assailed by an 'indescribable oppression . . . like a shadow; like a mist passing across her soul's summer day' (p. 8); Désirée wants to 'penetrate the threatening mist that she felt closing about her' (p. 195), to read, to understand, and to act: '"Tell me what it means!" she cried despairingly' (p. 196). In many, the keenest excitement comes as characters begin to break free, into new space, new forms of being: few readers ever forget Mrs Sommers' seduction by the glistening silk stockings, or Edna's first swim far out from the shore.

Whereas the *Century* and others demanded 'sweetness', and the sophisticated *Chap Book* never accepted a story, Chopin found that *Vogue*, again, allowed her scope to explore less than idealized images of human relationships. She often used a language of objectification and social expediency shared by the cartoons and jokes which surrounded the texts of her stories. 'Caline' was followed by the cynical exchange: 'To whom did you propose lawst night?' / 'To about fourteen yards of yellow silk, a lot of lace, some black hair, pair of slippers, and a bunch of roses. Don't know what her name was'. Two world-weary débutantes decorate the cover of 'The Father of Désirée's Baby': 'How do you like a man to propose?' / 'By mail' / 'But that is so prosaic' / 'Prose goes further than poetry in a breach of promise suit'. In this context, some of Chopin's stories themselves read as extended satirical anecdotes. Nathalie, in 'The Kiss', is quite at home in these pages, calculating her chances, as she plays men like chess pieces, and 'sees the game taking the course intended' (p. 280). With a more desperate edge, Dorothea rejects the prize, cycling (in 'The Unexpected'), 'as if Death himself pursued her', along a 'rough, unfrequented road' (p. 322) away from her expected sentimental ending (saintlinesss, marriage, and millions).

Chopin draws on this lexicon pervasively in *The Awakening*. Although always underpinned with more emotional notes, it enters the discourse of property and economic value which informs Edna's presentation, from the moment she arrives in the novel, as a 'white sunshade' (p. 4), fixed by her husband's gaze, up to the moment where she casts off 'the unpleasant, pricking garments' (p. 127) and disappears from the pages. It speaks through her rings, her hands, her skin, her clothes, her social routine, all of which sign her as her husband's exclusive possession, and most significant social asset. It is challenged, though some would argue never absolutely, in her attempt to shed social definitions, and to take ownership of her own body, her space, movement, time, gesture, and speech: 'I am no longer one of Mr. Pontellier's possessions to dispose of or not. I give myself where I choose' (p. 119).

Chopin never joins Edna's voice to that of any public women's movement; and some twentieth-century readers have regretted that New Women, such as Miss Mayblunt or Margaret Beaton ('A Point at Issue!') tend to remain as amusing sketches on the edges of Chopin's narratives. Unlike her contemporary, Charlotte Perkins Gilman, Chopin herself remained aloof from polemics and social activism. Her writing was informed, nevertheless, by topical controversies, particularly by the widely discussed 'Marriage Question', a label for a complex mesh of arguments about gender roles, sexual and artistic freedoms, women's rights, and the nature of parenthood. The *North American Review*, for example, in 1895 alone, printed a stream of articles on 'Nagging Women', 'The Matrimonial Puzzle', and 'The Modern Woman and Marriage', largely deploring what they saw as unsettling trends. As the well-known Louisiana writer, Elizabeth Bisland, lamented: 'The theory that marriage is a heavy bond, cramping the capacities of the sex, appears in the most unexpected quarters, held by women of ability and education. That loud cry for "the development of her individuality"—only a euphemistic phrase for the cruel and profligate modern creed, "Everything pleasant is yours by right: you have no duties"—has an ever increasing chorus of applause among women.'[15] (It was this kind of rhetoric that echoed in many reviews of *The Awakening*.) In contrast, *Vogue* exhorted poets and story-tellers to 'tell the truth about

---

[15] Elizabeth Bisland, 'The Modern Woman and Marriage', *North American Review*, 160:6 (June 1895), 755.

marriage'. Here, men were seldom 'Prince Charmings', few women 'Angels of Loveliness', and marriage 'not the union of two souls':

It is a union of two people drawn together by physical attraction, who look forward to a fool's paradise of happiness, but who find, to their disgust, a dull, commonplace world of wearying routine. . . . Its fundamental excuse for being is the perpetuation of the species, and not self-gratification of any kind. (3 Oct. 1895)

For Chopin, as critics have long realized, 'the truth' was never simple. Per Seyersted described her work as a 'running dialogue' with herself as she tested different possibilities.[16] The final sentence of 'The Kiss' lightly shrugs off the poignancy of 'Regret' written two days before; love, marriage, motherhood emerge as satisfying in some narratives, as they are debilitating in others. Time and again, however, Chopin questions fairy-tale dreams of romantic fulfilment. Self-appointed Prince Charmings seldom succeed in capturing the end of the story: Azélie resists 'Polyte's attempts to transform her. The more charismatic Grégoire emboldens 'Tite Reine ('little Queen'), to 'inward revolt' (p. 251): but, escaping the ogre, she and her knight ride off alone, in opposite directions. In Chopin's realist register, marriage is a disappointment. For Cazeau, it is nothing 'like w'at the story-books promise after the wedding' (p. 299); for Athénaïse, physically distasteful. She shudders at the thought of her husband's 'ugly bare feet' in her tub (p. 294), a hint about the actualities of married intimacy that offended some reviewers. Chopin sustains this note even in representing physical attraction: for Athénaïse, as for Edna, unromantic 'red blotches' (p. 316), not blushes, signal her awakening sensuality. In *The Awakening*, Chopin's critique intensifies. Edna sees a wedding as 'one of the most lamentable spectacles on earth' (p. 73), a note supported by sharp narratorial comments elsewhere. Edna's own marriage was an 'accident': a combination of frustration, self-delusion, and a chance to annoy her family, 'in this respect resembling many other marriages which masquerade as the decrees of Fate' (p. 21). But, more troubling still, perhaps, so too is her love affair, her passion— not, after all, as some readers would like to believe, Sleeping Beauty's awakening, or the transformation of a domestic prisoner into a

[16] Per Seyersted, *Kate Chopin: A Critical Biography* (1969; Baton Rouge: Louisiana State UP, 1980), 114.

divinity, but itself a chilly, mechanistic, Naturalist plot: in Doctor Mandelet's words, 'a decoy to secure mothers for the race' (p. 123).

Readers of *Vogue*'s profile in 1894 could turn to a new Chopin story in the same issue: 'The Dream of an Hour', which, now also known under Chopin's alternative title, 'The Story of an Hour', anthologized, adapted for screen, and endlessly explicated, represents the essence of her most daring and finished art. As a reader, Chopin disliked long-windedness, commenting in her diary on a story's slow opening: 'Those thousand words were all employed to tell how a black girl came in the possession of her name. It should have been told in five lines.' Having recently completed 'The Dream of an Hour' in '1000 words, 19 April, 1894',[17] her critique carries authority. In her concentrated narrative, occupying less than three columns on a single page, Chopin takes the kind of plot cliché she despised—the (false) report of a husband's death in a railroad wreck—and uses it to overturn the pieties of a culture. As a *Vogue* editorial had complained the previous month, traditional female fulfilment was 'epitomized in four words—Be wife and mother' (8 Nov. 1894). For Louise Mallard, however, the supreme relation becomes a supreme irrelevance: loving, or not loving, 'What did it matter!' (p. 260). It is the end of married life which brings visions of freedom, and it is her husband's return that kills her. The entire narrative works through swift reversals, as emotions (grief, loss, emptiness) lose their names, and swiftly become their opposite. Louise hears of the accident through 'broken sentences; veiled hints that revealed in half concealing' (p. 259), and her unexpected response, in turn, is presented as almost 'too subtle and elusive to name', indicated by carefully colourless descriptors, that seem to gather menace: 'it', 'something', 'this thing'. She 'fearfully' defers understanding, intuiting it only through 'the sounds, the scents, the color that filled the air'. These fragments cohere in an extraordinary mantra, said 'over and over under her breath: "free, free, free!"' (p. 260). This is a new language for untried emotions: 'There would be no one to live for during those coming years; she would live for herself,' Chopin wrote in the printed text (p. 260), later inserting one word, to try a different inflection: 'There would be no one to live for her during those coming years; she would

---

[17] Manuscript Account Books (Kate Chopin Papers: Missouri Historical Society), now transcribed in *KCPP*, 137–75.

live for herself.' Unsettling in either psychological variant, disturbing deep-held convictions about relationships and personal identity, this is a dream to be whispered behind closed doors, impossible for observers to guess at, far beyond the doctors' final crude efforts to diagnose.

Chopin seems not to have hesitated in choosing *Vogue* for her story (she wrote it one day and dispatched it the next), and she must have been disappointed when it was rejected within the week. Like *The Awakening* later, neither satire nor argument, but poetic, complex, exhilarating, the story perhaps seemed too intense and urgent even for *Vogue*. Accepting Chopin's resubmission in October, the magazine risked printing it, Emily Toth suggests, because of *Bayou Folk's* warm reviews. Later, Chopin planned to include it in *A Vocation and a Voice*, her final collection, which represents for many readers today some of her most ambitious writing. But, though initially accepted, the book did not appear in Chopin's lifetime and would wait almost a hundred years to be published.

Chopin's Narrative Uncertainties

Ironically anticipating her potential reception, Chopin fills her stories with references to stupid audiences, usually Society people. In 'Wiser than a God', and *The Awakening*, Paula and Mademoiselle Reisz despise ignorant enthusiasm, and popular art-forms. As dedicated women artists, they risk being typed as mad or warped. Chopin herself was a fine pianist, and her own true musicians play 'Chopin' for their truest listeners, coding for many critics the writer's private compact with her ideal readership. Listening to Mademoiselle's performance, Edna alone is shaken by the music, lost for words. Kate Chopin herself was taken aback by glib reviewers, puzzling in *Impressions* over those with no feeling 'for the spirit of . . . [Mary Wilkins'] work'; the misapplied praise for the soothing charm of her own stories. Only the rare reviewer mentioned the force of her writing, which, as one astutely noted, 'might remind some readers of certain of finished bits of Maupassant and other French "short story" masters'. In Chopin's fiction, art can calm and heal, as well as stir the soul (the Creoles' summer reading astonishes Edna), but that is very different from using it, as Paula exclaims, as 'the pleasing distraction of an idle moment' (p. 137). In *The Awakening*, those who treat it as such, Ben Knights suggests, are perhaps 'committing the nearest thing in the novel to sacrilege'.[18] Elsewhere, too, the most casual reactions are often the most disquieting. Chopin associates this kind of response with privilege and infantile narcissism. Doctor Chevalier's society trivializes the tragedy; Madame Delisle spends hours before her mirror, and settles for stagnation and safety on Bayou St John, using her nurse's stories to help her sleep.

Chopin disliked improving literature; she avoids obvious designs on her own readers, keeping her view oblique. But her texts provoke active readings, leaving interpretation open. Doctor Chevalier successfully rewrites a sordid death into a sentimental one, but his own motives and status remain ambiguous. Is he a 'chivalrous hero',[19] or a rescuer concealing his own contribution to the tragedy? In 'Athénaïse', as most critics point out, Chopin presents a sharp critique of patriarchy, embodied in the central symbol of the runaway slave, Black Gabe, who figures Athénaïse's bondage to her husband. But the story leaves few able to agree on the narrative direction, the dominant voice, or even whether Athénaïse is married to a tyrant, victim, or, finally, hero. (It would be so much easier, as the narrator implies, to picture Cazeau as 'unbearable' (p. 312).) Some readers feel let down, as Athénaïse's brother is, at the 'commonplace turn' (p. 319) of the ending. Others are moved by the slow, meditative, unfolding of the narrative: Cazeau's reflectiveness, Athénaïse's delight in a room of her own, Chopin's powerful metaphors of miracle and discovery.

Many stories set up cross-perspectives. In 'La Belle Zoraïde', Manna Loulou's story has one ending, Chopin's another. Manna Loulou's is, in effect, her tale 'of how a black girl came in the possession of her name': 'She was never known again as la belle Zoraïde, but ever after as Zoraïde la folle' (p. 227). It is a story, also, as critics remind us, which overturns polite conventions and racist assumptions about what black and white women feel, how they respond to sex, to passion, to motherhood. (Chopin, or her editors, perhaps felt afterwards that it was just too disconcerting for the wider public of *Bayou Folk*, and she inserted Mézor's declaration of love, giving Zoraïde's passion the 'excuse' of a conventional proposal.) Chopin's

[18] Ben Knights, *The Listening Reader: Fiction and Poetry for Counsellors and Psychotherapists* (London: Jessica Kingsley, 1995), 103.

[19] Seyersted, *Kate Chopin*, 114.

own broader story, too, speaks of the cruel contexts of white/black power relations, but also about tellers and listeners, about its own conventions and status as an artefact ('But this is the way Madame Delisle and Manna Loulou really talked to each other' (p. 228)). It is a written tale made out of an oral one, a translation from, and back into, a culture remote from most readers, and an intertextual response to another story—Chopin wrote it on the very day *Vogue* printed 'A Lady of Bayou St. John'.

All Chopin's endings complicate her fiction. In *The Awakening*, Robert tells Edna how her book ends, 'to save her the trouble of wading through it' (p. 118). It is unlikely that Edna is reading Chopin. It would be hard to sum up 'the end' of many of the stories in this selection, *The Awakening* included. Many seem noncommittal, even perfunctory, often fading away in Chopin's typical choice of the simple, indecisive words ('may . . . be', 'possibly', 'for some reason or other') that dissolve the emphasis of so many final paragraphs. Most avoid conclusions, like *The Awakening* lacking any final statements about events or motives. If they give reasons (as in 'The Dream of an Hour'), they are patently too simple. Even in the story where to tell the end might be to give most away, Désirée remains a blank, where others impose their desires. She arrives in the text as a mystery and walks out of it 'with no word of explanation' (p. 197). Few critics now agree on whether the famous final disclosure is inevitable, a cheat, or even a surprise; and recent re-readings dissolve any certainty about who the characters are, what happens to them, or what they (or the readers) can ever know at any stage through the narrative. Whose story is it, Désirée's or Armand's? (Neither title, 'The Father of Désirée's Baby' in *Vogue*, or 'Désirée's Baby' in *Bayou Folk*, gives primary place to Désirée.) Is it a political story, exposing the power structures of slavery, class, gender, and race? And, if so, does it disrupt those structures or reinforce them? (Is Désirée a stereotypical passive female victim? Does Armand's malignancy arise from nature or nurture?) Or, as others ask, do its Gothic intensities hint perhaps at a heart of darkness, deeper even than the immediate malaise of the South?

Chopin's 'refusal of endings', in Janet Beer's helpful phrase, turns readers back into all her stories, to speculate about more disruptive energies in the narratives. Chopin leaves us, like Edna reading Robert's letter, 'turn[ing] the pages this way and that way, looking for the reason, which was left untold' (p. 90). These stories unsettle meanings: what after all is 'respectability', 'spirituality', or 'Providence'? As Beer suggests, such questions reveal 'the impossibility of certainty' where any human being (or institution) is concerned.[20] 'What do you know of my life ... What can you guess of it?' exclaims Paula (p. 137). Louise Mallard comes to see that, well-intentioned or not, 'to impose a private will upon a fellow-creature' is 'a crime' (p. 260). Chopin's fiction is full of characters who are sure they know others: 'Polyte reads Azélie and her Acadian share-cropper family through the lens of social superiority and sexual fantasy, convinced of his power 'to awaken [her] to finer, better impulses when he should have her apart to himself' (p. 216); Uncle William pronounces to Elizabeth, 'I reckon you better stick to your dress making: this here aint no story' (p. 336); 'She's odd, she' not like herself' (p. 72), Léonce Pontellier tells his wife's doctor, seeking a cure. Frustrated, they act like the obsessed narrators in the stories Chopin translated from Maupassant. Locked in claustro-phobic projects of their own, they grow violent, like Bud Aiken ('In Sabine'), or desperate like the husband in 'Her Letters', holding a dead woman's papers to his brow in a mad telepathic effort to penetrate her secrets. Léonce rewrites Edna's private rebellion back into public conformity. He thinks up excuses for her non-attendance at her sister's wedding, and uses the newspaper personal column to transform potential social disgrace into self-advancement. Faced with characters like these, readers may be less quick to classify, to demand clear motives and tidy resolutions—in fiction or in the stories of their culture.

Genre, 'Local Colour', and Language

Modern readers, who are at home with indeterminacy and no longer troubled by Chopin's 'indelicate' subject matter, may feel more uneasy with other aspects of her fiction: broadly, two areas, which interfuse in many stories and linger even in *The Awakening*. The first encompasses Chopin's use of genre features—melodrama, senti-mentality, the child redeemers, reconciliations, and occasional moral-izing tags ('amid the shoots of Doubt and Misgiving, came the flower

---

[20] Janet Beer, *Kate Chopin, Edith Wharton and Charlotte Perkins Gilman: Studies in Short Fiction* (Basingstoke: Macmillan, 1997), 48.

of Truth' (p. 206))—which were the staple of so much nineteenth-century magazine fiction, and which constituted the 'charm' so praised by early reviewers. The second includes all those elements in the writing—the 'local colour', the conscious contemporary references, the typical narrative strategies—that inscribe Chopin's texts with the history and culture of her time. For some critics, these aspects are merely contingencies: the formulaic writing of her literary apprenticeship. Chopin transcends them: her stories express universal and timeless themes, or the inner dramas of human lives. Nevertheless, for many readers, these elements matter. 'Happenings, small in themselves, but big in their psychological comprehensiveness, held them with strange fascination', wrote Chopin in 'A Point at Issue!' (p. 143), and her fiction seldom separates individuals' stories from the wider stories of their time. Embedded, and often challenged within her own texts too, are the assumptions of her culture. It seems important and exciting now to read Chopin within her times, to keep discussion open. Only by exploring the entire spectrum of her writings as part of a broader expressive tradition can we reflect upon the multiple languages of her fictions.

If Chopin's earliest stories have always interested readers for their striking themes and independent-minded heroines, anticipating the rebellions of *The Awakening* a decade later, from the beginning she was also testing forms, leaving space for readers' interpretations. Read one way, 'Wiser than a God' is a traditional nineteenth-century story of filial transgression (Paula betrays her father's art; she plays cheap music at a party; she misses the last car home), punishment ('Dr. Sinn' is waiting (p. 134); her mother is dead), and reparation (she honours her father's wishes, and does credit to his name); read another, it is a revisionary tale, open-ended and formally innovative, which values Paula's choices as an independent artist, and, in the final sentences, directly draws in the reader ('You may have seen in the morning paper' (p. 137)), as part of the cosmopolitan audience. Similarly, 'A Point at Issue!' can be viewed as a conformist tale which brings Eleanor back into line: to home and wifehood, labelled by her husband as 'only a woman, after all'. A counter-plot, however, centring on Eleanor's apparently melodramatic gestures (p. 146) and self-display in the portrait, seems to deconstruct 'femininity' in what might now be seen as a self-conscious 'performance' of gender and desire'.[21] Here, Eleanor acts out her sensuality, as a creature governed by the body, and manœuvres her husband, and for a while the reader, into viewing her in stereotypical terms. In a further double-take, perhaps, anticipating 'A Respectable Woman', we might wonder about yet another layer of masking. Does Eleanor's trick conceal an actual rebellion in Paris? Who taught her the 'hundred little endearments', and just how *did* she come by her 'radiance' (p. 149)?

Chopin's sentiment is often strategy. 'The Christ Light' expresses untold, and perhaps untellable, stories. Here, Chopin makes her first attempt to write the narrative of a young wife leaving home and husband—a story that, as *The Awakening* showed, many did not want to hear. Like Edna, Liza-Jane is a reader, a woman 'who never were back'ard with her talk', a misfit in marriage, black-eyed in a blue-eyed family, linked in the story with all that is seen as 'Other': the city, the night, a dark unexplored continent, exotic and hunted animals. Chopin embeds her flight (as she would Edna's) within jolting and colliding discourses, drawn from male and female traditions, destabilizing too easy a reading. The language of religion and emotion, focused in the voice of the matriarch at the 'homely' fireside (p. 153), recaptures Liza as a repenting Magdalen, in a domestic Christmas tale of forgiveness, seeming to underwrite submission. But this is preceded by the more unsettling narration of Liza's revolt, told as a joke, in an intertextual echo of dialect fiction, through the men's voices, in the quintessential scene of rustic loafers gathered round the stove. Alfred Habegger has described American humour as developing out of 'a kind of border warfare between two cultures, vernacular and refined' and, he adds, 'between male and female'.[22] Liza-Jane's ambitions ('I hev that within me . . . thet craves to taste the joys of ixistence' (p. 153)) are recounted in the misogynistic language, malapropisms, and comic orthography adopted by 'Artemus Ward' and other dialect humourists intent on putting women back in their place. Reminiscent of Ward's satire on a 'feroshus' campaigner from the 'Bunkumville . . . Wimin's Rites Associashun', who screams about 'the yoke of tyrinny', and demands, 'what is the price that woman pays for her

[21] Judith Butler, *Gender Trouble: Feminism and the Subversion of Identity* (London: Routledge, 1990), *passim*.

[22] Alfred Habegger, *Gender, Fantasy, and Realism in American Literature* (New York: Columbia UP, 1982), 125.

expeeriunce!',[23] the passage may leave the reader uncomfortable. But always suspicious of authoritative, dismissive talk, here Chopin may well be turning the satire against the satirist. By the end of the story, Liza-Jane has indeed fallen silent (she is never heard speaking directly in her own voice), and her eyes (once 'fairly snappin' fire' (p. 152)) are half-closed. However, even this ending is inconclusive: Chopin avoids any predictable dialogue, but conducts the reconciliation through glances and silences. Liza-Jane's tears and gestures may well signify sorrow and enlightenment, endorsing conventional wisdom that a wife's place lies with hearth, husband, and home; or, instead, they may memorably hint (as in 'Athénaïse' and *The Awakening*) at enforced submission and resignation. Beyond this, again, they may suggest alternatives: Abner reprises the dominant male tone of the opening ('of all the voices that clamored in his soul to be heard, that of the outraged husband was the loudest' (p. 155)), then, guided by his mother, rejects it, recognizing, perhaps, that a soul has many voices, that there are other possible forms of relation.

Chopin's experiments with different genres compel attention, too, as arguments with her time and place. Her excursion into history with 'The Maid of Saint Phillippe' has been seen as a stilted attempt at costume drama, and, by Emily Toth, as a venture into family chronicles. In this edition, the Explanatory Notes point out its revisionary echoes of Longfellow's *Evangeline*; but it is also a spirited riposte to the narrowing 'booster' rhetoric of economic progress. As Chopin wrote, the St Louis year-books were promoting the 'Future Great City of the World' through heroic annals of its early years—a future rejected, from the moment of the city's founding, by the defiant Marianne, who resists all forms of colonization, choosing her destiny in the 'rising sun' of the frontier, and 'death rather than bondage' with the (doomed) Cherokees (p. 163). This Gilded Age discourse of 'push' reverberates through some of Chopin's darkest stories ('Miss McEnders', and the busy husband's realm in 'Her Letters') and is crucial to *The Awakening* in Léonce's gospel of capitalist investment and social advancement. Like Marianne and the rest, Edna repudiates it, seeking a space and languages beyond, and

---

[23] Charles F. Browne ('Artemus Ward'), *Complete Works* (London: Chatto, 1884), 84–5.

transmuted forms of treasure in the myth of pirate gold: not 'a thing
to be hoarded or utilized . . . something to squander and throw to the
four winds, for the fun of seeing the golden specks fly' (p. 39).

If this quest remains a fantasy (even Edna's day on the *Chênière*
ends in talk of stocks and shares), few critics question its force within
the stories. In Chopin's textual and social order, however, for some
readers, it is race which presents most problems: in *The Awakening*,
for these, Edna's struggles for self-expression take place within a
privileged world against a picturesque frieze of silent, often nameless, non-white characters (the 'quadroon', the little black girl who
works the sewing-machine, the servants, the much-reviled Mexicans). Even the dream-like Grand Isle setting, as Helen Taylor
points out, occludes its history of privilege as a former plantation.[24]
In Chopin's earlier fiction, it would not be difficult to read many
stories as uncritical celebrations of white mastery and the old plantation tradition. In 'Beyond the Bayou', for example, Jacqueline is
traumatized at the symbolic castration of the Old South, in the
injury of P'tit Maître, and recovers when her loyalty to the next
young master repairs the moment, figured in the repetition of the
original blooding. (Gun, curls, and red ribbon all underwrite the new
cycle of white masculine authority in Reconstruction.) She is
rewarded when her journey across the bayou takes her into a
reborn, idealized, plantation, seen as colour, light, scent and paradise, with all traces of labour and exploitation erased ('the white,
bursting cotton . . . gleamed . . . like frosted silver in the early dawn',
p. 171).

But many readers also see in Jacqueline's crossing of her
'imaginary line' (p. 166) a remarkable psychological study; and, in
the light of her representation, it becomes harder to sustain easy
labels of stereotyping and nostalgia elsewhere. In Jacqueline's
narrative, Chopin, at a time of hardening racism in the South, draws
white readers into an African-American woman's subjectivity. In
the *Youth's Companion* version (included in this selection), she
reinforces direct explanation for children with emotional, impressionistic, techniques of colour and light, revealing the world through
La Folle's eyes; and, further, offers the child reader a role in the
story—possibly to restore the old forms, but perhaps to enable new

---

[24] Helen Taylor, *Gender, Race, and Region in the Writings of Grace King, Ruth
McEnery Stuart, and Kate Chopin* (Baton Rouge: Louisiana State UP, 1989), 178, 195.

ones. In *Bayou Folk*, she followed Jacqueline's story with 'Old Aunt Peggy'—seen one way, a patronizing piece, expressing stereotypical white constructions of black folk as lazy, grasping, and manipulative; or, in Janet Beer's brilliant reading, an almost Brechtian confrontation of the white family with its own preconceptions, that might be extended to challenges throughout the fiction.[25] Chopin revised 'Regret', to remove the word 'darkies', with all its cheery, 'loyal black' associations. Again, she qualified cosy images of the Reconstruction South in 'Azélie', where a poor Acadian share-cropper's daughter takes on the heart of the plantation, both actually and symbolically. She gains control over the manager, and over the store, which here, as later in William Faulkner, is revealed as the controlling centre of the exploitative share-cropping cycle. (The key—here, the size of a pistol—is a potent symbol in this text, as in 'Athénaïse'.) Her 'unshaded, unmodulated voice' (p. 210) cuts through 'Polyte's insults, his threatening power. Most expressive of all, perhaps, is 'In Sabine'. At a time when groups such as the White League were intent on silencing black freedmen throughout the state, Uncle Mortimer helps a white woman, and foils her husband. He lifts up his axe before a white man, and passes 'the back of his black, knotty hand unctuously over his lips', not in flattery or in menace, but 'as though he relished in advance the words that were about to pass them' (p. 253)—astonishingly brave words, for any African-American man, or for a white writer of Chopin's time. Returning to *The Awakening* after these, some may still want to argue that Chopin writes Edna into a typical white-centred narrative, where these figures, at most, romantically reflect the dramas of a white psyche in crisis. Others, however, might emphasize that the text quietly notes the unspoken racial order. Its servants are not invisible; quotation marks destabilize its terminology; it observes individuals (the quadroon's role-playing (p. 60), the black women subjected to Victor's blustering management); and, in Léonce's narratives and the glimpses of Iberville, reveals the happy plantation as a construction, bound up with self-images of mastery, anticipated in Edna's father, already being reproduced in her sons.

In this light, Chopin's texts constantly resist attempts to present white social order as natural. Though seldom viewed as openly

---

[25] Beer, *Kate Chopin*, 70–2.

political, her stories question any 'progress' achieved through cancelling difference and denying others their narrative. They are full of reminders of the continuing contemporary efforts to assimilate and homogenize the diverse populations of the United States: movements to establish nationalistic symbols (Flag Day, or the adoption of State Flowers—a campaign dear to *Youth's Companion*), and the more alarming attempts to erase other languages, cultures and social groups. After the elimination of the German language from St Louis schools in 1888, Paula von Stoltz's route to international fame seems significant: she rejects her Ivy-League suitor and chooses her immigrant German-European heritage ('Wiser than a God' (1889)).

Chopin herself, with her Irish-American and French lineage, was, as Bernard Koloski reminds us, 'bilingual and bicultural'.[26] Her fiction seeks to celebrate difference, while steering clear of any attempt to colonize or deny other voices. In this project, Chopin's regional elements are of crucial significance. However, having rescued her from what even modern tourist guides call the 'trash-bin of local color', many of Chopin's most forceful critics have been eloquently dismissive of those who seem to be attempting to put her back there. Few, indeed, would want to associate her with the 'local color' label, as it was long popularly defined. At its narrowest, this conveyed an image of an art crafted for the entertainment of sophisticated metropolitan audiences, out of the lives of those inhabiting regions remote from the powerful centre. In such vignettes, the urban observer represents country people in a patronizing or nostalgic glow, as quaintly picturesque 'types', living in a simpler, but limited, culture. The subjects in such sketches seldom share the dominant language used by the artist, and are rarely assumed to have a stake in the work of which they are the focus. Other detractors connected the genre with the etiolated writing and fussy eccentricities of (often unmarried) provincial women which contributed nothing to the mainstream tradition of robust masculine art. In its contemporary contexts, much of Chopin's fiction blended seamlessly with local colour writing in the same issues: *Youth's Companion* placed 'Beyond the Bayou' alongside Grace Ellery Channing's 'Tuscan Peasants', and followed 'A Matter of Prejudice' with Mary E. Plummer Clemenceau's '. . . The Southerners of France, and their Queer

[26] Bernard Koloski, *Kate Chopin: A Study of the Short Fiction* (New York: Twayne, 1996), p. xi.

Ways'; and readers of 'Athénaïse' in the *Atlantic* could also enjoy, in the same issue, 'Some Yorkshire Good Cheer' by Eugenia Skelding. Chopin herself took increasing pains to dissociate herself from the regionalist frame, and to insist that her writing came from other creative sources: 'I have been taken to spots supposed to be alive with local color. I have been introduced to excruciating characters with frank permission to use them as I liked, but never, in any single instance, has such material been of the slightest service.'[27] Critics, who prefer to highlight her European affinities and her psychological penetration are respecting her own desire to seek the enduring values of 'human existence'.

Today, however, 'local colour' literature itself has been subject to re-readings, which open up its analogies with imperial and colonial fictions, as a complex project, where cultural identities are in contest, and which often destabilize the very hierarchies and stereotypes it appear to endorse. In terms of gender, the work of female local colourists is now strongly appreciated: fictions such as Freeman's 'A New England Nun' (1891) or Jewett's *The Country of the Pointed Firs* (1896) which calibrate the strength of even the most restrained and uneventful women's lives, and expose the limits of the society which discounts them. Koloski and others accent the way Chopin's texts, too, operate in crossing-places and border areas, sensitive to the lived details and the values of the racial, ethnic, and cultural communities her stories represent. Although early reviewers relished her characters as 'semi-aliens' who dwelt in 'taciturn wildernesses', in taking readers into the finely-drawn social classifications of the South, she preserves a space for others' voices: the Acadians, Creoles, African Americans, and people of mixed race, outside the dominant United States culture.

Unlike the desert of 'An Egyptian Cigarette' (a site for hallucinatory Orientalist fantasy), Chopin's Louisiana is seldom the reviewers' 'terra incognita'. She creates poetically doubled landscapes: the dream-like, labyrinthine Gulf or the private corners of New Orleans (Madame Carambeau's stockade, Athénaïse's balcony, the gardens where Edna meditates) or in the details of scents, darkness, light and air that express the characters' inner spaces. Her

---

[27] Untitled essay, *St. Louis Post-Dispatch* (26 Nov. 1899).

characters drift, like Mrs. Sommers in the depths of the department store, 'not thinking at all' (p. 329), or like Edna, 'lost in some inward maze of contemplation' (p. 5). On Grand Isle and the *Chênière*, time seems to go on for ever ('How many years have I slept?' reflects Edna (p. 42)). *The Awakening*, as a whole, is elusive about time; for some critics, this deliberate vagueness suggests the story is set in the realm of myth. But, even though exact dates are absent, in its references the text is often highly specific. Chopin overlays features of the New Orleans she remembered from the 1870s, with more recent elements, enabling her both to draw on details of a cultural milieu she knew well, and to take up contemporary issues. Whether idyll or routine, the *Chênière* and Grand Isle are finite: readers would have known that they would be devastated by a hurricane in 1893. Like these, many of Chopin's settings also exist on maps, or fit in between actual places; they have their own cultures, inhabitants, and atmosphere, written over with the signs of their changing histories.

Chopin realized that any act of representation may silence and harm its 'subjects'. 'Caline' and 'A Gentleman of Bayou Têche' both speak forcibly of artists as disruptive outsiders, potentially as culturally damaging as the Americans whose railroads penetrate the Louisiana countryside. Chopin's South is social text, and literary palimpsest, bearing traces of its treatment by other story-tellers, which pass into her fiction. Bayou Têche was already overwritten by Longfellow's *Evangeline: A Tale of Acadie* (1847)—the poet had never visited there, but waves of tourists would. The 1893 Baedeker introduced French New Orleans through G.W. Cable's popular stories. As L. M. Harris complained in 1898, 'Mr. Cable has made us an object of amusement to his American readers. Northern people come here to New Orleans to study us as curiosities. They walk up and down Royal Street with . . . "Old Creole Days" in their hands trying to identify the localities and types of persons.'[28] Visitors' guides presented the Gulf Coast through local legends (Madame Antoine's 'whispering voices of dead men and the click of muffled gold' (p. 44)); the Gulf seas, in all their moods, filled Lafcadio Hearn's *Chita: A Memory of Last Island* (1889).

All these, and more, enter *The Awakening*. The Appendix and Explanatory Notes offer further samples of the kind of contemporary

---

[28] Harris, 'The Creoles of New Orleans', *Southern Collegian*, 30 (Jan. 1898), 210.

observations which Chopin's fiction both parallels and revises. She works so closely with one of these, Alcée Fortier's descriptions of the 'Cadian Ball, as almost to suggest an actual source, but to say this is not to downplay her originality. Chopin infuses passion and inwardness into the professor's account, allowing characters their own life: just as, in 'A Gentleman of Bayou Têche', one of her most complexly self-referential stories, Acadian Martinette courageously expresses her 'bold and shrill' defiance of the patronizing Northern artist (p. 243) before an audience of amused men, and Evariste picks up his pen to write his own caption for the Northern magazines (p. 245). As a narrator, Chopin often keeps herself visible, pointing out features, putting local terms in italics, explaining customs. (If puzzled by dialect or Louisiana French, a reader usually only has to wait, and Chopin will make matters clear.) In this role as mediator and translator, she attempts to avoid judgement (the patronizing and colonizing discourse of the kind of artist she does not wish to become). Although she rejects extreme isolationism, her texts honour distinctive cultures. Even when she comically deploys the full force of a nineteenth-century 'change of heart' plot against Madame Carambeau's vigorous cultural defences in 'A Matter of Prejudice', she balances Madame's bold excursion into modern America by her son's emotional return to his Creole origins, his mother's voice, and his French title (p. 208).

Chopin's prime signifier of the inner life of a people is always language. The polyglot parrot whose voice opens *The Awakening* has attracted as much critical attention as anything else in the novel. But there are few stories in this selection which do not foreground language, whether in the briefest scatter of phrases, or in careful transcription of dialect and accent, and of individuated forms of non-English-American tongues. This is not the glib exoticism of the superior dialect writer, but a strong plea on behalf of multiple and diverse voices, allowing everyone the chance of expression. Time and again, even when the words have been represented in English, her stories remind us that they are translations of languages, perhaps now lost, or under threat: ('French was the language spoken at Valmondé in those days' (p. 194); 'La Folle said to herself in her dialect' (p. 167)). 'At the 'Cadian Ball' presents a spectrum of characters identified by social kind, purity of blood ('the young Acadian', 'the little Spanish vixen') and variety of spoken French. It is a love story, in which, as critics remark, like eventually speaks to like: Clarisse recalls Alcée with the voice of his own kin, which goes through his body 'like an electric shock' (p. 189). But it is also a story of gradual social change, instituted by the intrusive American rail-roaders, and precisely registered in Chopin's awareness of linguistic erosion: the old men mumble French proverbs, but the younger generation 'preferred to speak English' (p. 188). Alcée and Calixta remain divided by class, but talk in the more modern language. And Chopin opens newer languages yet, to express the experience the lovers eventually share—'at the very borderland of life's mystery' (p. 345)—in the story's hidden, passionate, utopian sequel, 'The Storm'.

Another fading language inspires 'La Belle Zoraïde', a narrative full of references to the dispossessed and silenced (the African dancers on Congo Square, the lovers, the mother). The 'half-forgotten' Creole romance that rises in Manna Loulou's memory (p. 223) and the women's speech that ends the story, is a transcription of patois, the variety of French acquired by black slaves in white French Creole families (see Appendix). Though opaque to northern audiences, this offers another telling form of speech. For Louisiana readers, far from being 'forgotten', patois had become the focus of vehement contemporary debate. This speech was a legacy of slavery and colonialism, and by the late nineteenth century, its forms were studied and argued over. For some it was a debased and slovenly tongue, transmitted to white children by their nurses, to be suppressed in adulthood; for others, flexible and creative, the hauntingly nostalgic language of childhood. (Old Celestine lingers 'to talk patois with Robert, whom she had known as a boy', p. 111). Whether Acadian dialect, aristocratic white Creole, or varieties of African-American speech, Chopin refuses to discredit any of these voices. Whereas G. W. Cable presented white Creoles, for example, as an anachronistic tribe, giving great offence through his rendering of their accents (and hints of mixed blood), Chopin pointedly avoids any attempt in *The Awakening* to spell their speech in idiosyncratic ways: the Ratignolles speak English 'with an accent which was only discernible through its un-English emphasis', Edna's husband 'with no accent whatever' (p. 62).

These voices all speak from distinct and different cultures. Chopin's fiction repeatedly turns on the shock of cultural collision.

Groups interpenetrate, characters gaze at their opposites, or travel over borders into others' territory. In 'Caline', the disruption begins when 'something awoke her as suddenly as if it had been a blow' (p. 199), and the country girl and the fashionable passengers stare at each other in the field, between the primal 'dense wood' and the glittering steel of the new railroad. This moment echoes in sudden awakenings throughout the stories, as Chopin traces the boundaries of characters' worlds, at moments of exit, entry, resistance, or 'melting'—a word, as Cynthia Griffin Wolff points out, of crucial significance in *The Awakening*.[29] The mirrored love-stories Chopin evokes in the sensuous summer landscape of 'Tonie' and *The Awakening* arise out of these gulfs of cultural division, as well as from the fatal erotics of sea, light, and air, and strange spirits of the isle. Revising 'Tonie' (as 'At Chênière Caminada'), she saw ways to use her characters in a new dimension in her novel. Like Tonie, but from an opposite social perspective, Edna peers into the Creole world; like him, she is deeply aroused by its difference, baffled by its languages. His story restores Tonie to 'rest and peace' (p. 236), though of a peculiarly ambiguous kind. In *The Awakening*, in the day upon the *Chênière*, he becomes, briefly, part of Edna's scenery. But Chopin takes Edna further, 'leaving her free to drift whithersoever she chose to set her sails' (p. 39).

'The Awakening'

Few readers agree about how far Edna travels, and what she, or the novel as a whole, expresses, whether she inaugurates a new language, is ensnared in an old one, or remains in some state of suspension in between: 'the beginning of things, of a world especially, is necessarily vague, tangled, chaotic, and exceedingly disturbing. How few of us ever emerge from such beginning!' (p. 16). But whether the last possible point of nineteenth-century realism, or a prototypical Modernist text, *The Awakening* continues to astonish readers as an extraordinarily moving narrative of discovery, which sets heroine and reader loose in strange, unwritten territory, the 'wild zone'[30] of

---

[29] Cynthia Griffin Wolff, 'The Fiction of Limits: "Désirée's Baby"', *Southern Literary Journal*, 10.2 (Spring 1978), 42.

[30] Elaine Showalter, 'Feminist Criticism in the Wilderness', in Showalter (ed.) *The New Feminist Criticism* (London: Virago, 1986), 262.

experience, beyond the apprehension of a dominant culture. For some years before Chopin began writing 'A Solitary Soul' (as she thought of her book), she had come to see herself primarily as the creator of short fiction. For modern readers, it seems ironical that it was the *Atlantic Monthly*'s Horace E. Scudder, the editor who had rejected Gilman's 'The Yellow Wall-Paper', who, in 1897, encouraged her to think of starting work on a novel. Like Gilman's story, *The Awakening* travels beyond acceptable forms of discourse, as Chopin tries to find new ways of expressing the self within society, and freeing it from social and textual limits. Her 'unwomanly' and 'unmentionable' subject matter releases Edna from nineteenth-century domestic plots that wrote women more firmly into home, marriage, motherhood, family, femininity. Asked '[w]here would they sleep, and where would papa sleep?' Edna promises her sons the traditional happy ending ('the fairies would fix it all right' (p. 105)); but the novel refuses it. (In its final sighting, the Pontellier mansion looks 'broken and half torn asunder', p. 109.) Instead, Chopin structures her narrative, in part, around a series of battles over territory, which take Edna further and further from home, husband and social obligation: from the first mute resistance over bed-time at the cottage, to the flight to the 'pigeon-house', and, finally, the walk into the unconfined space of the sea.

If Chopin dismantles the Doll's House, she also challenges motherhood. To choose a heroine who was not 'a mother-woman' (p. 10) took tremendous daring, in a society where many held, with Elizabeth Bisland, that: 'There are women lacking the [maternal] instinct as there are calves born with two heads, but for purposes of generalization these exceptions may be ignored.'[31] Edna, her husband, the narrator, and others, all examine her deficiencies, asking why she does not define herself by her children; and the text constantly reverts to images of maternity, focused above all in the Creole woman, Adèle Ratignolle: 'the embodiment of every womanly grace and charm' (p. 10). But, at the turn into a new century, there are 'no words' to describe Adèle except 'the old ones': and in a significant scene, as critics point out, Edna tries to paint her, but fails, and destroys the picture. Chopin's own efforts to represent the mother in less sanctified terms lead her into more controversial languages—the

---

[31] Bisland, 'The Modern Woman and Marriage', 753.

clinical 'ecstasy of pain, the heavy odor of chloroform' (p. 122), the Darwinian 'ways of Nature', the Gothic 'scene of torture' (p. 122). At the same time, the text tries to open up new, unknown roles beyond the 'delicious' one of the 'mother-woman'. Edna is seen at an increasing distance from her children: they are looked after by their 'quadroon' nurse, they play some way off, they are sent away to their grandmother, and finally—after Edna is urged by Adèle to 'think of the children!' (p. 122)—they become her 'antagonists', the image of 'the soul's slavery' (p. 127). And it is this image (not that of her husband or lover) that seems to trigger the final movement of the novel: Edna's effort to 'elude' them, by walking into the sea.

Readers remain deeply divided on whether Edna walks out of domesticity into an alternative space (sensually fulfilling, imaginatively satisfying), or simply entangles herself in other equally confining stories. Chopin gives her other roles—friend, lover, artist, at the everyday level, but touched with the sense of something more mysterious, 'the regal woman, the one who rules . . . who stands alone' (p. 98). Through Edna, she explores alternative constructions of the feminine, revising the emptied-out representations of woman as ornament and commodity, or as a 'peculiar and delicate organism' (p. 74). Edna is neither a fragile creature without desire or appetite—passionless, blank, and disembodied—nor a 'capricious' (p. 32) victim of dangerous instincts, who needs to be studied secretly by a doctor, and brought safely back into her husband's government. Some readers find compelling force in her female friendships, others in the scenes that suggest Edna's reclamation of her body: the growing 'ease' with which she handles her paint brushes, swims, walks, eats, experiences 'the fine, firm quality and texture of her flesh' (p. 41). Sensuality merges into sexuality, as Edna not only feels desire, but engages in sex entirely dissociated from marriage or even from romantic love. Such moments are replicated in the transgressive body of the text, which attempts to escape from the 'old' words, through the impressionistic repetitions of colour and sound, evocations of heat, languor, the scent of flowers, the short and fluid chapters that often end on a half-thought, a teasing cadence, a moment of arousal: 'The voice, the notes, the whole refrain haunted her memory' (p. 45). Chopin suffuses all these with a further language, heard above all in the voices of the sea. In Lafcadio Hearn's *Chita*, the narrator evokes Breton legend:

'the Voice of the Sea is never one voice, but a tumult of many voices—voices of drowned men, the muttering of the multitudinous dead'. A young girl learns 'how "the tears of women made the waves of the sea,"' and absorbs the lore of the Gulf: '*Si quieres aprender á orare, entra en el mar*. (If thou wouldst learn to pray, go to the sea.)'[32] Chopin, too, uses the sea as the language of the soul and of the senses, to write stories outside the social, unchaining Edna from her culturally written roles and scripted identity: 'As she swam she seemed to be reaching out for the unlimited in which to lose herself' (p. 32). And for many readers, this releases the novel from the rational domain of masculine authority into a realm of authenticity, liberatory in its rhythms, its energy, its openness.

For others, however, this language only echoes older ones. John Carlos Rowe warns against facile oppositions of a 'natural' and a socialized woman, pointing out that even the instincts are deeply inscribed by patriarchal structures. Patricia Yaeger suggests that adultery is an 'acceptable' transgression, only perpetuating traditional male/female relationships, predicated on hierarchical relationships of power.[33] As Robert merges into Arobin, so both merge back into Léonce, or even the Colonel: Edna cannot dent her wedding ring, she wears her husband's New York diamonds at her ceremonious dinner, she begins to talk like her father (p. 82); and, equally, she cannot break out of male definitions. In spite of the expressions of strength, the text persistently identifies Edna in terms of limit and lack. Much of her narrative is spent seeking to fill herself with images which substitute for the 'acme of bliss, which . . . was not for her in this world' (p. 21): photographs (of the tragedian, of Robert), reading, music, painting, letters, visits, talk, a lover. Even Robert, a gentle, almost feminized man who, critics notice, looks strangely like Edna, seems to be a substitute for the absence within her self, figured in her ever-returning 'ennui', the 'chill breath that seemed to issue from some vast cavern wherein discords wailed' (p. 98). In these terms, once Edna and the narrative cast themselves

[32] Lafcadio Hearn, *Chita. A Memory of Last Island* (New York: Harper, 1889), 19, 147.
[33] John Carlos Rowe, 'The Economics of the Body in Kate Chopin's *The Awakening*', in Kate Chopin International Conference, *Perspectives on Kate Chopin* (Natchitoches, La.: Northwestern State UP, 1990), 1–24; Patricia S. Yaeger, '"A Language Which Nobody Understood": Emancipatory Strategies in *The Awakening*', *Novel*, 20:3 (Spring 1987), 197–219.

loose from the defining languages of authority, the linear forms and the plots they prescribe, they move towards emptiness and extinction; or to stories, which cannot, by their very nature, be communicated.

For most readers, these debates are concentrated, above all, in discussion of Edna. As in so much of Chopin's fiction, the text puts its central character beyond conclusive understanding, and even beyond empathy. In some ways, certainly, readers know Edna through and through. The novel tells us about her blood and family history; it allows us to study her in scenes with her father, her husband and children, or alone, in her dreams and childhood memories, her thought-processes, her emotions, and even in the 'material pictures' (p. 29) of her imagination. But, as in so many other stories, Chopin leaves gaps, retreats from explanation. As the narrative follows Edna's solitary soul, from an outward to an inward existence, from a social self to some unnamed, unidentified form of being, she sets up endless speculation. The narrator becomes vague about her motives, other characters puzzle over her in their talk. Released from 'anchorage' (p. 39), she is at odds with herself, split and doubled: her thoughts travel somewhat in advance of her body (p. 33); her present self is in 'some way different from the other self' (p. 45); she is filled with 'strange, new voices' (p. 71), a 'thousand emotions' (p. 33), impulses, tears, passions she cannot understand or articulate ('It had crossed her thought like some unsought, extraneous impression', p. 63). But fragmented, she also seems most concentrated, most intensely herself, beginning to look 'with her own eyes' (p. 104), to swim, to speak, to paint, and to act.

As her story unfolds, it is recaptured by others' narratives: shaped into pathology by her husband, a case-study by the Doctor, and the dream-like legend of the Baratarian lovers by Edna herself. By the last chapter, she is already part of local folk-lore: 'Venus rising from the foam could have presented no more entrancing a spectacle than Mrs. Pontellier' (p. 125) Nobody holds the complete story of Edna, though in her own final reported thoughts, she projects omniscience onto the doctor: 'Perhaps Doctor Mandelet would have understood if she had seen him—' (p. 128). As the novel closes, readers take on the role of the absent physician, the potential all-seeing analyst, who can integrate the subject. Contemporary with Freud's early case-histories, here, the text gives us a case without an ending, one like 'Dora' (1905) where the subject simply vanishes. On the one hand, *The Awakening* draws readers into the desire to interpret, to penetrate, and solve Edna's mystery. The associative, metaphorical text seems to invite decoding: Chopin gives it the density and elusiveness of dream, in its doubled characters (Mlle Reisz/Mme Ratignolle, Robert/Arobin), its shadowy, unnamed figures (the woman in black, the lovers), its repeated motifs (flowers, songs, music, food, clothes, birds, sleeping, waking, gold), the dominant signifiers of the labyrinth, the night, the sea, that have interested so many critics. And Edna has been interpreted and reinterpreted, through widely varying analytical lenses, as a privileged white lady, a 'Creole Bovary' (as Willa Cather first called her), a New(ish) Woman, a redemptive Greek goddess (variously, Aphrodite, Athena, Artemis), a victim, a coward, a selfish narcissist, a prisoner, a rebel, a romantic pioneer.

On the other hand, the novel resists any single meaning. It is full of jolting discourses that never quite fuse, enacted within the narrative by the interrupted conversations, unfinished stories, broken promises, half-read books, jokes that fall flat. Chapters end on fading notes, with silences between, or in casual remarks, strong with implication. This hesitant mode is familiar from Chopin's stories, but here becomes more and more telling as one half-note echoes another, in partially repeated phrases and accumulating rhythms. It counters the loud bluster acquired by socially effective individuals, presented throughout the text in a spectrum of white male speakers at different stages of development, from Edna's young sons guarding their comics, 'making their authority felt' (p. 26), to Victor bullying black servants, and Léonce sortieing into the kitchen to rebuke the cook. Edna, too, can use this language—she can give orders and use servants, write breezy letters, command listeners with her stories ('She left them in heated argument, speculating about the conclusion of the tale' (p. 48))—but, even as she becomes more expressive, she abandons explanation ('She felt that her speech was voicing the incoherency of her thoughts, and stopped abruptly' (p. 123)). Her very indecisiveness and impulse reject the kind of dominating energies at large elsewhere: Léonce's ambitions, Victor's 'will which no ax could break' (p. 25). Although her night-time vigil is reported, its relevance to her final actions is immediately retracted: 'She was not thinking of these things when she walked down to the beach' (p. 127). And in a history of daring, this is one of Chopin's most radical refusals. Unlocking Edna from plot, time, and narrative closure, she leaves readers, like Edna in her meadow, 'believing that it had no beginning and no end' (p. 127), keeping open the multiple possibilities, the endless retellings of her story.

NOTE ON THE TEXTS

That there has been surprisingly little textual debate about Chopin's writings is a tribute to the openness and attentiveness of her founding editors. This edition would not have been possible without their work, and gratefully acknowledges its debts.

Here, I follow the general practice of previous editors of intervening as little as possible in Chopin's texts. I have made no attempt to standardize spelling or punctuation from story to story, or to regularize the use of upper-case (e.g. for 'Street', 'River'), or the use of italics for non-English terms. Although italicization may at times seem inconsistent, Chopin is often extremely precise about inflection, and I do not wish to erase possible critical implications that readers might wish to explore (e.g. questions of Chopin's construction of her audience). Occasional syntactical compressions or moments of disagreement of tense or number (e.g. 'their personality', p. 143) are also a feature of Chopin's writing, reflecting a frequent informal oral tone in her narration. Her punctuation, too, often marks speech patterns, not syntax. Some seeming misprints (e.g. 'Monsieur, l'Artist' for 'Monsieur, l'Artiste', p. 149) may represent deliberate 'Americanisms' or other intentional effects, and, if in any doubt, I have not altered these. I have, however, silently corrected obvious misprints, cross-checking with the book-version where one exists (e.g. 'walkinng' for 'walking', p. 134; 'luxurions' for 'luxurious', p. 178).

'The Awakening'

Editors have found little to argue about in the text of *The Awakening*, which was published by Herbert S. Stone & Company, Chicago & New York, on 22 April 1899. To date, no manuscript of the novel has been located, and, without later variants in Kate Chopin's lifetime, the first edition has served as the base for all subsequent reprintings, and is the one used here. Although the Stone text is remarkably clear of irritating errors, like most editors I have added a word ('of') to 'scene torture' (p. 122), and inserted two speech marks (pp. 69, 70); 'doctor' (p. 72, l. 31) has been changed to 'Doctor'. No further additions have been made to the text. The enigmatic comma after 'Good-by—because' (p.128) has been retained, spellings have been left unaltered (e.g. 'nugat', 'pompono', and 'Lucillean'), and there has been no attempt to regularize the use of italics for French terms. Chapters, however, no longer begin on a new page.

The Short Fiction

Choosing a version of Kate Chopin's short stories presents an editor with more options. Some editions adopt a compromise between representing Chopin's career chronologically and offering the final versions of her texts. Seyersted's *Complete Works*, for example, prints the stories in order of composition, but uses the book versions, or Chopin's hand-written alterations on her clippings, where they exist. This has the advantage of using Chopin's own revisions (although with the disadvantages suggested below), but, even with the excellent collations of variants in the Appendix, makes it a little difficult for readers who wish to follow Chopin through her earlier working life. (Although many of the stories in *Bayou Folk* (1894) were revised and collected fairly shortly after writing, several of those in *A Night in Acadie* (1897) were written before *Bayou Folk* and in their revised forms may represent Chopin's work from a later stage. Similarly, it is hard to tell just when Chopin made the changes on the magazine clippings of stories she hoped to collect later.) Another editorial option is to arrange stories, in their revised form, to represent the integrity of Chopin's collections (e.g. Nina Baym's Modern Library edition (1981)), and some critics (e.g. Barbara Ewell) have made out a strong thematic case for reading the stories within the book-context. (Placed in a collection, stories may suggest a kind of unity not there when published separately.)

Chopin was not the entirely spontaneous writer described in early accounts (including her own). She did revise, sometimes making slight changes to smooth a sentence (e.g. 'that' to 'which'), or to remove obvious genre features, change a title, or adjust a character's name or status for consistency within a collection. Although most often reprinted, the book versions should not, however, be regarded as altogether authoritative or improved. Mistakes creep in (e.g. the line 'famous lawyer who lived in New Orleans' (p. 231) was omitted when 'Tonie' was revised as 'At Chênière Caminada'). More

significantly, the earlier versions, although sometimes slightly
cruder, often seem, in the sum of many small impressions, fresher,
livelier, and more immediate. In revision, Chopin often (though by
no means always) made slight changes which turned her work, in
effect, from that of a spoken, story-telling mode into a more formal,
written one. See, for instance, the loss of the vivid italics for Athénaïse's revolt ('she would not, and she would not, and she would *not*
continue to enact the rôle of wife to Cazeau' (p. 297)), or for Calixta's charm, in 'At the 'Cadian Ball' ('Such animation! such *abandon!*', p. 188). Punctuation sometimes becomes muted, and less vital
(e.g. some of the dramatic dashes in *Vogue*'s 'The Father of Désirée's
Baby' (p. 196) give place to semi-colons in *Bayou Folk*'s 'Désirée's
Baby'). Sometimes Chopin distanced the narrator from the scene,
removing constructions which bear the trace of the story-teller's
voice—the 'stove which was there' (p. 151) (though she continued to
use this kind of scene-setting throughout her fiction—'the tiny
clock, which was there' ('An Egyptian Cigarette', p. 333)—or 'a
wicker rocker which was there' (*The Awakening*, p. 3)). Elsewhere
narrative energy diminishes: e.g. in Zoraïde's inserted apology, perhaps the result of editorial suggestion (see note to p. 225), or in the
removal of the impressionistic colour effects in 'Beyond the Bayou'
as Chopin rewrote her children's story for adults.

   For these reasons, and with the aim of offering readers the chance
to see the range of Chopin's writing, to follow her writing career as it
unfolded, to explore her excursions into different genres and literary
markets, and to gain insight into her working practices, I give the
first published versions (or, for unpublished fiction, the final manuscript version) throughout. Following *The Awakening*, the stories are
reprinted chronologically. I use the title of first publication in all
cases, but for readers' convenience, where the story is also well
known under an alternative, I give that in brackets. By-lines (such as
'Written for the Sunday Post-Dispatch') are omitted. Subtitles have
been retained. As Seyersted suggests, these were very likely editorial
additions, and critics have been interested in the way they seem in
some cases to defuse or distance potentially controversial material:
the critique of conventional marriage is described in 'A Point at
Issue!' as 'A Story of Love and Reason in Which Love Triumphs', in
'Athénaïse' as 'A Story of a Temperament'; the horrors of 'La Belle
Zoraïde' are explained as 'A Tragedy of the Old Régime'. By the same

token, however, the subtitles might also represent Kate Chopin's own, perhaps more ironic, presentation of such stories for magazine readers. (Although the subtitles did not appear in the book versions, Chopin did not cross them out on her clippings, even when she made other emendations.)

As this is a readers' edition, the Explanatory Notes indicate only the scope and nature of any substantive revisions Chopin made between magazine and book, or on her own clippings, outlining details of those believed potentially of most critical and interpretative interest. Readers are referred to *The Complete Works of Kate Chopin* (1969) for texts based on the revised versions to compare with those here, and for fuller details of variants. (Seyersted omits details of emended accents, italicization, misprints, or punctuation.) The texts fall broadly into these categories:

Uncollected Stories

(1) Early uncollected stories (written June 1889–March 1892; pub. in newspapers and magazines Dec. 1889–March 1897): 'Wiser Than a God', 'A Point at Issue!', 'The Christ Light', 'The Maid of Saint Phillippe',* 'Doctor Chevalier's Lie', 'Miss McEnders'.*
(2) 'A Pair of Silk Stockings' (written April 1896), pub. *Vogue* 10 (16 Sept. 1897).

Collected Stories

(1) Those that, with a few exceptions, Chopin published first in newspapers and magazines, then in the two collections which established her name:
Bayou Folk (Boston: Houghton Mifflin, March 1894): twenty-three stories, including (in order): 'In Sabine',† 'Beyond the Bayou', 'Old Aunt Peggy',† 'Désirée's Baby' (first pub. as 'The Father of Désirée's Baby'), 'At the 'Cadian Ball', 'La Belle Zoraïde', 'A Gentleman of Bayou Têche',† 'A Lady of Bayou St. John'. (Written Nov. 1891–Nov. 1893; first pub. in newspapers and magazines 1892–93.)

* These texts are those of Chopin's own clippings held in the Kate Chopin Papers, Missouri Historical Society, St Louis, Mo., and are published with kind permission of the Society.
† First pub. in *Bayou Folk*.

A Night in Acadie (Chicago, Way & Williams, Nov. 1897): twenty-one stories, including (in order): 'Athénaïse', 'Regret', 'A Matter of Prejudice', 'Caline', 'Azélie', 'At Chênière Caminada' (first pub. as 'Tonie'), 'A Respectable Woman', 'Ripe Figs'. (Written Feb. 1892–April 1895; first pub. newspapers and magazines, 1893–1896.)

(2)   Stories planned for *A Vocation and a Voice*: twenty-three listed stories, including (in order): 'Elizabeth Stock's One Story', 'An Egyptian Cigarette', 'The Dream of an Hour' (later title, 'The Story of an Hour'), 'The Unexpected', 'Her Letters', 'The Kiss', 'Lilacs'. (Written 1893–1900; all pub. in *Vogue* (1894–1900), except 'Lilacs' (*New Orleans Times-Democrat*, 20 Dec. 1896) and 'Elizabeth Stock's One Story' (written March 1898, unpub. in Chopin's lifetime.)

Chopin records the acceptance of this collection by Way & Williams (1898), its transfer to Herbert S. Stone (Nov. 1898), and its return (Feb. 1900), with no reason given. The reception of *The Awakening* might have prompted the rejection, but, so too, Emily Toth suggests, might cutbacks at the publishing firm. Daniel Rankin's list of the stories is that used by Toth in her excellent edition (Harmondsworth: Penguin, 1991) which at last presented readers with Chopin's third collection

Unpublished Stories

Stories unpub. in Chopin's lifetime: 'Vagabonds' (Dec. 1895); 'Elizabeth Stock's One Story' (March 1898) (see *A Vocation and a Voice*, above). The texts here are published, with kind permission, from the manuscripts held in the Kate Chopin Papers, Missouri Historical Society, St Louis, Mo.; 'The Storm' (19 July 1898) first appeared in Per Seyersted, *The Complete Works of Kate Chopin* (Baton Rouge: Louisiana State UP, 1969), and is reprinted here with kind permission of the publishers.

SELECT BIBLIOGRAPHY

Editions

The following make available Kate Chopin's known surviving writings (including unpublished fragments, personal statements, fiction, essays, diaries and letters):

Seyersted, Per (ed.), *The Complete Works of Kate Chopin* (Baton Rouge: Louisiana State UP, 1969).

Toth, Emily (ed.), *A Vocation and a Voice: Stories by Kate Chopin* (Harmondsworth: Penguin, 1991).

Seyersted, Per and Toth, Emily (eds.), *A Kate Chopin Miscellany* (Oslo: Universitetsforlaget and Natchitoches: Northwestern State Univ. of Louisiana, 1979). With useful bibliography.

Toth, Emily, Seyersted, Per, and Bonnell, Cheyenne (eds.), *Kate Chopin's Private Papers* (Bloomington, Ind.: Indiana UP, 1998). Updates and completes *Miscellany* above.

Bonner, Thomas, *The Kate Chopin Companion. With Chopin's Translations from French Fiction* (Westport, Conn.: Greenwood, 1988).

Editions of *The Awakening* reprint either the text of the first edition or that of *Complete Works*. The following contain especially helpful critical and contextual material:

Culley, Margo (ed.), *The Awakening. An Authoritative Text, Biographical and Historical Contexts, Criticism*, 2nd edn. (New York: Norton, 1994).

Walker, Nancy A. (ed.), *The Awakening* (Boston: Bedford Books of St Martin's Press; Basingstoke: Macmillan, 1993).

Biography and Selected Bibliographies

Nye, Lorraine M., 'Four Birth Dates for Kate Chopin', *Southern Studies*, 25:4 (1986), 375–6. (Argues for 1849 birthdate.)

Rankin, Daniel, *Kate Chopin and Her Creole Stories* (Philadelphia: Univ. of Pennsylvania, 1932). (Gives birthdate as 1851.) Now much criticized, but a pioneering study.

Seyersted, Per, *Kate Chopin: A Critical Biography* (1969; Baton Rouge: Louisiana State UP, 1980). (Gives birthdate as 1851.) Contributed immeasurably to Chopin's revival.

Toth, Emily, *Kate Chopin: A Life of the Author of 'The Awakening'* (1990; London: Century, 1991). (Settles 1850 birthdate.) Now the authoritative biography; shortened and rev. as *Kate Chopin Unveiled* (Jackson: UP of Mississippi, 1999). Useful bibliographies.

Wilson, Mary Helen, 'Kate Chopin's Family: Fallacies and Facts, Including Kate's True Birthdate', *Kate Chopin Newsletter*, 2 (Winter 1976–77), 25–31. (Argues for 1850 birthdate.)

Green, Suzanne and Caudle David, (eds.), *Kate Chopin: An Annotated Bibliography of Critical Works, 1976–1997* (Westport, Conn.: Greenwood, forthcoming).

Springer, Marlene, *Edith Wharton and Kate Chopin: A Reference Guide* (Boston: G. K. Hall, 1976).

Thomas, Heather Kirk, 'Kate Chopin: A Primary Bibliography, Alphabetically Arranged', *American Literary Realism 1870–1910*, 28:2 (Winter 1996), 71–88.

Critical Anthologies and Collections of Essays

These contain some of the most stimulating writing on Chopin, and many now 'classic' essays not listed below. Extremely helpful in giving a sense of the vast range of criticism written since her revival in the 1960s, and of some of the widely differing approaches to her work.

Bloom, Harold (ed.), *Kate Chopin* (New York: Chelsea House, 1987). Includes reprints of some of the best known critical essays, pre-1987.

Boren, Lynda S. and Davis, Sara deSaussure (eds.), *Kate Chopin Reconsidered: Beyond the Bayou* (Baton Rouge: Louisiana State UP, 1992).

Fick, Thomas H. and Gold, Eva (eds.), *Louisiana Literature*, 11:1, Special Section: Kate Chopin (Spring 1994), 8–171.

Koloski, Bernard (ed.), *Approaches to Teaching Chopin's* The Awakening (New York: Modern Language Association of America, 1988). Helpful for readers as well as teachers.

Martin, Wendy (ed.), *New Essays on* The Awakening (Cambridge: Cambridge UP, 1988).

Perspectives on Kate Chopin, Proceedings of Kate Chopin International Conference (Natchitoches, La.: Northwestern State Univ., 1990).

Petry, Alice Hall (ed.), *Critical Essays on Kate Chopin* (New York: G. K. Hall, 1996). Good introduction, contemporary essays, and a fine selection of reviews and of criticism pre-1969.

Introductions and Overviews

The following offer helpful introductions to Chopin's writings and critical history:

Allen, Priscilla, 'Old Critics and New: The Treatment of Chopin's *The Awakening*' in *The Authority of Experience: Essays in Feminist Criticism*, ed. Arlyn Diamond and Lee R. Edwards (Amherst: Univ. of Massachusetts Press, 1977), 224–38.

Arner, Robert, 'Kate Chopin', *Louisiana Studies* 14:1 (Spring 1975), 11–139.

Dyer, Joyce, The Awakening: *A Novel of Beginnings* (New York: Twayne, 1993).

Ewell, Barbara C., *Kate Chopin* (New York: Ungar, 1986).

Koloski, Bernard, *Kate Chopin: A Study of the Short Fiction* (New York: Twayne, 1996).

Skaggs, Peggy, *Kate Chopin* (Boston: Twayne, 1985).

Selected Books and Parts of Books

Ammons, Elizabeth, *Conflicting Stories: American Women Writers at the Turn into the Twentieth Century* (Oxford: Oxford UP, 1991).

Beer, Janet, *Kate Chopin, Edith Wharton and Charlotte Perkins Gilman: Studies in Short Fiction* (Basingstoke: Macmillan, 1997).

Chandler, Marilyn R., *Dwelling in the Text: Houses in American Fiction* (Berkeley and Los Angeles: Univ. of California Press, 1991).

Elfenbein, Anna Shannon, *Women on the Color Line: Evolving Stereotypes and the Writings of George Washington Cable, Grace King and Kate Chopin* (Charlottesville: UP of Virginia, 1989).

Fusco, Richard, *Maupassant and the American Short Story: The Influence of Form at the Turn of the Century* (University Park: Univ. of Pennsylvania Press, 1994).

Hoder-Salmon, Marilyn, *Kate Chopin's* The Awakening: *Screenplay as Interpretation* (Gainesville, Fla.: UP of Florida, 1992). A creative response, with theoretical commentary.

Huf, Linda, *A Portrait of the Artist as a Young Woman: The Writer as Heroine in American Literature* (New York: Ungar, 1983).

Jones, Anne Goodwyn, *Tomorrow is Another Day: The Woman Writer in the South, 1859–1936* (Baton Rouge: Louisiana State UP, 1981).

Kearns, Katherine, *Nineteenth-Century Literary Realism: Through the Looking-Glass* (Cambridge: Cambridge UP, 1996).

Knights, Ben, *The Listening Reader: Fiction and Poetry for Counsellors and Psychotherapists* (London: Jessica Kingsley, 1995). Also helpful for general readers.

Papke, Mary, *Verging on the Abyss: The Social Fiction of Kate Chopin and Edith Wharton* (Westport, Conn.: Greenwood, 1990).

Taylor, Helen, *Gender, Race, and Region in the Writings of Grace King, Ruth McEnery Stuart, and Kate Chopin* (Baton Rouge: Louisiana State UP, 1989).

Wyatt, Jean, *Reconstructing Desire*: *The Role of the Unconscious in Women's Reading and Writing* (Chapel Hill: Univ. of North Carolina Press, 1990).

Selected Essays and Articles

Bauer, Dale M., 'Kate Chopin's *The Awakening*: Having and Hating Tradition', in *Feminist Dialogics*: *A Theory of Failed Community* (Albany, NY: State Univ. of New York Press, 1988), 128–58.

Arner, Robert D., 'Pride and Prejudice: Kate Chopin's "Désirée's Baby"', *Mississippi Quarterly*, 25:2 (Spring 1972), 131–40.

Birnbaum, Michele A., '"Alien Hands": Kate Chopin and the Colonization of Race', *American Literature*, 66:2 (June 1994), 301–23.

Dawson, Hugh J., 'Kate Chopin's *The Awakening*: A Dissenting Opinion', *American Literary Realism 1870–1910*, 26:2 (Winter 1994), 1–18.

Dawson, Melanie, 'Edna and the Tradition of Listening: The Role of Romantic Music in *The Awakening*', *Southern Studies*, 3.2 (Summer 1992), 87–98.

Dimock, Wai-Chee, 'Rightful Subjectivity', *Yale Journal of Criticism*, 4:1 (1990), 25–51.

Dyer, Joyce Coyne, 'Night Images in the Work of Kate Chopin', *American Literary Realism, 1870–1910*, 14:2 (Autumn 1981), 216–230.

—— 'Lafcadio Hearn's *Chita* and Kate Chopin's *The Awakening*: Two Naturalistic Tales of the Gulf Islands', *Southern Studies*, 23:4 (Winter 1984), 412–26.

—— and Monroe, Robert Emmett, 'Texas and Texans in the Fiction of Kate Chopin', *Western American Literature*, 20 (1985), 3–15.

Franklin, Rosemary F., '*The Awakening* and the Failure of Psyche', *American Literature*, 56:4 (Dec. 1984), 510–26.

Gaudet, Marcia, 'Kate Chopin and the Lore of Cane River's Creoles of Color', *Xavier Review*, 6:1 (1986), 45–52.

Gunning, Sandra, 'Kate Chopin's Local Color Fiction and the Politics of White Supremacy', *Arizona Quarterly*, 51:3 (1995), 61–86.

Harrison, Antony H., 'Swinburne and the Critique of Ideology in *The Awakening*', in *Gender and Discourse in Victorian Literature and Art*, ed. Antony H. Harrison and Beverly Taylor (DeKalb, Ill.: Northern Illinois UP, 1992), 185–203.

Heath, Stephen, 'Chopin's Parrot', *Textual Practice*, 8:1 (1994), 11–32.

Hirsch, Marianne, 'Spiritual *Bildung*: The Beautiful Soul as Paradigm', in Elizabeth Abel *et al.* (eds.), *The Voyage In: Fictions of Female Development* (Hanover: Univ. Press of New England, 1983), 23–48.

Hochman, Barbara, '*The Awakening* and *The House of Mirth*: Plotting

Experience and Experiencing Plot', in Donald Pizer (ed.), *The Cambridge Companion to American Realism and Naturalism*: *Howells to London* (Cambridge: Cambridge UP, 1995), 211–35.

Kearns, Katherine, 'The Nullification of Edna Pontellier', *American Literature*, 63:1 (March 1991), 62–88.

Koloski, Bernard J., 'The Swinburne Lines in *The Awakening*', *American Literature*, 45 (1974), 608–10.

Kouidis, Virginia M., 'Prison into Prism: Emerson's "Many-Colored Lenses" and the Woman Writer of Early Modernism', in H. Daniel Peck (ed.), *The Green American Tradition*: *Essays and Poems for Sherman Paul* (Baton Rouge: Louisiana State University Press, 1989), 115–34.

Leary, Lewis, 'Kate Chopin and Walt Whitman' in *Southern Excursions*: *Essays on Mark Twain and Others* (Baton Rouge: Louisiana State UP, 1971), 169–74.

LeBlanc, Elizabeth, 'The Metaphorical Lesbian: Edna Pontellier in *The Awakening*', *Tulsa Studies in Women's Literature*, 15:2 (Fall 1996), 289–307.

Leder, Priscilla, 'An American Dilemma: Cultural Conflict in Kate Chopin's *The Awakening*', *Southern Studies*, 22 (Spring 1983), 97–104.

Linkin, Harriet Kramer, '"Call the Roller of Big Cigars": Smoking Out the Patriarchy in *The Awakening*', *Legacy*, 11:2 (1994), 130–42.

Peel, Ellen, 'Semiotic Subversion in "Désirée's Baby,"' *American Literature*, 62.2 (June 1990), 223–37.

Schulz, Dieter, 'Notes Toward a *fin-de-siécle* Reading of Kate Chopin's *The Awakening*', *American Literary Realism 1870–1910*, 25:3 (Spring 1993), 69–76.

Schweitzer, Ivy, 'Maternal Discourse and the Romance of Self-Possession in Kate Chopin's *The Awakening*', in Donald E. Pease (ed.), *Revisionary Interventions into the Americanist Canon* (Durham, NC: Duke UP, 1994), 158–86.

Shaw, Pat, 'Putting Audience in its Place: Psychosexuality and Perspective Shifts in *The Awakening*', *American Literary Realism 1870–1910*, 23:1 (1990), 61–9.

Shurbutt, Sylvia Bailey, 'The Cane River Characters and Revisionist Myth-Making in the Work of Kate Chopin', *Southern Literary Journal*, 25:2 (1993), 14–23.

Skaggs, Peggy, '"The Man-Instinct of Possession": A Persistent Theme in Kate Chopin's Stories', *Louisiana Studies*, 14:3 (Fall 1975), 277–85.

Smith-Rosenberg, Caroll, 'The Hysterical Woman: Sex Roles and Role Conflict in Nineteenth-Century America', in *Disorderly Conduct*: *Visions of Gender in Victorian America* (New York: Oxford UP, 1985). Useful discussion of medical discourses.

Stone, Carole, 'The Female Artist in Kate Chopin's *The Awakening*: Birth and Creativity', *Women's Studies*, 13 (1986), 23–32.

Taylor, Helen, 'Walking through New Orleans: Kate Chopin and the Female Flâneur', *Symbiosis* 1:1 (April 1997), 69–85.

Thomas, Heather Kirk, 'Kate Chopin's Scribbling Women and the American Literary Marketplace', *Studies in American Fiction*, 23:1 (1995), 19–34.

Thornton, Lawrence, '*The Awakening*: A Political Romance', *American Literature*, 52:1 (March 1980), 50–66.

Treichler, Paula A., 'The Construction of Ambiguity in *The Awakening*: A Linguistic Analysis', in Sally McConnell-Ginet *et al.* (eds.), *Women and Language in Literature and Society* (New York: Praeger, 1980), 239–57.

Vlasopolos, Anca, 'Staking Claims for No Territory: The Sea as Woman's Space', in Margaret R. Higonnet and Joan Templeton (eds.), *Reconfigured Spheres: Feminist Explorations of Literary Space* (Amherst: Univ. of Massachusetts Press, 1994), 72–88.

Walker, Nancy, 'Feminist or Naturalist: The Social Context of Kate Chopin's *The Awakening*', *Southern Quarterly*, 17:2 (1979), 95–103.

Toth, Emily, 'St. Louis and the Fiction of Kate Chopin', *Bulletin of the Missouri Historical Society*, 32 (October 1975), 33–50.

Wershoven, C. J., '*The Awakening* and *The House of Mirth*: Studies of Arrested Development', *American Literary Realism*, 19:3 (Spring 1987), 27–41.

Wolff, Cynthia Griffin, 'Un-Utterable Longing: The Discourse of Feminine Sexuality in *The Awakening*', *Studies in American Fiction*, 24:1 (1996), 3–22.

Yaeger, Patricia S., '"A Language Which Nobody Understood": Emancipatory Strategies in *The Awakening*', *Novel*, 20:3 (Spring 1987), 197–219.

Some Regional Contexts: Literary, Historical, Cultural

Ammons, Elizabeth and Rohy, Valerie (eds.), *American Local Color Writing, 1880–1920* (Harmondsworth: Penguin, 1998). An excellent anthology.

Benfey, Christopher, *Degas in New Orleans: Encounters in the Creole World of Kate Chopin and George Washington Cable* (New York: Knopf, 1997).

Brasseaux, Carl A., *Acadian to Cajun: Transformation of a People, 1803–1877* (Jackson: UP of Mississippi, 1992).

Brown, Dorothy and Ewell, Barbara (eds.), *Louisiana Women Writers: New Essays and a Comprehensive Bibliography* (Baton Rouge: Louisiana State UP, 1992).

Bryan, Violet Harrington, *The Myth of New Orleans in Literature*:

Dialogues of Race and Gender (Knoxville: Univ. of Tennessee Press, 1993).

Fetterley, Judith and Pryse, Marjorie, *American Women Regionalists 1850–1910* (New York: Norton, 1992). A richly illuminating selection.

Corbett, Katharine T. and Miller, Howard S., *Saint Louis in the Gilded Age* (St Louis: Missouri Historical Society, 1993).

Hirsch, Arnold R. and Logsdon, Joseph (eds.), *Creole New Orleans: Race and Americanization* (Baton Rouge: Louisiana State UP, 1992).

Jackson, Joy J., *New Orleans in the Gilded Age: Politics and Urban Progress, 1880–1896* (Baton Rouge: Louisiana State UP, 1969).

Pryse, Marjorie, ' "Distilling Essences": Regionalism and Women's Culture', *American Literary Realism 1870–1910*, 25:2 (Winter 1993), 1–15.

Wilds, John *et al.*, *Louisiana Yesterday and Today: A Historical Guide to the State* (Baton Rouge: Louisiana State UP, 1996).

Wood, Ann Douglas, 'The Literature of Impoverishment: The Woman Local Colorists in America 1865–1914', *Women's Studies*, 1 (1972), 3–45.

Further Reading in Oxford World's Classics

Cather, Willa, *Alexander's Bridge*, ed. Marilee Lindemann.

—— *O Pioneers!*, ed. Marilee Lindemann.

Flaubert, Gustave, *Madame Bovary*, tr. Gerard Hopkins.

Fuller, Margaret, *Woman in the Nineteenth Century and Other Writings*, ed. Donna Dickenson.

Gilman, Charlotte Perkins, *The Yellow Wall-Paper and Other Stories*, ed. Robert Shulman.

Ibsen, Henrik, *Four Major Plays*, trans. James McFarlane and Jens Arup, ed. James McFarlane.

Jewett, Sarah Orne, *The Country of the Pointed Firs and Other Fiction*, ed. Terry Heller.

Maupassant, Guy de, *A Day in the Country and Other Stories*, trans. and ed. David Coward.

——*Mademoiselle Fifi and Other Stories*, trans. and ed. David Coward.

Stowe, Harriet Beecher, *Uncle Tom's Cabin*, ed. Jean Fagan Yellin.

Wharton, Edith, *The Custom of the Country*, ed. Stephen Orgel.

—— *Ethan Frome*, ed. Elaine Showalter.

—— *The House of Mirth*, ed. Martha Banta.

—— *The Reef*, ed. Stephen Orgel.

A CHRONOLOGY OF KATE CHOPIN

1850   Catherine O'Flaherty (later Kate Chopin), born 8 Feb., St. Louis, Missouri. Daughter of successful Irish-born business-man, Thomas O'Flaherty (1805–55) and his second wife, Eliza (née Faris, 1828–85), a descendant, on her mother's side, from old St Louis French-speaking notables. Grows up in extended family in slave-holding household.

1855   1 Nov., father among guest dignitaries killed when Gasconade Bridge collapses under inaugural train. At 27, mother left a prosperous widow; she never remarries.

1855–68 Intermittently attends Academy of the Sacred Heart, sometimes as a boarder, following traditional 'Plan of Studies' and convent rituals. Learns French and piano from charismatic great-grandmother, Mme Charleville.

1861–65 Civil War divides St Louis, along French/German lines. Family sympathizes with Southern slaveholders and the Confederate cause. Half-brother George enlists with Missouri mounted infantry. Union headquarters set up in St Louis, close to family home. Kate is briefly arrested for tearing down a Yankee flag. George taken prisoner Aug. 1862, released Nov. In Louisiana, French-born Dr Victor Chopin sends family to France, to keep 17-year-old son Oscar out of the fighting.

1863   Jan., great-grandmother dies. Feb., George dies of typhoid aged 22. July, Union soldiers break into mother's garden after Confederate surrender at Vicksburg.

1864   Family slaves run off.

1866   Nov., elected as one of Children of Mary, the greatest Sacred Heart honour. Oscar Chopin (1844–82), a relation of the eminent St Louis Benoist dynasty, comes to the city from Natchitoches Parish, Louisiana, to study banking with the family firm.

1867–70 Keeps Commonplace Book, as literary record and diary.

1868   Graduates with highest honours from Sacred Heart. Reluctantly follows social season as a fashionable St Louis belle.

1869   Spring, visit to New Orleans. Diary breaks off, 24 May. Writes allegorical sketch, 'Emancipation. A Life Fable'. At some point, meets Oscar Chopin.

1870   Diary resumes, 24 May, announcing imminent marriage. 9 June, marries Oscar Chopin. June–Sept., honeymoon tour. Chopins visit Germany and Switzerland, but outbreak of Franco-Prussian war interrupts travel. Arrive in Paris as Second Empire falls (4 Sept.); leave for home shortly before the devastating siege.

1870–79 Chopins live in the American section of New Orleans, during restless years of Reconstruction (1865–77). Kate remains close to her mother who supports her through several confinements. May 1871, birth of son, Jean (d. 1911), delivered with aid of chloroform; followed by births of Oscar (1873–1933), George (1874–1952), Fred (1876–1953), and Felix (1878–1955). Oscar works with some success as cotton-factor and commission merchant. They twice upgrade their address, reaching 209 (now 1413) Louisiana Avenue in the Garden District in 1876. Summer vacations at Grand Isle.

1873   Brother, Tom, is thrown out of a runaway buggy, and dies aged 25.

1874   May–Nov., in St Louis for birth and baptism of George. Oscar spends summer in New Orleans, where he joins the militant Crescent City White League, and (14 Sept.) takes part in the violent conflict on Canal Street (known as the Battle of Liberty Place).

1879–81 New Orleans afflicted by post-war debts, made worse by deadly 1878 yellow fever epidemic. Chopins in financial difficulties leave city for northwest Louisiana. Settle in tiny French village, Cloutierville, in Natchitoches Parish. Lélia, only daughter, born 31 Dec. 1879 (d. 1962). Oscar (inefficiently) runs general store, where Kate occasionally helps. Oct. 1881, Kate departs for several months in St Louis without Oscar.

1882   Oscar succumbs to swamp fever (malaria). Dies, aged 38 (10 Dec.), leaving Kate with huge debts, overdue taxes, and threats to various mortgages.

1883–84 Manages own finances, pays debts and sells property. Proficiently runs store and remaining plantations. Settles accounts by March 1884. Possibly romantically involved with married planter, Albert Sampite (1844?–1913). Mid-1884, rents out Cloutierville house, returning to mother's home in St Louis.

1885   June, mother dies, aged 56.

1886–88 Buys house in St Louis for self and children. Lives on income from land and rental properties, but is encouraged to write by her obstetrician, Viennese-trained radical, Dr Frederick Kolbenheyer (one of several close male friends throughout her life). Revisits Natchitoches Parish. Begins first story (rev. as 'A No-Account Creole', 1894). 'Lilia. Polka for Piano', privately printed (1888). Begins 'Unfinished Story—Grand Isle' (later destroyed).

1889   First published writings. Jan., poem 'If It Might Be' appears in prestigious Chicago magazine, *America*. June, writes 'Wiser than a God' (pub. Dec.); Aug. writes 'A Point at Issue!' (pub. Oct.); July, begins first novel, *At Fault*, and continues writing short fiction, including first of many children's stories. Also (April), has Oscar's coffin shipped back from Louisiana for reburial in St Louis.

1890   April, completes *At Fault*, pub. at own expense (Sept.). May–Nov., writes novel, *Young Dr. Gosse* (later destroyed). Publishes first of many translations from French. Dec., becomes charter member of women's Wednesday Club of St Louis. (Charlotte Eliot, mother of future poet, T. S. Eliot, is one of its founders.)

1891   Completes more translations, sixteen stories, and a one-act comedy. Enters story contests and places work in national magazines. Nov.–Dec., revisits Louisiana.

1892   Maintains prolific output. March, draws on real-life St Louis scandal and on Wednesday Club's reform interests for satirical 'Miss McEnders' (pub. 1897); April, resigns from Club. Uses Louisiana material in 'At the 'Cadian Ball', 'Caline', and other stories.

1893   14 Jan., two stories in newly-founded *Vogue*. May, financial panic in New York leads to nationwide depression: Kate's rental incomes survive. Visits New York and Boston, in search of publishers. Aug., Houghton, Mifflin accept 'Collection of Creole Stories' (*Bayou Folk*). 1 Oct., hurricane devastates Grand Isle and Chênière Caminada. 21–23 Oct., uses Gulf setting in 'Tonie' (later retitled 'At Chênière Caminada').

1894   *Bayou Folk* pub. March, to praise in North and South. May, begins diary, *Impressions*. June, attends Western Association of Writers conference in Indiana; writes controversial essay criticizing the group. Writes 'The Dream of an Hour', translations from Maupassant (d. July 1893), and a dozen other stories. Becoming known for her Thursday evening gatherings.

1895–96 Possibly suffers from eye problems, but remains productive and experimental: writing includes 'Athénaïse', 'A Pair of Silk Stockings', 'The Unexpected', and 'Vagabonds'.

1897 Jan., death of grandmother, Athénaïse Charleville Faris. April, writes 'An Egyptian Cigarette'. (April–June?) Begins work on 'A Solitary Soul' (*The Awakening*). Brief visit to Louisiana. Nov., Way & Williams publish *A Night in Acadie*.

1898 Jan., finishes *The Awakening*: accepted by Way & Williams. March, unsuccessful visit to Chicago to find a literary agent. Fiction includes 'Elizabeth Stock's One Story', but devotes much of the year to poems. Feb.–Aug., insurrection in Cuba and Spanish-American war. Son, Fred, 22, enlists and leaves for military training. Kate helps organize benefits. War ends as Fred's company reaches Puerto Rico. July, writes 'The Storm'. Dec., sells house in Cloutierville and visits New Orleans.

1899 *The Awakening* and *A Vocation and a Voice*, transferred to Herbert S. Stone. *The Awakening* pub. 22 April. Reviews praise art and psychological acuity, but many censure distasteful themes. She prints ironic apology for her heroine's behaviour. Honoured at Wednesday Club literary afternoon, where she reads to nearly four hundred guests and her poems are sung to original settings. Dec., daughter, Lélia, presented as a debutante.

1900–1901 Works on long story, 'Charlie', and children's tales. Feb., publisher returns *A Vocation and a Voice*. *Vogue* prints 'An Egyptian Cigarette'. Features in census as a 'capitalist', with 1849 birthdate, and in *Who's Who in America* with 1851 birthdate. Begins selling Louisiana lands.

1902 Writes 'Polly's Opportunity' (final publication: *Youth's Companion*, July). June, marriage of son, Jean. Dec., makes will, dividing property between her five sons. Leaves daughter jewellery, clothes, and a valuable piece of city land, to be preserved from claims by a future husband.

1903 Moves house, along with Felix (now a lawyer), Fred (a superintendent), Oscar (a newspaper cartoonist), and Lélia (a society lady, later a professional bridge player and author of books on bridge and backgammon). July, daughter-in-law dies in childbirth along with the baby, Kate's first grandchild. Son, Jean, returns home in state of breakdown.

1904 30 April, World's Fair opens in St Louis. Visits on season ticket. 20 Aug., collapses after hot day at the Fair. 22 Aug., dies,

attended by physician son, George, and other children. 24 Aug.,
Cathedral Requiem Mass. Honoured in St Louis and New
Orleans obituaries. (Gravestone in St Louis Calvary Cemetery
records birthdate as 1851, and will long confuse biographers.)

THE AWAKENING
and Other Stories

THE AWAKENING

I

A green and yellow parrot, which hung in a cage outside the door, kept repeating over and over:

"*Allez vous-en! Allez vous-en! Sapristi!** That's all right!"

He could speak a little Spanish, and also a language which nobody understood, unless it was the mocking-bird that hung on the other side of the door, whistling his fluty notes out upon the breeze with maddening persistence.

Mr. Pontellier, unable to read his newspaper with any degree of comfort, arose with an expression and an exclamation of disgust. He walked down the gallery* and across the narrow "bridges" which connected the Lebrun cottages one with the other. He had been seated before the door of the main house. The parrot and the mocking-bird were the property of Madame Lebrun, and they had the right to make all the noise they wished. Mr. Pontellier had the privilege of quitting their society when they ceased to be entertaining.

He stopped before the door of his own cottage, which was the fourth one from the main building and next to the last. Seating himself in a wicker rocker which was there, he once more applied himself to the task of reading the newspaper. The day was Sunday; the paper was a day old. The Sunday papers had not yet reached Grand Isle.* He was already acquainted with the market reports, and he glanced restlessly over the editorials and bits of news which he had not had time to read before quitting New Orleans the day before.

Mr. Pontellier wore eye-glasses. He was a man of forty, of medium height and rather slender build; he stooped a little. His hair was brown and straight, parted on one side. His beard was neatly and closely trimmed.

Once in a while he withdrew his glance from the newspaper and looked about him. There was more noise than ever over at the house. The main building was called "the house," to distinguish it from the cottages. The chattering and whistling birds were still at it. Two young girls, the Farival twins, were playing a duet from "Zampa"* upon the piano. Madame Lebrun* was bustling in and out, giving orders in a high key to a yard-boy whenever she got inside the house, and directions in an equally high voice to a dining-room servant whenever she got outside. She was a fresh, pretty woman, clad always in white with elbow sleeves. Her starched skirts crinkled as she came and went. Farther down, before one of the cottages, a lady in black was walking demurely up and down, telling her beads. A good many persons of the *pension* had gone over to the *Chênière Caminada** in Beaudelet's lugger* to hear mass. Some young people were out under the water-oaks playing croquet. Mr. Pontellier's two children were there—sturdy little fellows of four and five. A quadroon* nurse followed them about with a far-away, meditative air.

Mr. Pontellier finally lit a cigar and began to smoke, letting the paper drag idly from his hand. He fixed his gaze upon a white sunshade that was advancing at snail's pace from the beach. He could see it plainly between the gaunt trunks of the water-oaks and across the stretch of yellow camomile. The gulf looked far away, melting hazily into the blue of the horizon. The sunshade continued to approach slowly. Beneath its pink-lined shelter were his wife, Mrs. Pontellier, and young Robert Lebrun. When they reached the cottage, the two seated themselves with some appearance of fatigue upon the upper step of the porch, facing each other, each leaning against a supporting post.

"What folly! to bathe at such an hour in such heat!" exclaimed Mr. Pontellier. He himself had taken a plunge at daylight. That was why the morning seemed long to him.

"You are burnt beyond recognition," he added, looking at his wife as one looks at a valuable piece of personal property which has suffered some damage. She held up her hands, strong, shapely hands, and surveyed them critically, drawing up her lawn* sleeves above the wrists. Looking at them reminded her of her rings, which she had given to her husband before leaving for the beach. She silently reached out to him, and he, understanding, took the rings from his vest pocket and dropped them into her open palm. She slipped them upon her fingers; then clasping her knees, she looked across at Robert and began to laugh. The rings sparkled upon her fingers. He sent back an answering smile.

"What is it?" asked Pontellier, looking lazily and amused from one to the other. It was some utter nonsense; some adventure out there in the water, and they both tried to relate it at once. It did not seem half so amusing when told. They realized this, and so did Mr. Pontellier. He yawned and stretched himself. Then he got up, saying he had half a mind to go over to Klein's hotel* and play a game of billiards.

"Come go along, Lebrun," he proposed to Robert. But Robert admitted quite frankly that he preferred to stay where he was and talk to Mrs. Pontellier.

"Well, send him about his business when he bores you, Edna," instructed her husband as he prepared to leave.

"Here, take the umbrella," she exclaimed, holding it out to him. He accepted the sunshade, and lifting it over his head descended the steps and walked away.

"Coming back to dinner?" his wife called after him. He halted a moment and shrugged his shoulders. He felt in his vest pocket; there was a ten-dollar bill there. He did not know; perhaps he would return for the early dinner and perhaps he would not. It all depended upon the company which he found over at Klein's and the size of "the game." He did not say this, but she understood it, and laughed, nodding good-by to him.

Both children wanted to follow their father when they saw him starting out. He kissed them and promised to bring them back bonbons and peanuts.

II

Mrs. Pontellier's eyes were quick and bright; they were a yellowish brown, about the color of her hair. She had a way of turning them swiftly upon an object and holding them there as if lost in some inward maze of contemplation or thought.

Her eyebrows were a shade darker than her hair. They were thick and almost horizontal, emphasizing the depth of her eyes. She was rather handsome than beautiful. Her face was captivating by reason of a certain frankness of expression and a contradictory subtle play of features. Her manner was engaging.

Robert rolled a cigarette. He smoked cigarettes because he could not afford cigars,* he said. He had a cigar in his pocket which Mr. Pontellier had presented him with, and he was saving it for his after-dinner smoke.

This seemed quite proper and natural on his part. In coloring he was not unlike his companion. A clean-shaved face made the resemblance more pronounced than it would otherwise have been. There rested no shadow of care upon his open countenance. His eyes gathered in and reflected the light and languor of the summer day.

Mrs. Pontellier reached over for a palm-leaf fan that lay on the porch and began to fan herself, while Robert sent between his lips light puffs from his cigarette. They chatted incessantly: about the things around them; their amusing adventure out in the water—it had again assumed its entertaining aspect; about the wind, the trees, the people who had gone to the *Chênière*; about the children playing croquet under the oaks, and the Farival twins, who were now performing the overture to "The Poet and the Peasant."*

Robert talked a good deal about himself. He was very young, and did not know any better. Mrs. Pontellier talked a little about herself for the same reason. Each was interested in what the other said. Robert spoke of his intention to go to Mexico in the autumn, where fortune awaited him. He was always intending to go to Mexico, but some way never got there. Meanwhile he held on to his modest position in a mercantile house in New Orleans, where an equal familiarity with English, French and Spanish gave him no small value as a clerk and correspondent.

He was spending his summer vacation, as he always did, with his mother at Grand Isle. In former times, before Robert could remember, "the house" had been a summer luxury of the Lebruns. Now, flanked by its dozen or more cottages, which were always filled with exclusive visitors from the "*Quartier Français*,"* it enabled Madame Lebrun to maintain the easy and comfortable existence which appeared to be her birthright.

Mrs. Pontellier talked about her father's Mississippi plantation and her girlhood home in the old Kentucky blue-grass country.* She was an American woman, with a small infusion of French* which seemed to have been lost in dilution. She read a letter from her sister, who was away in the East, and who had engaged herself to be married. Robert was interested, and wanted to know what manner of girls the sisters were, what the father was like, and how long the mother had been dead.

When Mrs. Pontellier folded the letter it was time for her to dress for the early dinner.

"I see Léonce isn't coming back," she said, with a glance in the direction whence her husband had disappeared. Robert supposed he was not, as there were a good many New Orleans club men* over at Klein's.

When Mrs. Pontellier left him to enter her room, the young man descended the steps and strolled over toward the croquet players, where, during the half-hour before dinner, he amused himself with the little Pontellier children, who were very fond of him.

III

It was eleven o'clock that night when Mr. Pontellier returned from Klein's hotel. He was in an excellent humor, in high spirits, and very talkative. His entrance awoke his wife, who was in bed and fast asleep when he came in. He talked to her while he undressed, telling her anecdotes and bits of news and gossip that he had gathered during the day. From his trousers pockets he took a fistful of crumpled bank notes and a good deal of silver coin, which he piled on the bureau indiscriminately with keys, knife, handkerchief, and whatever else happened to be in his pockets. She was overcome with sleep, and answered him with little half utterances.

He thought it very discouraging that his wife, who was the sole object of his existence, evinced so little interest in things which concerned him, and valued so little his conversation.

Mr. Pontellier had forgotten the bonbons and peanuts for the boys. Notwithstanding he loved them very much, and went into the adjoining room where they slept to take a look at them and make sure that they were resting comfortably. The result of his investigation was far from satisfactory. He turned and shifted the youngsters about in bed. One of them began to kick and talk about a basket full of crabs.

Mr. Pontellier returned to his wife with the information that Raoul had a high fever and needed looking after. Then he lit a cigar and went and sat near the open door to smoke it.

Mrs. Pontellier was quite sure Raoul had no fever. He had gone to bed perfectly well, she said, and nothing had ailed him all day. Mr. Pontellier was too well acquainted with fever symptoms to be mistaken. He assured her the child was consuming at that moment in the next room.

He reproached his wife with her inattention, her habitual neglect
of the children. If it was not a mother's place to look after children,
whose on earth was it? He himself had his hands full with his
brokerage business. He could not be in two places at once; making a
living for his family on the street, and staying at home to see that no
harm befell them. He talked in a monotonous, insistent way.

Mrs. Pontellier sprang out of bed and went into the next room.
She soon came back and sat on the edge of the bed, leaning her head
down on the pillow. She said nothing, and refused to answer her
husband when he questioned her. When his cigar was smoked out he
went to bed, and in half a minute he was fast asleep.

Mrs. Pontellier was by that time thoroughly awake. She began to
cry a little, and wiped her eyes on the sleeve of her *peignoir*. Blowing
out the candle, which her husband had left burning, she slipped her
bare feet into a pair of satin *mules* at the foot of the bed and went out
on the porch, where she sat down in the wicker chair and began to
rock gently to and fro.

It was then past midnight. The cottages were all dark. A single
faint light gleamed out from the hallway of the house. There was no
sound abroad except the hooting of an old owl in the top of a water-
oak, and the everlasting voice of the sea, that was not uplifted at that
soft hour. It broke like a mournful lullaby upon the night.

The tears came so fast to Mrs. Pontellier's eyes that the damp
sleeve of her *peignoir* no longer served to dry them. She was holding
the back of her chair with one hand; her loose sleeve had slipped
almost to the shoulder of her uplifted arm. Turning, she thrust her
face, steaming and wet, into the bend of her arm, and she went on
crying there, not caring any longer to dry her face, her eyes, her
arms. She could not have told why she was crying. Such experiences
as the foregoing were not uncommon in her married life. They
seemed never before to have weighed much against the abundance of
her husband's kindness and a uniform devotion which had come to
be tacit and self-understood.

An indescribable oppression, which seemed to generate in some
unfamiliar part of her consciousness, filled her whole being with a
vague anguish. It was like a shadow, like a mist passing across her
soul's summer day. It was strange and unfamiliar; it was a mood. She
did not sit there inwardly upbraiding her husband, lamenting at
Fate, which had directed her footsteps to the path which they had

taken. She was just having a good cry all to herself. The mosquitoes made merry over her, biting her firm, round arms and nipping at her bare insteps.

The little stinging, buzzing imps succeeded in dispelling a mood which might have held her there in the darkness half a night longer.

The following morning Mr. Pontellier was up in good time to take the rockaway* which was to convey him to the steamer at the wharf. He was returning to the city to his business, and they would not see him again at the Island till the coming Saturday. He had regained his composure, which seemed to have been somewhat impaired the night before. He was eager to be gone, as he looked forward to a lively week in Carondelet Street.*

Mr. Pontellier gave his wife half of the money which he had brought away from Klein's hotel the evening before. She liked money as well as most women, and accepted it with no little satisfaction.

"It will buy a handsome wedding present for Sister Janet!" she exclaimed, smoothing out the bills as she counted them one by one.

"Oh! we'll treat Sister Janet better than that, my dear," he laughed, as he prepared to kiss her good-by.

The boys were tumbling about, clinging to his legs, imploring that numerous things be brought back to them. Mr. Pontellier was a great favorite, and ladies, men, children, even nurses, were always on hand to say good-by to him. His wife stood smiling and waving, the boys shouting, as he disappeared in the old rockaway down the sandy road.

A few days later a box arrived for Mrs. Pontellier from New Orleans. It was from her husband. It was filled with *friandises*, with luscious and toothsome bits—the finest of fruits, *patés*, a rare bottle or two, delicious syrups, and bonbons in abundance.

Mrs. Pontellier was always very generous with the contents of such a box; she was quite used to receiving them when away from home. The *patés* and fruit were brought to the dining-room; the bonbons were passed around. And the ladies, selecting with dainty and discriminating fingers and a little greedily, all declared that Mr. Pontellier was the best husband in the world. Mrs. Pontellier was forced to admit that she knew of none better.

IV

It would have been a difficult matter for Mr. Pontellier to define to his own satisfaction or any one else's wherein his wife failed in her duty toward their children. It was something which he felt rather than perceived, and he never voiced the feeling without subsequent regret and ample atonement.

If one of the little Pontellier boys took a tumble whilst at play, he was not apt to rush crying to his mother's arms for comfort; he would more likely pick himself up, wipe the water out of his eyes and the sand out of his mouth, and go on playing. Tots as they were, they pulled together and stood their ground in childish battles with doubled fists and uplifted voices, which usually prevailed against the other mother-tots. The quadroon nurse was looked upon as a huge encumbrance, only good to button up waists and panties and to brush and part hair; since it seemed to be a law of society that hair must be parted and brushed.

In short, Mrs. Pontellier was not a mother-woman.* The mother-women seemed to prevail that summer at Grand Isle. It was easy to know them, fluttering about with extended, protecting wings when any harm, real or imaginary, threatened their precious brood. They were women who idolized their children, worshiped their husbands, and esteemed it a holy privilege to efface themselves as individuals and grow wings as ministering angels.

Many of them were delicious in the rôle; one of them was the embodiment of every womanly grace and charm. If her husband did not adore her, he was a brute, deserving of death by slow torture. Her name was Adèle Ratignolle. There are no words to describe her save the old ones that have served so often to picture the bygone heroine of romance and the fair lady of our dreams. There was nothing subtle or hidden about her charms; her beauty was all there, flaming and apparent: the spun-gold hair that comb nor confining pin could restrain; the blue eyes that were like nothing but sapphires; two lips that pouted, that were so red one could only think of cherries or some other delicious crimson fruit in looking at them. She was growing a little stout, but it did not seem to detract an iota from the grace of every step, pose, gesture. One would not have wanted her white neck a mite less full or her beautiful arms more slender. Never were hands more exquisite than hers, and it was a joy to look at them when she threaded her needle or adjusted her gold thimble to her taper middle finger as she sewed away on the little night-drawers or fashioned a bodice or a bib.

Madame Ratignolle was very fond of Mrs. Pontellier, and often she took her sewing and went over to sit with her in the afternoons. She was sitting there the afternoon of the day the box arrived from New Orleans. She had possession of the rocker, and she was busily engaged in sewing upon a diminutive pair of night-drawers.

She had brought the pattern of the drawers for Mrs. Pontellier to cut out—a marvel of construction, fashioned to enclose a baby's body so effectually that only two small eyes might look out from the garment, like an Eskimo's. They were designed for winter wear, when treacherous drafts came down chimneys and insidious currents of deadly cold found their way through key-holes.

Mrs. Pontellier's mind was quite at rest concerning the present material needs of her children, and she could not see the use of anticipating and making winter night garments the subject of her summer meditations. But she did not want to appear unamiable and uninterested, so she had brought forth newspapers, which she spread upon the floor of the gallery, and under Madame Ratignolle's directions she had cut a pattern of the impervious garment.

Robert was there, seated as he had been the Sunday before, and Mrs. Pontellier also occupied her former position on the upper step, leaning listlessly against the post. Beside her was a box of bonbons, which she held out at intervals to Madame Ratignolle.

That lady seemed at a loss to make a selection, but finally settled upon a stick of nugat, wondering if it were not too rich; whether it could possibly hurt her. Madame Ratignolle had been married seven years. About every two years she had a baby. At that time she had three babies, and was beginning to think of a fourth one. She was always talking about her "condition." Her "condition" was in no way apparent, and no one would have known a thing about it but for her persistence in making it the subject of conversation.

Robert started to reassure her, asserting that he had known a lady who had subsisted upon nugat during the entire—but seeing the color mount into Mrs. Pontellier's face he checked himself and changed the subject.

Mrs. Pontellier, though she had married a Creole, was not thoroughly at home in the society of Creoles;* never before had she been thrown so intimately among them. There were only Creoles that summer at Lebrun's. They all knew each other, and felt like one large family, among whom existed the most amicable relations. A characteristic which distinguished them and which impressed Mrs. Pontellier most forcibly was their entire absence of prudery. Their freedom of expression was at first incomprehensible to her, though she had no difficulty in reconciling it with a lofty chastity which in the Creole woman seems to be inborn and unmistakable.

Never would Edna Pontellier forget the shock with which she heard Madame Ratignolle relating to old Monsieur Farival the harrowing story of one of her *accouchements*, withholding no intimate detail. She was growing accustomed to like shocks, but she could not keep the mounting color back from her cheeks. Oftener than once her coming had interrupted the droll story with which Robert was entertaining some amused group of married women.

A book had gone the rounds of the *pension*. When it came her turn to read it, she did so with profound astonishment. She felt moved to read the book in secret and solitude, though none of the others had done so—to hide it from view at the sound of approaching footsteps. It was openly criticised and freely discussed at table. Mrs. Pontellier gave over being astonished, and concluded that wonders would never cease.

V

They formed a congenial group sitting there that summer afternoon—Madame Ratignolle sewing away, often stopping to relate a story or incident with much expressive gesture of her perfect hands; Robert and Mrs. Pontellier sitting idle, exchanging occasional words, glances or smiles which indicated a certain advanced stage of intimacy and *camaraderie*.

He had lived in her shadow during the past month. No one thought anything of it. Many had predicted that Robert would devote himself to Mrs. Pontellier when he arrived. Since the age of fifteen, which was eleven years before, Robert each summer at Grand Isle had constituted himself the devoted attendant of some fair dame or damsel. Sometimes it was a young girl, again a widow; but as often as not it was some interesting married woman.

For two consecutive seasons he lived in the sunlight of Mademoiselle Duvigné's presence.* But she died between summers; then Robert posed as an inconsolable, prostrating himself at the feet of Madame Ratignolle for whatever crumbs of sympathy and comfort she might be pleased to vouchsafe.

Mrs. Pontellier liked to sit and gaze at her fair companion as she might look upon a faultless Madonna.

"Could any one fathom the cruelty beneath that fair exterior?" murmured Robert. "She knew that I adored her once, and she let me adore her. It was 'Robert, come; go; stand up; sit down; do this; do that; see if the baby sleeps; my thimble, please, that I left God knows where. Come and read Daudet* to me while I sew.' "

"Par exemple! I never had to ask. You were always there under my feet, like a troublesome cat."

"You mean like an adoring dog. And just as soon as Ratignolle appeared on the scene, then it *was* like a dog. *'Passez! Adieu! Allez vous-en!'* "*

"Perhaps I feared to make Alphonse jealous," she interjoined, with excessive naïveté. That made them all laugh. The right hand jealous of the left! The heart jealous of the soul! But for that matter, the Creole husband is never jealous;* with him the gangrene passion is one which has become dwarfed by disuse.

Meanwhile Robert, addressing Mrs. Pontellier, continued to tell of his one time hopeless passion for Madame Ratignolle; of sleepless nights, of consuming flames till the very sea sizzled when he took his daily plunge. While the lady at the needle kept up a little running, contemptuous comment:

*"Blagueur—farceur—gros bête, va!"**

He never assumed this serio-comic tone when alone with Mrs. Pontellier. She never knew precisely what to make of it; at that moment it was impossible for her to guess how much of it was jest and what proportion was earnest. It was understood that he had often spoken words of love to Madame Ratignolle, without any thought of being taken seriously. Mrs. Pontellier was glad he had not assumed a similar rôle toward herself. It would have been unacceptable and annoying.

Mrs. Pontellier had brought her sketching materials, which she sometimes dabbled with in an unprofessional way. She liked the dabbling. She felt in it satisfaction of a kind which no other employment afforded her.

She had long wished to try herself on Madame Ratignolle. Never had that lady seemed a more tempting subject than at that moment, seated there like some sensuous Madonna, with the gleam of the fading day enriching her splendid color.

Robert crossed over and seated himself upon the step below Mrs. Pontellier, that he might watch her work. She handled her brushes with a certain ease and freedom which came, not from long and close acquaintance with them, but from a natural aptitude. Robert followed her work with close attention, giving forth little ejaculatory expressions of appreciation in French, which he addressed to Madame Ratignolle.

"*Mais ce n'est pas mal! Elle s'y connait, elle a de la force, oui.*"*

During his oblivious attention he once quietly rested his head against Mrs. Pontellier's arm. As gently she repulsed him. Once again he repeated the offense. She could not but believe it to be thoughtlessness on his part; yet that was no reason she should submit to it. She did not remonstrate, except again to repulse him quietly but firmly. He offered no apology.

The picture completed bore no resemblance to Madame Ratignolle. She was greatly disappointed to find that it did not look like her. But it was a fair enough piece of work, and in many respects satisfying.

Mrs. Pontellier evidently did not think so. After surveying the sketch critically she drew a broad smudge of paint across its surface, and crumpled the paper between her hands.

The youngsters came tumbling up the steps, the quadroon following at the respectful distance which they required her to observe. Mrs. Pontellier made them carry her paints and things into the house. She sought to detain them for a little talk and some pleasantry. But they were greatly in earnest. They had only come to investigate the contents of the bonbon box. They accepted without murmuring what she chose to give them, each holding out two chubby hands scoop-like, in the vain hope that they might be filled; and then away they went.

The sun was low in the west, and the breeze soft and languorous that came up from the south, charged with the seductive odor of the sea. Children, freshly befurbelowed, were gathering for their games under the oaks. Their voices were high and penetrating.

Madame Ratignolle folded her sewing, placing thimble, scissors and thread all neatly together in the roll, which she pinned securely. She complained of faintness. Mrs. Pontellier flew for the cologne water and a fan. She bathed Madame Ratignolle's face with cologne, while Robert plied the fan with unnecessary vigor.

The spell was soon over, and Mrs. Pontellier could not help wondering if there were not a little imagination responsible for its origin, for the rose tint had never faded from her friend's face.

She stood watching the fair woman walk down the long line of galleries with the grace and majesty which queens are sometimes supposed to possess. Her little ones ran to meet her. Two of them clung about her white skirts, the third she took from its nurse and with a thousand endearments bore it along in her own fond, encircling arms. Though, as everybody well knew, the doctor had forbidden her to lift so much as a pin!

"Are you going bathing?" asked Robert of Mrs. Pontellier. It was not so much a question as a reminder.

"Oh, no," she answered, with a tone of indecision. "I'm tired; I think not." Her glance wandered from his face away toward the Gulf, whose sonorous murmur reached her like a loving but imperative entreaty.

"Oh, come!" he insisted. "You mustn't miss your bath. Come on. The water must be delicious; it will not hurt you. Come."

He reached up for her big, rough straw hat that hung on a peg outside the door, and put it on her head. They descended the steps, and walked away together toward the beach. The sun was low in the west and the breeze was soft and warm.

VI

Edna Pontellier* could not have told why, wishing to go to the beach with Robert, she should in the first place have declined, and in the second place have followed in obedience to one of the two contradictory impulses which impelled her.

A certain light was beginning to dawn dimly within her,—the light which, showing the way, forbids it.

At that early period it served but to bewilder her. It moved her to dreams, to thoughtfulness, to the shadowy anguish which had overcome her the midnight when she had abandoned herself to tears.

In short, Mrs. Pontellier was beginning to realize her position in the universe as a human being, and to recognize her relations as an individual to the world within and about her. This may seem like a ponderous weight of wisdom to descend upon the soul of a young woman of twenty-eight—perhaps more wisdom than the Holy Ghost is usually pleased to vouchsafe to any woman.

But the beginning of things, of a world especially, is necessarily vague, tangled, chaotic, and exceedingly disturbing. How few of us ever emerge from such beginning! How many souls perish in its tumult!

The voice of the sea is seductive; never ceasing, whispering, clamoring, murmuring, inviting the soul to wander for a spell in abysses of solitude; to lose itself in mazes of inward contemplation.

The voice of the sea speaks to the soul. The touch of the sea is sensuous, enfolding the body in its soft, close embrace.

VII

Mrs. Pontellier was not a woman given to confidences, a characteristic hitherto contrary to her nature. Even as a child she had lived her own small life all within herself. At a very early period she had apprehended instinctively the dual life—that outward existence which conforms, the inward life which questions.

That summer at Grand Isle she began to loosen a little the mantle of reserve that had always enveloped her. There may have been—there must have been—influences, both subtle and apparent, working in their several ways to induce her to do this; but the most obvious was the influence of Adèle Ratignolle. The excessive physical charm of the Creole had first attracted her, for Edna had a sensuous susceptibility to beauty. Then the candor of the woman's whole existence, which every one might read, and which formed so striking a contrast to her own habitual reserve—this might have furnished a link. Who can tell what metals the gods use in forging the subtle bond which we call sympathy, which we might as well call love.

The two women went away one morning to the beach together, arm in arm, under the huge white sunshade. Edna had prevailed upon Madame Ratignolle to leave the children behind, though she could not induce her to relinquish a diminutive roll of needlework, which Adèle begged to be allowed to slip into the depths of her pocket. In some unaccountable way they had escaped from Robert.

The walk to the beach was no inconsiderable one, consisting as it did of a long, sandy path, upon which a sporadic and tangled growth that bordered it on either side made frequent and unexpected inroads. There were acres of yellow camomile reaching out on either hand. Further away still, vegetable gardens abounded, with frequent small plantations of orange or lemon trees intervening. The dark green clusters glistened from afar in the sun.

The women were both of goodly height, Madame Ratignolle possessing the more feminine and matronly figure. The charm of Edna Pontellier's physique stole insensibly upon you. The lines of her body were long, clean and symmetrical; it was a body which occasionally fell into splendid poses; there was no suggestion of the trim, stereotyped fashion-plate about it. A casual and indiscriminating observer, in passing, might not cast a second glance upon the figure. But with more feeling and discernment he would have recognized the noble beauty of its modeling, and the graceful severity of poise and movement, which made Edna Pontellier different from the crowd.

She wore a cool muslin that morning—white, with a waving vertical line of brown running through it; also a white linen collar and the big straw hat which she had taken from the peg outside the door. The hat rested any way on her yellow-brown hair, that waved a little, was heavy, and clung close to her head.

Madame Ratignolle, more careful of her complexion, had twined a gauze veil about her head. She wore dogskin gloves, with gauntlets that protected her wrists. She was dressed in pure white, with a fluffiness of ruffles that became her. The draperies and fluttering things which she wore suited her rich, luxuriant beauty as a greater severity of line could not have done.

There were a number of bath-houses along the beach, of rough but solid construction, built with small, protecting galleries facing the water. Each house consisted of two compartments, and each family at Lebrun's possessed a compartment for itself, fitted out with all the essential paraphernalia of the bath and whatever other conveniences the owners might desire. The two women had no intention of bathing; they had just strolled down to the beach for a walk and to be alone and near the water. The Pontellier and Ratignolle compartments adjoined one another under the same roof.

Mrs. Pontellier had brought down her key through force of habit. Unlocking the door of her bath-room she went inside, and soon emerged, bringing a rug, which she spread upon the floor of the gallery, and two huge hair pillows covered with crash,* which she placed against the front of the building.

The two seated themselves there in the shade of the porch, side by side, with their backs against the pillows and their feet extended. Madame Ratignolle removed her veil, wiped her face with a rather delicate handkerchief, and fanned herself with the fan which she always carried suspended somewhere about her person by a long, narrow ribbon. Edna removed her collar and opened her dress at the throat. She took the fan from Madame Ratignolle and began to fan both herself and her companion. It was very warm, and for a while they did nothing but exchange remarks about the heat, the sun, the glare. But there was a breeze blowing, a choppy, stiff wind that whipped the water into froth. It fluttered the skirts of the two women and kept them for a while engaged in adjusting, readjusting, tucking in, securing hair-pins and hat-pins. A few persons were sporting some distance away in the water. The beach was very still of human sound at that hour. The lady in black was reading her morning devotions on the porch of a neighboring bath-house. Two young lovers were exchanging their hearts' yearnings beneath the children's tent, which they had found unoccupied.

Edna Pontellier, casting her eyes about, had finally kept them at rest upon the sea. The day was clear and carried the gaze out as far as the blue sky went; there were a few white clouds suspended idly over the horizon. A lateen sail* was visible in the direction of Cat Island,* and others to the south seemed almost motionless in the far distance.

"Of whom—of what are you thinking?" asked Adèle of her companion, whose countenance she had been watching with a little amused attention, arrested by the absorbed expression which seemed to have seized and fixed every feature into a statuesque repose.

"Nothing," returned Mrs. Pontellier, with a start, adding at once: "How stupid! But it seems to me it is the reply we make instinctively to such a question. Let me see," she went on, throwing back her head and narrowing her fine eyes till they shone like two vivid points of light. "Let me see. I was really not conscious of thinking of anything; but perhaps I can retrace my thoughts."

"Oh! never mind!" laughed Madame Ratignolle. "I am not quite so exacting. I will let you off this time. It is really too hot to think, especially to think about thinking."

"But for the fun of it," persisted Edna. "First of all, the sight of the water stretching so far away, those motionless sails against the blue sky, made a delicious picture that I just wanted to sit and look at. The hot wind beating in my face made me think—without any connection that I can trace—of a summer day in Kentucky, of a meadow that seemed as big as the ocean to the very little girl walking through the grass, which was higher than her waist. She threw out her arms as if swimming when she walked, beating the tall grass as one strikes out in the water. Oh, I see the connection now!"

"Where were you going that day in Kentucky, walking through the grass?"

"I don't remember now. I was just walking diagonally across a big field. My sun-bonnet obstructed the view. I could see only the stretch of green before me, and I felt as if I must walk on forever, without coming to the end of it. I don't remember whether I was frightened or pleased. I must have been entertained."

"Likely as not it was Sunday," she laughed; "and I was running away from prayers, from the Presbyterian service, read in a spirit of gloom by my father that chills me yet to think of."

"And have you been running away from prayers ever since, *ma chère*?" asked Madame Ratignolle, amused.

"No! oh, no!" Edna hastened to say. "I was a little unthinking child in those days, just following a misleading impulse without question. On the contrary, during one period of my life religion took a firm hold upon me; after I was twelve and until—until—why, I suppose until now, though I never thought much about it—just driven along by habit. But do you know," she broke off, turning her quick eyes upon Madame Ratignolle and leaning forward a little so as to bring her face quite close to that of her companion, "sometimes I feel this summer as if I were walking through the green meadow again; idly, aimlessly, unthinking and unguided."

Madame Ratignolle laid her hand over that of Mrs. Pontellier, which was near her. Seeing that the hand was not withdrawn, she clasped it firmly and warmly. She even stroked it a little, fondly, with the other hand, murmuring in an undertone, "*Pauvre chérie.*"

The action was at first a little confusing to Edna, but she soon lent herself readily to the Creole's gentle caress. She was not accustomed to an outward and spoken expression of affection, either in herself or in others. She and her younger sister, Janet, had quarreled a good deal through force of unfortunate habit. Her older sister, Margaret, was matronly and dignified, probably from having assumed matronly and housewifely responsibilities too early in life, their mother having died when they were quite young. Margaret was not effusive; she was practical. Edna had had an occasional girl friend, but whether accidentally or not, they seemed to have been all of one type—the self-contained. She never realized that the reserve of her own character had much, perhaps everything, to do with this. Her most intimate friend at school* had been one of rather exceptional intellectual gifts, who wrote fine-sounding essays, which Edna admired and strove to imitate; and with her she talked and glowed over the English classics, and sometimes held religious and political controversies.

Edna often wondered at one propensity which sometimes had inwardly disturbed her without causing any outward show or manifestation on her part. At a very early age—perhaps it was when she traversed the ocean of waving grass—she remembered that she had been passionately enamored of a dignified and sad-eyed cavalry officer who visited her father in Kentucky. She could not leave his presence when he was there, nor remove her eyes from his face, which was something like Napoleon's,* with a lock of black hair falling across the forehead. But the cavalry officer melted imperceptibly out of her existence.

At another time her affections were deeply engaged by a young gentleman who visited a lady on a neighboring plantation. It was after they went to Mississippi to live. The young man was engaged to be married to the young lady, and they sometimes called upon Margaret, driving over of afternoons in a buggy. Edna was a little miss, just merging into her teens; and the realization that she herself was nothing, nothing, nothing to the engaged young man was a bitter affliction to her. But he, too, went the way of dreams.

She was a grown young woman when she was overtaken by what

she supposed to be the climax of her fate. It was when the face and figure of a great tragedian* began to haunt her imagination and stir her senses. The persistence of the infatuation lent it an aspect of genuineness. The hopelessness of it colored it with the lofty tones of a great passion.

The picture of the tragedian stood enframed upon her desk. Any one may possess the portrait of a tragedian without exciting suspicion or comment. (This was a sinister reflection which she cherished.) In the presence of others she expressed admiration for his exalted gifts, as she handed the photograph around and dwelt upon the fidelity of the likeness. When alone she sometimes picked it up and kissed the cold glass passionately.

Her marriage to Léonce Pontellier was purely an accident, in this respect resembling many other marriages which masquerade as the decrees of Fate. It was in the midst of her secret great passion that she met him. He fell in love, as men are in the habit of doing, and pressed his suit with an earnestness and an ardor which left nothing to be desired. He pleased her; his absolute devotion flattered her. She fancied there was a sympathy of thought and taste between them, in which fancy she was mistaken. Add to this the violent opposition of her father and her sister Margaret to her marriage with a Catholic, and we need seek no further for the motives which led her to accept Monsieur Pontellier for her husband.

The acme of bliss, which would have been a marriage with the tragedian, was not for her in this world. As the devoted wife of a man who worshiped her, she felt she would take her place with a certain dignity in the world of reality, closing the portals forever* behind her upon the realm of romance and dreams.

But it was not long before the tragedian had gone to join the cavalry officer and the engaged young man and a few others; and Edna found herself face to face with the realities. She grew fond of her husband, realizing with some unaccountable satisfaction that no trace of passion or excessive and fictitious warmth colored her affection, thereby threatening its dissolution.

She was fond of her children in an uneven, impulsive way. She would sometimes gather them passionately to her heart; she would sometimes forget them. The year before they had spent part of the summer with their grandmother Pontellier in Iberville.* Feeling secure regarding their happiness and welfare, she did not miss them except with an occasional intense longing. Their absence was a sort of relief, though she did not admit this, even to herself. It seemed to free her of a responsibility which she had blindly assumed and for which Fate had not fitted her.

Edna did not reveal so much as all this to Madame Ratignolle that summer day when they sat with faces turned to the sea. But a good part of it escaped her. She had put her head down on Madame Ratignolle's shoulder. She was flushed and felt intoxicated with the sound of her own voice and the unaccustomed taste of candor. It muddled her like wine, or like a first breath of freedom.

There was the sound of approaching voices. It was Robert, surrounded by a troop of children, searching for them. The two little Pontelliers were with him, and he carried Madame Ratignolle's little girl in his arms. There were other children beside, and two nurse-maids followed, looking disagreeable and resigned.

The women at once rose and began to shake out their draperies and relax their muscles. Mrs. Pontellier threw the cushions and rug into the bath-house. The children all scampered off to the awning, and they stood there in a line, gazing upon the intruding lovers, still exchanging their vows and sighs. The lovers got up, with only a silent protest, and walked slowly away somewhere else.

The children possessed themselves of the tent, and Mrs. Pontellier went over to join them.

Madame Ratignolle begged Robert to accompany her to the house; she complained of cramp in her limbs and stiffness of the joints. She leaned draggingly upon his arm as they walked.

VIII

"Do me a favor, Robert," spoke the pretty woman at his side, almost as soon as she and Robert had started on their slow, homeward way. She looked up in his face, leaning on his arm beneath the encircling shadow of the umbrella which he had lifted.

"Granted; as many as you like," he returned, glancing down into her eyes that were full of thoughtfulness and some speculation.

"I only ask for one; let Mrs. Pontellier alone."

"*Tiens!*" he exclaimed, with a sudden, boyish laugh. "*Voilà que Madame Ratignolle est jalouse!*"*

"Nonsense! I'm in earnest; I mean what I say. Let Mrs. Pontellier alone."

"Why?" he asked; himself growing serious at his companion's solicitation.

"She is not one of us; she is not like us. She might make the unfortunate blunder of taking you seriously."

His face flushed with annoyance, and taking off his soft hat he began to beat it impatiently against his leg as he walked. "Why shouldn't she take me seriously?" he demanded sharply. "Am I a comedian, a clown, a jack-in-the-box?* Why shouldn't she? You Creoles! I have no patience with you! Am I always to be regarded as a feature of an amusing programme? I hope Mrs. Pontellier does take me seriously. I hope she has discernment enough to find in me something besides the *blagueur*. If I thought there was any doubt—"

"Oh, enough, Robert!" she broke into his heated outburst. "You are not thinking of what you are saying. You speak with about as little reflection as we might expect from one of those children down there playing in the sand. If your attentions to any married women here were ever offered with any intention of being convincing, you would not be the gentleman we all know you to be, and you would be unfit to associate with the wives and daughters of the people who trust you."

Madame Ratignolle had spoken what she believed to be the law and the gospel. The young man shrugged his shoulders impatiently.

"Oh! well! That isn't it," slamming his hat down vehemently upon his head. "You ought to feel that such things are not flattering to say to a fellow."

"Should our whole intercourse consist of an exchange of compliments? *Ma foi!*"

"It isn't pleasant to have a woman tell you—" he went on, unheedingly, but breaking off suddenly: "Now if I were like Arobin—you remember Alcée Arobin and that story of the consul's wife at Biloxi?"* And he related the story of Alcée Arobin and the consul's wife; and another about the tenor of the French Opera,* who received letters which should never have been written; and still other stories, grave and gay, till Mrs. Pontellier and her possible propensity for taking young men seriously was apparently forgotten.

Madame Ratignolle, when they had regained her cottage, went in to take the hour's rest which she considered helpful. Before leaving her, Robert begged her pardon for the impatience—he called it rudeness—with which he had received her well-meant caution.

"You made one mistake, Adèle," he said, with a light smile; "there is no earthly possibility of Mrs. Pontellier ever taking me seriously. You should have warned me against taking myself seriously. Your advice might then have carried some weight and given me subject for some reflection. *Au revoir*. But you look tired," he added, solicitously. "Would you like a cup of bouillon? Shall I stir you a toddy? Let me mix you a toddy with a drop of Angostura."*

She acceded to the suggestion of bouillon, which was grateful and acceptable. He went himself to the kitchen, which was a building apart from the cottages and lying to the rear of the house. And he himself brought her the golden-brown bouillon, in a dainty Sèvres cup, with a flaky cracker or two on the saucer.

She thrust a bare, white arm from the curtain which shielded her open door, and received the cup from his hands. She told him he was a *bon garçon*, and she meant it. Robert thanked her and turned away toward "the house."

The lovers were just entering the grounds of the *pension*. They were leaning toward each other as the water-oaks bent from the sea. There was not a particle of earth beneath their feet. Their heads might have been turned upside-down, so absolutely did they tread upon blue ether. The lady in black, creeping behind them, looked a trifle paler and more jaded than usual. There was no sign of Mrs. Pontellier and the children. Robert scanned the distance for any such apparition. They would doubtless remain away till the dinner hour. The young man ascended to his mother's room. It was situated at the top of the house, made up of odd angles and a queer, sloping ceiling. Two broad dormer windows looked out toward the Gulf, and as far across it as a man's eye might reach. The furnishings of the room were light, cool, and practical.

Madame Lebrun was busily engaged at the sewing-machine. A little black girl sat on the floor, and with her hands worked the treadle of the machine. The Creole woman does not take any chances which may be avoided of imperiling her health.

Robert went over and seated himself on the broad sill of one of the dormer windows. He took a book from his pocket and began energetically to read it, judging by the precision and frequency with which he turned the leaves. The sewing-machine made a resounding clatter in the room; it was of a ponderous, by-gone make. In the lulls, Robert and his mother exchanged bits of desultory conversation.

"Where is Mrs. Pontellier?"

"Down at the beach with the children."

"I promised to lend her the Goncourt.* Don't forget to take it down when you go; it's there on the bookshelf over the small table." Clatter, clatter, clatter, bang! for the next five or eight minutes.

"Where is Victor going with the rockaway?"

"The rockaway? Victor?"

"Yes; down there in front. He seems to be getting ready to drive away somewhere."

"Call him." Clatter, clatter!

Robert uttered a shrill, piercing whistle which might have been heard back at the wharf.

"He won't look up."

Madame Lebrun flew to the window. She called "Victor!" She waved a handkerchief and called again. The young fellow below got into the vehicle and started the horse off at a gallop.

Madame Lebrun went back to the machine, crimson with annoyance. Victor was the younger son and brother—a *tête montée*, with a temper which invited violence and a will which no ax could break.

"Whenever you say the word I'm ready to thrash any amount of reason into him that he's able to hold."

"If your father had only lived!" Clatter, clatter, clatter, clatter, bang! It was a fixed belief with Madame Lebrun that the conduct of the universe and all things pertaining thereto would have been manifestly of a more intelligent and higher order had not Monsieur Lebrun been removed to other spheres during the early years of their married life.

"What do you hear from Montel?" Montel was a middle-aged gentleman whose vain ambition and desire for the past twenty years had been to fill the void which Monsieur Lebrun's taking off had left in the Lebrun household. Clatter, clatter, bang, clatter!

"I have a letter somewhere," looking in the machine drawer and finding the letter in the bottom of the work-basket. "He says to tell you he will be in Vera Cruz* the beginning of next month"—clatter, clatter!—"and if you still have the intention of joining him"—bang! clatter, clatter, bang!

"Why didn't you tell me so before, mother? You know I wanted—"
Clatter, clatter, clatter!

"Do you see Mrs. Pontellier starting back with the children? She
will be in late to luncheon again. She never starts to get ready for
luncheon till the last minute." Clatter, clatter! "Where are you
going?"

"Where did you say the Goncourt was?"

IX

Every light in the hall was ablaze; every lamp turned as high as it
could be without smoking the chimney or threatening explosion.
The lamps were fixed at intervals against the wall, encircling the
whole room. Some one had gathered orange and lemon branches,
and with these fashioned graceful festoons between. The dark green
of the branches stood out and glistened against the white muslin
curtains which draped the windows, and which puffed, floated, and
flapped at the capricious will of a stiff breeze that swept up from the
Gulf.

It was Saturday night a few weeks after the intimate conversation
held between Robert and Madame Ratignolle on their way from the
beach. An unusual number of husbands, fathers, and friends had
come down to stay over Sunday; and they were being suitably entertained by their families, with the material help of Madame Lebrun.
The dining tables had all been removed to one end of the hall, and
the chairs ranged about in rows and in clusters. Each little family
group had had its say and exchanged its domestic gossip earlier in
the evening. There was now an apparent disposition to relax; to
widen the circle of confidences and give a more general tone to the
conversation.

Many of the children had been permitted to sit up beyond
their usual bedtime. A small band of them were lying on their
stomachs on the floor looking at the colored sheets of the
comic papers which Mr. Pontellier had brought down. The little
Pontellier boys were permitting them to do so, and making their
authority felt.

Music, dancing, and a recitation or two were the entertainments
furnished, or rather, offered. But there was nothing systematic about

the programme, no appearance of prearrangement nor even premeditation.

At an early hour in the evening the Farival twins were prevailed upon to play the piano. They were girls of fourteen, always clad in the Virgin's colors, blue and white, having been dedicated to the Blessed Virgin at their baptism.* They played a duet from "Zampa," and at the earnest solicitation of every one present followed it with the overture to "The Poet and the Peasant."

"*Allez vous-en! Sapristi!*" shrieked the parrot outside the door. He was the only being present who possessed sufficient candor to admit that he was not listening to these gracious performances for the first time that summer. Old Monsieur Farival, grandfather of the twins, grew indignant over the interruption, and insisted upon having the bird removed and consigned to regions of darkness. Victor Lebrun objected; and his decrees were as immutable as those of Fate. The parrot fortunately offered no further interruption to the entertainment, the whole venom of his nature apparently having been cherished up and hurled against the twins in that one impetuous outburst.

Later a young brother and sister gave recitations, which every one present had heard many times at winter evening entertainments in the city.

A little girl performed a skirt dance in the center of the floor. The mother played her accompaniments and at the same time watched her daughter with greedy admiration and nervous apprehension. She need have had no apprehension. The child was mistress of the situation. She had been properly dressed for the occasion in black tulle* and black silk tights. Her little neck and arms were bare, and her hair, artificially crimped, stood out like fluffy black plumes over her head. Her poses were full of grace, and her little black-shod toes twinkled as they shot out and upward with a rapidity and suddenness which were bewildering.

But there was no reason why every one should not dance. Madame Ratignolle could not, so it was she who gaily consented to play for the others. She played very well, keeping excellent waltz time and infusing an expression into the strains which was indeed inspiring. She was keeping up her music on account of the children, she said; because she and her husband both considered it a means of brightening the home and making it attractive.

Almost every one danced but the twins, who could not be induced to separate during the brief period when one or the other should be whirling around the room in the arms of a man. They might have danced together, but they did not think of it.

The children were sent to bed. Some went submissively; others with shrieks and protests as they were dragged away. They had been permitted to sit up till after the ice-cream, which naturally marked the limit of human indulgence.

The ice-cream was passed around with cake—gold and silver cake arranged on platters in alternate slices; it had been made and frozen during the afternoon back of the kitchen by two black women, under the supervision of Victor. It was pronounced a great success— excellent if it had only contained a little less vanilla or a little more sugar, if it had been frozen a degree harder, and if the salt might have been kept out of portions of it.* Victor was proud of his achievement, and went about recommending it and urging every one to partake of it to excess.

After Mrs. Pontellier had danced twice with her husband, once with Robert, and once with Monsieur Ratignolle, who was thin and tall and swayed like a reed in the wind when he danced, she went out on the gallery and seated herself on the low window-sill, where she commanded a view of all that went on in the hall and could look out toward the Gulf. There was a soft effulgence in the east. The moon was coming up, and its mystic shimmer was casting a million lights across the distant, restless water.

"Would you like to hear Mademoiselle Reisz play?" asked Robert, coming out on the porch where she was. Of course Edna would like to hear Mademoiselle Reisz play; but she feared it would be useless to entreat her.

"I'll ask her," he said. "I'll tell her that you want to hear her. She likes you. She will come." He turned and hurried away to one of the far cottages, where Mademoiselle Reisz was shuffling away. She was dragging a chair in and out of her room, and at intervals objecting to the crying of a baby, which a nurse in the adjoining cottage was endeavoring to put to sleep. She was a disagreeable little woman, no longer young, who had quarreled with almost every one, owing to a temper which was self-assertive and a disposition to trample upon the rights of others. Robert prevailed upon her without any too great difficulty.

She entered the hall with him during a lull in the dance. She made an awkward, imperious little bow as she went in. She was a homely woman, with a small weazened face and body and eyes that glowed. She had absolutely no taste in dress, and wore a batch of rusty black lace with a bunch of artificial violets pinned to the side of her hair.

"Ask Mrs. Pontellier what she would like to hear me play," she requested of Robert. She sat perfectly still before the piano, not touching the keys, while Robert carried her message to Edna at the window. A general air of surprise and genuine satisfaction fell upon every one as they saw the pianist enter. There was a settling down, and a prevailing air of expectancy everywhere. Edna was a trifle embarrassed at being thus signaled out for the imperious little woman's favor. She would not dare to choose, and begged that Mademoiselle Reisz would please herself in her selections.

Edna was what she herself called very fond of music. Musical strains, well rendered, had a way of evoking pictures in her mind. She sometimes liked to sit in the room of mornings when Madame Ratignolle played or practiced. One piece which that lady played Edna had entitled "Solitude."* It was a short, plaintive, minor strain. The name of the piece was something else, but she called it "Solitude." When she heard it there came before her imagination the figure of a man standing beside a desolate rock on the seashore. He was naked. His attitude was one of hopeless resignation as he looked toward a distant bird winging its flight away from him.

Another piece called to her mind a dainty young woman clad in an Empire gown,* taking mincing dancing steps as she came down a long avenue between tall hedges. Again, another reminded her of children at play, and still another of nothing on earth but a demure lady stroking a cat.

The very first chords which Mademoiselle Reisz struck upon the piano sent a keen tremor down Mrs. Pontellier's spinal column. It was not the first time she had heard an artist at the piano. Perhaps it was the first time she was ready, perhaps the first time her being was tempered to take an impress of the abiding truth.

She waited for the material pictures which she thought would gather and blaze before her imagination. She waited in vain. She saw no pictures of solitude, of hope, of longing, or of despair. But the very passions themselves were aroused within her soul, swaying it, lashing it, as the waves daily beat upon her splendid body. She trembled, she was choking, and the tears blinded her.

Mademoiselle had finished. She arose, and bowing her stiff, lofty bow, she went away, stopping for neither thanks nor applause. As she passed along the gallery she patted Edna upon the shoulder.

"Well, how did you like my music?" she asked. The young woman was unable to answer; she pressed the hand of the pianist convulsively. Mademoiselle Reisz perceived her agitation and even her tears. She patted her again upon the shoulder as she said:

"You are the only one worth playing for. Those others? Bah!" and she went shuffling and sidling on down the gallery toward her room.

But she was mistaken about "those others." Her playing had aroused a fever of enthusiasm. "What passion!" "What an artist!" "I have always said no one could play Chopin* like Mademoiselle Reisz!" "That last prelude! Bon Dieu! It shakes a man!"

It was growing late, and there was a general disposition to disband. But some one, perhaps it was Robert, thought of a bath at that mystic hour and under that mystic moon.

X

At all events Robert proposed it, and there was not a dissenting voice. There was not one but was ready to follow when he led the way. He did not lead the way, however, he directed the way; and he himself loitered behind with the lovers, who had betrayed a disposition to linger and hold themselves apart. He walked between them, whether with malicious or mischievous intent was not wholly clear, even to himself.

The Pontelliers and Ratignolles walked ahead; the women leaning upon the arms of their husbands. Edna could hear Robert's voice behind them, and could sometimes hear what he said. She wondered why he did not join them. It was unlike him not to. Of late he had sometimes held away from her for an entire day, redoubling his devotion upon the next and the next, as though to make up for hours that had been lost. She missed him the days when some pretext served to take him away from her, just as one misses the sun on a cloudy day without having thought much about the sun when it was shining.

The people walked in little groups toward the beach. They talked and laughed; some of them sang. There was a band playing down at Klein's hotel, and the strains reached them faintly, tempered by the distance. There were strange, rare odors abroad—a tangle of the sea smell and of weeds and damp, new-plowed earth, mingled with the heavy perfume of a field of white blossoms somewhere near. But the night sat lightly upon the sea and the land. There was no weight of darkness; there were no shadows. The white light of the moon had fallen upon the world like the mystery and the softness of sleep.

Most of them walked into the water as though into a native element. The sea was quiet now, and swelled lazily in broad billows that melted into one another and did not break except upon the beach in little foamy crests that coiled back like slow, white serpents.

Edna had attempted all summer to learn to swim. She had received instructions from both the men and women; in some instances from the children. Robert had pursued a system of lessons almost daily; and he was nearly at the point of discouragement in realizing the futility of his efforts. A certain ungovernable dread hung about her when in the water, unless there was a hand near by that might reach out and reassure her.

But that night she was like the little tottering, stumbling, clutching child, who of a sudden realizes its powers, and walks for the first time alone, boldly and with over-confidence. She could have shouted for joy. She did shout for joy, as with a sweeping stroke or two she lifted her body to the surface of the water.

A feeling of exultation overtook her, as if some power of significant import had been given her to control the working of her body and her soul. She grew daring and reckless, overestimating her strength. She wanted to swim far out, where no woman had swum before.

Her unlooked-for achievement was the subject of wonder, applause, and admiration. Each one congratulated himself that his special teachings had accomplished this desired end.

"How easy it is!" she thought. "It is nothing," she said aloud; "why did I not discover before that it was nothing. Think of the time I have lost splashing about like a baby!" She would not join the groups in their sports and bouts, but intoxicated with her newly conquered power, she swam out alone.

She turned her face seaward to gather in an impression of space and solitude, which the vast expanse of water, meeting and melting with the moonlit sky, conveyed to her excited fancy. As she swam she seemed to be reaching out for the unlimited in which to lose herself.

Once she turned and looked toward the shore, toward the people she had left there. She had not gone any great distance—that is, what would have been a great distance for an experienced swimmer. But to her unaccustomed vision the stretch of water behind her assumed the aspect of a barrier which her unaided strength would never be able to overcome.

A quick vision of death smote her soul, and for a second of time appalled and enfeebled her senses. But by an effort she rallied her staggering faculties and managed to regain the land.

She made no mention of her encounter with death and her flash of terror, except to say to her husband, "I thought I should have perished out there alone."*

"You were not so very far, my dear; I was watching you," he told her.

Edna went at once to the bath-house, and she had put on her dry clothes and was ready to return home before the others had left the water. She started to walk away alone. They all called to her and shouted to her. She waved a dissenting hand, and went on, paying no further heed to their renewed cries which sought to detain her.

"Sometimes I am tempted to think that Mrs. Pontellier is capricious," said Madame Lebrun, who was amusing herself immensely and feared that Edna's abrupt departure might put an end to the pleasure.

"I know she is," assented Mr. Pontellier; "sometimes, not often."

Edna had not traversed a quarter of the distance on her way home before she was overtaken by Robert.

"Did you think I was afraid?" she asked him, without a shade of annoyance.

"No; I knew you weren't afraid."

"Then why did you come? Why didn't you stay out there with the others?"

"I never thought of it."

"Thought of what?"

"Of anything. What difference does it make?"

"I'm very tired," she uttered, complainingly.

"I know you are."

"You don't know anything about it. Why should you know? I never was so exhausted in my life. But it isn't unpleasant. A thousand emotions have swept through me to-night. I don't comprehend half of them. Don't mind what I'm saying; I am just thinking aloud. I wonder if I shall ever be stirred again as Mademoiselle Reisz's playing moved me to-night. I wonder if any night on earth will ever again be like this one. It is like a night in a dream. The people about me are like some uncanny, half-human beings. There must be spirits abroad to-night."

"There are," whispered Robert. "Didn't you know this was the twenty-eighth of August?"*

"The twenty-eighth of August?"

"Yes. On the twenty-eighth of August, at the hour of midnight, and if the moon is shining—the moon must be shining—a spirit that has haunted these shores for ages rises up from the Gulf. With its own penetrating vision the spirit seeks some one mortal worthy to hold him company, worthy of being exalted for a few hours into realms of the semi-celestials. His search has always hitherto been fruitless, and he has sunk back, disheartened, into the sea. But to-night he found Mrs. Pontellier. Perhaps he will never wholly release her from the spell. Perhaps she will never again suffer a poor, unworthy earthling to walk in the shadow of her divine presence."

"Don't banter me," she said, wounded at what appeared to be his flippancy. He did not mind the entreaty, but the tone with its delicate note of pathos was like a reproach. He could not explain; he could not tell her that he had penetrated her mood and understood. He said nothing except to offer her his arm, for, by her own admission, she was exhausted. She had been walking alone with her arms hanging limp, letting her white skirts trail along the dewy path. She took his arm, but she did not lean upon it. She let her hand lie listlessly, as though her thoughts were elsewhere—somewhere in advance of her body, and she was striving to overtake them.

Robert assisted her into the hammock which swung from the post before her door out to the trunk of a tree.

"Will you stay out here and wait for Mr. Pontellier?" he asked.

"I'll stay out here. Good-night."

"Shall I get you a pillow?"

"There's one here," she said, feeling about, for they were in the shadow.

"It must be soiled; the children have been tumbling it about."

"No matter." And having discovered the pillow, she adjusted it beneath her head. She extended herself in the hammock with a deep breath of relief. She was not a supercilious or an over-dainty woman. She was not much given to reclining in the hammock, and when she did so it was with no cat-like suggestion of voluptuous ease, but with a beneficent repose which seemed to invade her whole body.

"Shall I stay with you till Mr. Pontellier comes?" asked Robert, seating himself on the outer edge of one of the steps and taking hold of the hammock rope which was fastened to the post.

"If you wish. Don't swing the hammock. Will you get my white shawl which I left on the window-sill over at the house?"

"Are you chilly?"

"No; but I shall be presently."

"Presently?" he laughed. "Do you know what time it is? How long are you going to stay out here?"

"I don't know. Will you get the shawl?"

"Of course I will," he said, rising. He went over to the house, walking along the grass. She watched his figure pass in and out of the strips of moonlight. It was past midnight. It was very quiet.

When he returned with the shawl she took it and kept it in her hand. She did not put it around her.

"Did you say I should stay till Mr. Pontellier came back?"

"I said you might if you wished to."

He seated himself again and rolled a cigarette, which he smoked in silence. Neither did Mrs. Pontellier speak. No multitude of words could have been more significant than those moments of silence, or more pregnant with the first-felt throbbings of desire.

When the voices of the bathers were heard approaching, Robert said good-night. She did not answer him. He thought she was asleep. Again she watched his figure pass in and out of the strips of moonlight as he walked away.

XI

"What are you doing out here, Edna? I thought I should find you in bed," said her husband, when he discovered her lying there. He had walked up with Madame Lebrun and left her at the house. His wife did not reply.

"Are you asleep?" he asked, bending down close to look at her.

"No." Her eyes gleamed bright and intense, with no sleepy shadows, as they looked into his.

"Do you know it is past one o'clock? Come on," and he mounted the steps and went into their room.

"Edna!" called Mr. Pontellier from within, after a few moments had gone by.

"Don't wait for me," she answered. He thrust his head through the door.

"You will take cold out there," he said, irritably. "What folly is this? Why don't you come in?"

"It isn't cold; I have my shawl."

"The mosquitoes will devour you."

"There are no mosquitoes."

She heard him moving about the room; every sound indicating impatience and irritation. Another time she would have gone in at his request. She would, through habit, have yielded to his desire; not with any sense of submission or obedience to his compelling wishes, but unthinkingly, as we walk, move, sit, stand, go through the daily treadmill of the life which has been portioned out to us.

"Edna, dear, are you not coming in soon?" he asked again, this time fondly, with a note of entreaty.

"No; I am going to stay out here."

"This is more than folly," he blurted out. "I can't permit you to stay out there all night. You must come in the house instantly."

With a writhing motion she settled herself more securely in the hammock. She perceived that her will had blazed up, stubborn and resistant. She could not at that moment have done other than denied and resisted. She wondered if her husband had ever spoken to her like that before, and if she had submitted to his command. Of course she had; she remembered that she had. But she could not realize why or how she should have yielded, feeling as she then did.

"Léonce, go to bed," she said. "I mean to stay out here. I don't wish to go in, and I don't intend to. Don't speak to me like that again; I shall not answer you."

Mr. Pontellier had prepared for bed, but he slipped on an extra garment. He opened a bottle of wine, of which he kept a small and select supply in a buffet of his own. He drank a glass of the wine and went out on the gallery and offered a glass to his wife. She did not wish any. He drew up the rocker, hoisted his slippered feet on the rail, and proceeded to smoke a cigar. He smoked two cigars; then he went inside and drank another glass of wine. Mrs. Pontellier again declined to accept a glass when it was offered to her. Mr. Pontellier once more seated himself with elevated feet, and after a reasonable interval of time smoked some more cigars.

Edna began to feel like one who awakens gradually out of a dream, a delicious, grotesque, impossible dream, to feel again the realities pressing into her soul. The physical need for sleep began to overtake her; the exuberance which had sustained and exalted her spirit left her helpless and yielding to the conditions which crowded her in.

The stillest hour of the night had come, the hour before dawn, when the world seems to hold its breath. The moon hung low, and had turned from silver to copper in the sleeping sky. The old owl no longer hooted, and the water-oaks had ceased to moan as they bent their heads.

Edna arose, cramped from lying so long and still in the hammock. She tottered up the steps, clutching feebly at the post before passing into the house.

"Are you coming in, Léonce?" she asked, turning her face toward her husband.

"Yes, dear," he answered, with a glance following a misty puff of smoke. "Just as soon as I have finished my cigar."

XII

She slept but a few hours. They were troubled and feverish hours, disturbed with dreams that were intangible, that eluded her, leaving only an impression upon her half-awakened senses of something unattainable. She was up and dressed in the cool of the early morning. The air was invigorating and steadied somewhat her faculties. However, she was not seeking refreshment or help from any source, either external or from within. She was blindly following whatever impulse moved her, as if she had placed herself in alien hands for direction, and freed her soul of responsibility.

Most of the people at that early hour were still in bed and asleep. A few, who intended to go over to the *Chênière* for mass, were moving about. The lovers, who had laid their plans the night before, were already strolling toward the wharf. The lady in black, with her Sunday prayer-book, velvet and gold-clasped, and her Sunday silver beads, was following them at no great distance. Old Monsieur Farival was up, and was more than half inclined to do anything that suggested itself. He put on his big straw hat, and taking his umbrella from the stand in the hall, followed the lady in black, never overtaking her.

The little negro girl who worked Madame Lebrun's sewing-machine was sweeping the galleries with long, absent-minded strokes of the broom. Edna sent her up into the house to awaken Robert.

"Tell him I am going to the *Chênière*. The boat is ready; tell him to hurry."

He had soon joined her. She had never sent for him before. She had never asked for him. She had never seemed to want him before. She did not appear conscious that she had done anything unusual in commanding his presence. He was apparently equally unconscious of anything extraordinary in the situation. But his face was suffused with a quiet glow when he met her.

They went together back to the kitchen to drink coffee. There was no time to wait for any nicety of service. They stood outside the window and the cook passed them their coffee and a roll, which they drank and ate from the window-sill. Edna said it tasted good. She had not thought of coffee nor of anything. He told her he had often noticed that she lacked forethought.

"Wasn't it enough to think of going to the *Chênière* and waking you up?" she laughed. "Do I have to think of everything?—as Léonce says when he's in a bad humor. I don't blame him; he'd never be in a bad humor if it weren't for me."

They took a short cut across the sands. At a distance they could see the curious procession moving toward the wharf—the lovers, shoulder to shoulder, creeping; the lady in black, gaining steadily upon them; old Monsieur Farival, losing ground inch by inch, and a young barefooted Spanish girl, with a red kerchief on her head and a basket on her arm, bringing up the rear.

Robert knew the girl, and he talked to her a little in the boat. No one present understood what they said. Her name was Mariequita. She had a round, sly, piquant face and pretty black eyes. Her hands were small, and she kept them folded over the handle of her basket.

Her feet were broad and coarse. She did not strive to hide them. Edna looked at her feet, and noticed the sand and slime between her brown toes.

Beaudelet grumbled because Mariequita was there, taking up so much room. In reality he was annoyed at having old Monsieur Farival, who considered himself the better sailor of the two. But he would not quarrel with so old a man as Monsieur Farival, so he quarreled with Mariequita. The girl was deprecatory at one moment, appealing to Robert. She was saucy the next, moving her head up and down, making "eyes" at Robert and making "mouths" at Beaudelet.

The lovers were all alone. They saw nothing, they heard nothing. The lady in black was counting her beads for the third time. Old Monsieur Farival talked incessantly of what he knew about handling a boat, and of what Beaudelet did not know on the same subject.

Edna liked it all. She looked Mariequita up and down, from her ugly brown toes to her pretty black eyes, and back again.

"Why does she look at me like that?" inquired the girl of Robert.

"Maybe she thinks you are pretty. Shall I ask her?"

"No. Is she your sweetheart?"

"She's a married lady, and has two children."

"Oh! well! Francisco ran away with Sylvano's wife, who had four children. They took all his money and one of the children and stole his boat."

"Shut up!"

"Does she understand?"

"Oh, hush!"

"Are those two married over there—leaning on each other?"

"Of course not," laughed Robert.

"Of course not," echoed Mariequita, with a serious, confirmatory bob of the head.

The sun was high up and beginning to bite. The swift breeze seemed to Edna to bury the sting of it into the pores of her face and hands. Robert held his umbrella over her.

As they went cutting sidewise through the water, the sails bellied taut, with the wind filling and overflowing them. Old Monsieur Farival laughed sardonically at something as he looked at the sails, and Beaudelet swore at the old man under his breath.

Sailing across the bay to the *Chênière Caminada*, Edna felt as if she were being borne away from some anchorage which had held her fast, whose chains had been loosening—had snapped the night before when the mystic spirit was abroad, leaving her free to drift whithersoever she chose to set her sails. Robert spoke to her incessantly; he no longer noticed Mariequita. The girl had shrimps in her bamboo basket. They were covered with Spanish moss.* She beat the moss down impatiently, and muttered to herself sullenly.

"Let us go to Grande Terre* to-morrow?" said Robert in a low voice.

"What shall we do there?"

"Climb up the hill to the old fort and look at the little wriggling gold snakes, and watch the lizards sun themselves."

She gazed away toward Grande Terre and thought she would like to be alone there with Robert, in the sun, listening to the ocean's roar and watching the slimy lizards writhe in and out among the ruins of the old fort.

"And the next day or the next we can sail to the Bayou Brulow,"* he went on.

"What shall we do there?"

"Anything—cast bait for fish."

"No; we'll go back to Grande Terre. Let the fish alone."

"We'll go wherever you like," he said. "I'll have Tonie* come over and help me patch and trim my boat. We shall not need Beaudelet nor any one. Are you afraid of the pirogue?"

"Oh, no."

"Then I'll take you some night in the pirogue when the moon shines. Maybe your Gulf spirit will whisper to you in which of these islands the treasures are hidden—direct you to the very spot, perhaps."

"And in a day we should be rich!" she laughed. "I'd give it all to you, the pirate gold and every bit of treasure we could dig up. I think you would know how to spend it. Pirate gold isn't a thing to be hoarded or utilized. It is something to squander and throw to the four winds, for the fun of seeing the golden specks fly."

"We'd share it, and scatter it together," he said. His face flushed.

They all went together up to the quaint little Gothic church of Our Lady of Lourdes,* gleaming all brown and yellow with paint in the sun's glare.

Only Beaudelet remained behind, tinkering at his boat, and

Mariequita walked away with her basket of shrimps, casting a look of childish ill-humor and reproach at Robert from the corner of her eye.

XIII

A feeling of oppression and drowsiness overcame Edna during the service. Her head began to ache, and the lights on the altar swayed before her eyes. Another time she might have made an effort to regain her composure; but her one thought was to quit the stifling atmosphere of the church and reach the open air. She arose, climbing over Robert's feet with a muttered apology. Old Monsieur Farival, flurried, curious, stood up, but upon seeing that Robert had followed Mrs. Pontellier, he sank back into his seat. He whispered an anxious inquiry of the lady in black, who did not notice him or reply, but kept her eyes fastened upon the pages of her velvet prayer-book.

"I felt giddy and almost overcome," Edna said, lifting her hands instinctively to her head and pushing her straw hat up from her forehead. "I couldn't have stayed through the service." They were outside in the shadow of the church. Robert was full of solicitude.

"It was folly to have thought of going in the first place, let alone staying. Come over to Madame Antoine's; you can rest there." He took her arm and led her away, looking anxiously and continuously down into her face.

How still it was, with only the voice of the sea whispering through the reeds that grew in the salt-water pools! The long line of little gray, weather-beaten houses nestled peacefully among the orange trees. It must always have been God's day on that low, drowsy island, Edna thought. They stopped, leaning over a jagged fence made of sea-drift, to ask for water. A youth, a mild-faced Acadian,* was drawing water from the cistern, which was nothing more than a rusty buoy, with an opening on one side, sunk in the ground. The water which the youth handed to them in a tin pail was not cold to taste, but it was cool to her heated face, and it greatly revived and refreshed her.

Madame Antoine's cot* was at the far end of the village. She welcomed them with all the native hospitality, as she would have opened her door to let the sunlight in. She was fat, and walked heavily and clumsily across the floor. She could speak no English, but when Robert made her understand that the lady who accompanied him was ill and desired to rest, she was all eagerness to make Edna feel at home and to dispose of her comfortably.

The whole place was immaculately clean, and the big, four-posted bed, snow-white, invited one to repose. It stood in a small side room which looked out across a narrow grass plot toward the shed, where there was a disabled boat lying keel upward.

Madame Antoine had not gone to mass. Her son Tonie had, but she supposed he would soon be back, and she invited Robert to be seated and wait for him. But he went and sat outside the door and smoked. Madame Antoine busied herself in the large front room preparing dinner. She was boiling mullets over a few red coals in the huge fireplace.

Edna, left alone in the little side room, loosened her clothes, removing the greater part of them. She bathed her face, her neck and arms in the basin that stood between the windows. She took off her shoes and stockings and stretched herself in the very center of the high, white bed. How luxurious it felt to rest thus in a strange, quaint bed, with its sweet country odor of laurel lingering about the sheets and mattress! She stretched her strong limbs that ached a little. She ran her fingers through her loosened hair for a while. She looked at her round arms as she held them straight up and rubbed them one after the other, observing closely, as if it were something she saw for the first time, the fine, firm quality and texture of her flesh. She clasped her hands easily above her head, and it was thus she fell asleep.

She slept lightly at first, half awake and drowsily attentive to the things about her. She could hear Madame Antoine's heavy, scraping tread as she walked back and forth on the sanded floor. Some chickens were clucking outside the windows, scratching for bits of gravel in the grass. Later she half heard the voices of Robert and Tonie talking under the shed. She did not stir. Even her eyelids rested numb and heavily over her sleepy eyes. The voices went on—Tonie's slow, Acadian drawl, Robert's quick, soft, smooth French. She understood French imperfectly unless directly addressed, and the voices were only part of the other drowsy, muffled sounds lulling her senses.

When Edna awoke it was with the conviction that she had slept long and soundly. The voices were hushed under the shed. Madame Antoine's step was no longer to be heard in the adjoining room. Even the chickens had gone elsewhere to scratch and cluck. The mosquito bar was drawn over her; the old woman had come in while she slept and let down the bar. Edna arose quietly from the bed, and looking between the curtains of the window, she saw by the slanting rays of the sun that the afternoon was far advanced. Robert was out there under the shed, reclining in the shade against the sloping keel of the overturned boat. He was reading from a book. Tonie was no longer with him. She wondered what had become of the rest of the party. She peeped out at him two or three times as she stood washing herself in the little basin between the windows.

Madame Antoine had laid some coarse, clean towels upon a chair, and had placed a box of *poudre de riz* within easy reach. Edna dabbed the powder upon her nose and cheeks as she looked at herself closely in the little distorted mirror which hung on the wall above the basin. Her eyes were bright and wide awake and her face glowed.

When she had completed her toilet she walked into the adjoining room. She was very hungry. No one was there. But there was a cloth spread upon the table that stood against the wall, and a cover was laid for one, with a crusty brown loaf and a bottle of wine beside the plate. Edna bit a piece from the brown loaf, tearing it with her strong, white teeth. She poured some of the wine into the glass and drank it down. Then she went softly out of doors, and plucking an orange from the low-hanging bough of a tree, threw it at Robert, who did not know she was awake and up.

An illumination broke over his whole face when he saw her and joined her under the orange tree.

"How many years have I slept?" she inquired. "The whole island seems changed. A new race of beings must have sprung up, leaving only you and me as past relics. How many ages ago did Madame Antoine and Tonie die? and when did our people from Grand Isle disappear from the earth?"

He familiarly adjusted a ruffle upon her shoulder.

"You have slept precisely one hundred years. I was left here to guard your slumbers; and for one hundred years I have been out under the shed reading a book. The only evil I couldn't prevent was to keep a broiled fowl from drying up."

"If it has turned to stone, still will I eat it," said Edna, moving with him into the house. "But really, what has become of Monsieur Farival and the others?"

"Gone hours ago. When they found that you were sleeping they thought it best not to awake you. Any way, I wouldn't have let them. What was I here for?"

"I wonder if Léonce will be uneasy!" she speculated, as she seated herself at table.

"Of course not; he knows you are with me," Robert replied, as he busied himself among sundry pans and covered dishes which had been left standing on the hearth.

"Where are Madame Antoine and her son?" asked Edna.

"Gone to Vespers, and to visit some friends, I believe. I am to take you back in Tonie's boat whenever you are ready to go."

He stirred the smoldering ashes till the broiled fowl began to sizzle afresh. He served her with no mean repast, dripping the coffee anew and sharing it with her. Madame Antoine had cooked little else than the mullets, but while Edna slept Robert had foraged the island. He was childishly gratified to discover her appetite, and to see the relish with which she ate the food which he had procured for her.

"Shall we go right away?" she asked, after draining her glass and brushing together the crumbs of the crusty loaf.

"The sun isn't as low as it will be in two hours," he answered.

"The sun will be gone in two hours."

"Well, let it go; who cares!"

They waited a good while under the orange trees, till Madame Antoine came back, panting, waddling, with a thousand apologies to explain her absence. Tonie did not dare to return. He was shy, and would not willingly face any woman except his mother.

It was very pleasant to stay there under the orange trees, while the sun dipped lower and lower, turning the western sky to flaming copper and gold. The shadows lengthened and crept out like stealthy, grotesque monsters across the grass.

Edna and Robert both sat upon the ground—that is, he lay upon the ground beside her, occasionally picking at the hem of her muslin gown.

Madame Antoine seated her fat body, broad and squat, upon a bench beside the door. She had been talking all the afternoon, and had wound herself up to the story-telling pitch.

And what stories she told them! But twice in her life she had left the *Chênière Caminada*, and then for the briefest span. All her years she had squatted and waddled there upon the island, gathering legends of the Baratarians* and the sea. The night came on, with the moon to lighten it. Edna could hear the whispering voices of dead men and the click of muffled gold.

When she and Robert stepped into Tonie's boat, with the red lateen sail, misty spirit forms were prowling in the shadows and among the reeds, and upon the water were phantom ships, speeding to cover.

XIV

The youngest boy, Etienne, had been very naughty, Madame Ratignolle said, as she delivered him into the hands of his mother. He had been unwilling to go to bed and had made a scene; whereupon she had taken charge of him and pacified him as well as she could. Raoul had been in bed and asleep for two hours.

The youngster was in his long white nightgown, that kept tripping him up as Madame Ratignolle led him along by the hand. With the other chubby fist he rubbed his eyes, which were heavy with sleep and ill humor. Edna took him in her arms, and seating herself in the rocker, began to coddle and caress him, calling him all manner of tender names, soothing him to sleep.

It was not more than nine o'clock. No one had yet gone to bed but the children.

Léonce had been very uneasy at first, Madame Ratignolle said, and had wanted to start at once for the *Chênière*. But Monsieur Farival had assured him that his wife was only overcome with sleep and fatigue, that Tonie would bring her safely back later in the day; and he had thus been dissuaded from crossing the bay. He had gone over to Klein's, looking up some cotton broker whom he wished to see in regard to securities, exchanges, stocks, bonds, or something of the sort, Madame Ratignolle did not remember what. He said he would not remain away late. She herself was suffering from heat and oppression, she said. She carried a bottle of salts and a large fan. She would not consent to remain with Edna, for Monsieur Ratignolle was alone, and he detested above all things to be left alone.

When Etienne had fallen asleep Edna bore him into the back

room, and Robert went and lifted the mosquito bar that she might lay the child comfortably in his bed. The quadroon had vanished. When they emerged from the cottage Robert bade Edna good-night.

"Do you know we have been together the whole livelong day, Robert—since early this morning?" she said at parting.

"All but the hundred years when you were sleeping. Good-night."

He pressed her hand and went away in the direction of the beach. He did not join any of the others, but walked alone toward the Gulf.

Edna stayed outside, awaiting her husband's return. She had no desire to sleep or to retire; nor did she feel like going over to sit with the Ratignolles, or to join Madame Lebrun and a group whose animated voices reached her as they sat in conversation before the house. She let her mind wander back over her stay at Grand Isle; and she tried to discover wherein this summer had been different from any and every other summer of her life. She could only realize that she herself—her present self—was in some way different from the other self. That she was seeing with different eyes and making the acquaintance of new conditions in herself that colored and changed her environment, she did not yet suspect.

She wondered why Robert had gone away and left her. It did not occur to her to think he might have grown tired of being with her the livelong day. She was not tired, and she felt that he was not. She regretted that he had gone. It was so much more natural to have him stay, when he was not absolutely required to leave her.

As Edna waited for her husband she sang low a little song that Robert had sung as they crossed the bay. It began with "Ah! *Si tu savais*,"* and every verse ended with "*si tu savais*."

Robert's voice was not pretentious. It was musical and true. The voice, the notes, the whole refrain haunted her memory.

XV

When Edna entered the dining-room one evening a little late, as was her habit, an unusually animated conversation seemed to be going on. Several persons were talking at once, and Victor's voice was predominating, even over that of his mother. Edna had returned late from her bath, had dressed in some haste, and her face was flushed. Her head, set off by her dainty white gown, suggested a rich, rare blossom. She took her seat at table between old Monsieur Farival and Madame Ratignolle.

As she seated herself and was about to begin to eat her soup, which had been served when she entered the room, several persons informed her simultaneously that Robert was going to Mexico. She laid her spoon down and looked about her bewildered. He had been with her, reading to her all the morning, and had never even mentioned such a place as Mexico. She had not seen him during the afternoon; she had heard some one say he was at the house, upstairs with his mother. This she had thought nothing of, though she was surprised when he did not join her later in the afternoon, when she went down to the beach.

She looked across at him, where he sat beside Madame Lebrun, who presided. Edna's face was a blank picture of bewilderment, which she never thought of disguising. He lifted his eyebrows with the pretext of a smile as he returned her glance. He looked embarrassed and uneasy.

"When is he going?" she asked of everybody in general, as if Robert were not there to answer for himself.

"To-night!" "This very evening!" "Did you ever!" "What possesses him!" were some of the replies she gathered, uttered simultaneously in French and English.

"Impossible!" she exclaimed. "How can a person start off from Grand Isle to Mexico at a moment's notice, as if he were going over to Klein's or to the wharf or down to the beach?"

"I said all along I was going to Mexico; I've been saying so for years!" cried Robert, in an excited and irritable tone, with the air of a man defending himself against a swarm of stinging insects.

Madame Lebrun knocked on the table with her knife handle.

"Please let Robert explain why he is going, and why he is going tonight," she called out. "Really, this table is getting to be more and more like Bedlam every day, with everybody talking at once. Sometimes—I hope God will forgive me—but positively, sometimes I wish Victor would lose the power of speech."

Victor laughed sardonically as he thanked his mother for her holy wish, of which he failed to see the benefit to anybody, except that it might afford her a more ample opportunity and license to talk herself.

Monsieur Farival thought that Victor should have been taken out in mid-ocean in his earliest youth and drowned. Victor thought there would be more logic in thus disposing of old people with an established claim for making themselves universally obnoxious. Madame Lebrun grew a trifle hysterical; Robert called his brother some sharp, hard names.

"There's nothing much to explain, mother," he said; though he explained, nevertheless—looking chiefly at Edna—that he could only meet the gentleman whom he intended to join at Vera Cruz by taking such and such a steamer, which left New Orleans on such a day; that Beaudelet was going out with his lugger-load of vegetables that night, which gave him an opportunity of reaching the city and making his vessel in time.

"But when did you make up your mind to all this?" demanded Monsieur Farival.

"This afternoon," returned Robert, with a shade of annoyance.

"At what time this afternoon?" persisted the old gentleman, with nagging determination, as if he were cross-questioning a criminal in a court of justice.

"At four o'clock this afternoon, Monsieur Farival," Robert replied, in a high voice and with a lofty air, which reminded Edna of some gentleman on the stage.

She had forced herself to eat most of her soup, and now she was picking the flaky bits of a *court bouillon* with her fork.

The lovers were profiting by the general conversation on Mexico to speak in whispers of matters which they rightly considered were interesting to no one but themselves. The lady in black had once received a pair of prayer-beads of curious workmanship from Mexico, with very special indulgence attached to them, but she had never been able to ascertain whether the indulgence extended outside the Mexican border. Father Fochel of the Cathedral had attempted to explain it; but he had not done so to her satisfaction. And she begged that Robert would interest himself and discover, if possible, whether she was entitled to the indulgence accompanying the remarkably curious Mexican prayer-beads.

Madame Ratignolle hoped that Robert would exercise extreme caution in dealing with the Mexicans, who, she considered, were a treacherous people, unscrupulous and revengeful. She trusted she did them no injustice in thus condemning them as a race. She had known personally but one Mexican, who made and sold excellent tamales, and whom she would have trusted implicitly, so soft-spoken was he. One day he was arrested for stabbing his wife. She never knew whether he had been hanged or not.

Victor had grown hilarious, and was attempting to tell an anecdote about a Mexican girl who served chocolate one winter in a restaurant in Dauphine Street. No one would listen to him but old Monsieur Farival, who went into convulsions over the droll story.

Edna wondered if they had all gone mad, to be talking and clamoring at that rate. She herself could think of nothing to say about Mexico or the Mexicans.

"At what time do you leave?" she asked Robert.

"At ten," he told her. "Beaudelet wants to wait for the moon."

"Are you all ready to go?"

"Quite ready. I shall only take a hand-bag, and shall pack my trunk in the city."

He turned to answer some question put to him by his mother, and Edna, having finished her black coffee, left the table.

She went directly to her room. The little cottage was close and stuffy after leaving the outer air. But she did not mind; there appeared to be a hundred different things demanding her attention indoors. She began to set the toilet-stand to rights, grumbling at the negligence of the quadroon, who was in the adjoining room putting the children to bed. She gathered together stray garments that were hanging on the backs of chairs, and put each where it belonged in closet or bureau drawer. She changed her gown for a more comfortable and commodious wrapper. She rearranged her hair, combing and brushing it with unusual energy. Then she went in and assisted the quadroon in getting the boys to bed.

They were very playful and inclined to talk—to do anything but lie quiet and go to sleep. Edna sent the quadroon away to her supper and told her she need not return. Then she sat and told the children a story. Instead of soothing it excited them, and added to their wakefulness. She left them in heated argument, speculating about the conclusion of the tale which their mother promised to finish the following night.

The little black girl came in to say that Madame Lebrun would like to have Mrs. Pontellier go and sit with them over at the house till Mr. Robert went away. Edna returned answer that she had already undressed, that she did not feel quite well, but perhaps she would go over to the house later. She started to dress again, and got as far advanced as to remove her *peignoir*. But changing her mind once more she resumed the *peignoir*, and went outside and sat down before her door. She was overheated and irritable, and fanned herself energetically for a while. Madame Ratignolle came down to discover what was the matter.

"All that noise and confusion at the table must have upset me," replied Edna, "and moreover, I hate shocks and surprises. The idea of Robert starting off in such a ridiculously sudden and dramatic way! As if it were a matter of life and death! Never saying a word about it all morning when he was with me."

"Yes," agreed Madame Ratignolle. "I think it was showing us all—you especially—very little consideration. It wouldn't have surprised me in any of the others; those Lebruns are all given to heroics. But I must say I should never have expected such a thing from Robert. Are you not coming down? Come on, dear; it doesn't look friendly."

"No," said Edna, a little sullenly. "I can't go to the trouble of dressing again; I don't feel like it."

"You needn't dress; you look all right; fasten a belt around your waist. Just look at me!"

"No," persisted Edna; "but you go on. Madame Lebrun might be offended if we both stayed away."

Madame Ratignolle kissed Edna good-night, and went away, being in truth rather desirous of joining in the general and animated conversation which was still in progress concerning Mexico and the Mexicans.

Somewhat later Robert came up, carrying his hand-bag.

"Aren't you feeling well?" he asked.

"Oh, well enough. Are you going right away?"

He lit a match and looked at his watch. "In twenty minutes," he said. The sudden and brief flare of the match emphasized the darkness for a while. He sat down upon a stool which the children had left out on the porch.

"Get a chair," said Edna.

"This will do," he replied. He put on his soft hat and nervously took it off again, and wiping his face with his handkerchief, complained of the heat.

"Take the fan," said Edna, offering it to him.

"Oh, no! Thank you. It does no good; you have to stop fanning some time, and feel all the more uncomfortable afterward."

"That's one of the ridiculous things which men always say. I have never known one to speak otherwise of fanning. How long will you be gone?"

"Forever, perhaps. I don't know. It depends upon a good many things."

"Well, in case it shouldn't be forever, how long will it be?"

"I don't know."

"This seems to me perfectly preposterous and uncalled for. I don't like it. I don't understand your motive for silence and mystery, never saying a word to me about it this morning." He remained silent, not offering to defend himself. He only said, after a moment:

"Don't part from me in an ill-humor. I never knew you to be out of patience with me before."

"I don't want to part in any ill-humor," she said. "But can't you understand? I've grown used to seeing you, to having you with me all the time, and your action seems unfriendly, even unkind. You don't even offer an excuse for it. Why, I was planning to be together, thinking of how pleasant it would be to see you in the city next winter."

"So was I," he blurted. "Perhaps that's the—" He stood up suddenly and held out his hand. "Good-by, my dear Mrs. Pontellier; good-by. You won't—I hope you won't completely forget me." She clung to his hand, striving to detain him.

"Write to me when you get there, won't you, Robert?" she entreated.

"I will, thank you. Good-by."

How unlike Robert! The merest acquaintance would have said something more emphatic than "I will, thank you; good-by," to such a request.

He had evidently already taken leave of the people over at the house, for he descended the steps and went to join Beaudelet, who was out there with an oar across his shoulder waiting for Robert. They walked away in the darkness. She could only hear Beaudelet's voice; Robert had apparently not even spoken a word of greeting to his companion.

Edna bit her handkerchief convulsively, striving to hold back and to hide, even from herself as she would have hidden from another, the emotion which was troubling—tearing—her. Her eyes were brimming with tears.

For the first time she recognized anew the symptoms of infatuation which she had felt incipiently as a child, as a girl in her earliest teens, and later as a young woman. The recognition did not lessen the reality, the poignancy of the revelation by any suggestion or promise of instability. The past was nothing to her; offered no lesson which she was willing to heed. The future was a mystery which she never attempted to penetrate. The present alone was significant; was hers, to torture her as it was doing then with the biting conviction that she had lost that which she had held, that she had been denied that which her impassioned, newly awakened being demanded.

XVI

"Do you miss your friend greatly?" asked Mademoiselle Reisz one morning as she came creeping up behind Edna, who had just left her cottage on her way to the beach. She spent much of her time in the water since she had acquired finally the art of swimming. As their stay at Grand Isle drew near its close, she felt that she could not give too much time to a diversion which afforded her the only real pleasurable moments that she knew. When Mademoiselle Reisz came and touched her upon the shoulder and spoke to her, the woman seemed to echo the thought which was ever in Edna's mind; or, better, the feeling which constantly possessed her.

Robert's going had some way taken the brightness, the color, the meaning out of everything. The conditions of her life were in no way changed, but her whole existence was dulled, like a faded garment which seems to be no longer worth wearing. She sought him everywhere—in others whom she induced to talk about him. She went up in the mornings to Madame Lebrun's room, braving the clatter of the old sewing-machine. She sat there and chatted at intervals as Robert had done. She gazed around the room at the pictures and photographs hanging upon the wall, and discovered in some corner an old family album, which she examined with the keenest interest, appealing to Madame Lebrun for enlightenment concerning the many figures and faces which she discovered between its pages.

There was a picture of Madame Lebrun with Robert as a baby,

seated in her lap, a round-faced infant with a fist in his mouth. The eyes alone in the baby suggested the man. And that was he also in kilts, at the age of five, wearing long curls and holding a whip in his hand. It made Edna laugh, and she laughed, too, at the portrait in his first long trousers; while another interested her, taken when he left for college, looking thin, long-faced, with eyes full of fire, ambition and great intentions. But there was no recent picture, none which suggested the Robert who had gone away five days ago, leaving a void and wilderness behind him.

"Oh, Robert stopped having his pictures taken when he had to pay for them himself! He found wiser use for his money, he says," explained Madame Lebrun. She had a letter from him, written before he left New Orleans. Edna wished to see the letter, and Madame Lebrun told her to look for it either on the table or the dresser, or perhaps it was on the mantelpiece.

The letter was on the bookshelf. It possessed the greatest interest and attraction for Edna; the envelope, its size and shape, the post-mark, the handwriting. She examined every detail of the outside before opening it. There were only a few lines, setting forth that he would leave the city that afternoon, that he had packed his trunk in good shape, that he was well, and sent her his love and begged to be affectionately remembered to all. There was no special message to Edna except a postscript saying that if Mrs. Pontellier desired to finish the book which he had been reading to her, his mother would find it in his room, among other books there on the table. Edna experienced a pang of jealousy because he had written to his mother rather than to her.

Every one seemed to take for granted that she missed him. Even her husband, when he came down the Saturday following Robert's departure, expressed regret that he had gone.

"How do you get on without him, Edna?" he asked.

"It's very dull without him," she admitted. Mr. Pontellier had seen Robert in the city, and Edna asked him a dozen questions or more. Where had they met? On Carondelet Street, in the morning. They had gone "in" and had a drink and a cigar together. What had they talked about? Chiefly about his prospects in Mexico, which Mr. Pontellier thought were promising. How did he look? How did he seem—grave, or gay, or how? Quite cheerful, and wholly taken up with the idea of his trip, which Mr. Pontellier found altogether natural in a young fellow about to seek fortune and adventure in a strange, queer country.

Edna tapped her foot impatiently, and wondered why the children persisted in playing in the sun when they might be under the trees. She went down and led them out of the sun, scolding the quadroon for not being more attentive.

It did not strike her as in the least grotesque that she should be making of Robert the object of conversation and leading her husband to speak of him. The sentiment which she entertained for Robert in no way resembled that which she felt for her husband, or had ever felt, or ever expected to feel. She had all her life long been accustomed to harbor thoughts and emotions which never voiced themselves. They had never taken the form of struggles. They belonged to her and were her own, and she entertained the conviction that she had a right to them and that they concerned no one but herself. Edna had once told Madame Ratignolle that she would never sacrifice herself for her children, or for any one. Then had followed a rather heated argument; the two women did not appear to understand each other or to be talking the same language. Edna tried to appease her friend, to explain.

"I would give up the unessential; I would give my money, I would give my life for my children; but I wouldn't give myself. I can't make it more clear; it's only something which I am beginning to comprehend, which is revealing itself to me."

"I don't know what you would call the essential, or what you mean by the unessential," said Madame Ratignolle, cheerfully; "but a woman who would give her life for her children could do no more than that—your Bible tells you so.* I'm sure I couldn't do more than that."

"Oh, yes you could!" laughed Edna.

She was not surprised at Mademoiselle Reisz's question the morning that lady, following her to the beach, tapped her on the shoulder and asked if she did not greatly miss her young friend.

"Oh, good morning, Mademoiselle; is it you? Why, of course I miss Robert. Are you going down to bathe?"

"Why should I go down to bathe at the very end of the season when I haven't been in the surf all summer," replied the woman, disagreeably.

"I beg your pardon," offered Edna, in some embarrassment, for she should have remembered that Mademoiselle Reisz's avoidance of the water had furnished a theme for much pleasantry. Some among them thought it was on account of her false hair, or the dread of getting the violets wet, while others attributed it to the natural aversion for water sometimes believed to accompany the artistic temperament. Mademoiselle offered Edna some chocolates in a paper bag, which she took from her pocket, by way of showing that she bore no ill feeling. She habitually ate chocolates for their sustaining quality; they contained much nutriment in small compass, she said. They saved her from starvation, as Madame Lebrun's table was utterly impossible; and no one save so impertinent a woman as Madame Lebrun could think of offering such food to people and requiring them to pay for it.

"She must feel very lonely without her son," said Edna, desiring to change the subject. "Her favorite son, too. It must have been quite hard to let him go."

Mademoiselle laughed maliciously.

"Her favorite son! Oh, dear! Who could have been imposing such a tale upon you? Aline Lebrun lives for Victor, and for Victor alone. She has spoiled him into the worthless creature he is. She worships him and the ground he walks on. Robert is very well in a way, to give up all the money he can earn to the family, and keep the barest pittance for himself. Favorite son, indeed! I miss the poor fellow myself, my dear. I liked to see him and to hear him about the place— the only Lebrun who is worth a pinch of salt. He comes to see me often in the city. I like to play to him. That Victor! hanging would be too good for him. It's a wonder Robert hasn't beaten him to death long ago."

"I thought he had great patience with his brother," offered Edna, glad to be talking about Robert, no matter what was said.

"Oh! he thrashed him well enough a year or two ago," said Mademoiselle. "It was about a Spanish girl, whom Victor considered that he had some sort of claim upon. He met Robert one day talking to the girl, or walking with her, or bathing with her, or carrying her basket—I don't remember what;—and he became so insulting and abusive that Robert gave him a thrashing on the spot that has kept him comparatively in order for a good while. It's about time he was getting another."

"Was her name Mariequita?" asked Edna.

"Mariequita—yes, that was it; Mariequita. I had forgotten. Oh, she's a sly one, and a bad one, that Mariequita!"

Edna looked down at Mademoiselle Reisz and wondered how she could have listened to her venom so long. For some reason she felt depressed, almost unhappy. She had not intended to go into the water; but she donned her bathing suit, and left Mademoiselle alone, seated under the shade of the children's tent. The water was growing cooler as the season advanced. Edna plunged and swam about with an abandon that thrilled and invigorated her. She remained a long time in the water, half hoping that Mademoiselle Reisz would not wait for her.

But Mademoiselle waited. She was very amiable during the walk back, and raved much over Edna's appearance in her bathing suit. She talked about music. She hoped that Edna would go to see her in the city, and wrote her address with the stub of a pencil on a piece of card which she found in her pocket.

"When do you leave?" asked Edna.

"Next Monday; and you?"

"The following week," answered Edna, adding, "It has been a pleasant summer, hasn't it, Mademoiselle?"

"Well," agreed Mademoiselle Reisz, with a shrug, "rather pleasant, if it hadn't been for the mosquitoes and the Farival twins."

XVII

The Pontelliers possessed a very charming home on Esplanade Street* in New Orleans. It was a large, double cottage,* with a broad front veranda, whose round, fluted columns supported the sloping roof. The house was painted a dazzling white; the outside shutters, or jalousies, were green. In the yard, which was kept scrupulously neat, were flowers and plants of every description which flourishes in South Louisiana. Within doors the appointments were perfect after the conventional type. The softest carpets and rugs covered the floors; rich and tasteful draperies hung at doors and windows. There were paintings, selected with judgment and discrimination, upon the walls. The cut glass, the silver, the heavy damask which daily appeared upon the table were the envy of many women whose husbands were less generous than Mr. Pontellier.

Mr. Pontellier was very fond of walking about his house examining its various appointments and details, to see that nothing was amiss. He greatly valued his possessions, chiefly because they were his, and derived genuine pleasure from contemplating a painting, a statuette, a rare lace curtain—no matter what—after he had bought it and placed it among his household gods.

On Tuesday afternoons—Tuesday being Mrs. Pontellier's reception day*—there was a constant stream of callers—women who came in carriages or in the street cars, or walked when the air was soft and distance permitted. A light-colored mulatto boy, in dress coat and bearing a diminutive silver tray for the reception of cards, admitted them. A maid, in white fluted cap, offered the callers liqueur, coffee, or chocolate, as they might desire. Mrs. Pontellier, attired in a handsome reception gown, remained in the drawing-room the entire afternoon receiving her visitors. Men sometimes called in the evening with their wives.

This had been the programme which Mrs. Pontellier had religiously followed since her marriage, six years before. Certain evenings during the week she and her husband attended the opera or sometimes the play.

Mr. Pontellier left his home in the mornings between nine and ten o'clock, and rarely returned before half-past six or seven in the evening—dinner being served at half-past seven.

He and his wife seated themselves at table one Tuesday evening, a few weeks after their return from Grand Isle. They were alone together. The boys were being put to bed; the patter of their bare, escaping feet could be heard occasionally, as well as the pursuing voice of the quadroon, lifted in mild protest and entreaty. Mrs. Pontellier did not wear her usual Tuesday reception gown; she was in ordinary house dress. Mr. Pontellier, who was observant about such things, noticed it, as he served the soup and handed it to the boy in waiting.

"Tired out, Edna? Whom did you have? Many callers?" he asked. He tasted his soup and began to season it with pepper, salt, vinegar, mustard—everything within reach.*

"There were a good many," replied Edna, who was eating her soup with evident satisfaction. "I found their cards when I got home; I was out."

"Out!" exclaimed her husband, with something like genuine

consternation in his voice as he laid down the vinegar cruet and looked at her through his glasses. "Why, what could have taken you out on Tuesday? What did you have to do?"

"Nothing. I simply felt like going out, and I went out."

"Well, I hope you left some suitable excuse," said her husband, somewhat appeased, as he added a dash of cayenne pepper to the soup.

"No, I left no excuse. I told Joe to say I was out, that was all."

"Why, my dear, I should think you'd understand by this time that people don't do such things; we've got to observe *les convenances* if we ever expect to get on and keep up with the procession. If you felt that you had to leave home this afternoon, you should have left some suitable explanation for your absence.

"This soup is really impossible; it's strange that woman hasn't learned yet to make a decent soup. Any free-lunch stand* in town serves a better one. Was Mrs. Belthrop here?"

"Bring the tray with the cards, Joe. I don't remember who was here."

The boy retired and returned after a moment, bringing the tiny silver tray, which was covered with ladies' visiting cards. He handed it to Mrs. Pontellier.

"Give it to Mr. Pontellier," she said.

Joe offered the tray to Mr. Pontellier, and removed the soup.

Mr. Pontellier scanned the names of his wife's callers, reading some of them aloud, with comments as he read.

" 'The Misses Delasidas.' I worked a big deal in futures for their father this morning; nice girls; it's time they were getting married. 'Mrs. Belthrop.' I tell you what it is, Edna; you can't afford to snub Mrs. Belthrop. Why, Belthrop could buy and sell us ten times over. His business is worth a good, round sum to me. You'd better write her a note. 'Mrs. James Highcamp.' Hugh! the less you have to do with Mrs. Highcamp, the better. 'Madame Laforcé'. Came all the way from Carrolton,* too, poor old soul. 'Miss Wiggs,' 'Mrs. Eleanor Boltons.' " He pushed the cards aside.

"Mercy!" exclaimed Edna, who had been fuming. "Why are you taking the thing so seriously and making such a fuss over it?"

"I'm not making any fuss over it. But it's just such seeming trifles that we've got to take seriously; such things count."

The fish was scorched. Mr. Pontellier would not touch it. Edna said she did not mind a little scorched taste. The roast was in some way not to his fancy, and he did not like the manner in which the vegetables were served.

"It seems to me," he said, "we spend money enough in this house to procure at least one meal a day which a man could eat and retain his self-respect."

"You used to think the cook was a treasure," returned Edna, indifferently.

"Perhaps she was when she first came; but cooks are only human. They need looking after, like any other class of persons that you employ. Suppose I didn't look after the clerks in my office, just let them run things their own way; they'd soon make a nice mess of me and my business."

"Where are you going?" asked Edna, seeing that her husband arose from table without having eaten a morsel except a taste of the highly-seasoned soup.

"I'm going to get my dinner at the club. Good night." He went into the hall, took his hat and stick from the stand, and left the house.

She was somewhat familiar with such scenes. They had often made her very unhappy. On a few previous occasions she had been completely deprived of any desire to finish her dinner. Sometimes she had gone into the kitchen to administer a tardy rebuke to the cook. Once she went to her room and studied the cookbook during an entire evening, finally writing out a menu for the week, which left her harassed with a feeling that, after all, she had accomplished no good that was worth the name.

But that evening Edna finished her dinner alone, with forced deliberation. Her face was flushed and her eyes flamed with some inward fire that lighted them. After finishing her dinner she went to her room, having instructed the boy to tell any other callers that she was indisposed.

It was a large, beautiful room, rich and picturesque in the soft, dim light which the maid had turned low. She went and stood at an open window and looked out upon the deep tangle of the garden below. All the mystery and witchery of the night seemed to have gathered there amid the perfumes and the dusky and tortuous out-lines of flowers and foliage. She was seeking herself and finding herself in just such sweet, half-darkness which met her moods. But the voices were not soothing that came to her from the darkness and the sky above and the stars. They jeered and sounded mournful notes without promise, devoid even of hope. She turned back into the room and began to walk to and fro down its whole length, without stopping, without resting. She carried in her hands a thin hand-kerchief, which she tore into ribbons, rolled into a ball, and flung from her. Once she stopped, and taking off her wedding ring, flung it upon the carpet. When she saw it lying there, she stamped her heel upon it, striving to crush it. But her small boot heel did not make an indenture, not a mark upon the little glittering circlet.

In a sweeping passion she seized a glass vase from the table and flung it upon the tiles of the hearth. She wanted to destroy something. The crash and clatter were what she wanted to hear.

A maid, alarmed at the din of breaking glass, entered the room to discover what was the matter.

"A vase fell upon the hearth," said Edna. "Never mind; leave it till morning."

"Oh! you might get some of the glass in your feet, ma'am," insisted the young woman, picking up bits of the broken vase that were scattered upon the carpet. "And here's your ring, ma'am, under the chair."

Edna held out her hand, and taking the ring, slipped it upon her finger.

XVIII

The following morning Mr. Pontellier, upon leaving for his office, asked Edna if she would not meet him in town in order to look at some new fixtures for the library.

"I hardly think we need new fixtures, Léonce. Don't let us get anything new; you are too extravagant. I don't believe you ever think of saving or putting by."

"The way to become rich is to make money, my dear Edna, not to save it," he said. He regretted that she did not feel inclined to go with him and select new fixtures. He kissed her good-by, and told her she was not looking well and must take care of herself. She was unusually pale and very quiet.

She stood on the front veranda as he quitted the house, and absently picked a few sprays of jessamine that grew upon a trellis near by. She inhaled the odor of the blossoms and thrust them into the bosom of her white morning gown. The boys were dragging along the banquette a small "express wagon," which they had filled with blocks and sticks. The quadroon was following them with little quick steps, having assumed a fictitious animation and alacrity for the occasion. A fruit vender was crying his wares in the street.

Edna looked straight before her with a self-absorbed expression upon her face. She felt no interest in anything about her. The street, the children, the fruit vender, the flowers growing there under her eyes, were all part and parcel of an alien world which had suddenly become antagonistic.

She went back into the house. She had thought of speaking to the cook concerning her blunders of the previous night; but Mr. Pontellier had saved her that disagreeable mission, for which she was so poorly fitted. Mr. Pontellier's arguments were usually convincing with those whom he employed. He left home feeling quite sure that he and Edna would sit down that evening, and possibly a few subsequent evenings, to a dinner deserving of the name.

Edna spent an hour or two in looking over some of her old sketches. She could see their shortcomings and defects, which were glaring in her eyes. She tried to work a little, but found she was not in the humor. Finally she gathered together a few of the sketches— those which she considered the least discreditable; and she carried them with her when, a little later, she dressed and left the house. She looked handsome and distinguished in her street gown. The tan of the seashore had left her face, and her forehead was smooth, white, and polished beneath her heavy, yellow-brown hair. There were a few freckles on her face, and a small, dark mole near the under lip and one on the temple, half-hidden in her hair.

As Edna walked along the street she was thinking of Robert. She was still under the spell of her infatuation. She had tried to forget him, realizing the inutility of remembering. But the thought of him was like an obsession, ever pressing itself upon her. It was not that she dwelt upon details of their acquaintance, or recalled in any special or peculiar way his personality; it was his being, his existence, which dominated her thought, fading sometimes as if it would melt into the mist of the forgotten, reviving again with an intensity which filled her with an incomprehensible longing.

Edna was on her way to Madame Ratignolle's. Their intimacy,

begun at Grand Isle, had not declined, and they had seen each other with some frequency since their return to the city. The Ratignolles lived at no great distance from Edna's home, on the corner of a side street, where Monsieur Ratignolle owned and conducted a drug store which enjoyed a steady and prosperous trade. His father had been in the business before him, and Monsieur Ratignolle stood well in the community and bore an enviable reputation for integrity and clear-headedness. His family lived in commodious apartments over the store, having an entrance on the side within the *porte cochère*.* There was something which Edna thought very French, very foreign, about their whole manner of living. In the large and pleasant salon which extended across the width of the house, the Ratignolles entertained their friends once a fortnight with a *soirée musicale*,* sometimes diversified by card-playing. There was a friend who played upon the 'cello. One brought his flute and another his violin while there were some who sang and a number who performed upon the piano with various degrees of taste and agility. The Ratignolles' *soirées musicales* were widely known, and it was considered a privilege to be invited to them.

Edna found her friend engaged in assorting the clothes which had returned that morning from the laundry. She at once abandoned her occupation upon seeing Edna, who had been ushered without ceremony into her presence.

" 'Cité can do it as well as I; it is really her business," she explained to Edna, who apologized for interrupting her. And she summoned a young black woman, whom she instructed, in French, to be very careful in checking off the list which she handed her. She told her to notice particularly if a fine linen handkerchief of Monsieur Ratignolle's, which was missing last week, had been returned; and to be sure to set to one side such pieces as required mending and darning.

Then placing an arm around Edna's waist, she led her to the front of the house, to the salon, where it was cool and sweet with the odor of great roses that stood upon the hearth in jars.

Madame Ratignolle looked more beautiful than ever there at home, in a negligé which left her arms almost wholly bare and exposed the rich, melting curves of her white throat.

"Perhaps I shall be able to paint your picture some day," said Edna with a smile when they were seated. She produced the roll of sketches and started to unfold them. "I believe I ought to work again.

I feel as if I wanted to be doing something. What do you think of them? Do you think it worth while to take it up again and study some more? I might study for a while with Laidpore."

She knew that Madame Ratignolle's opinion in such a matter would be next to valueless, that she herself had not alone decided, but determined; but she sought the words of praise and encouragement that would help her to put heart into her venture.

"Your talent is immense, dear!"

"Nonsense!" protested Edna, well pleased.

"Immense, I tell you," persisted Madame Ratignolle, surveying the sketches one by one, at close range, then holding them at arm's length, narrowing her eyes, and dropping her head on one side. "Surely, this Bavarian peasant* is worthy of framing; and this basket of apples! never have I seen anything more lifelike. One might almost be tempted to reach out a hand and take one."

Edna could not control a feeling which bordered upon complacency at her friend's praise, even realizing, as she did, its true worth. She retained a few of the sketches, and gave all the rest to Madame Ratignolle, who appreciated the gift far beyond its value and proudly exhibited the pictures to her husband when he came up from the store a little later for his midday dinner.

Mr. Ratignolle was one of those men who are called the salt of the earth.* His cheerfulness was unbounded, and it was matched by his goodness of heart, his broad charity, and common sense. He and his wife spoke English with an accent which was only discernible through its un-English emphasis and a certain carefulness and deliberation. Edna's husband spoke English with no accent whatever.* The Ratignolles understood each other perfectly. If ever the fusion of two human beings into one has been accomplished on this sphere it was surely in their union.

As Edna seated herself at table with them she thought, "Better a dinner of herbs,"* though it did not take her long to discover that was no dinner of herbs, but a delicious repast, simple, choice, and in every way satisfying.

Monsieur Ratignolle was delighted to see her, though he found her looking not so well as at Grand Isle, and he advised a tonic. He talked a good deal on various topics, a little politics, some city news and neighborhood gossip. He spoke with an animation and earnestness that gave an exaggerated importance to every syllable he uttered. His wife was keenly interested in everything he said, laying down her fork the better to listen, chiming in, taking the words out of his mouth.

Edna felt depressed rather than soothed after leaving them. The little glimpse of domestic harmony which had been offered her, gave her no regret, no longing. It was not a condition of life which fitted her, and she could see in it but an appalling and hopeless ennui. She was moved by a kind of commiseration for Madame Ratignolle,—a pity for that colorless existence which never uplifted its possessor beyond the region of blind contentment, in which no moment of anguish ever visited her soul, in which she would never have the taste of life's delirium.* Edna vaguely wondered what she meant by "life's delirium." It had crossed her thought like some unsought, extraneous impression.

XIX

Edna could not help but think that it was very foolish, very childish, to have stamped upon her wedding ring and smashed the crystal vase upon the tiles. She was visited by no more outbursts, moving her to such futile expedients. She began to do as she liked and to feel as she liked. She completely abandoned her Tuesdays at home, and did not return the visits of those who had called upon her. She made no ineffectual efforts to conduct her household *en bonne ménagère*,* going and coming as it suited her fancy, and, so far as she was able, lending herself to any passing caprice.

Mr. Pontellier had been a rather courteous husband so long as he met a certain tacit submissiveness in his wife. But her new and unexpected line of conduct completely bewildered him. It shocked him. Then her absolute disregard for her duties as a wife angered him. When Mr. Pontellier became rude, Edna grew insolent. She had resolved never to take another step backward.

"It seems to me the utmost folly for a woman at the head of a household, and the mother of children, to spend in an atelier days which would be better employed contriving for the comfort of her family."

"I feel like painting," answered Edna. "Perhaps I shan't always feel like it."

"Then in God's name paint! but don't let the family go to the devil. There's Madame Ratignolle; because she keeps up her music, she doesn't let everything else go to chaos. And she's more of a musician than you are a painter."

"She isn't a musician, and I'm not a painter. It isn't on account of painting that I let things go."

"On account of what, then?"

"Oh! I don't know. Let me alone; you bother me."

It sometimes entered Mr. Pontellier's mind to wonder if his wife were not growing a little unbalanced mentally. He could see plainly that she was not herself. That is, he could not see that she was becoming herself and daily casting aside that fictitious self which we assume like a garment with which to appear before the world.

Her husband let her alone as she requested, and went away to his office. Edna went up to her atelier—a bright room in the top of the house. She was working with great energy and interest, without accomplishing anything, however, which satisfied her even in the smallest degree. For a time she had the whole household enrolled in the service of art. The boys posed for her. They thought it amusing at first, but the occupation soon lost its attractiveness when they discovered that it was not a game arranged especially for their entertainment. The quadroon sat for hours before Edna's palette, patient as a savage, while the house-maid took charge of the children, and the drawing-room went undusted. But the house-maid, too, served her term as model when Edna perceived that the young woman's back and shoulders were molded on classic lines, and that her hair, loosened from its confining cap, became an inspiration. While Edna worked she sometimes sang low the little air, "*Ah! si tu savais!*"

It moved her with recollections. She could hear again the ripple of the water, the flapping sail. She could see the glint of the moon upon the bay, and could feel the soft, gusty beating of the hot south wind. A subtle current of desire passed through her body, weakening her hold upon the brushes and making her eyes burn.

There were days when she was very happy without knowing why. She was happy to be alive and breathing, when her whole being seemed to be one with the sunlight, the color, the odors, the luxuriant warmth of some perfect Southern day. She liked then to wander alone into strange and unfamiliar places. She discovered many a sunny, sleepy corner, fashioned to dream in. And she found it good to dream and to be alone and unmolested.

There were days when she was unhappy, she did not know why,—when it did not seem worth while to be glad or sorry, to be alive or dead; when life appeared to her like a grotesque pandemonium and humanity like worms struggling blindly toward inevitable annihilation. She could not work on such a day, nor weave fancies to stir her pulses and warm her blood.

XX

It was during such a mood that Edna hunted up Mademoiselle Reisz. She had not forgotten the rather disagreeable impression left upon her by their last interview; but she nevertheless felt a desire to see her—above all, to listen while she played upon the piano. Quite early in the afternoon she started upon her quest for the pianist. Unfortunately she had mislaid or lost Mademoiselle Reisz's card, and looking up her address in the city directory, she found that the woman lived on Bienville Street, some distance away.* The directory which fell into her hands was a year or more old, however, and upon reaching the number indicated, Edna discovered that the house was occupied by a respectable family of mulattoes who had *chambres garnies* to let. They had been living there for six months, and knew absolutely nothing of a Mademoiselle Reisz. In fact, they knew nothing of any of their neighbors; their lodgers were all people of the highest distinction, they assured Edna. She did not linger to discuss class distinctions with Madame Pouponne, but hastened to a neighboring grocery store, feeling sure that Mademoiselle would have left her address with the proprietor.

He knew Mademoiselle Reisz a good deal better than he wanted to know her, he informed his questioner. In truth, he did not want to know her at all, or anything concerning her—the most disagreeable and unpopular woman who ever lived in Bienville Street. He thanked heaven she had left the neighborhood, and was equally thankful that he did not know where she had gone.

Edna's desire to see Mademoiselle Reisz had increased tenfold since these unlooked-for obstacles had arisen to thwart it. She was wondering who could give her the information she sought, when it suddenly occurred to her that Madame Lebrun would be the one most likely to do so. She knew it was useless to ask Madame Ratignolle, who was on the most distant terms with the musician, and preferred to know nothing concerning her. She had once been almost as emphatic in expressing herself upon the subject as the corner grocer.

Edna knew that Madame Lebrun had returned to the city, for it was the middle of November. And she also knew where the Lebruns lived, on Chartres Street.

Their home from the outside looked like a prison, with iron bars before the door and lower windows. The iron bars were a relic of the old *régime*,* and no one had ever thought of dislodging them. At the side was a high fence enclosing the garden. A gate or door opening upon the street was locked. Edna rang the bell at this side garden gate, and stood upon the banquette, waiting to be admitted.

It was Victor who opened the gate for her. A black woman, wiping her hands upon her apron, was close at his heels. Before she saw them Edna could hear them in altercation, the woman—plainly an anomaly—claiming the right to be allowed to perform her duties, one of which was to answer the bell.

Victor was surprised and delighted to see Mrs. Pontellier, and he made no attempt to conceal either his astonishment or his delight. He was a dark-browed, good-looking youngster of nineteen, greatly resembling his mother, but with ten times her impetuosity. He instructed the black woman to go at once and inform Madame Lebrun that Mrs. Pontellier desired to see her. The woman grumbled a refusal to do part of her duty when she had not been permitted to do it all, and started back to her interrupted task of weeding the garden. Whereupon Victor administered a rebuke in the form of a volley of abuse, which, owing to its rapidity and incoherence, was all but incomprehensible to Edna. Whatever it was, the rebuke was convincing, for the woman dropped her hoe and went mumbling into the house.

Edna did not wish to enter. It was very pleasant there on the side porch, where there were chairs, a wicker lounge, and a small table. She seated herself, for she was tired from her long tramp; and she began to rock gently and smooth out the folds of her silk parasol. Victor drew up his chair beside her. He at once explained that the black woman's offensive conduct was all due to imperfect training, as he was not there to take her in hand. He had only come up from the island the morning before, and expected to return next day. He stayed all winter at the island; he lived there, and kept the place in order and got things ready for the summer visitors.

But a man needed occasional relaxation, he informed Mrs. Pontellier, and every now and again he drummed up a pretext to bring him to the city. My! but he had had a time of it the evening before! He wouldn't want his mother to know, and he began to talk in a whisper. He was scintillant with recollections. Of course, he couldn't think of telling Mrs. Pontellier all about it, she being a woman and not comprehending such things. But it all began with a girl peeping and smiling at him through the shutters as he passed by. Oh! but she was a beauty! Certainly he smiled back, and went up and talked to her. Mrs. Pontellier did not know him if she supposed he was one to let an opportunity like that escape him. Despite herself, the youngster amused her. She must have betrayed in her look some degree of interest or entertainment. The boy grew more daring, and Mrs. Pontellier might have found herself, in a little while, listening to a highly colored story but for the timely appearance of Madame Lebrun.

That lady was still clad in white, according to her custom of the summer. Her eyes beamed an effusive welcome. Would not Mrs. Pontellier go inside? Would she partake of some refreshment? Why had she not been there before? How was that dear Mr. Pontellier and how were those sweet children? Had Mrs. Pontellier ever known such a warm November?

Victor went and reclined on the wicker lounge behind his mother's chair, where he commanded a view of Edna's face. He had taken her parasol from her hands while he spoke to her, and he now lifted it and twirled it above him as he lay on his back. When Madame Lebrun complained that it was *so* dull coming back to the city; that she saw *so* few people now; that even Victor, when he came up from the island for a day or two, had *so* much to occupy him and engage his time; then it was that the youth went into contortions on the lounge and winked mischievously at Edna. She somehow felt like a confederate in crime, and tried to look severe and disapproving.

There had been but two letters from Robert, with little in them, they told her. Victor said it was really not worth while to go inside for the letters, when his mother entreated him to go in search of them. He remembered the contents, which in truth he rattled off very glibly when put to the test.

One letter was written from Vera Cruz and the other from the City of Mexico. He had met Montel, who was doing everything toward his advancement. So far, the financial situation was no improvement over the one he had left in New Orleans, but of course the prospects were vastly better. He wrote of the City of Mexico, the buildings, the people and their habits, the conditions of life which he found there. He sent his love to the family. He inclosed a check to his mother, and hoped she would affectionately remember him to all his friends. That was about the substance of the two letters. Edna felt that if there had been a message for her, she would have received it. The despondent frame of mind in which she had left home began again to overtake her, and she remembered that she wished to find Mademoiselle Reisz.

Madame Lebrun knew where Mademoiselle Reisz lived. She gave Edna the address, regretting that she would not consent to stay and spend the remainder of the afternoon, and pay a visit to Mademoiselle Reisz some other day. The afternoon was already well advanced.

Victor escorted her out upon the banquette, lifted her parasol, and held it over her while he walked to the car* with her. He entreated her to bear in mind that the disclosures of the afternoon were strictly confidential. She laughed and bantered him a little, remembering too late that she should have been dignified and reserved.

"How handsome Mrs. Pontellier looked!" said Madame Lebrun to her son.

"Ravishing!" he admitted. "The city atmosphere has improved her. Some way she doesn't seem like the same woman."

XXI

Some people contended that the reason Mademoiselle Reisz always chose apartments up under the roof was to discourage the approach of beggars, peddlars and callers. There were plenty of windows in her little front room. They were for the most part dingy, but as they were nearly always open it did not make so much difference. They often admitted into the room a good deal of smoke and soot; but at the same time all the light and air that there was came through them. From her windows could be seen the crescent of the river, the masts of ships and the big chimneys of the Mississippi steamers. A magnificent piano crowded the apartment. In the next room she slept, and in the third and last she harbored a gasoline stove on which she cooked her meals when disinclined to descend to the neighboring restaurant. It was there also that she ate, keeping her belongings in a rare old buffet, dingy and battered from a hundred years of use.

When Edna knocked at Mademoiselle Reisz's front room door and entered, she discovered that person standing beside the window, engaged in mending or patching an old prunella gaiter.* The little musician laughed all over when she saw Edna. Her laugh consisted of a contortion of the face and all the muscles of the body. She seemed strikingly homely, standing there in the afternoon light. She still wore the shabby lace and the artificial bunch of violets on the side of her head.

"So you remembered me at last," said Mademoiselle. "I had said to myself, 'Ah, bah! she will never come.'"

"Did you want me to come?" asked Edna with a smile.

"I had not thought much about it," answered Mademoiselle. The two had seated themselves on a little bumpy sofa which stood against the wall. "I am glad, however, that you came. I have the water boiling back there, and was just about to make some coffee. You will drink a cup with me. And how is *la belle dame?** Always handsome! always healthy! always contented!" She took Edna's hand between her strong wiry fingers, holding it loosely without warmth, and executing a sort of double theme upon the back and palm.

"Yes," she went on; "I sometimes thought: 'She will never come. She promised as those women in society always do, without meaning it. She will not come.' For I really don't believe you like me, Mrs. Pontellier."

"I don't know whether I like you or not," replied Edna, gazing down at the little woman with a quizzical look.

The candor of Mrs. Pontellier's admission greatly pleased Mademoiselle Reisz. She expressed her gratification by repairing forthwith to the region of the gasoline stove and rewarding her guest with the promised cup of coffee. The coffee and the biscuit accompanying it proved very acceptable to Edna, who had declined refreshment at Madame Lebrun's and was now beginning to feel hungry. Mademoiselle set the tray which she brought in upon a small table near at hand, and seated herself once again on the lumpy sofa.

"I have had a letter from your friend," she remarked, as she poured a little cream into Edna's cup and handed it to her.

"My friend?"

"Yes, your friend Robert. He wrote to me from the City of Mexico."

"Wrote to *you*?" repeated Edna in amazement, stirring her coffee absently.

"Yes, to me. Why not? Don't stir all the warmth out of your coffee; drink it. Though the letter might as well have been sent to you; it was nothing but Mrs. Pontellier from beginning to end."

"Let me see it," requested the young woman, entreatingly.

"No; a letter concerns no one but the person who writes it and the one to whom it is written."

"Haven't you just said it concerned me from beginning to end?"

"It was written about you, not to you. 'Have you seen Mrs. Pontellier? How is she looking?' he asks. 'As Mrs. Pontellier says,' or 'as Mrs. Pontellier once said.' 'If Mrs. Pontellier should call upon you, play for her that Impromptu of Chopin's,* my favorite. I heard it here a day or two ago, but not as you play it. I should like to know how it affects her,' and so on, as if he supposed we were constantly in each other's society."

"Let me see the letter."

"Oh, no."

"Have you answered it?"

"No."

"Let me see the letter."

"No, and again, no."

"Then play the Impromptu for me."

"It is growing late; what time do you have to be home?"

"Time doesn't concern me. Your question seems a little rude. Play the Impromptu."

"But you have told me nothing of yourself. What are you doing?"

"Painting!" laughed Edna. "I am becoming an artist. Think of it!"

"Ah! an artist! You have pretensions, Madame."

"Why pretensions? Do you think I could not become an artist?"

"I do not know you well enough to say. I do not know your talent or your temperament. To be an artist includes much; one must possess many gifts—absolute gifts—which have not been acquired by one's own effort. And, moreover, to succeed, the artist must possess the courageous soul."

"What do you mean by the courageous soul?"

"Courageous, *ma foi!* The brave soul. The soul that dares and defies."

"Show me the letter and play for me the Impromptu. You see that I have persistence. Does that quality count for anything in art?"

"It counts with a foolish old woman whom you have captivated," replied Mademoiselle, with her wriggling laugh.

The letter was right there at hand in the drawer of the little table upon which Edna had just placed her coffee cup. Mademoiselle opened the drawer and drew forth the letter, the topmost one. She placed it in Edna's hands, and without further comment arose and went to the piano.

Mademoiselle played a soft interlude. It was an improvisation. She sat low at the instrument, and the lines of her body settled into ungraceful curves and angles that gave it an appearance of deformity. Gradually and imperceptibly the interlude melted into the soft opening minor chords of the Chopin Impromptu.

Edna did not know when the Impromptu began or ended. She sat in the sofa corner reading Robert's letter by the fading light. Mademoiselle had glided from the Chopin into the quivering love-notes of Isolde's song,* and back again to the Impromptu with its soulful and poignant longing.

The shadows deepened in the little room. The music grew strange and fantastic—turbulent, insistent, plaintive and soft with entreaty. The shadows grew deeper. The music filled the room. It floated out upon the night, over the housetops, the crescent of the river, losing itself in the silence of the upper air.

Edna was sobbing, just as she had wept one midnight at Grand Isle when strange, new voices awoke in her. She arose in some agitation to take her departure. "May I come again, Mademoiselle?" she asked at the threshold.

"Come whenever you feel like it. Be careful; the stairs and landings are dark; don't stumble."

Mademoiselle reëntered and lit a candle. Robert's letter was on the floor. She stooped and picked it up. It was crumpled and damp with tears. Mademoiselle smoothed the letter out, restored it to the envelope, and replaced it in the table drawer.

XXII

One morning on his way into town Mr. Pontellier stopped at the house of his old friend and family physician, Doctor Mandelet. The Doctor was a semi-retired physician, resting, as the saying is, upon his laurels. He bore a reputation for wisdom rather than skill— leaving the active practice of medicine to his assistants and younger contemporaries—and was much sought for in matters of consultation. A few families, united to him by bonds of friendship, he still attended when they required the services of a physician. The Pontelliers were among these.

Mr. Pontellier found the Doctor reading at the open window of his study. His house stood rather far back from the street, in the center of a delightful garden, so that it was quiet and peaceful at the old gentleman's study window. He was a great reader. He stared up disapprovingly over his eye-glasses as Mr. Pontellier entered, wondering who had the temerity to disturb him at that hour of the morning.

"Ah, Pontellier! Not sick, I hope. Come and have a seat. What news do you bring this morning?" He was quite portly, with a profusion of gray hair, and small blue eyes which age had robbed of much of their brightness but none of their penetration.

"Oh! I'm never sick, Doctor. You know that I come of tough fiber—of that old Creole race of Pontelliers that dry up and finally blow away.* I came to consult—no, not precisely to consult—to talk to you about Edna. I don't know what ails her."

"Madame Pontellier not well?" marveled the Doctor. "Why, I saw her—I think it was a week ago—walking along Canal Street,* the picture of health, it seemed to me."

"Yes, yes; she seems quite well," said Mr. Pontellier, leaning forward and whirling his stick between his two hands; "but she doesn't act well. She's odd, she's not like herself. I can't make her out, and I thought perhaps you'd help me."

"How does she act?" inquired the Doctor.

"Well, it isn't easy to explain," said Mr. Pontellier, throwing himself back in his chair. "She lets the housekeeping go to the dickens."

"Well, well; women are not all alike, my dear Pontellier. We've got to consider—"

"I know that; I told you I couldn't explain. Her whole attitude—toward me and everybody and everything—has changed. You know I have a quick temper, but I don't want to quarrel or be rude to a woman, especially my wife; yet I'm driven to it, and feel like ten thousand devils after I've made a fool of myself. She's making it devilishly uncomfortable for me," he went on nervously. "She's got some sort of notion in her head concerning the eternal rights of women; and—you understand—we meet in the morning at the breakfast table."

The old gentleman lifted his shaggy eyebrows, protruded his thick nether lip, and tapped the arms of his chair with his cushioned finger-tips.

"What have you been doing to her, Pontellier?"

"Doing! *Parbleu!*"

"Has she," asked the Doctor, with a smile, "has she been associating of late with a circle of pseudo-intellectual women—super-spiritual superior beings?* My wife has been telling me about them."

"That's the trouble," broke in Mr. Pontellier, "she hasn't been associating with any one. She has abandoned her Tuesdays at home, has thrown over all her acquaintances, and goes tramping about by herself, moping in the street-cars, getting in after dark. I tell you she's peculiar.* I don't like it; I feel a little worried over it."

This was a new aspect for the Doctor. "Nothing hereditary?"* he asked, seriously. "Nothing peculiar about her family antecedents, is there?"

"Oh, no, indeed! She comes of sound old Presbyterian Kentucky stock. The old gentleman, her father, I have heard, used to atone for his weekday sins with his Sunday devotions. I know for a fact, that his race horses literally ran away with the prettiest bit of Kentucky farming land I ever laid eyes upon. Margaret—you know Margaret—she has all the Presbyterianism undiluted. And the youngest is something of a vixen. By the way, she gets married in a couple of weeks from now."

"Send your wife up to the wedding," exclaimed the Doctor, foreseeing a happy solution. "Let her stay among her own people for a while; it will do her good."

"That's what I want her to do. She won't go to the marriage. She says a wedding is one of the most lamentable spectacles on earth.

Nice thing for a woman to say to her husband!" exclaimed Mr. Pontellier, fuming anew at the recollection.

"Pontellier," said the Doctor, after a moment's reflection, "let your wife alone for a while. Don't bother her, and don't let her bother you. Woman, my dear friend, is a very peculiar and delicate organism*—a sensitive and highly organized woman, such as I know Mrs. Pontellier to be, is especially peculiar. It would require an inspired psychologist to deal successfully with them. And when ordinary fellows like you and me attempt to cope with their idiosyncrasies the result is bungling. Most women are moody and whimsical. This is some passing whim of your wife, due to some cause or causes which you and I needn't try to fathom. But it will pass happily over, especially if you let her alone. Send her around to see me."

"Oh! I couldn't do that; there'd be no reason for it," objected Mr. Pontellier.

"Then I'll go around and see her," said the Doctor. "I'll drop in to dinner some evening *en bon ami*."

"Do! by all means," urged Mr. Pontellier. "What evening will you come? Say Thursday. Will you come Thursday?" he asked, rising to take his leave.

"Very well; Thursday. My wife may possibly have some engagement for me Thursday. In case she has, I shall let you know. Otherwise, you may expect me."

Mr. Pontellier turned before leaving to say:

"I am going to New York on business very soon. I have a big scheme on hand, and want to be on the field proper to pull the ropes and handle the ribbons. We'll let you in on the inside if you say so, Doctor," he laughed.

"No, I thank you, my dear sir," returned the Doctor. "I leave such ventures to you younger men with the fever of life still in your blood."

"What I wanted to say," continued Mr. Pontellier, with his hand on the knob; "I may have to be absent a good while. Would you advise me to take Edna along?"

"By all means, if she wishes to go. If not, leave her here. Don't contradict her. The mood will pass, I assure you. It may take a month, two, three months—possibly longer, but it will pass; have patience."

"Well, good-by, *à jeudi*," said Mr. Pontellier, as he let himself out.

The Doctor would have liked during the course of conversation to ask, "Is there any man in the case?" but he knew his Creole too well* to make such a blunder as that.

He did not resume his book immediately, but sat for a while meditatively looking out into the garden.

XXIII

Edna's father was in the city, and had been with them several days. She was not very warmly or deeply attached to him, but they had certain tastes in common, and when together they were companionable. His coming was in the nature of a welcome disturbance; it seemed to furnish a new direction for her emotions.

He had come to purchase a wedding gift for his daughter, Janet, and an outfit for himself in which he might make a creditable appearance at her marriage. Mr. Pontellier had selected the bridal gift, as every one immediately connected with him always deferred to his taste in such matters. And his suggestions on the question of dress—which too often assumes the nature of a problem—were of inestimable value to his father-in-law. But for the past few days the old gentleman had been upon Edna's hands, and in his society she was becoming acquainted with a new set of sensations. He had been a colonel in the Confederate army,* and still maintained, with the title, the military bearing which had always accompanied it. His hair and mustache were white and silky, emphasizing the rugged bronze of his face. He was tall and thin, and wore his coats padded, which gave a fictitious breadth and depth to his shoulders and chest. Edna and her father looked very distinguished together, and excited a good deal of notice during their perambulations. Upon his arrival she began by introducing him to her atelier and making a sketch of him. He took the whole matter very seriously. If her talent had been tenfold greater than it was, it would not have surprised him, convinced as he was that he had bequeathed to all of his daughters the germs of a masterful capability, which only depended upon their own efforts to be directed toward successful achievement.

Before her pencil he sat rigid and unflinching, as he had faced the cannon's mouth in days gone by. He resented the intrusion of the children, who gaped with wondering eyes at him, sitting so stiff up there in their mother's bright atelier. When they drew near he motioned them away with an expressive action of the foot, loath to disturb the fixed lines of his countenance, his arms, or his rigid shoulders.

Edna, anxious to entertain him, invited Mademoiselle Reisz to meet him, having promised him a treat in her piano playing; but Mademoiselle declined the invitation. So together they attended a *soirée musicale* at the Ratignolle's. Monsieur and Madame Ratignolle made much of the Colonel, installing him as the guest of honor and engaging him at once to dine with them the following Sunday, or any day which he might select. Madame coquetted with him in the most captivating and naïve manner, with eyes, gestures, and a profusion of compliments, till the Colonel's old head felt thirty years younger on his padded shoulders. Edna marveled, not comprehending. She herself was almost devoid of coquetry.

There were one or two men whom she observed at the *soirée musicale*; but she would never have felt moved to any kittenish display to attract their notice—to any feline or feminine wiles to express herself toward them. Their personality attracted her in an agreeable way. Her fancy selected them, and she was glad when a lull in the music gave them an opportunity to meet her and talk with her. Often on the street the glance of strange eyes had lingered in her memory, and sometimes had disturbed her.

Mr. Pontellier did not attend these *soirées musicales*. He considered them *bourgeois*,* and found more diversion at the club. To Madame Ratignolle he said the music dispensed at her *soirées* was too "heavy," too far beyond his untrained comprehension. His excuse flattered her. But she disapproved of Mr. Pontellier's club, and she was frank enough to tell Edna so.

"It's a pity Mr. Pontellier doesn't stay home more in the evenings. I think you would be more—well, if you don't mind my saying it—more united, if he did."

"Oh! dear no!" said Edna, with a blank look in her eyes. "What should I do if he stayed home? We wouldn't have anything to say to each other."

She had not much of anything to say to her father, for that matter; but he did not antagonize her. She discovered that he interested her, though she realized that he might not interest her long; and for the first time in her life she felt as if she were thoroughly acquainted with him. He kept her busy serving him and ministering to his wants. It amused her to do so. She would not permit a servant or one of the children to do anything for him which she might do herself. Her husband noticed, and thought it was the expression of a deep filial attachment which he had never suspected.

The Colonel drank numerous "toddies" during the course of the day, which left him, however, imperturbed. He was an expert at concocting strong drinks. He had even invented some, to which he had given fantastic names, and for whose manufacture he required diverse ingredients that it devolved upon Edna to procure for him.

When Doctor Mandelet dined with the Pontelliers on Thursday he could discern in Mrs. Pontellier no trace of that morbid condition which her husband had reported to him. She was excited and in a manner radiant. She and her father had been to the race course, and their thoughts when they seated themselves at table were still occupied with the events of the afternoon, and their talk was still of the track. The Doctor had not kept pace with turf affairs. He had certain recollections of racing in what he called "the good old times" when the Lecompte stables flourished, and he drew upon this fund of memories so that he might not be left out and seem wholly devoid of the modern spirit. But he failed to impose upon the Colonel, and was even far from impressing him with this trumped-up knowledge of bygone days.* Edna had staked her father on his last venture, with the most gratifying results to both of them. Besides, they had met some very charming people, according to the Colonel's impressions. Mrs. Mortimer Merriman and Mrs. James Highcamp, who were there with Alcée Arobin, had joined them and had enlivened the hours in a fashion that warmed him to think of.

Mr. Pontellier himself had no particular leaning toward horse-racing, and was even rather inclined to discourage it as a pastime, especially when he considered the fate of that blue-grass farm in Kentucky. He endeavored, in a general way, to express a particular disapproval, and only succeeded in arousing the ire and opposition of his father-in-law. A pretty dispute followed, in which Edna warmly espoused her father's cause and the Doctor remained neutral.

He observed his hostess attentively from under his shaggy brows, and noted a subtle change which had transformed her from the listless woman he had known into a being who, for the moment, seemed palpitant with the forces of life. Her speech was warm and energetic. There was no repression in her glance or gesture. She reminded him of some beautiful, sleek animal waking up in the sun.*

The dinner was excellent. The claret was warm and the champagne was cold, and under their beneficent influence the threatened unpleasantness melted and vanished with the fumes of the wine.

Mr. Pontellier warmed up and grew reminiscent. He told some amusing plantation experiences, recollections of old Iberville and his youth, when he hunted 'possum in company with some friendly darky; thrashed the pecan trees, shot the grosbec,* and roamed the woods and fields in mischievous idleness.

The Colonel, with little sense of humor and of the fitness of things, related a somber episode of those dark and bitter days, in which he had acted a conspicuous part and always formed a central figure. Nor was the Doctor happier in his selection, when he told the old, ever new and curious story of the waning of a woman's love, seeking strange, new channels, only to return to its legitimate source after days of fierce unrest. It was one of the many little human documents which had been unfolded to him during his long career as a physician. The story did not seem especially to impress Edna. She had one of her own to tell, of a woman who paddled away with her lover one night in a pirogue and never came back. They were lost amid the Baratarian Islands, and no one ever heard of them or found trace of them from that day to this. It was a pure invention. She said that Madame Antoine had related it to her. That, also, was an invention. Perhaps it was a dream she had had. But every glowing word seemed real to those who listened. They could feel the hot breath of the Southern night; they could hear the long sweep of the pirogue through the glistening moonlit water, the beating of birds' wings, rising startled from among the reeds in the salt-water pools; they could see the faces of the lovers, pale, close together, rapt in oblivious forgetfulness, drifting into the unknown.*

The champagne was cold, and its subtle fumes played fantastic tricks with Edna's memory that night.

Outside, away from the glow of the fire and the soft lamplight, the night was chill and murky. The Doctor doubled his old-fashioned cloak across his breast as he strode home through the darkness. He knew his fellow-creatures better than most men; knew that inner life which so seldom unfolds itself to unanointed eyes. He was sorry he had accepted Pontellier's invitation. He was growing old, and beginning to need rest and an imperturbed spirit. He did not want the secrets of other lives thrust upon him.

"I hope it isn't Arobin," he muttered to himself as he walked. "I hope to heaven it isn't Alcée Arobin."

XXIV

Edna and her father had a warm, and almost violent dispute upon the subject of her refusal to attend her sister's wedding. Mr. Pontellier declined to interfere, to interpose either his influence or his authority. He was following Doctor Mandelet's advice, and letting her do as she liked. The Colonel reproached his daughter for her lack of filial kindness and respect, her want of sisterly affection and womanly consideration. His arguments were labored and unconvincing. He doubted if Janet would accept any excuse— forgetting that Edna had offered none. He doubted if Janet would ever speak to her again, and he was sure Margaret would not.

Edna was glad to be rid of her father when he finally took himself off with his wedding garments and his bridal gifts, with his padded shoulders, his Bible reading, his "toddies" and ponderous oaths.

Mr. Pontellier followed him closely. He meant to stop at the wedding on his way to New York and endeavor by every means which money and love could devise to atone somewhat for Edna's incomprehensible action.

"You are too lenient, too lenient by far, Léonce," asserted the Colonel. "Authority, coercion are what is needed. Put your foot down good and hard; the only way to manage a wife. Take my word for it."

The Colonel was perhaps unaware that he had coerced his own wife into her grave. Mr. Pontellier had a vague suspicion of it which he thought it needless to mention at that late day.

Edna was not so consciously gratified at her husband's leaving home as she had been over the departure of her father. As the day approached when he was to leave her for a comparatively long stay, she grew melting and affectionate, remembering his many acts of consideration and his repeated expressions of an ardent attachment. She was solicitous about his health and his welfare. She bustled around, looking after his clothing, thinking about heavy underwear, quite as Madame Ratignolle would have done under similar circumstances. She cried when he went away, calling him her dear, good friend, and she was quite certain she would grow lonely before very long and go to join him in New York.

But after all, a radiant peace settled upon her when she at last found herself alone. Even the children were gone. Old Madame Pontellier had come herself and carried them off to Iberville with their quadroon. The old madame did not venture to say she was afraid they would be neglected during Léonce's absence; she hardly ventured to think so. She was hungry for them—even a little fierce in her attachment. She did not want them to be wholly "children of the pavement," she always said when begging to have them for a space. She wished them to know the country, with its streams, its fields, its woods, its freedom, so delicious to the young. She wished them to taste something of the life their father had lived and known and loved when he, too, was a little child.

When Edna was at last alone, she breathed a big, genuine sigh of relief. A feeling that was unfamiliar but very delicious came over her. She walked all through the house, from one room to another, as if inspecting it for the first time. She tried the various chairs and lounges, as if she had never sat and reclined upon them before. And she perambulated around the outside of the house, investigating, looking to see if windows and shutters were secure and in order. The flowers were like new acquaintances; she approached them in a familiar spirit, and made herself at home among them. The garden walks were damp, and Edna called to the maid to bring out her rubber sandals. And there she stayed, and stooped, digging around the plants, trimming, picking dead, dry leaves. The children's little dog came out, interfering, getting in her way. She scolded him, laughed at him, played with him. The garden smelled so good and looked so pretty in the afternoon sunlight. Edna plucked all the bright flowers she could find, and went into the house with them, she and the little dog.

Even the kitchen assumed a sudden interesting character which she had never before perceived. She went in to give directions to the cook, to say that the butcher would have to bring much less meat, that they would require only half their usual quantity of bread, of milk and groceries. She told the cook that she herself would be greatly occupied during Mr. Pontellier's absence, and she begged her to take all thought and responsibility of the larder upon her own shoulders.

That night Edna dined alone. The candelabra, with a few candles in the center of the table, gave all the light she needed. Outside the circle of light in which she sat, the large dining-room looked solemn and shadowy. The cook, placed upon her mettle, served a delicious repast—a luscious tenderloin broiled à point. The wine tasted good; the marron glacé seemed to be just what she wanted. It was so pleasant, too, to dine in a comfortable peignoir.

She thought a little sentimentally about Léonce and the children, and wondered what they were doing. As she gave a dainty scrap or two to the doggie, she talked intimately to him about Etienne and Raoul. He was beside himself with astonishment and delight over these companionable advances, and showed his appreciation by his little quick, snappy barks and a lively agitation.

Then Edna sat in the library after dinner and read Emerson until she grew sleepy.* She realized that she had neglected her reading, and determined to start anew upon a course of improving studies, now that her time was completely her own to do with as she liked.

After a refreshing bath, Edna went to bed. And as she snuggled comfortably beneath the eiderdown a sense of restfulness invaded her, such as she had not known before.

XXV

When the weather was dark and cloudy Edna could not work. She needed the sun to mellow and temper her mood to the sticking point. She had reached a stage when she seemed to be no longer feeling her way, working, when in the humor, with sureness and ease. And being devoid of ambition, and striving not toward accomplishment, she drew satisfaction from the work in itself.

On rainy or melancholy days Edna went out and sought the society of the friends she had made at Grand Isle. Or else she stayed indoors and nursed a mood with which she was becoming too familiar for her own comfort and peace of mind. It was not despair; but it seemed to her as if life were passing by, leaving its promise broken and unfulfilled. Yet there were other days when she listened, was led on and deceived by fresh promises which her youth held out to her.

She went again to the races, and again. Alcée Arobin and Mrs. Highcamp called for her one bright afternoon in Arobin's drag.* Mrs. Highcamp was a worldly but unaffected, intelligent, slim, tall blonde woman in the forties, with an indifferent manner and blue eyes that stared. She had a daughter who served her as a pretext for cultivating the society of young men of fashion. Alcée Arobin was one of them. He was a familiar figure at the race course, the opera, the fashionable clubs. There was a perpetual smile in his eyes, which seldom failed to awaken a corresponding cheerfulness in any one who looked into them and listened to his good-humored voice. His manner was quiet, and at times a little insolent. He possessed a good figure, a pleasing face, not overburdened with depth of thought or feeling; and his dress was that of the conventional man of fashion.

He admired Edna extravagantly, after meeting her at the races with her father. He had met her before on other occasions, but she had seemed to him unapproachable until that day. It was at his instigation that Mrs. Highcamp called to ask her to go with them to the Jockey Club* to witness the turf event of the season.

There were possibly a few track men out there who knew the race horse as well as Edna, but there was certainly none who knew it better. She sat between her two companions as one having authority to speak. She laughed at Arobin's pretensions, and deplored Mrs. Highcamp's ignorance. The race horse was a friend and intimate associate of her childhood. The atmosphere of the stables and the breath of the blue grass paddock* revived in her memory and lingered in her nostrils. She did not perceive that she was talking like her father as the sleek geldings ambled in review before them. She played for very high stakes, and fortune favored her. The fever of the game flamed in her cheeks and eyes, and it got into her blood and into her brain like an intoxicant. People turned their heads to look at her, and more than one lent an attentive ear to her utterances, hoping thereby to secure the elusive but ever-desired "tip." Arobin caught the contagion of excitement which drew him to Edna like a magnet. Mrs. Highcamp remained, as usual, unmoved, with her indifferent stare and uplifted eyebrows.

Edna stayed and dined with Mrs. Highcamp upon being urged to do so. Arobin also remained and sent away his drag.

The dinner was quiet and uninteresting, save for the cheerful efforts of Arobin to enliven things. Mrs. Highcamp deplored the absence of her daughter from the races, and tried to convey to her what she had missed by going to the "Dante reading"* instead of joining them. The girl held a geranium leaf up to her nose and said nothing, but looked knowing and noncommittal. Mr. Highcamp was a plain, bald-headed man, who only talked under compulsion. He was unresponsive. Mrs. Highcamp was full of delicate courtesy and consideration toward her husband. She addressed most of her conversation to him at table. They sat in the library after dinner and read the evening papers together under the droplight; while the younger people went into the drawing-room near by and talked. Miss Highcamp played some selections from Grieg* upon the piano. She seemed to have apprehended all of the composer's coldness and none of his poetry. While Edna listened she could not help wondering if she had lost her taste for music.

When the time came for her to go home, Mr. Highcamp grunted a lame offer to escort her, looking down at his slippered feet with tactless concern. It was Arobin who took her home. The car ride was long, and it was late when they reached Esplanade Street. Arobin asked permission to enter for a second to light his cigarette—his match safe was empty. He filled his match safe, but did not light his cigarette until he left her, after she had expressed her willingness to go to the races with him again.

Edna was neither tired nor sleepy. She was hungry again, for the Highcamp dinner, though of excellent quality, had lacked abundance. She rummaged in the larder and brought forth a slice of "Gruyère" and some crackers. She opened a bottle of beer which she found in the ice-box.* Edna felt extremely restless and excited. She vacantly hummed a fantastic tune as she poked at the wood embers on the hearth and munched a cracker.

She wanted something to happen—something, anything; she did not know what. She regretted that she had not made Arobin stay a half hour to talk over the horses with her. She counted the money she had won. But there was nothing else to do, so she went to bed, and tossed there for hours in a sort of monotonous agitation.

In the middle of the night she remembered that she had forgotten to write her regular letter to her husband; and she decided to do so next day and tell him about her afternoon at the Jockey Club. She lay wide awake composing a letter which was nothing like the one which she wrote next day. When the maid awoke her in the morning Edna was dreaming of Mr. Highcamp playing the piano at the entrance of a music store on Canal Street, while his wife was saying to Alcée Arobin, as they boarded an Esplanade Street car:

"What a pity that so much talent has been neglected! but I must go."

When, a few days later, Alcée Arobin again called for Edna in his drag, Mrs. Highcamp was not with him. He said they would pick her up. But as that lady had not been apprised of his intention of picking her up, she was not at home. The daughter was just leaving the house to attend the meeting of a branch Folk Lore Society,* and regretted that she could not accompany them. Arobin appeared nonplused, and asked Edna if there were any one else she cared to ask.

She did not deem it worth while to go in search of any of the fashionable acquaintances from whom she had withdrawn herself. She thought of Madame Ratignolle, but knew that her fair friend did not leave the house, except to take a languid walk around the block with her husband after nightfall. Mademoiselle Reisz would have laughed at such a request from Edna. Madame Lebrun might have enjoyed the outing, but for some reason Edna did not want her. So they went alone, she and Arobin.

The afternoon was intensely interesting to her. The excitement came back upon her like a remittent fever. Her talk grew familiar and confidential. It was no labor to become intimate with Arobin. His manner invited easy confidence. The preliminary stage of becoming acquainted was one which he always endeavored to ignore when a pretty and engaging woman was concerned.

He stayed and dined with Edna. He stayed and sat beside the wood fire. They laughed and talked; and before it was time to go he was telling her how different life might have been if he had known her years before. With ingenuous frankness he spoke of what a wicked, ill-disciplined boy he had been, and impulsively drew up his cuff to exhibit upon his wrist the scar from a saber cut which he had received in a duel outside of Paris* when he was nineteen. She touched his hand as she scanned the red cicatrice on the inside of his white wrist. A quick impulse that was somewhat spasmodic impelled her fingers to close in a sort of clutch upon his hand. He felt the pressure of her pointed nails in the flesh of his palm.

She arose hastily and walked toward the mantel.

"The sight of a wound or scar always agitates and sickens me," she said. "I shouldn't have looked at it."

"I beg your pardon," he entreated, following her; "it never occurred to me that it might be repulsive."

He stood close to her, and the effrontery in his eyes repelled the old, vanishing self in her, yet drew all her awakening sensuousness. He saw enough in her face to impel him to take her hand and hold it while he said his lingering good night.

"Will you go to the races again?" he asked.

"No," she said. "I've had enough of the races. I don't want to lose all the money I've won, and I've got to work when the weather is bright, instead of—"

"Yes; work; to be sure. You promised to show me your work. What morning may I come up to your atelier? To-morrow?"

"No!"

"Day after?"

"No, no."

"Oh, please don't refuse me! I know something of such things. I might help you with a stray suggestion or two."

"No. Good night. Why don't you go after you have said good night? I don't like you," she went on in a high, excited pitch, attempting to draw away her hand. She felt that her words lacked dignity and sincerity, and she knew that he felt it.

"I'm sorry you don't like me. I'm sorry I offended you. How have I offended you? What have I done? Can't you forgive me?" And he bent and pressed his lips upon her hand as if he wished never more to withdraw them.

"Mr. Arobin," she complained, "I'm greatly upset by the excitement of the afternoon; I'm not myself. My manner must have misled you in some way. I wish you to go, please." She spoke in a monotonous, dull tone. He took his hat from the table, and stood with eyes turned from her, looking into the dying fire. For a moment or two he kept an impressive silence.

"Your manner has not misled me, Mrs. Pontellier," he said finally. "My own emotions have done that. I couldn't help it. When I'm near you, how could I help it? Don't think anything of it, don't bother, please. You see, I go when you command me. If you wish me to stay away, I shall do so. If you let me come back, I—oh! you will let me come back?"

He cast one appealing glance at her, to which she made no response. Alcée Arobin's manner was so genuine that it often deceived even himself.

Edna did not care or think whether it were genuine or not. When she was alone she looked mechanically at the back of her hand which he had kissed so warmly. Then she leaned her head down on the mantelpiece. She felt somewhat like a woman who in a moment of passion is betrayed into an act of infidelity, and realizes the significance of the act without being wholly awakened from its glamour. The thought was passing vaguely through her mind, "What would he think?"

She did not mean her husband; she was thinking of Robert Lebrun. Her husband seemed to her now like a person whom she had married without love as an excuse.

She lit a candle and went up to her room. Alcée Arobin was absolutely nothing to her. Yet his presence, his manners, the warmth of his glances and above all the touch of his lips upon her hand had acted like a narcotic upon her.

She slept a languorous sleep, interwoven with vanishing dreams.

XXVI

Alcée Arobin wrote Edna an elaborate note of apology, palpitant with sincerity. It embarrassed her; for in a cooler, quieter moment it appeared to her absurd that she should have taken his action so seriously, so dramatically. She felt sure that the significance of the whole occurrence had lain in her own self-consciousness. If she ignored his note it would give undue importance to a trivial affair. If she replied to it in a serious spirit it would still leave in his mind the impression that she had in a susceptible moment yielded to his influence. After all, it was no great matter to have one's hand kissed. She was provoked at his having written the apology. She answered in as light and bantering a spirit as she fancied it deserved, and said she would be glad to have him look in upon her at work whenever he felt the inclination and his business gave him the opportunity.

He responded at once by presenting himself at her home with all his disarming naïveté. And then there was scarcely a day which followed that she did not see him or was not reminded of him. He was prolific in pretexts. His attitude became one of good-humored subservience and tacit adoration. He was ready at all times to submit to her moods, which were as often kind as they were cold. She grew accustomed to him. They became intimate and friendly by imperceptible degrees, and then by leaps. He sometimes talked in a way that astonished her at first and brought the crimson into her face; in a way that pleased her at last, appealing to the animalism that stirred impatiently within her.

There was nothing which so quieted the turmoil of Edna's senses as a visit to Mademoiselle Reisz. It was then, in the presence of that personality which was offensive to her, that the woman, by her divine art, seemed to reach Edna's spirit and set it free.

It was misty, with heavy, lowering atmosphere, one afternoon, when Edna climbed the stairs to the pianist's apartments under the roof. Her clothes were dripping with moisture. She felt chilled and pinched as she entered the room. Mademoiselle was poking at a rusty stove that smoked a little and warmed the room indifferently. She was endeavoring to heat a pot of chocolate on the stove. The room looked cheerless and dingy to Edna as she entered. A bust of Beethoven, covered with a hood of dust,* scowled at her from the mantelpiece.

"Ah! here comes the sunlight!" exclaimed Mademoiselle, rising from her knees before the stove. "Now it will be warm and bright enough; I can let the fire alone."

She closed the stove door with a bang, and approaching, assisted in removing Edna's dripping mackintosh.

"You are cold; you look miserable. The chocolate will soon be hot. But would you rather have a taste of brandy? I have scarcely touched the bottle which you brought me for my cold." A piece of red flannel was wrapped around Mademoiselle's throat; a stiff neck compelled her to hold her head on one side.

"I will take some brandy," said Edna, shivering as she removed her gloves and overshoes. She drank the liquor from the glass as a man would have done. Then flinging herself upon the uncomfortable sofa she said, "Mademoiselle, I am going to move away from my house on Esplanade Street."

"Ah!" ejaculated the musician, neither surprised nor especially interested. Nothing ever seemed to astonish her very much. She was endeavoring to adjust the bunch of violets which had become loose from its fastening in her hair. Edna drew her down upon the sofa, and taking a pin from her own hair, secured the shabby artificial flowers in their accustomed place.

"Aren't you astonished?"

"Passably. Where are you going? to New York? to Iberville? to your father in Mississippi? where?"

"Just two steps away," laughed Edna, "in a little four-room house around the corner. It looks so cozy, so inviting and restful, whenever I pass by; and it's for rent. I'm tired looking after that big house. It never seemed like mine, anyway—like home. It's too much trouble. I have to keep too many servants. I am tired bothering with them."

"That is not your true reason, *ma belle*. There is no use in telling me lies. I don't know your reason, but you have not told me the truth." Edna did not protest or endeavor to justify herself.

"The house, the money that provides for it, are not mine. Isn't that enough reason?"

"They are your husband's," returned Mademoiselle, with a shrug and a malicious elevation of the eyebrows.

"Oh! I see there is no deceiving you. Then let me tell you: It is a caprice. I have a little money of my own from my mother's estate, which my father sends me by driblets. I won a large sum this winter on the races, and I am beginning to sell my sketches. Laidpore is more and more pleased with my work; he says it grows in force and individuality. I cannot judge of that myself, but I feel that I have gained in ease and confidence. However, as I said, I have sold a good many through Laidpore. I can live in the tiny house for little or nothing, with one servant. Old Celestine, who works occasionally for me, says she will come stay with me and do my work. I know I shall like it, like the feeling of freedom and independence."

"What does your husband say?"

"I have not told him yet. I only thought of it this morning. He will think I am demented, no doubt. Perhaps you think so."

Mademoiselle shook her head slowly. "Your reason is not yet clear to me," she said.

Neither was it quite clear to Edna herself; but it unfolded itself as she sat for a while in silence. Instinct had prompted her to put away her husband's bounty in casting off her allegiance. She did not know how it would be when he returned. There would have to be an understanding, an explanation. Conditions would some way adjust themselves, she felt; but whatever came, she had resolved never again to belong to another than herself.

"I shall give a grand dinner before I leave the old house!" Edna exclaimed. "You will have to come to it, Mademoiselle. I will give you everything that you like to eat and to drink. We shall sing and laugh and be merry for once." And she uttered a sigh that came from the very depths of her being.

If Mademoiselle happened to have received a letter from Robert during the interval of Edna's visits, she would give her the letter unsolicited. And she would seat herself at the piano and play as her humor prompted her while the young woman read the letter.

The little stove was roaring; it was red-hot, and the chocolate in the tin sizzled and sputtered. Edna went forward and opened the stove door, and Mademoiselle rising, took a letter from under the bust of Beethoven and handed it to Edna.

"Another! so soon!" she exclaimed, her eyes filled with delight. "Tell me, Mademoiselle, does he know that I see his letters?"

"Never in the world! He would be angry and would never write to me again if he thought so. Does he write to you? Never a line. Does he send you a message? Never a word. It is because he loves you, poor fool, and is trying to forget you, since you are not free to listen to him or to belong to him."

"Why do you show me his letters, then?"

"Haven't you begged for them? Can I refuse you anything? Oh! you cannot deceive me," and Mademoiselle approached her beloved instrument and began to play. Edna did not at once read the letter. She sat holding it in her hand, while the music penetrated her whole being like an effulgence, warming and brightening the dark places of her soul. It prepared her for joy and exultation.

"Oh!" she exclaimed, letting the letter fall to the floor. "Why did you not tell me?" She went and grasped Mademoiselle's hands up from the keys. "Oh! unkind! malicious! Why did you not tell me?"

"That he was coming back? No great news, *ma foi*. I wonder he did not come long ago."

"But when, when?" cried Edna, impatiently. "He does not say when."

"He says 'very soon.' You know as much about it as I do; it is all in the letter."

"But why? Why is he coming? Oh, if I thought—" and she snatched the letter from the floor and turned the pages this way and that way, looking for the reason, which was left untold.

"If I were young and in love with a man," said Mademoiselle, turning on the stool and pressing her wiry hands between her knees as she looked down at Edna, who sat on the floor holding the letter, "it seems to me he would have to be some *grand esprit*;* a man with lofty aims and ability to reach them; one who stood high enough to attract the notice of his fellow-men. It seems to me if I were young and in love I should never deem a man of ordinary caliber worthy of my devotion."

"Now it is you who are telling lies and seeking to deceive me, Mademoiselle; or else you have never been in love, and know nothing about it. Why," went on Edna, clasping her knees and looking up into Mademoiselle's twisted face, "do you suppose a woman knows why she loves? Does she select? Does she say to herself: 'Go to! Here is a distinguished statesman with presidential possibilities; I shall proceed to fall in love with him.' Or, 'I shall set my heart upon this musician, whose fame is on every tongue?' Or, 'This financier, who controls the world's money markets?'"

"You are purposely misunderstanding me, *ma reine*. Are you in love with Robert?"

"Yes," said Edna. It was the first time she had admitted it, and a glow overspread her face, blotching it with red spots.

"Why?" asked her companion. "Why do you love him when you ought not to?"

Edna, with a motion or two, dragged herself on her knees before Mademoiselle Reisz, who took the glowing face between her two hands.

"Why? Because his hair is brown and grows away from his temples; because he opens and shuts his eyes, and his nose is a little out of drawing; because he has two lips and a square chin, and a little finger which he can't straighten from having played baseball too energetically in his youth. Because—"*

"Because you do, in short," laughed Mademoiselle. "What will you do when he comes back?" she asked.

"Do? Nothing, except feel glad and happy to be alive."

She was already glad and happy to be alive at the mere thought of his return. The murky, lowering sky, which had depressed her a few hours before, seemed bracing and invigorating as she splashed through the streets on her way home.

She stopped at a confectioner's and ordered a huge box of bonbons for the children in Iberville. She slipped a card in the box, on which she scribbled a tender message and sent an abundance of kisses.

Before dinner in the evening Edna wrote a charming letter to her husband, telling him of her intention to move for a while into the little house around the block, and to give a farewell dinner before leaving, regretting that he was not there to share it, to help her out with the menu and assist her in entertaining the guests. Her letter was brilliant and brimming with cheerfulness.

XXVII

"What is the matter with you?" asked Arobin that evening. "I never found you in such a happy mood." Edna was tired by that time, and was reclining on the lounge before the fire.

"Don't you know the weather prophet has told us we shall see the sun pretty soon?"

"Well, that ought to be reason enough," he acquiesced. "You wouldn't give me another if I sat here all night imploring you." He sat close to her on a low tabouret, and as he spoke his fingers lightly touched the hair that fell a little over her forehead. She liked the touch of his fingers through her hair, and closed her eyes sensitively.

"One of these days," she said, "I'm going to pull myself together for a while and think—try to determine what character of a woman I am; for, candidly, I don't know. By all the codes which I am acquainted with, I am a devilishly wicked specimen of the sex. But some way I can't convince myself that I am. I must think about it."

"Don't. What's the use? Why should you bother thinking about it when I can tell you what manner of woman you are." His fingers strayed occasionally down to her warm, smooth cheeks and firm chin, which was growing a little full and double.

"Oh, yes! You will tell me that I am adorable; everything that is captivating. Spare yourself the effort."

"No; I shan't tell you anything of the sort, though I shouldn't be lying if I did."

"Do you know Mademoiselle Reisz?" she asked irrelevantly.

"The pianist? I know her by sight. I've heard her play."

"She says queer things sometimes in a bantering way that you don't notice at the time and you find yourself thinking about afterward."

"For instance?"

"Well, for instance, when I left her to-day, she put her arms around me and felt my shoulder blades, to see if my wings were strong, she said. 'The bird that would soar above the level plain of tradition and prejudice must have strong wings.* It is a sad spectacle to see the weaklings bruised, exhausted, fluttering back to earth.' "

"Whither would you soar?"

"I'm not thinking of any extraordinary flights. I only half comprehend her."

"I've heard she's partially demented," said Arobin.

"She seems to me wonderfully sane," Edna replied.

"I'm told she's extremely disagreeable and unpleasant. Why have you introduced her at a moment when I desired to talk of you?"

"Oh! talk of me if you like," cried Edna, clasping her hands beneath her head; "but let me think of something else while you do."

"I'm jealous of your thoughts to-night. They're making you a little kinder than usual; but some way I feel as if they were wandering, as if they were not here with me." She only looked at him and smiled. His eyes were very near. He leaned upon the lounge with an arm extended across her, while the other hand still rested upon her hair. They continued silently to look into each other's eyes. When he leaned forward and kissed her, she clasped his head, holding his lips to hers.

It was the first kiss of her life to which her nature had really responded. It was a flaming torch that kindled desire.

XXVIII

Edna cried a little that night after Arobin left her. It was only one phase of the multitudinous emotions which had assailed her. There was with her an overwhelming feeling of irresponsibility. There was the shock of the unexpected and the unaccustomed. There was her husband's reproach looking at her from the external things around her which he had provided for her external existence. There was Robert's reproach making itself felt by a quicker, fiercer, more over-powering love, which had awakened within her toward him. Above all, there was understanding. She felt as if a mist had been lifted from her eyes, enabling her to look upon and comprehend the significance of life, that monster made up of beauty and brutality. But among the conflicting sensations which assailed her, there was neither shame nor remorse. There was a dull pang of regret because it was not the kiss of love which had inflamed her, because it was not love which had held this cup of life to her lips.

<h1 style="text-align:center">XXIX</h1>

Without even waiting for an answer from her husband regarding his opinion or wishes in the matter, Edna hastened her preparations for quitting her home on Esplanade Street and moving into the little house around the block. A feverish anxiety attended her every action in that direction. There was no moment of deliberation, no interval of repose between the thought and its fulfillment. Early upon the morning following those hours passed in Arobin's society, Edna set about securing her new abode and hurrying her arrangements for occupying it. Within the precincts of her home she felt like one who has entered and lingered within the portals of some forbidden temple in which a thousand muffled voices bade her begone.

Whatever was her own in the house, everything which she had acquired aside from her husband's bounty, she caused to be transported to the other house, supplying simple and meager deficiencies from her own resources.

Arobin found her with rolled sleeves, working in company with the house-maid when he looked in during the afternoon. She was splendid and robust, and had never appeared handsomer than in the old blue gown, with a red silk handkerchief knotted at random around her head to protect her hair from the dust. She was mounted upon a high step-ladder, unhooking a picture from the wall when he entered. He had found the front door open, and had followed his ring by walking in unceremoniously.

"Come down!" he said. "Do you want to kill yourself?" She

greeted him with affected carelessness, and appeared absorbed in her occupation.

If he had expected to find her languishing, reproachful, or indulging in sentimental tears, he must have been greatly surprised.

He was no doubt prepared for any emergency, ready for any one of the foregoing attitudes, just as he bent himself easily and naturally to the situation which confronted him.

"Please come down," he insisted, holding the ladder and looking up at her.

"No," she answered; "Ellen is afraid to mount the ladder. Joe is working over at the 'pigeon house'—that's the name Ellen gives it, because it's so small and looks like a pigeon house*—and some one has to do this."

Arobin pulled off his coat, and expressed himself ready and willing to tempt fate in her place. Ellen brought him one of her dust-caps, and went into contortions of mirth, which she found it impossible to control, when she saw him put it on before the mirror as grotesquely as he could. Edna herself could not refrain from smiling when she fastened it at his request. So it was he who in turn mounted the ladder, unhooking pictures and curtains, and dislodging ornaments as Edna directed. When he had finished he took off his dust-cap and went out to wash his hands.

Edna was sitting on the tabouret, idly brushing the tips of a feather duster along the carpet when he came in again.

"Is there anything more you will let me do?" he asked.

"That is all," she answered. "Ellen can manage the rest." She kept the young woman occupied in the drawing-room, unwilling to be left alone with Arobin.

"What about the dinner?" he asked; "the grand event, the *coup d'état*?"

"It will be day after to-morrow. Why do you call it the '*coup d'état*?' Oh! it will be very fine; all my best of everything—crystal, silver and gold, Sèvres, flowers, music, and champagne to swim in. I'll let Léonce pay the bills. I wonder what he'll say when he sees the bills."

"And you ask me why I call it a *coup d'état?*" Arobin had put on his coat, and he stood before her and asked if his cravat was plumb. She told him it was, looking no higher than the tip of his collar.

"When do you go to the 'pigeon house?'—with all due acknowledgment to Ellen."

"Day after to-morrow, after the dinner. I shall sleep there."

"Ellen, will you very kindly get me a glass of water?" asked Arobin. "The dust in the curtains, if you will pardon me for hinting such a thing, has parched my throat to a crisp."

"While Ellen gets the water," said Edna, rising, "I will say good-by and let you go. I must get rid of this grime, and I have a million things to do and think of."

"When shall I see you?" asked Arobin, seeking to detain her, the maid having left the room.

"At the dinner, of course. You are invited."

"Not before?—not to-night or to-morrow morning or to-morrow noon or night? or the day after morning or noon? Can't you see yourself, without my telling you, what an eternity it is?"

He had followed her into the hall and to the foot of the stairway, looking up at her as she mounted with her face half turned to him.

"Not an instant sooner," she said. But she laughed and looked at him with eyes that at once gave him courage to wait and made it torture to wait.

XXX

Though Edna had spoken of the dinner as a very grand affair, it was in truth a very small affair and very select, in so much as the guests invited were few and were selected with discrimination. She had counted upon an even dozen seating themselves at her round mahogany board, forgetting for the moment that Madame Ratignolle was to the last degree *souffrante* and unpresentable, and not foreseeing that Madame Lebrun would send a thousand regrets at the last moment. So there were only ten, after all, which made a cozy, comfortable number.

There were Mr. and Mrs. Merriman, a pretty, vivacious little woman in the thirties; her husband, a jovial fellow, something of a shallow-pate, who laughed a good deal at other people's witticisms, and had thereby made himself extremely popular. Mrs. Highcamp had accompanied them. Of course, there was Alcée Arobin; and Mademoiselle Reisz had consented to come. Edna had sent her a fresh bunch of violets with black lace trimmings for her hair. Monsieur Ratignolle brought himself and his wife's excuses. Victor Lebrun, who happened to be in the city, bent upon relaxation, had accepted with alacrity. There was a Miss Mayblunt, no longer in her teens, who looked at the world through lorgnettes and with the keenest interest. It was thought and said that she was intellectual; it was suspected of her that she wrote under a *nom de guerre*. She had come with a gentleman by the name of Gouvernail,* connected with one of the daily papers, of whom nothing special could be said, except that he was observant and seemed quiet and inoffensive. Edna herself made the tenth, and at half-past eight they seated themselves at table, Arobin and Monsieur Ratignolle on either side of their hostess.

Mrs. Highcamp sat between Arobin and Victor Lebrun. Then came Mrs. Merriman, Mr. Gouvernail, Miss Mayblunt, Mr. Merriman, and Mademoiselle Reisz next to Monsieur Ratignolle.

There was something extremely gorgeous about the appearance of the table, an effect of splendor conveyed by a cover of pale yellow satin under strips of lace-work. There were wax candles in massive brass candelabra, burning softly under yellow silk shades; full, fragrant roses, yellow and red, abounded. There were silver and gold, as she had said there would be, and crystal which glittered like the gems which the women wore.

The ordinary stiff dining chairs had been discarded for the occasion and replaced by the most commodious and luxurious which could be collected throughout the house. Mademoiselle Reisz, being exceedingly diminutive, was elevated upon cushions, as small children are sometimes hoisted at table upon bulky volumes.

"Something new, Edna?" exclaimed Miss Mayblunt, with lorgnette directed toward a magnificent cluster of diamonds that sparkled, that almost sputtered, in Edna's hair, just over the center of her forehead.

"Quite new; 'brand' new, in fact; a present from my husband. It arrived this morning from New York. I may as well admit that this is my birthday, and that I am twenty-nine. In good time I expect you to drink my health. Meanwhile, I shall ask you to begin with this cock-tail, composed—would you say 'composed?'" with an appeal to Miss Mayblunt—"composed by my father in honor of Sister Janet's wedding."

Before each guest stood a tiny glass that looked and sparkled like a garnet gem.

"Then, all things considered," spoke Arobin, "it might not be amiss to start out by drinking the Colonel's health in the cocktail which he composed,* on the birthday of the most charming of women—the daughter whom he invented."

Mr. Merriman's laugh at this sally was such a genuine outburst and so contagious that it started the dinner with an agreeable swing that never slackened.

Miss Mayblunt begged to be allowed to keep her cocktail untouched before her, just to look at. The color was marvelous! She could compare it to nothing she had ever seen, and the garnet lights which it emitted were unspeakably rare. She pronounced the Colonel an artist, and stuck to it.

Monsieur Ratignolle was prepared to take things seriously: the *mets*, the *entre-mets*, the service, the decorations, even the people. He looked up from his pompono* and inquired of Arobin if he were related to the gentleman of that name who formed one of the firm of Laitner and Arobin, lawyers. The young man admitted that Laitner was a warm personal friend, who permitted Arobin's name to decorate the firm's letterheads and to appear upon a shingle that graced Perdido Street.*

"There are so many inquisitive people and institutions abounding," said Arobin, "that one is really forced as a matter of convenience these days to assume the virtue of an occupation if he has it not."

Monsieur Ratignolle stared a little, and turned to ask Mademoiselle Reisz if she considered the symphony concerts up to the standard which had been set the previous winter. Mademoiselle Reisz answered Monsieur Ratignolle in French, which Edna thought a little rude, under the circumstances, but characteristic. Mademoiselle had only disagreeable things to say of the symphony concerts, and insulting remarks to make of all the musicians of New Orleans, singly and collectively. All her interest seemed to be centered upon the delicacies placed before her.

Mr. Merriman said that Mr. Arobin's remark about inquisitive people reminded him of a man from Waco the other day at the St. Charles Hotel*—but as Mr. Merriman's stories were always lame and lacking point, his wife seldom permitted him to complete them. She interrupted him to ask if he remembered the name of the author whose book she had bought the week before to send to a friend in Geneva.* She was talking "books" with Mr. Gouvernail and trying to draw from him his opinion upon current literary topics. Her husband told the story of the Waco man privately to Miss Mayblunt, who pretended to be greatly amused and to think it extremely clever.

Mrs. Highcamp hung with languid but unaffected interest upon the warm and impetuous volubility of her left-hand neighbor, Victor Lebrun. Her attention was never for a moment withdrawn from him after seating herself at table; and when he turned to Mrs. Merriman, who was prettier and more vivacious than Mrs. Highcamp, she waited with easy indifference for an opportunity to reclaim his attention. There was the occasional sound of music, of mandolins, sufficiently removed to be an agreeable accompaniment rather than an interruption to the conversation. Outside the soft, monotonous splash of a fountain could be heard; the sound penetrated into the room with the heavy odor of jessamine that came through the open windows.

The golden shimmer of Edna's satin gown spread in rich folds on either side of her. There was a soft fall of lace encircling her shoulders. It was the color of her skin, without the glow, the myriad living tints that one may sometimes discover in vibrant flesh. There was something in her attitude, in her whole appearance when she leaned her head against the high-backed chair and spread her arms, which suggested the regal woman, the one who rules, who looks on, who stands alone.

But as she sat there amid her guests, she felt the old ennui overtaking her; the hopelessness which so often assailed her, which came upon her like an obsession, like something extraneous, independent of volition. It was something which announced itself; a chill breath that seemed to issue from some vast cavern wherein discords wailed. There came over her the acute longing which always summoned into her spiritual vision the presence of the beloved one, overpowering her at once with a sense of the unattainable.

The moments glided on, while a feeling of good fellowship passed around the circle like a mystic cord, holding and binding these people together with jest and laughter. Monsieur Ratignolle was the first to break the pleasant charm. At ten o'clock he excused himself. Madame Ratignolle was waiting for him at home. She was *bien souffrante*, and she was filled with vague dread, which only her husband's presence could allay.

Mademoiselle Reisz arose with Monsieur Ratignolle, who offered to escort her to the car. She had eaten well; she had tasted the good, rich wines, and they must have turned her head, for she bowed pleasantly to all as she withdrew from table. She kissed Edna upon the shoulder, and whispered; "*Bonne nuit, ma reine; soyez sage.*"* She had been a little bewildered upon rising, or rather, descending from her cushions, and Monsieur Ratignolle gallantly took her arm and led her away.

Mrs. Highcamp was weaving a garland of roses, yellow and red. When she had finished the garland, she laid it lightly upon Victor's black curls. He was reclining far back in the luxurious chair, holding a glass of champagne to the light.

As if a magician's wand had touched him, the garland of roses transformed him into a vision of Oriental beauty.* His cheeks were the color of crushed grapes, and his dusky eyes glowed with a languishing fire.

"*Sapristi!*" exclaimed Arobin.

But Mrs. Highcamp had one more touch to add to the picture. She took from the back of her chair a white silken scarf, with which she had covered her shoulders in the early part of the evening. She draped it across the boy in graceful folds, and in a way to conceal his black, conventional evening dress. He did not seem to mind what she did to him, only smiled, showing a faint gleam of white teeth, while he continued to gaze with narrowing eyes at the light through his glass of champagne.

"Oh! to be able to paint in color rather than in words!" exclaimed Miss Mayblunt, losing herself in a rhapsodic dream as she looked at him.

> "'There was a graven image of Desire
> Painted with red blood on a ground of gold.'"*

murmured Gouvernail, under his breath.

The effect of the wine upon Victor was to change his accustomed volubility into silence. He seemed to have abandoned himself to a reverie, and to be seeing pleasing visions in the amber bead.

"Sing," entreated Mrs. Highcamp. "Won't you sing to us?"

"Let him alone," said Arobin.

"He's posing," offered Mr. Merriman; "let him have it out."

"I believe he's paralyzed," laughed Mrs. Merriman. And leaning over the youth's chair, she took the glass from his hand and held it to his lips. He sipped the wine slowly, and when he had drained the glass she laid it upon the table and wiped his lips with her little filmy handkerchief.

"Yes, I'll sing for you," he said, turning in his chair toward Mrs. Highcamp. He clasped his hands behind his head, and looking up at the ceiling began to hum a little, trying his voice like a musician tuning an instrument. Then, looking at Edna, he began to sing:

"Ah! si tu savais!"

"Stop!" she cried, "don't sing that. I don't want you to sing it," and she laid her glass so impetuously and blindly upon the table as to shatter it against a caraffe. The wine spilled over Arobin's legs and some of it trickled down upon Mrs. Highcamp's black gauze gown. Victor had lost all idea of courtesy, or else he thought his hostess was not in earnest, for he laughed and went on:

"Ah! si tu savais
Ce que tes yeux me disent"—*

"Oh! you mustn't! you mustn't," exclaimed Edna, and pushing back her chair she got up, and going behind him placed her hand over his mouth. He kissed the soft palm that pressed upon his lips.

"No, no, I won't, Mrs. Pontellier. I didn't know you meant it," looking up at her with caressing eyes. The touch of his lips was like a pleasing sting to her hand. She lifted the garland of roses from his head and flung it across the room.

"Come, Victor; you've posed long enough. Give Mrs. Highcamp her scarf."

Mrs. Highcamp undraped the scarf from about him with her own hands. Miss Mayblunt and Mr. Gouvernail suddenly conceived the notion that it was time to say good night. And Mr. and Mrs. Merriman wondered how it could be so late.

Before parting from Victor, Mrs. Highcamp invited him to call upon her daughter, who she knew would be charmed to meet him and talk French and sing French songs with him. Victor expressed his desire and intention to call upon Miss Highcamp at the first opportunity which presented itself. He asked if Arobin were going his way. Arobin was not.

The mandolin players had long since stolen away. A profound stillness had fallen upon the broad, beautiful street. The voices of Edna's disbanding guests jarred like a discordant note upon the quiet harmony of the night.

XXXI

"Well?" questioned Arobin, who had remained with Edna after the others had departed.

"Well," she reiterated, and stood up, stretching her arms, and feeling the need to relax her muscles after having been so long seated.

"What next?" he asked.

"The servants are all gone. They left when the musicians did. I have dismissed them. The house has to be closed and locked, and I shall trot around to the pigeon house, and shall send Celestine over in the morning to straighten things up."

He looked around, and began to turn out some of the lights.

"What about upstairs?" he inquired.

"I think it is all right; but there may he a window or two unlatched. We had better look; you might take a candle and see. And bring me my wrap and hat on the foot of the bed in the middle room."

He went up with the light, and Edna began closing doors and windows. She hated to shut in the smoke and the fumes of the wine. Arobin found her cape and hat, which he brought down and helped her to put on.

When everything was secured and the lights put out, they left through the front door, Arobin locking it and taking the key, which he carried for Edna. He helped her down the steps.

"Will you have a spray of jessamine?" he asked, breaking off a few blossoms as he passed.

"No; I don't want anything."

She seemed disheartened, and had nothing to say. She took his arm, which he offered her, holding up the weight of her satin train with the other hand. She looked down, noticing the black line of his leg moving in and out so close to her against the yellow shimmer of her gown. There was the whistle of a railway train somewhere in the distance, and the midnight bells were ringing. They met no one in their short walk.

The "pigeon-house" stood behind a locked gate, and a shallow *parterre* that had been somewhat neglected. There was a small front porch, upon which a long window and the front door opened. The door opened directly into the parlor; there was no side entry. Back in the yard was a room for servants, in which old Celestine had been ensconced.

Edna had left a lamp burning low upon the table. She had succeeded in making the room look habitable and homelike. There were some books on the table and a lounge near at hand. On the floor was a fresh matting, covered with a rug or two; and on the walls hung a few tasteful pictures. But the room was filled with flowers. These were a surprise to her. Arobin had sent them, and had had Celestine distribute them during Edna's absence. Her bedroom was adjoining, and across a small passage were the dining-room and kitchen.

Edna seated herself with every appearance of discomfort.

"Are you tired?" he asked.

"Yes, and chilled, and miserable. I feel as if I had been wound up to a certain pitch—too tight—and something inside of me had snapped." She rested her head against the table upon her bare arm.

"You want to rest," he said, "and to be quiet. I'll go; I'll leave you and let you rest."

"Yes," she replied.

He stood up beside her and smoothed her hair with his soft, magnetic hand. His touch conveyed to her a certain physical comfort. She could have fallen quietly asleep there if he had continued to pass his hand over her hair. He brushed the hair upward from the nape of her neck.

"I hope you will feel better and happier in the morning," he said. "You have tried to do too much in the past few days. The dinner was the last straw; you might have dispensed with it."

"Yes," she admitted; "it was stupid."

"No, it was delightful; but it has worn you out." His hand had strayed to her beautiful shoulders, and he could feel the response of her flesh to his touch. He seated himself beside her and kissed her lightly upon the shoulder.

"I thought you were going away," she said, in an uneven voice.

"I am, after I have said good night."

"Good night," she murmured.

He did not answer, except to continue to caress her. He did not say good night until she had become supple to his gentle, seductive entreaties.

XXXII

When Mr. Pontellier learned of his wife's intention to abandon her home and take up her residence elsewhere, he immediately wrote her a letter of unqualified disapproval and remonstrance. She had given reasons which he was unwilling to acknowledge as adequate. He hoped she had not acted upon her rash impulse; and he begged her to consider first, foremost, and above all else, what people would say. He was not dreaming of scandal when he uttered this warning; that was a thing which would never have entered into his mind to consider in connection with his wife's name or his own. He was simply thinking of his financial integrity. It might get noised about that the Pontelliers had met with reverses, and were forced to conduct their *ménage* on a humbler scale than heretofore. It might do incalculable mischief to his business prospects.

But remembering Edna's whimsical turn of mind of late, and foreseeing that she had immediately acted upon her impetuous determination, he grasped the situation with his usual promptness and handled it with his well-known business tact and cleverness.

The same mail which brought to Edna his letter of disapproval carried instructions—the most minute instructions—to a well-known architect concerning the remodeling of his home, changes which he had long contemplated, and which he desired carried forward during his temporary absence.

Expert and reliable packers and movers were engaged to convey the furniture, carpets, pictures—everything movable, in short—to places of security. And in an incredibly short time the Pontellier house was turned over to the artisans. There was to be an addition—a small snuggery; there was to be frescoing, and hardwood flooring was to be put into such rooms as had not yet been subjected to this improvement.

Furthermore, in one of the daily papers appeared a brief notice to the effect that Mr. and Mrs. Pontellier were contemplating a summer sojourn abroad, and that their handsome residence on Esplanade Street was undergoing sumptuous alterations, and would not be ready for occupancy until their return. Mr. Pontellier had saved appearances!*

Edna admired the skill of his maneuver, and avoided any occasion to balk his intentions. When the situation as set forth by Mr. Pontellier was accepted and taken for granted, she was apparently satisfied that it should be so.

The pigeon-house pleased her. It at once assumed the intimate character of a home, while she herself invested it with a charm which it reflected like a warm glow. There was with her a feeling of having descended in the social scale, with a corresponding sense of having risen in the spiritual. Every step which she took toward relieving herself from obligations added to her strength and expansion as an individual. She began to look with her own eyes;* to see and to apprehend the deeper undercurrents of life. No longer was she content to "feed upon opinion"* when her own soul had invited her.

After a little while, a few days, in fact, Edna went up and spent a week with her children in Iberville. They were delicious February days, with all the summer's promise hovering in the air.

How glad she was to see the children! She wept for very pleasure when she felt their little arms clasping her; their hard, ruddy cheeks pressed against her own glowing cheeks. She looked into their faces with hungry eyes that could not be satisfied with looking. And what stories they had to tell their mother! About the pigs, the cows, the mules! About riding to the mill behind Gluglu; fishing back in the lake with their Uncle Jasper; picking pecans with Lidie's little black brood, and hauling chips in their express wagon. It was a thousand times more fun to haul real chips for old lame Susie's real fire than to drag painted blocks along the banquette on Esplanade Street!

She went with them herself to see the pigs and the cows, to look at the darkies laying the cane, to thrash the pecan trees, and catch fish in the back lake. She lived with them a whole week long, giving them all of herself, and gathering and filling herself with their young existence. They listened, breathless, when she told them the house in Esplanade Street was crowded with workmen, hammering, nailing, sawing, and filling the place with clatter. They wanted to know where their bed was; what had been done with their rocking-horse; and where did Joe sleep, and where had Ellen gone, and the cook? But, above all, they were fired with a desire to see the little house around the block. Was there any place to play? Were there any boys next door? Raoul, with pessimistic foreboding, was convinced that there were only girls next door. Where would they sleep, and where would papa sleep? She told them the fairies would fix it all right.

The old Madame was charmed with Edna's visit, and showered all manner of delicate attentions upon her. She was delighted to know that the Esplanade Street house was in a dismantled condition. It gave her the promise and pretext to keep the children indefinitely.

It was with a wrench and a pang that Edna left her children. She carried away with her the sound of their voices and the touch of their cheeks. All along the journey homeward their presence lingered with her like the memory of a delicious song. But by the time she had regained the city the song no longer echoed in her soul. She was again alone.

XXXIII

It happened sometimes when Edna went to see Mademoiselle Reisz that the little musician was absent, giving a lesson or making some small necessary household purchase. The key was always left in a secret hiding-place in the entry, which Edna knew. If Mademoiselle happened to be away, Edna would usually enter and wait for her return.

When she knocked at Mademoiselle Reisz's door one afternoon there was no response; so unlocking the door, as usual, she entered and found the apartment deserted, as she had expected. Her day had been quite filled up, and it was for a rest, for a refuge, and to talk about Robert, that she sought out her friend.

She had worked at her canvas—a young Italian character study— all the morning, completing the work without the model; but there had been many interruptions, some incident to her modest house-keeping, and others of a social nature.

Madame Ratignolle had dragged herself over, avoiding the too public thoroughfares, she said. She complained that Edna had neglected her much of late. Besides, she was consumed with curiosity to see the little house and the manner in which it was conducted. She wanted to hear all about the dinner party; Monsieur Ratignolle had left *so* early. What had happened after he left? The champagne and grapes which Edna sent over were *too* delicious. She had so little appetite; they had refreshed and toned her stomach. Where on earth was she going to put Mr. Pontellier in that little house, and the boys? And then she made Edna promise to go to her when her hour of trial overtook her.

"At any time—any time of the day or night, dear," Edna assured her.

Before leaving Madame Ratignolle said:

"In some way you seem to me like a child, Edna. You seem to act without a certain amount of reflection which is necessary in this life. That is the reason I want to say you mustn't mind if I advise you to be a little careful while you are living here alone. Why don't you have some one come and stay with you? Wouldn't Mademoiselle Reisz come?"

"No; she wouldn't wish to come, and I shouldn't want her always with me."

"Well, the reason—you know how evil-minded the world is— some one was talking of Alcée Arobin visiting you. Of course, it wouldn't matter if Mr. Arobin had not such a dreadful reputation. Monsieur Ratignolle was telling me that his attentions alone are considered enough to ruin a woman's name."

"Does he boast of his successes?" asked Edna, indifferently, squinting at her picture.

"No, I think not. I believe he is a decent fellow as far as that goes. But his character is so well known among the men. I shan't be able to come back and see you; it was very, very imprudent to-day."

"Mind the step!" cried Edna.

"Don't neglect me," entreated Madame Ratignolle; "and don't mind what I said about Arobin, or having some one to stay with you."

"Of course not," Edna laughed. "You may say anything you like to me." They kissed each other good-by. Madame Ratignolle had not far to go, and Edna stood on the porch a while watching her walk down the street.

Then in the afternoon Mrs. Merriman and Mrs. Highcamp had made their "party call."* Edna felt that they might have dispensed with the formality. They had also come to invite her to play *vingt-et-un* one evening at Mrs. Merriman's. She was asked to go early, to dinner, and Mr. Merriman or Mr. Arobin would take her home. Edna accepted in a half-hearted way. She sometimes felt very tired of Mrs. Highcamp and Mrs. Merriman.

Late in the afternoon she sought refuge with Mademoiselle Reisz, and stayed there alone, waiting for her, feeling a kind of repose invade her with the very atmosphere of the shabby, unpretentious little room.

Edna sat at the window, which looked out over the house-tops and across the river. The window frame was filled with pots of flowers, and she sat and picked the dry leaves from a rose geranium. The day was warm, and the breeze which blew from the river was very pleasant. She removed her hat and laid it on the piano. She went on picking the leaves and digging around the plants with her hat pin. Once she thought she heard Mademoiselle Reisz approaching. But it was a young black girl, who came in, bringing a small bundle of laundry, which she deposited in the adjoining room, and went away.

Edna seated herself at the piano, and softly picked out with one hand the bars of a piece of music which lay open before her. A half-hour went by. There was the occasional sound of people going and coming in the lower hall. She was growing interested in her occupation of picking out the aria, when there was a second rap at the door. She vaguely wondered what these people did when they found Mademoiselle's door locked.

"Come in," she called, turning her face toward the door. And this time it was Robert Lebrun who presented himself. She attempted to rise; she could not have done so without betraying the agitation which mastered her at sight of him, so she fell back upon the stool, only exclaiming, "Why, Robert!"

He came and clasped her hand, seemingly without knowing what he was saying or doing.

"Mrs. Pontellier! How do you happen—oh! how well you look! Is Mademoiselle Reisz not here? I never expected to see you."

"When did you come back?" asked Edna in an unsteady voice, wiping her face with her handkerchief. She seemed ill at ease on the piano stool, and he begged her to take the chair by the window. She did so, mechanically, while he seated himself on the stool.

"I returned day before yesterday," he answered, while he leaned his arm on the keys, bringing forth a crash of discordant sound.

"Day before yesterday!" she repeated, aloud; and went on thinking to herself, "day before yesterday," in a sort of an uncomprehending way. She had pictured him seeking her at the very first hour, and he had lived under the same sky since day before yesterday; while only by accident had he stumbled upon her. Mademoiselle must have lied when she said, "Poor fool, he loves you."

"Day before yesterday," she repeated, breaking off a spray of Mademoiselle's geranium; "then if you had not met me here to-day you wouldn't—when—that is, didn't you mean to come and see me?"

"Of course, I should have gone to see you. There have been so many things—" he turned the leaves of Mademoiselle's music nervously. "I started in at once yesterday with the old firm. After all there is as much chance for me here as there was there—that is, I might find it profitable some day. The Mexicans were not very congenial."

So he had come back because the Mexicans were not congenial; because business was as profitable here as there; because of any reason, and not because he cared to be near her. She remembered the day she sat on the floor, turning the pages of his letter, seeking the reason which was left untold.

She had not noticed how he looked—only feeling his presence; but she turned deliberately and observed him. After all, he had been absent but a few months, and was not changed. His hair—the color of hers—waved back from his temples in the same way as before. His skin was not more burned than it had been at Grand Isle. She found in his eyes, when he looked at her for one silent moment, the same tender caress, with an added warmth and entreaty which had not been there before—the same glance which had penetrated to the sleeping places of her soul and awakened them.

A hundred times Edna had pictured Robert's return, and imagined their first meeting. It was usually at her home, whither he had sought her out at once. She always fancied him expressing or betraying in some way his love for her. And here, the reality was that they sat ten feet apart, she at the window, crushing geranium leaves in her hand and smelling them, he twirling around on the piano stool, saying:

"I was very much surprised to hear of Mr. Pontellier's absence; it's a wonder Mademoiselle Reisz did not tell me; and your moving—mother told me yesterday. I should think you would have gone to New York with him, or to Iberville with the children, rather than be bothered here with housekeeping. And you are going abroad, too, I hear. We shan't have you at Grand Isle next summer; it won't seem—do you see much of Mademoiselle Reisz? She often spoke of you in the few letters she wrote."

"Do you remember that you promised to write to me when you went away?" A flush overspread his whole face.

"I couldn't believe that my letters would be of any interest to you."

"That is an excuse; it isn't the truth." Edna reached for her hat on the piano. She adjusted it, sticking the hat pin through the heavy coil of hair with some deliberation.

"Are you not going to wait for Mademoiselle Reisz?" asked Robert.

"No; I have found when she is absent this long, she is liable not to come back till late." She drew on her gloves, and Robert picked up his hat.

"Won't you wait for her?" asked Edna.

"Not if you think she will not be back till late," adding, as if suddenly aware of some discourtesy in his speech, "and I should miss the pleasure of walking home with you." Edna locked the door and put the key back in its hiding-place.

They went together, picking their way across muddy streets and side-walks encumbered with the cheap display of small tradesmen. Part of the distance they rode in the car, and after disembarking, passed the Pontellier mansion, which looked broken and half torn asunder. Robert had never known the house, and looked at it with interest.

"I never knew you in your home," he remarked.

"I am glad you did not."

"Why?" She did not answer. They went on around the corner, and it seemed as if her dreams were coming true after all, when he followed her into the little house.

"You must stay and dine with me, Robert. You see I am all alone, and it is so long since I have seen you. There is so much I want to ask you."

She took off her hat and gloves. He stood irresolute, making some excuse about his mother who expected him; he even muttered something about an engagement. She struck a match and lit the lamp on the table; it was growing dusk. When he saw her face in the lamp-light, looking pained, with all the soft lines gone out of it, he threw his hat aside and seated himself.

"Oh! you know I want to stay if you will let me!" he exclaimed. All the softness came back. She laughed, and went and put her hand on his shoulder.

"This is the first moment you have seemed like the old Robert. I'll go tell Celestine." She hurried away to tell Celestine to set an extra place. She even sent her off in search of some added delicacy which she had not thought of for herself. And she recommended great care in dripping the coffee and having the omelet done to a proper turn.

When she reëntered, Robert was turning over magazines, sketches, and things that lay upon the table in great disorder. He picked up a photograph, and exclaimed:

"Alcée Arobin! What on earth is his picture doing here?"

"I tried to make a sketch of his head one day," answered Edna, "and he thought the photograph might help me. It was at the other house. I thought it had been left there. I must have packed it up with my drawing materials."

"I should think you would give it back to him if you have finished with it."

"Oh! I have a great many such photographs. I never think of returning them. They don't amount to anything." Robert kept on looking at the picture.

"It seems to me—do you think his head worth drawing? Is he a friend of Mr. Pontellier's? You never said you knew him."

"He isn't a friend of Mr. Pontellier's; he's a friend of mine. I always knew him—that is, it is only of late that I know him pretty well. But I'd rather talk about you, and know what you have been seeing and doing and feeling out there in Mexico." Robert threw aside the picture.

"I've been seeing the waves and the white beach of Grand Isle; the quiet, grassy street of the *Chênière*; the old fort at Grande Terre. I've been working like a machine, and feeling like a lost soul. There was nothing interesting."

She leaned her head upon her hand to shade her eyes from the light.

"And what have you been seeing and doing and feeling all these days?" he asked.

"I've been seeing the waves and the white beach of Grand Isle; the quiet, grassy street of the *Chênière Caminada*; the old sunny fort at Grande Terre. I've been working with a little more comprehension than a machine, and still feeling like a lost soul. There was nothing interesting."

"Mrs. Pontellier, you are cruel," he said, with feeling, closing his eyes and resting his head back in his chair. They remained in silence till old Celestine announced dinner.

XXXIV

The dining-room was very small. Edna's round mahogany would have almost filled it. As it was there was but a step or two from the little table to the kitchen, to the mantel, the small buffet, and the side door that opened out on the narrow brick-paved yard.

A certain degree of ceremony settled upon them with the announcement of dinner. There was no return to personalities. Robert related incidents of his sojourn in Mexico, and Edna talked of events likely to interest him, which had occurred during his absence. The dinner was of ordinary quality, except for the few delicacies which she had sent out to purchase. Old Celestine, with a bandana *tignon* twisted about her head, hobbled in and out, taking a personal interest in everything; and she lingered occasionally to talk patois with Robert, whom she had known as a boy.*

He went out to a neighboring cigar stand to purchase cigarette papers, and when he came back he found that Celestine had served the black coffee in the parlor.

"Perhaps I shouldn't have come back," he said. "When you are tired of me, tell me to go."

"You never tire me. You must have forgotten the hours and hours at Grand Isle in which we grew accustomed to each other and used to being together."

"I have forgotten nothing at Grand Isle," he said, not looking at her, but rolling a cigarette. His tobacco pouch, which he laid upon the table, was a fantastic embroidered silk affair, evidently the handiwork of a woman.

"You used to carry your tobacco in a rubber pouch," said Edna, picking up the pouch and examining the needlework.

"Yes; it was lost."

"Where did you buy this one? In Mexico?"

"It was given to me by a Vera Cruz girl; they are very generous," he replied, striking a match and lighting his cigarette.

"They are very handsome, I suppose, those Mexican women; very picturesque, with their black eyes and their lace scarfs."

"Some are; others are hideous. Just as you find women everywhere."

"What was she like—the one who gave you the pouch? You must have known her very well."

"She was very ordinary. She wasn't of the slightest importance. I knew her well enough."

"Did you visit at her house? Was it interesting? I should like to know and hear about the people you met, and the impressions they made on you."

"There are some people who leave impressions not so lasting as the imprint of an oar upon the water."

"Was she such a one?"

"It would be ungenerous for me to admit that she was of that order and kind." He thrust the pouch back in his pocket, as if to put away the subject with the trifle which had brought it up.

Arobin dropped in with a message from Mrs. Merriman, to say that the card party was postponed on account of the illness of one of her children.

"How do you do, Arobin?" said Robert, rising from the obscurity.

"Oh! Lebrun. To be sure! I heard yesterday you were back. How did they treat you down in Mexique?"

"Fairly well."

"But not well enough to keep you there. Stunning girls, though, in Mexico.* I thought I should never get away from Vera Cruz when I was down there a couple of years ago."

"Did they embroider slippers and tobacco pouches and hat-bands and things for you?" asked Edna.

"Oh! my! no! I didn't get so deep in their regard. I fear they made more impression on me than I made on them."

"You were less fortunate than Robert, then."

"I am always less fortunate than Robert. Has he been imparting tender confidences?"

"I've been imposing myself long enough," said Robert, rising, and shaking hands with Edna. "Please convey my regards to Mr. Pontellier when you write."

He shook hands with Arobin and went away.

"Fine fellow, that Lebrun," said Arobin when Robert had gone. "I never heard you speak of him."

"I knew him last summer at Grand Isle," she replied. "Here is that photograph of yours. Don't you want it?"

"What do I want with it? Throw it away." She threw it back on the table.

"I'm not going to Mrs. Merriman's," she said. "If you see her, tell her so. But perhaps I had better write. I think I shall write now, and say that I am sorry her child is sick, and tell her not to count on me."

"It would be a good scheme," acquiesced Arobin. "I don't blame you; stupid lot!"

Edna opened the blotter, and having procured paper and pen, began to write the note. Arobin lit a cigar and read the evening paper, which he had in his pocket.

"What is the date?" she asked. He told her.

"Will you mail this for me when you go out?"

"Certainly." He read to her little bits out of the newspaper, while she straightened things on the table.

"What do you want to do?" he asked, throwing aside the paper. "Do you want to go out for a walk or a drive or anything? It would be a fine night to drive."

"No; I don't want to do anything but just be quiet. You go away and amuse yourself. Don't stay."

"I'll go away if I must; but I shan't amuse myself. You know that I only live when I am near you."

He stood up to bid her good night.

"Is that one of the things you always say to women?"

"I have said it before, but I don't think I ever came so near meaning it," he answered with a smile. There were no warm lights in her eyes; only a dreamy, absent look.

"Good night. I adore you. Sleep well," he said, and he kissed her hand and went away.

She stayed alone in a kind of reverie—a sort of stupor. Step by step she lived over every instant of the time she had been with Robert after he had entered Mademoiselle Reisz's door. She recalled his words, his looks. How few and meager they had been for her hungry heart! A vision—a transcendently seductive vision of a Mexican girl arose before her. She writhed with a jealous pang. She wondered when he would come back. He had not said he would come back. She had been with him, had heard his voice and touched his hand. But some way he had seemed nearer to her off there in Mexico.

XXXV

The morning was full of sunlight and hope. Edna could see before her no denial—only the promise of excessive joy. She lay in bed awake, with bright eyes full of speculation. "He loves you, poor fool." If she could but get that conviction firmly fixed in her mind, what mattered about the rest? She felt she had been childish and unwise the night before in giving herself over to despondency. She recapitulated the motives which no doubt explained Robert's reserve. They were not insurmountable; they would not hold if he really loved her; they could not hold against her own passion, which he must come to realize in time. She pictured him going to his business that morning. She even saw how he was dressed; how he walked down one street, and turned the corner of another; saw him bending over his desk, talking to people who entered the office, going to his lunch, and perhaps watching for her on the street. He would come to her in the afternoon or evening, sit and roll his cigarette, talk a little, and go away as he had done the night before. But how delicious it would be to have him there with her! She would have no regrets, nor seek to penetrate his reserve if he still chose to wear it.

Edna ate her breakfast only half dressed. The maid brought her a delicious printed scrawl from Raoul, expressing his love, asking her to send him some bonbons, and telling her they had found that morning ten tiny white pigs all lying in a row beside Lidie's big white pig.

A letter also came from her husband, saying he hoped to be back early in March, and then they would get ready for that journey abroad which he had promised her so long, which he felt now fully able to afford; he felt able to travel as people should, without any thought of small economies—thanks to his recent speculations in Wall Street.

Much to her surprise she received a note from Arobin, written at midnight from the club. It was to say good morning to her, to hope that she had slept well, to assure her of his devotion, which he trusted she in some faintest manner returned.

All these letters were pleasing to her. She answered the children in a cheerful frame of mind, promising them bonbons, and congratulating them upon their happy find of the little pigs.

She answered her husband with friendly evasiveness,—not with any fixed design to mislead him, only because all sense of reality had gone out of her life; she had abandoned herself to Fate, and awaited the consequences with indifference.

To Arobin's note she made no reply. She put it under Celestine's stove-lid.

Edna worked several hours with much spirit. She saw no one but a picture dealer, who asked her if it were true that she was going abroad to study in Paris.

She said possibly she might, and he negotiated with her for some Parisian studies to reach him in time for the holiday trade in December.

Robert did not come that day. She was keenly disappointed. He did not come the following day, nor the next. Each morning she awoke with hope, and each night she was a prey to despondency. She was tempted to seek him out. But far from yielding to the impulse, she avoided any occasion which might throw her in his way. She did not go to Mademoiselle Reisz's nor pass by Madame Lebrun's, as she might have done if he had still been in Mexico.

When Arobin, one night, urged her to drive with him, she went—out to the lake, on the Shell Road.* His horses were full of mettle, and even a little unmanageable. She liked the rapid gait at which they spun along and the quick, sharp sound of the horses' hoofs on the hard road. They did not stop anywhere to eat or to drink. Arobin was not needlessly imprudent. But they ate and they drank when they regained Edna's little dining-room—which was comparatively early in the evening.

It was late when he left her. It was getting to be more than a passing whim with Arobin to see her and be with her. He had detected the latent sensuality, which unfolded under his delicate sense of her nature's requirements like a torpid, torrid, sensitive blossom.

There was no despondency when she fell asleep that night; nor was there hope when she awoke in the morning.

XXXVI

There was a garden out in the suburbs; a small, leafy corner, with a few green tables under the orange trees. An old cat slept all day on the stone step in the sun, and an old *mulatresse* slept her idle hours away in her chair at the open window, till some one happened to knock on one of the green tables. She had milk and cream cheese to sell, and bread and butter. There was no one who could make such excellent coffee or fry a chicken so golden brown as she.

The place was too modest to attract the attention of people of fashion, and so quiet as to have escaped the notice of those in search of pleasure and dissipation. Edna had discovered it accidentally one day when the high-board gate stood ajar. She caught sight of a little green table, blotched with the checkered sunlight that filtered through the quivering leaves overhead. Within she had found the slumbering *mulatresse*, the drowsy cat, and a glass of milk which reminded her of the milk she had tasted in Iberville.

She often stopped there during her perambulations; sometimes taking a book with her, and sitting an hour or two under the trees when she found the place deserted. Once or twice she took a quiet dinner there alone, having instructed Celestine beforehand to prepare no dinner at home. It was the last place in the city where she would have expected to meet any one she knew.

Still she was not astonished when, as she was partaking of a modest dinner late in the afternoon, looking into an open book, stroking the cat, which had made friends with her—she was not greatly astonished to see Robert come in at the tall garden gate.

"I am destined to see you only by accident," she said, shoving the cat off the chair beside her. He was surprised, ill at ease, almost embarrassed at meeting her thus so unexpectedly.

"Do you come here often?" he asked.

"I almost live here," she said.

"I used to drop in very often for a cup of Catiche's good coffee. This is the first time since I came back."

"She'll bring you a plate, and you will share my dinner. There's always enough for two—even three." Edna had intended to be indifferent and as reserved as he when she met him; she had reached the determination by a laborious train of reasoning, incident to one of her despondent moods. But her resolve melted when she saw him before her, seated there beside her in the little garden, as if a designing Providence had led him into her path.

"Why have you kept away from me, Robert?" she asked, closing the book that lay open upon the table.

"Why are you so personal, Mrs. Pontellier? Why do you force me to idiotic subterfuges?" he exclaimed with sudden warmth. "I suppose there's no use telling you I've been very busy, or that I've been sick, or that I've been to see you and not found you at home. Please let me off with any one of these excuses."

"You are the embodiment of selfishness," she said. "You save yourself something—I don't know what—but there is some selfish motive, and in sparing yourself you never consider for a moment what I think, or how I feel your neglect and indifference. I suppose this is what you would call unwomanly; but I have got into a habit of expressing myself. It doesn't matter to me, and you may think me unwomanly if you like."

"No; I only think you cruel, as I said the other day. Maybe not intentionally cruel; but you seem to be forcing me into disclosures which can result in nothing; as if you would have me bare a wound for the pleasure of looking at it, without the intention or power of healing it."

"I'm spoiling your dinner, Robert; never mind what I say. You haven't eaten a morsel."

"I only came in for a cup of coffee." His sensitive face was all disfigured with excitement.

"Isn't this a delightful place?" she remarked. "I am so glad it has never actually been discovered. It is so quiet, so sweet, here. Do you notice there is scarcely a sound to be heard? It's so out of the way; and a good walk from the car. However, I don't mind walking. I always feel so sorry for women who don't like to walk;* they miss so much—so many rare little glimpses of life; and we women learn so little of life on the whole.

"Catiche's coffee is always hot. I don't know how she manages it, here in the open air. Celestine's coffee gets cold bringing it from the kitchen to the dining-room. Three lumps! How can you drink it so sweet? Take some of the cress with your chop; it's so biting and crisp. Then there's the advantage of being able to smoke with your coffee out here. Now, in the city—aren't you going to smoke?"

"After a while," he said, laying a cigar on the table.

"Who gave it to you?" she laughed.

"I bought it. I suppose I'm getting reckless; I bought a whole box."

She was determined not to be personal again and make him uncomfortable.

The cat made friends with him, and climbed into his lap when he smoked his cigar. He stroked her silky fur, and talked a little about her. He looked at Edna's book, which he had read; and he told her the end, to save her the trouble of wading through it, he said.

Again he accompanied her back to her home; and it was after dusk when they reached the little "pigeon-house." She did not ask him to remain, which he was grateful for, as it permitted him to stay without the discomfort of blundering through an excuse which he had no intention of considering. He helped her to light the lamp; then she went into her room to take off her hat and to bathe her face and hands.

When she came back Robert was not examining the pictures and magazines as before; he sat off in the shadow, leaning his head back on the chair as if in a reverie. Edna lingered a moment beside the table, arranging the books there. Then she went across the room to where he sat. She bent over the arm of his chair and called his name.

"Robert," she said, "are you asleep?"

"No," he answered, looking up at her.

She leaned over and kissed him—a soft, cool, delicate kiss, whose voluptuous sting penetrated his whole being—then she moved away from him. He followed, and took her in his arms, just holding her close to him. She put her hand up to his face and pressed his cheek against her own. The action was full of love and tenderness. He sought her lips again. Then he drew her down upon the sofa beside him and held her hand in both of his.

"Now you know," he said, "now you know what I have been

fighting against since last summer at Grand Isle; what drove me away and drove me back again."

"Why have you been fighting against it?" she asked. Her face glowed with soft lights.

"Why? Because you were not free; you were Léonce Pontellier's wife. I couldn't help loving you if you were ten times his wife; but so long as I went away from you and kept away I could help telling you so." She put her free hand up to his shoulder, and then against his cheek, rubbing it softly. He kissed her again. His face was warm and flushed.

"There in Mexico I was thinking of you all the time, and longing for you."

"But not writing to me," she interrupted.

"Something put into my head that you cared for me; and I lost my senses. I forgot everything but a wild dream of your some way becoming my wife."

"Your wife!"

"Religion, loyalty, everything would give way if only you cared."

"Then you must have forgotten that I was Léonce Pontellier's wife."

"Oh! I was demented, dreaming of wild, impossible things, recalling men who had set their wives free, we have heard of such things."

"Yes, we have heard of such things."

"I came back full of vague, mad intentions. And when I got here—"

"When you got here you never came near me!" She was still caressing his cheek.

"I realized what a cur I was to dream of such a thing, even if you had been willing."

She took his face between her hands and looked into it as if she would never withdraw her eyes more. She kissed him on the forehead, the eyes, the cheeks, and the lips.

"You have been a very, very foolish boy, wasting your time dreaming of impossible things when you speak of Mr. Pontellier setting me free! I am no longer one of Mr. Pontellier's possessions to dispose of or not. I give myself where I choose. If he were to say, 'Here, Robert, take her and be happy; she is yours,' I should laugh at you both."

His face grew a little white. "What do you mean?" he asked.

There was a knock at the door. Old Celestine came in to say that Madame Ratignolle's servant had come around the back way with a message that Madame had been taken sick and begged Mrs. Pontellier to go to her immediately.

"Yes, yes," said Edna, rising; "I promised. Tell her yes—to wait for me. I'll go back with her."

"Let me walk over with you," offered Robert.

"No," she said; "I will go with the servant." She went into her room to put on her hat, and when she came in again she sat once more upon the sofa beside him. He had not stirred. She put her arms about his neck.

"Good-by, my sweet Robert. Tell me good-by." He kissed her with a degree of passion which had not before entered into his caress, and strained her to him.

"I love you," she whispered, "only you; no one but you. It was you who awoke me last summer out of a life-long, stupid dream. Oh! you have made me so unhappy with your indifference. Oh! I have suffered, suffered! Now you are here we shall love each other, my Robert. We shall be everything to each other. Nothing else in the world is of any consequence. I must go to my friend; but you will wait for me? No matter how late; you will wait for me, Robert?"

"Don't go; don't go! Oh! Edna, stay with me," he pleaded. "Why should you go? Stay with me, stay with me."

"I shall come back as soon as I can; I shall find you here." She buried her face in his neck, and said good-by again. Her seductive voice, together with his great love for her, had enthralled his senses, had deprived him of every impulse but the longing to hold her and keep her.

XXXVII

Edna looked in at the drug store. Monsieur Ratignolle was putting up a mixture himself very carefully, dropping a red liquid into a tiny glass. He was grateful to Edna for having come; her presence would be a comfort to his wife. Madame Ratignolle's sister, who had always been with her at such trying times, had not been able to come up from the plantation, and Adèle had been inconsolable until Mrs.

Pontellier so kindly promised to come to her. The nurse had been with them at night for the past week, as she lived a great distance away. And Dr. Mandelet had been coming and going all the afternoon. They were then looking for him any moment.

Edna hastened upstairs by a private stairway that led from the rear of the store to the apartments above. The children were all sleeping in a back room. Madame Ratignolle was in the salon, whither she had strayed in her suffering impatience. She sat on the sofa, clad in an ample white *peignoir*, holding a handkerchief tight in her hand with a nervous clutch. Her face was drawn and pinched, her sweet blue eyes haggard and unnatural. All her beautiful hair had been drawn back and plaited. It lay in a long braid on the sofa pillow, coiled like a golden serpent. The nurse, a comfortable looking *Griffe* woman in white apron and cap, was urging her to return to her bedroom.

"There is no use, there is no use," she said at once to Edna. "We must get rid of Mandelet; he is getting too old and careless. He said he would be here at half-past seven; now it must be eight. See what time it is, Joséphine."

The woman was possessed of a cheerful nature, and refused to take any situation too seriously, especially a situation with which she was so familiar. She urged Madame to have courage and patience. But Madame only set her teeth hard into her under lip, and Edna saw the sweat gather in beads on her white forehead. After a moment or two she uttered a profound sigh and wiped her face with the handkerchief rolled in a ball. She appeared exhausted. The nurse gave her a fresh handkerchief, sprinkled with cologne water.

"This is too much!" she cried. "Mandelet ought to be killed! Where is Alphonse? Is it possible I am to be abandoned like this—neglected by every one?"

"Neglected, indeed!" exclaimed the nurse. Wasn't she there? And here was Mrs. Pontellier leaving, no doubt, a pleasant evening at home to devote to her? And wasn't Monsieur Ratignolle coming that very instant through the hall? And Joséphine was quite sure she had heard Doctor Mandelet's coupé. Yes, there it was, down at the door.

Adèle consented to go back to her room. She sat on the edge of a little low couch next to her bed.

Doctor Mandelet paid no attention to Madame Ratignolle's upbraidings. He was accustomed to them at such times, and was too well convinced of her loyalty to doubt it.

He was glad to see Edna, and wanted her to go with him into the salon and entertain him. But Madame Ratignolle would not consent that Edna should leave her for an instant. Between agonizing moments, she chatted a little, and said it took her mind off her sufferings.

Edna began to feel uneasy. She was seized with a vague dread. Her own like experiences seemed far away, unreal, and only half remembered. She recalled faintly an ecstasy of pain, the heavy odor of chloroform, a stupor which had deadened sensation, and an awakening to find a little new life to which she had given being,* added to the great unnumbered multitude of souls that come and go.

She began to wish she had not come; her presence was not necessary. She might have invented a pretext for staying away; she might even invent a pretext now for going. But Edna did not go. With an inward agony, with a flaming, outspoken revolt against the ways of Nature, she witnessed the scene of torture.

She was still stunned and speechless with emotion when later she leaned over her friend to kiss her and softly say good-by. Adèle, pressing her cheek, whispered in an exhausted voice: "Think of the children, Edna. Oh think of the children!* Remember them!"

XXXVIII

Edna still felt dazed when she got outside in the open air. The Doctor's coupé had returned for him and stood before the *porte cochère*. She did not wish to enter the coupé and told Doctor Mandelet she would walk; she was not afraid, and would go alone. He directed his carriage to meet him at Mrs. Pontellier's, and he started to walk home with her.

Up—away up, over the narrow street between the tall houses, the stars were blazing. The air was mild and caressing, but cool with the breath of spring and the night. They walked slowly, the Doctor with a heavy, measured tread and his hands behind him; Edna, in an absent-minded way, as she had walked one night at Grand Isle, as if her thoughts had gone ahead of her and she was striving to overtake them.

"You shouldn't have been there, Mrs. Pontellier," he said. "That was no place for you. Adèle is full of whims at such times. There were a dozen women she might have had with her, unimpressionable women. I felt that it was cruel, cruel. You shouldn't have gone."

"Oh, well!" she answered, indifferently. "I don't know that it matters after all. One has to think of the children some time or other; the sooner the better."

"When is Léonce coming back?"

"Quite soon. Some time in March."

"And you are going abroad?"

"Perhaps—no, I am not going. I'm not going to be forced into doing things. I don't want to go abroad. I want to be let alone. Nobody has any right—except children, perhaps—and even then, it seems to me—or it did seem—" She felt that her speech was voicing the incoherency of her thoughts, and stopped abruptly.

"The trouble is," sighed the Doctor, grasping her meaning intuitively, "that youth is given up to illusions. It seems to be a provision of Nature; a decoy to secure mothers for the race.* And Nature takes no account of moral consequences, of arbitrary conditions which we create, and which we feel obliged to maintain at any cost."

"Yes," she said. "The years that are gone seem like dreams—if one might go on sleeping and dreaming—but to wake up and find— oh! well! perhaps it is better to wake up after all, even to suffer, rather than to remain a dupe to illusions all one's life."

"It seems to me, my dear child," said the Doctor at parting, holding her hand, "you seem to me to be in trouble. I am not going to ask for your confidence. I will only say that if ever you feel moved to give it to me, perhaps I might help you. I know I would understand, and I tell you there are not many who would—not many, my dear."

"Some way I don't feel moved to speak of things that trouble me. Don't think I am ungrateful or that I don't appreciate your sympathy. There are periods of despondency and suffering which take possession of me. But I don't want anything but my own way. That is wanting a good deal, of course, when you have to trample upon the lives, the hearts, the prejudices of others—but no matter—still, I shouldn't want to trample upon the little lives. Oh! I don't know what I'm saying, Doctor. Good night. Don't blame me for anything."

"Yes, I will blame you if you don't come and see me soon. We will talk of things you never have dreamt of talking about before. It will do us both good. I don't want you to blame yourself, whatever comes. Good night, my child."

She let herself in at the gate, but instead of entering she sat upon the step of the porch. The night was quiet and soothing. All the tearing emotion of the last few hours seemed to fall away from her like a somber, uncomfortable garment, which she had but to loosen to be rid of. She went back to that hour before Adèle had sent for her; and her senses kindled afresh in thinking of Robert's words, the pressure of his arms, and the feeling of his lips upon her own. She could picture at that moment no greater bliss on earth than possession of the beloved one. His expression of love had already given him to her in part. When she thought that he was there at hand, waiting for her, she grew numb with the intoxication of expectancy. It was so late; he would be asleep perhaps. She would awaken him with a kiss. She hoped he would be asleep that she might arouse him with her caresses.

Still, she remembered Adèle's voice whispering, "Think of the children; think of them." She meant to think of them; that determination had driven into her soul like a death wound—but not to-night. To-morrow would be time to think of everything.

Robert was not waiting for her in the little parlor. He was nowhere at hand. The house was empty. But he had scrawled on a piece of paper that lay in the lamplight:

"I love you. Good-by—because I love you."

Edna grew faint when she read the words. She went and sat on the sofa. Then she stretched herself out there, never uttering a sound. She did not sleep. She did not go to bed. The lamp sputtered and went out. She was still awake in the morning, when Celestine unlocked the kitchen door and came in to light the fire.

XXXIX

Victor, with hammer and nails and scraps of scantling, was patching a corner of one of the galleries. Mariequita sat near by, dangling her legs, watching him work, and handing him nails from the tool-box. The sun was beating down upon them. The girl had covered her head with her apron folded into a square pad. They had been talking for an hour or more. She was never tired of hearing Victor describe the dinner at Mrs. Pontellier's. He exaggerated every detail, making it appear a veritable Lucillean feast.* The flowers were in tubs, he said. The champagne was quaffed from huge golden goblets. Venus rising from the foam could have presented no more entrancing a spectacle than Mrs. Pontellier, blazing with beauty and diamonds at the head of the board, while the other women were all of them youthful houris,* possessed of incomparable charms.

She got it into her head that Victor was in love with Mrs. Pontellier, and he gave her evasive answers, framed so as to confirm her belief. She grew sullen and cried a little, threatening to go off and leave him to his fine ladies. There were a dozen men crazy about her at the *Chênière*; and since it was the fashion to be in love with married people, why, she could run away any time she liked to New Orleans with Célina's husband.

Célina's husband was a fool, a coward, and a pig, and to prove it to her, Victor intended to hammer his head into a jelly the next time he encountered him. This assurance was very consoling to Mariequita. She dried her eyes, and grew cheerful at the prospect.

They were still talking of the dinner and the allurements of city life when Mrs. Pontellier herself slipped around the corner of the house. The two youngsters stayed dumb with amazement before what they considered to be an apparition. But it was really she in flesh and blood, looking tired and a little travel-stained.

"I walked up from the wharf," she said, "and heard the hammering. I supposed it was you, mending the porch. It's a good thing. I was always tripping over those loose planks last summer. How dreary and deserted everything looks!"

It took Victor some little time to comprehend that she had come in Beaudelet's lugger, that she had come alone, and for no purpose but to rest.

"There's nothing fixed up yet, you see. I'll give you my room; it's the only place."

"Any corner will do," she assured him.

"And if you can stand Philomel's cooking," he went on, "though I might try to get her mother while you are here. Do you think she would come?" turning to Mariequita.

Mariequita thought that perhaps Philomel's mother might come for a few days, and money enough.

Beholding Mrs. Pontellier make her appearance, the girl had at once suspected a lovers' rendezvous. But Victor's astonishment was so genuine, and Mrs. Pontellier's indifference so apparent, that the disturbing notion did not lodge long in her brain. She contemplated with the greatest interest this woman who gave the most sumptuous dinners in America, and who had all the men in New Orleans at her feet.

"What time will you have dinner?" asked Edna. "I'm very hungry; but don't get anything extra."

"I'll have it ready in little or no time," he said, bustling and packing away his tools. "You may go to my room to brush up and rest yourself. Mariequita will show you."

"Thank you," said Edna. "But, do you know, I have a notion to go down to the beach and take a good wash and even a little swim, before dinner?"

"The water is too cold!" they both exclaimed. "Don't think of it."

"Well, I might go down and try—dip my toes in. Why, it seems to me the sun is hot enough to have warmed the very depths of the ocean. Could you get me a couple of towels? I'd better go right away, so as to be back in time. It would be a little too chilly if I waited till this afternoon."

Mariequita ran over to Victor's room, and returned with some towels, which she gave to Edna.

"I hope you have fish for dinner," said Edna, as she started to walk away; "but don't do anything extra if you haven't."

"Run and find Philomel's mother," Victor instructed the girl. "I'll go to the kitchen and see what I can do. By Gimminy! Women have no consideration! She might have sent me word."

Edna walked on down to the beach rather mechanically, not noticing anything special except that the sun was hot. She was not dwelling upon any particular train of thought. She had done all the thinking which was necessary after Robert went away, when she lay awake upon the sofa till morning.

She had said over and over to herself: "To-day it is Arobin; to-morrow it will be some one else. It makes no difference to me, it doesn't matter about Léonce Pontellier—but Raoul and Etienne!" She understood now clearly what she had meant long ago when she said to Adèle Ratignolle that she would give up the unessential, but she would never sacrifice herself for her children.

Despondency had come upon her there in the wakeful night, and had never lifted. There was no one thing in the world that she desired. There was no human being whom she wanted near her except Robert; and she even realized that the day would come when he, too, and the thought of him would melt out of her existence, leaving her alone. The children appeared before her like antagonists who had overcome her; who had overpowered and sought to drag her into the soul's slavery for the rest of her days. But she knew a way to elude them. She was not thinking of these things when she walked down to the beach.

The water of the Gulf stretched out before her, gleaming with the million lights of the sun. The voice of the sea is seductive, never ceasing, whispering, clamoring, murmuring, inviting the soul to wander in abysses of solitude. All along the white beach, up and down, there was no living thing in sight. A bird with a broken wing was beating the air above, reeling, fluttering, circling disabled down, down to the water.

Edna had found her old bathing suit still hanging, faded, upon its accustomed peg.

She put it on, leaving her clothing in the bath-house. But when she was there beside the sea, absolutely alone, she cast the unpleasant, pricking garments from her, and for the first time in her life she stood naked in the open air, at the mercy of the sun, the breeze that beat upon her, and the waves that invited her.

How strange and awful it seemed to stand naked under the sky! how delicious! She felt like some new-born creature, opening its eyes in a familiar world that it had never known.

The foamy wavelets curled up to her white feet, and coiled like serpents about her ankles. She walked out. The water was chill, but she walked on. The water was deep, but she lifted her white body and reached out with a long, sweeping stroke. The touch of the sea is sensuous, enfolding the body in its soft, close embrace.

She went on and on. She remembered the night she swam far out, and recalled the terror that seized her at the fear of being unable to regain the shore. She did not look back now, but went on and on, thinking of the blue-grass meadow that she had traversed when a little child, believing that it had no beginning and no end.

Her arms and legs were growing tired.

She thought of Léonce and the children. They were a part of her life. But they need not have thought that they could possess her, body and soul. How Mademoiselle Reisz would have laughed, perhaps sneered, if she knew! "And you call yourself an artist! What pretensions, Madame! The artist must possess the courageous soul that dares and defies."

Exhaustion was pressing upon and overpowering her.

"Good-by—because, I love you." He did not know; he did not understand. He would never understand. Perhaps Doctor Mandelet would have understood if she had seen him—but it was too late; the shore was far behind her, and her strength was gone.

She looked into the distance, and the old terror flamed up for an instant, then sank again. Edna heard her father's voice and her sister Margaret's. She heard the barking of an old dog that was chained to the sycamore tree. The spurs of the cavalry officer clanged as he walked across the porch. There was the hum of bees, and the musky odor of pinks filled the air.*

WISER THAN A GOD

"To love and be wise is scarcely granted even to a god."*

—Latin Proverb

I

"You might at least show some distaste for the task, Paula," said Mrs. Von Stoltz, in her querulous invalid voice, to her daughter who stood before the glass bestowing a few final touches of embellishment upon an otherwise plain toilet.

"And to what purpose, Mutterchen?* The task is not entirely to my liking, I'll admit; but there can be no question as to its results, which you even must concede are gratifying."

"Well, it's not the career your poor father had in view for you. How often he has told me when I complained that you were kept too closely at work, 'I want that Paula shall be at the head,' " with appealing look through the window and up into the gray, November sky into that far "somewhere," which might be the abode of her departed husband.

"It isn't a career at all, mamma; it's only a make-shift," answered the girl, noting the happy effect of an amber pin that she had thrust through the coils of her lustrous yellow hair. "The pot must be kept boiling at all hazards, pending the appearance of that hoped for career. And you forget that an occasion like this gives me the very opportunities I want."

"I can't see the advantages of bringing your talent down to such banale servitude. Who are those people, anyway?"

The mother's question ended in a cough which shook her into speechless exhaustion.

"Ah! I have let you sit too long by the window, mother," said Paula, hastening to wheel the invalid's chair nearer the grate fire that was throwing genial light and warmth into the room, turning its plainness to beauty as by a touch of enchantment. "By the way," she added, having arranged her mother as comfortably as might be, "I haven't yet qualified for that 'banale servitude,' as you call it." And approaching the piano which stood in a distant alcove of the room, she took up a roll of music that lay curled up on the instrument, straightened it out before her. Then, seeming to remember the question which her mother had asked, turned on the stool to answer it. "Don't you know? The Brainards, very swell people, and awfully rich. The daughter is that girl whom I once told you about, having gone to the Conservatory to cultivate her voice and old Engfelder told her in his brusque way to go back home, that his system was not equal to overcoming impossibilities."

"Oh, those people."

"Yes; this little party is given in honor of the son's return from Yale or Harvard, or some place or other." And turning to the piano she softly ran over the dances, whilst the mother gazed into the fire with unresigned sadness, which the bright music seemed to deepen.

"Well, there'll be no trouble about *that*," said Paula, with comfortable assurance, having ended the last waltz. "There's nothing here to tempt me into flights of originality; there'll be no difficulty in keeping to the hand-organ effect."

"Don't leave me with those dreadful impressions, Paula; my poor nerves are on edge."

"You are too hard on the dances, mamma. There are certain strains here and there that I thought not bad."

"It's your youth that finds it so; I have outlived such illusions."

"What an inconsistent little mother it is!" the girl exclaimed, laughing. "You told me only yesterday it was my youth that was so impatient with the commonplace happenings of everyday life. That age, needing to seek its delights, finds them often in unsuspected places, wasn't that it?"

"Don't chatter, Paula; some music, some music!"

"What shall it be?" asked Paula, touching a succession of harmonious chords. "It must be short."

"The 'Berceuse,'* then; Chopin's. But soft, soft and a little slowly as your dear father used to play it."

Mrs. Von Stoltz leaned her head back amongst the cushions, and with eyes closed, drank in the wonderful strains that came like an ethereal voice out of the past, lulling her spirit into the quiet of sweet memories.

When the last soft notes had melted into silence, Paula approached her mother and looking into the pale face saw that tears stood beneath the closed eyelids. "Ah! mamma, I have made you unhappy," she cried, in distress.

"No, my child; you have given me a joy that you don't dream of. I have no more pain. Your music has done for me what Faranelli's singing did for poor King Philip of Spain;* it has cured me."

There was a glow of pleasure on the warm face and the eyes with almost the brightness of health. "Whilst I listened to you, Paula, my soul went out from me and lived again through an evening long ago. We were in our pretty room at Leipsic.* The soft air and the moonlight came through the open-curtained window, making a quivering fret-work along the gleaming waxed floor. You lay in my arms and I felt again the pressure of your warm, plump little body against me. Your father was at the piano playing the 'Berceuse,' and all at once you drew my head down and whispered, 'Ist es nicht wonderschen, mama?'* When it ended, you were sleeping and your father took you from my arms and laid you gently in bed."

Paula knelt beside her mother, holding the frail hands which she kissed tenderly.

"Now you must go, liebchen.* Ring for Berta, she will do all that is needed. I feel very strong to-night. But do not come back too late."

"I shall be home as early as possible; likely in the last car, I couldn't stay longer or I should have to walk. You know the house in case there should be need to send for me?"

"Yes, yes; but there will be no need."

Paula kissed her mother lovingly and went out into the drear November night with the roll of dances under her arm.

II

The door of the stately mansion at which Paula rang, was opened by a footman, who invited her to "kindly walk upstairs."

"Show the young lady into the music room, James," called from some upper region a voice, doubtless the same whose impossibilities had been so summarily dealt with by Herr Engfelder, and Paula was led through a suite of handsome apartments, the warmth and mellow light of which were very grateful, after the chill out-door air.

Once in the music room, she removed her wraps and seated herself comfortably to await developments. Before her stood the magnificent "Steinway",* on which her eyes rested with greedy admiration, and her fingers twitched with a desire to awaken its inviting possibilities. The odor of flowers impregnated the air like a subtle intoxicant and over everything hung a quiet smile of expectancy, disturbed by an occasional feminine flutter above stairs, or muffled suggestions of distant household sounds.

Presently, a young man entered the drawing-room,—no doubt, the college student, for he looked critically and with an air of proprietorship at the festive arrangements, venturing the bestowal of a few improving touches. Then, gazing with pardonable complacency at his own handsome, athletic figure in the mirror, he saw reflected Paula looking at him, with a demure smile lighting her blue eyes.

"By Jove!" was his startled exclamation. Then, approaching, "I beg pardon, Miss—Miss—"

"Von Stoltz."

"Miss Von Stoltz," drawing the right conclusion from her simple toilet and the roll of music. "I hadn't seen you when I came in. Have you been here long? and sitting all alone, too? That's certainly rough."

"Oh, I've been here but a few moments, and was very well entertained."

"I dare say," with a glance full of prognostic complimentary utterances, which a further acquaintance might develop.

As he was lighting the gas of a side bracket that she might better see to read her music, Mrs. Brainard and her daughter came into the room, radiantly attired and both approached Paula with sweet and polite greeting.

"George, in mercy!" exclaimed his mother, "put out that gas, you are killing the effect of the candle light."

"But Miss Von Stoltz can't read her music without it, mother."

"I've no doubt Miss Von Stoltz knows her pieces by heart," Mrs. Brainard replied, seeking corroboration from Paula's glance.

"No, madam; I'm not accustomed to playing dance music, and this is quite new to me," the girl rejoined, touching the loose sheets that George had conveniently straightened out and placed on the rack.

"Oh, dear! 'not accustomed'?" said Miss Brainard. "And Mr. Sohmeir told us he knew you would give satisfaction."

Paula hastened to re-assure the thoroughly alarmed young lady on the point of her ability to give perfect satisfaction.

The door bell now began to ring incessantly. Up the stairs, tripped fleeting opera-cloaked figures, followed by their black robed attendants. The rooms commenced to fill with the pretty hub-bub that a bevy of girls can make when inspired by a close masculine proximity; and Paula, not waiting to be asked, struck the opening bars of an inspiring waltz.

Some hours later, during a lull in the dancing, when the men were making vigorous applications of fans and handkerchiefs; and the girls beginning to throw themselves into attitudes of picturesque exhaustion—save for the always indefatigable few—a proposition was ventured, backed by clamorous entreaties, which induced George to bring forth his banjo. And an agreeable moment followed, in which that young man's skill met with a truly deserving applause. Never had his audience beheld such proficiency as he displayed in the handling of his instrument, which was now behind him, now over-head, and again swinging in mid-air like the pendulum of a clock and sending forth the sounds of stirring melody. Sounds so inspiring that a pretty little black-eyed fairy, an acknowledged votary of Terpsichore,* and George's particular admiration, was moved to contribute a few passes of a Virginia breakdown, as she had studied it from life on a Southern plantation. The act closing amid a spontaneous babel of hand clapping and admiring bravos.

It must be admitted that this little episode, however graceful, was hardly a fitting prelude to the magnificent "Jewel Song from 'Faust,'"* with which Miss Brainard next consented to regale the company. That Miss Brainard possessed a voice, was a fact that had existed as matter of tradition in the family as far back almost as the days of that young lady's baby utterances, in which loving ears had already detected the promise which time had so recklessly fulfilled.

True genius is not to be held in abeyance, though a host of Engfelders would rise to quell it with their mundane protests!

Miss Brainard's rendition was a triumphant achievement of sound, and with the proud flush of success moving her to kind condescension, she asked Miss Von Stoltz to "please play something."

Paula amiably consented, choosing a selection from the Modern Classic.* How little did her auditors appreciate in the performance the results of a life study, of a drilling that had made her amongst the knowing an acknowledged mistress of technique. But to her skill she added the touch and interpretation of the artist; and in hearing her, even Ignorance paid to her genius the tribute of a silent emotion.

When she arose there was a moment of quiet, which was broken by the black-eyed fairy, always ready to cast herself into a breach, observing, flippantly, "How pretty!" "Just lovely!" from another; and "What wouldn't I give to play like that." Each inane compliment falling like a dash of cold water on Paula's ardor.

She then became solicitous about the hour, with reference to her car, and George who stood near looked at his watch and informed her that the last car had gone by a full half hour before.

"But," he added, "if you are not expecting any one to call for you, I will gladly see you home."

"I expect no one, for the car that passes here would have set me down at my door," and in this avowal of difficulties, she tacitly accepted George's offer.

The situation was new. It gave her a feeling of elation to be walking through the quiet night with this handsome young fellow. He talked so freely and so pleasantly. She felt such a comfort in his strong protective nearness. In clinging to him against the buffets of the staggering wind she could feel the muscles of his arms, like steel.

He was so unlike any man of her acquaintance. Strictly unlike Poldorf, the pianist, the short rotundity of whose person could have been less objectionable, if she had not known its cause to lie in an inordinate consumption of beer. Old Engfelder, with his long hair, his spectacles and his loose, disjointed figure, was hors de combat in comparison. And of Max Kuntzler, the talented composer, her teacher of harmony, she could at the moment think of no positive point of objection against him, save the vague, general, serious one of his unlikeness to George.

Her new-awakened admiration, though, was not deaf to a little inexplicable wish that he had not been so proficient with the banjo.*

On they went chatting gaily, until turning the corner of the street in which she lived, Paula saw that before the door stood Dr. Sinn's buggy.

Brainard could feel the quiver of surprised distress that shook her frame, as she said, hurrying along, "Oh! mamma must be ill—worse; they have called the doctor."

Reaching the house, she threw open wide the door that was unlocked, and he stood hesitatingly back. The gas in the small hall

burned at its full, and showed Berta at the top of the stairs, speechless, with terrified eyes, looking down at her. And coming to meet
her, was a neighbor, who strove with well-meaning solicitude to keep
her back, to hold her yet a moment in ignorance of the cruel blow
that fate had dealt her whilst she had in happy unconsciousness
played her music for the dance.

III

Several months had passed since the dreadful night when death had
deprived Paula for the second time of a loved parent.

After the first shock of grief was over, the girl had thrown all her
energies into work, with the view of attaining that position in the
musical world which her father and mother had dreamed might be
hers.

She had remained in the small home occupying now but the half
of it; and here she kept house with the faithful Berta's aid.

Friends were both kind and attentive to the stricken girl. But there
had been two, whose constant devotion spoke of an interest deeper
than mere friendly solicitude.

Max Kuntzler's love for Paula was something that had taken hold
of his sober middle age with an enduring strength which was not to
be lessened or shaken, by her rejection of it. He had asked leave to
remain her friend, and while holding the tender, watchful privileges
which that comprehensive title may imply, had refrained from
further thrusting a warmer feeling on her acceptance.

Paula one evening was seated in her small sitting-room, working
over some musical transpositions, when a ring at the bell was followed
by a footstep in the hall which made her hand and heart tremble.

George Brainard entered the room, and before she could rise to
greet him, had seated himself in the vacant chair beside her.

"What an untiring worker you are," he said, glancing down at the
scores before her. "I always feel that my presence interrupts you; and
yet I don't know that a judicious interruption isn't the wholesomest
thing for you sometimes."

"You forget," she said, smiling into his face, "that I was trained to
it. I must keep myself fitted to my calling. Rest would mean
deterioration."

"Would you not be willing to follow some other calling?" he asked, looking at her with unusual earnestness in his dark, handsome eyes.

"Oh, never!"

"Not if it were a calling that asked only for the labor of loving?"

She made no answer, but kept her eyes fixed on the idle traceries that she drew with her pencil on the sheets before her.

He arose and made a few impatient turns about the room, then coming again to her side, said abruptly:

"Paula, I love you. It isn't telling you something that you don't know, unless you have been without bodily perceptions. To-day there is something driving me to speak it out in words. Since I have known you," he continued, striving to look into her face that bent low over the work before her, "I have been mounting into higher and always higher circles of Paradise, under a blessed illusion that you— cared for me. But to-day, a feeling of dread has been forcing itself upon me—dread that with a word you might throw me back into a gulf that would now be one of everlasting misery. Say if you love me, Paula. I believe you do, and yet I wait with indefinable doubts for your answer."

He took her hand which she did not withdraw from his.

"Why are you speechless? Why don't you say something to me!" he asked desperately.

"I am speechless with joy and misery," she answered. "To know that you love me, gives me happiness enough to brighten a lifetime. And I am miserable, feeling that you have spoken the signal that must part us."

"You love me, and speak of parting. Never! You will be my wife. From this moment we belong to each other. Oh, my Paula," he said, drawing her to his side, "my whole existence will be devoted to your happiness."

"I can't marry you," she said shortly, disengaging his hand from her waist.

"Why?" he asked abruptly. They stood looking into each other's eyes.

"Because it doesn't enter into the purpose of my life."

"I don't ask you to give up anything in your life. I only beg you to let me share it with you."

George had known Paula only as the daughter of the undemonstrative American woman. He had never before seen her with the father's emotional nature aroused in her. The color mounted into her cheeks, and her blue eyes were almost black with intensity of feeling.

"Hush," she said; "don't tempt me further." And she cast herself on her knees before the table near which they stood, gathering the music that lay upon it into an armful, and resting her hot cheek upon it.

"What do you know of my life," she exclaimed passionately. "What can you guess of it? Is music anything more to you than the pleasing distraction of an idle moment? Can't you feel that with me, it courses with the blood through my veins? That it's something dearer than life, than riches, even than love?" with a quiver of pain.

"Paula listen to me; don't speak like a mad woman."

She sprang up and held out an arm to ward away his nearer approach.

"Would you go into a convent, and ask to be your wife a nun who has vowed herself to the service of God?"

"Yes, if that nun loved me; she would owe to herself, to me and to God to be my wife."

Paula seated herself on the sofa, all emotion seeming suddenly to have left her; and he came and sat beside her.

"Say only that you love me, Paula," he urged persistently.

"I love you," she answered low and with pale lips.

He took her in his arms, holding her in silent rapture against his heart and kissing the white lips back into red life.

"You will be my wife?"

"You must wait. Come back in a week and I will answer you." He was forced to be content with the delay.

The days of probation being over, George went for his answer, which was given him by the old lady who occupied the upper story.

"Ach Gott! Fräulein Von Stoltz ist schon im Leipsic gegangen!"*—All that has not been many years ago. George Brainard is as handsome as ever, though growing a little stout in the quiet routine of domestic life. He has quite lost a pretty taste for music that formerly distinguished him as a skilful banjoist. This loss his little black-eyed wife deplores; though she has herself made concessions to the advancing years, and abandoned Virginia break-downs as incompatible with the serious offices of wifehood and matrimony.

You may have seen in the morning paper, that the

renowned pianist, Fräulein Paula Von Stoltz, is resting in Leipsic, after an extended and remunerative concert tour.

Professor Max Kuntzler* is also in Leipsic—with the ever persistent will—the dogged patience that so often wins in the end.

A POINT AT ISSUE!

A Story of Love and Reason in Which Love Triumphs.

MARRIED—On Tuesday, May 11, Eleanor Gail to Charles Faraday.

Nothing bearing the shape of a wedding announcement could have been less obtrusive than the foregoing hidden in a remote corner of the Plymdale *Promulgator*, clothed in the palest and smallest of type, and modestly wedged in between the big, black-lettered offer of the *Promulgator* to mail itself free of extra charge to subscribers leaving home for the summer months, and an equally somber-clad notice (doubtless astray as to place and application) that Hammersmith & Co. were carrying a large and varied assortment of marble and granite monuments!

Yet notwithstanding its sandwiched condition, that little marriage announcement seemed to Eleanor to parade the whole street.

Whichever way she turned her eyes, it glowered at her with scornful reproach.

She felt it to be an indelicate thrusting of herself upon the public notice; and at the sight she was plunged in regret at having made to the proprieties the concession of permitting it.

She hoped now that the period for making concessions was ended. She had endured long and patiently the trials that beset her path when she chose to diverge from the beaten walks of female Plymdaledom. Had stood stoically enough the questionable distinction of being relegated to a place amid that large and ill-assorted family of "cranks,"* feeling the discomfit and attending opprobrium to be far outbalanced by the satisfying consciousness of roaming the heights of free thought, and tasting the sweets of a spiritual emancipation.

The closing act of Eleanor's young ladyhood, when she chose to be married without pre-announcement, without the paraphernalia of accessories so dear to a curious public—had been in keeping with previous methods distinguishing her career. The disappointed public cheated of its entertainment, was forced to seek such compensation for the loss as was offered in reflections that while condemning her present, were unsparing of her past, and full with damning prognostic of her future.

Charles Faraday, who added to his unembellished title that of Professor of Mathematics of the Plymdale University, had found in Eleanor Gail his ideal woman.

Indeed, she rather surpassed that ideal, which had of necessity been but an adorned picture of woman as he had known her. A mild emphasizing of her merits, a soft toning down of her defects had served to offer to his fancy a prototype of that bequoted creature.

"Not too good for human nature's daily food,"* yet so good that he had cherished no hope of beholding such a one in the flesh. Until Eleanor had come, supplanting his ideal, and making of that fanciful creation a very simpleton by contrast. In the beginning he had found her extremely good to look at, with her combination of graceful womanly charms, unmarred by self-conscious mannerisms that was as rare as it was engaging. Talking with her, he had caught a look from her eyes into his that he recognized at once as a free masonry of intellect.* And the longer he knew her, the greater grew his wonder at the beautiful revelations of her mind that unfurled itself to his, like the curling petals of some hardy blossom that opens to the inviting warmth of the sun. It was not that Eleanor knew many things. According to her own modest estimate of herself, she knew nothing. There were school girls in Plymdale who surpassed her in the amount of their positive knowledge. But she was possessed of a clear intellect: sharp in its reasoning, strong and unprejudiced in its outlook. She was that *rara avis*,* a logical woman—something which Faraday had not encountered in his life before. True, he was not hoary with age. At 30 the types of women he had met with were not legion; but he felt safe in doubting that the hedges of the future would grow logical women for him, more than they had borne such prodigies in the past.

He found Eleanor ready to take broad views of life and humanity; able to grasp a question and anticipate conclusions by a quick intuition which he himself reached by the slower, consecutive steps of reason.

During the months that shaped themselves into the cycle of a year these two dwelt together in the harmony of a united purpose.

Together they went looking for the good things of life, knocking at the closed doors of philosophy; venturing into the open fields of science, she, with uncertain steps, made steady by his help.

Whithersoever he led she followed, oftentimes in her eagerness taking the lead into unfamiliar ways in which he, weighted with a lingering conservatism, had hesitated to venture.

So did they grow in their oneness of thought to belong each so absolutely to the other that the idea seemed not to have come to them that this union might be made faster by marriage. Until one day it broke upon Faraday, like a revelation from the unknown, the possibility of making her his wife.

When he spoke, eager with the new awakened impulse, she laughingly replied:

"Why not?" She had thought of it long ago.

In entering upon their new life they decided to be governed by no precedential methods. Marriage was to be a form, that while fixing legally their relation to each other, was in no wise to touch the individuality of either; that was to be preserved intact. Each was to remain a free integral of humanity, responsible to no dominating exactions of so-called marriage laws. And the element that was to make possible such a union was trust in each other's love, honor, courtesy, tempered by the reserving clause of readiness to meet the consequences of reciprocal liberty.

Faraday appreciated the need of offering to his wife advantages for culture which had been of impossible attainment during her girlhood.

Marriage, which marks too often the closing period of a woman's intellectual existence, was to be in her case the open portal* through which she might seek the embellishments that her strong, graceful mentality deserved.

An urgent desire with Eleanor was to acquire a thorough speaking knowledge of the French language. They agreed that a lengthy sojourn in Paris could be the only practical and reliable means of accomplishing such an end.

Faraday's three months of vacation were to be spent by them in the idle happiness of a loitering honeymoon through the continent of Europe, then he would leave his wife in the French capital for a stay that might extend indefinitely—two, three years—as long as should be found needful, he returning to join her with the advent of each summer, to renew their love in a fresh and re-strengthened union.

And so, in May, they were married, and in September we find Eleanor established in the pension of the old couple Clairegobeau and comfortably ensconced in her pretty room that opened on to the Rue Rivoli, her heart full of sweet memories that were to cheer her coming solitude.

On the wall, looking always down at her with his quiet, kind glance, hung the portrait of her husband. Beneath it stood the fanciful little desk at which she hoped to spend many happy hours.

Books were everywhere, giving character to the graceful furnishings which their united taste had evolved from the paucity of the Clairegobeau germ, and out of the window was Paris!

Eleanor was supremely satisfied amid her new and attractive surroundings. The pang of parting from her husband seeming to lend sharp zest to a situation that offered the fulfillment of a cherished purpose.

Faraday, with the stronger man-nature, felt more keenly the discomfit of giving up a companionship that in its brief duration had been replete with the duality of accomplished delight and growing promise.

But to him also was the situation made acceptable by its involving a principle which he felt it incumbent upon him to uphold. He returned to Plymdale and to his duties at the university, and resumed his bachelor existence as quietly as though it had been interrupted but by the interval of a day.

The small public with which he had acquaintance, and which had forgotten his existence during the past few months, was fired anew with indignant astonishment at the effrontery of the situation which his singular coming back offered to their contemplation.

That two young people should presume to introduce such innovations into matrimony!

It was uncalled for!

It was improper!

It was indecent!

He must have already tired of her idiosyncrasies, since he had left her in Paris.

And in Paris, of all places, to leave a young woman alone! Why not at once in Hades?

She had been left in Paris forsooth to learn French. And since when was Mme. Belaire's French, as it had been taught to select generations of Plymdalions, considered insufficient for the practical needs of existence as related by that foreign tongue?

But Faraday's life was full with occupation and his brief moments of leisure were too precious to give to heeding the idle gossip that floated to his hearing and away again without holding his thoughts an instant.

He lived uninterruptedly a certain existence with his wife through the medium of letters. True, an inadequate substitute for her actual presence, but there was much satisfaction in this constant communion of thought between them.

They told such details of their daily lives as they thought worth the telling.

Their readings were discussed. Opinions exchanged. Newspaper cuttings sent back and forth, bearing upon questions that interested them. And what did not interest them?

Nothing was so large that they dared not look at it. Happenings, small in themselves, but big in their psychological comprehensiveness, held them with strange fascination. Her earnestness and intensity in such matters were extreme; but happily, Faraday brought to this union humorous instincts, and an optimism that saved it from a too monotonous sombreness.

The young man had his friends in Plymdale. Certainly none that ever remotely approached the position which Eleanor held in that regard. She stood pre-eminent. She was himself.

But his nature was genial. He invited companionship from his fellow beings, who, however short that companionship might be, carried always away a gratifying consciousness of having made their personality felt.

The society in Plymdale which he most frequented was that of the Beatons.

Beaton père was a fellow professor, many years older than Faraday, but one of those men with whom time, after putting its customary stamp upon his outward being, took no further care.

The spirit of his youth had remained untouched, and formed the nucleus around which the family gathered, drawing the light of their own cheerfulness.

Mrs. Beaton was a woman whose aspirations went not further

than the desire for her family's good, and her bearing announced in its every feature, the satisfaction of completed hopes.

Of the daughters, Margaret, the eldest, was looked upon as slightly erratic, owing to a timid leaning in the direction of Woman's Suffrage.*

Her activity in that regard, taking the form of a desultory correspondence with members of a certain society of protest; the fashioning and donning of garments of mysterious shape,* which, while stamping their wearer with the distinction of a quasi-emancipation, defeated the ultimate purpose of their construction by inflicting a personal discomfort that extended beyond the powers of long endurance. Miss Kitty Beaton, the youngest daughter, and just returned from boarding-school, while clamoring for no privileges doubtful of attainment and of remote and questionable benefit, with a Napoleonic grip, possessed herself of such rights as were at hand and exercised them in keeping the household under her capricious command.

She was at that age of blissful illusion when a girl is in love with her own youth and beauty and happiness. That age which heeds no purpose in the scope of creation further than may touch her majesty's enjoyment. Who would not smilingly endure with that charming selfishness of youth, knowing that the rough hand of experience is inevitably descending to disturb the short-lived dream?

They were all clever people, bright and interesting, and in this family circle Faraday found an acceptable relaxation from work and enforced solitude.

If they ever doubted the wisdom or expediency of his domestic relations, courtesy withheld the expression of any such doubts. Their welcome was always complete in its friendliness, and the interest which they evinced in the absent Eleanor proved that she was held in the highest esteem.

With Beaton Faraday enjoyed that pleasant intercourse which may exist between men whose ways, while not too divergent, are yet divided by an appreciable interval.

But it remained for Kitty to touch him with her girlish charms in a way, which, though not too usual with Faraday, meant so little to the man that he did not take the trouble to resent it.

Her laughter and song, the restless motions of her bubbling

happiness, he watched with the casual pleasure that one follows the playful gambols of a graceful kitten.

He liked the soft shining light of her eyes. When she was near him the velvet smoothness of her pink cheeks stirred him with a feeling that could have found satisfying expression in a kiss.

It is idle to suppose that even the most exemplary men go through life with their eyes closed to woman's beauty and their senses steeled against its charm.

Faraday thought little of this feeling (and so should we if it were not outspoken).

In writing one day to his wife, with the cold-blooded impartiality of choosing a subject which he thought of neither more nor less prominence than the next, he descanted at some length upon the interesting emotions which Miss Kitty's pretty femininity aroused in him.

If he had given serious thought to the expediency of touching upon such a theme with one's wife, he still would not have been deterred. Was not Eleanor's large comprehensiveness far above the littleness of ordinary women?

Did it not enter into the scheme of their lives, to keep free from prejudices that hold their sway over the masses?

But he thought not of that, for, after all, his interest in Kitty and his interest in his university class bore about an equal reference to Eleanor and his love for her.

His letter was sent, and he gave no second thought to the matter of its contents.

The months went by for Faraday with few distinctive features to mark them outside the enduring desire for his wife's presence.

There had been a visit of sharp disturbance once when her customary letter failed him, and the tardy missive coming, carried an inexplicable coldness that dealt him a pain which, however, did not long survive a little judicious reflection and a very deluge of letters from Paris that shook him with their unusual ardor.

May had come again, and at its approach Faraday with the impatience of a hundred lovers hastened across the seas to join his Eleanor.

It was evening and Eleanor paced to and fro in her room, making the last of a series of efforts that she had been putting forth all day to fight down a misery of the heart, against which her reason was in armed rebellion. She had tried the strategy of simply ignoring its presence, but the attempt had failed utterly. During her daily walk it had embodied itself in every object that her eyes rested upon. It had enveloped her like a smoke mist, through which Paris looked more dull than the desolation of Sahara.

She had thought to displace it with work, but, like the disturbing element in the chemist's crucible, it rose again and again overspreading the surface of her labor.

Alone in her room, the hour had come when she meant to succeed by the unaided force of reason—proceeding first to make herself bodily comfortable in the folds of a majestic flowing gown, in which she looked a distressed goddess.

Her hair hung heavy and free about her shoulders, for those reasoning powers were to be spurred by a plunging of white fingers into the golden mass.

In this dishevelled state Eleanor's presence seemed too large for the room and its delicate furnishings. The place fitted well an Eleanor in repose but not an Eleanor who swept the narrow confines like an incipient cyclone.

Reason did good work and stood its ground bravely, but against it were the too great odds of a woman's heart, backed by the soft prejudices of a far-reaching heredity.

She finally sank into a chair before her pretty writing desk. The golden head fell upon the outspread arms waiting to receive it, and she burst into a storm of sobs and tears. It was the signal of surrender.

It is a gratifying privilege to be permitted to ignore the reason of such unusual disturbance in a woman of Eleanor's high qualifications. The cause of that abandonment of grief will never be learned unless she chooses to disclose it herself.

When Faraday first folded his wife in his arms he saw but the Eleanor of his constant dreams. But he soon began to perceive how more beautiful she had grown; with a richness of coloring and fullness of health that Plymdale had never been able to bestow. And the object of her stay in Paris was gaining fast to accomplishment, for she had already acquired a knowledge of French that would not require much longer to perfect.

They sat together in her room discussing plans for the summer, when a timid knock at the door caused Eleanor to look up, to see the little housemaid eyeing her with the glance of a fellow conspirator and holding in her hand a card that she suffered to be but partly visible.

Eleanor hastily approached her, and reading the name upon the card thrust it into her pocket, exchanging some whispered words with the girl, among which were audible, "excuse me," "engaged," "another time." She came back to her husband looking a little flustered, to resume the conversation where it had been interrupted and he offered no inquiries about her mysterious caller.

Entering the salon not many days later he found that in doing so he interrupted a conversation between his wife and a very striking looking gentleman who seemed on the point of taking his leave.

They were both disconcerted; she especially, in bowing, almost thrusting him out, had the appearance of wanting to run away; to do any thing but meet her husband's glance.

He asked with assumed indifference whom her friend might be.

"Oh, no one special," with a hopeless attempt at brazenness.

He accepted the situation without protest, only indulging the reflection that Eleanor was losing something of her frankness.

But when his wife asked him on another occasion to dispense with her company for a whole afternoon, saying that she had an urgent call upon her time, he began to wonder if there might not be modifications to this marital liberty of which he was so staunch an advocate.

She left him with a hundred little endearments that she seemed to have acquired with her French.

He forced himself to the writing of a few urgent letters, but his restlessness did not permit him to do more.

It drove him to ugly thoughts, then to the means of dispelling them.

He gazed out of the window, wondered why he was remaining indoors, and followed up the reflection by seizing his hat and plunging out into the street.

The Paris boulevards of a day in early summer are calculated to dispel almost any ache but one of that nature, which was making itself incipiently felt with Faraday.

It was at that stage when it moves a man to take exception at the inadequacy of every thing that is offered to his contemplation or entertainment.

The sun was too hot.

The shop windows were vulgar; lacking artistic detail in their make-up.

How could he ever have found the Paris women attractive? They had lost their chic. Most of them were scrawny—not worth looking at.

He thought to go and stroll through the galleries of art. He knew Eleanor would wish to be with him; then he was tempted to go alone.

Finally, more tired from inward than outward restlessness, he took refuge at one of the small tables of a café, called for a "Mazarain,"* and, so seated for an unheeded time, let the panorama of Paris pass before his indifferent eyes.

When suddenly one of the scenes in this shifting show struck him with stunning effect.

It was the sight of his wife riding in a fiacre with her caller of a few days back, both conversing and in high spirits.

He remained for a moment enervated, then the blood came tingling back into his veins like fire, making his finger ends twitch with a desire (full worthy of any one of the "prejudiced masses") to tear the scoundrel from his seat and paint the boulevard red with his villainous blood.

A rush of wild intentions crowded into his brain.

Should he follow and demand an explanation? Leave Paris without ever looking into her face again? and more not worthy of the man.

It is right to say that his better self and better senses came quickly back to him.

That first revolt was like the unwilling protest of the flesh against the surgeon's knife before a man has steeled himself to its endurance.

Everything came back to him from their short, common past— their dreams, their large intentions for the shaping of their lives. Here was the first test, and should he be the one to cry out, "I cannot endure it."

When he returned to the pension, Eleanor was impatiently waiting for him in the entry, radiant with gladness at his coming.

She was under a suppressed excitement that prevented her noting his disturbed appearance.

She took his listless hand and led him into the small drawing-room that adjoined their sleeping chamber.

There stood her companion of the fiacre, smiling as was she at the pleasure of introducing him to another Eleanor disposed on the wall in the best possible light to display the gorgeous radiance of her wonderful beauty and the skill of the man who had portrayed it.

The most sanguine hopes of Eleanor and her artist could not have anticipated anything like the rapture with which Faraday received this surprise.

"Monsieur l'Artist" went away with his belief in the undemonstrativeness of the American very much shaken; and in his pocket substantial evidence of American appreciation of art.

Then the story was told how the portrait was intended as a surprise for his arrival. How there had been delay in its completion. The artist had required one more sitting, which she gave him that day, and the two had brought the picture home in the fiacre, he to give it the final advantages of a judicious light; to witness its effect upon Mons. Faraday and finally the excusable wish to be presented to the husband of the lady who had captivated his deepest admiration and esteem.

"You shall take it home with you," said Eleanor.

Both were looking at the lovely creation by the soft light of a reckless expenditure of bougie.

"Yes, dearest," he answered, with feeble elation at the prospect of returning home with that exquisite piece of inanimation.

"Have you engaged your return passage?" she asked.

She sat at his knee, arrayed in the gown that had one evening clothed such a goddess in distress.

"Oh, no. There's plenty time for that," was his answer. "Why do you ask?"

"I'm sure I don't know," and after a while:

"Charlie, I think—I mean, don't you think—I have made wonderful progress in French?"

"You've done marvels, Nellie. I find no difference between your French and Mme. Clairegobeau's, except that yours is far prettier."

"Yes?" she rejoined, with a little squeeze of the hand.

"I mayn't be right and I want you to give me your candid opinion. I believe Mme. Belaire—now that I have gone so far—don't you think—hadn't you better engage passage for two?"

His answer took the form of a pantomimic rapture of assenting gratefulness, during which each gave speechless assurance of a love that could never more take a second place.

"Nellie," he asked, looking into the face that nestled in close reach of his warm kisses, "I have often wanted to know, though you needn't tell it if it doesn't suit you," he added, laughing, "why you once failed to write to me, and then sent a letter whose coldness gave me a week's heart trouble?"

She flushed, and hesitated, but finally answered him bravely, "It was when—when you cared so much for that Kitty Beaton."

Astonishment for a moment deprived him of speech.

"But Eleanor! In the name of reason! It isn't possible!"

"I know all you would say," she replied, "I have been over the whole ground myself, over and over, but it is useless. I have found that there are certain things which a woman can't philosophize about, any more than she can about death when it touches that which is near to her."

"But you don't think—"

"Hush! don't speak of it ever again. I think nothing!" closing her eyes, and with a little shudder drawing closer to him.

As he kissed his wife with passionate fondness, Faraday thought, "I love her none the less for it, but my Nellie is only a woman, after all."

With man's usual inconsistency, he had quite forgotten the episode of the portrait.

THE CHRIST LIGHT

The south-bound mail and express had just pulled away from
Bludgitt* station. There had been an exchange of mail bags; sundry
freight marked "Abner Rydon, Bludgitt Station, Missouri" had been
deposited upon the platform and that was all. It was Christmas eve,
a raw, chill, Christmas eve, and the air was thick with promise
of snow.

A few weazened, shivering men stood with hands plunged in
their trouser pockets, watching the train come and go. When the
station-master dragged the freight under shelter, depositing some
of it within the waiting-room, they all tramped into the room too
and proceeded to lounge round the rusty red-hot stove which was
there.

Presently a light cart drove up along-side the platform, and one of
this leisurely band craning his neck to peer through the begrimed
window panes, remarked :

"Thur's Abner, now."

Abner Rydon was a stalwart fellow of thirty; one type of the
western farmer who puts his own hand to the plow. He was stern-
visaged, with stubborn determination in the set of his square jaw.
The casual glance which he offered the assembled group was neither
friendly nor inviting.

"It's a wonder you wouldn't of took the two horse wagon, Ab,
with them roads." He paid no attention to the gentle insinuation.

"Seems to me you'd fix that thur road and throw a bridge acrost
Bludgitt creek," suggested a second. "If I had your money—"

"If you had my money you wouldn't run the country with it more
'an you do your own," replied Abner as he quitted the room, bearing
an armful of freight. Returning for more he was met by further
friendly advances:

"I seen a man the other day, Ab, says he run acrost Liza-Jane a
couple o'weeks ago in town."

Abner turned quickly upon the speaker, and with a sharp blow of
his clenched fist sent him sprawling to the floor. He then continued
towards the cart, mounted it, and drove rapidly away over the rough
and frost-hardening road, and into the woods beyond.

A burst of hilarity greeted the discomfiture of this too daring speaker.

"Oh, Whillikens! *you* seen a man that run acrost Liza-Jane, did you!" "Anything more to say on the subject of Liza-Jane, Si? Ab ain't got so fur you can't ketch up with him."

Si had risen and was rubbing his injured back as best he could.

"The plague-on-it-fool," he muttered; "if he thinks so much o' that red-cheeked huzzy, what in tarnation did he want to turn her loose to Satan fur!"

When the mirth occasioned by this quickly acted scene had subsided, it left the assembly in a pleasant, reminiscent mood that led naturally to the quiet discussion of Abner Rydon's domestic drama.

"I always said thet harm would come o' the match," remarked the traditional prophet, "time Almiry told me thet Liza-Jane was goin' to marry Abner Rydon. Why, a blind un could 'a seen they wasn't a matched team. First place, thet gal was all fur readin'—constant readin' in them paper-covered books thet come to her through the mail, an' readin's boun' to fill the mind up with one thing another in time.*

"When she'd come an' see Almiry she'd out en' tell by the hour how folks lives in town. How the ladies sets in rockin-cheers by the winders all day a imbroidryin' things with their white, jewel fingers; an' how they walks up an' down drawing-rooms disdinful; an' rides in open kerridges along the boulyvards, bowin' languid to gents a horseback. She got it all out o' them books, an' she called it the higher life, an' said she hankered fur it, to Almiry."

"I was down here to Bludgitt the mornin' she left," interrupted one whose information was more to the point. "Time I seen her I knowed somethin' was up. Her black eyes was fairly snappin' fire, an' her cheeks was blazin' most as red as the ribband round her nake. She never were back'ard with her talk, en' when I ast whur she was bound fur, she up an' let loose again' Ab, an' mother Rydon, an' thur life of drudgery what was no ixistance."

"Ab never turned her out, did he?"

"Turn her out! Abner Rydon ain't the man to turn a dog from his door. No; they had one o' them everlastin' quarrels what's been a imbitterin' their married life. She out with the hull thing that day down here to Bludgitt. How they fussed, an' how she endid by tellin' him that no woman born could keep on lovin' a man that hadn't

no soul above the commonplaces.* How he got as grey as ashes an'
flung back at her that a woman better quit livin' with a man when she
quit kerrin' fur him. She said she didn't ask no better, 'fur,' sa' she,
'I hev that within me, Mr. MicBride, thet craves to taste the joys of
ixistence.* I hev gathered my belongings; my own incompetence is in
my pocket, an' I hev shook the dust of the Rydon threshold from off
of my feet forever,' was her own words. An' Si Smith might's well
learn to-day as tomorrow that Ab Rydon's goin' to knock any man
down that mentions the name o' Liza-Jane to him."

*

At every fresh gust of wind that struck the north-west angle of the
old Rydon farm-house that night, mother Rydon would give a little
jump and clasp the arms of her comfortable chair that she occupied
at the fire-side.

"Lands, Abner! I hain't hered the wind a blowin' so since the
night the pasture fence was laid low, what's it a doin' out o' doors,
anyway. Before dark the hull country was covered with snow. Now
the sleet's a strikin' like pebbles again' the window panes."

"That's just it, mother; sleet an' snow an' wind a tryin' to outdo
thurselves."

"I don't know as the Christ Light'll hold through it, Abner."

"It's been through worse, mother, if you'll try an' remember," said
Abner, throwing upon the fire a fresh stick that he had brought from
the porch, where a pile of evenly-cut fire wood was stacked. He had
also strung a blazing lantern high up above the house-top. It was an
old tradition—a homely family custom of these Rydons, hanging the
Christ Light out on Christmas eve to swing like a star in the darkness
till the stroke of mid-night. It was a beacon to the weary, the weak,
the foot-sore,* telling that the spirit of Christ dwelt within.

Abner sat down beside the table upon which a lamp burned
brightly, and opened his newspaper. His features seemed much less
harsh than when he faced the roomful of loafers down at Bludgitt.
There was a kind ring in his voice and a look in his blue eyes that told
they had been merry once.

The two seated so cozily together amid their homely surroundings,
resembled each other closely. Not a feature in the one but finds its
counterpart in the other. Only the steadfast look in the eyes of the
woman had grown patient with age.

"It's a mercy you went fur the goods to-day, Abner, what with Moll's lame foot, an' the mules loaned fur old man Buckthorn's funeral, you never would hev got the cart through them roads tomorrow. Who'd you see down to Bludgitt?"

"The same old lot at the station, mother, a settin' round the stove. It's a puzzle to me how they live. That McBride don't do work enough to keep him in tobacco. Old Joseph—I guess he ain't able to work. But that Si Smith—why!" he exclaimed excitedly, "the government ought to take holt of it."

"That's thur business Abner; 'taint none o'ours," his mother replied rebukingly. "I'd like if you'd read me the noos, now. An' read about them curious pictures of them animals.* Miraculous things happens nowadays, if you've got the papers to belive."

Abner stretched his fine legs out towards the blaze and began to read from the conglomerate contents of his weekly paper. Old Mother Rydon sat upright, knitting and listening, often stopping in her work to look at him intently, which she could not always do, apt as he was to resent such close scrutiny when unguarded.

Her thoughts easily wandered then to the time he had brought his pretty wife home, when he was happy, and when it had taken them such a little while to learn that she not did fit into their lives. Abner's mother wished sometimes that he had been more patient; for he was not always so, during those stormy scenes in which the man's love and pride were often wounded to the quick by the taunts and insults of his young and foolish wife.

Now, Mother Rydon knitted, listened, and mused. Abner was reading slowly and carefully:

"This singular animal has seldom been seen by the eye of civilized man, familiar as are the native blacks with his habits and peculiar haunts. The writer—fortunately armed with his trusty—"

"Hold, Abner! Hark!"

"What is it, mother'?"

"My years ain't as good as they was once, but seems like I heard something at the door latch, and a movin' on the porch."

"The dogs would bark if any one as much as opened the gate, mother. This talk about the animals has got you worked up."

"No such thing. Thur! I hered it again. Go see, Abner; 'taint goin' to hurt nothin' to look."

Abner approached the door and opened it abruptly. A wild gust of wind came blowing into the room; beating and lashing as it did so, the bedraggled garments of a young woman who was clinging to the door-post.

"My God!" cried Abner starting back. Mother Rydon in astonishment could only utter: "Liza-Jane! for the land sakes!"

The wind literally drove the woman into the room. Abner stayed there with his hand upon the latch, shaken at what seemed this apparition before him.

Liza-Jane stood, like a hunted and hungry thing in the great glow of the fire-light, her big dark eyes greedily seizing upon every detail of homely and honest comfort that surrounded her. Her cheeks were not round nor red as they had been once. Whatever sin or suffering had swept over her had left its impress upon her plastic being.

As Abner looked at her, of all the voices that clamored in his soul to be heard, that of the outraged husband was the loudest.*

When mother Rydon endeavored to remove Liza-Jane's wet and tattered shawl the woman clutched it firmly, turning a frightened and beseeching face upon her husband.

"Abner, son, what air you a waitin' fur?" demanded mother Rydon, standing back.

Mother and son looked for a long instant into each other's eyes. Then Abner approached his wife. With unsteady hands he lifted the soaking garment from her shoulders. He did not belong to a class nor to a row that talks when the heart is moved; but when he saw that Liza-Jane's arms fell to her side at his approach, and that two shining tears hung beneath the half closed lids, then he knelt upon the floor and took the wet and torn shoes from off her feet.

THE MAID OF SAINT PHILLIPPE

An historical incident furnishes the ground-work of this story, the heroine of which is a girl of lofty character and noble purpose. The tale describes the abandonment of Saint Phillippe in favor of the rival village of St. Louis, and shows how the latter settlement forthwith started to become a great city.

Marianne was tall, supple, and strong. Dressed in her worn buckskin trappings she looked like a handsome boy rather than like the French girl of seventeen that she was. As she stepped from the woods the glimmer of the setting sun dazzled her. An instant she raised her hand—palm outward—to shield her eyes from the glare, then she continued to descend the gentle slope and make her way toward the little village of Saint Phillippe that lay before her, close by the waters of the Mississippi.

Marianne carried a gun across her shoulder as easily as a soldier might. Her stride was as untrammelled as that of the stag who treads his native hill-side unmolested. There was something stag-like, too, in the poise of her small head as she turned it from side to side, to snuff the subtle perfume of the Indian summer. But against the red western sky curling columns of thin blue smoke began to ascend from chimneys in the village.* This meant that housewives were already busy preparing the evening meal; and the girl quickened her steps, singing softly as she strode along over the tufted meadow where sleek cattle were grazing in numbers.

Less than a score of houses formed the village of Saint Phillippe, and they differed in no wise from one another except in the matter of an additional room when the prosperity of the owner admitted of such. All were of upright logs, standing firmly in the ground, or rising from a low foundation of stone, with two or more rooms clustering round a central stone chimney. Before each was an inviting porch, topped by the projection of the shingled roof.

Gathered upon such a porch, when Marianne walked into the village, were groups of men talking eagerly and excitedly together with much gesture and intensity of utterance.

The place was Sans-Chagrin's tavern; and Marianne stopped

beside the fence, seeing that her father, Picoté Laronce, was among the number who crowded the gallery. But it was not he, it was young Jacques Labrie who when he saw her there came down to where she stood.

"Well, what luck, Marianne?" he asked, noting her equipment.

"Oh, not much," she replied, slapping the game-bag that hung rather slack at her side. "Those idle soldiers down at the fort have no better employment than to frighten the game away out of reach. But what does this talk and confusion mean? I thought all the trouble with monsieur le curé was settled. My father stands quiet there in a corner; he seems to be taking no part. What is it all about?"

"The old grievance of a year ago, Marianne. We were content to grumble only so long as the English did not come to claim what is theirs. But we hear to-day they will soon be at Fort Chartres to take possession."

"Never!" she exclaimed. "Have not the Natchez* driven them back each time they attempted to ascend the river? And do you think that watchful tribe will permit them now to cross the line?"

"They have not attempted the river this time. They have crossed the great mountains and are coming from the east."

"Ah," muttered the girl with pale exasperation, "that is a monarch to be proud of! Your Louis who sits in his palace at Versailles* and gives away his provinces and his people as if they were baubles! Well, what next?"

"Come, Marianne," said the young man as he joined her outside. "Let me walk to your home with you, I will tell you as we go along. Sans-Chagrin, you know, returned this morning from the West Illinois, and he tells astonishing things of the new trading-post over there—Laclede's village."*

"The one they call Saint Louis?" she asked half-heartedly, "where old Toussaint of Kaskaskia has taken his family to live?"

"Old Toussaint is far seeing, Marianne, for Sans-Chagrin says the town across the water is growing as if by enchantment. Already it is double the size of Saint Phillippe and Kaskaskia put together. When the English reach Fort Chartres, St. Ange de Bellerive* will relinquish the fort to them, and with his men will cross to Laclede's village—all but Captain Vaudry,* who has leave to return to France."

"Capt. Alexis Vaudry will return to France!" she echoed in tones that rose and fell like a song of lamentation. "The English are coming from the east! And all this news has come to-day while I hunted in the forest."

"Do you not see what is in the air, Marianne?" he asked, giving her a sideward cautious glance.

They were at her portal now, and as he followed her into the house she half turned to say to him:

"No, Jacques, I can see no way out of it." She sat down languidly at the table, as though heavy fatigue had suddenly weighted her limbs.

"We hate the English," Jacques began emphatically; leaning upon the table as he stood beside her.

"To be sure, we hate the English," she returned, as though the fact were a self-evident one that needed no comment.

"Well, it is only the eastern province of Louisiana that has been granted to England.* There is hardly a man in Saint Phillippe who would not rather die than live subject to that country. But there is no reason to do either," he added smiling. "In a week from now, Marianne, Saint Phillippe will be deserted."

"You mean that the people will abandon their homes, and go to the new trading-post?"

"Yes, that is what I mean."

"But I have heard—I am sure I have heard, long ago, that King Louis made a gift of his Louisiana possessions to his cousin of Spain; that they jointly granted the East Illinois to England. So that leaves the West under the Spanish dominion,* Jacques."

"But Spain is not England," he explained, a little disconcerted. "No Frenchman who respects himself will live subject to England," he added fiercely. "All are of one mind—to quit Saint Phillippe at once. All save one, Marianne."

"And that one?"

"Your father."

"My father! Ah, I might have known. What does he say?" she questioned eagerly.

"He says he is old; that he has dwelt here many years—"

"That is true," the girl mused. "I was born here in Saint Phillippe; so were you, Jacques."

"He says," continued the young man, "that he could not dispose of his mill and that he would not leave it."

"His mill—his mill! no!" exclaimed Marianne, rising abruptly, "it is not that. Would you know why my father will never leave Saint Phillippe?" approaching as she said this a rear window whose shutters were partly closed, and throwing them wide open. "Come here, Jacques. That is the reason," pointing with her strong shapely arm to where a wooden cross marked the presence of a grave out under the wide-spreading branches of a maple.

They both stood for a while silently gazing across the grassy slope that reflected the last flickering gleams of the setting sun. Then Jacques muttered as if in answer to some unspoken thought:

"Yes, he loved her very dearly. Surely the better part of himself went with her. And you, Marianne?" he questioned gently.

"I, Jacques? Oh, it is only the old whose memories dwell in graves,"* she replied a little wearily. "My life belongs to my father. I have but to follow his will; whatever that may be."

Then Marianne left Jacques standing by the open window, and went into the adjoining room to divest herself of her hunting raiment. When she returned she was dressed in the garments that had been her mother's once—a short camlet skirt of sober hue; a green laced bodice whose scantiness was redeemed by a muslin kerchief laid in deep folds across the bosom; and upon her head was the white cap of the French working-woman.*

Jacques had lighted the fire for her in the big stone chimney, and gone silently away.

It was indeed true. During that autumn of 1765, a handful of English, under command of Captain Sterling of the Highlanders, crossed the Alleghanies and were coming to take peaceful possession of their hitherto inaccessible lands in the Illinois.

To none did this seem a more hated intrusion than to the people of Saint Phillippe. After the excited meeting at Sans-Chagrin's tavern, all went to work with feverish haste to abandon the village which had been the only home that many of them had ever known. Men, women, and children seemed suddenly possessed with demoniac strength to demolish. Doors, windows, and flooring; everything that could serve in building up the new was rifled from the old. For days there was gathering together and hauling away in rough carts constructed for the sole purpose. Cattle were called from the pasture lands and driven in herds to the northward.*

When the last of these rebellious spirits was gone, Saint Phillippe stood like the skeleton of its former self; and Picoté Laronce with his daughter found themselves alone amid the desolate hearthstones.

"It will be a dreary life, my child, for you," said the old man, gathering Marianne in a close embrace.

"It will not be dreary," she assured him, disengaging herself to look into his eyes. "I shall have much work to do. We shall forget— try to forget—that the English are at our door. And some time when we are rich in peltries,* we will go to visit our friends in that great town that they talk so much about. Do not ever think that I am sad, father, because we are alone."

But the silence was very desolate. So was the sight of those abandoned homes, where smiling faces no longer looked from windows, and where the music of children's laughter was heard no more.

Marianne worked and hunted and grew strong and stronger. The old man was more and more like a child to her. When she was not with him, he would sit for hours upon a rude seat under the maple-tree, with a placid look of content in his old, dim eyes.

One day when Captain Vaudry rode up from Fort Chartres, fine as could be in his gay uniform of a French officer, he found Picoté and Marianne sitting in the solitude hand in hand. He had heard how they had remained alone in Saint Phillippe, and he had come to know if it was true, and to persuade them, if he could, to return with him to France—to La Rochelle,* where Picoté had formerly lived. But he urged in vain. Picoté knew no home save that in which his wife had dwelt with him, and no resting-place on earth except where she lay. And Marianne said always the same thing—that her father's will was hers.

But when she came in from her hunt one evening and found him stretched in the eternal sleep out under the maple, at once she felt that she was alone, with no will to obey in the world but her own. Then her heart was as strong as oak and her nerves were like iron. Lovingly she carried him into the house. And when she had wept because he was dead, she lit two blessed candles and placed them at his head and she watched with him all through the still night.

At the break of day she barred the doors and windows, and mounting her fleet Indian pony, away she galloped to the fort, five miles below, to seek the aid she needed.

Captain Vaudry, and others as well, made all haste to Saint

Phillippe when they learned this sad thing that had befallen Marianne. Word was sent to the good curé of Kaskaskia, and he came too, with prayer and benediction. Jacques was in Kaskaskia when the tidings of Picoté's death reached there, and with all the speed at his command he hurried to Marianne to help her in her need.

So Marianne was not alone. Good and staunch friends were about her.

When Picoté had been laid to rest—under the maple—and the last blessing had been spoken, the good curé turned to Marianne and said:

"My daughter, you will return with me to Kaskaskia. Your father had many friends in that village, and there is not a door but will open to receive you. It would be unseemly, now he is gone, to live alone in Saint Phillippe."

"I thank you, my father," she answered, "but I must pass this night alone, and in thought. If I decide to go to my good friends in Kaskaskia, I shall ride into town early, upon my pony."

Jacques, too, spoke to her, with gentle persuasion: "You know, Marianne, what I want to say, and what my heart is full of. It is not I alone but my father and mother as well to whom you are dear, and who long to have you with us—one of us. Over there in the new village of Saint Louis a new life has begun for all of us. Let me beg that you will not refuse to share it till you have at least tried—"

She held up her hand in token that she had heard enough and turned resolutely from him. "Leave me, my friend," she said, "leave me alone. Follow the curé, there where he goes. If I so determine, you shall hear from me, if not, then think no longer of Marianne."

So another silent night fell upon Saint Phillippe, with Marianne alone in her home. Not even the dead with her now. She did not know that under the shelter of a neighboring porch Captain Vaudry lay like a sentinel wrapped in his mantle.

Near the outer road, but within the inclosure of Marianne's home, was "the great tree of Saint Phillippe" under which a rude table and benches stood. Here Picoté and his daughter had often taken their humble meals, shared with any passer-by that chose to join them.

Seated there in the early morning was Captain Vaudry when Marianne stepped from her door, in her jerkin of buckskin and her gun across her shoulder.

"What are you doing here, Captain Vaudry?" she asked with startled displeasure when she saw him there.

"I have waited, Marianne. You cannot turn me from you as lightly as you have the others." And then with warm entreaty in his voice he talked to her of France:

"Ah, Marianne, you do not know what life is, here in this wild America. Let the curé of Kaskaskia say the words that will make you my wife, and I will take you to a land, child, where men barter with gold, and not with hides and peltries. Where you shall wear jewels and silks and walk upon soft and velvet carpets. Where life can be a round of pleasure. I do not say these things to tempt you; but to let you know that existence holds joys you do not dream of—that may be yours if you will."

"Enough, Captain Alexis Vaudry! I have sometimes thought I should like to know what it is that men call luxury; and sometimes have felt that I should like to live in sweet and gentle intercourse with men and women. Yet these have been but fleeting wishes. I have passed the night in meditation and my choice is made."

"I love you, Marianne." He sat with hands clasped upon the table, and his handsome enraptured eyes gazing up into her face, as she stood before him. But she went on unheedingly:

"I could not live here in Saint Phillippe or there in Kaskaskia. The English shall never be masters of Marianne. Over the river it is no better. The Spaniards may any day they choose give a rude awakening to those stolid beings who are living on in a half-slumber of content—"

"I love you; oh, I love you, Marianne!"

"Do you not know, Captain Vaudry," she said with savage resistance, "I have breathed the free air of forest and stream, till it is in my blood now. I was not born to be the mother of slaves."*

"Oh, how can you think of slaves and motherhood! Look into my eyes, Marianne, and think of love."

"I will not look into your eyes, Captain Vaudry," she murmured, letting the quivering lids fall upon her own, "with your talk and your looks of love—of love! You have looked it before, and you have spoken it before till the strength would go from my limbs and leave me feeble as a little child, till my heart would beat like that of one who has been stricken. Go away, with your velvet and your jewels and your love. Go away to your France and to your treacherous kings; they are not for me."

"What do you mean, Marianne?" demanded the young man, grown pale with apprehension. "You deny allegiance to England and Spain; you spurn France with contempt; what is left for you?"

"Freedom is left for me!" exclaimed the girl, seizing her gun that she lifted upon her shoulder. "Marianne goes to the Cherokees.* You cannot stay me; you need not try to. Hardships may await me, but let it be death rather than bondage."

While Vaudry sat dumb with pain and motionless with astonishment; while Jacques was hoping for a message; while the good curé was looking eagerly from his door-step for signs of the girl's approach, Marianne had turned her back upon all of them.

With gun across her shoulder she walked up the gentle slope; her brave, strong face turned to the rising sun.

DOCTOR CHEVALIER'S LIE

The quick report of a pistol rang through the quiet autumn night. It was no unusual sound in the unsavory quarter where Dr. Chevalier had his office. Screams commonly went with it. This time there had been none.

Midnight had already rung in the old cathedral tower.

The doctor closed the book over which he had lingered so late, and awaited the summons that was almost sure to come.

As he entered the house to which he had been called he could not but note the ghastly sameness of detail that accompanied these oft-recurring events. The same scurrying; the same groups of tawdry, frightened women bending over banisters—hysterical, some of them; morbidly curious, others; and not a few shedding womanly tears; with a dead girl stretched somewhere, as this one was.

And yet it was not the same. Certainly she was dead: there was the hole in the temple where she had sent the bullet through. Yet it was different. Other such faces had been unfamiliar to him, except so far as they bore the common stamp of death. This one was not.

Like a flash he saw it again amid other surroundings. The time was little more than a year ago. The place, a homely cabin down in Arkansas, in which he and a friend had found shelter and hospitality during a hunting expedition.

There were others beside. A little sister or two; a father and mother—coarse, and bent with toil, but proud as archangels of their handsome girl, who was too clever to stay in an Arkansas cabin, and who was going away to seek her fortune in the big city.

"The girl is dead," said Doctor Chevalier. "I knew her well, and charge myself with her remains and decent burial."

The following day he wrote a letter. One, doubtless, to carry sorrow, but no shame to the cabin down there in the forest.

It told that the girl had sickened and died. A lock of hair was sent and other trifles with it. Tender last words were even invented.

Of course it was noised about that Doctor Chevalier had cared for the remains of a woman of doubtful repute.

Shoulders were shrugged. Society thought of cutting him. Society did not, for some reason or other, so the affair blew over.

BEYOND THE BAYOU

The bayou* curved like a crescent around the point of land on which La Folle's cabin stood. Between the stream and the hut lay a big abandoned field, where cattle were pastured when the bayou supplied them with water enough. Through the woods that spread back into unknown regions the woman who lived in the hut had drawn an imaginary line, and past this circle she never stepped. All was flaming red beyond there, La Folle believed. This was the form of her only mania.

She was now a large, gaunt, black woman, past thirty-five years of age. Her real name was Jacqueline, but every one on the plantation called her La Folle, or the Crazy Woman, because she had been frightened literally "out of her senses" in childhood.

On that far-past day, which was in the time of the Civil War,* there had been skirmishing and sharpshooting all day in the woods. Evening was near when P'tit Maître,—the young master,—black with powder and crimson with blood, had staggered into the cabin of Jacqueline's mother. His pursuers were close at his heels.

The horror of that spectacle had stunned Jacqueline's childish reason. And so all across the bayou seemed to her aflame with blood color, alternating with black.

Alone she dwelt in her solitary cabin. The rest of the quarters had long since been removed* beyond her sight and knowledge. She had more physical strength than most men, and made her patch of cotton and corn and tobacco like the best of them. Of the world beyond the bayou she had long known nothing, save what her morbid imagination conceived.

People across the bayou at Bellissime* had grown used to her and her way, and they thought nothing of it. Even when "Old Mis'" died, La Folle had not crossed the bayou. She had stood upon her side of it, wailing and lamenting. This did not astonish the people at Bellissime. They would have been amazed had she overcome her fear of everything beyond the water.

P'tit Maître was now the owner of Bellissime. He was a middle-aged man, with a family of beautiful daughters about him, and a little son whom La Folle loved as if he had been her own. He had often been carried across the bayou as a tiny baby, that Jacqueline might be comforted by the sight of him. The child took to her from the first. Scarcely could he toddle when he began his demands to be taken across the bayou to be fondled by La Folle. She called him Chéri, and so did every one else because she did.

None of the girls had ever been to her what Chéri was. They had each and all loved to be with her, and to listen to her wondrous stories of things that always happened "yonda, beyon' de bayou."

But none of them had stroked her black hand quite as Chéri did, nor rested their heads against her knee so confidingly, nor fallen asleep in her arms as he used to do.

"He used to kiss me so lovingly!" La Folle said to herself in her dialect. "Ah, he used to!" For Chéri hardly did such things now, since he had become the proud possessor of a gun, and had had his black curls cut off.

But Chéri gave La Folle two of his black curls, tied with a knot of red ribbon. That was in the heat of summer, when the water ran so low in the bayou that even the little children at Bellissime were able to cross it on foot.

All the cattle were sent to pasture down by the river. La Folle was sorry they were gone, for she loved these dumb companions well, and liked to feel that they were there, and to hear them browsing by night up to her own inclosure.

It was Saturday afternoon, when the fields were deserted. The men had flocked to a neighboring village to do their week's trading, and the women were occupied with household affairs, — La Folle as well as the others.

It was then she mended and washed her handful of clothes, scoured her house, and did her baking.

In this last employment she never forgot Chéri. To-day she had fashioned *croquignoles* of the most fantastic and alluring shapes for him. So when she saw the boy come trudging across the old field with his gleaming little new rifle on his shoulder, she called out gaily to him, "Chéri! Chéri!"

But Chéri did not need the summons, for he was coming straight to her. His pockets all bulged out with almonds and raisins and an orange that he had secured for her from the very fine dinner that had been given that day up at his father's house.

He was a sunny-faced youngster of ten. When he had emptied his pockets, La Folle patted his round red cheek, wiped his soiled hands on her apron, and smoothed his hair. He let her kiss him as a special favor, and with the air of one who is getting too old to think it proper to treat him as a baby.

Then she watched him as, with his cakes in his hands, he crossed her strip of cotton back of the cabin, and disappeared into the wood.

He had boasted of the things he was going to do with his gun out there.

"You think they got plenty deer in the wood, La Folle?" he had inquired, with a look of profound intention to distinguish himself as a hunter.

"*Non, non!*" the woman laughed. "Don't you look fo' no deer, Chéri. Dat's too big. But you bring La Folle one good fat squirrel fo' her dinner to-morrow, an' she goin' be satisfy."

"One squirrel aint a bite. I'll bring you mo' 'an one, La Folle," he had boasted pompously as he went away.

When the woman, an hour later, heard the report of the boy's rifle close to the wood's edge, she would have thought nothing of it if a sharp cry of distress had not followed the sound.

She withdrew her arms from the tub of suds in which they had been plunged, dried them upon her apron, and as quickly as her trembling limbs would bear her, hurried to the spot where the ominous report had come.

It was as she feared. There she found Chéri stretched upon the ground, with his rifle beside him. He moaned piteously:

"I'm dead, La Folle! I'm dead! I'm gone!"

"*Non, non!*" she said resolutely, as she knelt beside him. "Put you' arm 'roun La Folle's nake, Chéri. Dat's nuttin'; dat goin' be nuttin'." She lifted him in her powerful arms.

Chéri had carried his gun muzzle downward. He had stumbled,— he did not know how. He only knew that he had a ball lodged somewhere in his leg, and he thought that his end was at hand. Now, with his head upon the woman's shoulder, he moaned and wept with pain and fright.

"Oh, La Folle! La Folle! it hurt so bad! I can' stan' it, La Folle!"

"Don't cry, *mon bébé, mon bébé, mon Chéri!*" The woman spoke soothingly as she covered the ground with long strides. "La Folle goin' mine you; Doctor Bonfils goin' come make *mon Chéri* well agin."

She had reached the abandoned field. As she crossed it with her precious burden, she looked constantly and restlessly from side to side. A terrible fear was upon her—the fear of the world beyond the bayou, the morbid and insane dread she had been under since childhood.

When she was at the bayou's edge she stood there, and shouted for help as if a life depended upon it:

"Oh, P'tit Maître! P'tit Maître! *Venez donc*! Come! come! *Au secours*! Help! help! *Au secours*!"

No voice responded. Chéri's hot tears were scalding her neck. She called for each and every one upon the place, and still no answer came.

She shouted, she wailed; but whether her voice remained unheard or unheeded, no reply came to her frenzied cries. And all the while Chéri moaned and wept and entreated to be taken home to his mother.

La Folle gave a last despairing look around her. Extreme terror was upon her. But love struggled more powerfully to impel her forward. She clasped the child close against her breast, where he could feel her heart beat like a muffled hammer.

La Folle shut her eyes, ran suddenly down the shallow bank of the bayou, and never stopped till she had climbed the opposite shore.

She stood quivering an instant as she opened her eyes. Then she plunged into the foot-path through the fearful trees.

She spoke no more to Chéri, but muttered constantly, "*Bon Dieu, ayes pitié La Folle*! (O good God, pity La Folle!) *Bon Dieu, ayes pitié moi*! Good God, help me."

Instinct seemed to guide her. When the pathway spread clear and smooth enough before her, she again closed her eyes tightly against the sight of that unknown and terrifying world that to her looked more crimson than flame.

A child, playing in some weeds, caught sight of her as she neared the quarters. The little one uttered a cry of dismay.

"La Folle!" she screamed, in her piercing treble. "La Folle done cross de bayou!"

As quick as light the cry passed down the line of cabins.

"Yonda, La Folle done cross de bayou!"

Children, old men, old women, young ones with infants in their arms, flocked to doors and windows to see this awe-inspiring spectacle. Most of them shuddered with superstitious dread of what it might portend. "She totin' Chéri!" the cry rose.

Some of the more daring gathered about her, and followed at her heels, only to fall back with new terror when she turned her distorted face upon them. Her eyes were bloodshot.*

Some one had run ahead of her to where P'tit Maître sat with his family and guests upon the broad veranda.

"P'tit Maître! La Folle done cross de bayou! Look her! Look her yonda totin' Chéri!" The family at Bellissime rose. This startling intimation was the first which they had of the woman's approach.

She was now near at hand. She walked with long strides. Her eyes were fixed desperately before her, and she breathed heavily, as a tired ox.

At the foot of the stairway, which she could not have mounted, she laid the boy in his father's arms. Then the world that had looked red to La Folle suddenly turned black, —like that day she had seen powder and blood.

She reeled for an instant. Before a sustaining arm could reach her, she fell heavily to the ground.

When La Folle regained consciousness, she was at home again in her own cabin and upon her own bed. The moon rays, streaming in through the open door and windows, gave what light was needed to the old black mammy who stood at the table concocting a tisane of fragrant herbs.* It was very late.

Others who had come, and found that the stupor clung to her, had gone again. P'tit Maître had been there, and with him Doctor Bonfils, who said that La Folle might die.

But death had passed her by. The voice was very clear and steady with which she spoke to Tante Lizette, brewing her tisane there in a corner.

"Ef you will give me one good drink tisane, Tante Lizette, I b'lieve I'm goin' sleep, me."

And she did sleep; so soundly, so healthfully, that old Lizette without compunction stole softly away, to creep back through the moonlit fields to her own cabin in the new quarters.

The first touch of the cool gray morning awoke La Folle. She arose, calmly, as if no tempest had shaken and threatened her existence but yesterday.

She donned her new blue cottonade and white apron, for she remembered that this was Sunday. When she had made for herself a cup of strong black coffee, and drunk it with relish, she quitted the cabin and walked across the old familiar field to the bayou's edge again.

She did not stop there as she had always done before, but crossed with a long, steady stride as if she had done this all her life.

When she had made her way through the brush and scrub-cottonwood trees that lined the opposite bank, she found herself upon the border of a field where the white, bursting cotton, with the dew upon it, gleamed for acres and acres like frosted silver in the early dawn.

La Folle drew a long, deep breath as she gazed across the country. She walked slowly and uncertainly, like one who hardly knows how, looking about her as she went.

The cabins, that yesterday had sent a clamor of voices to pursue her, were quiet now. No one was yet astir at Bellissime. Only the birds that darted here and there from hedges were awake, and singing their matins.

When La Folle came to the broad stretch of velvety lawn that surrounded the house, she moved slowly and with delight over the springy turf that was delicious beneath her tread. More and more slowly she went, with clear senses and fear dead, and joy at her heart.

She stopped to find whence came those perfumes that were stealing over her with memories from a time far gone.

Sweet odors swooned to her from the thousand blue violets that peeped out from green, luxuriant beds. Fragrance showered down from the big waxen bells of the magnolias far above her head, and from the jessamine clumps around her.

There were roses, too, without number. To right and left palms spread in broad and graceful curves. It all looked like enchantment beneath the sparkling sheen of dew.

When La Folle had slowly and cautiously mounted the many steps that led up to the veranda, she turned to look back at the perilous ascent she had made. Now she caught sight of the river, bending like a silver bow at the foot of Bellissime. Exultation possessed her soul. All the world was fair about her, and green and white and blue and silvery shinings had come again instead of that frightful fancy of interminable red!

La Folle rapped softly upon a door near at hand. Chéri's mother soon cautiously opened it. Quickly and cleverly she dissembled the astonishment she felt at seeing La Folle.

"Ah, La Folle! Is it you? so early?"

"*Oui*, madame. I come ax how my po' li'le Chéri to, s'mo'nin'."

"He is feeling easier, thank you, La Folle. Dr. Bonfils says it will be nothing serious. He's sleeping now. Will you come back when he awakes?"

"*Non*, madame. I'm goin' wait zair tell Chéri wake up." La Folle seated herself upon the topmost step of the veranda.

A look of wonder and deep content crept into her face as she watched for the first time the sun rise upon this new, this beautiful world beyond the bayou.

OLD AUNT PEGGY*

When the war was over, old Aunt Peggy went to Monsieur, and said:—

"Massa; I ain't never gwine to quit yer. I'm gittin' ole an' feeble, an' my days is few in dis heah lan' o' sorrow an' sin. All I axes is a li'le co'ner whar I kin set down an' wait peaceful fu de en'."

Monsieur and Madame were very much touched at this mark of affection and fidelity from Aunt Peggy. So, in the general reconstruction of the plantation which immediately followed the surrender, a nice cabin, pleasantly appointed, was set apart for the old woman. Madame did not even forget the very comfortable rocking-chair in which Aunt Peggy might "set down," as she herself feelingly expressed it, "an' wait fu de en'."

She has been rocking ever since.

At intervals of about two years Aunt Peggy hobbles up to the house, and delivers the stereotyped address which has become more than familiar:—

"Mist'ess, I 's come to take a las' look at you all. Le' me look at you good. Le' me look at de chillun,—de big chillun an' de li'le chillun. Le' me look at de picters an' de photygraphts an' de pianny, an' eve'ything 'fo' it's too late. One eye is done gone, an' de udder's a-gwine fas'. Any mo'nin' yo' po' ole Aunt Peggy gwine wake up an' fin' herse'f stone-bline."

After such a visit Aunt Peggy invariably returns to her cabin with a generously filled apron.

The scruple which Monsieur one time felt in supporting a woman for so many years in idleness has entirely disappeared. Of late his attitude towards Aunt Peggy is simply one of profound astonishment,—wonder at the surprising age which an old black woman may attain when she sets her mind to it, for Aunt Peggy is a hundred and twenty-five, so she says.

It may not be true, however. Possibly she is older.

RIPE FIGS

(An Idyl)

Maman-Nainaine said that when the figs were ripe Babette might go to visit her cousins down on Bayou-Bœuf,* where the sugar cane grows. Not that the ripening of figs had the least thing to do with it, but that is the way Maman-Nainaine was.

It seemed to Babette a very long time to wait; for the leaves upon the trees were tender yet, and the figs were like little hard, green marbles.

But warm rains came along and plenty of strong sunshine; and though Maman-Nainaine was as patient as the statue of la Madone, and Babette as restless as a humming-bird, the first thing they both knew it was hot summer-time. Every day Babette danced out to where the fig-trees were in a long line against the fence. She walked slowly beneath them, carefully peering between the gnarled, spreading branches. But each time she came disconsolate away again. What she saw there finally was something that made her sing and dance the whole day long.

When Maman-Nainaine sat down in her stately way to breakfast, the following morning, her muslin cap standing like an aureole about her white, placid face, Babette approached. She bore a dainty porcelain platter, which she set down before her godmother. It contained a dozen purple figs, fringed around with their rich, green leaves.

"Ah," said Maman-Nainaine, arching her eye-brows, "how early the figs have ripened this year!"

"Oh," said Babette, "I think they have ripened very late."

"Babette," continued Maman-Nainaine, as she peeled the very plumpest figs with her pointed silver fruit-knife, "you will carry my love to them all down on Bayou-Bœuf. And tell your tante Frosine I shall look for her at Toussaint—when the chrysanthemums are in bloom."

MISS McENDERS

An Episode

I

When Miss Georgie McEnders had finished an elaborately simple toilet* of gray and black, she divested herself completely of rings, bangles, brooches—everything to suggest that she stood in friendly relations with fortune. For Georgie was going to read a paper upon "The Dignity of Labor" before the Woman's Reform Club;* and if she was blessed with an abundance of wealth, she possessed a no less amount of good taste.

Before entering the neat victoria that stood at her father's too-sumptuous door—and that was her special property—she turned to give certain directions to the coachman. First upon the list from which she read was inscribed: "Look up Mademoiselle Salambre."

"James," said Georgie, flushing a pretty pink, as she always did with the slightest effort of speech, "we want to look up a person named Mademoiselle Salambre, in the southern part of town, on Arsenal street,"* indicating a certain number and locality. Then she seated herself in the carriage, and as it drove away proceeded to study her engagement list further and to knit her pretty brows in deep and complex thought.

"Two o'clock—look up M. Salambre," said the list. "Three-thirty—read paper before Woman's Ref. Club. Four-thirty—" and here followed cabalistic abbreviations which meant: "Join committee of ladies to investigate moral condition of St. Louis factory-girls.* Six o'clock—dine with papa. Eight o'clock—hear Henry George's lecture on Single Tax."*

So far, Mademoiselle Salambre was only a name to Georgie McEnders, one of several submitted to her at her own request by her furnishers, Push and Prodem, an enterprising firm charged with the construction of Miss McEnder's very elaborate trousseau. Georgie liked to know the people who worked for her, as far as she could.

She was a charming young woman of twenty-five, though almost too white-souled for a creature of flesh and blood. She possessed ample wealth and time to squander, and a burning desire to do good—to elevate the human race, and start the world over again on a comfortable footing for everybody.

When Georgie had pushed open the very high gate of a very small yard she stood confronting a robust German woman, who, with dress tucked carefully between her knees, was in the act of noisily "redding" the bricks.

"Does M'selle Salambre live here?" Georgie's tall, slim figure was very erect. Her face suggested a sweet peach blossom, and she held a severely simple lorgnon up to her short-sighted blue eyes.

"Ya! ya! aber oop stairs!"* cried the woman brusquely and impatiently. But Georgie did not mind. She was used to greetings that lacked the ring of cordiality.

When she had ascended the stairs that led to an upper porch she knocked at the first door that presented itself, and was told to enter by Mlle. Salambre herself.

The woman sat at an opposite window, bending over a bundle of misty white goods that lay in a fluffy heap in her lap. She was not young. She might have been thirty, or she might have been forty. There were lines about her round, piquante face that denoted close acquaintance with struggles, hardships and all manner of unkind experiences.

Georgie had heard a whisper here and there touching the private character of Mlle. Salambre which had determined her to go in person and make the acquaintance of the woman and her surroundings; which latter were poor and simple enough, and not too neat. There was a little child at play upon the floor.

Mlle. Salambre had not expected so unlooked-for an apparition as Miss McEnders, and seeing the girl standing there in the door she removed the eye-glasses that had assisted her in the delicate work, and stood up also.

"Mlle. Salambre, I suppose?" said Georgie, with a courteous inclination.

"Ah! Mees McEndairs! What an agree'ble surprise! Will you be so kind to take a chair." Mademoiselle had lived many years in the city, in various capacities, which brought her in touch with the fashionable set. There were few people in polite society whom Mademoiselle did not know—by sight, at least; and their private histories were as familiar to her as her own.

"You 'ave come to see your the work?" the woman went on with smile that quite brightened her face. "It is a pleasure to handle such fine, such delicate quality of goods, Mees," and she went and laid several pieces of her handiwork upon the table beside Georgie, at the same time indicating such details as she hoped would call forth her visitor's approval.

There was something about the woman and her surroundings, and the atmosphere of the place, that affected the girl unpleasantly. She shrank instinctively, drawing her invisible mantle of chastity closely about her. Mademoiselle saw that her visitor's attention was divided between the lingerie and the child upon the floor, who was engaged in battering a doll's unyielding head against the unyielding floor.

"The child of my neighbor, down-stairs," said Mademoiselle, with a wave of the hand which expressed volumes of unutterable ennui. But at that instant the little one, with instinctive mistrust, and in seeming defiance of the repudiation, climbed to her feet and went rolling and toddling towards her mother, clasping the woman about the knees, and calling her by the endearing title which was her own small right.

A spasm of annoyance passed over Mademoiselle's face, but still she called the child "*Chérie*"* as she grasped its arm to keep it from falling. Miss McEnders turned every shade of carmine.

"Why did you tell me an untruth?" she asked, looking indignantly into the woman's lowered face. "Why do you call yourself 'Mademoiselle' if this child is yours?"

"For the reason that it is more easy to obtain employment. For reasons that you would not understand," she continued, with a shrug of the shoulders that expressed some defiance and a sudden disregard for consequences. "Life is not all *couleur de rose*, Mees McEndairs; you do not know what life is, you!" And drawing a handkerchief from an apron pocket she mopped an imaginary tear from the corner of her eye, and blew her nose till it glowed again.

Georgie could hardly recall the words or actions with which she quitted Mademoiselle's presence. As much as she wanted to, it had been impossible to stand and read the woman a moral lecture. She had simply thrown what disapproval she could into her hasty leave-taking, and that was all for the moment. But as she drove away, a more practical form of rebuke suggested itself to her not too nimble intelligence—one that she promised herself to act upon as soon as her home was reached.

When she was alone in her room, during an interval between her many engagements, she then attended to the affair of Mlle. Salambre.

Georgie believed in discipline. She hated unrighteousness. When it pleased God to place the lash in her hand she did not hesitate to apply it. Here was this Mlle. Salambre living in her sin. Not as one who is young and blinded by the glamour of pleasure, but with cool and deliberate intention. Since she chose to transgress, she ought to suffer, and be made to feel that her ways were iniquitous and invited rebuke. It lay in Georgie's power to mete out a small dose of that chastisement which the woman deserved, and she was glad that the opportunity was hers.

She seated herself forthwith at her writing table, and penned the following note to her furnishers:

"MESSRS. PUSH & PRODEM.

"*Gentlemen*—Please withdraw from Mademoiselle Salambre all work of mine, and return same to me at once—finished or unfinished.

Yours truly,

GEORGIE MCENDERS."

II

On the second day following this summary proceeding, Georgie sat at her writing-table, looking prettier and pinker than ever, in a luxurious and soft-toned robe de chambre that suited her own delicate coloring, and fitted the pale amber tints of her room decorations.

There were books, pamphlets, and writing material set neatly upon the table before her. In the midst of them were two framed photographs, which she polished one after another with a silken scarf that was near.

One of these was a picture of her father, who looked like an Englishman, with his clean-shaved mouth and chin, and closely-cropped side-whiskers, just turning gray. A good-humored shrewdness shone in his eyes. From the set of his thin, firm lips one might guess that he was in the foremost rank in the interesting game of "push" that occupies mankind.* One might further guess that his cleverness in using opportunities had brought him there, and that a dexterous management of elbows had served him no less. The other picture was that of Georgie's fiancé, Mr. Meredith Holt, approaching more closely than he liked to his forty-fifth year and an unbecoming corpulence. Only one who knew beforehand that he was a *viveur* could have detected evidence of such in his face, which told little more than that he was a good-looking and amiable man of the world, who might be counted on to do the gentlemanly thing always. Georgie was going to marry him because his personality pleased her; because his easy knowledge of life—such as she apprehended it—commended itself to her approval; because he was likely to interfere in no way with her "work." Yet she might not have given any of these reasons if asked for one. Mr. Meredith Holt was simply an eligible man, whom almost any girl in her set would have accepted for a husband.

Georgie had just discovered that she had yet an hour to spare before starting out with the committee of four to further investigate the moral condition of the factory-girl, when a maid appeared with the announcement that a person was below who wished to see her.

"A person? Surely not a visitor at this hour?"

"I left her in the hall, miss, and she says her name is Mademoiselle Sal–Sal—"

"Oh, yes! Ask her to kindly walk up to my room, and show her the way, please, Hannah."

Mademoiselle Salambre came in with a sweep of skirts that bristled defiance, and a poise of the head that was aggressive in its backward tilt. She seated herself and with an air of challenge waited to be questioned or addressed.

Georgie felt at ease amid her own familiar surroundings. While she made some idle tracings with a pencil upon a discarded envelope, she half turned to say:

"This visit of yours is very surprising, madam, and wholly useless. I suppose you guess my motive in recalling my work, as I have done."

"Maybe I do, and maybe I do not, Mees McEndairs," replied the woman, with an impertinent uplifting of the eyebrows.

Georgie felt the same shrinking which had overtaken her before in the woman's presence. But she knew her duty, and from that there was no shrinking.

"You must be made to understand, madam, that there is a right way to live, and that there is a wrong way," said Georgie with more condescension than she knew. "We cannot defy God's laws with impunity, and without incurring His displeasure. But in His infinite justice and mercy He offers forgiveness, love and protection to those who turn away from evil and repent. It is for each of us to follow the divine way as well as may be. And I am only humbly striving to do His will."

"A most charming sermon, Mees McEndairs!" mademoiselle interrupted with a nervous laugh; "it seems a great pity to waste it upon so small an audience. And it grieves me, I cannot express, that I have not the time to remain and listen to its close."

She arose and began to talk volubly, swiftly, in a jumble of French and English, and with a wealth of expression and gesture which Georgie could hardly believe was natural, and not something acquired and rehearsed.

She had come to inform Miss McEnders that she did not want her work; that she would not touch it with the tips of her fingers. And her little, gloved hands recoiled from an imaginary pile of lingerie with unspeakable disgust. Her eyes had traveled nimbly over the room, and had been arrested by the two photographs on the table. Very small, indeed, were her worldly possessions, she informed the young lady; but as Heaven was her witness—not a mouthful of bread that she had not earned. And her parents over yonder in France! As honest as the sunlight! Poor, ah! for that— poor as rats. God only knew how poor; and God only knew how honest. Her eyes remained fixed upon the picture of Horace McEnders. Some people might like fine houses, and servants, and horses, and all the luxury which dishonest wealth brings. Some people might enjoy such surroundings. As for her!—and she drew up her skirts ever so carefully and daintily, as though she feared contamination to her petticoats from the touch of the rich rug upon which she stood.

Georgie's blue eyes were filled with astonishment as they followed the woman's gestures. Her face showed aversion and perplexity.

"Please let this interview come to an end at once," spoke the girl. She would not deign to ask an explanation of the mysterious allusions to ill-gotten wealth. But mademoiselle had not yet said all that she had come there to say.

"If it was only me to say so," she went on, still looking at the likeness, "but, *cher maître*! Go, yourself Mees McEndairs, and stand for a while on the street and ask the people passing by how your dear papa has made his money, and see what they will say."

Then shifting her glance to the photograph of Meredith Holt, she stood in an attitude of amused contemplation, with a smile of commiseration playing about her lips.

"Mr. Meredith Holt!" she pronounced with quiet, surpressed emphasis—"ah! *c'est un propre, celui la**! You know him very well, no doubt, Mees McEndairs. You would not care to have my opinion of Mr. Meredith Holt. It would make no difference to you, Mees McEndairs, to know that he is not fit to be the husband of a self-respecting bar-maid. Oh! you know a good deal, my dear young lady. You can preach sermons in *merveille!*"

When Georgie was finally alone, there came to her, through all her disgust and indignation, an indefinable uneasiness. There was no misunderstanding the intention of the woman's utterances in regard to the girl's fiancé and her father. A sudden, wild, defiant desire came to her to test the suggestion which Mademoiselle Salambre had let fall.

Yes, she would go stand there on the corner and ask the passers-by how Horace McEnders made his money. She could not yet collect her thoughts for calm reflection; and the house stifled her. It was fully time for her to join her committee of four, but she would meddle no further with morals till her own were adjusted, she thought. Then she quitted the house, very pale, even to her lips that were tightly set.

Georgie stationed herself on the opposite side of the street, on the corner, and waited there as though she had appointed to meet some one.

The first to approach her was a kind-looking old gentleman, very much muffled for the pleasant spring day. Georgie did not hesitate an instant to accost him:

"I beg pardon, sir. Will you kindly tell me whose house that is?" pointing to her own domicile across the way.

"That is Mr. Horace McEnder's residence, Madame," replied the old gentleman, lifting his hat politely.

"Could you tell me how he made the money with which to build so magnificent a home?"

"You should not ask indiscreet questions, my dear young lady," answered the mystified old gentleman, as he bowed and walked away.

The girl let one or two persons pass her. Then she stopped a plumber, who was going cheerily along with his bag of tools on his shoulder.

"I beg pardon," began Georgie again; "but may I ask whose residence that is across the street?"

"Yes'um. That's the McEnderses."

"Thank you; and can you tell me how Mr. McEnders made such an immense fortune?"

"Oh, that aint my business; but they say he made the biggest pile of it in the Whisky Ring.*"

So the truth would come to her somehow! These were the people from whom to seek it—who had not learned to veil their thoughts and opinions in polite subterfuge.

When a careless little news-boy came strolling along, she stopped him with the apparent intention of buying a paper from him.

"Do you know whose house that is?" she asked him, handing him a piece of money and nodding over the way.

"W'y, dats ole MicAndrus' house."

"I wonder where he got the money to build such a fine house."

"He stole it; dats w'ere he got it. Thank you," pocketing the change which Georgie declined to take, and he whistled a popular air as he disappeared around the corner.

Georgie had heard enough. Her heart was beating violently now, and her cheeks were flaming. So everybody knew it; even to the street gamins! The men and women who visited her and broke bread at her father's table, knew it. Her co-workers, who strove with her in Christian endeavor, knew. The very servants who waited upon her doubtless knew this, and had their jests about it.

She shrank within herself as she climbed the stairway to her room.

Upon the table there she found a box of exquisite white spring blossoms that a messenger had brought from Meredith Holt, during her absence. Without an instant's hesitation, Georgie cast the spotless things into the wide, sooty, fire-place. Then she sank into a chair and wept bitterly.

AT THE 'CADIAN BALL

Bobinôt—that big, brown, good-natured Bobinôt—had no intention of going to the ball, even though he knew Calixta would be there. For what came of those balls but heartache, and a sickening disinclination for work the whole week through, till Saturday night came again and his tortures began afresh? Why could he not have loved Ozéina, who would marry him to-morrow; or Fronie,* or any one of a dozen others, rather than that little Spanish vixen? Calixta's slender foot had never touched Cuban soil; but her mother's had, and the Spanish was in her blood all the same. For that reason the prairie people* forgave her much that they would not have overlooked in their own daughters and sisters.

Her eyes—Bobinôt thought of her eyes, and weakened—the bluest, the drowsiest, most tantalizing that ever looked into a man's; her flaxen hair that kinked worse than a mulatto's close to her head; that broad, smiling mouth and tip-tilted nose, that full figure; that voice like a rich contralto song, with cadences in it that must have been taught by Satan, for there had been no one else to teach her tricks on that 'Cadian prairie. Bobinôt thought of them all as he ploughed his rows of cane.

There had even been a breath of scandal whispered about her a year ago, when she went to Assumption*—but why talk of it? No one did now. "*C'est Espagnol, ça*,"* most of them said with lenient shoulder-shrugs. "*Bon chien tient de race*,"* the old men mumbled over their pipes, stirred by recollections. Nothing was made of it, except that Fronie threw it up to Calixta when the two quarrelled and fought on the church steps after mass one Sunday, about a lover. Calixta swore roundly in fine 'Cadian French and with true Spanish spirit, and slapped Fronie's face. Fronie had slapped her back: "*Tiens, cocotte, va!*" "*Espèce de lionèse: prends ça, et ça!*"* till the curé himself was obliged to hasten and make peace between them. Bobinôt thought of it all, and would not go to the ball.

But in the afternoon, over at Friedheimer's store, where he was buying a trace-chain,* he heard some one say that Alcée Laballière* would be there. Then wild horses could not have kept him away. He knew how it would be—or rather he did not know how it would be—if the handsome young planter came over to the ball as he sometimes did. If Alcée happened to be in a serious mood, he might only go to the card-room and play a round or two; or he might stand out on the galleries talking crops and politics with the old people. But there was no telling. A drink or two could put the devil in his head—that was what Bobinôt said to himself, as he wiped the sweat from his brow with his red bandanna; a gleam from Calixta's eyes, a flash of her ankle, a twirl of her skirts could do the same. Yes, Bobinôt would go to the ball.

*

That was the year Alcée Laballière put nine hundred acres in rice. It was putting a good deal of money into the ground, but the returns promised to be glorious. Old Madame Laballière, sailing about the spacious galleries in her white *volante*,* figured it all out in her head. Clarisse, her god-daughter, helped her a little, and together they built more air-castles than enough. Alcée worked like a mule that time; and if he did not kill himself, it was because his constitution was an iron one. It was an every-day affair for him to come in from the field well nigh exhausted, and wet to the waist. He did not mind if there were visitors; he left them to his mother and Clarisse. There were often visitors. Young men and women who came up from the city, which was but a few hours away, to see his beautiful kinswoman. She was worth going a good deal farther than that to see. Dainty as a lily; hardy as a sunflower; slim, tall, graceful like one of the reeds that grew in the marsh. Cold and kind and cruel by turn, and everything that was aggravating to Alcée.

He would have liked to sweep the place of those visitors, often. The men above all, with their ways and their manners; their swaying of fans like women, and dandling about hammocks. He could have pitched them over the levee into the river, if it hadn't meant murder. That was Alcée. But he must have been crazy the day he came in from the rice-field, and, toil-stained as he was, clasped Clarisse by the arms and panted a volley of hot, blistering love-words into her face. No man had ever spoken love to her like that.

"Monsieur!" she exclaimed, looking him full in the eyes, without a quiver. Alcée's hands dropped and his glance wavered before the chill of her calm, clear eyes.

"*Par exemple!*" she muttered disdainfully, as she turned from him, deftly adjusting the careful toilet that he had so brutally disarranged.

That happened a day or two before the cyclone came that cut into the rice like fine steel.* It was an awful thing—coming so swiftly, without a moment's warning in which to light a holy candle or set a piece of blessed palm burning. Old madame wept openly and said her beads, just as her son Lidié, the New Orleans one, would have done. If such a thing had happened to Alphonse, the Laballière planting cotton up in Natchitoches,* he would have raved and stormed like a second cyclone and made his surroundings unbearable for a day or two. But Alcée took the misfortune differently. He looked ill and gray, after it, and said nothing. His speechlessness was frightful. Clarisse's heart grew as tender as a kitten's; but when she offered her soft, purring words of condolence, he accepted them with mute indifference. Then she and nainaine wept afresh in each other's arms.

A night or two later, when Clarisse went to her window to kneel there in the moonlight and say her prayers before retiring, she saw that Bruce, Alcée's negro servant, had led his master's saddle-horse noiselessly along the edge of the sward that bordered the gravel-path, and stood holding him near by. Presently, she heard Alcée quit his room, which was beneath her own, and traverse the lower portico. As he emerged from the shadow and crossed the strip of moonlight, she perceived that he carried a pair of well-filled saddle-bags which he at once flung across the animal's back. He then lost no time in mounting, and after a brief exchange of words with Bruce, went cantering away, taking no precaution to avoid the noisy gravel as the negro had done.

Clarisse had never suspected that it might be Alcée's custom to sally forth from the plantation secretly, and at such an hour; for it was nearly midnight. And had it not been for the tell-tale saddle-bags, she would only have crept to bed, to wonder, to fret and dream unpleasant dreams. But her impatience and anxiety would not be held in check. Hastily unbolting the shutters of her door that opened upon the gallery, she stepped outside and called softly to the old negro.

"Gre't Peter! Miss Clarisse. I wasn' sho it was a ghos' o' w'at, stan'in' up dah, plumb in de night,* dataway."

He mounted half-way up the long, broad flight of stairs. She was standing at the top of them.

"Bruce, w'ere has Monsieur Alcée gone?" she asked.

"W'y, he gone 'bout he business, I reckin," replied Bruce, striving to be non-commital at the outset.

"W'ere has Monsieur Alcée gone?" she reiterated, stamping her bare foot. "I won't stan' any nonsense or any lies; mine, Bruce."

I don' ric'lic ez I eva tole you lie *yit*, Miss Clarisse. Mista Alcée, he all broke up, sho."

"W'ere—has—he gone? *Ah Sainte Vierge! faut de la patience! butor, va!*"*

"W'en I was in he room, a-breshin' off he clo'es to-day," the darkey began, settling himself against the stair-rail, "he look dat speechless an' down, I say, 'You 'pear tu me like some pussun w'at gwine have a spell o' sickness, Mista Alcée.' He say, 'You reckin.' An' he git up, go look hisse'f stidy in de glass. Den he go to de chimbly an' jerk up de quinine bottle* an po' a gre't hoss-dose onto he han'. An' he swalla dat mess in a wink, an' wash hit down wid a big dram o' whisky w'at he keep in he room, agin he come all soppin' wet outen de fiel'.

"He lows,* 'No I ain' gwine be sick, Bruce.' Den he square off. He say, 'I kin mak out to stan' up an' gi' an' take wid any man I knows, lessen hit's John L. Sulvun.* But w'en God A'mighty an' a 'oman jines fo'ces agin me, dats one too many fur me.' I tell 'im jis so, whils' I'se makin' out to bresh a spot off w'at ain'dah, on he coat colla. I tell 'im, 'You wants li'le res', suh.' He say, 'No, I wants li'le fling; dats w'at I wants; an I gwine git it. Pitch me a fis'ful o' clo'es in dem 'ar saddle-bags.' Dat w'at he say. Don't you bodda, missy. He jis gone a caperin' yonda tu de Cajun ball. Uh—uh—de skeeters is fair' a-swarmin' like bees roun' yo' foots!"

The mosquitoes were indeed attacking Clarisse's white feet savagely. She had unconsciously been alternately rubbing one foot over the other while hearing the darkey's recital.

"The 'Cadian ball," she repeated contemptuously. "Humph! *Par exemple!* Nice conduc' for a Laballière. An' he needs a saddle-bag, fill' with clothes to go to the 'Cadian ball!"

"Oh, Miss Clarisse; you go on tu bed, chile; git yo' soun' sleep. He 'low he come back in couple weeks o' so. I kiarn be repeatin' lot o' truck w'at young mans say, out heah face o' a young gol."

Clarisse said no more but flashed back into the house.

"You done talk too much wid yo' mouf a'ready, you ole fool nigga, you," muttered Bruce to himself as he walked away.

*

Alcée reached the ball very late, of course—too late for the chicken gombo* which had been served at midnight.

The big, low-ceiled room—they called it a hall—was packed with men and women dancing to the music of three fiddles. There were broad galleries all around it. There was a room at one side where sober-faced men were playing cards. Another in which babies were sleeping, called *le parc aux petits*.* Any one who is white may go to a 'Cadian ball, but he must pay for his lemonade, his coffee and chicken gombo. And he must behave himself like a 'Cadian. Grosbœuf was giving this ball. He had been giving them since he was a young man, and he was a middle-aged one, now. In that time he could recall but one disturbance, and that was caused by American railroaders, who were not in touch with their surroundings and had no business there. "*Ces maudits gens du raiderode*,"* Grosbœuf called them.

Alcée Laballière's presence at the ball caused a flutter even among the men, who could not but admire his grit* after such a misfortune befalling him. To be sure, they knew the Laballières were rich—that there were resources East, and more again in the city. But they felt it took a *brave homme* to stand a blow like that philosophically. One old gentleman, who was in the habit of reading a Paris newspaper and knew things, chuckled gleefully to everybody that Alcée's conduct was altogether *chic, mais chic*. That he had more *panache* than Boulanger.* Well, perhaps he had.

But what he did not show outwardly was that he was in a mood for ugly things to-night. Poor Bobinôt alone felt it, vaguely. He discerned a gleam of it in Alcée's handsome eyes as the young planter stood in the doorway looking with rather feverish glance upon the assembly, while he laughed and talked with a 'Cadian farmer who was beside him.

Bobinôt himself was dull-looking and clumsy. Most of the men were. But the young women were very beautiful. The eyes that glanced into Alcée's as they passed him, were big, dark, soft as those of the young heifers standing out in the cool prairie grass.

But the belle was Calixta. Her white dress was not nearly so handsome or well made as Fronie's (she and Fronie had quite forgotten the battle on the church steps, and were friends again), nor were her slippers so stylish as those of Ozéina; and she fanned herself with a handkerchief, since she had broken her red fan at the last ball, and her aunts and uncles were not willing to give her another. But all the men agreed she was at her best to-night. Such animation! such *abandon!* such flashes of wit!

"Né, Bobinôt! *Mais* w'ats the matta? W'at you standin' *planté là**
like ole Ma'ame Tina's cow in the bog, you?"

That was good. That was an excellent thrust at Bobinôt, who had forgotten the figure of the dance, with his mind bent on other things, and it started a clamor of laughter at his expense. He joined good-naturedly. It was better to receive even such notice as that from Calixta than none at all. But Madame Suzonne, sitting in a corner, whispered to her neighbor that if Ozéina were to conduct herself in such manner, she should immediately be taken out to the mule-cart and driven home. The women did not always approve of Calixta.

Now and then were short lulls in the dance, when couples flocked out upon the galleries for a brief respite and a breath of air. The moon had gone down pale in the west, and in the east was yet no promise of day. After such an interval, when the dancers again assembled to resume the interrupted quadrille, Calixta was not among them.

She was sitting out upon a bench in the shadow, with Alcée beside her. They were acting like fools. He had attempted to take a little gold ring from her finger; just for the fun of it, for there was nothing he could have done with the ring but replace it again. But she clinched her hand tight. He had pretended that it was a very difficult matter to open it. Then he kept the hand in his. They seemed to forget about it. He played with her ear-ring, a thin crescent of gold hanging from her small, brown ear. He caught a whisp of the kinky hair that had escaped its fastening, and rubbed the ends of it against his shaven cheek.

"You know, last year in Assumption, Calixta." They belonged to the younger generation, so preferred to speak English.*

"Don't come say Assumption to me, M'sieur Alcée. I done yeard Assumption till I'm plumb sick."

"Yes, I know. The idiots! Because you were in Assumption, and I happened to go to Assumption, they must have it that we went to-gether. But it was nice—*hein*, Calixta?—in Assumption?"

They saw Bobinôt emerge from the hall and stand a moment outside the lighted doorway, peering uneasily and searchingly into the darkness. He did not see them, and went slowly back.

"There is Bobinôt looking for you. You are going to set poor Bobinôt crazy. You'll marry him some day; *hein*, Calixta?"

"I don't say, no, me," she replied, striving to withdraw her hand, which he held more firmly for the attempt.

"But, come, Calixta; you know you said you would go back to Assumption, just to spite them."

"No, I never said that, me. You mus' dreamt that."

"Oh, I thought you did. You know I'm going down to the city."

"W'en?"

"To-night."

"You betta make has'e, then; it's mos' day."

"Well, to-morrow 'll do."

"W'at you goin' do, yonda?"

"I don't know. Drown myself in the lake, maybe; unless you go down there to visit your uncle."

Calixta's senses were reeling; and they well-nigh left her when she felt Alcée's lips brush her ear like the touch of a rose.

"Mista Alcée! Is dat Mista Alcée?" the thick voice of a negro was asking, who stood on the ground holding to the banister-rails near which the couple sat.

"W'at do you want, now?" cried Alcée impatiently. "Can't I have a moment of peace?"

"I ben huntin' you high an' low, suh," said the man. "Dey—dey some one in de road, onda de mulbare-tree, want see you a minute."

"I wouldn't go out to the road to see the Angel Gabriel. And if you come back here with any more talk, I'll have to break your neck." The negro turned mumbling away.

Alcée and Calixta laughed softly about it. Her boisterousness was all gone. They talked low, and laughed softly, as lovers do.

"Alcée! Alcée Laballière!"

It was not the negro's voice this time; but one that went through Alcée's body like an electric shock, bringing him to his feet.

It was Clarisse standing there in her riding-habit, where the negro had stood. For an instant confusion reigned in Alcée's thoughts, like one who awakes suddenly from a dream. But he felt that something of serious import had brought her to the ball in the dead of night.

"W'at does this mean, Clarisse?" he asked.

"It means something has happen' at home. You mus' come."

"Happened to maman?" he questioned, in alarm.

"No; nainaine is well, and asleep. It is something else. Not to fr'ghten you. But you mus' come. Come with me, Alcée."

There was no need for the imploring note. He would have followed the voice anywhere.

She had now recognized the girl sitting back on the bench.

"*Ah, c'est vous, Calixta? Comment ça va, mon enfant?*"

"*Tcha va b'en; et vous, mam'zélle?*"*

Alcée swung himself over the low rail and startcd to follow Clarisse, without a word, without a glance back at the girl. He had forgotten he was leaving her there. But Clarisse whispered something to him and he turned back to say "good night, Calixta" and offer his hand to press through the railing. She pretended not to see it.

*

"How come that? You settin' yere by yo'se'f, Calixta?" It was Bobinôt who had found her there alone. The dancers had not yet come out. She looked ghastly in the faint, gray light that was struggling out of the east.

"Yes, that's me. Go yonda in the *parc aux petits* an' ask aunt Olisse fu' my hat. She knows w'ere 'tis. I want ter go home, me."

"How you came?"

"I come afoot, with the Cateaus. But I'm goin' now. I ent goin' wait fu' 'em. I'm plumb wo' out, me."

They went together across the open prairie and along the edge of the fields, stumbling in the uncertain light. He told her to lift her dress that was getting wet and bedraggled; for she was pulling at the weeds and grasses with her hands.

"I don' care; it's got to go in the tub, anyway. You been sayin' all along you want to marry me, Bobinôt. Well, if you want, yet, I don' care, me."

The glow of a sudden and overwhelming happiness shone out in the brown, rugged face of the young Acadian. He could not speak, for very joy. It choked him.

"Oh well, if you don' want," snapped Calixta, flippantly, pretending to be piqued at his silence.

"*Bon Dieu!* You know that makes me crazy, w'at you sayin'. You mean that, Calixta? You ent goin' to turn roun' agin?"

"I neva tole you that much *yet*, Bobinôt. I mean that. *Tiens*," and she held out her hand in the business-like manner of a man who clinches a bargain with a hand-clasp. Bobinôt grew bold with happiness and asked Calixta to kiss him. She turned her face, that looked almost ugly after the night's dissipation, and looked steadily into his.

"I don' want ter kiss you, Bobinôt," she said, turning away again, "not to-day. Some other time. *Bonté divine!* ent you satisfy, *yet!*"

"Oh, I'm satisfy, Calixta," he said.

*

Riding through a patch of wood, Clarisse's saddle became ungirted, and she and Alcée dismounted to readjust it.

For the twentieth time he asked her what had happened at home.

"But, Clarisse, w'at is it? Is it a misfortune?"

"*Ah, Dieu sait!* It's only something that happen' to me."

"To you!"

"I saw you go away las' night, Alcée, with those saddle-bags," she said, haltingly, striving to arrange something about the saddle, "an' I made Bruce tell me. He said you had gone to the ball, an' wouldn' be home for weeks an' weeks. I thought, Alcée—maybe you were going to—to Assumption. I got wild. An' then I knew if you didn't come back, *now*, to-night, I would die. I couldn' stan' it—again."

She had her face hidden in her arm that she was resting against the saddle when she said that.

He began to wonder if this meant love. But she had to tell him so, before he believed it. And when she told him, he thought the face of the Universe was changed—just like Bobinôt. Was it last week the cyclone had well-nigh ruined him? The cyclone seemed a huge joke, now. It was he, then, who, an hour ago was kissing little Calixta's ear and whispering nonsense into it. Calixta was like a myth, now. The one, only, great reality in the world was Clarisse standing before him, telling him that she loved him.

In the distance they heard the rapid discharge of pistol-shots; but it did not disturb them. They knew it was only the negro musicians who had gone into the yard to fire their pistols into the air, as the custom is, and to announce *"le bal est fini."**

THE FATHER OF
DÉSIRÉE'S BABY

(DÉSIRÉE'S BABY)

As the day was pleasant Madame Valmondé drove over to L'Abri* to see Désirée and the baby.

It made her laugh to think of Désirée with a baby. Why, it seemed but yesterday that Désirée was little more than a baby herself; when Monsieur in riding through the gateway of Valmondé had found her lying asleep in the shadow of the big stone pillar.

The little one awoke in his arms and began to cry for "Dada." That was as much as she could do or say. Some people thought she might have strayed there of her own accord, for she was of the toddling age. The prevailing belief was that she had been purposely left by a party of Texans,* whose canvas-covered wagon, late in the day had crossed the ferry that Coton-Maïs kept, just below the plantation. In time Madame Valmondé abandoned every speculation but the one that Désirée had been sent to her by a beneficent Providence to be the child of her affection, seeing that she was without child of the flesh. For the girl grew to be beautiful and gentle, affectionate and sincere; the idol of Valmondé.

It was no wonder, when she stood one day against the stone pillar in whose shadow she had lain asleep, eighteen years before, that Armand Aubigny riding by and seeing her there, had fallen in love with her. That was the way all the Aubignys fell in love, as if struck by a pistol shot. The wonder was, that he had not loved her before; for he had known her since his father brought him home from Paris, a boy of eight, after his mother died there. The passion that awoke in him that day, when he saw her at the gate, swept along like an avalanche, or like a prairie fire, or like anything that drives headlong over all obstacles.

Monsieur Valmondé grew practical and wanted things well considered: that is, the girl's obscure origin. Armand looked into her eyes and did not care. He was reminded that she was nameless. What did it matter about a name when he could give her one of the oldest and proudest in Louisiana? He ordered the corbeille* from Paris, and contained himself with what patience he could until it arrived, then they were married.

Madame Valmondé had not seen Désirée and the baby for four weeks. When she reached L'Abri she shuddered at the first sight of it, as she always did. It was a sad looking place, which for many years had not known the gentle presence of a mistress. Old Monsieur Aubigny having married and buried his wife in France, and she having loved her own land too well ever to leave it. The roof came down steep and black like a cowl reaching out beyond the wide galleries that encircled the yellow stuccoed house. Big, solemn oaks grew close to it, and their thick-leaved, far-reaching branches shadowed it like a pall. Young Aubigny's rule was a strict one, too, and under it his negroes had forgotten how to be gay, as they had been during the old master's easy-going and indulgent lifetime.

The young mother was recovering slowly, and lay full length, in her soft white muslins and laces, upon a couch. The baby was beside her, upon her arm, where he had fallen asleep at her breast. The yellow nurse woman* sat beside a window fanning herself.

Madame Valmondé bent her portly figure over Désirée and kissed her, holding her an instant tenderly in her arms. Then she turned to the child.

"This is not the baby!" she exclaimed, in startled tones. French was the language spoken at Valmondé in those days.

"I knew you would be astonished," laughed Désirée, "at the way he has grown. The little cochon de lait!* Look at his legs, mamma, and his hands and finger-nails,—real finger-nails.* Zandrine had to cut them this morning. Isn't it so, Zandrine?"

The woman bowed her turbaned head majestically, "Mais si, madame."

"And the way he cries," went on Désirée, "is deafening. Armand heard him the other day as far away as La Blanche's cabin."

Madame Valmondé had never removed her eyes from the child. She picked it up and walked with it over to the window that was lightest. She scanned it narrowly, then looked as searchingly at Zandrine, whose face was turned to look across the fields.

"Yes, the child has grown, has changed," said Madame Valmondé, slowly, as she replaced it beside its mother. "What does Armand say?"

Désirée's face became suffused with a glow that was happiness itself.

"Oh, Armand is the proudest father in the parish, I believe, chiefly because it is a boy, to bear his name; though he says, not—that he would have loved a girl as well. But I know it isn't true. I know he says that to please me. And, mamma," she added, drawing Madame Valmondé's head down to her, and speaking in a whisper, "he hasn't punished one of them—not one of them—since baby is born. Even Négrillon,* who pretended to have burnt his leg that he might rest from work—he only laughed, and said Négrillon was a great scamp. Oh, mamma, I'm so happy; it frightens me."

What Désirée said was true. Marriage, and later the birth of his son, had softened Armand Aubigny's imperious and exacting nature greatly. This was what made the gentle Désirée so happy, for she loved him desperately. When he frowned she trembled, but loved him. When he smiled, she asked no greater blessing of God. But Armand's dark, handsome face had not often been disfigured by frowns since the day he fell in love with her.

When the baby was about three months old Désirée awoke one day to the conviction that there was something in the air menacing her peace. It was at first too subtle to grasp. It had only been a disquieting suggestion; an air of mystery among the blacks; unexpected visits from far-off neighbors who could hardly account for their coming. Then a strange, an awful change in her husband's manner, which she dared not ask him to explain. When he spoke to her, it was with averted eyes, from which the old love-light seemed to have gone out. He absented himself from home; and when there, avoided her presence and that of her child, without excuse. And the very spirit of Satan seemed suddenly to take hold of him in his dealings with the slaves. Désirée was miserable enough to die.

She sat in her room, one hot afternoon, in her peignoir, listlessly drawing through her fingers the strands of her long, silky brown hair that hung about her shoulders. The baby, half naked, lay asleep upon her own great mahogany bed, that was like a sumptuous throne, with its satin-lined half-canopy. One of La Blanche's little quadroon boys*—half naked too—stood fanning the child slowly with a fan of peacock feathers. Désirée's eyes had been fixed absently and sadly upon the baby, while she was striving to penetrate the threatening mist that she felt closing about her. She looked from her child to the boy who stood beside him, and back again; over and over. "Ah!" It was a cry that she could not help; which she was not conscious of having uttered. The blood turned like ice in her veins, and a clammy moisture gathered upon her face.

She tried to speak to the little quadroon boy; but no sound would come, at first. When he heard his name uttered, he looked up, and his mistress was pointing to the door. He laid aside the great, soft fan, and obediently stole away, over the polished floor, on his bare tiptoes.

She stayed motionless, with gaze riveted upon her child, and her face the picture of fright.

Presently her husband entered the room, and without noticing her, went to a table and began to search among some papers which covered it.

"Armand," she called to him, in a voice which must have stabbed him, if he was human. But he did not notice. "Armand," she said again. Then she rose and tottered towards him. "Armand," she panted once more, clutching his arm, "look at our child. What does it mean? tell me."

He coldly but gently loosened her fingers from about his arm and thrust the hand away from him. "Tell me what it means!" she cried despairingly.

"It means," he answered lightly, "that the child is not white; it means that you are not white."

A quick conception of all that this accusation meant for her, nerved her with unwonted courage to deny it. 'It is a lie—it is not true, I am white! Look at my hair, it is brown; and my eyes are gray, Armand, you know they are gray. And my skin is fair," seizing his wrist. "Look at my hand—whiter than yours, Armand," she laughed hysterically.

"As white as La Blanche's," he said cruelly; and went away leaving her alone with their child.

When she could hold a pen in her hand, she sent a despairing letter to Madame Valmondé.

"My mother, they tell me I am not white. Armand has told me I am not white. For God's sake tell them it is not true. You must know it is not true. I shall die. I must die. I cannot be so unhappy, and live."

The answer that came was as brief:

"My own Désirée: Come home to Valmondé —back to your mother who loves you. Come with your child."

When the letter reached Désirée she went with it to her husband's study, and laid it open upon the desk before which he sat. She was like a stone image: silent, white, motionless after she placed it there.

In silence he ran his cold eyes over the written words. He said nothing. "Shall I go, Armand?" she asked in tones sharp with agonized suspense.

"Yes, go."

"Do you want me to go?"

"Yes, I want you to go."

He thought Almighty God had dealt cruelly and unjustly with him; and felt, somehow, that he was paying Him back in kind when he stabbed thus into his wife's soul. Moreover he no longer loved her, because of the unconscious injury she had brought upon his home and his name.

She turned away like one stunned by a blow, and walked slowly towards the door, hoping he would call her back.

"Good-bye, Armand," she moaned.

He did not answer her. That was his last blow at fate. After it was dealt he felt like a remorseless murderer.*

Désirée went in search of her child. Zandrine was pacing the sombre gallery with it. She took the little one from the nurse's arms with no word of explanation, and descending the steps, walked away, under the live oak branches.

It was an October afternoon. Out in the still fields the negroes were picking cotton; and the sun was just sinking.

Désirée had not changed the thin white garment nor the slippers which she wore. Her head was uncovered and the sun's rays brought a golden gleam from its brown meshes. She did not take the broad, beaten road which led to the far-off plantation of Valmondé. She walked across a deserted field, where the stubble bruised her tender feet, so delicately shod, and tore her thin gown to shreds.

She disappeared among the reeds and willows that grew thick along the banks of the deep, sluggish bayou; and she did not come back again.

*

Some weeks later there was a curious scene enacted at L'Abri. In the centre of the smoothly swept back-yard was a great bonfire. Armand Aubigny sat in the wide hallway that commanded a view of the spectacle; and it was he who dealt out to a half-dozen negroes the material which kept this fire ablaze.

A graceful cradle of willow, with all its dainty furbishings, was laid upon the pyre, which had already been fed with the richness of a priceless layette. Then there were silk gowns, and velvet and satin ones added to these; laces, too, and embroideries; bonnets and gloves—for the corbeille had been of rare quality.

The last thing to go was a tiny bundle of letters; innocent little scribblings that Désirée had sent to him during the days of their espousal. There was the remnant of one back in the drawer from which he took them. But it was not Désirée's; it was part of an old letter from his mother to his father. He read it. She was thanking God for the blessing of her husband's love;

"But, above all," she wrote, "night and day, I thank the good God for having so arranged our lives that our dear Armand will never know that his mother, who adores him, belongs to the race that is cursed with the brand of slavery."

CALINE

The sun was just far enough in the west to send inviting shadows. In the centre of a small field, and in the shade of a haystack which was there, a girl lay sleeping. She had slept long and soundly, when something awoke her as suddenly as if it had been a blow. She opened her eyes and stared a moment up in the cloudless sky. She yawned and stretched her strong brown legs and arms, lazily. Then she arose, never minding the bits of straw that clung to her black hair, to her red bodice, and blue cotonade skirt that did not reach her naked ankles.

The log cabin in which she dwelt with her parents was just outside the enclosure in which she had been sleeping. Beyond was a small clearing that did duty as a cotton field. All else was dense wood, except the long stretch that curved round the brow of the hill, and in which glittered the steel rails of the Texas and Pacific road.*

When Caline emerged from the shadow she saw a long train of passenger coaches standing in view, where they must have stopped abruptly. It was that sudden stopping which had awakened her; for such a thing had not happened before within her recollection and she looked stupid, at first, with astonishment. There seemed to be something wrong with the engine; and some of the passengers who dismounted went forward to investigate the trouble. Others came strolling along in the direction of the cabin, where Caline stood under an old gnarled mulberry tree, staring. Her father had halted his mule at the end of the cotton row, and stood staring also, leaning upon his plough.

There were ladies in the party. They walked awkwardly in their high-heeled boots over the rough, uneven ground, and held up their skirts mincingly. They twirled parasols over their shoulders, and laughed immoderately at the funny things which their masculine companions were saying.

They tried to talk to Caline, but could not understand the French patois with which she answered them.

One of the men—a pleasant-faced youngster—drew a sketch book from his pocket and began to make a picture of the girl. She stayed motionless, her hands behind her, and her wide eyes fixed earnestly upon him.

Before he had finished there was a summons from the train; and all went scampering hurriedly away. The engine screeched, it sent a few lazy puffs into the still air, and in another moment or two had vanished, bearing its human cargo with it.

Caline could not feel the same after that. She looked with new and strange interest upon the trains of cars that passed so swiftly back and forth across her vision, each day; and wondered whence those people came, and whither they were going.

Her mother and father could not tell her, except to say that they came from loin la bas, and were going "Djieu sait é ou."*

One day she walked miles down the track to talk with the old flagman,* who stayed down there by the big water tank. Yes, he knew. Those people came from the great cities in the north, and were going to the city in the south.* He knew all about the city; it was a grand place. He had lived there once. His sister lived there now; and she would be glad enough to have so fine a girl as Caline to help her cook and scrub, and tend the babies. And he thought Caline might earn as much as five dollars a month, in the city.

So she went; in a new cotonade,* and her Sunday shoes; and a sacredly guarded scrawl, that the flagman sent to his sister.

The woman lived in a tiny, stuccoed house, with green blinds, and three wooden steps leading down to the banquette. There seemed to be hundreds like it along the street. Over the house tops loomed the tall masts of ships, and the hum of the French market* could be heard on a still morning.

Caline was at first bewildered. She had to re-adjust all her pre-conceptions to fit the reality of it. The flagman's sister was a kind and gentle task-mistress. At the end of a week or two she wanted to know how the girl liked it all. Caline liked it very well, for it was pleasant, on Sunday afternoons, to stroll with the children under the great, solemn sugar sheds; or to sit upon the compressed cotton bales, watching the stately steamers, the graceful boats, and noisy little tugs that plied the waters of the Mississippi. And it filled her with agreeable excitement to go to the French market, where the handsome Gascon butchers* were eager to present their compliments and little Sunday bouquets to the pretty Acadian girl; and to throw fistsful of lagniappe* in her basket.

When the woman asked her again after another week or two if she were still pleased, she was not so sure. And again when she questioned Caline the girl turned away, and went to sit behind the big, yellow cistern, to cry unobserved. For she knew now that it was not the great city and its crowds of people she had so eagerly sought; but the pleasant-faced boy, who had made her picture that day under the mulberry tree.

A MATTER OF PREJUDICE

The Strange Result of Disturbing Madame Carambeau.

Madame Carambeau wanted it strictly understood that she was not to be disturbed by Gustave's birthday party. They carried her big rocking-chair from the back gallery, that looked out upon the garden where the children were going to play, around to the front gallery, which closely faced the green levee bank* and the Mississippi coursing almost flush with the top of it.

The house—an old Spanish one,* broad, low and completely encircled by a wide gallery—was far down in the French quarter of New Orleans.* It stood upon a square of ground that was covered thick with a semi-tropical growth of plants and flowers. An impenetrable board fence, edged with a formidable row of iron spikes, shielded the garden from the prying glances of the occasional passer-by.

Madame Carambeau's widowed daughter, Madame Cécile Lalonde, lived with her. This annual party, given to her little son, Gustave, was the one defiant act of Madame Lalonde's existence. She persisted in it, to her own astonishment and the wonder of those who knew her and her mother.

For old Madame Carambeau was a woman of many prejudices—so many, in fact, that it would be difficult to name them all. She detested dogs, cats, organ-grinders, white servants* and children's noises. She despised Americans, Germans* and all people of a different faith from her own. Anything not French had, in her opinion, little right to existence.*

She had not spoken to her son Henri for ten years because he had married an American girl from Prytania street.* She would not permit green tea to be introduced into her house, and those who could not or would not drink coffee might drink tisane of *fleur de Laurier** for all she cared.

Nevertheless, the children seemed to be having it all their own way that day, and the organ-grinders were let loose. Old madame, in her retired corner, could hear the screams, the laughter and the music far more distinctly than she liked. She rocked herself noisily, and hummed "*Partant pour la Syrie.*"*

She was straight and slender. Her hair was white, and she wore it in puffs on the temples. Her skin was fair, and her eyes blue and cold.

Suddenly she became aware that footsteps were approaching, and threatening to invade her privacy—not only footsteps, but screams! Then two little children, one in hot pursuit of the other, darted wildly around the corner near which she sat.

The child in advance, a pretty little girl, sprang excitedly into Madame Carambeau's lap, and threw her arms convulsively around the old lady's neck. Her companion lightly struck her a "last tag," and ran laughing gleefully away.

The most natural thing for the child to do then would have been to wriggle down from madame's lap, without a "thank you" or a "by your leave," after the manner of small and thoughtless children. But she did not do this. She stayed there, panting and fluttering, like a frightened bird.

Madame was greatly annoyed. She moved as if to put the child away from her, and scolded her sharply for being boisterous and rude. The little one, who did not understand French,* was not disturbed by the reprimand, and stayed on in madame's lap. She rested her plump little cheek, that was hot and flushed, against the soft white linen of the old lady's gown.

The cheek was very hot and very flushed. It was dry, too, and so were the hands. The child's breathing was quick and irregular. Madame was not long in detecting these signs of disturbance.

Though she was a creature of prejudice, she was nevertheless a skilful and accomplished nurse, and a connoisseur in all matters pertaining to health. She prided herself upon this talent, and never lost an opportunity of exercising it. She would have treated an organ-grinder with tender consideration if one had presented himself in the character of an invalid.

Madame's manner toward the little one changed immediately. Her arms and her lap were at once adjusted so as to become the most comfortable of resting places. She rocked very gently to and fro. She fanned the child softly with her palm leaf fan, and sang "*Partant pour la Syrie*" in a low and agreeable tone.

The child was perfectly content to lie still and prattle a little in that language that madame thought hideous. But the brown eyes were soon swimming in drowsiness, and the little body grew heavy with sleep in madame's clasp.

When the little girl slept Madame Carambeau arose, and treading carefully and deliberately, entered her room, that opened near at hand upon the gallery. The room was large, airy and inviting, with its cool matting upon the floor, and its heavy, old, polished mahogany furniture. Madame, with the child still in her arms, pulled a bell-cord; then she stood waiting, swaying gently back and forth. Presently an old black woman answered the summons. She wore gold hoops in her ears, and a bright bandanna knotted fantastically on her head.

"Louise, turn down the bed," commanded madame. "Place that small, soft pillow below the bolster. Here is a poor little unfortunate creature whom Providence must have driven into my arms." She laid the child carefully down.

"Ah, those Americans! Do they deserve to have children? Understanding as little as they do how to take care of them!" said madame, while Louise was mumbling an accompanying assent that would have been unintelligible to any one unacquainted with the negro patois.*

"There, you see, Louise, she is burning up," remarked madame; "she is consumed. Unfasten the little bodice while I lift her. Ah, talk to me of such parents! So stupid as not to perceive a fever like that coming on, but must dress their child up like a monkey to go play and dance to the music of organ-grinders!

"Haven't you better sense, Louise, than to take off a child's shoe as if you were removing the boot from the leg of a cavalry officer?" Madame would have required fairy fingers to minister to the sick. "Now go to Mamzelle Cécile, and tell her to send me one of those old, soft, thin nightgowns that Gustave wore two summers ago."

When the woman retired, madame busied herself with concocting a cooling pitcher of orange-flower water, and mixing a fresh supply of *eau sédative** with which agreeably to sponge the little invalid.

Madame Lalonde came herself with the old, soft nightgown. She was a pretty, blonde, plump little woman, with the deprecatory air of one whose will has become flaccid from want of use. She was mildly distressed at what her mother had done.

"But, mamma! But, mamma, the child's parents will be sending the carriage for her in a little while. Really, there was no use. Oh dear! oh dear!"

If the bedpost had spoken to Madame Carambeau, she would have paid more attention, for speech from such a source would have been at least surprising if not convincing. Madame Lalonde did not possess the faculty of either surprising or convincing her mother.

"Yes, the little one will be quite comfortable in this," said the old lady, taking the garment from her daughter's irresolute hands.

"But, mamma! What shall I say, what shall I do when they send? Oh, dear; oh, dear!"

"That is your business," replied madame, with lofty indifference. "My concern is solely with a sick child that happens to be under my roof. I think I know my duty at this time of life, Cécile."

As Madame Lalonde predicted, the carriage soon came, with a stiff English coachman driving it, and a red-cheeked Irish nursemaid seated inside. Madame would not even permit the maid to see her little charge. She had an original theory that the Irish voice is distressing to the sick.*

Madame Lalonde sent the girl away with a long letter of explanation that must have satisfied the parents; for the child was left undisturbed in Madame Carambeau's care. She was a sweet child, gentle and affectionate. And, though she cried and fretted a little throughout the night for her mother, she seemed, after all, to take kindly to madame's gentle nursing. It was not much of a fever that afflicted her, and after two days she was well enough to be sent back to her parents.

Madame, in all her varied experience with the sick, had never before nursed so objectionable a character as an American child. But the trouble was that after the little one went away, she could think of nothing really objectionable against her except the accident of her birth, which was, after all, her misfortune; and her ignorance of the French language, which was not her fault.

But the touch of the caressing baby arms; the pressure of the soft little body in the night; the tones of the voice, and the feeling of the hot lips when the child kissed her, believing herself to be with her mother, were impressions that had sunk through the crust of madame's prejudice and reached her heart.

She often walked the length of the gallery, looking out across the wide, majestic river. Sometimes she trod the mazes of her garden where the solitude was almost that of a tropical jungle. It was during such moments that the seed began to work in her soul—the seed planted by the innocent and undesigning hands of a little child.*

The first shoot that it sent forth was Doubt. Madame plucked it away once or twice. But it sprouted again, and with it, Mistrust and Dissatisfaction. Then from the heart of the seed, and amid the shoots of Doubt and Misgiving, came the flower of Truth. It was a very beautiful flower, and it bloomed on Christmas morning.

As Madame Carambeau and her daughter were about to enter her carriage on that Christmas morning, to be driven to church, the old lady stopped to give an order to her black coachman, François. François had been driving these ladies every Sunday morning to the French Cathedral* for so many years—he had forgotten exactly how many, but ever since he had entered their service, when Madame Lalonde was a little girl. His astonishment may therefore be imagined when Madame Carambeau said to him:

"François, to-day you will drive us to one of the American churches."

"*Plait-il, madame?*"* the negro stammered, doubting the evidence of his hearing.

"I say, you will drive us to one of the American churches. Any one of them," she added, with a sweep of her hand. "I suppose they are all alike," and she followed her daughter into the carriage.

Madame Lalonde's surprise and agitation were painful to see, and they deprived her of the ability to question, even if she had possessed the courage to do so.

François, left to his fancy, drove them to St. Patrick's Church on Camp street.* Madame Lalonde looked and felt like the proverbial fish out of its element as they entered the edifice. Madame Carambeau, on the contrary, looked as if she had been attending St. Patrick's church all her life. She sat with unruffled calm through the long service and through a lengthy English sermon, of which she did not understand a word.

When the mass was ended and they were about to enter the carriage again, Madame Carambeau turned, as she had done before, to the coachman.

"François," she said, coolly, "you will now drive us to the residence of my son, M. Henri Carambeau. No doubt Mamzelle Cécile can inform you where it is," she added, with a sharply penetrating glance that caused Madame Lalonde to wince.

Yes, her daughter Cécile knew, and so did François, for that matter. They drove out St. Charles avenue—very far out. It was like a strange city to old madame, who had not been in the American quarter since the town had taken on this new and splendid growth.*

The morning was a delicious one, soft and mild; and the roses were all in bloom. They were not hidden behind spiked fences. Madame appeared not to notice them, or the beautiful and striking residences that lined the avenue along which they drove. She held a bottle of smelling-salts to her nostrils, as though she were passing through the most unsavory instead of the most beautiful quarter of New Orleans.

Henri's house was a very modern and very handsome one, standing a little distance away from the street. A well-kept lawn, studded with rare and charming plants, surrounded it. The ladies, dismounting, rang the bell, and stood out upon the banquette, waiting for the iron gate to be opened.

A white maid-servant admitted them. Madame did not seem to mind. She handed her a card with all proper ceremony, and followed with her daughter to the house.

Not once did she show a sign of weakness; not even when her son, Henri, came and took her in his arms and sobbed and wept upon her neck as only a warm-hearted Creole could. He was a big, good-looking, honest-faced man, with tender brown eyes like his dead father's and a firm mouth like his mother's.

Young Mrs. Carambeau came, too, her sweet, fresh face transfigured with happiness. She led by the hand her little daughter, the "American child" whom madame had nursed so tenderly a month before, never suspecting the little one to be other than an alien to her.

"What a lucky chance was that fever! What a happy accident!" gurgled Madame Lalonde.

"Cécile, it was no accident, I tell you; it was Providence," spoke madame, reprovingly, and no one contradicted her.

They all drove back together to eat Christmas dinner in the old house by the river. Madame held her little granddaughter upon her lap; her son Henri sat facing her, and beside her was her daughter-in-law.

Henri sat back in the carriage and could not speak. His soul was possessed by a pathetic joy that would not admit of speech. He was going back again to the home where he was born, after a banishment of ten long years.

He would hear again the water beat against the green levee-bank with a sound that was not quite like any other that he could remember. He would sit within the sweet and solemn shadow of the deep and overhanging roof; and roam through the wild, rich solitude of the old garden, where he had played his pranks of boyhood and dreamed his dreams of youth. He would listen to his mother's voice calling him, "*mon fils*," as it had always done before that day he had had to choose between mother and wife. No; he could not speak.

But his wife chatted much and pleasantly—in a French, however, that must have been trying to old madame to listen to.

"I am so sorry, *ma mère*," she said, "that our little one does not speak French. It is not my fault, I assure you," and she flushed and hesitated a little. "It—it was Henri who would not permit it."

"That is nothing," replied madame, amiably, drawing the child close to her. "Her grandmother will teach her French; and she will teach her grandmother English. You see, I have no prejudices. I am not like my son. Henri was always a stubborn boy. Heaven only knows how he came by such a character!"

AZÉLIE

Azélie crossed the yard with slow, hesitating steps. She wore a pink sunbonnet and a faded calico* dress that had been made the summer before, and was now too small for her in every way. She carried a large tin pail on her arm. When within a few yards of the house she stopped under a chinaberry-tree,* quite still, except for the occasional slow turning of her head from side to side.

Mr. Mathurin, from his elevation upon the upper gallery, laughed when he saw her; for he knew she would stay there, motionless, till some one noticed and questioned her.

The planter was just home from the city, and was therefore in an excellent humor, as he always was, on getting back to what he called *le grand air,** the space and stillness of the country, and the scent of the fields. He was in shirt-sleeves, walking around the gallery that encircled the big square white house. Beneath was a brick-paved portico upon which the lower rooms opened. At wide intervals were large whitewashed pillars that supported the upper gallery.

In one corner of the lower house was the store, which was in no sense a store for the general public, but maintained only to supply the needs of Mr. Mathurin's "hands."*

"*Eh bien!* what do you want, Azélie?" the planter finally called out to the girl in French. She advanced a few paces, and, pushing back her sunbonnet, looked up at him with a gentle, inoffensive face—"to which you would give the good God without confession," he once described it.

"*Bon jou', M'si' Mathurin,*" she replied; and continued in English: "I come git a li'le piece o' meat. We plumb out o' meat home."

"Well, well, the meat is n' going to walk to you, my chile: it has n' got feet. Go fine Mr. 'Polyte. He's yonda mending his buggy unda the shed." She turned away with an alert little step, and went in search of Mr. 'Polyte.

"That's you again!" the young man exclaimed, with a pretended air of annoyance, when he saw her. He straightened himself, and looked down at her and her pail with a comprehending glance. The sweat was standing in shining beads on his brown, good-looking face. He was in his shirt-sleeves, and the legs of his trousers were thrust into the tops of his fine, high-heeled boots. He wore his straw hat very much on one side, and had an air that was altogether *fanfaron*. He reached to a back pocket for the store key, which was as large as the pistol that he sometimes carried in the same place. She followed him across the thick, tufted grass of the yard with quick, short steps that strove to keep pace with his longer, swinging ones.

When he had unlocked and opened the heavy door of the store, there escaped from the close room the strong, pungent odor of the varied wares and provisions massed within. Azélie seemed to like the odor, and, lifting her head, snuffed the air as people sometimes do upon entering a conservatory filled with fragrant flowers.

A broad ray of light streamed in through the open door, illumining the dingy interior. The double wooden shutters of the windows were all closed, and secured on the inside by iron hooks.

"Well, w'at you want, Azélie?" asked 'Polyte, going behind the counter with an air of hurry and importance. "I ain't got time to fool. Make has'e; say w'at you want."

Her reply was precisely the same that she had made to Mr. Mathurin.

"I come git a li'le piece o' meat. We plumb out o' meat home."

He seemed exasperated.

"*Bonté!* w'at you all do with meat yonda? You don't reflec' you about to eat up yo' crop befo' it's good out o' the groun',* you all. I like to know w'y yo' pa don't go he'p with the killin' once aw'ile, an' git some fresh meat fo' a change."

She answered in an unshaded, unmodulated voice that was penetrating, like a child's: "Popa he do go he'p wid the killin'; but he say he can't work 'less he got salt meat.* He got plenty to feed—him. He's got to hire he'p wid his crop, an' he's boun' to feed 'em; they won't year no diffe'nt. An' he's got gra'ma to feed, an' Sauterelle, an' me—"

"An' all the lazy-bone 'Cadians* in the country that know w'ere they goin' to fine coffee-pot always in the corna of the fire," grumbled 'Polyte.

With an iron hook he lifted a small piece of salt meat from the pork-barrel, weighed it, and placed it in her pail. Then she wanted a little coffee. He gave it to her reluctantly. He was still more loath to let her have sugar; and when she asked for lard, he refused flatly.

She had taken off her sunbonnet, and was fanning herself with it, as she leaned with her elbows upon the counter, and let her eyes travel lingeringly along the well-lined shelves. 'Polyte stood staring into her face with a sense of aggravation that her presence, her manner, always stirred up in him.

The face was colorless but for the red, curved line of the lips. Her eyes were dark, wide, innocent, questioning eyes, and her black hair was plastered smooth back from the forehead and temples. There was no trace of any intention of coquetry in her manner. He resented this as a token of indifference toward his sex, and thought it inexcusable.

"Well, Azélie, if it's anything you don't see, ask fo' it," he suggested, with what he flattered himself was humor. But there was no responsive humor in Azélie's composition. She seriously drew a small flask from her pocket.

"Popa say, if you want to let him have a li'le dram, 'count o' his pains that's 'bout to cripple him."

"Yo' pa knows as well as I do we don't sell whisky. Mr. Mathurin don't carry no license."

"I know. He say if you want to give 'im a li'le dram, he's willin' to do some work fo' you."

"No! Once fo' all, no!" And 'Polyte reached for the day-book, in which to enter the articles he had given to her.

But Azélie's needs were not yet satisfied. She wanted tobacco;* he would not give it to her. A spool of thread; he rolled one up, together with two sticks of peppermint candy, and placed it in her pail. When she asked for a bottle of coal-oil,* he grudgingly consented, but assured her it would be useless to cudgel her brain further, for he would positively let her have nothing more. He disappeared toward the coal-oil tank, which was hidden from view behind the piled-up boxes on the counter. When she heard him searching for an empty quart bottle, and making a clatter with the tin funnels, she herself withdrew from the counter against which she had been leaning.

After they quitted the store, 'Polyte, with a perplexed expression upon his face, leaned for a moment against one of the whitewashed pillars, watching the girl cross the yard. She had folded her sunbonnet into a pad, which she placed beneath the heavy pail that she balanced upon her head. She walked upright, with a slow, careful tread. Two of the yard dogs that had stood a moment before upon the threshold of the store door, quivering and wagging their tails, were following her now, with a little businesslike trot. 'Polyte called them back.

The cabin which the girl occupied with her father, her grandmother, and her little brother Sauterelle, was removed some distance from the plantation house, and only its pointed roof could be discerned like a speck far away across the field of cotton, which was all in bloom. Her figure soon disappeared from view, and 'Polyte emerged from the shelter of the gallery, and started again toward his interrupted task. He turned to say to the planter, who was keeping up his measured tramp above:

"Mr. Mathurin, ain't it 'mos' time to stop givin' credit to Arsène Pauché? Look like that crop o' his ain't goin' to start to pay his account. I don't see, me, anyway, how you come to take that triflin' Li'le River* gang on the place."

"I know it was a mistake, 'Polyte, but *que voulez-vous?*"* the planter returned, with a good-natured shrug. "Now they are yere, we can't let them starve, my frien'. Push them to work all you can. Hole back all supplies that are not necessary, an' nex' year we will let some one else enjoy the privilege of feeding them," he ended, with a laugh.

"I wish they was all back on Li'le River," 'Polyte muttered under his breath as he turned and walked slowly away.

Directly back of the store was the young man's sleeping-room. He had made himself quite comfortable there in his corner. He had screened his windows and doors; planted Madeira vines,* which now formed a thick green curtain between the two pillars that faced his room; and had swung a hammock out there, in which he liked well to repose himself after the fatigues of the day.

He lay long in the hammock that evening, thinking over the day's happenings and the morrow's work,—half dozing, half dreaming, and wholly possessed by the charm of the night, the warm, sweeping air that blew through the long corridor, and the almost unbroken stillness that enveloped him.

At times his random thoughts formed themselves into an almost inaudible speech: "I wish she would go 'way f'om yere."

One of the dogs came and thrust his cool, moist muzzle against 'Polyte's cheek. He caressed the fellow's shaggy head. "I don' know w'at's the matta with her," he sighed; "I don' b'lieve she's got good sense."

It was a long time afterward that he murmured again: "I wish to God she'd go 'way f'om yere!"

The edge of the moon crept up—a keen, curved blade of light above the dark line of the cotton-field. 'Polyte roused himself when he saw it. "I did n' know it was so late," he said to himself—or to his dog. He entered his room at once, and was soon in bed, sleeping soundly.

It was some hours later that 'Polyte was roused from his sleep by—he did not know what; his senses were too scattered and confused to determine at once. There was at first no sound; then so faint a one that he wondered how he could have heard it. A door of his room communicated with the store, but this door was never used, and was almost completely blocked by wares piled up on the other side. The faint noise that 'Polyte heard, and which came from within the store, was followed by a flare of light that he could discern through the chinks, and that lasted as long as a match might burn.

He was now fully aware that some one was in the store. How the intruder had entered he could not guess, for the key was under his pillow with his watch and his pistol.

As cautiously as he could he donned an extra garment, thrust his bare feet into slippers, and crept out into the portico, pistol in hand.

The shutters of one of the store windows were open. He stood close to it, and waited, which he considered surer and safer than to enter the dark and crowded confines of the store to engage in what might prove a bootless struggle with the intruder.

He had not long to wait. In a few moments some one darted through the open window as nimbly as a cat. 'Polyte staggered back as if a heavy blow had stunned him. His first thought and his first exclamation were: "My God! how close I come to killin' you!"

It was Azélie. She uttered no cry, but made one quick effort to run when she saw him. He seized her arm and held her with a brutal grip. He put the pistol back into his pocket. He was shaking like a man with the palsy. One by one he took from her the parcels she was carrying, and flung them back into the store. There were not many: some packages of tobacco, a cheap pipe, some fishing-tackle, and the flask which she had brought with her in the afternoon. This he threw into the yard. It was still empty, for she had not been able to find the whisky-barrel.

"So—so, you a thief!" he muttered savagely under his breath.

"You hurtin' me, Mr. 'Polyte," she complained, squirming. He somewhat relaxed, but did not relinquish, his hold upon her.

"I ain't no thief," she blurted.

"You was stealin'," he contradicted her sharply.

"I was n' stealin'. I was jus' takin' a few li'le things you all too mean to gi' me. You all treat my popa like he was a dog. It's on'y las' week Mr. Mathurin sen' 'way to the city to fetch a fine buckboa'd fo' Son Ambroise, an' he's on'y a nigga, *après tout*.* An' my popa he want a picayune tobacca? It's 'No'—" She spoke loud in her monotonous, shrill voice. 'Polyte kept saying: "Hush, I tell you! Hush! Somebody'll hear you. Hush! It's enough you broke in the sto'—how you got in the sto'?" he added, looking from her to the open window.

"It was w'en you was behine the boxes to the coal-oil tank—I unhook' it," she explained sullenly.

"An' you don' know I could sen' you to Baton Rouge* fo' that?" He shook her as though trying to rouse her to a comprehension of her grievous fault.

"Jus' fo' a li'le picayune o' tobacca!" she whimpered.

He suddenly abandoned his hold upon her, and left her free. She mechanically rubbed the arm that he had grasped so violently.

Between the long row of pillars the moon was sending pale beams of light. In one of these they were standing.

"Azélie," he said, "go 'way f'om yere quick; some one might fine you yere. W'en you want something in the sto', fo' yo'se'f or fo' yo' pa—I don' care—ask me fo' it. But you—but you can't neva set yo' foot inside that sto' again. Go 'way f'om yere quick as you can, I tell you!"

She tried in no way to conciliate him. She turned and walked away over the same ground she had crossed before. One of the big dogs started to follow her. 'Polyte did not call him back this time. He knew no harm could come to her, going through those lonely fields, while the animal was at her side.

He went at once to his room for the store key that was beneath his pillow. He entered the store, and refastened the window. When he had made everything once more secure, he sat dejectedly down upon a bench that was in the portico. He sat for a long time motionless. Then, overcome by some powerful feeling that was at work within him, he buried his face in his hands and wept, his whole body shaken by the violence of his sobs.

After that night 'Polyte loved Azélie desperately. The very action which should have revolted him had seemed, on the contrary, to inflame him with love. He felt that love to be a degradation— something that he was almost ashamed to acknowledge to himself; and he knew that he was hopelessly unable to stifle it.

He watched now in a tremor for her coming. She came very often, for she remembered every word he had said; and she did not hesitate to ask him for those luxuries which she considered necessities to her "popa's" existence. She never attempted to enter the store, but always waited outside, of her own accord, laughing, and playing with the dogs. She seemed to have no shame or regret for what she had done, and plainly did not realize that it was a disgraceful act. 'Polyte often shuddered with disgust to discern in her a being so wholly devoid of moral sense.

He had always been an industrious, bustling fellow, never idle. Now there were hours and hours in which he did nothing but long for the sight of Azélie. Even when at work there was that gnawing want at his heart to see her, often so urgent that he would leave everything to wander down by her cabin with the hope of seeing her. It was even something if he could catch a glimpse of Sauterelle playing in the weeds, or of Arsène lazily dragging himself about, and smoking the pipe which rarely left his lips now that he was kept so well supplied with tobacco.

Once, down the bank of the bayou, when 'Polyte came upon Azélie unexpectedly, and was therefore unprepared to resist the shock of her sudden appearance, he seized her in his arms, and covered her face with kisses. She was not indignant; she was not flustered or agitated, as might have been a susceptible, coquettish girl; she was only astonished and annoyed.

"W'at you doin', Mr. 'Polyte?" she cried, struggling. "Let me 'lone, I say! Let me go!"

"I love you, I love you, I love you!" he stammered helplessly over and over in her face.

"You mus' los' yo' head," she told him, red from the effort of the struggle, when he released her.

"You right, Azélie; I b'lieve I los' my head," and he climbed up the bank of the bayou as fast as he could.

After that his behavior was shameful, and he knew it, and he did not care. He invented pretexts that would enable him to touch her hand with his. He wanted to kiss her again, and told her she might come into the store as she used to do. There was no need for her to unhook a window now; he gave her whatever she asked for, charging it always to his own account on the books. She permitted his caresses without returning them, and yet that was all he seemed to live for now. He gave her a little gold ring.

He was looking eagerly forward to the close of the season, when Arsène would go back to Little River. He had arranged to ask Azélie to marry him. He would keep her with him when the others went away. He longed to rescue her from what he felt to be the demoralizing influences of her family and her surroundings. 'Polyte believed he would be able to awaken Azélie to finer, better impulses when he should have her apart to himself.

But when the time came to propose it, Azélie looked at him in amazement. "*Ah, b'en*, no. I ain't goin' to stay yere wid you, Mr. 'Polyte; I'm goin' yonda on Li'le River wid my popa."

This resolve frightened him, but he pretended not to believe it.

"You jokin', Azélie; you mus' care a li'le about me. It looked to me all along like you cared some about me."

"An' my popa, *donc? Ah, b'en*, no."

"You don' rememba how lonesome it is on Li'le River, Azélie," he pleaded. "W'enever I think 'bout Li'le River it always make me sad—like I think about a graveyard. To me it's like a person mus' die, one way or otha, w'en they go on Li'le River. Oh, I hate it! Stay with me, Azélie; don' go 'way f'om me."

She said little, one way or the other, after that, when she had fully understood his wishes, and her reserve led him to believe, since he hoped it, that he had prevailed with her, and that she had determined to stay with him and be his wife.

It was a cool, crisp morning in December that they went away. In a ramshackle wagon, drawn by an ill-mated team, Arsène Pauché and his family left Mr. Mathurin's plantation for their old familiar haunts on Little River. The grandmother, looking like a witch, with a black shawl tied over her head, sat upon a roll of bedding in the bottom of the wagon. Sauterelle's bead-like eyes glittered with mischief as he peeped over the side. Azélie, with the pink sunbonnet completely hiding her round young face, sat beside her father, who drove.

'Polyte caught one glimpse of the group as they passed in the road. Turning, he hurried into his room, and locked himself in.

It soon became evident that 'Polyte's services were going to count for little. He himself was the first to realize this. One day he approached the planter, and said: "Mr. Mathurin, befo' we start anotha year togetha, I betta tell you I'm goin' to quit." 'Polyte stood upon the steps, and leaned back against the railing. The planter was a little above on the gallery.

"W'at in the name o' sense are you talking about, 'Polyte!" he exclaimed in astonishment.

"It's jus' that; I'm boun' to quit."

"You had a better offer?"

"No; I ain't had no offa."

"Then explain yo'se'f, my frien'—explain yo'se'f," requested Mr. Mathurin, with something of offended dignity. "If you leave me, w'ere are you going?"

'Polyte was beating his leg with his limp felt hat. "I reckon I jus' as well go yonda on Li'le River—w'ere Azélie," he said.

A LADY OF BAYOU ST. JOHN

The days and the nights were very lonely for Madame Delisle. Gustave, her husband, was away yonder in Virginia somewhere with Beauregard,* and she was here in the old house on Bayou St. John,* alone with her slaves.

Madame was very beautiful. So beautiful that she found much diversion in sitting for hours before the mirror, contemplating her own loveliness; admiring the brilliancy of her golden hair, the sweet languor of her blue eyes, the graceful contours of her figure and the peach-like bloom of her flesh. She was very young. So young that she romped with the dogs, teased the parrot, and could not fall asleep at night unless old black Manna-Lulu* sat beside her bed and told her stories.

In short, she was a child, not able to realize the significance of the tragedy whose unfolding kept the civilized world in suspense. It was only the immediate effect of the awful drama that moved her: the gloom that, spreading on all sides, penetrated her own existence and deprived it of joyousness.

Sépincourt found her looking very lonely* and disconsolate one day when he stopped to talk with her. She was pale, and her blue eyes were dim with unwept tears. He was a Frenchman who lived near by. He shrugged his shoulders over this strife between brothers, this quarrel which was none of his;* and he resented it chiefly upon the ground that it made life uncomfortable; yet he was young enough to have had quicker and hotter blood in his veins.

When he left Madame Delisle that day, her eyes were no longer dim, and a something of the dreariness that weighted her had been lifted away. That mysterious, that treacherous bond called sympathy had revealed them to each other.

He came to her very often that summer, clad always in cool white duck, with a flower in his buttonhole. His pleasant brown eyes sought hers with warm, friendly glances that comforted her as a caress might comfort a disconsolate child. She took to watching for his slim figure, a little bent, walking lazily up the avenue between the double line of magnolias.

They would sit sometimes during whole afternoons in the

vine-sheltered corner of the gallery; sipping the black coffee that Manna-Lulu brought to them at intervals; and talking, talking incessantly during the first days when they were unconsciously unfolding themselves to each other. Then a time came—it came very quickly—when they seemed to have nothing more to say to one another.

He brought her news of the war; and they talked about it listlessly, between long intervals of silence of which neither took account. An occasional letter came by roundabout ways from Gustave—guarded and saddening in its tone. They would read it and sigh over it together.

Once they stood before his portrait that hung in the drawing-room and that looked out at them with kind, indulgent eyes. Madame wiped the picture with her gossamer handkerchief and impulsively pressed a tender kiss upon the painted canvas. For months past the living image of her husband had been receding further and further into a mist which she could penetrate with no faculty or power that she possessed.

One day at sunset, when she and Sépincourt stood silently side by side, looking across the marais, aflame with the western light, he said to her: "M'amie, let us go away from this country that is so triste. Let us go to Paris, you and me."

She thought that he was jesting and she laughed nervously. "Yes, Paris would surely be gayer than Bayou St. John," she answered. But he was not jesting. She saw it at once in the glance that penetrated her own; in the quiver of his sensitive lip and the quick beating of a swollen vein in his brown throat.

"Paris, or anywhere—with you—ah, bon Dieu!" he whispered, seizing her hands. But she withdrew from him, frightened, and hurried away into the house, leaving him alone.

That night, for the first time, Madame did not want to hear Manna-Lulu's stories, and she blew out the wax candle that till now had burned nightly in her sleeping-room, under its tall, crystal globe. She had suddenly become a woman capable of love or sacrifice. She would not hear Manna-Lulu's stories. She wanted to be alone, to tremble and to weep.

In the morning her eyes were dry, but she would not see Sépincourt when he came. Then he wrote her a letter.

"I have offended you and I would rather die!" it read. "Do not banish me from your presence that is life to me. Let me lie at your feet, if only for a moment, in which to hear you say that you forgive me."

Men have written just such letters before, but Madame did not know it. To her it was a voice from the unknown, like music, awaking in her a delicious tumult that seized and held possession of her whole being.

When they met he had but to look into her face to know that he need not lie at her feet craving forgiveness. She was waiting for him beneath the spreading branches of a live oak that guarded the gate of her home like a sentinel.

For a brief moment he held her hands, which trembled. Then he folded her in his arms and kissed her many times. "You will go with me, m'amie? I love you—oh, I love you! Will you not go with me, m'amie?"

"Anywhere, anywhere," she told him in a fainting voice that he could scarcely hear.

But she did not go with him. Chance willed it otherwise. That night a courier brought her a message from Beauregard, telling her that Gustave, her husband, was dead.

When the new year was still young Sépincourt decided that, all things considered, he might, without any appearance of indecent haste, speak again of his love to Madame Delisle. That love was quite as acute as ever; perhaps a little sharper, from the long period of silence and waiting to which he had subjected it. He found her, as he had expected, clad in deepest mourning. She greeted him precisely as she had welcomed the curé when the kind old priest had brought to her the consolations of religion—clasping his two hands warmly, and calling him "chèr ami." Her whole attitude and bearing brought to Sépincourt the poignant, the bewildering conviction that he held no place in her thoughts.

They sat in the drawing-room before the portrait of Gustave,* which was draped with his scarf. Above the picture hung his sword, and beneath it was an embankment of flowers. Sépincourt felt an almost irresistible impulse to bend his knee before this altar upon which he saw foreshadowed the immolation of his hopes.

There was a soft air blowing gently over the marais. It came to them through the open window, laden with a hundred subtle sounds and scents of the springtime. It seemed to remind Madame of something far, far away, for she gazed dreamily out into the blue firmament. It fretted Sépincourt with impulses to speech and action which he found it impossible to control.

"You must know what has brought me," he began impulsively, drawing his chair nearer to hers. "Through all these months I have never ceased to love you and to long for you. Night and day the sound of your dear voice has been with me; your eyes——"

She held out her hand deprecatingly. He took it and held it. She let it lie unresponsive in his.

"You cannot have forgotten that you loved me not long ago," he went on eagerly, "that you were ready to follow me anywhere— anywhere; do you remember? I have come now to ask you to fulfil that promise; to ask you to be my wife, my companion, the dear treasure of my life."

She heard his warm and pleading tones as though listening to a strange language, imperfectly understood.

She withdrew her hand from his, and leaned her brow thoughtfully upon it.

"Can you not feel—can you not understand, mon ami," she said calmly, "that now, such a thing—such a thought, is impossible to me?"

"Impossible?"

"Yes, impossible. Can you not see that now my heart, my soul, my thought—my very life must belong to another? It could not be different."

"Would you have me believe that you can wed your young existence to the dead?" he exclaimed with something like horror. Her glance was sunk deep in the embankment of flowers before her.

"My husband has never been so living to me as he is now," she replied with a faint smile of commiseration for Sépincourt's fatuity. "Every object that surrounds me speaks to me of him. I look yonder across the marais, and I see him coming toward me, tired and toil-stained from the hunt. I see him again sitting in this chair or in that one. I hear his familiar voice—his footsteps upon the galleries. We walk once more together beneath the magnolias; and at night in dreams I feel that he is there, there, near me. How could it be different! Ah! I have memories, memories to crowd and fill my life, if I live a hundred years!"

Sépincourt was wondering why she did not take the sword down from her altar and thrust it through his body here and there. The effect would have been infinitely more agreeable than her words, penetrating his soul like fire. He arose confused, enraged with pain.

"Then, Madame," he stammered, "there is nothing left for me but to take my leave. I bid you adieu."

"Do not be offended, mon ami," she said kindly, holding out her hand. "You are going to Paris, I suppose?"

"What does it matter," he exclaimed desperately, "where I go?"

"Oh, I only wanted to wish you bon voyage," she assured him amiably.

Many days after that Sépincourt spent in the fruitless mental effort of trying to comprehend that psychological enigma, a woman's heart.

Madame still lives in Bayou St. John. She is rather an old lady now, a very pretty old lady, against whose long years of widowhood there has never been a breath of reproach. The memory of Gustave still fills and satisfies her day. She has never failed, once a year, to have a solemn high mass said for the repose of his soul.

LA BELLE ZORAÏDE

A Tragedy of the Old Régime.

The summer night was hot and still; not a ripple of air swept over the marais. Yonder, across Bayou St. John* lights twinkled here and there in the darkness, and in the dark sky above a few stars were blinking. A lugger that had come out of the lake was moving with slow, lazy motion down the bayou. A man in the boat was singing a song.

The notes of the song came faintly to the ears of old Manna Loulou—herself as black as the night—who had gone out upon the gallery to open the shutters wide.

Something in the refrain reminded the woman of an old half-forgotten Creole romance, and she began to sing it low to herself while she threw the shutters open:

> "Lisett' to kité la plaine,*
> Mo perdi bonhair à moué;
> Ziés à moué semblé fontaine,
> Dépi mo pa miré toué."

And then this old song—a lover's lament for the loss of his mistress—floating into her memory, brought with it the story she would tell to Madame, who lay in her sumptuous mahogany bed waiting to be fanned and put to sleep to the sound of one of Manna Loulou's stories. The old negress had already bathed her mistress's pretty white feet and kissed them lovingly, one then the other. She had brushed her mistress's beautiful hair, that was as soft and shining as satin, and was the color of Madame's wedding ring. Now, when she re-entered the room, she moved softly toward the bed, and seating herself there began gently to fan Madame Delisle.

Manna Loulou was not always ready with her story, for Madame would hear none but those that were true. But to-night the story was all there in Manna Loulou's head—the story of la belle Zoraïde—and she told it to her mistress in the soft Creole patois, whose music and charm no English words can convey.*

"La belle Zoraïde had eyes that were so dusky, so beautiful, that any man so unfortunate as to gaze too long into their depths was sure to lose his head, and even his heart sometimes. Her soft, smooth skin was the color of café-au-lait.* As for her elegant manners, her svelte and graceful figure, they were the envy of half the ladies who visited her mistress, Madame Delarivière.

"No wonder Zoraïde was as charming and as dainty as the finest lady of la rue Royale:* from a toddling thing she had been brought up at her mistress's side; her fingers had never done rougher work than sewing a fine muslin seam; and she even had her own little black servant to wait upon her. Madame, who was her godmother as well as her mistress, would often say to her:

"'Remember, Zoraïde, when you are ready to marry it must be in a way to do honor to your bringing up. It will be at the Cathedral.* Your wedding gown, your corbeille,* all will be of the best; I shall see to that myself. You know, M'sieur Ambroise is ready whenever you say the word; and his master is willing to do as much for him as I shall do for you. It is a union that will please me in every way.' M'sieur Ambroise was then the body servant of Doctor Langlé. La belle Zoraïde detested the little mulatto, with his shining whiskers like a white man's, and his small eyes, that were cruel and false as a snake's. She would cast down her own mischievous eyes, and say:

"'Ah, Nénaine, I am so happy, so contented here at your side just as I am. I don't want to marry now; next year, perhaps, or the next.' And Madame would smile indulgently and remind Zoraïde that a woman's charms are not everlasting.

"But the truth of the matter was, Zoraïde had seen le beau Mézor dance the Bamboula in Congo Square.* That was a sight to hold one rooted to the ground. Mézor was as straight as a cypress-tree and as proud looking as a king.* His body, bare to the waist, was like a column of ebony and it glistened like oil.

"Poor Zoraïde's heart grew sick in her bosom with love for le beau Mézor from the moment she saw the fierce gleam of his eye, lighted by the inspiring strains of the Bamboula, and beheld the stately movements of his splendid body swaying and quivering through the figures of the dance.

"But when she knew him later and he came near her to speak with her all the fierceness was gone out of his eyes, and she saw only kindness in them and heard only gentleness in his voice; for love had taken possession of him also, and Zoraïde was more distracted than ever. When Mézor was not dancing Bamboula in Congo Square he was hoeing sugar-cane,* barefooted and half naked, in his master's field outside of the city. Doctor Langlé was his master as well as M'sieur Ambroise's.

"One day, when Zoraïde kneeled before her mistress, drawing on Madame's silken stockings, that were of the finest, she said:

"'Nénaine, you have spoken to me often of marrying. Now, at last, I have chosen a husband, but it is not M'sieur Ambroise; it is le beau Mézor that I want and no other.' And Zoraïde hid her face in her hands when she had said that, for she guessed, rightly enough, that her mistress would be very angry. And, indeed, Madame Delarivière was at first speechless with rage. When she finally spoke it was only to gasp out, exasperated:

"'That negro! that negro! Ah, Seigneur, but this is too much!'

"'Am I white, Nénaine?' pleaded Zoraïde.

"'You white! Malheureuse! You deserve to have the lash laid upon you like any other slave; you have proven yourself no better than they.'

"'I am not white,' persisted Zoraïde, respectfully and gently. 'Dr. Langlé gives me his slave to marry, but he would not give me his son. Then, since I am not white, let me have from out of my own race the one that my heart has chosen.'

"However, you may well believe that Madame would not hear to that. Zoraïde was forbidden to speak to Mézor and Mézor was cautioned against seeing Zoraïde again. But you know how the negroes are, Ma'zélle Titite,*" added Manna Loulou, smiling a little sadly. "There is no mistress, no master, no king nor priest who can hinder them from loving when they will. And these two found ways and means.

"When months had passed by, Zoraïde, who had grown unlike herself—sober and preoccupied—said again to her mistress:

"'Nénaine, you would not let me have Mézor for my husband; but I have disobeyed you, I have sinned. Kill me if you wish, Nénaine: forgive me if you will;* I could not help it.'

"This time Madame Delarivière was so actually pained, so wounded at hearing Zoraïde's confession, that there was no place left in her heart for anger. She could utter only confused reproaches. But she was a woman of action rather than of words, and she acted promptly. Her first step was to induce Doctor Langlé to sell Mézor.

Doctor Langlé, who was a widower, had long wanted to marry Madame Delarivière, and he would willingly have walked on all fours at noon through the Place d'Armes if she wanted him to. Naturally he lost no time in disposing of le beau Mézor, who was sold away into Georgia,* or the Carolinas, or one of those distant countries far away, where he would no longer hear his Creole tongue spoken, nor dance Calinda,* nor hold la belle Zoraïde in his arms.

"The poor thing was heartbroken when Mézor was sent away from her, but she took comfort and hope in the thought of her baby that she would soon be able to clasp to her breast.

"La belle Zoraïde's sorrows had now begun in earnest. Not only sorrows but sufferings, and with the anguish of maternity came the shadow of death. But there is no agony that a mother will not forget when she holds her first-born to her heart, and presses her lips upon the baby flesh that is her own, and yet far more precious than her own.*

"So, instinctively, when Zoraïde came out of the awful shadow she gazed questioningly about her and felt with her trembling hands upon either side of her. 'Ou li, mo piti a moné? where is my little one?' she asked imploringly. Madame who was there and the nurse who was there both told her in turn, 'To piti à toné, li mouri' ('Your little one is dead'), which was a wicked falsehood that must have caused the angels in heaven to weep. For the baby was living and well and strong. It had at once been removed from its mother's side, to be sent away to Madame's plantation, far up the coast. Zoraïde could only moan in reply, 'Li mouri, li mouri,' and she turned her face to the wall.

"Madame had hoped, in thus depriving Zoraïde of her child, to have her young waiting-maid again at her side free, happy and beautiful as of old. But there was a more powerful will than Madame's at work—the will of the good God, who had already designed that Zoraïde should grieve with a sorrow that was never more to be lifted in this world. La belle Zoraïde was no more. In her stead was a sad woman who mourned night and day for her baby. 'Li mouri, li mouri,' she would sigh over and over again to those about her and to herself, when others grew weary of her complaint.

"Yet in spite of all, M'sieur Ambroise was still in the notion to marry her. A sad wife or a merry one was all the same to him so long as that wife was Zoraïde. And she seemed to consent, or rather submit, to the approaching marriage as though nothing mattered any longer in this world.

"One day, a black servant entered a little noisily the room in which Zoraïde sat sewing. With a look of strange and vacuous happiness upon her face, Zoraïde arose hastily. 'Hush, hush,' she whispered, lifting a warning finger, 'my little one is asleep; you must not awaken her.'

"Upon the bed was a senseless bundle of rags shaped like an infant in swaddling clothes. Over this dummy the woman had drawn the mosquito bar, and she was sitting contentedly beside it. In short, from that day Zoraïde was demented. Night nor day did she lose sight of the doll that lay in her bed or in her arms.

"And now was Madame stung with sorrow and remorse at seeing this terrible affliction that had befallen her dear Zoraïde. Consulting with Doctor Langlé, they decided to bring back to the mother the real baby of flesh and blood that was now toddling about, and kicking its heels in the dust yonder upon the plantation.

"It was Madame herself who led the pretty, tiny little griffe girl to her mother. Zoraïde was sitting upon a stone bench in the courtyard, listening to the soft splashing of the fountain, and watching the fitful shadows of the palm leaves upon the broad, white flagging.

" 'Here,' said Madame, approaching, 'here, my poor dear Zoraïde, is your own little child. Keep her; she is yours. No one will ever take her from you again.'

"Zoraïde looked with sullen suspicion upon her mistress and the child before her. Reaching out a hand she thrust the little one mistrustfully away from her. With the other hand she clasped the rag bundle fiercely to her breast; for she suspected a plot to deprive her of it.

"Nor could she ever be induced to let her own child approach her; and finally the little one was sent back to the plantation, where she was never to know the love of mother or father.

"And now this is the end of Zoraïde's story. She was never known again as la belle Zoraïde, but ever after as Zoraïde la folle,* whom no one ever wanted to marry—not even M'sieur Ambroise. She lived to be an old woman, whom some people pitied and others laughed at— always clasping her bundle of rags—her 'mo piti.'

"Are you asleep, Ma'zélle Titite?"

"No, I am not asleep; I was thinking. Ah, the poor little one, Man Loulou, the poor little one! better had she died!"

But this is the way Madame Delisle and Manna Loulou really talked to each other:

"Vou pré droumi, Ma'zélle Titite?"

"Non, pa pré droumi; mo yapré zongler. Ah, la pauv' piti, Man Loulou. La pauv' piti! Mieux li mouri!"

TONIE

(AT CHÊNIÈRE CAMINADA)

I

There was no clumsier looking fellow in church that Sunday morning than Antoine Bocaze—the one they called Tonie. But Tonie did not really care if he were clumsy or not. He felt that he could speak intelligibly to no woman save his mother; but since he had no desire to inflame the hearts of any of the island maidens, what difference did it make?

He knew there was no better fisherman on the Chênière Caminada than himself, if his face was too long and bronzed, his limbs too unmanageable and his eyes too earnest—almost too honest.

It was a midsummer day, with a lazy, scorching breeze blowing from the Gulf straight into the church windows. The ribbons on the young girls' hats fluttered like the wings of birds, and the old women clutched the flapping ends of the veils that covered their heads.

A few mosquitoes, floating through the blistering air, with their nipping and humming fretted the people to a certain degree of attention and consequent devotion. The measured tones of the priest at the altar rose and fell like a song: "Credo in unum Deum patrem omnipotentem"* he chanted. And then the people all looked at one another, suddenly electrified.

Some one was playing upon the organ whose notes no one on the whole island was able to awaken; whose tones had not been heard during the many months since a passing stranger had one day listlessly dragged his fingers across its idle keys. A long, sweet strain of music floated down from the loft and filled the church.

It seemed to most of them—it seemed to Tonie standing there beside his old mother—that some heavenly being must have descended upon the Church of Our Lady of Lourdes and chosen this celestial way of communicating with its people.

But it was no creature from a different sphere; it was only a young lady from Grand Isle. A rather pretty young person with blue eyes and nut-brown hair, who wore a dotted lawn of fine texture and fashionable make, and a white Leghorn sailor-hat.

Tonie saw her standing outside of the church after mass, receiving the priest's voluble praises and thanks for her graceful service.

She had come over to mass from Grand Isle in Baptiste Beaudelet's lugger, with a couple of young men, and two ladies who kept a pension over there. Tonie knew these two ladies—Mme. Lebrun and her daughter*—but he did not attempt to speak with them; he would not have known what to say. He stood aside gazing at the group, as others were doing, his serious eyes fixed earnestly upon the fair organist.

Tonie was late at dinner that day. His mother must have waited an hour for him, sitting patiently with her coarse hands folded in her lap, in that little still room with its "brick-painted" floor, its gaping chimney and homely furnishings.

He told her that he had been walking—walking he hardly knew where, and he did not know why. He must have tramped from one end of the island to the other; but he brought her no bit of news or gossip. He did not know if the Cotures had stopped for dinner with the Avendettes; whether old Pierre François was worse, or better, or dead: or if lame Philibert was drinking again this morning. He knew nothing; yet he had crossed the village, and passed every one of its small houses that stood close together in a long jagged line facing the sea; they were gray and battered by time and the rude buffets of the salt sea winds.

He knew nothing though the Cotures had all bade him "good day" as they filed into Avendette's, where a steaming plate of crab gumbo was waiting for each. He had heard some woman screaming, and others saying it was because old Pierre François had just passed away. But he did not remember this, nor did he recall the fact that lame Philibert had staggered against him when he stood absently watching a "fiddler"* sidling across the sun-baked sand. He could tell his mother nothing of all this; but he said he had noticed that the wind was fair and must have driven Baptiste's boat, like a flying bird, across the water.

Well, that was something to talk about, and old Ma'me Antoine, who was fat, leaned comfortably upon the table after she had helped Tonie to his courtbouillon, and remarked that she found Madame Lebrun was getting old. Tonie thought that perhaps she was aging and her hair was getting whiter. He seemed glad to talk about her, and reminded his mother of Madame Lebrun's kindness and sympathy at the time his father and brothers had perished. It was when he was a little fellow, ten years before, during a squall in Barataria Bay.

Ma'me Antoine declared that she could never forget that sympathy, if she lived till Judgment Day; but all the same she was sorry to see that Mamzelle Lebrun was also not so young nor fresh as she used to be. Her chances of getting a husband were surely lessening every year; especially with the young girls around her, budding each spring like flowers to be plucked. The one who had played upon the organ was Mademoiselle Duvigné, Claire Duvigné, a great belle, the daughter of the famous lawyer who lived in New Orleans, on Rampart street. Ma'me Antoine had found that out during the ten minutes she and others had stopped after mass to gossip with the priest.

"Claire Duvigné," muttered Tonie, not even making a pretense to taste his courtbouillon, but picking little bits from the half loaf of crusty brown bread that lay beside his plate. "Claire Duvigné; that is a pretty name. Don't you think so, mother? I can't think of anyone on the Chênière who has so pretty a one, nor at Grand Isle, either, for that matter. And you say she lives on Rampart street?"

It appeared to him a matter of great importance that he should have his mother repeat all that the priest had told her.

II

Early the following morning Tonie went out in search of lame Philibert, than whom there was no cleverer workman on the island when he could be caught sober.

Tonie had tried to work on his big lugger that lay bottom upward under the shed, but it had seemed impossible. His mind, his hands, his tools refused to do their office, and in sudden desperation he desisted. He found Philibert and set him to work in his own place under the shed. Then he got into his small boat with the red lateen sail and went over to Grand Isle.

There was no one at hand to warn Tonie that he was acting the part of a fool. He had, singularly, never felt those premonitory symptoms of love which afflict the greater portion of mankind before they

reach the age which he had attained. He did not at first recognize
this powerful impulse that had, without warning, possessed itself of
his entire being. He obeyed it without a struggle, as naturally as he
would have obeyed the dictates of hunger and thirst.

Tonie left his boat at the wharf and proceeded at once to Mme.
Lebrun's pension, which consisted of a group of plain, stoutly built
cottages that stood in mid island, about half a mile from the sea.

The day was bright and beautiful with soft, velvety gusts of wind
blowing from the water. From a cluster of orange trees a flock of
doves ascended, and Tonie stopped to listen to the beating of their
wings and follow their flight toward the water oaks whither he himself was moving.

He walked with a dragging, uncertain step through the yellow,
fragrant camomile, his thoughts traveling before him. In his mind
was always the vivid picture of the girl as it had stamped itself there
yesterday, connected in some mystical way with that celestial music
which had thrilled him and was vibrating yet in his soul.

But she did not look the same to-day. She was returning from the
beach when Tonie first saw her, leaning upon the arm of one of the
men who had accompanied her yesterday. She was dressed
differently—in a dainty blue cotton gown. Her companion held a big
white sunshade over them both. They had exchanged hats and were
laughing with great abandonment.

Two young men walked behind them and were trying to engage
her attention. She glanced at Tonie, who was leaning against a tree
when the group passed by; but of course she did not know him. She
was speaking English, a language which he hardly understood.*

There were other young people gathered under the water oaks—
girls who were, many of them, more beautiful than Mlle. Duvigné;
but for Tonie they simply did not exist. His whole universe had
suddenly become converted into a glamorous background for the
person of Mlle. Duvigné, and the shadowy figures of men who were
about her.

Tonie went to Mme. Lebrun and told her he would bring
her oranges next day from the Chênière. She was well pleased, and
commissioned him to bring her other things from the stores there,
which she could not procure at Grand Isle. She did not question his
presence, knowing that these summer days were idle ones for the
Chênière fishermen. Nor did she seem surprised when he told

her that his boat was at the wharf, and would be there every day at her service. She knew his frugal habits, and supposed he wished to hire it, as others did. He intuitively felt that this could be the only way.

And that is how it happened that Tonie spent so little of his time at the Chênière Caminada that summer. Old Ma'me Antoine grumbled enough about it. She herself had been twice in her life to Grand Isle and once to Grand Terre, and each time had been more than glad to get back to the Chênière. And why Tonie should want to spend his days, and even his nights, away from home, was a thing she could not comprehend, especially as he would have to be away the whole winter: and meantime there was much work to be done at his own hearthside and in the company of his own mother. She did not know that Tonie had much, much more to do at Grand Isle than at the Chênière Caminada.

He had to see how Claire Duvigné sat upon the gallery in the big rocking chair that she kept in motion by the impetus of her slender, slippered foot; turning her head this way and that way to speak to the men who were always near her. He had to follow her lithe motions at tennis or croquet, that she often played with the children under the trees. Some days he wanted to see how she spread her bare, white arms, and walked out to meet the foam-crested waves. Even here there were men with her. And then at night, standing alone like a still shadow under the stars, did he not have to listen to her voice when she talked and laughed and sang? Did he not have to follow her slim figure whirling through the dance, in the arms of men who must have loved her and wanted her as he did. He did not dream that they could help it more than he could help it. But the days when she stepped into his boat, the one with the red lateen sail, and sat for hours within a few feet of him, were days that he would have given up for nothing else that he could think of.

III

There were always others in her company at such times, young people with jests and laughter on their lips. Only once she was alone.

She had foolishly brought a book with her, thinking she would want to read. But with the breath of the sea stinging her she could not read a line. She looked precisely as she had looked the day he first saw her, standing outside of the church at Chênière Caminada.

She laid the book down in her lap, and let her soft eyes sweep dreamily along the line of the horizon where the sky and water met. Then she looked straight at Tonie, and for the first time spoke directly to him.

She called him Tonie, as she had heard others do, and questioned him about his boats and his work. He trembled, and answered her vaguely and stupidly. She did not mind, but spoke to him anyhow, satisfied to talk herself when she found that he could not or would not. She spoke French, and talked about the Chênière Caminada, its people and its church. She talked of the day she had played upon the organ there, and complained of the instrument being woefully out of tune.

Tonie was perfectly at home in the familiar task of guiding his boat before the wind that bellied its taut, red sail. He did not seem clumsy and awkward as when he sat in church. The girl noticed that he appeared as strong as an ox.

As she looked at him and surprised one of his shifting glances, a glimmer of the truth began to dawn faintly upon her. She remembered how she had encountered him daily in her path, with his earnest, devouring eyes always seeking her out. She recalled—but there was no need to recall anything. There are women whose perception of passion is very keen; they are the women who most inspire it.

A feeling of complacency took possession of her with this conviction. There was some softness and sympathy mingled with it. She would have liked to lean over and pat his big, brown hand, and tell him she felt sorry and would have helped it if she could. With this belief he ceased to be an object of complete indifference in her eyes. She had thought, awhile before, of having him turn about and take her back home. But now it was really piquant to pose for an hour longer before a man—even a rough fisherman—to whom she felt herself to be an object of silent and consuming devotion. She could think of nothing more interesting to do on shore.

She was incapable of conceiving the full force and extent of his infatuation. She did not dream that under the rude, calm exterior before her a man's heart was beating clamorously, and his reason yielding to the savage instinct of his blood.

"I hear the Angelus ringing at Chênière, Tonie," she said. "I didn't know it was so late; let us go back to the island." There had been a long silence which her musical voice interrupted.

Tonie could now faintly hear the Angelus bell* himself. A vision of the church came with it, the odor of incense and the sound of the organ. The girl before him was again that celestial being whom Our Lady of Lourdes* had once offered to his immortal vision.

It was growing dusk when they landed at the pier, and frogs had begun to croak among the reeds in the pools. There were two of Mlle. Duvigné's usual attendants anxiously awaiting her return. But she chose to let Tonie assist her out of the boat. The touch of her hand fired his blood again.

She said to him very low and half-laughing: "I have no money tonight, Tonie; take this instead," pressing into his palm a delicate silver chain, which she had worn twined about her bare wrist. It was purely a spirit of coquetry that prompted the action, and a touch of the sentimentality which most women possess. She had read in some romance of a young girl doing something like that.

As she walked away between her two attendants she fancied Tonie pressing the chain to his lips. But he was standing quite still, and held it buried in his tightly-closed hand; wanting to hold as long as he might the warmth of the body that still penetrated the bauble when she thrust it into his hand.

He watched her retreating figure like a blotch against the fading sky. He was stirred by a terrible, an overmastering regret, that he had not clasped her in his arms when they were out there alone, and sprung with her into the sea. It was what he had vaguely meant to do when the sound of the Angelus had weakened and palsied his resolution. Now she was going from him, fading away into the mist with those figures on either side of her, leaving him alone. He resolved within himself that if ever again she were out there on the sea at his mercy, she would have to perish in his arms. He would go far, far out, where the sound of no bell could reach him. There was some comfort for him in the thought.

But as it happened, Mlle. Duvigné never went out alone in the boat with Tonie again.

IV

It was one morning in January. Tonie had been collecting a bill from one of the fishmongers at the French Market, in New Orleans, and had turned his steps toward St. Philip street. The day was chilly; a keen wind was blowing. Tonie mechanically buttoned his rough, warm coat and crossed over into the sun.

There was perhaps not a more wretched-hearted being in the whole district, that morning, than he. For months the woman he so hopelessly loved had been lost to his sight. But all the more she dwelt in his thoughts, preying upon his mental and bodily forces until his unhappy condition became apparent to all who knew him. Before leaving his home for the winter fishing grounds he had opened his whole heart to his mother, and told her of the trouble that was killing him. She hardly expected that he would ever come back to her when he went away. She feared that he would not, for he had spoken wildly of the rest and peace that he craved, and that could only come to him with death.

That morning when Tonie had crossed St. Philip street he found himself accosted by Madame Lebrun and her daughter. He had not noticed them approaching, and, moreover, their figures in winter garb appeared unfamiliar to him. He had never seen them elsewhere than at Grand Isle and the Chênière during the summer. They were glad to meet him, and shook his hand cordially. He stood as usual a little helplessly before them. A pulse in his throat was beating and almost choking him, so poignant were the recollections which their presence stirred up.

They were staying in the city this winter, they told him. Mademoiselle wanted to hear the opera as often as she could, and the island was really too dreary with everyone gone. She had left her son there to keep order and superintend repairs, and so on.

"You are both well," stammered Tonie.

"In perfect health, my dear Tonie," madame replied. She was wondering at his haggard eyes and thin, gaunt cheeks; but possessed too much tact to mention them.

"And—and the young lady who used to go sailing—is she well?" he inquired lamely.

"You mean Mlle. Favette? She was married just after leaving Grand Isle."

"No; I mean the one you called Claire—Mamzelle Duvigné—is she well?"

Mother and daughter exclaimed together: "Impossible! You haven't heard? Why, Tonie," madame continued, "Mlle. Duvigné died three weeks ago. But that was something sad, I tell you! . . . Her family heartbroken. . . . Simply from a cold caught by standing in thin slippers, waiting for her carriage after the opera. . . . What a warning!"

Madame and her daughter were talking at once. Tonie kept looking from one to the other. He did not know what they were saying, after madame had told him, "Elle est morte."

As in a dream he finally heard that they said good-by to him, and sent their love to his mother.

He stood still in the middle of the banquette when they had left him, watching them go toward the market. He could not stir. Something had happened to him—he did not know what. He wondered if the news was killing him.

Some women passed by, laughing coarsely. He noticed how they laughed and tossed their heads. A mockingbird was singing in a cage which hung from a window above his head. He had not heard it before.

Just beneath the window was the entrance to a barroom. Tonie turned and plunged through its swinging doors. He asked the bartender for whisky. The man thought he was already drunk, but pushed the bottle toward him nevertheless. Tonie poured a great quantity of the fiery liquor into a glass and swallowed it at a draught. The rest of the day he spent among the fishermen and Barataria oystermen; and that night he slept soundly and peacefully until morning.

He did not know why it was so; he could not understand. But from that day he felt that he began to live again, to be once more a part of the moving world about him. He would ask himself over and over again why it was so, and stay bewildered before this truth that he could not answer or explain, and which he began to accept as a holy mystery.

One day in early spring Tonie sat with his mother upon a piece of drift-wood close to the sea.

He had returned that day to the Chênière Caminada. At first she thought he was like his former self again, for all his old strength and courage had returned. But she found that there was a new brightness in his face which had not been there before. It made her think of the Holy Ghost descending and bringing some kind of light to a man.

She knew that Mademoiselle Duvigné was dead, and all along had feared that this knowledge would be the death of Tonie. When she saw him come back to her like a new being, at once she dreaded that he did not know. All day the doubt had been fretting her, and she could bear the uncertainty no longer.

"You know, Tonie—that young lady whom you cared for—well, some one read it to me in the papers—she died last winter." She had tried to speak as cautiously as she could.

"Yes, I know she is dead. I am glad."

It was the first time he had said this in words, and it made his heart beat quicker.

Ma'me Antoine shuddered and drew aside from him. To her it was somehow like murder to say such a thing.

"What do you mean? Why are you glad?" she demanded, indignantly.

Tonie was sitting with his elbows on his knees. He wanted to answer his mother, but it would take time; he would have to think. He looked out across the water that glistened gem-like with the sun upon it, but there was nothing there to open his thought. He looked down into his open palm and began to pick at the callous flesh that was hard as a horse's hoof. Whilst he did this his ideas began to gather and take form.

"You see, while she lived I could never hope for anything," he began, slowly feeling his way. "Despair was the only thing for me. There were always men about her. She walked and sang and danced with them. I knew it all the time, even when I didn't see her. But I saw her often enough. I knew that some day one of them would please her and she would give herself to him—she would marry him. That thought haunted me like an evil spirit."

Tonie passed his hand across his forehead as if to sweep away anything of the horror that might have remained there.

"It kept me awake at night," he went on. "But that was not so bad; the worst torture was to sleep, for then I would dream that it was all true.

"Oh, I could see her married to one of them—his wife—coming

year after year to Grand Isle and bringing her little children with her! I can't tell you all that I saw—all that was driving me mad. But now"—and Tonie clasped his hands together and smiled as he looked again across the water—"She is where she belongs; there is no difference up there; the curé has often told us there is no difference between men. It is with the soul that we approach each other there. Then she will know who has loved her best. That is why I am so contented. Who knows what may happen up there?"

Ma'me Antoine could not answer. She only took her son's big, rough hand and pressed it against her.

"And now, ma mère," he exclaimed, cheerfully, rising, "I shall go light the fire for your bread; it is a long time since I have done anything for you," and he stooped and pressed a warm kiss on her withered old cheek.

With misty eyes she watched him walk away in the direction of the big brick oven that stood open-mouthed under the lemon trees.

A GENTLEMAN OF BAYOU TÊCHE*

It was no wonder Mr. Sublet, who was staying at the Hallet plantation, wanted to make a picture of Evariste. The 'Cadian was rather a picturesque subject in his way, and a tempting one to an artist looking for bits of "local color" along the Têche.*

Mr. Sublet had seen the man on the back gallery just as he came out of the swamp, trying to sell a wild turkey to the housekeeper. He spoke to him at once, and in the course of conversation engaged him to return to the house the following morning and have his picture drawn. He handed Evariste a couple of silver dollars to show that his intentions were fair, and that he expected the 'Cadian to keep faith with him.

"He tell' me he want' put my picture in one fine '*Mag*'zine,'"* said Evariste to his daughter, Martinette, when the two were talking the matter over in the afternoon. "W'at fo' you reckon he want' do dat?" They sat within the low, homely cabin of two rooms, that was not quite so comfortable as Mr. Hallet's negro quarters.

Martinette pursed her red lips that had little sensitive curves to them, and her black eyes took on a reflective expression.

"Mebbe he yeard 'bout that big fish w'at you ketch las' winta in Carancro* lake. You know it was all wrote about in the 'Suga Bowl.'" Her father set aside the suggestion with a deprecatory wave of the hand.

"Well, anyway, you got to fix yo'se'f up," declared Martinette, dismissing further speculation; "put on yo' otha pant'loon an' yo' good coat; an' you betta ax Mr. Léonce to cut yo' hair, an' yo' w'sker' a li'le bit."

"It 's w'at I say," chimed in Evariste. "I tell dat gent'man I 'm goin' make myse'f fine. He say', 'No, no,' like he ent please'. He want' me like I come out de swamp. So much betta if my pant'loon' an' coat is tore, he say, an' color' like de mud." They could not understand these eccentric wishes on the part of the strange gentleman, and made no effort to do so.

An hour later Martinette, who was quite puffed up over the affair, trotted across to Aunt Dicey's cabin* to communicate the news to her. The negress was ironing; her irons stood in a long row before the fire of logs that burned on the hearth. Martinette seated herself in the chimney corner and held her feet up to the blaze; it was damp and a little chilly out of doors. The girl's shoes were considerably worn and her garments were a little too thin and scant for the winter season. Her father had given her the two dollars he had received from the artist, and Martinette was on her way to the store to invest them as judiciously as she knew how.

"You know, Aunt Dicey," she began a little complacently after listening awhile to Aunt Dicey's unqualified abuse of her own son, Wilkins, who was dining-room boy at Mr. Hallet's, "you know that stranger gentleman up to Mr. Hallet's? he want' to make my popa's picture; an' he say' he goin' put it in one fine *Mag*'zine yonda."

Aunt Dicey spat upon her iron to test its heat. Then she began to snicker. She kept on laughing inwardly, making her whole fat body shake, and saying nothing.

"W'at you laughin' 'bout, Aunt Dice?" inquired Martinette mistrustfully.

"I is n' laughin', chile!"

"Yas, you' laughin'."

"Oh, don't pay no 'tention to me. I jis studyin' how simple you an' yo' pa is. You is bof de simplest somebody I eva come 'crost."

"You got to say plumb out w'at you mean, Aunt Dice," insisted the girl doggedly, suspicious and alert now.

"Well, dat w'y I say you is simple," proclaimed the woman, slamming down her iron on an inverted, battered pie pan, "jis like you says, dey gwine put yo' pa's picture yonda in de picture paper. An' you know w'at readin' dey gwine sot down on'neaf dat picture?" Martinette was intensely attentive. "Dey gwine sot down on'neaf: 'Dis heah is one dem low-down 'Cajuns o' Bayeh Têche!'"*

The blood flowed from Martinette's face, leaving it deathly pale; in another instant it came beating back in a quick flood, and her eyes smarted with pain as if the tears that filled them had been fiery hot.

"I knows dem kine o' folks," continued Aunt Dicey, resuming her interrupted ironing. "Dat stranger he got a li'le boy w'at ain't none too big to spank. Dat li'le imp he come a hoppin' in heah yistiddy wid a kine o' box on'neaf his arm. He say' 'Good mo'nin', madam. Will you be so kine an' stan' jis like you is dah at yo' i'onin', an' lef me take yo' picture?' I 'lowed I gwine make a picture outen him wid dis heah flati'on, ef he don' cl'ar hisse'f quick. An' he say he baig my pardon fo' his intrudement. All dat kine o' talk to a ole nigga 'oman! Dat plainly sho' he don' know his place."

"W'at you want 'im to say, Aunt Dice?" asked Martinette, with an effort to conceal her distress.

"I wants 'im to come in heah an' say: 'Howdy, Aunt Dicey! will you be so kine and go put on yo' noo calker dress an' yo' bonnit w'at you w'ars to meetin', an' stan' 'side f'om dat i'onin'-boa'd w'ilse I gwine take yo photygraph.' Dat de way fo' a boy to talk w'at had good raisin'."

Martinette had arisen, and began to take slow leave of the woman. She turned at the cabin door to observe tentatively: "I reckon it 's Wilkins tells you how the folks they talk, yonda up to Mr. Hallet's."

She did not go to the store as she had intended, but walked with a dragging step back to her home. The silver dollars clicked in her pocket as she walked. She felt like flinging them across the field; they seemed to her somehow the price of shame.*

The sun had sunk, and twilight was settling like a silver beam upon the bayou and enveloping the fields in a gray mist. Evariste, slim and slouchy, was waiting for his daughter in the cabin door. He had lighted a fire of sticks and branches, and placed the kettle before it to boil. He met the girl with his slow, serious, questioning eyes, astonished to see her empty-handed.

"How come you did n' bring nuttin' f'om de sto', Martinette?"

She entered and flung her gingham sunbonnet upon a chair. "No, I did n' go yonda;" and with sudden exasperation: "You got to go take back that money; you mus' n' git no picture took."

"But, Martinette," her father mildly interposed, "I promise 'im; an' he 's goin' give me some mo' money w'en he finish."

"If he give you a ba'el o' money, you mus' n' git no picture took. You know w'at he want to put un'neath that picture, fo' ev'body to read?" She could not tell him the whole hideous truth as she had heard it distorted from Aunt Dicey's lips; she would not hurt him that much. "He 's goin' to write: 'This is one *'Cajun* o' the Bayou Têche.'" Evariste winced.*

"How you know?" he asked.

"I yeard so. I know it 's true."

The water in the kettle was boiling. He went and poured a small quantity upon the coffee which he had set there to drip. Then he said to her: "I reckon you jus' as well go care dat two dolla' back, tomo' mo'nin'; me, I'll go yonda ketch a mess o' fish in Carancro lake."

Mr. Hallet and a few masculine companions were assembled at a rather late breakfast the following morning. The dining-room was a big, bare one, enlivened by a cheerful fire of logs that blazed in the wide chimney on massive andirons. There were guns, fishing tackle, and other implements of sport lying about. A couple of fine dogs strayed unceremoniously in and out behind Wilkins, the negro boy who waited upon the table. The chair beside Mr. Sublet, usually occupied by his little son, was vacant, as the child had gone for an early morning outing and had not yet returned.

When breakfast was about half over, Mr. Hallet noticed Martinette standing outside upon the gallery. The dining-room door had stood open more than half the time.

"Is n't that Martinette out there, Wilkins?" inquired the jovial-faced young planter.

"Dat's who, suh," returned Wilkins. "She ben standin' dah sence mos' sun-up; look like she studyin' to take root to de gall'ry."

"What in the name of goodness does she want? Ask her what she wants. Tell her to come in to the fire."

Martinette walked into the room with much hesitancy. Her small, brown face could hardly be seen in the depths of the gingham sun-bonnet. Her blue cottonade skirt scarcely reached the thin ankles that it should have covered.

"Bonjou'," she murmured, with a little comprehensive nod that took in the entire company. Her eyes searched the table for the "stranger gentleman," and she knew him at once, because his hair was parted in the middle and he wore a pointed beard. She went and laid the two silver dollars beside his plate and motioned to retire without a word of explanation.

"Hold on, Martinette!" called out the planter, "what 's all this pantomime business? Speak out, little one."

"My popa don't want any picture took," she offered, a little timorously. On her way to the door she had looked back to say this. In that fleeting glance she detected a smile of intelligence pass from one to the other of the group. She turned quickly, facing them all, and spoke out, excitement making her voice bold and shrill: "My popa ent one low-down 'Cajun. He ent goin' to stan' to have that kine o' writin' put down un'neath his picture!"

She almost ran from the room, half blinded by the emotion that had helped her to make so daring a speech.

Descending the gallery steps she ran full against her father who was ascending, bearing in his arms the little boy, Archie Sublet. The child was most grotesquely attired in garments far too large for his diminutive person—the rough jeans clothing of some negro boy. Evariste himself had evidently been taking a bath without the preliminary ceremony of removing his clothes, that were now half dried upon his person by the wind and sun.

"Yere you' li'le boy," he announced, stumbling into the room. "You ought not lef dat li'le chile go by hisse'f *comme ça* in de pirogue." Mr. Sublet darted from his chair; the others following suit almost as hastily. In an instant, quivering with apprehension, he had his little son in his arms. The child was quite unharmed, only somewhat pale and nervous, as the consequence of a recent very serious ducking.

Evariste related in his uncertain, broken English how he had been fishing for an hour or more in Carancro lake, when he noticed the boy paddling over the deep, black water in a shell-like pirogue. Nearing a clump of cypress-trees that rose from the lake, the pirogue became entangled in the heavy moss that hung from the tree limbs and trailed upon the water. The next thing he knew, the boat had overturned, he heard the child scream, and saw him disappear beneath the still, black surface of the lake.

"W'en I done swim to de sho' wid 'im," continued Evariste, "I hurry yonda to Jake Baptiste's cabin, an' we rub 'im an' warm 'im up, an' dress 'im up dry like you see. He all right now, M'sieur; but you mus'n lef 'im go no mo' by hisse'f in one pirogue."

Martinette had followed into the room behind her father. She was feeling and tapping his wet garments solicitously, and begging him in French to come home. Mr. Hallet at once ordered hot coffee and a warm breakfast for the two; and they sat down at the corner of the table, making no manner of objection in their perfect simplicity. It was with visible reluctance and ill-disguised contempt that Wilkins served them.*

When Mr. Sublet had arranged his son comfortably, with tender care, upon the sofa, and had satisfied himself that the child was quite uninjured, he attempted to find words with which to thank Evariste for this service which no treasure of words or gold could pay for. These warm and heartfelt expressions seemed to Evariste to exaggerate the importance of his action, and they intimidated him. He attempted shyly to hide his face as well as he could in the depths of his bowl of coffee.

"You will let me make your picture now, I hope, Evariste," begged Mr. Sublet, laying his hand upon the 'Cadian's shoulder. "I want to place it among things I hold most dear, and shall call it 'A hero of Bayou Têche.'" This assurance seemed to distress Evariste greatly.

"No, no," he protested, "it 's nuttin' hero' to take a li'le boy out de water. I jus' as easy do dat like I stoop down an' pick up a li'le chile w'at fall down in de road. I ent goin' to 'low dat, me. I don't git no picture took, *va*!"

Mr. Hallet, who now discerned his friend's eagerness in the matter, came to his aid.

"I tell you, Evariste, let Mr. Sublet draw your picture, and you yourself may call it whatever you want. I'm sure he 'll let you."

"Most willingly," agreed the artist.

Evariste glanced up at him with shy and child-like pleasure. "It 's a bargain?" he asked.

"A bargain," affirmed Mr. Sublet.

"Popa," whispered Martinette, "you betta come home an' put on yo' otha pant'loon' an' yo' good coat."

"And now, what shall we call the much talked-of picture?" cheerily inquired the planter, standing with his back to the blaze.

Evariste in a business-like manner began carefully to trace on the tablecloth imaginary characters with an imaginary pen; he could not have written the real characters with a real pen—he did not know how.*

'You will put on'neat' de picture," he said, deliberately, "'Dis is one picture of Mista Evariste Anatole Bonamour, a gent'man of de Bayou Têche.'"

IN SABINE

The sight of a human habitation, even if it was a rude log cabin with a mud chimney at one end, was a very gratifying one to Grégoire.*

He had come out of Natchitoches parish, and had been riding a great part of the day through the big lonesome parish of Sabine. He was not following the regular Texas road, but, led by his erratic fancy, was pushing toward the Sabine River* by circuitous paths through the rolling pine forests.

As he approached the cabin in the clearing, he discerned behind a palisade of pine saplings an old negro man chopping wood.

"Howdy, Uncle," called out the young fellow, reining his horse. The negro looked up in blank amazement at so unexpected an apparition, but he only answered: "How you do, suh," accompanying his speech by a series of polite nods.

"Who lives yere?"

"Hit 's Mas' Bud Aiken w'at live' heah, suh."

"Well, if Mr. Bud Aiken c'n affo'd to hire a man to chop his wood, I reckon he won't grudge me a bite o' suppa an' a couple hours' res' on his gall'ry. W'at you say, ole man?"

"I say dit Mas' Bud Aiken don't hires me to chop 'ood. Ef I don't chop dis heah, his wife got it to do. Dat w'y I chops 'ood, suh. Go right 'long in, suh; you g'ine fine Mas' Bud some'eres roun', ef he ain't drunk an' gone to bed."

Grégoire, glad to stretch his legs, dismounted, and led his horse into the small inclosure which surrounded the cabin. An unkempt, vicious-looking little Texas pony stopped nibbling the stubble there to look maliciously at him and his fine sleek horse, as they passed by. Back of the hut, and running plumb up against the pine wood, was a small, ragged specimen of a cotton-field.

Grégoire was rather undersized, with a square, well-knit figure, upon which his clothes sat well and easily. His corduroy trousers were thrust into the legs of his boots; he wore a blue flannel shirt; his coat was thrown across the saddle. In his keen black eyes had come a puzzled expression, and he tugged thoughtfully at the brown moustache that lightly shaded his upper lip.

He was trying to recall when and under what circumstances he had before heard the name of Bud Aiken. But Bud Aiken himself saved Grégoire the trouble of further speculation on the subject. He appeared suddenly in the small doorway, which his big body quite filled; and then Grégoire remembered. This was the disreputable so-called "Texan" who a year ago had run away with and married Baptiste Choupic's pretty daughter, 'Tite Reine, yonder on Bayou Pierre, in Natchitoches parish.* A vivid picture of the girl as he remembered her appeared to him: her trim rounded figure; her piquant face with its saucy black coquettish eyes; her little exacting, imperious ways that had obtained for her the nickname of 'Tite Reine, little queen. Grégoire had known her at the 'Cadian balls that he sometimes had the hardihood to attend.

These pleasing recollections of 'Tite Reine lent a warmth that might otherwise have been lacking to Grégoire's manner, when he greeted her husband.

"I hope I fine you well, Mr. Aiken," he exclaimed cordially, as he approached and extended his hand.

"You find me damn' porely, suh; but you 've got the better o' me, ef I may so say." He was a big good-looking brute, with a straw-colored "horse-shoe" moustache quite concealing his mouth, and a several days' growth of stubble on his rugged face. He was fond of reiterating that women's admiration had wrecked his life, quite forgetting to mention the early and sustained influence of "Pike's Magnolia" and other brands, and wholly ignoring certain inborn propensities capable of wrecking unaided any ordinary existence. He had been lying down, and looked frouzy and half asleep.

"Ef I may so say, you 've got the better o' me, Mr.—er"—

"Santien, Grégoire Santien. I have the pleasure o' knowin' the lady you married, suh; an' I think I met you befo',—somew'ere o' 'nother," Grégoire added vaguely.

"Oh," drawled Aiken, waking up, "one o' them Red River Sanchuns!"* and his face brightened at the prospect before him of enjoying the society of one of the Santien boys. "Mortimer!" he called in ringing chest tones worthy a commander at the head of his troop. The negro had rested his axe and appeared to be listening to their talk, though he was too far to hear what they said.

"Mortimer, come along here an' take my frien' Mr. Sanchun's hoss. Git a move thar, git a move!" Then turning toward the entrance of the cabin he called back through the open door: "Rain!"

it was his way of pronouncing 'Tite Reine's name. "Rain!" he cried again peremptorily; and turning to Grégoire: "she 's 'tendin' to some or other housekeepin' truck."* 'Tite Reine was back in the yard feeding the solitary pig which they owned, and which Aiken had mysteriously driven up a few days before, saying he had bought it at Many.

Grégoire could hear her calling out as she approached: "I 'm comin', Bud. Yere I come. W'at you want, Bud?" breathlessly, as she appeared in the door frame and looked out upon the narrow sloping gallery where stood the two men. She seemed to Grégoire to have changed a good deal. She was thinner, and her eyes were larger, with an alert, uneasy look in them; he fancied the startled expression came from seeing him there unexpectedly. She wore cleanly homespun garments, the same she had brought with her from Bayou Pierre; but her shoes were in shreds. She uttered only a low, smothered exclamation when she saw Grégoire.

"Well, is that all you got to say to my frien' Mr. Sanchun? That 's the way with them Cajuns," Aiken offered apologetically to his guest; "ain't got sense enough to know a white man when they see one." Grégoire took her hand.

"I 'm mighty glad to see you, 'Tite Reine," he said from his heart. She had for some reason been unable to speak; now she panted somewhat hysterically: —

"You mus' escuse me, Mista Grégoire. It 's the truth I did n' know you firs', stan'in' up there." A deep flush had supplanted the former pallor of her face, and her eyes shone with tears and ill-concealed excitement.

"I thought you all lived yonda in Grant," remarked Grégoire carelessly, making talk for the purpose of diverting Aiken's attention away from his wife's evident embarrassment, which he himself was at a loss to understand.

"Why, we did live a right smart while in Grant; but Grant ain't no parish to make a livin' in. Then I tried Winn and Caddo* a spell; they was n't no better. But I tell you, suh, Sabine 's a damn' sight worse than any of 'em. Why, a man can't git a drink o' whiskey here without going out of the parish fer it, or across into Texas. I 'm fixin' to sell out an' try Vernon."*

Bud Aiken's household belongings surely would not count for much in the contemplated "selling out." The one room that constituted his home was extremely bare of furnishing,—a cheap bed, a pine table, and a few chairs, that was all. On a rough shelf were some paper parcels representing the larder. The mud daubing had fallen out here and there from between the logs of the cabin; and into the largest of these apertures had been thrust pieces of ragged bagging and wisps of cotton. A tin basin outside on the gallery offered the only bathing facilities to be seen. Notwithstanding these drawbacks, Grégoire announced his intention of passing the night with Aiken.

"I 'm jus' goin' to ask the privilege o' layin' down yere on yo' gall'ry to-night, Mr. Aiken. My hoss ain't in firs'-class trim; an' a night's res' ain't goin' to hurt him o' me either." He had begun by declaring his intention of pushing on across the Sabine, but an imploring look from 'Tite Reine's eyes had stayed the words upon his lips. Never had he seen in a woman's eyes a look of such heart-broken entreaty. He resolved on the instant to know the meaning of it before setting foot on Texas soil. Grégoire had never learned to steel his heart against a woman's eyes, no matter what language they spoke.

An old patchwork quilt folded double and a moss pillow which 'Tite Reine gave him out on the gallery made a bed that was, after all, not too uncomfortable for a young fellow of rugged habits.

Grégoire slept quite soundly after he laid down upon his impro-vised bed at nine o'clock. He was awakened toward the middle of the night by some one gently shaking him. It was 'Tite Reine stooping over him; he could see her plainly, for the moon was shining. She had not removed the clothing she had worn during the day; but her feet were bare and looked wonderfully small and white. He arose on his elbow, wide awake at once. "W'y, 'Tite Reine! w'at the devil you mean? w'ere 's yo' husban'?"

"The house kin fall on 'im, 't en goin' wake up Bud w'en he 's sleepin'; he drink' too much." Now that she had aroused Grégoire, she stood up, and sinking her face in her bended arm like a child, began to cry softly. In an instant he was on his feet.

"My God, 'Tite Reine! w'at 's the matta? you got to tell me w'at 's the matta." He could no longer recognize the imperious 'Tite Reine, whose will had been the law in her father's household. He led her to the edge of the low gallery and there they sat down.

Grégoire loved women. He liked their nearness, their atmosphere; the tones of their voices and the things they said; their ways of moving and turning about; the brushing of their garments when they passed him by pleased him. He was fleeing now from the pain that a woman had inflicted upon him.* When any overpowering sorrow came to Grégoire he felt a singular longing to cross the Sabine River and lose himself in Texas. He had done this once before when his home, the old Santien place, had gone into the hands of creditors. The sight of 'Tite Reine's distress now moved him painfully.

"W'at is it, 'Tite Reine? tell me w'at it is," he kept asking her. She was attempting to dry her eyes on her coarse sleeve. He drew a handkerchief from his back pocket and dried them for her.

"They all well, yonda?" she asked, haltingly, "my popa? my moma? the chil'en?" Grégoire knew no more of the Baptiste Choupic family than the post beside him. Nevertheless he answered: "They all right well, 'Tite Reine, but they mighty lonesome of you."

"My popa, he got a putty good crop this yea'?"

"He made right smart o' cotton fo' Bayou Pierre."

"He done haul it to the relroad?"

"No, he ain't quite finish pickin'."

"I hope they all ent sole 'Putty Girl'?" she inquired solicitously.

"Well, I should say not! Yo' pa says they ain't anotha piece o' hossflesh in the pa'ish he 'd want to swap fo' 'Putty Girl.'" She turned to him with vague but fleeting amazement,—"Putty Girl" was a cow!

The autumn night was heavy about them. The black forest seemed to have drawn nearer; its shadowy depths were filled with the gruesome noises that inhabit a southern forest at night time.

"Ain't you 'fraid sometimes yere, 'Tite Reine?" Grégoire asked, as he felt a light shiver run through him at the weirdness of the scene.

"No," she answered promptly, "I ent 'fred o' nothin' 'cep Bud."

"Then he treats you mean? I thought so!"

"Mista Grégoire," drawing close to him and whispering in his face, "Bud 's killin' me." He clasped her arm, holding her near him, while an expression of profound pity escaped him. "Nobody don' know, 'cep' Unc' Mort'mer," she went on. "I tell you, he beats me; my back an' arms—you ought to see—it 's all blue. He would 'a' choke' me to death one day w'en he was drunk, if Unc' Mort'mer had n' make 'im lef go—with his axe ov' his head." Grégoire glanced back over his shoulder toward the room where the man lay sleeping. He was wondering if it would really be a criminal act to go then and there and shoot the top of Bud Aiken's head off. He himself would hardly have considered it a crime,* but he was not sure of how others might regard the act.

"That 's w'y I wake you up, to tell you," she continued. "Then sometime' he plague me mos' crazy; he tell me 't ent no preacher, it 's a Texas drummer* w'at marry him an' me; an' w'en I don' know w'at way to turn no mo', he say no, it 's a Meth'dis' archbishop, an' keep on laughin' 'bout me, an' I don' know w'at the truth!"

Then again, she told how Bud had induced her to mount the vicious little mustang "Buckeye," knowing that the little brute would n't carry a woman; and how it had amused him to witness her distress and terror when she was thrown to the ground.

"If I would know how to read an' write, an' had some pencil an' paper, it 's long 'go I would wrote to my popa. But it 's no pos'office, it 's no relroad,—nothin' in Sabine. An' you know, Mista Grégoire, Bud say he 's goin' carry me yonda to Vernon, an' fu'ther off yet,— 'way yonda, an' he 's goin' turn me loose. Oh, don' leave me yere, Mista Grégoire! don' leave me behine you!" she entreated, breaking once more into sobs.

"'Tite Reine," he answered, "do you think I 'm such a low-down scound'el as to leave you yere with that"—He finished the sentence mentally, not wishing to offend the ears of 'Tite Reine.

They talked on a good while after that. She would not return to the room where her husband lay; the nearness of a friend had already emboldened her to inward revolt. Grégoire induced her to lie down and rest upon the quilt that she had given to him for a bed. She did so, and broken down by fatigue was soon fast asleep.

He stayed seated on the edge of the gallery and began to smoke cigarettes which he rolled himself of périque tobacco.* He might have gone in and shared Bud Aiken's bed, but preferred to stay there near 'Tite Reine. He watched the two horses, tramping slowly about the lot, cropping the dewy wet tufts of grass.

Grégoire smoked on. He only stopped when the moon sank down behind the pine-trees, and the long deep shadow reached out and enveloped him. Then he could no longer see and follow the filmy smoke from his cigarette, and he threw it away. Sleep was pressing heavily upon him. He stretched himself full length upon the rough bare boards of the gallery and slept until day-break.

Bud Aiken's satisfaction was very genuine when he learned that

Grégoire proposed spending the day and another night with him. He had already recognized in the young creole a spirit not altogether uncongenial to his own.

'Tite Reine cooked breakfast for them. She made coffee; of course there was no milk to add to it, but there was sugar. From a meal bag that stood in the corner of the room she took a measure of meal, and with it made a pone of corn bread. She fried slices of salt pork.* Then Bud sent her into the field to pick cotton with old Uncle Mortimer. The negro's cabin was the counterpart of their own, but stood quite a distance away hidden in the woods. He and Aiken worked the crop on shares.*

Early in the day Bud produced a grimy pack of cards from behind a parcel of sugar on the shelf. Grégoire threw the cards into the fire and replaced them with a spic and span new "deck" that he took from his saddlebags. He also brought forth from the same receptacle a bottle of whiskey, which he presented to his host, saying that he himself had no further use for it, as he had "sworn off" since day before yesterday, when he had made a fool of himself in Cloutierville.*

They sat at the pine table smoking and playing cards all the morning, only desisting when 'Tite Reine came to serve them with the gumbo-filé* that she had come out of the field to cook at noon. She could afford to treat a guest to chicken gumbo, for she owned a half dozen chickens that Uncle Mortimer had presented to her at various times. There were only two spoons, and 'Tite Reine had to wait till the men had finished before eating her soup. She waited for Grégoire's spoon, though her husband was the first to get through. It was a very childish whim.

In the afternoon she picked cotton again; and the men played cards, smoked, and Bud drank.

It was a very long time since Bud Aiken had enjoyed himself so well, and since he had encountered so sympathetic and appreciative a listener to the story of his eventful career. The story of 'Tite Reine's fall from the horse he told with much spirit, mimicking quite skillfully the way in which she had complained of never being permitted "to teck a li'le pleasure," whereupon he had kindly suggested horseback riding. Grégoire enjoyed the story amazingly, which encouraged Aiken to relate many more of a similar character. As the afternoon wore on, all formality of address between the two had disappeared: they were "Bud" and "Grégoire" to each other, and

Grégoire had delighted Aiken's soul by promising to spend a week with him. 'Tite Reine was also touched by the spirit of recklessness in the air; it moved her to fry two chickens for supper. She fried them deliciously in bacon fat. After supper she again arranged Grégoire's bed out on the gallery.

The night fell calm and beautiful, with the delicious odor of the pines floating upon the air. But the three did not sit up to enjoy it. Before the stroke of nine, Aiken had already fallen upon his bed unconscious of everything about him in the heavy drunken sleep that would hold him fast through the night. It even clutched him more relentlessly than usual, thanks to Grégoire's free gift of whiskey.

The sun was high when he awoke. He lifted his voice and called imperiously for 'Tite Reine, wondering that the coffee-pot was not on the hearth, and marveling still more that he did not hear her voice in quick response with its, "I 'm comin', Bud. Yere I come." He called again and again. Then he arose and looked out through the back door to see if she were picking cotton in the field, but she was not there. He dragged himself to the front entrance. Grégoire's bed was still on the gallery, but the young fellow was nowhere to be seen.

Uncle Mortimer had come into the yard, not to cut wood this time, but to pick up the axe which was his own property, and lift it to his shoulder.

"Mortimer," called out Aiken, "whur 's my wife?" at the same time advancing toward the negro. Mortimer stood still, waiting for him. "Whur 's my wife an' that Frenchman? Speak out, I say, before I send you to h—l."

Uncle Mortimer never had feared Bud Aiken; and with the trusty axe upon his shoulder, he felt a double hardihood in the man's presence. The old fellow passed the back of his black, knotty hand unctuously over his lips, as though he relished in advance the words that were about to pass them. He spoke carefully and deliberately:

"Miss Reine," he said, "I reckon she mus' of done struck Natchitoches pa'ish sometime to'ard de middle o' de night, on dat 'ar swif' hoss o' Mr. Sanchun's."

Aiken uttered a terrific oath. "Saddle up Buckeye," he yelled, "before I count twenty, or I'll rip the black hide off yer. Quick, thar!

Thur ain't nothin' fourfooted top o' this earth that Buckeye can't run down." Uncle Mortimer scratched his head dubiously, as he answered:—

"Yas, Mas' Bud, but you see, Mr. Sanchun, he done cross de Sabine befo' sun-up on Buckeye."*

A RESPECTABLE WOMAN

Mrs. Baroda was a little provoked to learn that her husband expected his friend, Gouvernail, up to spend a week or two on the plantation.

They had entertained a good deal during the winter; much of the time had also been passed in New Orleans in various forms of mild dissipation. She was looking forward to a period of unbroken rest, now, and undisturbed tête-à-tête with her husband, when he informed her that Gouvernail* was coming up to stay a week or two.

This was a man she had heard much of but never seen. He had been her husband's college friend; was now a journalist, and in no sense a Society man or "a man about town," which were, perhaps, some of the reasons she had never met him. But she had unconsciously formed an image of him in her mind. She pictured him tall, slim, cynical; with eye-glasses, and his hands in his pockets; and she did not like him. Gouvernail was slim enough, but he wasn't very tall nor very cynical; neither did he wear eye-glasses nor carry his hands in his pockets. And she rather liked him when he first presented himself.

But why she liked him she could not explain satisfactorily to herself when she partly attempted to do so. She could discover in him none of those brilliant and promising traits which Gaston, her husband, had often assured her that he possessed. On the contrary, he sat rather mute and receptive before her chatty eagerness to make him feel at home, and in face of Gaston's frank and wordy hospitality. His manner was as courteous toward her as the most exacting woman could require; but he made no direct appeal to her approval or even esteem.

Once settled at the plantation he seemed to like to sit upon the wide portico in the shade of one of the big Corinthian pillars,* smoking his cigar lazily and listening attentively to Gaston's experience as a sugar planter.

"This is what I call living," he would utter with deep satisfaction, as the air that swept across the sugar field caressed him with its warm and scented velvety touch. It pleased him also to get on familiar terms with the big dogs that came about him, rubbing themselves sociably against his legs. He did not care to fish, and displayed no eagerness to go out and kill grosbecs* when Gaston proposed doing so.

Gouvernail's personality puzzled Mrs. Baroda, but she liked him. Indeed, he was a lovable, inoffensive fellow. After a few days, when she could understand him no better than at first, she gave over being puzzled and remained piqued. In this mood she left her husband and her guest, for the most part, alone together. Then finding that Gouvernail took no manner of exception to her action, she imposed her society upon him, accompanying him in his idle strolls to the mill and walks along the batture.* She persistently sought to penetrate the reserve in which he had unconsciously enveloped himself.

"When is he going—your friend?" she one day asked her husband. "For my part, he tires me frightfully."

"Not for a week yet, dear. I can't understand; he gives you no trouble."

"No. I should like him better if he did; if he were more like others, and I had to plan somewhat for his comfort and enjoyment."

Gaston took his wife's pretty face between his hands and looked tenderly and laughingly into her troubled eyes. They were making a bit of toilet sociably together in Mrs. Baroda's dainty dressing-room.

"You are full of surprises, ma belle," he said to her. "Even I can never count upon how you are going to act under given conditions." He kissed her and turned to fasten his cravat before the mirror.

"Here you are," he went on, "taking poor Gouvernail seriously and making a commotion over him, the last things he would desire or expect."

"Commotion!" she hotly resented. "Nonsense! How can you say such a thing? Commotion, indeed! But, you know, you said he was clever."

"So he is. But the poor fellow is run down by overwork now. That's why I asked him here to take a rest."

"You used to say he was a man of ideas," she retorted, unconciliated. "I expected him to be interesting, at least. I'm going to the city in the morning to have my spring gowns fitted. Let me know when Mr. Gouvernail is gone; I shall be at my Aunt Octavie's."

That night she went and sat alone upon a bench that stood beneath a live oak tree at the edge of the gravel walk.

She had never known her thoughts or her intentions to be so

confused. She could gather nothing from them but the feeling of a distinct necessity to quit home in the morning.

Mrs. Baroda heard footsteps crunching the gravel; but could discern in the darkness only the approaching red point of a lighted cigar. She knew it was Gouvernail, for her husband did not smoke. She hoped to remain unnoticed, but her white gown revealed her to him. He threw away his cigar and seated himself upon the bench beside her; without a suspicion that she might object to his presence.

"Your husband told me to bring this to you, Mrs. Baroda," he said, handing her a filmy, white scarf with which she sometimes enveloped her head and shoulders. She accepted the scarf from him with a murmur of thanks, and let it lie in her lap.

He made some commonplace observation upon the baneful effect of the night air at that season. Then as his gaze reached out into the darkness, he murmured, half to himself:

> "'Night of south winds—night of the large few stars!
> Still nodding night——'"*

She made no reply to this apostrophe to the night, which indeed, was not addressed to her.

Gouvernail was in no sense a diffident man, for he was not a self-conscious one. His periods of reserve were not constitutional, but the result of moods. Sitting there beside Mrs. Baroda, his silence melted for the time.

He talked freely and intimately in a low, hesitating drawl that was not unpleasant to hear. He talked of the old college days when he and Gaston had been a good deal to each other; of the days of keen and blind ambitions and large intentions. Now there was left with him, at least, a philosophic acquiescence to the existing order—only a desire to be permitted to exist, with now and then a little whiff of genuine life, such as he was breathing now.

Her mind only vaguely grasped what he was saying. Her physical being was for the moment predominant. She was not thinking of his words, only drinking in the tones of his voice. She wanted to reach out her hand in the darkness and touch him with the sensitive tips of her fingers upon the face or the lips. She wanted to draw close to him and whisper against his cheek—she did not care what—as she might have done if she had not been a respectable woman.

The stronger the impulse grew to bring herself near him, the further, in fact, did she draw away from him. As soon as she could do so without an appearance of too great rudeness, she rose and left him there alone.

Before she reached the house, Gouvernail had lighted a fresh cigar and ended his apostrophe to the night.

Mrs. Baroda was greatly tempted that night to tell her husband—who was also her friend—of this folly that had seized her. But she did not yield to the temptation. Beside being a respectable woman she was a very sensible one; and she knew there are some battles in life which a human being must fight alone.

When Gaston arose in the morning, his wife had already departed. She had taken an early morning train to the city. She did not return till Gouvernail was gone from under her roof.

There was some talk of having him back during the summer that followed. That is, Gaston greatly desired it; but this desire yielded to his wife's strenuous opposition.

However, before the year ended, she proposed, wholly from herself, to have Gouvernail visit them again. Her husband was surprised and delighted with the suggestion coming from her.

"I am glad, chère amie, to know that you have finally overcome your dislike for him; truly he did not deserve it."

"Oh," she told him laughingly, after pressing a long, tender kiss upon his lips, "I have overcome everything! you will see. This time I shall be very nice to him."

THE DREAM OF AN HOUR
(THE STORY OF AN HOUR)

Knowing that Mrs. Mallard was afflicted with a heart trouble, great care was taken to break to her as gently as possible the news of her husband's death.

It was her sister Josephine who told her, in broken sentences; veiled hints that revealed in half concealing. Her husband's friend Richards was there, too, near her. It was he who had been in the newspaper office when intelligence of the railroad disaster* was received, with Brently Mallard's name leading the list of "killed." He had only taken the time to assure himself of its truth by a second telegram, and had hastened to forestall any less careful, less tender friend in bearing the sad message.

She did not hear the story as many women have heard the same, with a paralyzed inability to accept its significance. She wept at once, with sudden, wild abandonment, in her sister's arms. When the storm of grief had spent itself she went away to her room alone. She would have no one follow her.

There stood, facing the open window, a comfortable, roomy arm-chair. Into this she sank, pressed down by a physical exhaustion that haunted her body and seemed to reach into her soul.

She could see in the open square before her house the tops of trees that were all aquiver with the new spring life. The delicious breath of rain was in the air. In the street below a peddler was crying his wares. The notes of a distant song which some one was singing reached her faintly, and countless sparrows were twittering in the eaves.

There were patches of blue sky showing here and there through the clouds that had met and piled one above the other in the west facing her window.

She sat with her head thrown back upon the cushion of the chair, quite motionless, except when a sob came up into her throat and shook her, as a child who has cried itself to sleep continues to sob in its dreams.

She was young, with a fair, calm face, whose lines bespoke repression and even a certain strength. But now there was a dull stare in her eyes, whose gaze was fixed away off yonder on one of those patches of blue sky. It was not a glance of reflection, but rather indicated a suspension of intelligent thought.

There was something coming to her and she was waiting for it, fearfully. What was it? She did not know; it was too subtle and elusive to name. But she felt it, creeping out of the sky, reaching toward her through the sounds, the scents, the color that filled the air.

Now her bosom rose and fell tumultuously. She was beginning to recognize this thing that was approaching to possess her, and she was striving to beat it back with her will—as powerless as her two white slender hands would have been.

When she abandoned herself a little whispered word escaped her slightly parted lips. She said it over and over under her breath: "free, free, free!" The vacant stare and the look of terror that had followed it went from her eyes. They stayed keen and bright. Her pulses beat fast, and the coursing blood warmed and relaxed every inch of her body.

She did not stop to ask if it were or were not a monstrous joy that held her. A clear and exalted perception enabled her to dismiss the suggestion as trivial.

She knew that she would weep again when she saw the kind, tender hands folded in death; the face that had never looked save with love upon her, fixed and gray and dead. But she saw beyond that bitter moment a long procession of years to come that would belong to her absolutely. And she opened and spread her arms out to them in welcome.

There would be no one to live for during those coming years; she would live for herself. There would be no powerful will bending hers in that blind persistence with which men and women believe they have a right to impose a private will upon a fellow-creature. A kind intention or a cruel intention made the act seem no less a crime as she looked upon it in that brief moment of illumination.

And yet she had loved him—sometimes. Often she had not. What did it matter! What could love, the unsolved mystery, count for in face of this possession of self-assertion which she suddenly recognized as the strongest impulse of her being!

"Free! Body and soul free!" she kept whispering.

Josephine was kneeling before the closed door with her lips to the keyhole, imploring for admission. "Louise, open the door! I beg; open the door—you will make yourself ill. What are you doing, Louise? For heaven's sake open the door."

"Go away. I am not making myself ill." No; she was drinking in a very elixir of life through that open window.

How fancy* was running riot along those days ahead of her. Spring days, and summer days, and all sorts of days that would be her own. She breathed a quick prayer that life might be long. It was only yesterday she had thought with a shudder that life might be long.

She arose at length and opened the door to her sister's importunities. There was a feverish triumph in her eyes, and she carried herself unwittingly like a goddess of Victory.* She clasped her sister's waist, and together they descended the stairs. Richards stood waiting for them at the bottom.

Some one was opening the front door with a latch key. It was Brently Mallard who entered, a little travel-stained, composedly carrying his grip-sack and umbrella. He had been far from the scene of accident, and did not even know there had been one. He stood amazed at Josephine's piercing cry; at Richards' quick motion to screen him from the view of his wife.

But Richards was too late.

When the doctors came they said she had died of heart disease— of joy that kills.

LILACS

I

Mme. Adrienne Farival never announced her coming; but the good nuns knew very well when to look for her. When the scent of the lilac blossoms began to permeate the air, Sister Agathe would turn many times during the day to the window; upon her face the happy, beatific expression with which pure and simple souls watch for the coming of those they love.

But it was not Sister Agathe; it was Sister Marceline who first espied her crossing the beautiful lawn that sloped up to the convent. Her arms were filled with great bunches of lilacs which she had gathered along her path. She was clad all in brown; like one of the birds that come with the spring, the nuns used to say. Her figure was rounded and graceful, and she walked with a happy, buoyant step. The cabriolet which had conveyed her to the convent moved slowly up the gravel drive that led to the imposing entrance. Beside the driver was her modest little black trunk, with her name and address printed in white letters upon it: "Mme. A. Farival, Paris." It was the crunching of the gravel which had attracted Sister Marceline's attention. And then the commotion began.

White-capped heads appeared suddenly at the windows; she waved her parasol and her bunch of lilacs at them. Sister Marceline and Sister Marie Anne appeared, fluttered and expectant at the doorway. But Sister Agathe, more daring and impulsive than all, descended the steps and flew across the grass to meet her. What embraces, in which the lilacs were crushed between them! What ardent kisses! What pink flushes of happiness mounting the cheeks of the two women!

Once within the convent Adrienne's soft brown eyes moistened with tenderness as they dwelt caressingly upon the familiar objects about her, and noted the most trifling details. The white, bare boards of the floor had lost nothing of their lustre. The stiff, wooden chairs, standing in rows against the walls of hall and parlor, seemed to have taken on an extra polish since she had seen them, last lilac time. And there was a new picture of the Sacré-Coeur* hanging over the hall table. What had they done with Ste. Catherine de Sienne,* who had occupied that position of honor for so many years? In the chapel—it was no use trying to deceive her—she saw at a glance that St. Joseph's mantle had been embellished with a new coat of blue, and the aureole about his head freshly gilded. And the Blessed Virgin there neglected!* Still wearing her garb of last spring, which looked almost dingy by contrast. It was not just—such partiality! The Holy Mother had reason to be jealous and to complain.

But Adrienne did not delay to pay her respects to the Mother Superior, whose dignity would not permit her to so much as step outside the door of her private apartments to welcome this old pupil. Indeed, she was dignity in person; large, uncompromising, unbending. She kissed Adrienne without warmth, and discussed conventional themes learnedly and prosaically during the quarter of an hour which the young woman remained in her company.

It was then that Adrienne's latest gift was brought in for inspection. For Adrienne always brought a handsome present for the chapel in her little black trunk. Last year it was a necklace of gems for the Blessed Virgin, which the Good Mother was only permitted to wear on extra occasions, such as great feast days of obligation. The year before it had been a precious crucifix—an ivory figure of Christ suspended from an ebony cross, whose extremities were tipped with wrought silver. This time it was a linen embroidered altar-cloth of such rare and delicate workmanship that the Mother Superior, who knew the value of such things, chided Adrienne for the extravagance.

"But, dear Mother, you know it is the greatest pleasure I have in life—to be with you all once a year, and to bring some such trifling token of my regard."

The Mother Superior dismissed her with the rejoinder: "Make yourself at home, my child. Sister Thérèse will see to your wants. You will occupy Sister Marceline's bed in the end room, over the chapel. You will share the room with Sister Agathe."

There was always one of the nuns detailed to keep Adrienne company during her fortnight's stay at the convent. This had become almost a fixed regulation. It was only during the hours of recreation that she found herself with them all together. Those were hours of much harmless merrymaking under the trees or in the nuns' refectory.

This time it was Sister Agathe who waited for her outside of the Mother Superior's door. She was taller and slenderer than Adrienne, and perhaps ten years older. Her fair blonde face flushed and paled with every passing emotion that visited her soul. The two women linked arms and went together out into the open air.

There was so much which Sister Agathe felt that Adrienne must see. To begin with, the enlarged poultry yard, with its dozens upon dozens of new inmates. It took now all the time of one of the lay-sisters to attend to them. There had been no change made in the vegetable garden, but—yes, there had; Adrienne's quick eye at once detected it. Last year old Philippe had planted his cabbages in a large square to the right. This year they were set out in an oblong bed to the left. How it made Sister Agathe laugh to think Adrienne should have noticed such a trifle! And old Philippe, who was nailing a broken trellis not far off, was called forward to be told about it.

He never failed to tell Adrienne how well she looked, and how she was growing younger each year. And it was his delight to recall certain of her youthful and mischievous escapades. Never would he forget that day she disappeared; and the whole convent in a hubbub about it! And how at last it was he who discovered her perched among the tallest branches of the highest tree on the grounds, where she had climbed to see if she could get a glimpse of Paris! And her punishment afterward!—half of the Gospel of Palm Sunday to learn by heart!

"We may laugh over it, my good Philippe, but we must remember that Madame is older and wiser now."

"I know well, Sister Agathe, that one ceases to commit follies after the first days of youth." And Adrienne seemed greatly impressed by the wisdom of Sister Agathe and old Philippe, the convent gardener.

A little later when they sat upon a rustic bench which overlooked the smiling landscape about them, Adrienne was saying to Sister Agathe, who held her hand and stroked it fondly:

"Do you remember my first visit, four years ago, Sister Agathe? and what a surprise it was to you all!"

"As if I could forget it, dear child!"

"And I! Always shall I remember that morning as I walked along the boulevard with a heaviness of heart—oh, a heaviness which I hate to recall. Suddenly there was wafted to me the sweet odor of lilac blossoms. A young girl had passed me by, carrying a great bunch of them. Did you ever know, Sister Agathe, that there is nothing which so keenly revives a memory as a perfume—an odor?"

"I believe you are right, Adrienne. For now that you speak of it, I can feel how the odor of fresh bread—when Sister Jeanne bakes—always makes me think of the great kitchen of ma tante de Sierge,* and crippled Julie, who sat always knitting at the sunny window. And I never smell the sweet scented honeysuckle without living again through the blessed day of my first communion."

"Well, that is how it was with me, Sister Agathe, when the scent of the lilacs at once changed the whole current of my thoughts and my despondency. The boulevard, its noises, its passing throng, vanished from before my senses as completely as if they had been spirited away. I was standing here with my feet sunk in the green sward as they are now. I could see the sunlight glancing from that old white stone wall, could hear the notes of birds, just as we hear them now, and the humming of insects in the air. And through all I could see and could smell the lilac blossoms, nodding invitingly to me from their thick-leaved branches. It seems to me they are richer than ever this year, Sister Agathe. And do you know, I became like an enragée; nothing could have kept me back. I do not remember now where I was going; but I turned and retraced my steps homeward in a perfect fever of agitation: 'Sophie! my little trunk—quick—the black one! A mere handful of clothes! I am going away. Don't ask me any questions. I shall be back in a fortnight.' And every year since then it is the same. At the very first whiff of a lilac blossom, I am gone! There is no holding me back."

"And how I wait for you, and watch those lilac bushes, Adrienne! If you should once fail to come, it would be like the spring coming without the sunshine or the song of birds.

"But do you know, dear child, I have sometimes feared that in moments of despondency such as you have just described, I fear that you do not turn as you might to our Blessed Mother in heaven, who is ever ready to comfort and solace an afflicted heart with the precious balm of her sympathy and love."

"Perhaps I do not, dear Sister Agathe. But you cannot picture the annoyances which I am constantly submitted to. That Sophie alone, with her detestable ways! I assure you she of herself is enough to drive me to St. Lazare."*

"Indeed, I do understand that the trials of one living in the world must be very great, Adrienne; particularly for you, my poor child, who have to bear them alone, since Almighty God was pleased to call to himself your dear husband. But on the other hand, to live one's life along the lines which our dear Lord traces for each one of us, must bring with it resignation and even a certain comfort. You have your household duties, Adrienne, and your music, to which, you say, you continue to devote yourself. And then, there are always good works—the poor—who are always with us—to be relieved; the afflicted to be comforted."

"But, Sister Agathe! Will you listen! Is it not La Rose that I hear moving down there at the edge of the pasture? I fancy she is reproaching me with being an ingrate, not to have pressed a kiss yet on that white forehead of hers. Come, let us go."

The two women arose and walked again, hand in hand this time, over the tufted grass down the gentle decline where it sloped toward the broad, flat meadow, and the limpid stream that flowed cool and fresh from the woods. Sister Agathe walked with her composed, nunlike tread; Adrienne with a balancing motion, a bounding step, as though the earth responded to her light footfall with some subtle impulse all its own.

They lingered long upon the foot-bridge that spanned the narrow stream which divided the convent grounds from the meadow beyond. It was to Adrienne indescribably sweet to rest there in soft, low converse with this gentle-faced nun, watching the approach of evening. The gurgle of the running water beneath them; the lowing of cattle approaching in the distance, were the only sounds that broke upon the stillness, until the clear tones of the angelus bell* pealed out from the convent tower. At the sound both women instinctively sank to their knees, signing themselves with the sign of the cross. And Sister Agathe repeated the customary invocation, Adrienne responding in musical tones:

> "The Angel of the Lord declared unto Mary,
> And she conceived by the Holy Ghost—"

and so forth, to the end of the brief prayer, after which they arose and retraced their steps toward the convent.

It was with subtle and naïve pleasure that Adrienne prepared herself that night for bed. The room which she shared with Sister Agathe was immaculately white. The walls were a dead white, relieved only by one florid print depicting Jacob's dream* at the foot of the ladder, upon which angels mounted and descended. The bare floors, a soft yellow-white, with two little patches of gray carpet beside each spotless bed. At the head of the white-draped beds were two bénitiers* containing holy water absorbed in sponges.

Sister Agathe disrobed noiselessly behind her curtains and glided into bed without having revealed, in the faint candlelight, as much as a shadow of herself. Adrienne pattered about the room, shook and folded her garments with great care, placing them on the back of a chair as she had been taught to do when a child at the convent. It secretly pleased Sister Agathe to feel that her dear Adrienne clung to the habits acquired in her youth.

But Adrienne could not sleep. She did not greatly desire to do so. These hours seemed too precious to be cast into the oblivion of slumber.

"Are you not asleep, Adrienne?"

"No, Sister Agathe. You know it is always so the first night. The excitement of my arrival—I don't know what—keeps me awake."

"Say your 'Hail, Mary,' dear child, over and over."

"I have done so, Sister Agathe: it does not help."

"Then lie quite still on your side and think of nothing but your own respiration. I have heard that such inducement to sleep seldom fails."

"I will try. Good night, Sister Agathe."

"Good night, dear child. May the Holy Virgin guard you."

An hour later Adrienne was still lying with wide, wakeful eyes, listening to the regular breathing of Sister Agathe. The trailing of the passing wind through the treetops, the ceaseless babble of the rivulet were some of the sounds that came to her faintly through the night.

The days of the fortnight which followed were in character much like the first peaceful, uneventful day of her arrival, with the exception only that she devoutly heard mass every morning at an early hour in the convent chapel, and on Sundays sang in the choir in her agreeable, cultivated voice, which was heard with delight and the warmest appreciation.

When the day of her departure came, Sister Agathe was not satisfied to say good-by at the portal as the others did. She walked down the drive beside the creeping old cabriolet, chattering her pleasant last words. And then she stood—it was as far as she might go*—at the edge of the road, waving good-by in response to the fluttering of Adrienne's handkerchief. Four hours later Sister Agathe, who was instructing a class of little girls for their first communion, looked up at the classroom clock and murmured: "Adrienne is at home now."

Yes, Adrienne was at home. Paris had engulfed her.

II

At the very hour when Sister Agathe looked up at the clock, Adrienne, clad in a charming négligé, was reclining indolently in the depths of a luxurious armchair. The bright room was in its accustomed state of picturesque disorder. Musical scores were scattered upon the open piano. Thrown carelessly over the backs of chairs were puzzling and astonishing-looking garments.

In a large gilded cage near the window perched a clumsy green parrot. He blinked stupidly at a young girl in street dress who was exerting herself to make him talk.

In the centre of the room stood Sophie, that thorn in her mistress's side. With hands plunged in the deep pockets of her apron, her white starched cap quivering with each emphatic motion of her grizzled head, she was holding forth, to the evident ennui of the two young women. She was saying:

"Heaven knows I have stood enough in the six years I have been with Mademoiselle; but never such indignities as I have had to endure in the past two weeks at the hands of that man who calls himself a manager! The very first day—and I, good enough to notify him at once of Mademoiselle's flight—he arrives like a lion; I tell you, like a lion. He insists upon knowing Mademoiselle's whereabouts. How can I tell him any more than the statue out there in the square? He calls me a liar! Me, me—a liar! He declares he is ruined. The public will not stand La Petite Gilberta in the role which Mademoiselle has made so famous—La Petite Gilberta, who dances like a jointed wooden figure and sings like a traînée of a café chantant.* If I were to tell La Gilberta that, as I easily might, I guarantee it would not be well for the few straggling hairs which he has left on that miserable head of his!

"What could he do? He was obliged to inform the public that

Mademoiselle was ill; and then began my real torment! Answering this one and that one with their cards, their flowers, their dainties in covered dishes! which, I must admit, saved Florine and me much cooking. And all the while having to tell them that the physician had advised for Mademoiselle a rest of two weeks at some watering-place, the name of which I had forgotten!"

Adrienne had been contemplating old Sophie with quizzical, half-closed eyes, and pelting her with hothouse roses which lay in her lap, and which she nipped off short from their graceful stems for that purpose. Each rose struck Sophie full in the face; but they did not disconcert her or once stem the torrent of her talk.

"Oh, Adrienne!" entreated the young girl at the parrot's cage. "Make her hush; please do something. How can you ever expect Zozo to talk?* A dozen times he has been on the point of saying something! I tell you, she stupefies him with her chatter."

"My good Sophie," remarked Adrienne, not changing her attitude, "you see the roses are all used up. But I assure you, anything at hand goes," carelessly picking up a book from the table beside her. "What is this? Mons. Zola!* Now I warn you, Sophie, the weightiness, the heaviness of Mons. Zola are such that they cannot fail to prostrate you; thankful you may be if they leave you with energy to regain your feet."

"Mademoiselle's pleasantries are all very well; but if I am to be shown the door for it—if I am to be crippled for it—I shall say that I think Mademoiselle is a woman without conscience and without heart. To torture a man as she does! A man? No, an angel!

"Each day he has come with sad visage and drooping mien. 'No news, Sophie?'

"'None, Monsieur Henri.' 'Have you no idea where she has gone?' 'Not any more than the statue in the square, Monsieur.' 'Is it perhaps possible that she may not return at all?' with his face blanching like that curtain.

"I assure him you will be back at the end of the fortnight. I entreat him to have patience. He drags himself, désolé, about the room, picking up Mademoiselle's fan, her gloves, her music, and turning them over and over in his hands. Mademoiselle's slipper, which she took off to throw at me in the impatience of her departure, and which I purposely left lying where it fell on the chiffonier—he kissed it—I saw him do it—and thrust it into his pocket, thinking himself unobserved.

"The same song each day. I beg him to eat a little good soup which I have prepared. 'I cannot eat, my dear Sophie.' The other night he came and stood long gazing out of the window at the stars. When he turned he was wiping his eyes; they were red. He said he had been riding in the dust, which had inflamed them. But I knew better; he had been crying.

"Ma foi! his place I would snap my finger at such cruelty. I would go out and amuse myself. What is the use of being young!"

Adrienne arose with a laugh. She went and seizing old Sophie by the shoulders shook her till the white cap wobbled on her head.

"What is the use of all this litany, my good Sophie? Year after year the same! Have you forgotten that I have come a long, dusty journey by rail, and that I am perishing of hunger and thirst? Bring us a bottle of Château Yquem* and a biscuit and my box of cigarettes." Sophie had freed herself, and was retreating toward the door. "And, Sophie! If Monsieur Henri is still waiting, tell him to come up."

III

It was precisely a year later. The spring had come again, and Paris was intoxicated.

Old Sophie sat in her kitchen discoursing to a neighbor who had come in to borrow some trifling kitchen utensil from the old bonne.

"You know, Rosalie, I begin to believe it is an attack of lunacy which seizes her once a year. I wouldn't say it to everyone, but with you I know it will go no further. She ought to be treated for it; a physician should be consulted; it is not well to neglect such things and let them run on.

"It came this morning like a thunder clap. As I am sitting here, there had been no thought or mention of a journey. The baker had come into the kitchen—you know what a gallant he is—with always a girl in his eye. He laid the bread down upon the table and beside it a bunch of lilacs. I didn't know they had bloomed yet. 'For Mam'selle Florine, with my regards,' he said with his foolish simper.

"Now, you know I was not going to call Florine from her work in order to present her the baker's flowers. All the same, it would not do to let them wither. I went with them in my hand into the dining room to get a majolica pitcher which I had put away in the closet there, on an upper shelf, because the handle was broken. Mademoiselle, who rises early, had just come from her bath, and was crossing the hall that opens into the dining room. Just as she was, in her white peignoir, she thrust her head into the dining room, snuffing the air and exclaiming, 'What do I smell?'

"She espied the flowers in my hand and pounced upon them like a cat upon a mouse. She held them up to her, burying her face in them for the longest time, only uttering a long 'Ah!'

"'Sophie, I am going away. Get out the little black trunk; a few of the plainest garments I have; my brown dress that I have not yet worn.'

"'But, Mademoiselle,' I protested, 'you forget that you have ordered a breakfast of a hundred francs for tomorrow.'

"'Shut up!' she cried, stamping her foot.

"'You forget how the manager will rave,' I persisted, 'and vilify me. And you will go like that without a word of adieu to Monsieur Paul, who is an angel if ever one trod the earth.'

"I tell you, Rosalie, her eyes flamed.

"'Do as I tell you this instant,' she exclaimed, 'or I will strangle you—with your Monsieur Paul and your manager and your hundred francs!'"

"Yes," affirmed Rosalie, "it is insanity. I had a cousin seized in the same way one morning, when she smelled calf's liver frying with onions. Before night it took two men to hold her."

"I could well see it was insanity, my dear Rosalie, and I uttered not another word as I feared for my life. I simply obeyed her every command in silence. And now—whiff, she is gone! God knows where. But between us, Rosalie—I wouldn't say it to Florine—but I believe it is for no good. I, in Monsieur Paul's place, should have her watched. I would put a detective upon her track.

"Now I am going to close up; barricade the entire establishment. Monsieur Paul, the manager, visitors, all—all may ring and knock and shout themselves hoarse. I am tired of it all. To be vilified and called a liar—at my age, Rosalie!"

IV

Adrienne left her trunk at the small railway station, as the old cabriolet was not at the moment available; and she gladly walked the mile
or two of pleasant roadway which led to the convent. How infinitely
calm, peaceful, penetrating was the charm of the verdant, undulating country spreading out on all sides of her! She walked along the
clear smooth road, twirling her parasol; humming a gay tune; nipping here and there a bud or a wax-like leaf from the hedges along
the way; and all the while drinking deep draughts of complacency
and content.

She stopped, as she had always done, to pluck lilacs in her
path.

As she approached the convent she fancied that a white-capped
face had glanced fleetingly from a window; but she must have been
mistaken. Evidently she had not been seen, and this time would take
them by surprise. She smiled to think how Sister Agathe would utter
a little joyous cry of amazement, and in fancy she already felt the
warmth and tenderness of the nun's embrace. And how Sister
Marceline and the others would laugh, and make game of her puffed
sleeves! For puffed sleeves had come into fashion since last year; and
the vagaries of fashion always afforded infinite merriment to the
nuns. No, they surely had not seen her.

She ascended lightly the stone steps and rang the bell. She could
hear the sharp metallic sound reverberate through the halls. Before
its last note had died away the door was opened very slightly, very
cautiously by a lay Sister who stood there with downcast eyes and
flaming cheeks. Through the narrow opening she thrust forward
toward Adrienne a package and a letter, saying, in confused tones:
"By order of our Mother Superior." After which she closed the door
hastily and turned the heavy key in the great lock.

Adrienne remained stunned. She could not gather her faculties to
grasp the meaning of this singular reception. The lilacs fell from her
arms to the stone portico on which she was standing. She turned the
note and the parcel stupidly over in her hands, instinctively dreading
what their contents might disclose.

The outlines of the crucifix were plainly to be felt through the wrapper of the bundle, and she guessed, without having courage to assure herself, that the jeweled necklace and the altar cloth accompanied it.

Leaning against the heavy oaken door for support, Adrienne opened the letter. She did not seem to read the few bitter reproachful lines word by word—the lines that banished her forever from this haven of peace, where her soul was wont to come and refresh itself. They imprinted themselves as a whole upon her brain, in all their seeming cruelty—she did not dare to say injustice.

There was no anger in her heart; that would doubtless possess her later, when her nimble intelligence would begin to seek out the origin of this treacherous turn. Now, there was only room for tears. She leaned her forehead against the heavy oaken panel of the door and wept with the abandonment of a little child.

She descended the steps with a nerveless and dragging tread. Once as she was walking away, she turned to look back at the imposing façade of the convent, hoping to see a familiar face, or a hand, even, giving a faint token that she was still cherished by some one faithful heart. But she saw only the polished windows looking down at her like so many cold and glittering and reproachful eyes.

In the little white room above the chapel, a woman knelt beside the bed on which Adrienne had slept. Her face was pressed deep in the pillow in her efforts to smother the sobs that convulsed her frame. It was Sister Agathe.

After a short while, a lay Sister came out of the door with a broom, and swept away the lilac blossoms* which Adrienne had let fall upon the portico.

REGRET

Mamzelle Aurélie possessed a good strong figure, ruddy cheeks, hair that was changing from brown to gray, and a determined eye. She wore a man's hat about the farm, and an old blue army overcoat* when it was cold, and sometimes top-boots.

Mamzelle Aurélie had never thought of marrying. She had never been in love. At the age of twenty she had received a proposal, which she had promptly declined, and at the age of fifty she had not yet lived to regret it.

So she was quite alone in the world, except for her dog Ponto,* and the negroes who lived in her cabins and worked her crops, and the fowls, a few cows, a couple of mules, her gun (with which she shot chicken-hawks), and her religion.

One morning Mamzelle Aurélie stood upon her gallery, contemplating, with arms akimbo, a small band of very small children who, to all intents and purposes, might have fallen from the clouds, so unexpected and bewildering was their coming, and so unwelcome. They were the children of her nearest neighbor, Odile, who was not such a near neighbor, after all.

The young woman had appeared but five minutes before, accompanied by these four children. In her arms she carried little Élodie; she dragged Ti Nomme* by an unwilling hand; while Marcéline and Marcélette followed with irresolute steps.

Her face was red and disfigured from tears and excitement. She had been summoned to a neighboring parish by the dangerous illness of her mother; her husband was away in Texas—it seemed to her a million miles away; and Valsin was waiting with the mule-cart to drive her to the station.

"It's no question, Mamzelle Aurélie; you jus' got to keep those youngsters fo' me tell I come back. *Dieu sait*, I would n' botha you with 'em if it was any otha way to do! Make 'em mine you, Mamzelle Aurélie; don' spare 'em. Me, there, I'm half crazy between the chil'ren, an' Léon not home, an' maybe not even to fine po' *maman* alive *encore*!"*—a harrowing possibility which drove Odile to take a final hasty and convulsive leave of her disconsolate family.

She left them crowded into the narrow strip of shade on the porch of the long, low house; the white sunlight was beating in on the white old boards; some chickens were scratching in the grass at the foot of the steps, and one had boldly mounted, and was stepping heavily, solemnly, and aimlessly across the gallery. There was a pleasant odor of pinks in the air, and the sound of negroes' laughter was coming across the flowering cotton-field.

Mamzelle Aurélie stood contemplating the children. She looked with a critical eye upon Marcéline, who had been left staggering beneath the weight of the chubby Élodie. She surveyed with the same calculating air Marcélette mingling her silent tears with the audible grief and rebellion of Ti Nomme. During those few contemplative moments she was collecting herself, determining upon a line of action which should be identical with a line of duty. She began by feeding them.

If Mamzelle Aurélie's responsibilities might have begun and ended there, they could easily have been dismissed; for her larder was amply provided against an emergency of this nature. But little children are not little pigs; they require and demand attentions which were wholly unexpected by Mamzelle Aurélie, and which she was ill prepared to give.

She was, indeed, very inapt in her management of Odile's children during the first few days. How could she know that Marcélette always wept when spoken to in a loud and commanding tone of voice? It was a peculiarity of Marcélette's. She became acquainted with Ti Nomme's passion for flowers only when he had plucked all the choicest gardenias and pinks for the apparent purpose of critically studying their botanical construction.

"'T ain't enough to tell 'im, Mamzelle Aurélie," Marcéline instructed her; "you got to tie 'im in a chair. It's w'at *maman* all time do w'en he's bad: she tie 'im in a chair." The chair in which Mamzelle Aurélie tied Ti Nomme was roomy and comfortable, and he seized the opportunity to take a nap in it, the afternoon being warm.

At night, when she ordered them one and all to bed as she would have shooed the chickens into the hen-house, they stayed uncomprehending before her. What about the little white night-gowns that had to be taken from the pillow-slip in which they were brought over, and shaken by some strong hand till they snapped like ox-whips? What about the tub of water which had to be brought and set in the middle of the floor, in which the little tired, dusty, sun-browned feet had every one to be washed sweet and clean? And it made Marcéline and Marcélette laugh merrily—the idea that Mamzelle Aurélie should for a moment have believed that Ti Nomme could fall asleep without being told the story of Croque-mitaine or Loup-garou,* or both; or that Élodie could fall asleep at all without being rocked and sung to.

"I tell you, Aunt Ruby," Mamzelle Aurélie informed her cook in confidence; "me, I'd rather manage a dozen plantation' than fo' chil'ren. It's *terrassent*! *Bonté!* Don't talk to me about chil'ren!"

"'T ain' ispected sich as you would know airy thing 'bout 'em, Mamzelle Aurélie. I see dat plainly yistiddy w'en I spy dat li'le chile playin' wid yo' baskit o' keys. You don' know dat makes chillun grow up hard-headed, to play wid keys? Des like it make 'em teeth hard to look in a lookin'-glass.* Them's the things you got to know in the raisin' an' manigement o' chillun."

Mamzelle Aurélie certainly did not pretend or aspire to such subtle and far-reaching knowledge on the subject as Aunt Ruby possessed, who had "raised five an' bared [buried] six" in her day. She was glad enough to learn a few little mother-tricks to serve the moment's need.

Ti Nomme's sticky fingers compelled her to unearth white aprons that she had not worn for years, and she had to accustom herself to his moist kisses—the expressions of an affectionate and exuberant nature. She got down her sewing-basket, which she seldom used, from the top shelf of the armoire, and placed it within the ready and easy reach which torn slips and buttonless waists demanded. It took her some days to become accustomed to the laughing, the crying, the chattering that echoed through the house and around it all day long. And it was not the first or the second night that she could sleep comfortably with little Élodie's hot, plump body pressed close against her, and the little one's warm breath beating her cheek like the fanning of a bird's wing.

But at the end of two weeks Mamzelle Aurélie had grown quite used to these things, and she no longer complained.

It was also at the end of two weeks that Mamzelle Aurélie, one evening, looking away toward the crib where the cattle were being fed, saw Valsin's blue cart turning the bend of the road. Odile sat beside the mulatto, upright and alert. As they drew near, the young woman's beaming face indicated that her homecoming was a happy one.

But this coming, unannounced and unexpected, threw Mamzelle Aurélie into a flutter that was almost agitation. The children had to be gathered. Where was Ti Nomme? Yonder in the shed, putting an edge on his knife at the grindstone. And Marcéline and Marcélette? Cutting and fashioning doll-rags in the corner of the gallery. As for Élodie, she was safe enough in Mamzelle Aurélie's arms; and she had screamed with delight at sight of the familiar blue cart which was bringing her mother back to her.

The excitement was all over, and they were gone. How still it was when they were gone! Mamzelle Aurélie stood upon the gallery, looking and listening. She could no longer see the cart; the red sunset and the blue-gray twilight had together flung a purple mist across the fields and road that hid it from her view. She could no longer hear the wheezing and creaking of its wheels. But she could still faintly hear the shrill, glad voices of the children.

She turned into the house. There was much work awaiting her, for the children had left a sad disorder behind them; but she did not at once set about the task of righting it. Mamzelle Aurélie seated herself beside the table. She gave one slow glance through the room, into which the evening shadows were creeping and deepening around her solitary figure. She let her head fall down upon her bended arm, and began to cry. Oh, but she cried! Not softly, as women often do. She cried like a man, with sobs that seemed to tear her very soul. She did not notice Ponto licking her hand.

THE KISS

It was still quite light out of doors, but inside with the curtains drawn and the smouldering fire sending out a dim, uncertain glow, the room was full of deep shadows.

Brantain sat in one of these shadows; it had overtaken him and he did not mind. The obscurity lent him courage to keep his eyes fastened as ardently as he liked upon the girl who sat in the firelight.

She was very handsome, with a certain fine, rich coloring that belongs to the healthy brune type. She was quite composed, as she idly stroked the satiny coat of the cat that lay curled in her lap, and she occasionally sent a slow glance into the shadow where her companion sat. They were talking low, of indifferent things which plainly were not the things that occupied their thoughts. She knew that he loved her—a frank, blustering fellow without guile enough to conceal his feelings, and no desire to do so. For two weeks past he had sought her society eagerly and persistently. She was confidently waiting for him to declare himself and she meant to accept him. The rather insignificant and unattractive Brantain was enormously rich; and she liked and required the entourage which wealth could give her.

During one of the pauses between their talk of the last tea and the next reception the door opened and a young man entered whom Brantain knew quite well. The girl turned her face toward him. A stride or two brought him to her side, and bending over her chair—before she could suspect his intention, for she did not realize that he had not seen her visitor—he pressed an ardent, lingering kiss upon her lips.

Brantain slowly arose; so did the girl arise, but quickly, and the newcomer stood between them, a little amusement and some defiance struggling with the confusion in his face.

"I believe," stammered Brantain, "I see that I have stayed too long. I—I had no idea—that is, I must wish you good-by." He was clutching his hat with both hands, and probably did not perceive that she was extending her hand to him, her presence of mind had not completely deserted her; but she could not have trusted herself to speak.

"Hang me if I saw him sitting there, Nattie! I know it's deuced awkward for you. But I hope you'll forgive me this once—this very first break. Why, what's the matter?"

"Don't touch me; don't come near me," she returned angrily. "What do you mean by entering the house without ringing?"

"I came in with your brother, as I often do," he answered coldly, in self-justification. "We came in the side way. He went upstairs and I came in here hoping to find you. The explanation is simple enough and ought to satisfy you that the misadventure was unavoidable. But do say that you forgive me, Nathalie," he entreated, softening.

"Forgive you! You don't know what you are talking about. Let me pass. It depends upon—a good deal whether I ever forgive you."

At that next reception which she and Brantain had been talking about she approached the young man with a delicious frankness of manner when she saw him there.

"Will you let me speak to you a moment or two, Mr. Brantain?" she asked with an engaging but perturbed smile. He seemed extremely unhappy; but when she took his arm and walked away with him, seeking a retired corner, a ray of hope mingled with the almost comical misery of his expression. She was apparently very outspoken.

"Perhaps I should not have sought this interview, Mr. Brantain; but—but, oh, I have been very uncomfortable, almost miserable since that little encounter the other afternoon. When I thought how you might have misinterpreted it, and believed things"—hope was plainly gaining the ascendancy over misery in Brantain's round, guileless face—"of course, I know it is nothing to you, but for my own sake I do want you to understand that Mr. Harvy is an intimate friend of long standing. Why, we have always been like cousins—like brother and sister, I may say. He is my brother's most intimate associate and often fancies that he is entitled to the same privileges as the family. Oh, I know it is absurd, uncalled for, to tell you this; undignified even," she was almost weeping, "but it makes so much difference to me what you think of—of me." Her voice had grown very low and agitated. The misery had all disappeared from Brantain's face.

"Then you do really care what I think, Miss Nathalie? May I call you Miss Nathalie?" They turned into a long, dim corridor that was lined on either side with tall, graceful plants. They walked slowly to the very end of it. When they turned to retrace their steps Brantain's face was radiant and hers was triumphant.

*

Harvy was among the guests at the wedding; and he sought her out in a rare moment when she stood alone.

"Your husband," he said, smiling, "has sent me over to kiss you."

A quick blush suffused her face and round polished throat. "I suppose it's natural for a man to feel and act generously on an occasion of this kind. He tells me he doesn't want his marriage to interrupt wholly that pleasant intimacy which has existed between you and me. I don't know what you've been telling him," with an insolent smile, "but he has sent me here to kiss you."

She felt like a chess player who, by the clever handling of his pieces, sees the game taking the course intended. Her eyes were bright and tender with a smile as they glanced up into his; and her lips looked hungry for the kiss which they invited.

"But, you know," he went on quietly, "I didn't tell him so, it would have seemed ungrateful, but I can tell you. I've stopped kissing women; it's dangerous."

Well, she had Brantain and his million left. A person can't have everything in this world; and it was a little unreasonable of her to expect it.

HER LETTERS

I

She had given orders that she wished to remain undisturbed and moreover had locked the doors of her room.

The house was very still. The rain was falling steadily from a leaden sky in which there was no gleam, no rift, no promise. A generous wood fire had been lighted in the ample fireplace and it brightened and illumined the luxurious apartment to its furthermost corner.

From some remote nook of her writing desk the woman took a thick bundle of letters, bound tightly together with strong, coarse twine, and placed it upon the table in the centre of the room.

For weeks she had been schooling herself for what she was about to do. There was a strong deliberation in the lines of her long, thin, sensitive face; her hands, too, were long and delicate and blue-veined.

With a pair of scissors she snapped the cord binding the letters together. Thus released the ones which were top-most slid down to the table and she, with a quick movement thrust her fingers among them, scattering and turning them over till they quite covered the broad surface of the table.

Before her were envelopes of various sizes and shapes, all of them addressed in the handwriting of one man and one woman. He had sent her letters all back to her one day when, sick with dread of possibilities, she had asked to have them returned. She had meant, then, to destroy them all, his and her own. That was four years ago, and she had been feeding upon them ever since; they had sustained her, she believed, and kept her spirit from perishing utterly.

But now the days had come when the premonition of danger could no longer remain unheeded. She knew that before many months were past she would have to part from her treasure, leaving it unguarded. She shrank from inflicting the pain, the anguish which the discovery of those letters would bring to others; to one, above all, who was near to her, and whose tenderness and years of devotion had made him, in a manner, dear to her.

She calmly selected a letter at random from the pile and cast it into the roaring fire.* A second one followed almost as calmly, with the third her hand began to tremble; when, in a sudden paroxysm she cast a fourth, a fifth, and a sixth into the flames in breathless succession.

Then she stopped and began to pant—for she was far from strong, and she stayed staring into the fire with pained and savage eyes. Oh, what had she done! What had she not done! With feverish apprehension she began to search among the letters before her. Which of them had she so ruthlessly, so cruelly put out of her existence? Heaven grant, not the first, that very first one, written before they had learned, or dared to say to each other "I love you." No, no; there it was, safe enough. She laughed with pleasure, and held it to her lips. But what if that other most precious and most imprudent one were missing! in which every word of untempered passion had long ago eaten its way into her brain; and which stirred her still to-day, as it had done a hundred times before when she thought of it. She crushed it between her palms when she found it. She kissed it again and again. With her sharp white teeth she tore the far corner from the letter, where the name was written; she bit the torn scrap and tasted it between her lips and upon her tongue like some god-given morsel.

What unbounded thankfulness she felt at not having destroyed them all! How desolate and empty would have been her remaining days without them; with only her thoughts, illusive thoughts that she could not hold in her hands and press, as she did these, to her cheeks and her heart.

This man had changed the water in her veins to wine,* whose taste had brought delirium to both of them. It was all one and past now, save for these letters that she held encircled in her arms. She stayed breathing softly and contentedly, with the hectic cheek resting upon them.

She was thinking; thinking of a way to keep them without possible ultimate injury to that other one whom they would stab more cruelly than keen knife blades.

At last she found the way. It was a way that frightened and bewildered her to think of at first, but she had reached it by deduction too sure to admit of doubt. She meant, of course, to destroy them herself before the end came. But how does the end come and when? Who may tell? She would guard against the possibility of accident by leaving them in charge of the very one who, above all, should be spared a knowledge of their contents.

She roused herself from the stupor of thought and gathered the scattered letters once more together, binding them again with the rough twine. She wrapped the compact bundle in a thick sheet of white polished paper. Then she wrote in ink upon the back of it, in large, firm characters:

"I leave this package to the care of my husband. With perfect faith in his loyalty and his love, I ask him to destroy it unopened."

It was not sealed; only a bit of string held the wrapper, which she could remove and replace at will whenever the humor came to her to pass an hour in some intoxicating dream of the days when she felt she had lived.

II

If he had come upon that bundle of letters in the first flush of his poignant sorrow there would not have been an instant's hesitancy. To destroy it promptly and without question would have seemed a welcome expression of devotion—a way of reaching her, of crying out his love to her while the world was still filled with the illusion of her presence. But months had passed since that spring day when they had found her stretched upon the floor, clutching the key of her writing desk, which she appeared to have been attempting to reach when death overtook her.

The day was much like that day a year ago when the leaves were falling and rain pouring steadily from a leaden sky which held no gleam, no promise. He had happened accidentally upon the package in that remote nook of her desk. And just as she herself had done a year ago, he carried it to the table and laid it down there, standing, staring with puzzled eyes at the message which confronted him:

"I leave this package to the care of my husband. With perfect faith in his loyalty and his love, I ask him to destroy it unopened."

She had made no mistake; every line of his face—no longer young—spoke loyalty and honesty, and his eyes were as faithful as a dog's and as loving. He was a tall, powerful man, standing there in the firelight, with shoulders that stooped a little, and hair that was growing somewhat thin and gray, and a face that was distinguished, and must have been handsome when he smiled. But he was slow. "Destroy it unopened," he re-read, half aloud; "but why unopened?"

He took the package again in his hands, and turning it about and feeling it, discovered that it was composed of many letters tightly packed together.

So here were letters which she was asking him to destroy unopened. She had never seemed in her lifetime to have had a secret from him. He knew her to have been cold and passionless, but true, and watchful of his comfort and his happiness. Might he not be holding in his hands the secret of some other one, which had been confided to her and which she had promised to guard? But, no, she would have indicated the fact by some additional word or line. The secret was her own, something contained in these letters, and she wanted it to die with her.

If he could have thought of her as on some distant shadowy shore waiting for him throughout the years with outstretched hands to come and join her again, he would not have hesitated. With hopeful confidence he would have thought "in that blessed meeting-time, soul to soul, she will tell me all; till then I can wait and trust." But he could not think of her in any far-off paradise awaiting him. He felt that there was no smallest part of her anywhere in the universe, more than there had been before she was born into the world. But she had embodied herself with terrible significance in an intangible wish, uttered when life still coursed through her veins; knowing that it would reach him when the annihilation of death was between them, but uttered with all confidence in its power and potency. He was moved by the splendid daring, the magnificence of the act, which at the same time exalted him and lifted him above the head of common mortals.

What secret save one could a woman choose to have die with her? As quickly as the suggestion came to his mind, so swiftly did the man-instinct of possession creep into his blood. His fingers cramped about the package in his hands, and he sank into a chair beside the table. The agonizing suspicion that perhaps another had shared with him her thoughts, her affections, her life, deprived him for a swift instant of honor and reason. He thrust the end of his strong thumb beneath the string which, with a single turn would have yielded— "with perfect faith in your loyalty and your love." It was not the written characters addressing themselves to the eye; it was like a voice speaking to his soul. With a tremor of anguish he bowed his head down upon the letters.

He had once seen a clairvoyant hold a letter to his forehead and purport in so doing to discover its contents. He wondered for a wild moment if such a gift, for force of wishing it, might not come to him. But he was only conscious of the smooth surface of the paper, cold against his brow, like the touch of a dead woman's hand.*

A half-hour passed before he lifted his head. An unspeakable conflict had raged within him, but his loyalty and his love had conquered. His face was pale and deep-lined with suffering, but there was no more hesitancy to be seen there.

He did not for a moment think of casting the thick package into the flames to be licked by the fiery tongues, and charred and half-revealed to his eyes. That was not what she meant. He arose, and taking a heavy bronze paper-weight from the table, bound it securely to the package. He walked to the window and looked out into the street below. Darkness had come, and it was still raining. He could hear the rain dashing against the window-panes, and could see it falling through the dull yellow rim of light cast by the lighted street lamp.

He prepared himself to go out, and when quite ready to leave the house thrust the weighted package into the deep pocket of his top-coat.

He did not hurry along the street as most people were doing at that hour, but walked with a long, slow, deliberate step, not seeming to mind the penetrating chill and rain driving into his face despite the shelter of his umbrella.

His dwelling was not far removed from the business section of the city; and it was not a great while before he found himself at the entrance of the bridge that spanned the river*—the deep, broad, swift, black river dividing two States. He walked on and out to the very centre of the structure. The wind was blowing fiercely and keenly. The darkness where he stood was impenetrable. The thousands of lights in the city he had left seemed like all the stars of heaven massed together, sinking into some distant mysterious horizon, leaving him alone in a black, boundless universe.

He drew the package from his pocket and leaning as far as he could over the broad stone rail of the bridge, cast it from him into the river. It fell straight and swiftly from his hand. He could not follow its descent through the darkness, nor hear its dip into the water far below. It vanished silently; seemingly into some inky unfathomable space. He felt as if he were flinging it back to her in that unknown world whither she had gone.

III

An hour or two later he sat at his table in the company of several men whom he had invited that day to dine with him. A weight had settled upon his spirit, a conviction, a certitude that there could be but one secret which a woman would choose to have die with her. This one thought was possessing him. It occupied his brain, keeping it nimble and alert with suspicion. It clutched his heart, making every breath of existence a fresh moment of pain.

The men about him were no longer the friends of yesterday; in each one he discerned a possible enemy. He attended absently to their talk. He was remembering how she had conducted herself toward this one and that one; striving to recall conversations, subtleties of facial expression that might have meant what he did not suspect at the moment, shades of meaning in words that had seemed the ordinary interchange of social amenities.

He led the conversation to the subject of women, probing these men for their opinions and experiences. There was not one but claimed some infallible power to command the affections of any woman whom his fancy might select. He had heard the empty boast before from the same group and had always met it with good-humored contempt. But to-night every flagrant, inane utterance was charged with a new meaning, revealing possibilities that he had hitherto never taken into account.

He was glad when they were gone. He was eager to be alone, not from any desire or intention to sleep. He was impatient to regain her room, that room in which she had lived a large portion of her life, and where he had found those letters. There must surely be more of them somewhere, he thought; some forgotten scrap, some written thought or expression lying unguarded by an inviolable command.

At the hour when he usually retired for the night he sat himself down before her writing desk and began the search of drawers, slides, pigeon-holes, nooks and corners. He did not leave a scrap of anything unread. Many of the letters which he found were old; some he had read before; others were new to him. But in none did he find a faintest evidence that his wife had not been the true and loyal woman he had always believed her to be. The night was nearly spent before the fruitless search ended. The brief troubled sleep which he snatched before his hour for rising was freighted with feverish, grotesque dreams, through all of which he could hear and could see dimly the dark river rushing by, carrying away his heart, his ambitions, his life.

But it was not alone in letters that women betrayed their emotions, he thought. Often he had known them, especially when in love, to mark fugitive, sentimental passages in books of verse or prose, thus expressing and revealing their own hidden thought. Might she not have done the same?

Then began a second and far more exhausting and arduous quest than the first, turning, page by page, the volumes that crowded her room—books of fiction, poetry, philosophy. She had read them all; but nowhere, by the shadow of a sign, could he find that the author had echoed the secret of her existence—the secret which he had held in his hands and had cast into the river.

He began cautiously and gradually to question this one and that one, striving to learn by indirect ways what each had thought of her. Foremost he learned she had been unsympathetic because of her coldness of manner. One had admired her intellect; another her accomplishments; a third had thought her beautiful before disease claimed her, regretting, however, that her beauty had lacked warmth of color and expression. She was praised by some for gentleness and kindness, and by others for cleverness and tact. Oh, it was useless to try to discover anything from men! he might have known. It was women who would talk of what they knew.

They did talk, unreservedly. Most of them had loved her; those who had not had held her in respect and esteem.

IV

And yet, and yet, "there is but one secret which a woman would choose to have die with her," was the thought which continued to haunt him and deprive him of rest. Days and nights of uncertainty began slowly to unnerve him and to torture him. An assurance of the worst that he dreaded would have offered him peace most welcome, even at the price of happiness.

It seemed no longer of any moment to him that men should come and go; and fall or rise in the world; and wed and die. It did not signify if money came to him by a turn of chance or eluded him. Empty and meaningless seemed to him all devices which the world offers for man's entertainment. The food and the drink set before him had lost their flavor. He did not longer know or care if the sun shone or the clouds lowered about him. A cruel hazard had struck him there where he was weakest, shattering his whole being, leaving him with but one wish in his soul, one gnawing desire, to know the mystery which he had held in his hands and had cast into the river.

One night when there were no stars shining he wandered, restless, upon the streets. He no longer sought to know from men and women what they dared not or could not tell him. Only the river knew. He went and stood again upon the bridge where he had stood many an hour since that night when the darkness then had closed around him and engulfed his manhood.

Only the river knew. It babbled, and he listened to it, and it told him nothing, but it promised all. He could hear it promising him with caressing voice, peace and sweet repose. He could hear the sweep, the song of the water inviting him.

A moment more and he had gone to seek her, and to join her and her secret thought in the immeasurable rest.

ATHÉNAÏSE

A Story of a Temperament.

I

Athénaïse went away in the morning to make a visit to her parents, ten miles back on rigolet du Bon Dieu.* She did not return in the evening, and Cazeau, her husband, fretted not a little. He did not worry much about Athénaïse, who, he suspected, was resting only too content in the bosom of her family; his chief solicitude was manifestly for the pony she had ridden. He felt sure those "lazy pigs," her brothers, were capable of neglecting it seriously. This misgiving Cazeau communicated to his servant, old Félicité, who waited upon him at supper.

His voice was low pitched, and even softer than Félicité's. He was tall, sinewy, swarthy, and altogether severe looking. His thick black hair waved, and it gleamed like the breast of a crow. The sweep of his mustache, which was not so black, outlined the broad contour of the mouth. Beneath the under lip grew a small tuft which he was much given to twisting, and which he permitted to grow, apparently, for no other purpose. Cazeau's eyes were dark blue, narrow and over-shadowed. His hands were coarse and stiff from close acquaintance with farming tools and implements, and he handled his fork and knife clumsily. But he was distinguished looking, and succeeded in commanding a good deal of respect, and even fear sometimes.

He ate his supper alone, by the light of a single coal-oil lamp that but faintly illumined the big room, with its bare floor and huge rafters, and its heavy pieces of furniture that loomed dimly in the gloom of the apartment. Félicité, ministering to his wants, hovered about the table like a little, bent, restless shadow.

She served him a dish of sunfish fried crisp and brown. There was nothing else set before him beside the bread and butter and the bottle of red wine which she locked carefully in the buffet after he had poured his second glass. She was occupied with her mistress's absence, and kept reverting to it after he had expressed his solicitude about the pony.

"Dat beat me! on'y marry two mont', an' got de head turn' a'ready to go 'broad. Ce n'est pas Chrétien, ténez!"*

Cazeau shrugged his shoulders for answer, after he had drained his glass and pushed aside his plate. Félicité's opinion of the unchristian-like behavior of his wife in leaving him thus alone after two months of marriage weighed little with him. He was used to solitude, and did not mind a day or a night or two of it. He had lived alone ten years, since his first wife died, and Félicité might have known better than to suppose that he cared. He told her she was a fool. It sounded like a compliment in his modulated, caressing voice. She grumbled to herself as she set about clearing the table, and Cazeau arose and walked outside on the gallery; his spur, which he had not removed upon entering the house, jangled at every step.

The night was beginning to deepen, and to gather black about the clusters of trees and shrubs that were grouped in the yard. In the beam of light from the open kitchen door a black boy stood feeding a brace of snarling, hungry dogs; further away, on the steps of a cabin, some one was playing the accordion; and in still another direction a little negro baby was crying lustily. Cazeau walked around to the front of the house, which was square, squat and one-story.

A belated wagon was driving in at the gate, and the impatient driver was swearing hoarsely at his jaded oxen. Félicité stepped out on the gallery, glass and polishing-towel in hand, to investigate, and to wonder, too, who could be singing out on the river. It was a party of young people paddling around, waiting for the moon to rise, and they were singing Juanita,* their voices coming tempered and melodious through the distance and the night.

Cazeau's horse was waiting, saddled, ready to be mounted, for Cazeau had many things to attend to before bed-time; so many things that there was not left to him a moment in which to think of Athénaïse. He felt her absence, though, like a dull, insistent pain.

However, before he slept that night he was visited by the thought of her, and by a vision of her fair young face with its drooping lips and sullen and averted eyes. The marriage had been a blunder; he had only to look into her eyes to feel that, to discover her growing aversion. But it was a thing not by any possibility to be undone. He was quite prepared to make the best of it, and expected no less than a like effort on her part. The less she revisited the rigolet, the better. He would find means to keep her at home hereafter.

These unpleasant reflections kept Cazeau awake far into the night, notwithstanding the craving of his whole body for rest and sleep. The moon was shining, and its pale effulgence reached dimly into the room, and with it a touch of the cool breath of the spring night. There was an unusual stillness abroad; no sound to be heard save the distant, tireless, plaintive notes of the accordion.

II

Athénaïse did not return the following day, even though her husband sent her word to do so by her brother, Montéclin, who passed on his way to the village early in the morning.

On the third day Cazeau saddled his horse and went himself in search of her. She had sent no word, no message, explaining her absence, and he felt that he had good cause to be offended. It was rather awkward to have to leave his work, even though late in the afternoon,—Cazeau had always so much to do; but among the many urgent calls upon him, the task of bringing his wife back to a sense of her duty seemed to him for the moment paramount.

The Michés, Athénaïse's parents, lived on the old Gotrain place.* It did not belong to them; they were "running" it for a merchant in Alexandria. The house was far too big for their use. One of the lower rooms served for the storing of wood and tools; the person "occupying" the place before Miché having pulled up the flooring in despair of being able to patch it. Upstairs, the rooms were so large, so bare, that they offered a constant temptation to lovers of the dance, whose importunities Madame Miché was accustomed to meet with amiable indulgence. A dance at Miché's and a plate of Madame Miché's gumbo filé at midnight* were pleasures not to be neglected or despised, unless by such serious souls as Cazeau.

Long before Cazeau reached the house his approach had been observed, for there was nothing to obstruct the view of the outer road; vegetation was not yet abundantly advanced, and there was but a patchy, straggling stand of cotton and corn in Miché's field.

Madame Miché, who had been seated on the gallery in a rocking-chair, stood up to greet him as he drew near. She was short and fat, and wore a black skirt and loose muslin sack fastened at the throat with a hair brooch. Her own hair, brown and glossy, showed but a few threads of silver. Her round pink face was cheery, and her eyes were bright and good humored. But she was plainly perturbed and ill at ease as Cazeau advanced.

Montéclin, who was there too, was not ill at ease, and made no attempt to disguise the dislike with which his brother-in-law inspired him. He was a slim, wiry fellow of twenty-five, short of stature like his mother, and resembling her in feature. He was in shirt-sleeves, half leaning, half sitting, on the insecure railing of the gallery, and fanning himself with his broad-rimmed felt hat.

"Cochon!" he muttered under his breath as Cazeau mounted the stairs,—"sacré cochon!"*

"Cochon" had sufficiently characterized the man who had once on a time declined to lend Montéclin money. But when this same man had had the presumption to propose marriage to his well-beloved sister, Athénaïse, and the honor to be accepted by her, Montéclin felt that a qualifying epithet was needed fully to express his estimate of Cazeau.

Miché and his oldest son were absent. They both esteemed Cazeau highly, and talked much of his qualities of head and heart, and thought much of his excellent standing with city merchants.

Athénaïse had shut herself up in her room. Cazeau had seen her rise and enter the house at perceiving him. He was a good deal mystified, but no one could have guessed it when he shook hands with Madame Miché. He had only nodded to Montéclin, with a muttered "Comment ça va?"

"Tiens! something tole me you were coming to-day!" exclaimed Madame Miché, with a little blustering appearance of being cordial and at ease, as she offered Cazeau a chair.

He ventured a short laugh as he seated himself.

"You know, nothing would do," she went on, with much gesture of her small, plump hands, "nothing would do but Athénaïse mus' stay las' night fo' a li'le dance. The boys wouldn' year to their sister leaving."

Cazeau shrugged his shoulders significantly, telling as plainly as words that he knew nothing about it.

"Comment! Montéclin didn' tell you we were going to keep Athénaïse?" Montéclin had evidently told nothing.

"An' how about the night befo'," questioned Cazeau, " an' las' night? It is n't possible you dance every night out yere on the Bon Dieu!"

Madame Miché laughed, with amiable appreciation of the sarcasm; and turning to her son, "Montéclin, my boy, go tell yo' sister that Monsieur Cazeau is yere."

Montéclin did not stir except to shift his position and settle himself more securely on the railing.

"Did you year me, Montéclin?"

"Oh yes, I yeard you plain enough," responded her son, "but you know as well as me it's no use to tell 'Thénaïse anything. You been talkin' to her yo'se'f since Monday; an' pa's preached himse'f hoa'se on the subject; an' you even had uncle Achille down yere yesterday to reason with her. W'en 'Thénaïse said she wasn' goin' to set her foot back in Cazeau's house, she meant it."

This speech, which Montéclin delivered with thorough unconcern, threw his mother into a condition of painful but dumb embarrassment. It brought two fiery red spots to Cazeau's cheeks, and for the space of a moment he looked wicked.

What Montéclin had spoken was quite true, though his taste in the manner and choice of time and place in saying it were not of the best. Athénaïse, upon the first day of her arrival, had announced that she came to stay, having no intention of returning under Cazeau's roof. The announcement had scattered consternation, as she knew it would. She had been implored, scolded, entreated, stormed at, until she felt herself like a dragging sail that all the winds of heaven had beaten upon. Why in the name of God had she married Cazeau? Her father had lashed her with the question a dozen times. Why indeed? It was difficult now for her to understand why, unless because she supposed it was customary for girls to marry when the right opportunity came. Cazeau, she knew, would make life more comfortable for her; and again, she had liked him, and had even been rather flustered when he pressed her hands and kissed them, and kissed her lips and cheeks and eyes, when she accepted him.

Montéclin himself had taken her aside to talk the thing over. The turn of affairs was delighting him.

"Come, now, 'Thénaïse, you mus' explain to me all about it, so we can settle on a good cause, an' secu' a separation fo' you. Has he been mistreating an' abusing you, the sacré cochon?" They were alone

together in her room, whither she had taken refuge from the angry
domestic elements.

"You please to reserve yo' disgusting expressions, Montéclin. No,
he has not abused me in any way that I can think."

"Does he drink? Come 'Thénaïse, think well over it. Does he ever
get drunk?"

"Drunk! Oh, mercy, no,—Cazeau never gets drunk."

"I see; it's jus' simply you feel like me; you hate him."

"No, I don't hate him," she returned reflectively; adding with a
sudden impulse, "It's jus' being married that I detes' an' despise. I
hate being Mrs. Cazeau, an' would want to be Athénaïse Miché
again. I can't stan' to live with a man: to have him always there; his
coats an' pantaloons hanging in my room; his ugly bare feet—
washing them in my tub, befo' my very eyes, ugh!" She shuddered
with recollections, and resumed, with a sigh that was almost a sob:
"Mon Dieu, mon Dieu! Sister Marie Angélique knew w'at she was
saying; she knew me better than myse'f w'en she said God had sent
me a vocation an' I was turning deaf ears. W'en I think of a blessed
life in the convent, at peace! Oh, w'at was I dreaming of!" and then
the tears came.

Montéclin felt disconcerted and greatly disappointed at having
obtained evidence that would carry no weight with a court of justice.
The day had not come when a young woman might ask the court's
permission to return to her mamma on the sweeping grounds of a
constitutional disinclination for marriage. But if there was no way of
untying this Gordian knot* of marriage, there was surely a way
of cutting it.

"Well, 'Thénaïse, I'm mighty durn sorry you got no better
groun's 'an w'at you say. But you can count on me to stan' by you
w'atever you do. God knows I don' blame you fo' not wantin' to live
with Cazeau."

And now there was Cazeau himself, with the red spots flaming in
his swarthy cheeks, looking and feeling as if he wanted to thrash
Montéclin into some semblance of decency. He arose abruptly,
and approaching the room which he had seen his wife enter, thrust
open the door after a hasty preliminary knock. Athénaïse, who was
standing erect at a far window, turned at his entrance.

She appeared neither angry nor frightened, but thoroughly
unhappy, with an appeal in her soft dark eyes and a tremor on

her lips that seemed to him expressions of unjust reproach, that wounded and maddened him at once. But whatever he might feel, Cazeau knew only one way to act toward a woman.

"Athénaïse, you are not ready?" he asked in his quiet tones. "It's getting late; we havn' any time to lose."

She knew that Montéclin had spoken out, and she had hoped for a wordy interview, a stormy scene, in which she might have held her own as she had held it for the past three days against her family, with Montéclin's aid. But she had no weapon with which to combat subtlety. Her husband's looks, his tones, his mere presence, brought to her a sudden sense of hopelessness, an instinctive realization of the futility of rebellion against a social and sacred institution.

Cazeau said nothing further, but stood waiting in the doorway. Madame Miché had walked to the far end of the gallery, and pretended to be occupied with having a chicken driven from her parterre. Montéclin stood by, exasperated, fuming, ready to burst out.

Athénaïse went and reached for her riding-skirt that hung against the wall. She was rather tall, with a figure which, though not robust, seemed perfect in its fine proportions. "La fille de son père,"* she was often called, which was a great compliment to Miché. Her brown hair was brushed all fluffily back from her temples and low forehead, and about her features and expression lurked a softness, a prettiness, a dewiness, that were perhaps too childlike, that savored of immaturity.

She slipped the riding-skirt, which was of black alpaca,* over her head, and with impatient fingers hooked it at the waist over her pink linen-lawn. Then she fastened on her white sunbonnet and reached for her gloves on the mantelpiece.

"If you don' wan' to go, you know w'at you got to do, 'Thénaïse," fumed Montéclin. "You don' set yo' feet back on Cane River,* by God, unless you want to,—not w'ile I'm alive."

Cazeau looked at him as if he were a monkey whose antics fell short of being amusing.

Athénaïse still made no reply, said not a word. She walked rapidly past her husband, past her brother; bidding good-by to no one, not even to her mother. She descended the stairs, and without assistance from any one mounted the pony, which Cazeau had ordered to be saddled upon his arrival. In this way she obtained a fair start of her husband, whose departure was far more leisurely, and for the greater part of the way she managed to keep an appreciable gap between them. She rode almost madly at first, with the wind inflating her skirt balloon-like about her knees, and her sunbonnet falling back between her shoulders.

At no time did Cazeau make an effort to overtake her until traversing an old fallow meadow that was level and hard as a table. The sight of a great solitary oak-tree, with its seemingly immutable outlines, that had been a landmark for ages—or was it the odor of elderberry stealing up from the gully to the south? or what was it that brought vividly back to Cazeau, by some association of ideas, a scene of many years ago? He had passed that old live-oak hundreds of times, but it was only now that the memory of one day came back to him. He was a very small boy that day, seated before his father on horseback. They were proceeding slowly, and Black Gabe was moving on before them at a little dog-trot. Black Gabe had run away, and had been discovered back in the Gotrain Swamp. They had halted beneath this big oak to enable the negro to take breath; for Cazeau's father was a kind and considerate master, and every one had agreed at the time that Black Gabe was a fool, a great idiot indeed, for wanting to run away from him.

The whole impression was for some reason hideous,* and to dispel it Cazeau spurred his horse to a swift gallop. Overtaking his wife, he rode the remainder of the way at her side in silence.

It was late when they reached home. Félicité was standing on the grassy edge of the road, in the moonlight, waiting for them.

Cazeau once more ate his supper alone; for Athénaïse went to her room, and there she was crying again.

III

Athénaïse was not one to accept the inevitable with patient resignation, a talent born in the souls of many women; neither was she the one to accept it with philosophical resignation, like her husband. Her sensibilities were alive and keen and responsive. She met the pleasurable things of life with frank, open appreciation, and against distasteful conditions she rebelled. Dissimulation was as foreign to her nature as guile to the breast of a babe, and her rebellious outbreaks, by no means rare, had hitherto been quite open and above-board. People often said that Athénaïse would know her own mind some day, which was equivalent to saying that she was at present unacquainted with it. If she ever came to such knowledge, it would be by no intellectual research, by no subtle analyses or tracing the motives of actions to their source. It would come to her as the song to the bird, the perfume and color to the flower.

Her parents had hoped—not without reason and justice—that marriage would bring the poise, the desirable pose, so glaringly lacking in Athénaïse's character. Marriage they knew to be a wonderful and powerful agent in the development and formation of a woman's character; they had seen its effect too often to doubt it.

"And if this marriage does nothing else," exclaimed Miché in an outburst of sudden exasperation, "it will rid us of Athénaïse; for I am at the end of my patience with her! You have never had the firmness to manage her,"—he was speaking to his wife,—"I have not had the time, the leisure, to devote to her training; and what good we might have accomplished, that maudit Montéclin—Well, Cazeau is the one! It takes just such a steady hand to guide a disposition like Athénaïse's, a master hand, a strong will that compels obedience."

And now, when they had hoped for so much, here was Athénaïse, with gathered and fierce vehemence, beside which her former outbursts appeared mild, declaring that she would not, and she would not, and she would *not* continue to enact the rôle of wife to Cazeau. If she had had a reason! as Madame Miché lamented; but it could not be discovered that she had any sane one. He had never scolded, or called names, or deprived her of comforts, or been guilty of any of the many reprehensible acts commonly attributed to objectionable husbands. He did not slight nor neglect her. Indeed, Cazeau's chief offense seemed to be that he loved her, and Athénaïse was not the woman to be loved against her will. She called marriage a trap set for the feet of unwary and unsuspecting girls, and in round, unmeasured terms reproached her mother with treachery and deceit.

"I told you Cazeau was the man," chuckled Miché, when his wife had related the scene that had accompanied and influenced Athénaïse's departure.

Athénaïse again hoped, in the morning, that Cazeau would scold or make some sort of a scene, but he apparently did not dream of it. It was exasperating that he should take her acquiescence so for granted. It is true he had been up and over the fields and across the river and back long before she was out of bed, and he may have been thinking of something else, which was no excuse, which was even in some sense an aggravation. But he did say to her at breakfast, "That brother of yo's, that Montéclin, is unbearable."

"Montéclin? Par exemple!"

Athénaïse, seated opposite to her husband, was attired in a white morning wrapper. She wore a somewhat abused, long face, it is true,—an expression of countenance familiar to some husbands,—but the expression was not sufficiently pronounced to mar the charm of her youthful freshness. She had little heart to eat, only playing with the food before her, and she felt a pang of resentment at her husband's healthy appetite.

"Yes, Montéclin," he reasserted. "He's developed into a firs'-class nuisance; an' you better tell him, Athénaïse,—unless you want me to tell him,—to confine his energies after this to matters that concern him. I have no use fo' him or fo' his interference in w'at regards you an' me alone."

This was said with unusual asperity. It was the little breach that Athénaïse had been watching for, and she charged rapidly: "It's strange, if you detes' Montéclin so heartily, that you would desire to marry his sister." She knew it was a silly thing to say, and was not surprised when he told her so. It gave her a little foothold for further attack, however. "I don't see, anyhow, w'at reason you had to marry me, w'en there were so many others," she complained, as if accusing him of persecution and injury. "There was Marianne running after you fo' the las' five years till it was disgraceful; an' any one of the Dortrand girls would have been glad to marry you. But no, nothing would do; you mus' come out on the rigolet fo' me." Her complaint was pathetic, and at the same time so amusing that Cazeau was forced to smile.

"I can't see w'at the Dortrand girls or Marianne have to do with it," he rejoined; adding, with no trace of amusement, "I married you because I loved you; because you were the woman I wanted to marry, an' the only one. I reckon I tole you that befo'. I thought—of co'se I was a fool fo' taking things fo' granted—but I did think that I might make you happy in making things easier an' mo' comfortable fo' you. I expected—I was even that big a fool—I believed that yo' coming yere to me would be like the sun shining out of the clouds, an' that our days would be like w'at the story-books promise after the wedding. I was mistaken. But I can't imagine w'at induced you to marry me. W'atever it was, I reckon you foun' out you made a mistake, too. I don' see anything to do but make the best of a bad bargain, an' shake han's over it." He had arisen from the table, and, approaching, held out his hand to her. What he had said was commonplace enough, but it was significant, coming from Cazeau, who was not often so unreserved in expressing himself.

Athénaïse ignored the hand held out to her. She was resting her chin in her palm, and kept her eyes fixed moodily upon the table. He rested his hand, that she would not touch, upon her head for an instant, and walked away out of the room.

She heard him giving orders to workmen who had been waiting for him out on the gallery, and she heard him mount his horse and ride away. A hundred things would distract him and engage his attention during the day. She felt that he had perhaps put her and her grievance from his thoughts when he crossed the threshold; whilst she—

Old Félicité was standing there holding a shining tin pail, asking for flour and lard and eggs from the storeroom, and meal for the chicks.

Athénaïse seized the bunch of keys which hung from her belt and flung them at Félicité's feet.

"Tiens! tu vas les garder comme tu as jadis fait. Je ne veux plus de ce train là, moi!"*

The old woman stooped and picked up the keys from the floor. It was really all one to her that her mistress returned them to her keeping, and refused to take further account of the ménage.

IV

It seemed now to Athénaïse that Montéclin was the only friend left to her in the world. Her father and mother had turned from her in what appeared to be her hour of need. Her friends laughed at her, and refused to take seriously the hints which she threw out,—feeling her way to discover if marriage were as distasteful to other women as to herself. Montéclin alone understood her. He alone had always been ready to act for her and with her, to comfort and solace her with his sympathy and support. Her only hope for rescue from her hateful surroundings lay in Montéclin. Of herself she felt powerless to plan, to act, even to conceive a way out of this pitfall into which the whole world seemed to have conspired to thrust her.

She had a great desire to see her brother, and wrote asking him to come to her. But it better suited Montéclin's spirit of adventure to appoint a meeting-place at the turn of the lane, where Athénaïse might appear to be walking leisurely for health and recreation, and where he might seem to be riding along, bent on some errand of business or pleasure.

There had been a shower, a sudden downpour, short as it was sudden, that had laid the dust in the road. It had freshened the pointed leaves of the live-oaks, and brightened up the big fields of cotton on either side of the lane till they seemed carpeted with green, glittering gems.

Athénaïse walked along the grassy edge of the road, lifting her crisp skirts with one hand, and with the other twirling a gay sunshade over her bare head. The scent of the fields after the rain was delicious. She inhaled long breaths of their freshness and perfume, that soothed and quieted her for the moment. There were birds splashing and spluttering in the pools, pluming themselves on the fence-rails, and sending out little sharp cries, twitters, and shrill rhapsodies of delight.

She saw Montéclin approaching from a great distance,—almost as far away as the turn of the woods. But she could not feel sure it was he; it appeared too tall for Montéclin, but that was because he was riding a large horse. She waved her parasol to him; she was so glad to see him. She had never been so glad to see Montéclin before; not even the day when he had taken her out of the convent, against her parents' wishes, because she had expressed a desire to remain there no longer. He seemed to her, as he drew near, the embodiment of kindness, of bravery, of chivalry, even of wisdom; for she had never known Montéclin at a loss to extricate himself from a disagreeable situation.

He dismounted, and, leading his horse by the bridle, started to walk beside her, after he had kissed her affectionately and asked her what she was crying about. She protested that she was not crying, for she was laughing, though drying her eyes at the same time on her handkerchief, rolled in a soft mop for the purpose.

She took Montéclin's arm, and they strolled slowly down the lane; they could not seat themselves for a comfortable chat, as they would have liked, with the grass all sparkling and bristling wet.

Yes, she was quite as wretched as ever, she told him. The week which had gone by since she saw him had in no wise lightened the burden of her discontent. There had even been some additional provocations laid upon her, and she told Montéclin all about them,—about the keys, for instance, which in a fit of temper she had returned to Félicité's keeping; and she told how Cazeau had brought them back to her as if they were something she had accidentally lost, and he had recovered; and how he had said, in that aggravating tone of his, that it was not the custom on Cane River for the negro servants to carry the keys, when there was a mistress at the head of the household.

But Athénaïse could not tell Montéclin anything to increase the disrespect which he already entertained for his brother-in-law; and it was then he unfolded to her a plan which he had conceived and worked out for her deliverance from this galling matrimonial yoke.

It was not a plan which met with instant favor, which she was at once ready to accept, for it involved secrecy and dissimulation, hateful alternatives, both of them. But she was filled with admiration for Montéclin's resources and wonderful talent for contrivance. She accepted the plan; not with the immediate determination to act upon it, rather with the intention to sleep and to dream upon it.

Three days later she wrote to Montéclin that she had abandoned herself to his counsel. Displeasing as it might be to her sense of honesty, it would yet be less trying than to live on with a soul full of bitterness and revolt, as she had done for the past two months.

V

When Cazeau awoke, one morning at his usual very early hour, it was to find the place at his side vacant. This did not surprise him until he discovered that Athénaïse was not in the adjoining room, where he had often found her sleeping in the morning on the lounge. She had perhaps gone out for an early stroll, he reflected, for her jacket and hat were not on the rack where she had hung them the night before. But there were other things absent,—a gown or two from the armoire; and there was a great gap in the piles of lingerie on the shelf; and her traveling-bag was missing, and so were her bits of jewelry from the toilet tray—and Athénaïse was gone!

But the absurdity of going during the night, as if she had been a prisoner, and he the keeper of a dungeon! So much secrecy and mystery, to go sojourning out on the Bon Dieu! Well, the Michés might keep their daughter after this. For the companionship of no woman on earth would he again undergo the humiliating sensation of baseness that had overtaken him in passing the old oak-tree in the fallow meadow.

But a terrible sense of loss overwhelmed Cazeau. It was not new or sudden; he had felt it for weeks growing upon him, and it seemed to culminate with Athénaïse's flight from home. He knew that he could again compel her return as he had done once before,— compel her return to the shelter of his roof, compel her cold and unwilling submission to his love and passionate transports; but the loss of self-respect seemed to him too dear a price to pay for a wife.

He could not comprehend why she had seemed to prefer him above others; why she had attracted him with eyes, with voice, with a hundred womanly ways, and finally distracted him with love which she seemed, in her timid, maidenly fashion, to return. The great sense of loss came from the realization of having missed a chance for happiness,—a chance that would come his way again only through a miracle. He could not think of himself loving any other woman, and could not think of Athénaïse ever—even at some remote date—caring for him.

He wrote her a letter, in which he disclaimed any further intention of forcing his commands upon her. He did not desire her presence ever again in his home unless she came of her free will, uninfluenced by family or friends; unless she could be the companion he had hoped for in marrying her, and in some measure return affection and respect for the love which he continued and would always continue to feel for her. This letter he sent out to the rigolet by a messenger early in the day. But she was not out on the rigolet, and had not been there.

The family turned instinctively to Montéclin, and almost literally fell upon him for an explanation; he had been absent from home all night. There was much mystification in his answers, and a plain desire to mislead in his assurances of ignorance and innocence.

But with Cazeau there was no doubt or speculation when he accosted the young fellow. "Montéclin, w'at have you done with Athénaïse?" he questioned bluntly. They had met in the open road on horseback, just as Cazeau ascended the river bank before his house.

"W'at have you done to Athénaïse?" returned Montéclin for answer.

"I don't reckon you 've considered yo' conduct by any light of decency an' propriety in encouraging yo' sister to such an action, but let me tell you"—

"Voyons! you can let me alone with yo' decency an' morality an' fiddlesticks. I know you mus' 'a' done Athénaïse pretty mean that she can't live with you; an' fo' my part, I'm mighty durn glad she had the spirit to quit you."

"I ain't in the humor to take any notice of yo' impertinence, Montéclin; but let me remine you that Athénaïse is nothing but a chile in character; besides that, she's my wife, an' I hole you responsible fo' her safety an' welfare. If any harm of any description happens to her, I'll strangle you, by God, like a rat, and fling you in Cane River, if I have to hang fo' it!" He had not lifted his voice. The only sign of anger was a savage gleam in his eyes.

"I reckon you better keep yo' big talk fo' the women, Cazeau," replied Montéclin, riding away.

But he went doubly armed after that, and intimated that the precaution was not needless, in view of the threats and menaces that were abroad touching his personal safety.

VI

Athénaïse reached her destination sound of skin and limb, but a good deal flustered, a little frightened, and altogether excited and interested by her unusual experiences.

Her destination was the house of Sylvie, on Dauphine Street,* in New Orleans,—a three-story gray brick, standing directly on the banquette, with three broad stone steps leading to the deep front entrance. From the second-story balcony swung a small sign, conveying to passers-by the intelligence that within were "chambres garnies."*

It was one morning in the last week of April that Athénaïse presented herself at the Dauphine Street house. Sylvie was expecting her, and introduced her at once to her apartment, which was in the second story of the back ell,* and accessible by an open, outside gallery. There was a yard below, paved with broad stone flagging; many fragrant flowering shrubs and plants grew in a bed along the side of the opposite wall, and others were distributed about in tubs and green boxes.

It was a plain but large enough room into which Athénaïse was ushered, with matting on the floor, green shades and Nottingham-lace curtains at the windows that looked out on the gallery, and furnished with a cheap walnut suit. But everything looked exquisitely clean, and the whole place smelled of cleanliness.

Athénaïse at once fell into the rocking-chair, with the air of exhaustion and intense relief of one who has come to the end of her troubles. Sylvie, entering behind her, laid the big traveling-bag on the floor and deposited the jacket on the bed.

She was a portly quadroon of fifty or thereabout, clad in an ample volante of the old-fashioned purple calico so much affected by her class. She wore large golden hoop-earrings, and her hair was combed plainly, with every appearance of effort to smooth out the kinks. She had broad, coarse features, with a nose that turned up, exposing the wide nostrils, and that seemed to emphasize the loftiness and command of her bearing,—a dignity that in the presence of white people assumed a character of respectfulness, but never of obsequiousness. Sylvie believed firmly in maintaining the color-line,* and would not suffer a white person, even a child, to call her "Madame Sylvie," —a title which she exacted religiously, however, from those of her own race.

"I hope you be please' wid yo' room, madame," she observed amiably. "Dat's de same room w'at yo' brother, M'sieur Miché, all time like w'en he come to New Orlean'. He well, M'sieur Miché? I receive' his letter las' week, an' dat same day a gent'man want I give 'im dat room. I say, 'No, dat room already ingage'.' Ev'body like dat room on 'count it so quite [quiet].* M'sieur Gouvernail, dere in nax' room, you can't pay 'im! He been stay t'ree year' in dat room; but all fix' up fine wid his own furn'ture an' books, 'tel you can't see! I say to 'im plenty time', 'M'sieur Gouvernail, w'y you don' take dat t'ree-story front, now, long it's empty?' He tell me, 'Leave me 'lone, Sylvie; I know a good room w'en I fine it, me.'"

She had been moving slowly and majestically about the apartment, straightening and smoothing down bed and pillows, peering into ewer and basin, evidently casting an eye around to make sure that everything was as it should be.

"I sen' you some fresh water, madame," she offered upon retiring from the room. "An' w'en you want an't'ing, you jus' go out on de gall'ry an' call Pousette: she year you plain,—she right down dere in de kitchen."

Athénaïse was really not so exhausted as she had every reason to be after that interminable and circuitous way by which Montéclin had seen fit to have her conveyed to the city.

Would she ever forget that dark and truly dangerous midnight ride along the "coast"* to the mouth of Cane River! There Montéclin had parted with her, after seeing her aboard the St. Louis and Shreveport packet which he knew would pass there before dawn. She had received instructions to disembark at the mouth of Red River, and there transfer to the first south-bound steamer for New Orleans; all of which instructions she had followed implicitly, even to making her way at once to Sylvie's upon her arrival in the city. Montéclin had enjoined secrecy and much caution; the clandestine nature of the affair gave it a savor of adventure which was highly pleasing to him. Eloping with his sister was only a little less engaging than eloping with some one else's sister.

But Montéclin did not do the grand seigneur by halves. He had paid Sylvie a whole month in advance for Athénaïse's board and lodging. Part of the sum he had been forced to borrow, it is true, but he was not niggardly.

Athénaïse was to take her meals in the house, which none of the other lodgers did;* the one exception being that Mr. Gouvernail was served with breakfast on Sunday mornings.

Sylvie's clientèle came chiefly from the southern parishes;* for the most part, people spending but a few days in the city. She prided herself upon the quality and highly respectable character of her patrons, who came and went unobtrusively.

The large parlor opening upon the front balcony was seldom used. Her guests were permitted to entertain in this sanctuary of elegance,—but they never did. She often rented it for the night to parties of respectable and discreet gentlemen desiring to enjoy a quiet game of cards outside the bosom of their families. The second-story hall also led by a long window out on the balcony. And Sylvie advised Athénaïse, when she grew weary of her back room, to go and sit on the front balcony, which was shady in the afternoon, and where she might find diversion in the sounds and sights of the street below.

Athénaïse refreshed herself with a bath, and was soon unpacking her few belongings, which she ranged neatly away in the bureau drawers and the armoire.

She had revolved certain plans in her mind during the past hour or so. Her present intention was to live on indefinitely in this big, cool, clean back room on Dauphine Street. She had thought seriously, for moments, of the convent, with all readiness to embrace the vows of poverty and chastity; but what about obedience? Later, she intended, in some roundabout way, to give her parents and her husband the assurance of her safety and welfare; reserving the right to remain unmolested and lost to them. To live on at the expense of Montéclin's generosity was wholly out of the question, and Athénaïse meant to look about for some suitable and agreeable employment.

The imperative thing to be done at present, however, was to go out in search of material for an inexpensive gown or two; for she found herself in the painful predicament of a young woman having almost literally nothing to wear. She decided upon pure white for one, and some sort of a sprigged muslin for the other.

VII

On Sunday morning, two days after Athénaïse's arrival in the city, she went in to breakfast somewhat later than usual, to find two covers laid at table instead of the one to which she was accustomed. She had been to mass, and did not remove her hat, but put her fan, parasol, and prayer-book aside. The dining-room was situated just beneath her own apartment, and, like all the rooms of the house, was large and airy; the floor was covered with a glistening oil-cloth.

The small, round table, immaculately set, was drawn near the open window. There were some tall plants in boxes on the gallery outside; and Pousette, a little, old, intensely black woman, was splashing and dashing buckets of water on the flagging, and talking loud in her Creole patois to no one in particular.

A dish piled with delicate river-shrimps* and crushed ice was on the table; a caraffe of crystal-clear water, a few hors d'œuvres, beside a small golden-brown crusty loaf of French bread at each plate. A half-bottle of wine and the morning paper were set at the place opposite Athénaïse.

She had almost completed her breakfast when Gouvernail came in and seated himself at table. He felt annoyed at finding his cherished privacy invaded. Sylvie was removing the remains of a mutton-chop from before Athénaïse, and serving her with a cup of café au lait.

"M'sieur Gouvernail," offered Sylvie in her most insinuating and impressive manner, "you please leave me make you acquaint' wid Madame Cazeau. Dat's M'sieur Miché's sister; you meet 'im two t'ree time', you rec'lec', an' been one day to de race wid 'im. Madame Cazeau, you please leave me make you acquaint' wid M'sieur Gouvernail."

Gouvernail expressed himself greatly pleased to meet the sister of Monsieur Miché, of whom he had not the slightest recollection. He inquired after Monsieur Miché's health, and politely offered Athénaïse a part of his newspaper,—the part which contained the Woman's Page and the social gossip.

Athénaïse faintly remembered that Sylvie had spoken of a Monsieur Gouvernail occupying the room adjoining hers, living amid luxurious surroundings and a multitude of books. She had not thought of him further than to picture him a stout, middle-aged gentleman, with a bushy beard turning gray, wearing large gold-rimmed spectacles, and stooping somewhat from much bending over books and writing material. She had confused him in her mind with the likeness of some literary celebrity that she had run across in the advertising pages of a magazine.

Gouvernail's appearance was, in truth, in no sense striking. He looked older than thirty and younger than forty, was of medium height and weight, with a quiet, unobtrusive manner which seemed to ask that he be let alone. His hair was light brown, brushed carefully and parted in the middle. His mustache was brown, and so were his eyes, which had a mild, penetrating quality. He was neatly dressed in the fashion of the day; and his hands seemed to Athénaïse remarkably white and soft for a man's.

He had been buried in the contents of his newspaper, when he suddenly realized that some further little attention might be due to Miché's sister. He started to offer her a glass of wine, when he was surprised and relieved to find that she had quietly slipped away while he was absorbed in his own editorial on Corrupt Legislation.*

Gouvernail finished his paper and smoked his cigar out on the gallery. He lounged about, gathered a rose for his buttonhole, and had his regular Sunday-morning confab with Pousette, to whom he paid a weekly stipend for brushing his shoes and clothing. He made a great pretense of haggling over the transaction, only to enjoy her uneasiness and garrulous excitement.

He worked or read in his room for a few hours, and when he quitted the house, at three in the afternoon, it was to return no more till late in the night. It was his almost invariable custom to spend Sunday evenings out in the American quarter, among a congenial set of men and women,—des esprits forts,* all of them, whose lives were irreproachable, yet whose opinions would startle even the traditional "sapeur," for whom "nothing is sacred." But for all his "advanced" opinions, Gouvernail was a liberal-minded fellow; a man or woman lost nothing of his respect by being married.

When he left the house in the afternoon, Athénaïse had already ensconced herself on the front balcony. He could see her through the jalousies when he passed on his way to the front entrance. She had not yet grown lonesome or homesick; the newness of her surroundings made them sufficiently entertaining. She found it diverting to sit there on the front balcony watching people pass by, even though there was no one to talk to. And then the comforting, comfortable sense of not being married!

She watched Gouvernail walk down the street, and could find no fault with his bearing. He could hear the sound of her rockers for some little distance. He wondered what the "poor little thing" was doing in the city, and meant to ask Sylvie about her when he should happen to think of it.

VIII

The following morning, towards noon, when Gouvernail quitted his room, he was confronted by Athénaïse, exhibiting some confusion and trepidation at being forced to request a favor of him at so early a stage of their acquaintance. She stood in her doorway, and had evidently been sewing, as the thimble on her finger testified, as well as a long-threaded needle thrust in the bosom of her gown. She held a stamped but unaddressed letter in her hand.

And would Mr. Gouvernail be so kind as to address the letter to her brother, Mr. Montéclin Miché? She would hate to detain him with explanations this morning,—another time, perhaps,—but now she begged that he would give himself the trouble.

He assured her that it made no difference, that it was no trouble whatever; and he drew a fountain pen from his pocket and addressed the letter at her dictation, resting it on the inverted rim of his straw hat. She wondered a little at a man of his supposed erudition stumbling over the spelling of "Montéclin" and "Miché."

She demurred at overwhelming him with the additional trouble of posting it, but he succeeded in convincing her that so simple a task as the posting of a letter would not add an iota to the burden of the day. Moreover, he promised to carry it in his hand, and thus avoid any possible risk of forgetting it in his pocket.

After that, and after a second repetition of the favor, when she had told him that she had had a letter from Montéclin, and looked as if she wanted to tell him more, he felt that he knew her better. He felt that he knew her well enough to join her out on the balcony, one night, when he found her sitting there alone. He was not one who deliberately sought the society of women, but he was not wholly a bear. A little commiseration for Athénaïse's aloneness, perhaps some curiosity to know further what manner of woman she was, and the natural influence of her feminine charm were equal unconfessed factors in turning his steps towards the balcony when he discovered the shimmer of her white gown through the open hall window.

It was already quite late, but the day had been intensely hot, and neighboring balconies and doorways were occupied by chattering groups of humanity, loath to abandon the grateful freshness of the outer air. The voices about her served to reveal to Athénaïse the feeling of loneliness that was gradually coming over her. Notwithstanding certain dormant impulses, she craved human sympathy and companionship.

She shook hands impulsively with Gouvernail, and told him how glad she was to see him. He was not prepared for such an admission, but it pleased him immensely, detecting as he did that the expression was as sincere as it was outspoken. He drew a chair up within comfortable conversational distance of Athénaïse, though he had no intention of talking more than was barely necessary to encourage Madame— He had actually forgotten her name!

He leaned an elbow on the balcony rail, and would have offered an opening remark about the oppressive heat of the day, but Athénaïse did not give him the opportunity. How glad she was to talk to some one, and how she talked!

An hour later she had gone to her room, and Gouvernail stayed smoking on the balcony. He knew her quite well after that hour's talk. It was not so much what she had said as what her half saying had revealed to his quick intelligence. He knew that she adored Montéclin, and he suspected that she adored Cazeau without being herself aware of it. He had gathered that she was self-willed, impulsive, innocent, ignorant, unsatisfied, dissatisfied; for had she not complained that things seemed all wrongly arranged in this world, and no one was permitted to be happy in his own way? And he told her he was sorry she had discovered that primordial fact of existence so early in life.

He commiserated her loneliness, and scanned his bookshelves next morning for something to lend her to read, rejecting everything that offered itself to his view. Philosophy was out of the question, and so was poetry; that is, such poetry as he possessed. He had not sounded her literary tastes, and strongly suspected she had none; that she would have rejected The Duchess as readily as Mrs. Humphry Ward.* He compromised on a magazine.

It had entertained her passably, she admitted, upon returning it. A New England story had puzzled her, it was true, and a Creole tale had offended her,* but the pictures had pleased her greatly, especially one which had reminded her so strongly of Montéclin after a hard day's ride that she was loath to give it up. It was one of Remington's

Cowboys,* and Gouvernail insisted upon her keeping it,—keeping the magazine.

He spoke to her daily after that, and was always eager to render her some service or to do something towards her entertainment.

One afternoon he took her out to the lake end.* She had been there once, some years before, but in winter, so the trip was comparatively new and strange to her. The large expanse of water studded with pleasure-boats, the sight of children playing merrily along the grassy palisades, the music, all enchanted her. Gouvernail thought her the most beautiful woman he had ever seen. Even her gown—the sprigged muslin—appeared to him the most charming one imaginable. Nor could anything be more becoming than the arrangement of her brown hair under the white sailor hat, all rolled back in a soft puff from her radiant face. And she carried her parasol and lifted her skirts and used her fan in ways that seemed quite unique and peculiar to herself and which he considered almost worthy of study and imitation.

They did not dine out there at the water's edge, as they might have done, but returned early to the city to avoid the crowd. Athénaïse wanted to go home, for she said Sylvie would have dinner prepared and would be expecting her. But it was not difficult to persuade her to dine instead in the quiet little restaurant that he knew and liked, with its sanded floor, its secluded atmosphere, its delicious menu, and its obsequious waiter wanting to know what he might have the honor of serving to "monsieur et madame." No wonder he made the mistake, with Gouvernail assuming such an air of proprietorship. But Athénaïse was very tired after it all; the sparkle went out of her face, and she hung draggingly on his arm in walking home.

He was reluctant to part from her when she bade him good-night at her door and thanked him for the agreeable evening. He had hoped she would sit outside until it was time for him to regain the newspaper office. He knew that she would undress and get into her peignoir and lie upon her bed; and what he wanted to do, what he would have given much to do, was to go and sit beside her, read to her something restful, soothe her, do her bidding, whatever it might be. Of course there was no use in thinking of that. But he was surprised at his growing desire to be serving her. She gave him an opportunity sooner than he looked for.

"Mr. Gouvernail," she called from her room, "will you be so kine as to call Pousette an' tell her she fo'got to bring my ice-water?"

He was indignant at Pousette's negligence, and called severely to her over the banisters. He was sitting before his own door, smoking. He knew that Athénaïse had gone to bed, for her room was dark, and she had opened the slats of the door and windows. Her bed was near a window.

Pousette came flopping up with the ice-water, and with a hundred excuses: "Mo pa oua vou à tab c'te lanuite, mo cri vou pé gagni déja là-bas; parole! Vou pas cri conté ça Madame Sylvie?"* She had not seen Athénaïse at table, and thought she was gone. She swore to this, and hoped Madame Sylvie would not be informed of her remissness.

A little later Athénaïse lifted her voice again: "Mr. Gouvernail, did you remark that young man sitting on the opposite side from us, coming in, with a gray coat an' a blue ban' aroun' his hat?"

Of course Gouvernail had not noticed any such individual, but he assured Athénaïse that he had observed the young fellow particularly.

"Don't you think he looked something,—not *very* much, of co'se,—but don't you think he had a little faux-air of Montéclin?"

"I think he looked strikingly like Montéclin," asserted Gouvernail, with the one idea of prolonging the conversation. "I meant to call your attention to the resemblance, and something drove it out of my head."

"The same with me," returned Athénaïse. "Ah, my dear Montéclin! I wonder w'at he is doing now?"

"Did you receive any news, any letter from him to-day?" asked Gouvernail, determined that if the conversation ceased it should not be through lack of effort on his part to sustain it.

"Not today, but yesterday. He tells me that maman was so distracted with uneasiness that finally, to pacify her, he was fo'ced to confess that he knew w'ere I was, but that he was boun' by a vow of secrecy not to reveal it. But Cazeau has not noticed him or spoken to him since he threaten' to throw po' Montéclin in Cane River. You know Cazeau wrote me a letter the morning I lef', thinking I had gone to the rigolet. An' maman opened it, an' said it was full of the mos' noble sentiments, an' she wanted Montéclin to sen' it to me; but Montéclin refuse' poin' blank, so he wrote to me."

Gouvernail preferred to talk of Montéclin. He pictured Cazeau as unbearable, and did not like to think of him.

A little later Athénaïse called out, "Good-night, Mr. Gouvernail."

"Good-night," he returned reluctantly. And when he thought that she was sleeping, he got up and went away to the midnight pandemonium of his newspaper office.

IX

Athénaïse could not have held out through the month had it not been for Gouvernail. With the need of caution and secrecy always uppermost in her mind, she made no new acquaintances, and she did not seek out persons already known to her; however, she knew so few, it required little effort to keep out of their way. As for Sylvie, almost every moment of her time was occupied in looking after her house; and, moreover, her deferential attitude towards her lodgers forbade anything like the gossipy chats in which Athénaïse might have condescended sometimes to indulge with her landlady. The transient lodgers, who came and went, she never had occasion to meet. Hence she was entirely dependent upon Gouvernail for company.

He appreciated the situation fully; and every moment that he could spare from his work he devoted to her entertainment. She liked to be out of doors, and they strolled together in the summer twilight through the mazes of the old French quarter. They went again to the lake end, and stayed for hours on the water; returning so late that the streets through which they passed were silent and deserted. On Sunday morning he arose at an unconscionable hour to take her to the French market,* knowing that the sights and sounds there would interest her. And he did not join the intellectual coterie in the afternoon, as he usually did, but placed himself all day at the disposition and service of Athénaïse.

Notwithstanding all, his manner toward her was tactful, and evinced intelligence and a deep knowledge of her character, surprising upon so brief an acquaintance. For the time he was everything to her that she would have him; he replaced home and friends. Sometimes she wondered if he had ever loved a woman. She could not fancy him loving any one passionately, rudely, offensively, as Cazeau loved her. Once she was so naive as to ask him outright if he had ever been in love, and he assured her promptly that he had not. She thought it an admirable trait in his character, and esteemed him greatly therefor.

He found her crying one night, not openly or violently. She was leaning over the gallery rail, watching the toads that hopped about in the moonlight, down on the damp flagstones of the courtyard. There was an oppressively sweet odor rising from the cape jessamine. Pousette was down there, mumbling and quarreling with some one, and seeming to be having it all her own way,—as well she might, when her companion was only a black cat that had come in from a neighboring yard to keep her company.

Athénaïse did admit feeling heart-sick, body-sick, when he questioned her; she supposed it was nothing but homesick. A letter from Montéclin had stirred her all up. She longed for her mother, for Montéclin; she was sick for a sight of the cotton-fields, the scent of the ploughed earth, for the dim, mysterious charm of the woods, and the old tumble-down home on the Bon Dieu.

As Gouvernail listened to her, a wave of pity and tenderness swept through him. He took her hands and pressed them against him. He wondered what would happen if he were to put his arms around her.

He was hardly prepared for what happened, but he stood it courageously. She twined her arms around his neck and wept outright on his shoulder; the hot tears scalding his cheek and neck, and her whole body shaken in his arms. The impulse was powerful to strain her to him; the temptation was fierce to seek her lips; but he did neither.

He understood a thousand times better than she herself understood it that he was acting as substitute for Montéclin. Bitter as the conviction was, he accepted it. He was patient; he could wait. He hoped some day to hold her with a lover's arms. That she was married made no particle of difference to Gouvernail. He could not conceive or dream of its making a difference. When the time came that she wanted him,—as he hoped and believed it would come,—he felt he would have a right to her. So long as she did not want him, he had no right to her,—no more than her husband had. It was very hard to feel her warm breath and tears upon his cheek, and her struggling bosom pressed against him and her soft arms clinging to him and his whole body and soul aching for her, and yet to make no sign.

He tried to think what Montéclin would have said and done, and to act accordingly. He stroked her hair, and held her in a gentle embrace, until the tears dried and the sobs ended. Before releasing herself she kissed him against the neck; she had to love somebody in her own way! Even that he endured like a stoic. But it was well he left her, to plunge into the thick of rapid, breathless, exacting work till nearly dawn.

Athénaïse was greatly soothed, and slept well. The touch of friendly hands and caressing arms had been very grateful. Henceforward she would not be lonely and unhappy, with Gouvernail there to comfort her.

X

The fourth week of Athénaïse's stay in the city was drawing to a close. Keeping in view the intention which she had of finding some suitable and agreeable employment, she had made a few tentatives in that direction. But with the exception of two little girls who had promised to take piano lessons at a price that it would be embarrassing to mention, these attempts had been fruitless. Moreover, the homesickness kept coming back, and Gouvernail was not always there to drive it away.

She spent much of her time weeding and pottering among the flowers down in the courtyard. She tried to take an interest in the black cat, and a mockingbird that hung in a cage outside the kitchen door, and a disreputable parrot that belonged to the cook next door, and swore hoarsely all day long in bad French.

Beside, she was not well; she was not herself, as she told Sylvie. The climate of New Orleans did not agree with her. Sylvie was distressed to learn this, as she felt in some measure responsible for the health and well-being of Monsieur Miché's sister; and she made it her duty to inquire closely into the nature and character of Athénaïse's malaise.

Sylvie was very wise, and Athénaïse was very ignorant. The extent of her ignorance and the depth of her subsequent enlightenment were bewildering. She stayed a long, long time quite still, quite stunned, except for the short, uneven breathing that ruffled her bosom. Her whole being was steeped in a wave of ecstasy. When she finally arose from the chair in which she had been seated, and looked at herself in the mirror, a face met hers which she seemed to see for the first time, so transfigured was it with wonder and rapture.

One mood quickly followed another, in this new turmoil of her senses, and the need of action became uppermost. Her mother must know at once, and her mother must tell Montéclin. And Cazeau must know. As she thought of him, the first purely sensuous tremor of her life swept over her. She half whispered his name, and the sound of it brought red blotches into her cheeks. She spoke it over and over, as if it were some new, sweet sound born out of darkness and confusion, and reaching her for the first time. She was impatient to be with him. Her whole passionate nature was aroused as if by a miracle.

She seated herself to write to her husband. The letter he would get in the morning, and she would be with him at night. What would he say? How would he act? She knew that he would forgive her, for had he not written a letter?—and a pang of resentment toward Montéclin shot through her. What did he mean by withholding that letter? How dared he not have sent it?

Athénaïse attired herself for the street, and went out to post the letter which she had penned with a single thought, a spontaneous impulse. It would have seemed incoherent to most people, but Cazeau would understand.

She walked along the street as if she had fallen heir to some magnificent inheritance. On her face was a look of pride and satisfaction that passers-by noticed and admired. She wanted to talk to some one, to tell some person; and she stopped at the corner and told the oyster-woman, who was Irish, and who God-blessed her, and wished prosperity to the race of Cazeaus for generations to come. She held the oyster-woman's fat, dirty little baby in her arms and scanned it curiously and observingly, as if a baby were a phenomenon that she encountered for the first time in life. She even kissed it!

Then what a relief it was to Athénaïse to walk the streets without dread of being seen and recognized by some chance acquaintance from Red River! No one could have said now that she did not know her own mind.

She went directly from the oyster-woman's to the office of Harding & Offdean,* her husband's merchants; and it was with such an air of partnership, almost proprietorship, that she demanded a sum of money on her husband's account, they gave it to her as unhesitatingly as they would have handed it over to Cazeau himself. When Mr. Harding, who knew her, asked politely after her health, she turned so rosy and looked so conscious, he thought it a great pity for so pretty a woman to be such a little goose.

Athénaïse entered a dry-goods store and bought all manner of things,—little presents for nearly everybody she knew. She bought whole bolts of sheerest, softest, downiest white stuff; and when the clerk, in trying to meet her wishes, asked if she intended it for infant's use, she could have sunk through the floor, and wondered how he might have suspected it.

As it was Montéclin who had taken her away from her husband, she wanted it to be Montéclin who should take her back to him. So she wrote him a very curt note,—in fact it was a postal card,—asking that he meet her at the train on the evening following. She felt convinced that after what had gone before, Cazeau would await her at their own home; and she preferred it so.

Then there was the agreeable excitement of getting ready to leave, of packing up her things. Pousette kept coming and going, coming and going; and each time that she quitted the room it was with something that Athénaïse had given her,—a handkerchief, a petticoat, a pair of stockings with two tiny holes at the toes, some broken prayer-beads, and finally a silver dollar.

Next it was Sylvie who came along bearing a gift of what she called "a set of pattern',"*—things of complicated design which never could have been obtained in any new-fangled bazaar or pattern-store, that Sylvie had acquired of a foreign lady of distinction whom she had nursed years before at the St. Charles Hotel. Athénaïse accepted and handled them with reverence, fully sensible of the great compliment and favor, and laid them religiously away in the trunk which she had lately acquired.

She was greatly fatigued after the day of unusual exertion, and went early to bed and to sleep. All day long she had not once thought of Gouvernail, and only did think of him when aroused for a brief instant by the sound of his foot-falls on the gallery, as he passed in going to his room. He had hoped to find her up, waiting for him.

But the next morning he knew. Some one must have told him. There was no subject known to her which Sylvie hesitated to discuss in detail with any man of suitable years and discretion.

Athénaïse found Gouvernail waiting with a carriage to convey her to the railway station. A momentary pang visited her for having forgotten him so completely, when he said to her, "Sylvie tells me you are going away this morning."

He was kind, attentive, and amiable, as usual, but respected to the utmost the new dignity and reserve that her manner had developed since yesterday. She kept looking from the carriage window, silent, and embarrassed as Eve after losing her ignorance.* He talked of the muddy streets and the murky morning, and of Montéclin. He hoped she would find everything comfortable and pleasant in the country, and trusted she would inform him whenever she came to visit the city again. He talked as if afraid or mistrustful of silence and himself.

At the station she handed him her purse, and he bought her ticket, secured for her a comfortable section, checked her trunk, and got all the bundles and things safely aboard the train. She felt very grateful. He pressed her hand warmly, lifted his hat, and left her. He was a man of intelligence, and took defeat gracefully; that was all. But as he made his way back to the carriage, he was thinking, "By Heaven, it hurts, it hurts!"

XI

Athénaïse spent a day of supreme happiness and expectancy. The fair sight of the country unfolding itself before her was balm to her vision and to her soul. She was charmed with the rather unfamiliar, broad, clean sweep of the sugar plantations, with their monster sugar-houses, their rows of neat cabins like little villages of a single street, and their impressive homes standing apart amid clusters of trees. There were sudden glimpses of a bayou curling between sunny, grassy banks, or creeping sluggishly out from a tangled growth of wood, and brush, and fern, and poison-vines, and palmettos. And passing through the long stretches of monotonous woodlands, she would close her eyes and taste in anticipation the moment of her meeting with Cazeau. She could think of nothing but him.

It was night when she reached her station.* There was Montéclin, as she had expected, waiting for her with a two-seated buggy, to which he had hitched his own swift-footed, spirited pony. It was good, he felt, to have her back on any terms; and he had no fault to find since she came of her own choice. He more than suspected the cause of her coming; her eyes and her voice and her foolish little manner went far in revealing the secret that was brimming over in her heart. But after he had deposited her at her own gate, and as he continued his way toward the rigolet, he could not help feeling that the affair had taken a very disappointing, an ordinary, a most commonplace turn, after all. He left her in Cazeau's keeping.

Her husband lifted her out of the buggy, and neither said a word until they stood together within the shelter of the gallery. Even then they did not speak at first. But Athénaïse turned to him with an appealing gesture. As he clasped her in his arms, he felt the yielding of her whole body against him. He felt her lips for the first time respond to the passion of his own.

The country night was dark and warm and still, save for the distant notes of an accordion which some one was playing in a cabin away off. A little negro baby was crying somewhere. As Athénaïse withdrew from her husband's embrace, the sound arrested her.

"Listen, Cazeau! How Juliette's baby is crying! Pauvre ti chou,* I wonder w'at is the matter with it?"

THE UNEXPECTED

When Randall, for a brief absence, left his Dorothea, whom he was to marry after a time, the parting was bitter; the enforced separation seemed to them too cruel an ordeal to bear. The good-bye dragged with lingering kisses and sighs, and more kisses and more clinging till the last wrench came.

He was to return at the close of the month. Daily letters, impassioned and interminable, passed between them.

He did not return at the close of the month; he was delayed by illness. A heavy cold, accompanied by fever, contracted in some unaccountable way, held him to his bed. He hoped it would be over and that he would rejoin her in a week. But this was a stubborn cold, that seemed not to yield to familiar treatment; yet the physician was not discouraged, and promised to have him on his feet in a fortnight.

All this was torture to the impatient Dorothea; and if her parents had permitted, she surely would have hastened to the bedside of her beloved.

For a long interval he could not write himself. One day he seemed better; another day a "fresh cold" seized him with relentless clutch; and so a second month went by, and Dorothea had reached the limit of her endurance.

Then a tremulous scrawl came from him, saying he would be obliged to pass a season at the south; but he would first revisit his home, if only for a day, to clasp his dearest one to his heart, to appease the hunger for her presence, the craving for her lips that had been devouring him through all the fever and pain of this detestable illness.

Dorothea had read his impassioned letters almost to tatters. She had sat daily gazing for hours upon his portrait, which showed him to be an almost perfect specimen of youthful health, strength and manly beauty.

She knew he would be altered in appearance—he had prepared her, and had even written that she would hardly know him. She expected to see him ill and wasted; she would not seem shocked; she would not let him see astonishment or pain in her face. She was in a quiver of anticipation, a sensuous fever of expectancy till he came.

She sat beside him on the sofa, for after the first delirious embrace he had been unable to hold himself upon his tottering feet, and had sunk exhausted in a corner of the sofa. He threw his head back upon the cushions and stayed, with closed eyes, panting; all the strength of his body had concentrated in the clasp—the grasp with which he clung to her hand.

She stared at him as one might look upon a curious apparition which inspired wonder and mistrust rather than fear. This was not the man who had gone away from her; the man she loved and had promised to marry. What hideous transformation had he undergone, or what devilish transformation was she undergoing in contemplating him? His skin was waxy and hectic, red upon the cheek-bones. His eyes were sunken; his features pinched and prominent; and his clothing hung loosely upon his wasted frame. The lips with which he had kissed her so hungrily, and with which he was kissing her now, were dry and parched, and his breath was feverish and tainted.

At the sight and the touch of him something within her seemed to be shuddering, shrinking, shriveling together, losing all semblance of what had been. She felt as if it was her heart; but it was only her love.

"This is the way my uncle Archibald went—in a gallop—you know." He spoke with a certain derision and in little gasps, as if breath were failing him. "There's no danger of that for me, of course, once I get south; but the doctors won't answer for me if I stay here during the coming fall and winter."

Then he held her in his arms with what seemed to be a frenzy of passion; a keen and quickened desire beside which his former and healthful transports were tempered and lukewarm by comparison.

"We need not wait, Dorothea," he whispered. "We must not put it off. Let the marriage be at once, and you will come with me and be with me. Oh, God! I feel as if I would never let you go; as if I must hold you in my arms forever, night and day, and always!"

She attempted to withdraw from his embrace. She begged him not to think of it, and tried to convince him that it was impossible.

"I would only be a hindrance, Randall. You will come back well and strong; it will be time enough then," and to herself she was saying: "never, never, never!" There was a long silence, and he had closed his eyes again.

"For another reason, my Dorothea," and then he waited again, as one hesitates through shame or through fear, to speak. "I am quite—almost sure I shall get well; but the strongest of us cannot count upon life. If the worst should come I want you to have all I possess; what fortune I have must be yours, and marriage will make my wish secure. Now I'm getting morbid." He ended with a laugh that died away in a cough which threatened to wrench the breath from his body, and which brought the attendant, who had waited without, quickly to his side.

Dorothea watched him from the window descend the steps, leaning upon the man's arm, and saw him enter his carriage and fall helpless and exhausted as he had sunk an hour before in the corner of her sofa.

She was glad there was no one present to compel her to speak. She stayed at the window as if dazed, looking fixedly at the spot where the carriage had stood. A clock on the mantel striking the hour finally roused her, and she realized that there would soon be people appearing whom she would be forced to face and speak to.

Fifteen minutes later Dorothea had changed her house gown, had mounted her "wheel,"* and was fleeing as if Death himself pursued her.

She sped along the familiar roadway, seemingly borne on by some force other than mechanical—some unwonted energy—a stubborn impulse that lighted her eyes, set her cheeks aflame, bent her supple body to one purpose—that was, swiftest flight.

How far, and how long did she go? She did not know; she did not care. The country about her grew unfamiliar. She was on a rough, unfrequented road, where the birds in the wayside brooks seemed unafraid. She could perceive no human habitation; an old fallow field, a stretch of wood, great trees bending thick-leaved branches, languidly, and flinging long, inviting shadows about the road; the woody smell of summer; the drone of the insects; the sky and the clouds, and the quivering, lambent air. She was alone with nature; her pulses beating in unison with its sensuous throb, as she stopped and stretched herself upon the sward. Every muscle, nerve, fibre abandoned itself to the delicious sensation of rest that overtook and crept tingling through the whole length of her body.

She had never spoken a word after bidding him good-bye; but now she seemed disposed to make confidants of the tremulous leaves, or the crawling and hopping insects, or the big sky into which she was staring.

"Never!" she whispered, "not for all his thousands! Never, never! not for millions!"

VAGABONDS

Valcour was waiting. A negro who had come to the store for rations told me that he was down below around the bend and wanted to see me. It never would have entered my mind to put myself the least bit out of the way for the sake of a rendez-vous with Valcour; he might have waited till the crack of doom. But it was the hour for my afternoon walk and I did not mind stopping on the way, to see what the vagabond wanted with me.

The weather was a little warm for April, and of course it had been raining. But with the shabby skirt which I wore and the clumsy old boots, the wet and the mud distressed me not at all; beside, I walked along the grassy edge of the road. The river was low and sluggish between its steep embankments that were like slimy pit-falls. Valcour was sitting on the fallen trunk of a tree near the water, waiting.

I saw at a glance that he was sober; though his whole appearance gave evidence of his having been drunk at no very remote period. His clothes, his battered hat, his skin, his straggling beard which he never shaved, were all of one color—the color of clay. He made but the faintest offer to rise at my approach; and I saved him the complete effort by seating myself at once beside him on the log. I was glad that he showed no disposition to shake hands, for his hands were far from clean; and moreover he might have discovered the dollar bill which I had slipped into my glove in case of emergencies. He greeted me with his usual:

"How you come on, cousin?"

There exists a tradition outside the family that Valcour is a relation of ours. I am the only one, somehow, who does not strenuously deny the charge.

"Me, I'm well enough, Valcour."

I long ago discovered that there is no need of wasting fine language on Valcour. Such effort could only evince a pride and affectation from which I am happily free.

"W'at you mean," I continued, "by sending me word you want to see me. You don' think fo' an instant I'd come down here o' purpose to see an object like you."

Valcour laughed. He is the only soul who discovers any intention of humor in my utterances. He refuses to take me seriously.

"An' w'at you doing with yo'self these days?" I asked.

"Oh, me, I been jobbin' roun' some, up the coas'. But I yeard 'bout a chance down in Alexandria if I c'n make out to git down there."

"Of course not a picayune in sight," I grumbled. "An' I tell you, I aint much better off myself. Look at those shoes," holding my feet out for his inspection, "an' this dress; an' take a look at those cabins an' fences—ready to fall to pieces."

"I ent no mine to ask you fo' money, cousin," he cheerfully assured me.

"All the same, I bet you a' plumb broke," I insisted. With some little difficulty—for his grasp was unsteady—he drew from his trousers pocket a few small coins which he held out before me. I was glad to see them and thrust the dollar bill further into my glove.

"Just about the price of a quart, Valcour," I calculated. "I reckon it's no use warning a *vaurien* like you agains' whiskey. It's boun' to be the end of you some o' these days."

"It make' a man crazy, that w'iskey," he admitted. "Wouldn' been fo' that w'iskey, I neva would got in that peck o' trouble yonda on Bayou Derbonne. Me, I don' rec'lec' a thing till I fine myse'f layin' on doctor Jureau's gall'ry."

"That *was* a nice mess," I told him, "getting yo'self filled plumb full of buckshot fo' trying to kiss another man's wife. You must a' been pretty drunk anyway, to want to kiss Joe Poussin's wife."

Valcour, again mistaking cynicism for humor, almost rolled off the log in his hilarious appreciation of the insinuation. His laugh was contagious and I could not help joining him. "*Hein*, Valcour?" I persisted, "a man mus' be pretty drunk, or mighty hard pushed, *va!*"

"You right," he returned between attacks of mirth, "a man got to be hard push', sho', that want' to kiss Joe Poussin's wife; 'less he been blin' drunk like me."

At the end of a half hour (how could I have stood the vagabond so long!) I reminded Valcour that the way to Alexandria lay across the river; and I expressed a hope that the walking was fair.

I had asked him how he fared, what he ate and where, and how he slept. There was his gun beside him—for a wonder he had never sold it for drink—and were the woods not filled with feathered and antlered game? And sometimes there was a chicken roosting low, and always there was a black wench ready to cook it. As for sleeping—in the winter time, better not have asked him. Grand Dieu! that was hard. But with the summer coming on, why, a man could sleep anywhere that the mosquitoes would let him.

I called him names; but all the same I could not help thinking that it must be good to prowl sometimes; to get close to the black night and lose oneself in its silence and mystery.*

He waited for the flat that had been crossing and re-crossing a little distance away, and when it touched the bank he said good-by— as he had greeted me—stolidly and indifferently. He went slipping and slumping down the slimy embankment, ankle deep in mud.

I stayed for pure idleness watching the flat cross the river. Valcour made no offer to help the ferryman with an oar; but rested his arms indolently on the rail of the boat and stared into the muddy stream.

I turned to continue my walk. I was glad the vagabond did not want money. But for the life of me I don't know what he wanted, or why he wanted to see me.

A PAIR OF SILK STOCKINGS

Little Mrs. Sommers one day found herself the unexpected possessor of fifteen dollars. It seemed to her a very large amount of money,*
and the way in which it stuffed and bulged her worn old porte-
monnaie gave her a feeling of importance such as she had not
enjoyed for years.

The question of investment was one that occupied her greatly. For
a day or two she walked about apparently in a dreamy state, but really
absorbed in speculation and calculation. She did not wish to act
hastily, to do anything she might afterward regret. But it was during
the still hours of the night when she lay awake revolving plans in her
mind that she seemed to see her way clearly toward a proper and
judicious use of the money.

A dollar or two should be added to the price usually paid for
Janie's shoes, which would insure their lasting an appreciable time
longer than they usually did. She would buy so and so many yards of
percale for new shirt waists* for the boys and Janie and Mag. She had
intended to make the old ones do by skilful patching. Mag should
have another gown. She had seen some beautiful patterns, veritable
bargains in the shop windows. And still there would be left enough
for new stockings—two pairs apiece—and what darning that would
save for a while! She would get caps for the boys and sailor-hats for
the girls. The vision of her little brood looking fresh and dainty and
new for once in their lives excited her and made her restless and
wakeful with anticipation.

The neighbors sometimes talked of certain "better days" that
little Mrs. Sommers had known before she had ever thought of being
Mrs. Sommers. She herself indulged in no such morbid retrospec-
tion. She had no time—no second of time to devote to the past. The
needs of the present absorbed her every faculty. A vision of the
future like some dim, gaunt monster sometimes appalled her, but
luckily to-morrow never comes.

Mrs. Sommers was one who knew the value of bargains; who
could stand for hours making her way inch by inch toward the
desired object that was selling below cost. She could elbow her way if
need be; she had learned to clutch a piece of goods and hold it and

stick to it with persistence and determination till her turn came to be served, no matter when it came.

But that day she was a little faint and tired. She had swallowed a light luncheon—no! when she came to think of it, between getting the children fed and the place righted, and preparing herself for the shopping bout, she had actually forgotten to eat any luncheon at all!

She sat herself down upon a revolving stool before a counter that was comparatively deserted, trying to gather strength and courage to charge through an eager multitude that was besieging breastworks of shirting and figured lawn. An all-gone limp feeling had come over her and she rested her hand aimlessly upon the counter. She wore no gloves. By degrees she grew aware that her hand had encountered something very soothing, very pleasant to touch. She looked down to see that her hand lay upon a pile of silk stockings. A placard near by announced that they had been reduced in price from two dollars and fifty cents to one dollar and ninety-eight cents; and a young girl who stood behind the counter asked her if she wished to examine their line of silk hosiery. She smiled, just as if she had been asked to inspect a tiara of diamonds with the ultimate view of purchasing it. But she went on feeling the soft, sheeny luxurious things—with both hands now, holding them up to see them glisten, and to feel them glide serpent-like through her fingers.

Two hectic blotches came suddenly into her pale cheeks. She looked up at the girl.

"Do you think there are any eights-and-a-half among these?"

There were any number of eights-and-a-half. In fact, there were more of that size than any other. Here was a light-blue pair; there were some lavender, some all black and various shades of tan and gray. Mrs. Sommers selected a black pair and looked at them very long and closely. She pretended to be examining their texture, which the clerk assured her was excellent.

"A dollar and ninety-eight cents," she mused aloud. "Well, I'll take this pair." She handed the girl a five-dollar bill and waited for her change and for her parcel. What a very small parcel it was! It seemed lost in the depths of her shabby old shopping-bag.

Mrs. Sommers after that did not move in the direction of the bargain counter. She took the elevator, which carried her to an upper floor into the region of the ladies' waiting-rooms.* Here, in a retired corner, she exchanged her cotton stockings for the new silk ones which she had just bought. She was not going through any acute mental process or reasoning with herself, nor was she striving to explain to her satisfaction the motive of her action. She was not thinking at all. She seemed for the time to be taking a rest from that laborious and fatiguing function and to have abandoned herself to some mechanical impulse that directed her actions and freed her of responsibility.

How good was the touch of the raw silk to her flesh! She felt like lying back in the cushioned chair and reveling for a while in the luxury of it. She did for a little while. Then she replaced her shoes, rolled the cotton stockings together and thrust them into her bag. After doing this she crossed straight over to the shoe department and took her seat to be fitted.

She was fastidious. The clerk could not make her out; he could not reconcile her shoes with her stockings, and she was not too easily pleased. She held back her skirts and turned her feet one way and her head another way as she glanced down at the polished, pointed-tipped boots. Her foot and ankle looked very pretty. She could not realize that they belonged to her and were a part of herself. She wanted an excellent and stylish fit, she told the young fellow who served her, and she did not mind the difference of a dollar or two more in the price so long as she got what she desired.

It was a long time since Mrs. Sommers had been fitted with gloves. On rare occasions when she had bought a pair they were always "bargains," so cheap that it would have been preposterous and unreasonable to have expected them to be fitted to the hand.

Now she rested her elbow on the cushion of the glove counter, and a pretty, pleasant young creature, delicate and deft of touch, drew a long-wristed "kid" over Mrs. Sommer's hand. She smoothed it down over the wrist and buttoned it neatly, and both lost themselves for a second or two in admiring contemplation of the little symmetrical gloved hand. But there were other places where money might be spent.

There were books and magazines piled up in the window of a stall a few paces down the street. Mrs. Sommers bought two high-priced magazines* such as she had been accustomed to read in the days when she had been accustomed to do other pleasant things. She carried them without wrapping. As well as she could she lifted her skirts at the crossings. Her stockings and boots and well fitting gloves had worked marvels in her bearing—had given her a feeling of assurance, a sense of belonging to the well-dressed multitude.

She was very hungry. Another time she would have stilled the cravings for food until reaching her own home, where she would have brewed herself a cup of tea and taken a snack of anything that was available. But the impulse that was guiding her would not suffer her to entertain any such thought.

There was a restaurant at the corner. She had never entered its doors; from the outside she had sometimes caught glimpses of spotless damask and shining crystal, and soft-stepping waiters serving people of fashion.

When she entered her appearance created no surprise, no consternation, as she had half feared it might. She seated herself at a small table alone, and an attentive waiter at once approached to take her order. She did not want a profusion; she craved a nice and tasty bite—a half dozen blue-points,* a plump chop with cress, a something sweet—a crème-frappée,* for instance; a glass of Rhine wine, and after all a small cup of black coffee.

While waiting to be served she removed her gloves very leisurely and laid them beside her. Then she picked up a magazine and glanced through it, cutting the pages with the blunt edge of her knife. It was all very agreeable. The damask was even more spotless than it had seemed through the window, and the crystal more sparkling. There were quiet ladies and gentlemen, who did not notice her, lunching at the small tables like her own. A soft, pleasing strain of music could be heard, and a gentle breeze was blowing through the window. She tasted a bite, and she read a word or two, and she sipped the amber wine and wiggled her toes in the silk stockings. The price of it made no difference. She counted the money out to the waiter and left an extra coin on his tray, whereupon he bowed before her as before a princess of royal blood.

There was still money in her purse, and her next temptation presented itself in the shape of a matinée poster.

It was a little later when she entered the theatre, the play had begun and the house seemed to her to be packed. But there were vacant seats here and there, and into one of them she was ushered, between brilliantly dressed women who had gone there to kill time and eat candy and display their gaudy attire. There were many others who were there solely for the play and acting. It is safe to say there was no one present who bore quite the attitude which Mrs. Sommers did to her surroundings. She gathered in the whole—stage and players and people in one wide impression, and absorbed it and enjoyed it. She laughed at the comedy and wept—she and the gaudy woman next to her wept over the tragedy. And they talked a little together over it. And the gaudy woman wiped her eyes and sniffled on a tiny square of filmy, perfumed lace and passed little Mrs. Sommers her box of candy.

The play was over, the music ceased, the crowd filed out. It was like a dream ended. People scattered in all directions. Mrs. Sommers went to the corner and waited for the cable car.

A man with keen eyes, who sat opposite to her, seemed to like the study of her small, pale face. It puzzled him to decipher what he saw there. In truth, he saw nothing—unless he were wizard enough to detect a poignant wish, a powerful longing that the cable car would never stop anywhere, but go on and on with her forever.

AN EGYPTIAN CIGARETTE

My friend, the Architect, who is something of a traveler, was showing us various curios which he had gathered during a visit to the
Orient.

"Here is something for you," he said, picking up a small box and
turning it over in his hand. "You are a cigarette-smoker; take this
home with you. It was given to me in Cairo by a species of fakir, who
fancied I had done him a good turn."

The box was covered with glazed, yellow paper,* so skillfully
gummed as to appear to be all one piece. It bore no label, no stamp—
nothing to indicate its contents.

"How do you know they are cigarettes?" I asked, taking the box
and turning it stupidly around as one turns a sealed letter and specu-
lates before opening it.

"I only know what he told me," replied the Architect, "but it is
easy enough to determine the question of his integrity." He handed
me a sharp, pointed paper-cutter, and with it I opened the lid as
carefully as possible.

The box contained six cigarettes, evidently hand-made. The
wrappers were of pale-yellow paper, and the tobacco was almost the
same color. It was of finer cut than the Turkish or ordinary Egyptian,
and threads of it stuck out at either end.

"Will you try one now, Madam?" asked the Architect, offering to
strike a match.

"Not now and not here," I replied, "after the coffee, if you will
permit me to slip into your smoking-den. Some of the women here
detest the odor of cigarettes."

The smoking-room lay at the end of a short, curved passage. Its
appointments were exclusively Oriental. A broad, low window
opened out upon a balcony that overhung the garden. From the
divan upon which I reclined, only the swaying tree-tops could be
seen. The maple leaves glistened in the afternoon sun. Beside the
divan was a low stand which contained the complete paraphernalia
of a smoker. I was feeling quite comfortable, and congratulated
myself upon having escaped for a while the incessant chatter of the
women that reached me faintly.

I took a cigarette and lit it, placing the box upon the stand just as the tiny clock, which was there, chimed in silvery strokes the hour of five.

I took one long inspiration* of the Egyptian cigarette. The gray-green smoke arose in a small puffy column that spread and broadened, that seemed to fill the room. I could see the maple leaves dimly, as if they were veiled in a shimmer of moonlight. A subtle, disturbing current passed through my whole body and went to my head like the fumes of disturbing wine. I took another deep inhalation of the cigarette.

*

"Ah! the sand has blistered my cheek!* I have lain here all day with my face in the sand. To-night, when the everlasting stars are burning, I shall drag myself to the river."

He will never come back.

Thus far I followed him; with flying feet; with stumbling feet; with hands and knees, crawling; and outstretched arms, and here I have fallen in the sand.

The sand has blistered my cheek; it has blistered all my body, and the sun is crushing me with hot torture. There is shade beneath yonder cluster of palms.

I shall stay here in the sand till the hour and the night comes.

I laughed at the oracles and scoffed at the stars when they told that after the rapture of life I would open my arms inviting death, and the waters would envelop me.

Oh! how the sand blisters my cheek! and I have no tears to quench the fire. The river is cool and the night is not far distant.

I turned from the gods and said: "There is but one; Bardja is my god." That was when I decked myself with lilies and wove flowers into a garland and held him close in the frail, sweet fetters.

He will never come back. He turned upon his camel as he rode away. He turned and looked at me crouching here and laughed, showing his gleaming white teeth.

Whenever he kissed me and went away he always came back again. Whenever he flamed with fierce anger and left me with stinging words, he always came back. But to-day he neither kissed me nor was he angry. He only said:

"Oh! I am tired of fetters, and kisses, and you. I am going away.

You will never see me again. I am going to the great city where men swarm like bees. I am going beyond, where the monster stones are rising heavenward in a monument for the unborn ages. Oh! I am tired. You will see me no more."

And he rode away on his camel. He smiled and showed his cruel white teeth as he turned to look at me crouching here.

How slow the hours drag! It seems to me that I have lain here for days in the sand, feeding upon despair. Despair is bitter and it nourishes resolve.

I hear the wings of a bird flapping above my head, flying low, in circles.

The sun is gone.

The sand has crept between my lips and teeth and under my parched tongue.

If I raise my head, perhaps I shall see the evening star.

Oh! the pain in my arms and legs! My body is sore and bruised as if broken. Why can I not rise and run as I did this morning? Why must I drag myself thus like a wounded serpent, twisting and writhing?

The river is near at hand. I hear it——I see it—— Oh! the sand! Oh! the shine! How cool! how cold!

The water! the water! In my eyes, my ears, my throat! It strangles me! Help! will the gods not help me?

Oh! the sweet rapture of rest! There is music in the Temple. And here is fruit to taste. Bardja came with the music—— The moon shines and the breeze is soft—— A garland of flowers——let us go into the King's garden and look at the blue lily, Bardja.

*

The maple leaves looked as if a silvery shimmer enveloped them. The gray-green smoke no longer filled the room. I could hardly lift the lids of my eyes. The weight of centuries seemed to suffocate my soul that struggled to escape, to free itself and breathe.

I had tasted the depths of human despair.

The little clock upon the stand pointed to a quarter past five. The cigarettes still reposed in the yellow box. Only the stub of the one I had smoked remained. I had laid it in the ash tray.

As I looked at the cigarettes in their pale wrappers, I wondered what other visions they might hold for me; what might I not find in their mystic fumes? Perhaps a vision of celestial peace; a dream of hopes fulfilled; a taste of rapture, such as had not entered into my mind to conceive.

I took the cigarettes and crumpled them between my hands. I walked to the window and spread my palms wide. The light breeze caught up the golden threads and bore them writhing and dancing far out among the maple leaves.

My friend, the Architect, lifted the curtain and entered, bringing me a second cup of coffee.

"How pale you are!" he exclaimed, solicitously. "Are you not feeling well?"

"A little the worse for a dream," I told him.

ELIZABETH STOCK'S ONE STORY

Elizabeth Stock, an unmarried woman of thirty-eight, died of consumption during the past winter at the St. Louis City Hospital. There were no unusually pathetic features attending her death. The physicians say she showed hope of rallying till placed in the incurable ward, when all courage seemed to leave her, and she relapsed into a silence that remained unbroken till the end.

In Stonelift, the village where Elizabeth Stock was born and raised, and where I happen to be sojourning this summer, they say she was much given over to scribbling. I was permitted to examine her desk, which was quite filled with scraps and bits of writing in bad prose and impossible verse. In the whole conglomerate mass, I discovered but the following pages which bore any semblance to a connected or consecutive narration.

Since I was a girl I always felt as if I would like to write stories. I never had that ambition to shine or make a name; first place because I knew what time and labor it meant to acquire a literary style. Second place, because whenever I wanted to write a story I never could think of a plot. Once I wrote about old Si Shepard that got lost in the woods and never came back, and when I showed it to Uncle William he said:

"Why, Elizabeth, I reckon you better stick to your dress making: this here aint no story;* everybody knows about old Si Shepard."

No, the trouble was with plots. Whenever I tried to think of one, it always turned out to be something that some one else had thought about* before me. But here back awhile, I heard of great inducements offered for an acceptable story, and I said to myself:

"Elizabeth Stock, this is your chance. Now or never!" And I laid awake most a whole week; and walked about days in a kind of dream, turning and twisting things in my mind just like I often saw old ladies twisting quilt patches around to compose a design. I tried to think of a railroad story with a wreck, but couldn't. No more could I make a tale out of a murder, or money getting stolen, or even mistaken identity; for the story had to be original, entertaining, full of action and Goodness knows what all. It was no use. I gave it up. But now that I got my pen in my hand and sitting here kind of quiet and peaceful at the south window, and the breeze so soft carrying the autumn leaves along, I feel as I'd like to tell how I lost my position, mostly through my own negligence, I'll admit that.

My name is Elizabeth Stock. I'm thirty-eight years old and unmarried, and not afraid or ashamed to say it. Up to a few months ago I been postmistress of this village of Stonelift* for six years, through one administration and a half—up to a few months ago.

Often seems like the village was most too small; so small that people were bound to look into each other's lives, just like you see folks in crowded tenements looking into each other's windows. But I was born here in Stonelift and I got no serious complaints. I been pretty comfortable and contented most of my life. There aint more than a hundred houses all told, if that, counting stores, churches, postoffice, and even Nathan Brightman's palatial mansion up on the hill. Looks like Stonelift wouldn't be anything without that.

He's away a good part of the time, and his family; but he's done a lot for this community, and they always appreciated it, too.

But I leave it to any one—to any woman especially, if it aint human nature in a little place where everybody knows every one else, for the postmistress to glance at a postal card once in a while. She could hardly help it. And besides, seems like if a person had anything very particular and private to tell, they'd put it under a sealed envelope.

Anyway, the train was late that day. It was the breaking up of winter, or the beginning of spring; kind of betwixt and between; along in March. It was most night when the mail came in that ought have been along at 5:15. The Brightman girls had been down with their pony-cart, but had got tired waiting and had been gone more than an hour.

It was chill and dismal in the office. I had let the stove go out for fear of fire. I was cold and hungry and anxious to get home to my supper. I gave out everybody's mail that was waiting; and for the thousandth time told Vance Wallace there was nothing for him. He'll come and ask as regular as clockwork. I got that mail assorted and put aside in a hurry. There was no dilly dallying with postal cards, and how I ever come to give a second look at Nathan Brightman's postal, Heaven only knows!

It was from St. Louis, written with pencil in large characters and signed, "Collins," nothing else; just "Collins." It read:

"Dear Brightman:

Be on hand tomorrow, Tuesday at 10. A. M. promptly. Important meeting of the board. Your own interest demands your presence. Whatever you do, don't fail.

In haste,
Collins."

I went to the door to see if there was anyone left standing around: but the night was so raw and chill, every last one of the loungers had disappeared. Vance Wallace would of been willing enough to hang about to see me home; but that was a thing I'd broken him of long ago. I locked things up and went on home, just ashivering as I went, it was that black and penetrating—worse than a downright freeze, I thought.

After I had had my supper and got comfortably fixed front of the fire, and glanced over the St. Louis paper and was just starting to read my Seaside Library novel,* I got thinking, somehow, about that postal card of Nath Brightman's. To a person that knew B. from bull's foot,* it was just as plain as day that if that card laid on there in the office, Mr. Brightman would miss that important meeting in St. Louis in the morning. It wasn't anything to me, of course, except it made me uncomfortable and I couldn't rest or get my mind fixed on the story I was reading. Along about nine o'clock, I flung aside the book and says to myself:

"Elizabeth Stock, you a fool, and you know it." There aint much use telling how I put on my rubbers and waterproof, covered the fire with ashes, took my umbrella and left the house.

I carried along the postoffice key and went on down and got out that postal card—in fact, all of the Brightman's mail—wasn't any use leaving part of it, and started for "the house on the hill" as we mostly call it. I don't believe anything could of induced me to go if I had known before hand what I was undertaking. It was drizzling and the rain kind of turned to ice when it struck the ground. If it hadn't been for the rubbers, I'd of taken more than one fall. As it was, I took one good and hard one on the footbridge. The wind was sweeping down so swiftly from the Northwest, looked like it carried me clean off my feet before I could clutch the handrail. I found out about that time that the stitches had come out of my old rubbers that I'd sewed about a month before, and letting the water in soaking my feet through and through. But I'd got more than good and started and I wouldn't think of turning around.

Nathan Brightman has got kind of steps cut along the side of the hill, going zig-zag. What you would call a gradual ascent, and making it easy like to climb. That is to say, in good weather. But Lands! There wasn't anything easy that night, slipping back one step for every two; clutching at the frozen twigs along the path; and having to use my umbrella half the time for a walking stick; like a regular Alpine climber. And my heart would most stand still at the way the cedar trees moaned and whistled like doleful organ tones; and sometimes sighing deep and soft like dying souls in pain.

Then I was a fool for not putting on something warm underneath that mackintosh. I could of put on my knitted wool jacket just as easy as not. But the day had been so mild, it bamboozled us into thinking spring was here for good; especially when we were all looking and longing for it; and the orchards ready to bud, too.

But I forgot all the worry and unpleasantness of the walk when I saw how Nath Brightman took on over me bringing him that postal card. He made me sit down longside the fire and dry my feet, and kept saying:

"Why, Miss Elizabeth, it was exceedingly obliging of you; on such a night, too. Margaret, my dear"—that was his wife—"mix a good stiff toddy for Miss Elizabeth, and see that she drinks it."

I never could stand the taste or smell of alcohol. Uncle William says if I'd of had any sense and swallowed down that toddy like medicine, it might of saved the day.

Anyhow, Mr. Brightman had the girls scampering around getting his grip packed; one bringing his big top coat, another his muffler and umbrella; and at the same time here they were all three making up a list of a thousand and one things they wanted him to bring down from St. Louis.

Seems like he was ready in a jiffy, and by that time I was feeling sort of thawed out and I went along with him. It was a mighty big comfort to have him, too. He was as polite as could be, and kept saying:

"Mind out, Miss Elizabeth! Be careful here; slow now. My! but it's cold! Goodness knows what damage this won't do to the fruit trees." He walked to my very door with me, helping me along. Then he went on to the station. When the midnight express came tearing around the bend, rumbling like thunder and shaking the very house, I'd got my clothes changed and was drinking a hot cup of tea side the fire I'd started up. There was a lot of comfort knowing that Mr. Brightman had got aboard that train. Well, we all more or less selfish creatures in this world! I don't believe I'd of slept a wink that night if I'd of left that postal card lying in the office.

Uncle William will have it that this heavy cold all came of that walk; though he got to admit with me that this family been noted for weak lungs as far back as I ever heard of.

Anyway, I'd been sick on and off all spring; sometimes hardly able to stand on my feet when I'd drag myself down to that postoffice. When one morning, just like lightning out of a clear sky, here comes an official document from Washington, discharging me from my position as postmistress of Stonelift. I shook all over when I read it, just like I had a chill; and I felt sick at my stomach and my teeth chattered. No one was in the office when I opened that document except Vance Wallace, and I made him read it and I asked him what he made out it meant. Just like when you can't understand a thing because you don't want to. He says:

"You've lost your position, Lizabeth. That what it means; they've passed you up."

I took it away from him kind of dazed, and says:

"We got to see about it. We got to go see Uncle William; see what he says. Maybe it's a mistake."

"Uncle Sam* don't make mistakes," said Vance. "We got to get up a petition in this here community; that's what I reckon we better do, and send it on to the gover'ment."

Well, it don't seem like any use to dwell on this subject. The whole community was indignant, and pronounced it an outrage. They decided, in justice to me, I had to find out what I got that dismissal for. I kind of thought it was for my poor health, for I would of had to send in my resignation sooner or later, with these fevers and cough. But we got information it was for incompetence and negligence in office, through certain accusations of me reading postal cards and permitting people to help themselves to their own mail. Though I don't know as that ever happened except with Nathan Brightman always reaching over and saying:

"Don't disturb yourself, Miss Elizabeth," when I'd be sorting out letters and he could reach his mail in the box just as well as not.

But that's all over and done for. I been out of office two months now, on the 26th. There's a young man named Collins, got the position. He's the son of some wealthy, influential St. Louis man; a kind of delicate, poetical-natured young fellow that can't get along in business, and they used their influence to get him the position when it was vacant. They think it's the very place for him. I reckon it is. I hope in my soul he'll prosper. He's a quiet, nice-mannered young man. Some of the community thought of boycotting him. It was Vance Wallace started the notion. I told them they must be demented, and I up and told Vance Wallace he was a fool.

"I know I'm a fool, Lizbeth Stock," he said. "I always been a fool for hanging round you for the past twenty years."

The trouble with Vance is, he's got no intellect. I believe in my soul Uncle William's got more. Uncle William advised me to go up to St. Louis and get treated. I been up there. The doctor said, with this cough and short breath, if I know what's good for me I'll spend the winter in the South. But the truth is, I got no more money, or so little it don't count.* Putting Danny to school and other things here lately, hasn't left me much to brag of. But I oughtn't be blamed about Danny; he's the only one of sister Martha's boys that seemed to me capable. And full of ambition to study as he was! it would have felt sinful of me, not to. Of course, I've taken him out, now I've lost my position. But I got him in with Filmore Green to learn the grocery trade, and maybe it's all for the best; who knows!

But indeed, indeed, I don't know what to do. Seems like I've come to the end of the rope. O! it's mighty pleasant here at this south window. The breeze is just as soft and warm as May, and the leaves look like birds flying. I'd like to sit right on here and forget every thing and go to sleep and never wake up. Maybe it's sinful to make that wish. After all, what I got to do is to leave everything in the hands of Providence, and trust to luck.

THE STORM
A SEQUEL TO "THE 'CADIAN BALL"

I

The leaves were so still that even Bibi thought it was going to
rain. Bobinôt, who was accustomed to converse on terms of perfect
equality with his little son, called the child's attention to certain
sombre clouds that were rolling with sinister intention from the
west, accompanied by a sullen, threatening roar. They were at
Friedheimer's store and decided to remain there till the storm had
passed. They sat within the door on two empty kegs. Bibi was four
years old and looked very wise.

"Mama'll be 'fraid, yes," he suggested with blinking eyes.

"She'll shut the house. Maybe she got Sylvie helpin' her this
evenin'," Bobinôt responded reassuringly.

"No; she ent got Sylvie. Sylvie was helpin' her yistiday," piped
Bibi.

Bobinôt arose and going across to the counter purchased a can of
shrimps, of which Calixta was very fond. Then he returned to his
perch on the keg and sat stolidly holding the can of shrimps while
the storm burst. It shook the wooden store and seemed to be ripping
great furrows in the distant field. Bibi laid his little hand on his
father's knee and was not afraid.

II

Calixta, at home, felt no uneasiness for their safety. She sat at a side
window sewing furiously on a sewing machine. She was greatly
occupied and did not notice the approaching storm. But she felt very
warm and often stopped to mop her face on which the perspiration
gathered in beads. She unfastened her white sacque at the throat. It
began to grow dark, and suddenly realizing the situation she got up
hurriedly and went about closing windows and doors.

Out on the small front gallery she had hung Bobinôt's Sunday clothes to air and she hastened out to gather them before the rain fell. As she stepped outside, Alcée Laballière rode in at the gate. She had not seen him very often since her marriage, and never alone. She stood there with Bobinôt's coat in her hands, and the big rain drops began to fall. Alcée rode his horse under the shelter of a side projection where the chickens had huddled and there were plows and a harrow piled up in the corner.

"May I come and wait on your gallery till the storm is over, Calixta?" he asked.

"Come 'long in, M'sieur Alcée."

His voice and her own startled her as if from a trance, and she seized Bobinôt's vest. Alcée, mounting to the porch, grabbed the trousers and snatched Bibi's braided jacket that was about to be carried away by a sudden gust of wind. He expressed an intention to remain outside, but it was soon apparent that he might as well have been out in the open: the water beat in upon the boards in driving sheets, and he went inside, closing the door after him. It was even necessary to put something beneath the door to keep the water out.

"My! what a rain! It's good two years sence it rain' like that," exclaimed Calixta as she rolled up a piece of bagging and Alcée helped her to thrust it beneath the crack.

She was a little fuller of figure than five years before when she married; but she had lost nothing of her vivacity. Her blue eyes still retained their melting quality; and her yellow hair, dishevelled by the wind and rain, kinked more stubbornly than ever about her ears and temples.

The rain beat upon the low, shingled roof with a force and clatter that threatened to break an entrance and deluge them there. They were in the dining room—the sitting room—the general utility room. Adjoining was her bed room, with Bibi's couch along side her own. The door stood open, and the room with its white, monumental bed, its closed shutters, looked dim and mysterious.

Alcée flung himself into a rocker and Calixta nervously began to gather up from the floor the lengths of a cotton sheet which she had been sewing.

"If this keeps up, *Dieu sait* if the levees goin' to stan' it!" she exclaimed.

"What have you got to do with the levees?"

"I got enough to do! An' there's Bobinôt with Bibi out in that storm—if he only didn' left Friedheimer's!"

"Let us hope, Calixta, that Bobinôt's got sense enough to come in out of a cyclone."

She went and stood at the window with a greatly disturbed look on her face. She wiped the frame that was clouded with moisture. It was stiflingly hot. Alcée got up and joined her at the window, looking over her shoulder. The rain was coming down in sheets obscuring the view of far-off cabins and enveloping the distant wood in a gray mist. The playing of the lightning was incessant. A bolt struck a tall chinaberry tree at the edge of the field. It filled all visible space with a blinding glare and the crash seemed to invade the very boards they stood upon.

Calixta put her hands to her eyes, and with a cry, staggered backward. Alcée's arm encircled her, and for an instant he drew her close and spasmodically to him.

"*Bonté!*" she cried, releasing herself from his encircling arm and retreating from the window, "the house'll go next! If I only knew w'ere Bibi was!" She would not compose herself; she would not be seated. Alcée clasped her shoulders and looked into her face. The contact of her warm, palpitating body when he had unthinkingly drawn her into his arms, had aroused all the old-time infatuation and desire for her flesh.

"Calixta," he said, "don't be frightened. Nothing can happen. The house is too low to be struck, with so many tall trees standing about. There! aren't you going to be quiet? say, aren't you?" He pushed her hair back from her face that was warm and steaming. Her lips were as red and moist as pomegranate seed. Her white neck and a glimpse of her full, firm bosom disturbed him powerfully. As she glanced up at him the fear in her liquid blue eyes had given place to a drowsy gleam that unconsciously betrayed a sensuous desire. He looked down into her eyes and there was nothing for him to do but to gather her lips in a kiss. It reminded him of Assumption.

"Do you remember—in Assumption, Calixta?" he asked in a low voice broken by passion. Oh! she remembered; for in Assumption he had kissed her and kissed and kissed her; until his senses would well nigh fail, and to save her he would resort to a desperate flight. If she was not an immaculate dove in those days, she was still inviolate; a passionate creature whose very defenselessness had made her defense, against which his honor forbade him to prevail. Now—well, now—her lips seemed in a manner free to be tasted, as well as her round, white throat and her whiter breasts.

They did not heed the crashing torrents, and the roar of the elements made her laugh as she lay in his arms. She was a revelation in that dim, mysterious chamber; as white as the couch she lay upon. Her firm, elastic flesh that was knowing for the first time its birthright, was like a creamy lily that the sun invites to contribute its breath and perfume to the undying life of the world.

The generous abundance of her passion, without guile or trickery, was like a white flame which penetrated and found response in depths of his own sensuous nature that had never yet been reached.

When he touched her breasts they gave themselves up in quivering ecstasy, inviting his lips. Her mouth was a fountain of delight. And when he possessed her, they seemed to swoon together at the very borderland of life's mystery.

He stayed cushioned upon her, breathless, dazed, enervated, with his heart beating like a hammer upon her. With one hand she clasped his head, her lips lightly touching his forehead. The other hand stroked with a soothing rhythm his muscular shoulders.

The growl of the thunder was distant and passing away. The rain beat softly upon the shingles, inviting them to drowsiness and sleep. But they dared not yield.

The rain was over; and the sun was turning the glistening green world into a palace of gems. Calixta, on the gallery, watched Alcée ride away. He turned and smiled at her with a beaming face; and she lifted her pretty chin in the air and laughed aloud.

III

Bobinôt and Bibi, trudging home, stopped without at the cistern to make themselves presentable.

"My! Bibi, w'at will yo' mama say! You ought to be ashame'. You oughtn' put on those good pants. Look at 'em! An' that mud on yo' collar! How you got that mud on yo' collar, Bibi? I never saw such a boy!" Bibi was the picture of pathetic resignation. Bobinôt was the embodiment of serious solicitude as he strove to remove from his own person and his son's the signs of their tramp over heavy roads and through wet fields. He scraped the mud off Bibi's bare legs and feet with a stick and carefully removed all traces from his heavy brogans. Then, prepared for the worst—the meeting with an over-scrupulous housewife, they entered cautiously at the back door.

Calixta was preparing supper. She had set the table and was dripping coffee at the hearth. She sprang up as they came in.

"Oh, Bobinôt! You back! My! but I was uneasy. W'ere you been during the rain? An' Bibi? he ain't wet? he ain't hurt?" She had clasped Bibi and was kissing him effusively. Bobinôt's explanations and apologies which he had been composing all along the way, died on his lips as Calixta felt him to see if he were dry, and seemed to express nothing but satisfaction at their safe return.

"I brought you some shrimps, Calixta," offered Bobinôt, hauling the can from his ample side pocket and laying it on the table.

"Shrimps! Oh, Bobinôt! you too good fo' anything! and she gave him a smacking kiss on the cheek that resounded. "*J'vous réponds,** we'll have a feas' to night! umph-umph!"

Bobinôt and Bibi began to relax and enjoy themselves, and when the three seated themselves at table they laughed much and so loud that anyone might have heard them as far away as Laballière's.

IV

Alcée Laballière wrote to his wife, Clarisse, that night. It was a loving letter, full of tender solicitude. He told her not to hurry back, but if she and the babies liked it at Biloxi, to stay a month longer. He was getting on nicely; and though he missed them, he was willing to bear the separation a while longer—realizing that their health and pleasure were the first things to be considered.

V

As for Clarisse, she was charmed upon receiving her husband's let-ter. She and the babies were doing well. The society was agreeable; many of her old friends and acquaintances were at the bay. And the first free breath since her marriage seemed to restore the pleasant liberty of her maiden days. Devoted as she was to her husband, their intimate conjugal life was something which she was more than willing to forego for a while.

So the storm passed and every one was happy.

APPENDIX

Louisiana Observed: Regional Writing and Kate Chopin's People and Languages

In the revival of Chopin's reputation, many critics have chosen to down-play her associations with nineteenth-century regional writing. New readers, however, often inquire about these very elements, which can be particularly striking, even baffling, at first encounter.

Chopin's Louisiana stories tap into a rich vein of interest in southern people and places, exploited in literature, journalism, and travel-writing from the end of the Civil War onwards, waning to some extent by the mid-nineties. As Alcée Fortier wrote in 1891, 'Everything concerning French Louisiana seems at this time to possess an interest for the public' ('The Acadians of Louisiana and their Dialect', *PMLA* 6:1 (1891), 64). In New Orleans itself, promotional literature for the Cotton Centennial Exposition of 1884 played on romanticized images of Louisiana, as the city turned to advantage its unique differences from the rest of the nation. The colourful social geographies of New Orleans, the mysterious Gulf Coast, comparisons between Creoles and Americans, accounts of the Creole woman, comments on patois, descriptions of the Acadian way of life, all became standard features, repeated from text to text often in near-identical phrasing. Writing by outsiders varied in tone, however, from the openly patronizing to the sympathetic and excited. (One of the most notable commentators was Chopin's exact contemporary, the versatile Lafcadio Hearn (1850–1904), a British-Irish/Greek-born cosmopolitan, later a Japanese subject, whose lyrical prose-poems and down-to-earth observations of everyday New Orleans life contributed much to positive constructions of the city. His romantic images of the Gulf in *Chita* may also have influenced Chopin.) Southerners themselves frequently took up similar tropes, but some were more vigorously defensive. The work of George Washington Cable (1844–1925), which for many came quintessen-tially to define the old regime, caused offence among the Creoles of his native New Orleans. Cable drew heavily on the standard *History of Louisiana* (1879) by Judge Charles Gayarré (1805–1895), which represented French Louisiana culture as the summit of civilization. His own work was more critical, hinting at the oppression and embedded racial injustices of that society. His *Old Creole Days* (1879), *The Grandissimes* (1880), and his articles in national periodicals such as the *Century* were received with enthusiasm in the North, as stories of a fascinating and exotic foreign realm. But they were deemed by many locals to portray the Creoles as a proud but decadent caste, deeply prejudiced against the 'black' blood which Cable suggested ran in their own veins. In 1885, Gayarré himself gave a well-attended public lecture to refute Cable's representations of Creole life. Other local writers, such as Ruth McEnery Stuart (1849–1917) and Grace King (1852–1932), attempted to counter these images in their own stories, even as, at the same time, they recognized Cable's force in giving regional subject-matter value in fiction.

Although regionalism was not in itself of primary interest to Chopin, aspects of her representation of Louisiana peoples appear to be a direct rebuttal of negative or sentimental stereotypes. When read against the extracts below, her work, in general, strikes a distinctive note, drawing on readers' expectations, but also marking itself out from the prevailing conventions: the treatment of Louisiana as the merely picturesque or quaint, the distanced view of the local people, and the superior stance of the detached observer.

I. New Orleans

In the nineteenth century, as now, city guides made much of the distinctive atmosphere created by the unique divisions of the town, created during the varied phases of its history. The *Quartier Français* (French Quarter), also known as the *Vieux Carré* ('Old Square'), was the heart of old New Orleans, first laid out as a walled city in the 1720s by the founding French colonists. After a period of Spanish control (1762–1803), Louisiana was transferred to the United States (30 Nov. 1803) as part of Napoleon's sale of vast lands in North America (the 'Louisiana Purchase'). English then officially replaced French as the city's language. A neutral ground (which became Canal Street) divided the old French quarter from the rapidly expanding American section of the city. Chopin makes full use of these divisions in 'A Matter of Prejudice', and her evocations of the city's character are important in *The Awakening*, 'Athénaïse', and many other stories.

(i) [*the picturesque French Quarter*] from James F. Muirhead (ed.), *The United States . . .: A Handbook for Travellers, 1893* (Leipzig: Karl Baedeker, 1893), 368.

New Orleans is in many ways one of the most picturesque and interesting cities in America, owing to the survival of the buildings, manners and customs of its original French and Spanish inhabitants. It has been described by *Mr. G. W. Cable* as 'a city of villas and cottages . . shaded by forest trees, haunted by song-birds, fragrant with a wealth of flowers that never fails a day in the year, and abundant, in season, with fruit— the fig, the plum, the pomegranate, the orange'. . . . Among the foreign-looking features of this quarter are the walls of adobé, the limewashed stucco façades, the jalousies, the gratings, the small-paned windows, the portes-cochères, the arcades and balconies, the tiled roofs, and the inner courts—the whole embosomed in bright-flowering semi-tropical plants.

(ii) [*the divided city*] from Carl E. Groenevelt, *New Orleans. Illustrated in Photo Etching* (New Orleans: F. F. Hansell, 1892), 5.

New Orleans may be said to be divided into two quarters, the French or Creole and the American, Canal street being the dividing line. Upon that general thoroughfare, the Broadway of New Orleans, and at which point all the numerous lines of horsecars have their starting point, all society goes shopping, to see and to be seen. And yet, take half a dozen steps either way from Canal street and you are in a town as widely different in race, language, custom and ideas as two races of people living close to each other, and separated only by an imaginary line, can well be. Up town, as the American portion of the city is called, all is bustle and hurry, partaking of the activity of Northern cities. Cross that magic line toward Creole town, and one hears the foreign tongue and sees the signs in French, while groups of men chatter over their cigarettes and gesticulate as only the men can through whose veins Gallic blood flows. Sauntering further into the Latin quarter through open doors and windows are revealed beautiful gardens, ivy-clad walls and bubbling, sparkling fountains.

(iii) *Grand Isle* (some sixty miles South of New Orleans, and a popular summer resort for wealthy Creoles and their families). From Lafcadio Hearn, who stayed on the island in the mid-1880s.

[T]he plantation residences have been converted into rustic hotels, and the negro-quarters remodelled into villages of cozy cottages for the reception of guests. But with its imposing groves of live oak, its golden wealth of orange trees, its odorous lanes of oleander, its broad grazing-meadows yellow-starred with wild camomile, Grande Isle remains the prettiest island of the gulf and its loveliness is exceptional. (*Chita: A Memory of Last Isle* (New York: Harper, 1889), 11.)

It makes a curious impression on me: the old plantation cabins, standing in rows like village streets, and neatly remodelled for more cultivated inhabitants, have a delightfully rural aspect under their shadowing trees: and there is a veritable country calm by day and night . . . An absolutely ancient purity of morals appears to prevail here:—no one thinks of bolts or locks or keys, everything is left open and nothing is ever touched. Nobody has ever been robbed on this island. There is no inequity. . . . There are no temptations—except the perpetual and delicious temptation of the sea. (*Life and Letters of Lafcadio Hearn*, I, ed. Elizabeth Bisland (Boston: Houghton Mifflin, 1906), 87–8.)

II. The Creoles of Louisiana

'Creole' has undergone many different definitions, and was a much contested term in the late nineteenth century. Originally meaning any Louisiana-born descendants of early colonists, by the 1890s it had come to be applied (as it is in *The Awakening*), to the exclusive members of white New Orleans society, of French and Spanish descent. Cable's definition, which included those of mixed race, was bitterly rejected by this group, which inhabited a very different, privileged, social rank. However, other members of the native-born population (e.g. Germans and citizens of colour) continued to regard themselves as 'Creole'; the word was also used as an adjective for any local products, including dialect, eggs, horses, and vegetables. The 'characteristics' of Creoles, a source of pride to Creoles themselves, fascinated observers, and were much canvassed. *The Awakening* is full of explicit and embedded allusions to Creole character and social life, whose differences from Edna's more austere American Presbyterian background are of crucial importance in her story. It is also interesting to read Chopin's presentations of the bustling, Americanized, Léonce, and of the two handsome dilettantes, Robert and Arobin, in the light of such commentaries. (The Darwinian notes hint that the Creoles may be a dying breed.) Chopin's depiction of Creole girls and women is touched with irony in some instances (the Farival twins), admiring, searching, and troubled in others (Edna's relationship with Madame Ratignolle). Although Léonce may have chosen an American wife as a career move, his exaggerated expectations of feminine behaviour are coloured by the dominating images of purity and compliant sociability in these extracts, very different from the 'solitary soul' who attempts to escape them.

(i) *Creole Men:* from Albert Rhodes, 'The Louisiana Creoles', *Galaxy: A Magazine of Entertaining Reading*, 16:2 (Aug. 1873), 252–60.

The American criticises his Creole neighbor with severity. He avers that he is neither practical, energetic, nor able; that he is a stumbling-block in the way of progress. . . . If the deficiencies exist which are charged to his account, the Creole has compensating qualities for which his critical neighbor does not give him credit. If happiness is to be taken as a guide and test of excellence in man, the Creole is nearer the right path than the American, for the latter compared with him is a sombre, perturbed soul. . . . The Creole still lingers in the past, dallying with the flowers of love and sentiment, while the American hurries

forward with unhappy haste to pluck the thorns of ambition and pelf.
One is like a steam-tug, wheezing, tugging, and tossing; the other like a
Nile-boat loitering along the shores of lotus-land. . . . There is general
integrity of character in the Creole. . . . He lives long. Fair food and
wine, easy digestion, and a pleasant life, generally carry him, with but
little incidental sickness, past the line of fourscore. Thus his death
follows with the natural sequence of night to day. A Creole proverb
puts it that at last he dries up and blows away. (pp. 253–4)

. . . This race of Creoles has lost the virility of its prime, and is sinking
into old age. . . [T]he young gentlemen whom one sees in the Crescent
City are sadly in need . . . of a practical education, which would enable
them to hold their ground in the battle of life. The mind of the young
Creole dwells much on being well booted and gloved, on handsome
execution in piano playing and waltzing; and such preoccupation is
hardly of a nature to gird him for that strife which is generally the
inheritance of every American citizen. Artistic qualities should be
encouraged, but they are not everything. Ices and charlotte-russe may
be nice eating, but they will not supply the place of bread and beef.
(p. 256)

from Edwin L. Jewell, *Jewell's Crescent City Illustrated* (New Orleans:
1873), 5.

They form the foundation, on which the superstructure of what is
termed 'society' is erected. They are remarkably exclusive in their
intercourse with others, and, with strangers, enter into business
arrangements with extreme caution. They were once, and very properly, considered as the patricians of the land. But they are not more
distinguished for their exclusiveness, and pride of family, than for their
habits of punctuality, temperance and good faith.

(ii) *Creole Women*, from *Historical Sketch Book and Guide to New Orleans*
(New York: W. H. Coleman, 1885).

[*The maiden*] The pretty Creole maiden . . . returns from the convent
where she had gone for her education, to spend the summer vacation at
home. . . . [She] takes kindly to music. She has been as it were cradled
in song. It is mother's milk to her. Her earliest lullabies were operatic
airs. She comes of a musical family, and would be untrue to its traditions if she were not a lover of the *art musical*. (p. 151)

. . . [*The mother*] Her motherly virtue is her cardinal virtue. Care for
her children seems to have contributed indeed to the number and the
sensibility of the chords of sympathy and affection. . . . She is all the
fonder of what many deem frivolities, because of her children. For

them the gay reception, and the graceful dance are pleasant and harmless pastime. In such indulgences her children learn that ease of manner, grace of movement, and the thousand little prettinesses which are so adorable in after years. (p. 152)

... [*The matron*] The Creole matron grows old, as she does everything else, gracefully. She has not been shaken by the blasts of many passions, or enervated by the stimulants of violent sensations. There is no paled reflex of her youthful warmth in the glance she gives to the past, with its buried joys, or the present, with its all-pervading contentment and happiness. (p. 153)

III. Patois

This version of French spoken by the black population of the Creole sections of Louisiana, descendants of French-owned slaves, was the subject of considerable attention in the late nineteenth century. Many held that it was a barbaric jargon, an unsophisticated mish-mash of crude verbal gestures (nick-named 'Gombo', after the local stew). The numerous instances of patois in Chopin's fiction, however, suggest that she was keen to promote the view she shared with contemporaries such as Hearn, Cable, Fortier, and others, that this was a valuable tongue, worth capturing in written form. Although Fortier and later linguists attempted to clarify basic linguistic features, they made clear that there was no standard way of writing down patois. Chopin's attempts to render this predominantly oral form are impressive in their care and respect for a 'minority' tongue: both the language of black New Orleans and the language of white children, cared for by African-American servants. The extracts below give samples of both positive and racially contemptuous attitudes to patois voices, and offer a version of 'Lizette', the 'old half-forgotten Creole romance' (p. 223): Manna Loulou's inspiration for the story of 'La Belle Zoraïde'.

(i) [*a horrible jargon*] from *Historical Sketch Book and Guide to New Orleans* (New York: W. H. Coleman, 1885), 21.

The old colored nurse, the Creole 'mammy' was the ideal servant—a good cook, a thorough nurse, a second mother to the children, but teaching them to prattle a horrible jargon, sometimes called '*gombo*', and again 'Creole'. . . . Whether it was that French was a language too difficult for their tongues, or whether it was due to the presence of so many *négres brutes*, wild negroes of African birth, in the colony, cannot be said; it is only known that they spoke a distinct patois—another language from that of their masters, made up of about equal parts of French and African words, and absolutely incomprehensible to an ordinary Frenchman. Who was to know that '*ma pe couri*' was gombo for '*je m'en vais*', 'I am going away' . . . '*me ganyé choue*', for '*j'ai un*

cheval', 'I have a horse'? The whole gibberish contained but a few
hundred words and was without tense, mood or grammar. One word
did duty for a hundred, and the very animals and trees were without
distinctive titles, because the language was not rich enough to give
them names.

(ii) [*the sweet maternal tongue*] from Lafcadio Hearn, 'New Orleans'
(1877), collected in *Occidental Gleanings* i, ed. Albert Mordell (London:
1925), 223–34; and 'The Creole Patois' (1885), collected in *The American
Miscellany* (New York: 1925), 144–53.

I think it is very strange that so little has been written in regard to the
curiosities of Creole grammar, and the peculiar poetical adaptation of
the dialect. English antiquaries have produced elaborate treatises on
the dialects of Devonshire, Lancashire, and Cornwall. . . . Yet there is
certainly no European patois owning greater curiosities of construction, greater beauties of melody and rhythm than this Creole speech;
there is no provincial dialect of the mother country wealthier in romantic tradition and ballad legends than this almost unwritten tongue of
Louisiana. (p. 228)
. . . But creole is the maternal speech; it is the tongue in which the baby
first learns to utter its thoughts; it is the language of family and of
home. The white creole child learns it from the lips of his swarthy
nurse; and creole adults still use it in speaking to servants or to their
little ones. At a certain age the white boys or girls are trained to converse in French; judicious petting, or even mild punishment, is given
to enforce the use of the less facile but more polite medium of expression. But the young creole who remains in Louisiana seldom forgets
the sweet patois, the foster-mother tongue, the household words which
are lingual caresses. (p. 145)

(iii) *'Lizette'* from *Historical Sketch Book and Guide to New Orleans* (New
York: W. H. Coleman, 1885), 157–8.

This is one of a number of Creole songs transcribed in Coleman's
guide, presumably from an oral rendering. Even the author of the
derogatory comments in (i) above recalls 'those Creole ballads whose
simple and touching melody goes right to the heart and makes you
dream of unknown worlds' (p. 21). The songs are introduced with a
reference to the interest aroused by G.W. Cable's reading tour with
Mark Twain (1884–85), and exemplify 'a few of the most ancient and
popular among them'. Translations are given for several of the songs,
but not, unfortunately, for 'Lizette'. The version of 'Lisett' used by
Chopin is closer to the rendering given by the pioneer dialect scholar,
Alcée Fortier (see notes to 'La Belle Zoraïde'), but only the first stanza

is given. G. William Knott, who writes 'No less touching is the plaintive refrain of "Lizette"' also translates only the opening stanza, in the Coleman version ('The Haunting Melodies of Creole Songs', New Orleans *Times-Picayune*, 18 July 1926, p. 3). Fortier comments that the *Guide to New Orleans* songs are 'so completely disfigured by errors . . . that it is difficult for a stranger to understand them', 'Bits of Louisiana Folk-Lore', *PMLA* 3 (1887), 162. Nevertheless, with that warning in mind, I hope that even a free version, with some lines in doubt (indicated *[ ]*), might be of interest to readers of 'La Belle Zoraïde' and other stories. (The bird, the cage, the dance, are repeated images in Chopin's fiction.) I am deeply grateful to Michael Watts for the version that follows. Any further patois versions, or alternative translations, would be welcomed.

Lizette

Lizette quitté la plaine | Mon perdi bonher a moué; | Gié a moin semblé fontaine | Dipi mon pas mué toué | La jour quand mon coupé canne, | Mon songé zamone a moué | La nuit quand mon dans cabane | Dans dromi mon quimbé toué,

Lizette has fled the plains | My happiness has flown, | My tears like a fountain | Have flowed to your footsteps. | By day, when I'm cutting cane | I think deeply of your charms | At night, in my cabin, | In my sleep you are in my arms.

Si to allé la ville | Yo trouvé jeune Candio | Qui gagné pour tromper fille | Bouche doux passé sirop. | Yo va crer yo bin sincère | Pendant quior yo coquin tro; | C'est serpent qui contrefair | Crier rat pour tromper yo.

If you go into town | You will find young Candio | With a mouth sweeter than | Cane syrup, to lead girls astray. | You will think him very sincere | While he flirts with you too much; | He is a snake, pretending to be a | Rat, just to fool you.

Dipi mon perdi Lizette | Mon pas souchié calinda | Mon quitte Bram bram sonnette | Mon pas batte Bamboula | Quand mo contré l'aut'négresse | Mon pas gagne gié pone li. | Font qui chose à moin mourri.

Since I lost Lizette | I do not dance calinda | I left the beat of the drum | I do not beat the Bamboula | When I meet another black girl | I cannot look at her | Something in me dies.

Mon maigne tant com' gnon
souche | Jambe a moin tant
comme roseau, | Mangé na pa
doux dans bouche, | Tafia même
c'est comme dyo. | Quand mon
sagé toné Lizette, | Dyo toujours
dans gié moin. | Magnel moin vin
trop bete | A force chagrin mangé
moin.

My hands and knees are
numb | My legs are like
reeds, | Food does not taste
sweet | Even ratafia is like
water. | When I think Lizette
may return | There is always water
in my eyes. | I am weak and
foolish | Sorrow is eating me up.

Lizet' mon taudé nouvelle, | To
Compté bientôt tourné; | Vini
donc toujours fidèle | Miré bon
passé tandé, | N'a pas tardé
davantage, | To fai moin assez
chagrin— | Mon tant com' zozo
dans cage | Quand yo fait li
mourri faim.

*[Lizette the news reached
me | Soon that you left Comp-
té]* | I remain always true | My
past happiness | Has not lasted
long | You bring me a lot of
sorrow. | I am like a bird in a
cage | When you starve it to death.

IV.　The Acadians of Louisiana

The Acadians (now commonly 'Cajuns') were the descendants of the
French population of Nova Scotia (French, '*L'Acadie*'). Having refused to
swear loyalty to the British crown and the Anglican faith, they were
expelled in their thousands by the British in a series of moves from 1755.
The exiles who survived the disastrous '*le grand dérangement*' ('the great
disturbance') were widely scattered. Groups began to settle in southern
Louisiana from about 1763 until the 1780s, occupying the backwaters and
prairies known generically as 'Acadiana' on the west of the Mississippi
and along the Bayous (Têche, Lafourche) mentioned by Chopin. Romanticized by Longfellow in his epic love-poem, *Evangeline: A Tale of Acadie*
(1847), one dominant image of Acadians was of a pastoral folk, living in a
happy state of innocence. In contrast, despised by Creoles and Americans
as ill-educated and primitive, there developed a stereotype of 'Cajuns' as
lazy, ignorant swamp-dwellers. These images persisted late into the twentieth century, being gradually driven back only by the resurgence of
Acadian self-pride, and the international spread of interest in the lively
Acadian culture and music. In the nineteenth century, aware that these
communities were on the edge of change, some of Chopin's contemporaries, such as Alcée Fortier and A. R. Waud (1828–91), tried to document
Acadian life: Waud through his drawings, and Fortier through detailed
studies of customs and dialect. G. W. Cable, too, produced several
'Acadian' stories, drawing them together in the novel, *Bonaventure: A
Prose Pastoral of Acadian Louisiana* (1888). In 'A Gentleman of Bayou

Têche', 'Azélie', 'Tonie', and elsewhere, Chopin is keen to represent Acadians as distinct individuals, valuing their emotions, relationships and dialect, respecting their independence and potential, yet hinting at the impact of a new 'grand dérangement': the disturbances of modern America.

(i) [*'these peculiar people'*] from R.L. Daniels, 'The Acadians of Louisiana', *Scribner's Monthly* 19 (Nov. 1879–April 1880), 383.

> Among themselves they are '*Créole Français*'; and Acadian—or rather its corruption 'Cajun', as they pronounce it—is regarded as implying contempt. Indeed, the educated classes habitually designate those whom they regard as their social inferiors by the objectionable epithet. With the lower orders it is bandied from one to another in the same spirit; and none are so humble as not to feel the implied insult . . .
>
> These peculiar people are often spoken of as 'passing away' . . . On the Mississippi River, for instance, where they once owned large and valuable tracts of land, they have mostly yielded before the more enterprising, energetic American . . . while the more intelligent that remain are rapidly becoming Americanized—losing their distinctive characteristics through English education, social intercourse, and intermarriages with their American compatriots. But go back from the Mississippi . . . to the smaller bayous, where steamboats never come; to the extensive prairies where the whistle of the engine has not yet been heard, and you find genuine Acadians everywhere, unchanged, too, in character and mode of living from what they were fifty—perhaps one hundred years ago.

(ii) [*the 'dreamer and idler'*] from Albert Rhodes, 'The Louisiana Creoles', *Galaxy: A Magazine of Entertaining Reading*, 16: 2 (Aug. 1873), 254.

> The American employs the word Acadian in an uncomplimentary sense. A Utopian dreamer and idler is implied—one who sits on the skirts of progress. The reproaching American delves and digs in the shadow of life while his cheerful neighbor pleasantly basks in the sunshine. To one, the world is a workshop; to the other, a great fair. The Acadians are the least intelligent of the Creole population, and occupy small patches of land along bayous and the coast, which are just sufficient in extent to satisfy the wants of their simple lives.

(iii) [*'this earthly paradise'*] from Richard Taylor, *Destruction and Reconstruction. Personal Experiences of the Late War in the United States* (Edinburgh: Blackwood, 1879), 133–5.

> The upper or northern Teche waters the parishes of St Landry, Lafayette, and St Martin's—the Attakapas, home of the 'Acadians' . . . Their little *cabanes* dotted the broad prairie in all directions, and it was

pleasant to see the smoke curling from their chimneys, while herds of cattle and ponies grazed at will. . . . Mounted on his pony, with lariat in hand, he herded his cattle, or shot and fished; but so gentle was his nature, that lariat and rifle seemed transformed into pipe and crook of shepherd. . . . It was to this earthly paradise, and upon this simple race, that the war came, like the tree of the knowledge of evil to our early parents.

(iv) [*At the 'Cadian Ball*] from Alcée Fortier, 'The Acadians of Louisiana', *PMLA* 6:1 (1891), 64–94; rpt. *Louisiana Studies. Literature, Customs, Dialects, History and Education* (New Orleans: 1894), 176–9.

Outsiders were interested in Acadian entertainments, conventionally commenting on similar features. This piece is striking, nevertheless, for a number of observations, also found in 'At the 'Cadian Ball' (written 15–17 July 1892; pub. 22 Oct. 1892), close enough, perhaps, to suggest a direct stimulus. Although I have no evidence that Chopin read *PMLA*, she could well have had the article drawn to her attention by someone who knew of her interest in Louisiana life. (At the time, she was a member of the Wednesday Club; she may also have known James Kendall Hosmer, Prof. of English and German Literature at Washington University, St Louis, and an MLA member. As Emily Toth points out, Chopin used his daughter's name (Melicent Hosmer) for a major character in *At Fault*, 1890.) Fortier's study celebrates a people looking forward to new opportunities, but urges the preservation of their culture. Chopin's story similarly pays tribute to Acadian life and notes the onset of change, but, within that framework, concentrates on the characters' passions and the dynamics of their relationships.

Having heard that every Saturday evening there was a ball in the prairie, I requested one of my friends to take me to see one. We arrived at eight o'clock, but already the ball had begun. In the yard were vehicles of all sorts, but three-mule carts were most numerous. The ball room was a large hall with galleries all around it. When we entered it was crowded with persons dancing to the music of three fiddles. I was astonished to see that nothing was asked for entrance, but I was told that any white person decently dressed could come in. The man giving the entertainment derived his profits from the sale of refreshments. My friend, a wealthy young planter, born in the neighborhood, introduced me to many persons and I had a good chance to hear the Acadian dialect, as everybody there belonged to the Acadian race. I asked a pleasant looking man: "Votre fille est-elle ici?" He corrected me by replying: "Oui, ma *demoiselle* est là." However, he did not say *mes messieurs* for his sons but spoke of them as *mes garçons*, although he showed me his *dame*. We went together to the refreshment room where were beer and lemonade, but I observed that the favorite drink was black coffee, which indeed was excellent. At midnight supper was served; it was chicken gombo with rice, the national Creole dish.

Most of the men appeared uncouth and awkward, but the young girls were really charming. They were elegant, well-dressed and exceedingly handsome. They had large and soft black eyes and beautiful black hair. Seeing how well they looked I was astonished and grieved to hear that probably very few of them could read or write. On listening to the conversation I could easily see that they had no education. French was spoken by all, but occasionally English was heard.

After supper my friend asked me if I wanted to see *le parc aux petits*. I followed him without knowing what he meant and he took me to a room adjoining the dancing hall, where I saw a number of little children thrown on a bed and sleeping. The mothers who accompanied their daughters had left the little ones in the *parc aux petits* before passing to the dancing room, where I saw them the whole evening assembled together in one corner of the hall and watching over their daughters. *Le parc aux petits* interested me very much, but I found the gambling room stranger still. There were about a dozen men at a table playing cards. One lamp suspended from the ceiling threw a dim light upon the players who appeared at first sight very wild, with their broad brimmed felt hats on their heads and their long untrimmed sun burnt faces. There was, however, a kindly expression on every face, and everything was so quiet that I saw that the men were not professional gamblers. I saw the latter a little later, in a barn near by where they had taken refuge. About half a dozen men, playing on a rough board by the light of two candles. I understood that these were the black sheep of the crowd and we merely cast a glance at them.

I was desirous to see the end of the ball, but having been told that the break-up would only take place at four or five o'clock in the morning, we went away at one o'clock. I was well-pleased with my evening and I admired the perfect order that reigned, considering that it was a public affair and open to all who wished to come, without any entrance fee. My friend told me that when the dance was over the musicians would rise, and going out in the yard would fire several pistol shots in the air, crying out at the same time: *le bal est fini*.

EXPLANATORY NOTES

These notes attempt to clarify details of some of Chopin's explicit and embedded literary, historical, and cultural allusions. Scattered, often repeated, throughout the stories are short, foreign words and phrases: these are translated in the glossary. Longer phrases and words requiring more explanation are marked in the text and translated here (all from varieties of French, unless noted otherwise). Racial classifications are explained in the glossary.

All references to Chopin's manuscripts and clippings are to those held in the Kate Chopin Papers, Missouri Historical Society (MHS), St Louis, Mo. Her Commonplace Book (*CB*), diary (*Impressions*), and MS account books recording her story submissions and earnings (1888–95; 1888–1902) are cited from these papers (Box 1/Folders 2 and 14; Box 3/Folders 19 and 20). These have now been transcribed in Emily Toth and Per Seyersted (eds.), *Kate Chopin's Private Papers* (1998). If not specified, full publication details for other references will be found in the Select Bibliography. I use the following abbreviations: KC = Kate Chopin; *BF* = *Bayou Folk*; *NA* = *A Night in Acadie*; ET = Emily Toth, *Kate Chopin: A Life of the Author of 'The Awakening'* (1990); Baedeker = James F. Muirhead (ed.), *The United States . . . 1893* (Leipzig: Karl Baedeker, 1893); *Coleman = Historical Sketch Book and Guide to New Orleans* (New York: W. H. Coleman, 1885).

THE AWAKENING

Written April/June(?) 1897–Jan. 1898. Pub. by Herbert S. Stone & Company (Chicago: 22 April 1899). (Text here.) Working title: 'A Solitary Soul'.

3 *"Allez vous-en! . . . Sapristi!"*: 'Go away! Go away! For heaven's sake!' KC shared Mr Pontellier's impatience with parrots: 'I have no leaning towards a parrot. I think them detestable birds with their blinking stupid eyes and heavy clumsy motions. I could never become attached to one. I have never in my life heard one talk' (*Impressions*, May 1894). This unusually vocal parrot has been much discussed, as an image of the novel's multiple voices, and for the metaphors of caging and freedom it introduces.

gallery: (of a house) a long balcony or open porch.

Grand Isle: one of a number of semi-tropical islands lying in the Gulf of Mexico about sixty miles south of New Orleans, now linked by a bridge to the mainland, but then accessible only by boat, and inhabited largely by shrimp fishers and trappers, many of whom were believed to be descendants of pirates. After the Civil War, the former plantation grounds became a select summer resort for New Orleans residents. KC and her children are said to have spent summer vacations here.

Zampa: or *La Fiancée de Marbre* (*The Marble Fiancée*), an opera by the French composer Ferdinand (Louis Joseph) Hérold (1791–1833): in one of its many popular arrangements for amateur musicians, this is the first of several instances of debased artistic performance in the novel. Irritating though the twins become, their musical choice is appropriate for the Gulf setting: Zampa, a pirate chief in seventeenth-century Sicily, sets in train a romantic plot of love, betrayal, violence, and death in the sea.

Madame Lebrun: developed from a character in 'Tonie' (1893) ('At Chênière Caminada').

4 *Chênière Caminada*: a coastal settlement, opposite Grand Isle. Actually a peninsula, it was often described as an island (a point of symbolic force in the novel), because a large grove of oak trees at its tip made it look like an island from the perspective of sailing ships. Its name derives from '*chênière*', a mound emerging from a swamp, covered with live-oaks (from *chêne*, French for oak), and from the name of the Spanish merchant, Francisco Caminada, who owned the land in the later eighteenth century.

lugger: a small working sailing vessel, with one mast and a simple rigging.

quadroon: a person with one black grand-parent and three white, the first of many racial classifications in the novel, and in other stories. (See Glossary for further instances.)

lawn: a light, fine cotton or linen fabric.

5 *Klein's hotel*: generally believed to be based on J. Krantz's 'Grand Isle Hotel'. Founded on a former Creole plantation, its guest rooms had formed part of the slave quarters.

he could not afford cigars: for some critics, also a sign of Robert's insignificance in the masculine hierarchy in the novel.

6 *"The Poet and the Peasant"*: an operetta (1846), with incidental music by Franz von Suppé (1819–95), and, to judge by the number of adaptations for home performance, another hugely popular standard for amateur display.

The "Quartier Français": the old French section of New Orleans, still home for many French-speaking Creoles (see Appendix). Madame Lebrun's own Creole credentials presumably help to attract the 'exclusive visitors'.

the old Kentucky blue-grass country: the undulating plateau of Northern Kentucky, known for its rich soil and celebrated pastures of 'Blue Grass'. (See also note to p. 82.)

an American woman, with a small infusion of French: Mrs Pontellier, although well-born, is an outsider, an 'American', marked as different from the aristocratic Creoles of French descent. On her own marriage to a Louisiana Creole, KC herself had entered New Orleans society at a time when definitions of caste, class, and race were hardening along exclusive lines. In her heroine's origins, KC touches on Creole fears that

French was indeed becoming diluted by the increasing Americanization of the city.

7 *New Orleans club men*: KC repeatedly emphasizes Mr Pontellier's desire to keep in with the prosperous men of the city. First founded in the 1830s, clubs flourished, recovering from the set-backs of the Civil War to become again, by the 1880s, powerful social organizations for well-to-do (and aspiring) commercial and professional men.

9 *rockaway*: (after Rockaway, New Jersey) a light open-sided carriage, with cross-wise seats, for six to nine passengers.

Carondelet Street: with the large Cotton Exchange on its corner was the financial and commercial centre of New Orleans. In the 1872 city directory, the street boasted half of the entire city's listed brokers (dealers in money, plantations, ships, stocks, exchange, etc.). The 1873 directory records Oscar Chopin's progression to 65 Carondelet from the less prosperous Union St where he started in business in 1870.

10 *Mrs. Pontellier was not a mother-woman*: a daring statement that places KC's heroine at odds with prevailing orthodoxies, as expressed, for example, by Elizabeth Bisland (later Wetmore, 1861–1929), a well-known Louisiana writer of the day: 'Woman simply may not eat her cake and have it too. Using all her energies for her own needs she can not give vigor to her children. If she employ for her own ends her store of life she robs the child,' 'The Modern Woman and Marriage', *North American Review*, 160:6 (June 1895), 755.

12 *the society of Creoles*: these paragraphs draw on a widespread interest in discussing the Creole 'characteristics' (see Appendix) which KC exploits in her heroine's awakening.

13 *Mademoiselle Duvigné's presence*: KC here adds another story to the one she had already told about Mlle Duvigné in 'Tonie' (1893).

Daudet: Alphonse Daudet (b. 1840) French novelist, whose impressionist prose KC admired. He died on 16 December 1897, as KC was reaching the end of *The Awakening*.

'Passez! Adieu! Allez vous-en!': 'Get along! Good-bye! Go away!'

never jealous: because he can trust his wife's honour absolutely (see Appendix).

"Blageur—farceur—gros bête, va!": 'Clown—buffoon—big idiot, get along with you!'

14 *"Mais ce n'est pas mal! Elle s'y connait, elle a de la force, oui"*: 'But it's not at all bad! Yes, she knows what she's doing, she's got some real ability'. For non-French speakers, KC skilfully gives the sense of Robert's 'little ejaculatory expressions of appreciation'.

15 *Edna Pontellier*: the heroine's full name is suggestive: 'Pontellier', a bridge-maker, and 'Edna', an echo of two popular earlier heroines: Edna Earl of *St. Elmo* (1866), by Augusta Jane Evans (later Wilson,

1835–1909); and Edna Kenderdine of *The Woman's Kingdom* (1868), by Dinah Mulock (later Craik, 1826–87). (See Elaine Showalter, *Sister's Choice: Tradition and Change in American Women's Writing* (Oxford: 1991), 71.) Emily Toth has discussed an even more intriguing possibility: that through the painter, Degas (see note to p. 55), KC may have known of Berthe Morisot's sister: an artist, who gave up her painting on marriage, and whose name was Edma Pontillon (*Unveiling Kate Chopin*, 74).

18 *crash*: strong coarse cotton or linen fabric.

lateen sail: a triangular sail, simply rigged to a yard at the head of a short mast, and for many writers, a distinctively picturesque feature of the Gulf coastal seas.

Cat Island: according to G.W. Cable, the site of an encounter between a British sloop-of-war and two privateers: 'the pirates stood ground and repulsed them with considerable loss' (*The Creoles of Louisiana*, ch. xxiv).

20 *Her most intimate friend at school*: believed to be based on Kitty Gareschéé, who gave KC's first biographer, Daniel Rankin, details of the girls' favourite books, including Dickens, Scott, and Bunyan.

something like Napoleon's: paintings such as those by Jacques-Louis David (1748–1825) offered a romantic image of the charismatic French ruler, Napoleon Bonaparte (1769–1821), whose life featured significantly in New Orleans history and legend.

21 *a great tragedian*: generally considered to be modelled on Edwin Booth (1833–93). KC had reviewed *Century*'s selection of his letters, paying tribute to the 'magnetic power' of his art ('The Real Edwin Booth', *St. Louis Life* 10 (13 Oct. 1894), 11).

closing the portals forever: an image KC repeats in similar contexts; see, e.g. 'A Point at Issue!' (p. 141).

Iberville: one of the wealthy River Parishes (counties) spreading north-west of New Orleans along the Mississippi, it boasted vast cane plantations and palatial houses. This countryside is evoked more fully in ch. xxxii below.

22 *"Tiens! . . . est jalouse!"*: 'Well! . . so Madame Ratignolle's jealous!'

23 *a comedian . . . jack-in-the-box*: Robert has clearly been stung by Madame Ratignolle's affectionate 'little running, contemptuous comment' (p. 13 above).

Biloxi: a popular resort on the Mississippi coast, celebrated for its bathing, fishing, and fine oysters, it was a discreet eighty miles from New Orleans, served by a coast train.

the French Opera: (founded 1859, destroyed by fire, 1919) one of the finest opera houses in North America and the most fashionable cultural and social centre in New Orleans.

24 *Angostura*: extract of bitter bark, added to liquids as a tonic, or to enliven

a drink. Creoles were noted for their extensive knowledge of herbs, spices, and seasonings.

25 *the Goncourt*: sustaining the theme of the Creoles' daring taste in summer reading. The French brothers, Edmond (1822–96) and Jules de Goncourt (1830–70), who collaborated on many books, were notable for presenting the artist as an exceptional being, and for their attempts to convey in highly refined descriptive prose and stylized patterns of colour, a finely tuned, aesthetic response to existence. Their sexually and emotionally restless heroines (e.g. in *Germinie Lacerteux* (1864) and *Madame Gervaisais* (1869)) shocked many readers.

Vera Cruz: for Robert, not perhaps the most attractive prospect. According to Baedeker (1893), this 'seaport on the *Gulf of Mexico*, with 24,000 inhab., lies in a dreary sandy plain and contains comparatively little of interest to the tourist. Its commerce has declined since the opening of railway communication with the United States. The climate is hot and very unhealthy in summer' (p. 494).

27 *At an early hour . . . their baptism*: though taking up conventional representations of the piety, musicality, and accomplishments of young Creole girls (see Appendix), KC's depiction is distinctly tinged with irony.

tulle: fabric of soft, fine net; in the nineteenth century, generally silk.

28 *if the salt might have been kept out of portions of it*: even with the advent of the patent 'freezer', ice-cream making involved skill and hard work. Salt was essential to keep the ingredients at the right temperature, and the mixture had to be kept moving: 'Turn the crank of your freezer briskly if you have a five-minute freezer; if not, turn the can with your hand for fifteen minutes, and then pack round again with ice and salt,' instructed *La Cuisine Creole* (New Orleans: Hansell, 1885), 181. Recipes gave tips about how to cover the tub adequately, but clearly there was much room for error—especially for any servant, like these two black women, working under Victor's supervision. (KC's satirical eye falls on Victor's blustering management of servants again on p. 66.)

29 *"Solitude"*: echoing KC's working title for the novel, and recalling her translation of Guy de Maupassant's story, 'Solitude,' pub. *St. Louis Life* (28 Dec. 1895). Although the Paris setting seems remote from Grand Isle, the story voices meditations on 'the isolation of self' and images (e.g. of 'portals', the sea, the sanctuary) to which KC returns in her novel.

Empire gown: dainty, high-waisted dress, reminiscent of those worn in the first (1804–14) French empire, again linking Edna's fantasies with romanticized images of an unattainable world.

30 *Chopin*: Frédéric Chopin (1810–49), Polish composer of French descent, whose haunting music KC used at significant moments from 'Wiser than a God' onwards.

32 *"I thought I should have perished out there alone"*: sustaining the 'solitude' theme, Edna's words recall William Cowper's poem, 'The Cast-away'

(1799): 'We perish'd, each alone: | But I beneath a rougher sea, | And whelm'd in deeper gulfs than he.' Edna may also have had in mind Cowper's vivid lines about struggling to swim in 'the whelming brine'.

33 *the twenty-eighth of August*: the associations here may spring entirely from Robert's imagination. For some critics, the date has wider significance: e.g. as part of an extended allusion to *Song of Myself*, linking Edna's age (28), with Whitman's vision of a young woman ('Twenty-eight years of womanly life and all so lonesome'), bathing with twenty-eight young men (Bert Bender, 'The Teeth of Desire: *The Awakening* and *The Descent of Man*', 1991; rpt. in Alice Hall Petry (ed.), *Critical Essays on Kate Chopin* (1996), 117–28).

39 *Spanish moss*: a long, grey, velvety, soft moss, which, hanging from trees, was an instantly recognizable feature of Louisiana scenes.

Grande Terre: this beautiful small island, across the Barataria Pass to the east of Grand Isle, had poetic associations as 'the retreat of the dread corsair of the Gulf, whom the genius of Byron has immortalized' (*Coleman*, 188). Fort Livingstone, never completed and abandoned during the Civil War, was a romantic ruin, threatened by the encroaching waves.

Bayou Brulow: or 'Bruleau', a tiny fishing and shrimping settlement, built on stilts above the waters, with drying platforms for the shrimp catch.

Tonie: unknown to Robert, once his rival for Mlle Duvigné's love. See 'Tonie'.

the ... church of Our Lady of Lourdes: at Caminadaville: named after the relatively recent miracles of healing at the grotto of Lourdes, France, where the Virgin Mary appeared to Bernadette Soubirous (1844–79) in Feb. 1858. Besides its symbolic associations, the reference bears on the question of when the novel is set: the church was destroyed in the 1893 hurricane, but built after KC left New Orleans in 1879. (I have seen 1881 and 1883 given for its founding, but no earlier. Gaston D'Espinose, its presiding priest, arrived in 1883.)

40 *Acadian*: a French-speaking Louisiana settler. See Appendix.

cot: cottage (normally a poetic usage, in keeping here with the pastoral and fairy-tale notes).

44 *the Baratarians*: famous outlaws and local heroes, led by Jean Lafitte (1780?–?, reputedly Byron's Corsair) and his brother, Pierre, who had their headquarters in the islands and sea-marshes of Barataria Bay. KC draws on the romantic legends of the Baratarians, rather than on the stories of their dealings in the slave trade, and rumoured links with Napoleon and Karl Marx. However, some critics have read the presence of Lafitte as part of the novel's general critique of corrupt economic forms.

45 *"Ah! Si tu savais"*: untraced in exactly the version given in *The*

Awakening. The song is generally held to echo the popular 'Si Tu Savais' (1864; 'Didst Thou But Know') by Michael William Balfe (1808–70). This certainly employs the phrase as an insistent refrain, but, in the versions I have seen, does not contain the further line given later (p. 100). As in the many similar songs with this title, however, the phrase serves as prelude to a passionate declaration of love, and to emotionally climactic descriptions of the overwhelming consequences which would be unleashed if the woman only knew the man's true state of heart.

53 *your Bible tells you so*: specific passage unidentified, but Mme Ratignolle evokes the spirit of many Biblical texts on the virtues of selflessness: e.g. 'the good shepherd giveth his life for the sheep' (John 10: 11) and 'Greater love have no man than this, that a man lay down his life for his friends' (John 15: 13).

55 *Esplanade Street*: (later renamed 'Avenue') KC gives the socially ambitious Mr Pontellier a more exclusive address than the Chopins' own: equivalent to St Charles Avenue in the American section, this broad, tree-lined street was home to the most prosperous Creole élite, and was recommended for 'desirable locations, that may be purchased by those who wish to establish themselves in the Crescent City' (J. Curtis Waldo, *Illustrated Visitors' Guide to New Orleans* (New Orleans: 1879), 56). The French painter Edgar Degas (1834–1917) visited his uncle and his brother's family here in 1872–3.

double cottage: an urban development of a traditional style, the steep-roofed creole cottage was usually built directly on to the street front, with gardens (the 'yard') and separate service buildings at the back. Grand versions, built in the mid- to late-nineteenth century, often of two storeys, might include three bays, and incorporate the servants' rooms. Today's architectural guides direct visitors to the Esplanade Ridge area for some of the finest of the type.

56 *reception day*: visitors to the city were warned that the etiquette of calling 'is rigorously adhered to, and strangers should be careful to observe these customs. Reception days for ladies are kept very generally, and the hours are from 1 to 6 P.M. . . . Gentlemen, if strangers, also call on these days': James S. Zacharie, *New Orleans Guide* (New Orleans, 1893), 32.

He tasted his soup . . . everything within reach: here, Edna again offends the household gods. *La Cuisine Creole* (1885), aimed at the Creole housewife, opened with a section which urged women to 'keep one vessel sacred to soup as nearly as possible', warning that 'domestic contentment depends upon the successful preparation of the meal', and that 'food rendered indigestible through ignorance in cooking often creates discord and unhappiness' (p. 1). As well as conveying the general pepperiness of Mr Pontellier's mood, however, KC has fun with the Creoles' reputation for relishing spicy food. Among suggested seasonings for soups were mushroom catsup [ketchup], red pepper, Madeira wine, curry powder, a pint of sherry, French mustard, cayenne, garlic, and 'strong vinegar or brandy' flavoured with herbs (p. 102).

57 *free-lunch stand*: a well-known New Orleans institution, copied in major cities elsewhere. Inaugurated in bar rooms in the 1830s, to save businessmen a journey home at midday, lavish free spreads were offered between half-past eleven and one o'clock, to tempt men to patronize the saloons and conduct business deals over drinks.

Carrolton: a suburb on the river bend, west of New Orleans. A former plantation area, divided by the railroad in 1833, it underwent rapid development after the Cotton Centennial Exposition of 1884, merging with the rest of the city. In 1893, according to Zacharie, streetcars took 35 minutes to make the journey into the city (p. 20). Mr Pontellier is clearly keen to build up connections in all areas of the city.

61 *porte cochère*: a traditional feature of many French Quarter buildings, this was a large arched carriage entrance, built into the front of the house, leading through into a rear courtyard. Generally lined with flagstones, it provided sheltered off-street access to the house.

soirée musicale: an evening party, featuring various informal musical contributions, a popular form of sociability among the Creoles.

62 *Bavarian peasant*: contributing to the theme of art and representation in the novel, this seems to be intended as a cliché of genre painting. (Even by the 1880s, art critics were expressing weariness with the fashion for depicting sentimentalized European peasants.)

salt of the earth: 'Ye are the salt of the earth: but if the salt have lost his savour, wherewith shall it be salted? it is thenceforth good for nothing, but to be cast out, and to be trodden under the foot of men', Matthew 5:13. The first part of the verse seems most applicable to Mr Ratignolle. Edna echoes the narrator's tone below, in one of several Biblical allusions that appear in the ambience of this worthy couple.

. . . spoke English with no accent whatever: comments implicitly challenging G.W. Cable's representation of Creole speech, endorsed even in city guides: 'Try speaking English to any of the dwellers in this neighborhood, and one is answered in the carressing accents and delicious dialect that makes so large a part of the charm of Cable's books' (*Coleman*, 149). Whether viewed as delicious or decadent, the Creole community took general offence at this depiction. KC here offers more evidence, too, of Mr Pontellier's efforts at Americanization.

"Better a dinner of herbs": 'Better is a dinner of herbs where love is, than a stalled ox and hatred therewith', Proverbs 15:17. Here, some editors insert a word, to smooth a slight syntactic awkwardness ('it did not take her long to discover that [it/here] was no dinner of herbs'). I have left the text as it stands in the first edition. KC frequently uses compressed oral inflections, and any difficulty vanishes if the passage is read aloud.

63 *life's delirium*: KC's short poem, 'An Ecstasy of Madness' (written 10 July

1898) similarly evokes 'A delirium of gladness | Too wild to tell'; see, too, 'Her Letters' (p. 282).

63 *en bonne ménagère*: as a good housewife.

65 *some distance away*: even at the closest points, to reach Bienville Street from Esplanade Avenue would have entailed a walk of some twelve main blocks to the far side of the French Quarter (about three-quarters of a mile).

66 *the old régime*: the city's years under Spanish rule (1762–1803). French Quarter architecture often combined Spanish and French features. Buildings presented a dead face to the street, concealing beautiful private courtyards and gardens at the rear.

68 *the car*: the street car, presumably on Canal Street, the centre of the city transport system. At that stage of the day, even Edna seems disinclined to walk; she would not have required an escort on the car: 'the utmost decorum is strictly enforced, so that ladies unattended can ride with safety to every part of the city' (Zacharie, *New Orleans Guide*, 37).

69 *prunella gaiter*: a foot covering, of strong twill fabric, another example of Mlle Reisz's disregard for style.

la belle dame: the beautiful lady, possibly with an echo of John Keats's 'La Belle Dame sans Merci' (1819), identifying Edna as a *femme fatale*.

70 *that Impromptu of Chopin's*: see note to p. 30. Chopin composed three romantic pieces under this title, which suggests the kind of improvised playing Mlle Reisz uses to such powerful effect below.

71 *Isolde's song*: an allusion to *Tristan and Isolde* (1865), the opera by Richard Wagner (1813–83), notable for its Romantic conflation of Love and Death.

72 *that old Creole race . . . that dry up and finally blow away*: Mr Pontellier prides himself on conforming to type. For this proverb, see Appendix, II. i. Ironically, sometimes it was also attributed to the Acadians, viewed by the Creoles as decidedly inferior.

Canal Street: a broad, lively thoroughfare, running at right angles to the river, this was New Orleans' famous highstreet, dividing the French and American sections. See Appendix, I. ii.

73 *a circle . . . super-spiritual superior beings*: an allusion to new clubs for women. The Doctor's wife would have read arguments for female superiority, even if she had not met any New Women in person. (The *New Orleans Times-Democrat* (9 April 1893) printed KC's story 'A Shameful Affair', in the same issue as a spirited column scorning those who had yet to accept the 'Undeniable proofs of the mental equality—or superiority—of the gentler sex.' (p. 7).)

she's peculiar: Mr Pontellier's worries may be set in a general context by the following advertisement (for a female tonic), typical of hundreds in publications of the day, including those where KC appeared: 'Women are by nature happy, cheerful, unselfish, attractive. When a woman becomes fretful, peevish, languid and careless: when she complains of everyone and everything: when she is nervous day and night, and can obtain no rest, she is not well. . . . She needs attention' (*St. Louis Republic*, 4 April 1896, 5).

"Nothing hereditary?": a question echoing the growing interest in eugenics during the 1890s. It is not unlikely that Mr Pontellier considered Edna's 'stock' before marrying her.

74 *a very peculiar and delicate organism*: echoing Mme Lebrun's anxiety that Edna may be 'capricious' (p. 32), and fusing older myths of feminine irrationality with more contemporary medical discourse. Widely read treatises, such as George M. Beard's *American Nervousness* (1881), represented women's bodies as 'highly organized' (i.e. finely tuned) structures, easily put under strain. As critics note, an 'inspired psychologist', was indeed then working on similar cases: Sigmund Freud had published *Studies on Hysteria* in 1895. *The Interpretation of Dreams* appeared in the same year as *The Awakening*, at the end of 1899.

75 *he knew his Creole too well*: i.e. he is aware of the offence to honour. KC refers to 'an almost Creolean sensitiveness to criticism' in 'The Western Association of Writers', *Critic* (7 July 1894).

colonel in the Confederate army: he had supported the secessionist cause and the slave-holding Southern Confederate States during the Civil War (1861–65). By bestowing on him a military title, KC sustains the novel's satire on forms of male power, but also succeeds in keeping Edna's birth name a secret.

76 *He considered them bourgois*: for the social-climbing Mr Pontellier, the Ratignolles, living over their drug-store, are middle-class, with no connections worth cultivating.

77 *trumped-up knowledge of bygone days*: although the Doctor's story falls flat, New Orleans long recalled the racing glories of antebellum days when the city boasted five courses 'upon all of which the music of flying feet was regularly heard' (*Coleman*, 241). The 'giants of the turf' (p. 242) were Lexington and Lecompte, both foaled in the Colonel's own Blue Grass Country: their celebrated contests (April 1854–55) could still rouse discussion decades later.

78 *some beautiful, sleek animal waking up in the sun*: recalling KC's allegorical sketch, 'Emancipation. A Life Fable' (*c*.1869), where a beautiful animal relishes life outside its comfortable cage.

grosbec: probably not the large-beaked finch or bunting of this name, but the night-heron, classified as a game bird, which could be hunted from Sept. to Feb. KC's carefully judged use of the term 'friendly darky' in this sentence colours Mr Pontellier's plantation reminiscences with the nostalgic sentimentality found in many southern stories of the period.

drifting into the unknown: Edna's invention echoes (but brilliantly transforms) popular romance drawing on the atmospheric southern landscape.

Contrast for instance this moonlit scene with the noon-time flight of the summer lovers who drift out of New Orleans (and visit a romantic fort), in 'Down the Bayou' (1882), by the then famous Mary Ashley Townsend ('Xariffa', 1836–1901): 'Once more, as in a vision, seem | To rise before me lake and stream; | Once more a semi-tropic noon, | A boat upon a long lagoon; | Two figures there, as in a dream' (*'Down the Bayou'* . . . *And Other Poems* (Philadelphia: 1896), 25).

81 . . . *read Emerson until she grew sleepy*: Ralph Waldo Emerson (1803–82), writer, lecturer, and thinker, was one of the dominant men of letters in nineteenth-century America. Associated with various philosophies of reform and a belief in a higher individualism, some of his ideas seem to be echoed in Edna's narrative. Critics also recall his strong endorsement of separate spheres for men and women and relish KC's passing satire at his expense. Elizabeth Gaskell enjoys a similar moment in *Mary Barton* (1848) where one of the listless Miss Carsons 'tried to read "Emerson's Essays," and fell asleep in the attempt' (ch. 18).

82 *drag*: a vehicle, like a coach, usually drawn by four horses.

the Jockey Club: chartered in May 1871, the New Louisiana Jockey Club, at the top of Esplanade St, quickly gained a reputation as an exclusive social venue. Members and guests enjoyed parlours, reading rooms, restaurants, and beautiful gardens: 'the benefits of a princely private establishment, adorned with all that taste or comfort could suggest or wealth command', Edwin L. Jewell (ed.), *Jewell's Crescent City* . . . (New Orleans: 1873), 123.

the breath of the blue grass paddock: the Kentucky Blue Grass region was renowned for its racing and its excellence in horse-breeding, 'the blood horses of Kentucky exhibiting a remarkable combination of speed and endurance' (Baedeker, 317). Edna's own 'sound old . . . Kentucky stock' (p. 73) seems to be emerging in a pronounced form here.

83 *"Dante reading"*: a reading, possibly in the original Italian, of the work of Dante Alighieri (1265–1321), Florentine poet. The activity is characteristic of intellectual women's clubs of the period (satirized by KC in *At Fault*)—over one season, the St Louis Wednesday Club heard essays on Dante and Giotto, his 'philosophy and symbolism', and 'place and influence in literature' (30 Nov. 1892–8 Feb. 1893: Wednesday Club Pubs., 1890–92, held at MHS). 'The Vision—Dante' appears in a list of KC's reading in *CB* (p. 204).

Grieg: Edvard Grieg (1843–1907), Norwegian composer, who is betrayed by yet another of the novel's failed pianists.

the ice-box: New Orleans was known for its commercial ice-manufacture, and impressed outsiders such as Mark Twain with its ability to maintain domestic supplies. Long before the advent of electrical versions in the 1920s, the well-to-do enjoyed the benefits of the 'Jewett's Labrador' and other similarly well-advertised 'refrigerators'.

84 *a branch Folk Lore Society*: New Orleans was home of the President of the American Folklore Society, Professor Alcée Fortier (1856–1914), author of *Louisiana Folk-Tales* (1894) and other significant works. Although KC associates this society with the satirically treated Miss Highcamp, she entered 'The Maid of Saint Phillippe' for a *Youth's Companion* folk-lore contest (April 1891), and various elements in her writing reflect the interests of 1890s folklorists. Miss Highcamp's appointment leaves Edna without the required lady companion.

a duel outside of Paris: Louisiana Creoles were known for their duelling tradition. As late as 1876, the London *Times* reported a 'duel [outside New Orleans] fought between two gentlemen, Creoles' (26 Oct., 9), but by the 1890s the practice was virtually defunct.

87 *A bust of Beethoven, covered with . . . dust*: a less than reverent treatment of Ludwig van Beethoven (1770–1827), the most esteemed of nineteenth-century European composers.

90 *grand esprit*: an outstanding character, someone destined to rise above the ordinary: a phrase thoroughly glossed here for Edna by Mlle Reisz herself.

"Why? . . . Because—": in a commissioned piece, 'Is Love Divine?', printed as she was finishing *The Awakening*, KC quotes this passage (possibly from memory). She adds, 'One really never knows the exact, definite thing which excites love for any one person, and one can never truly know whether this love is the result of circumstances or whether it is predestination,' *St. Louis Post-Dispatch* (16 Jan. 1898), 17.

92 *'The bird . . . must have strong wings'*: while most critics view this as a positive note in the novel's signifying scheme of restraint, flight, and freedom, Stephen Heath hears echoes of Flaubert's list of clichés, *Le Dictionnaire des idées reçues*: 'Bird—Wanting to be one and sighing for "wings, wings" is the mark of a poetic soul' ('Chopin's Parrot' (1994), 21).

94 *pigeon house*: dovecote, or *pigeonnier*, a shelter and nesting house for ornamental doves, a common architectural feature, particularly on plantations.

96 *Gouvernail*: a character with a significant role in 'A Respectable Woman' and 'Athénaïse'. His name may play on *gouvernail*, in Mississippi Valley French, the steersman of a canoe (or a rudder): perhaps one whose editorials steer opinion.

97 *the cocktail which he composed*: an appropriate drink for this company, who could appreciate its artistry. Although the Colonel is a Kentuckian, New Orleans claimed to be the inventor of the cocktail (and its name), and still celebrates the arrival in the city of the originators of Peychaud bitters (1793), Sazerac (1859), and the Ramos gin fizz (1888).

pompono: (usually 'pompano') this dish alone substantiates Edna's promise of a 'very fine' dinner. This was the most expensive and prized fish,

costing up to five dollars in the markets, where a red snapper, large
enough for ten people, could be had for 50 cents. Guide-books called it a
'delightful morsel from old Neptune's table' (*Coleman*, 86); and for Mark
Twain it was 'delicious as the less criminal forms of sin' (*Life on the
Mississippi* (1883), ch. 44).

97 *Perdido Street*: in the American section, running parallel with Canal
Street. For critics, a name with symbolic resonance: literally, 'lost' in
Spanish, because, as legend recalled, it had once lost itself in a cypress
swamp. Here, Arobin's gentlemanly disdain for a profession reflects
observers' views of young Creole men (see Appendix).

St. Charles Hotel: the city's principal hotel; mentioned here in another of
the novel's many interrupted stories.

98 *Geneva*: a town on the beautiful Seneca Lake, New York.

99 *"Bonne nuit, ma reine; soyez sage"*: 'Good night, my queen; be good'
(literally 'wise').

a vision of Oriental beauty: Mrs Highcamp turns Victor into a *tableau-
vivant* (living picture): possibly, with the addition of the white silken
scarf, the famous *Bacchus* by Caravaggio (?1571–1610).

"'There was a graven image of Desire | ... ground of gold'": the opening
lines of 'A Cameo', a sonnet by Algernon Charles Swinburne (1837–
1909), an often controversial English poet. Critics emphasize the eroticism, the fatality, and the cynicism of the association.

100 *"Ah! si tu savais | Ce que tes yeux me disent"*: 'Ah! if you knew | What
your eyes are telling me'. (The second line may be KC's invention.)

104 *Mr. Pontellier had saved appearances!*: a satire in touch with the social
realities of Gilded Age New Orleans, where aspiring men needed to
maintain a strong profile within the commercial community. Daily newspapers detailed their families' activities, and city guides often featured
their photographs, with comments on their social standing. Mr Pontellier
clearly endorses the spirit of 'Emulation and Enterprise', and his
schemes of improvement declare his solidity. His choice of an American
wife may have been part of the same set of ambitions.

to look with her own eyes: echoing KC's tribute to Guy de Maupassant
(1850–93) who played a crucial role in her own awakening as a writer:
'Here was a man who had escaped from tradition and authority, who had
entered into himself and looked out upon life through his own being and
with his own eyes', 'Confidences' (Sept. 1896), *Complete Works*, 700–1.

"feed upon opinion": source untraced, but a long-standing commonplace:
as in Francis Quarles, 'The Shepheards Oracles' (1646): 'Opinion | 'Tis
a curious feed that sheep doe most delight in' (Eclogue VII).

106 *"party call"*: follow-up visit, demanded by etiquette after attending a
dinner.

111 *she lingered to talk patois with Robert, whom she had known as a boy*: an

allusion to the language shared by Creole children and their black servants: here tinged with affection, a contrast with the disparaging comments of many observers (see Appendix, III).

112 *Stunning girls, though, in Mexico*: Baedeker confirms this kind of generalization about Mexican women: 'The women of Jalapa are distinguished for their beauty' (p. 494).

115 *out to the lake, on the Shell Road*: Lake Pontchartrain was a popular drive from the city, especially as the smooth, level white road (made of broken shells) allowed owners of fast teams to show off their horses. Discretion prevents Arobin being seen with Edna at one of the garden restaurants for which the lake was famous.

117 *I always feel so sorry for women who don't like to walk*: on her honeymoon, KC enjoyed taking time to herself in Zurich: 'I wonder what people thought of me—a young woman strolling about alone. I even took a glass of beer at a friendly little beer garden quite on the edge of the lake' (*CB* 188).

122 *She recalled faintly ... to which she had given being*: as ET remarks (127–8), an unusually explicit description, which echoes KC's own memories of her first confinement (*Impressions*, 11–12).

Oh think of the children!: an echo of the impassioned pleas of the traditionalists, especially in the wake of *A Doll's House* (1879) by the Norwegian dramatist, Henrik Ibsen (1828–1906), and a reminder of just how much KC risked in her novel: 'This enmity to and destructive criticism of that fair temple of life called marriage—built by women's hands out of women's hearts—seems like a madness. . . . [W]omen are not and never can be free. They are all under bonds to the new generation. If she were alone, she might choose to make herself homeless—but how of the little children?' (Bisland: 'The Modern Woman and Marriage', 755).

123 *a provision of Nature ... for the race*: a remark coloured by Darwinian accounts of the processes of human survival, which KC reputedly read in the years of her early widowhood.

125 *Lucillean feast*: (usually, 'Lucullan' or 'Lucullian') lavish, luxurious, deriving from the reputation of the Roman general, Lucius Licinius Lucullus (*c.*114–57 BC), notorious for his prodigal banquets.

Venus ... youthful houris: to impress Mariequita, Victor creates an extravagant cocktail of allusion. Venus, a goddess of gardens and fertility, became identified in classical Rome with Aphrodite, the goddess of Love, who was said to have been born rising from the foam of the sea; houris were beautiful young women, who awaited men in the Muslim paradise.

128 *Filled the air*: critical interpretations of the ending have been wideranging. Among them, the realistic (Edna sets up careful alibis, to allow her children to believe it an accident); the clinical (she is confused and depressed); the theoretical and political (this is part of her struggle with

patriarchal language and limits); the psychoanalytical (she returns to childhood, or the pre-Oedipal); the mythic (Edna swims triumphantly out of time into the sphere of the goddess).

WISER THAN A GOD

Written June 1889; pub. *Philadelphia Musical Journal*, 4:12 (Dec. 1889), 38–40. (Paid $5.00. Text here.)

129 *"To love and be wise . . . a god"*: from the Latin, *'Amare et sapere vix deo conceditur'*, in the *Sententiae* of Publilius Syrus (first century BC), a sentiment much repeated: e.g. Shakespeare ('To be wise, and love, | Exceeds man's might' *Troilus and Cressida*, III. ii. 163); Edmund Spenser (*The Shepheard's Calendar*, March, 19–20); and Edmund Burke ('To tax and to please, no more than to love and to be wise, is not given to men', 'Speech on American Taxation', 1774).

Mutterchen: literally, 'little mother' (German), an endearment. Already KC uses scattered words to suggest other languages, accents, or dialects: here to sketch Paula's German–American origins at a time of threat to the German language. St Louis had a substantial German population, supporting German-language newspapers. Although she joined a German Reading Club (1869), KC never became entirely at ease in the tongue and refers to the excruciating efforts the Chopins made to speak German while on honeymoon (*CB* 194).

130 *'Berceuse'*: cradle song or lullaby (from French, 'bercer', meaning 'to rock to sleep'). Fréderic Chopin's gentle *Berceuse* for piano (D flat major, Op. 57) is one of the most famous.

131 *Faranelli's singing . . . poor King Philip of Spain*: more usually 'Farinelli', this famous Italian castrato (1705–82) was director of the royal music at the court of Philip V of Spain (1700–46). A supremely dedicated artist, during the last ten years of Philip's life he was forbidden to sing in public, having to reserve his voice to perform to the king. In hearing the same four songs nightly, Philip found some relief from his severe depression.

Leipsic: renowned as a musical centre, Leipzig in south-eastern Germany was associated particularly with J. S. Bach (1685–1750), and was famous for its Conservatory, founded by Felix Mendelssohn (1809–47) in 1843. The family ambitions for Paula may have been fired by the precedent of Clara Schumann (1819–96), who gave her first piano concert in Leipzig, aged 11. KC, herself a fine pianist, delivered a paper on 'Typical Forms of German Music' to the St Louis Wednesday Club (9 Dec. 1891).

'Ist es nicht wonderschen, mama?': 'Isn't it wonderful, mother?'

liebchen: darling.

132 *the magnificent "Steinway"*: a prestigious make of piano: also, here, another reminder of the creativity of German immigrants. Like the Von

Stoltz family, Henry Engelhard Steinweg (1797–1871) and his five sons
had emigrated to the United States from Germany, founding their famous piano manufactory in New York in 1853.

133 *votary of Terpsichore*: a follower of the Greek Muse of dancing and
poetry. The show on the banjo, and the mimicry of a 'Virginia
breakdown', a lively black American slave dance, reflects white society's
fashion for crude pastiche of African–American plantation culture. The
comic inflections of this passage emphasize the contrast with Paula, here,
for KC, the true votary of (European) high-art.

the magnificent "Jewel Song from 'Faust'": a soprano aria from the enormously popular opera (*Faust*, 1859) by Charles François Gounod (1818–
93). Performed by Marguérite in Act III, as she excitedly admires the
jewels in a casket given her by Faust and Mephistophiles, the song lent
itself as a show-piece for the ostentatious voice.

the Modern Classic: unfortunately, in spite of best efforts, untraced.

134 *a . . . wish that he had not been so proficient with the banjo*: given the satiric
thrust of KC's remark, it seems mischievous of the editor to have
followed the story with a column by the Philadelphia Banjo Club.
Listing 'Selections from "Faust"' as the highlight of a recent concert, the
column assured readers that 'The people of Germantown are very
enthusiastic over the banjo' ('The Banjo', 40).

137 *"Ach Gott! . . . ist schon im Leipsic gegangen!"*: 'Good Heavens [literally,
Oh God]! Miss Von Stoltz has already left for Leipzig'. Paula takes the
direction KC dreamed of as a schoolgirl, when having read Longfellow's
'Hyperion', she wrote of her passion to visit Germany, 'that cradle and
repository of genius' (*CB* 43).

138 *Kuntzler*: like 'Dr Sinn' earlier, a play on a name. Here, KC hints that
Paula may both marry and stay wedded to her art: '*Künstler*' (German),
an 'artist'. That he is a 'teacher of harmony' may also be significant.

A POINT AT ISSUE!

Written Aug. 1889; pub. *St. Louis Post-Dispatch* (27 Oct. 1889), 22. (Paid
$16.00. Text here.)

139 *"cranks"*: all-purpose term for reformers and eccentrics, from vegetarians
to velocipedists. The omission of Eleanor's title, 'Miss', is probably an
index here of her 'cranky' tendencies.

140 *"Not too good for human nature's daily food"*: echoing the widely (mis)-
quoted 'She was a Phantom of Delight' (1807) by William Wordsworth:
'A Creature not too bright or good | For human nature's daily food' (lines
17–18).

free masonry of intellect: suggesting Faraday's desire to seek an alternative
to the world of men's clubs and business-centred secret societies dominant at the time.

140 *rara avis*: (Latin, rare bird) unique being: by implication here, for Faraday, also a freak of nature. An early instance, too, of KC's repeated metaphor of the rare bird, caged and free.

141 *Marriage . . . open portal*: on her own honeymoon, KC met one of the women's activist Claflin sisters and promised not to 'fall into the useless degrading life of most married ladies' (*CB*, 165).

144 *Woman's Suffrage*: in spite of this story's interest in the topical 'Marriage Question', KC seems to have shown no concern with the right to vote, and often treats New Women with humour.

garments of mysterious shape: alluding to 'dress reform' movements which sought healthy alternatives to the constraints of corsets and elaborate gowns. KC's son Felix recalled his mother's intellectual friends wearing eccentric garments, of a style unspecified (Interview, 19 Jan. 1949; in *A Kate Chopin Miscellany*, 166–8). In 'Charlie' (1900), KC's heroine cycles in 'something between bloomers and a divided skirt, which she called her "trouserlets."'

148 *"Mazarain"*: (more usually 'Mazarin'), a small fancy sponge confection, filled with a number of sweet ingredients, including apricot preserve and almonds (possibly after Jules Mazarin (1602–61), Sicilian-born French statesman). However, the misprint here offers the possibility that what Faraday really ordered was a 'mazagran': a glass of cold black coffee.

THE CHRIST LIGHT

Written 4 April 1891. Submitted to prestigious magazines (e.g. *Century*, *Scribners*, the *Atlantic*) and entered, unsuccessfully, for a *Short Stories* contest; twelve rejections. Syndicated American Press Association (paid $6.00); pub. Dec. 1892, as 'The Christ Light'. KC tested various titles (e.g. 'A Woman Goes and Comes', 'Liza Jane', and 'The Going and Coming of Liza Jane'). Seyersted called the story 'The Going Away of Liza', printing the text as cut on KC's clipping. I use the original version and title on the clipping (Box 4/Folder 2). KC's main revisions remove all references to the Christ Light, which she crosses out with the energetic zigzag she often adopts for her most decisive erasures.

151 *Bludgitt*: there is a Blodgett in south-eastern Missouri, near the Illinois/Kentucky state border, and the confluence of the Mississippi and Ohio rivers: a rare instance in KC of a Missouri rural setting, not as marketable as Louisiana material, but used later to great effect in 'Elizabeth Stock's One Story'.

152 *readin's boun' to fill the mind . . . in time*: KC was always interested in the power of reading, including the detrimental effects of cheap literature: the alcoholic Fanny in *At Fault* is victim of 'those prolific female writers who turn out their unwholesome intellectual sweets so tirelessly, to be devoured by the girls and women of the age' (II. ii).

153 *no soul above the commonplaces*: an idea echoed by Mlle Reisz: *The Awakening* (p. 90).

'*I hev that within me . . . thet craves . . . the joys of ixistence*': like Edna, she wants to taste of 'life's delirium'. The voice KC gives Liza-Jane's detractor here echoes the vindictive belittling of independent women in the work of dialect humourists such as 'Artemus Ward' (Charles Farrar Browne, 1834–67). See Introduction (p. xxviii).

It was a beacon . . . the foot-sore: the symbolic Christ Light may have helped to market the story in Christmas issues, but KC may also be evoking associations with the Statue of Liberty unveiled four years before (26 Oct. 1886), to enormous public interest. Emma Lazarus's verses to the 'tired', the 'poor', were inscribed rather later, however, in 1903.

154 *them animals*: the clipping is damaged, but the remnant is interesting. (Extent of omissions may be judged by the remaining full lines of the newspaper column): 'An read about them curious | pictures of them animals that look some | thing twixt sn [. . .] | glin' crost the paper. [. . .] | miraculous things happens nowadays, if | you've got the papers to belive.

155 *the loudest*: followed on same line by damaged sentences: 'loudest. The thought that this woman | might have dragged his name [. . .] | not know, he dare not [. . .] | like fire in his blood. [. . .] Mother Rydon ha[. . .] | hand and led her to t[h][. . .] | Abner had been sea[t] [. . .] | she said, "you're as [. . .] | as if you'd fell in Blu[. . .] | lieve in my soul you did.[. . .] | them feet. Fur pity sake!" || When she endeavored to [continues as text, with 'she' cancelled and 'MOTHER RYDON' inserted].

THE MAID OF SAINT PHILLIPPE

Written 19 April 1891. Four rejections. Entered, unsuccessfully, for a *Youth's Companion* folk-lore competition; pub. *Short Stories*, 11:3 (New York, Nov. 1892), 257–64. (Paid $10.00. Text here.) Usually assumed to be the story which KC later humorously described as the failed outcome of painstaking historical research; but no direct evidence for the association (*Atlantic Monthly*, 83, January 1899).

KC may have intended a Missouri equivalent of Longfellow's famous poem *Evangeline* (1847), an epic wrought out of the Acadians' expulsion from Nova Scotia (a subject KC herself never treated directly). Like Longfellow, she chooses an emotionally charged moment of historical dispossession. Saint Phillippe, Fort Chartres, and Kaskaskia, in what is now southern Illinois, were all small French frontier trading posts on the Mississippi River, which were caught up in key moments of the European colonizers' struggles over the continent. Through a number of secret treaties in Europe (e.g. The Treaty of Paris, 1763), the Spanish, French and English powers exchanged North American lands over the heads of the early settlers and of the Native American tribes. Writing in St Louis in the 1890s, KC creates a heroine who questions the dominant rhetoric of progress, and a historical narrative which challenges contemporary celebrations of the city's heroic origins and glorious future.

156 *curling columns . . . chimneys in the village*: echoes the pastoral notes of *Evangeline* (I. i.), representing the Acadians, on the eve of their similarly sudden expulsion from Nova Scotia by English colonial overlords: 'Columns of pale blue smoke, like clouds of incense ascending, | Rose from a hundred hearths, the homes of peace and contentment. | Thus dwelt together in love these simple Acadian farmers, – | . . . Alike were they free from | Fear, that reigns with the tyrant, and envy, the vice of republics.'

157 *Natchez*: a Native American tribe, already believed to be extinct ('among the noblest specimens of Red Men in America', Baedeker (1893), 325). In the 'French and Indian' wars, one of the colonial struggles of the so-called 'Seven Years War' (1756–63), the tribes maintained a temporary foothold by promising assistance to one or other of the opposing European powers. United States historians in the 1880s–90s tended to emphasize their enmity to the British and, in contrast, their strong support for the American city founders.

Louis . . . at Versailles: Louis XV of France (reigned 1715–74): his high-handed secret treaties rouse Marianne's growing antipathy to all forms of government and constraint.

Laclede's village: St Louis, KC's birthplace and home-town. Its founder Pierre Laclede Liguest (c.1724–78), French colonist and merchant, explored the river territory above Fort Chartres, selecting the site as a trading-post in Feb. 1764. St Louis 'boosters' gave the moment great weight when promoting the city's prospects: 'The future has in store for her a place among the marvellous cities of the world that will surprise even the wildest dream of her founder's prophetic vision,' G. W. Orear, *Commercial and Architectural St Louis* ([St Louis], 1891), 6. KC, however, makes Marianne less than enthusiastic.

St. Ange de Bellerive: (c.1705–74) military commander who became acting governor of St Louis, after handing over the East side of the river to the English. He is represented in late nineteenth-century histories as a wise leader, beloved by the Indians and by the French settlers.

Captain Vaudry: echoes the name 'Vaudreuil', the Canadian governor-general in the French and Indian wars; also, ET suggests (p. 450), that of a founder of the White League. 'Vaudry' (or 'Vodry') was also a local Mississippi Valley name: the marriage of a Toussaint Vaudry to a Marianne Pre appears in the Chartres parish records (in *The Village of Chartres in Colonial Illinois, 1720–65*, ed. Margaret Kimball Brown *et al.* (New Orleans, 1977).

158 *only the Eastern province . . . has been granted to England*: KC exploits the historical irony here: this was a key moment in the expansion

of English-speaking powers on the continent, culminating in the crucial Louisiana Purchase of 1803.

So that leaves the West under the Spanish dominion: although Marianne has missed the morning's news, she is more politically acute than Jacques, understanding the dynamics of the colonial power deals (here the Spanish land-accession, implemented 3 Nov. 1762).

159 *it is only the old whose memories dwell in graves*: later, in *Impressions* (22 May 1894), KC wrote that she could not connect her mother or husband with 'mounds of earth' in the cemetery, but in April 1889, she had arranged for Oscar's body to be moved from Cloutierville and reburied in St Louis's Calvary Cemetery.

the garments . . . of the French working-woman: in her French mother's clothes, Marianne at seventeen resembles a favourite literary heroine, the exiled Evangeline: 'Fair was she to behold, that maiden of seventeen summers. | . . . Wearing her Norman cap, and her kirtle of blue, and the ear-rings, | Brought down in the olden times from France, and since, as an heirloom, | Handed down from mother to child, through long generations' (I. i.).

For days . . . to the northward: recalls a similarly harrowing scene in *Evangeline*, as the stricken peasants move their households, 'Driving in ponderous wains their household goods to the sea-shore' (I. v). KC's emphasis on 'building up the new' perhaps gives a slightly more positive colouring to this disaster.

160 *peltries*: furs and skins, a crucial commercial factor in the contested territory.

La Rochelle: a town on the western seaboard of France.

162 *I was not born to be the mother of slaves*: perhaps a subtle reminder that, as ET (p. 40) points out, Saint Phillippe was the first village in the 'Illinois country' to institute slavery.

163 *the Cherokees*: KC seems to have shared the common white belief that Cherokees, expert farmers, were migrant hunters—a label which excused politicians for turning the tribes off their land; but Marianne's sentiments echo those of the tribal leaders, who denied that their ancestral lands could be expropriated by impersonal powers. Settlements over the next decade effectively removed the land rights of the Cherokees and other Mississippi Valley tribes. How much KC knew of this, or of the recent Allotment Act of 1887, which dealt the final blow to tribal lands, is uncertain. Her only Native American central characters are a young girl in 'Loka' and a pony in 'Ti Démon' ('A Horse Story'), and both are associated, conventionally, with cravings for freedom.

DOCTOR CHEVALIER'S LIE

Written 12 Sept., 1891. One rejection; pub. *Vogue*, 2 (5 Oct. 1893), 174, 178, attributed to 'K.C.' (Paid $4.00. Text here.) According to Rankin, the story was based upon an actual incident in the life of a New Orleans physician, perhaps explaining KC's anonymity. The story's opposition between city and country needs no specific location. However, the references to the cabin 'down in Arkansas' would also fit a St Louis setting.

BEYOND THE BAYOU

Written 7 Nov. 1891. Accepted 11 Dec. 1891; pub. *Youth's Companion*, 66 (15 June 1893). (Paid $30.00. Text here.) Fifth story in *BF*; KC revised the text for adults, reducing details of Chéri's growing-up, removing some explanations and the glosses of French words for younger readers, and much of the colour symbolism. French dialect spelling was regularized (169: *ayes → ayez*) and several shorter sentences were combined, becoming more formal and elaborate, but losing the dramatic immediacy of the children's version.

166 *bayou*: a very general term for a stream, a natural canal or creek, here probably a branch of a larger river. For many Northern readers, 'bayou' instantly triggered exotic images of the remote South. ET (p. 225) points out how reviews perpetuated the stereotype that a bayou was an over-grown swamp, but KC's use is much more varied.

in the time of the Civil War: without knowing Jacqueline's age on this traumatic occasion, it is impossible to date the year in which the story is set, but twenty-five to thirty years after the Civil War (1861–65), brings it into the late 1880s or early 1890s, the time of reading: a chronology KC observes in another retrospective Civil War story, 'Ma'ame Pélagie' (1893).

the rest of the quarters had long . . . been removed: in Reconstruction, after the Civil War. Jacqueline continues to live in the old slave quarters. The plantation is still worked by black labour, presumably in some form of share-cropping (see 'Azélie'), and so is both changed and remains the same—an ambiguity reflected in much white plantation fiction of this period.

Bellissime: (from Latin) 'the most beautiful'. Plantations were often given names suggesting an ideal classical civilization or a pastoral idyll: a trad-ition memorably exposed in Toni Morrison's 'Sweet Home' in *Beloved* (1987).

170 *Her eyes were bloodshot*: in *BF*, KC intensified this, adding, 'and the saliva had gathered in a white foam on her black lips'.

tisane of fragrant herbs: a calming infusion of soothing herbs, flowers, or leaves, the opposite of the stimulating cup of strong black coffee Jacque-line later makes for herself.

OLD AUNT PEGGY

Written 8 Jan. 1892. Accepted but never pub. by *Harper's Young People*, 28 Jan. 1892 (Paid $3.00.) Sixth story in *BF* (text here).

173 *Title*: like slaves on antebellum plantations, long after the war African Americans were conventionally known to whites by their first names, older persons often being called by the familiar titles, 'Aunt' and 'Uncle'. The term avoided the respect of a second name, while implying close and friendly relationships.

RIPE FIGS

Written 26 Feb. 1892. Working title: 'Babette's Visit'. Two rejections; pub. *Vogue*, 2 (19 Aug. 1893), 90. (Paid $3.00. Text here.) Twentieth story in *NA*. Title (and theme) recalls a Louisiana proverb: '*Can vou jéne et joli, ça passé vité com la saison dé figue*': 'When you are young and pretty, it passes quickly like the season of the figs' (Alcée Fortier, 'Bits of Louisiana Folk-Lore', *PMLA* 3 (1887), 161).

174 *Bayou Boeuf*: in central Louisiana, described by Fortier as a 'beautiful stream' ('The Acadians of Louisiana', *PMLA* 6:1 (1891), 73). In *BF*, possibly in the interests of euphony, or to increase the scale of Babette's adventure, KC substituted 'Bayou Lafourche', moving the cousins much further South to a coastal parish (county) in the southeast.

MISS McENDERS

Written 7 March 1892. Five rejections, 1892–3; pub. *St. Louis Criterion*, 13 (6 March 1897), 16–18. (Paid $10.00. Text here.) Signed 'La Tour', a pseudonym KC also used for 'The Falling in Love of Fedora' (1895). Based on a St Louis scandal of the 1870s, the story took five years to find a publisher and caused comment when it appeared. It was common knowledge, as ET (pp. 290–3) points out, that Miss McEnders' original, though much older, was Miss Ellen McKee, a well-known St Louis philanthropist and patron of the *Criterion*, which printed the story. However, the paper was proud of its impartiality, reminding readers, in this issue: ' "The Criterion" is the only paper whose dramatic critics pay for their seats at the theaters. Our criticisms are always fair, unprejudiced and fearless.'

175 *an elaborately simple toilet*: a recognizable satire on the wealthy Miss McKee who had a reputation for personal austerity. Even her obituary commented on her modest tastes (Necrology 8, MHS).

the Woman's Reform Club: a growing movement in the 1890s: 'It has been only a few years since the majority of women were shocked at the very mention of a woman's club; now every small town and village can boast something of the kind ... Women realize that instead of meeting to gossip about dress or servants they can discuss the interesting topics of the day' (*St. Louis Republic*, 25 Dec. 1892). KC's writing often casts an amused glance at earnest club women. Briefly a member of the St Louis 'Wednesday Club', here she draws closely on its programme. On 1 April 1891, a Mrs E. C. Stirling had read an essay on 'The Dignity of Labor' followed by discussion of 'Relation of Woman of Wealth and Position to the Wage-Earner' (Wednesday Club Publications, 1890–92, MHS). KC resigned from the club in April 1892: less than one month, as ET points out (pp. 185–6, 292), after writing this story.

175 *Arsenal street*: a long street running west from the vast Anheuser-Busch brewery in downtown St Louis: ethnically diverse, with a mixture of lodging houses, small businesses, and saloons, it represented in the 1890s an extreme contrast with the 'too-sumptuous' McEnders home. Georgie, presumably, would have been pictured as living in one of the exclusive 'private streets', the preserve of the St Louis élite. Miss McKee herself lived at 3028 Pine Street (St Louis City Directory, 1893–4), not a private street, but a smart neighbourhood.

to investigate moral condition of St. Louis factory-girls: a typical charitable project of the day: such as the St Louis White Cross Home, founded in 1888 to aid 'young women who have been misled in the ways of evil, and might be glad . . . to retrace their steps and regain their self-respect'; and the 'Travelers' Aid', to place 'a motherly woman at the Union Railway Depot . . . to look after the lonely and unprotected young women who were in danger from the many evil-disposed persons who were constantly laying snares for the unwary', William Hyde and Howard L. Conard (eds.), *Encyclopaedia of the History of St. Louis*, iv (New York: 1899), 2537.

Henry George's lecture on Single Tax: another topical item culled from the Wednesday Club programme, which heard and discussed an essay on 'The Single Tax' on 29 April 1891. The 'St. Louis Single Tax League' worked to spread the doctrines of Henry George (1839–97), author of the influential *Progress and Poverty* (1879). George contested the 'aggrandizement of an aristocracy of wealth and power' (Mayoralty Contest, New York, 1886), aiming to improve city communities through a 'Single Tax' on land-ownership, the prime source of wealth for privileged individuals. As most of KC's income in the 1890s came from land and property, it is unlikely that she was a 'Georgist' (see ET, p. 258).

176 *"Ya! Ya! aber oop stairs"*: (representing German-American speech) 'Yes! Yes! but up the stairs'.

177 *"Chérie"*: (French) dear. Given as '*Chene*' ('oak'), which I take as a misprint, although, like others in this story, KC did not correct it on her clipping (Box 2/Folder 5).

179 *the . . . game of 'push' that occupies mankind*: like 'Push and Prodem' above, topical slang, and a barbed allusion to 'booster' rhetoric. This justified aggressive business practices by 'men of push and power' in the name of civic enterprise: 'The merchants, manufacturers, bankers, and business men at large of St. Louis, have always been pre-eminent in

"tact, push and principle"; and are now employing *push* in excess of their predecessors, whilst carrying forward all the great interest of this city with such energy and ability as is not overmatched elsewhere! . . . [S]ordidness is not a characteristic of Saint Louis men!', M. M. Yeakle, *The City of St. Louis . . . Its Progress and Prospects . . .* (St Louis, 1889), 45, 48.

181 *"c'est un propre, celui la!"*: (sarcasm) 'he's a good one, that one'.

182 *the Whisky Ring*: like Oedipus, Georgie discovers the answer to her riddle in her own tainted origins. In May 1875, William McKee, father of Ellen, and proprietor of the *Globe-Democrat*, was indicted as one of the main conspirators in an elaborate tax fraud to avoid paying liquor revenue. (The Ring crossed several states, involving distillers, revenue collectors, and government officers, and over three hundred and fifty arrests were made.) McKee, a chief beneficiary, was said to have taken up to one thousand dollars a week. The national press highlighted the trial (1875–76), using cartoons to clarify the chain of deceit, and explain its political force. McKee was sentenced to a ten thousand dollar fine and two years in jail, but after a presidential pardon was released within six months. (See Mary E. Seematter, 'The St. Louis Whiskey Ring', *Gateway Heritage*, 8:4, Spring 1988, 32–42; *Frank Leslie's Illustrated Newspaper*, 26 Feb. 1876; and ET, pp. 291–2.)

AT THE 'CADIAN BALL

Written 15–17 July 1892. Sold at first attempt; pub. in *Two Tales* (Boston) 3 (22 Oct. 1892), 145–52. (Paid $40.00. Text here.) Twentieth story in *BF*, with small changes.

183 *Ozéina . . . or Fronie*: Acadian names, 'as strange as the old Biblical names among the early Puritans, but much more harmonious' (Fortier, 'The Acadians of Louisiana', *PMLA* 6:1 (1891), 82: a comment immediately following his description of the ball, Appendix, IV. iv).

the prairie people: Acadians of the grass region of southern Louisiana ('the 'Cadian prairie' below) particularly in the parishes (counties) north of Lafayette. Like the 'Cadian wetlands, its beauty struck many observers, and with its undulating landscape, small round ponds, and 'islands' of wooded ground, was often compared with a vast ocean.

Assumption: a parish in southeast Louisiana, along the Bayou Lafourche.

"C'est Espagnol, ça": 'well, that's the Spanish!'

"Bon chien tient de race": a version of the French proverb, *'bon chien chasse de race'*. Literally 'a good dog hunts from natural instincts': a good dog shows its breeding (or runs true to type): i.e. Calixta takes after her Spanish mother.

"Tiens . . . prends ça, et ça!": (idiomatic and near untranslatable insults): 'I'm telling you, slut, get out of here'; 'You big cat [literally, 'type of lioness']; take that, and that!' Fortier gives 'Une *lionèse*, a lioness, from

the English' as a specific dialect form of St Mary Parish (in southern Louisiana on the Bayou Têche), 'Acadians of Louisiana', p. 87.

183 *a trace-chain*: part of the harness connecting a draft animal to a plough or wagon: attached to the breast-strap and passed along the animal's sides. KC plays with the image in the next sentence, and throughout the story associates 'big, brown, good-natured Bobinôt' with large, plodding animals. (Compare the hapless lover, Tonie, another Acadian, in 'Tonie'.)

Alcée Laballière: Alcée and Clarisse are mentioned in 'In and Out of Old Natchitoches', written five months earlier (pub. *Two Tales*, April 1893), and appear again in 'The Storm'. Alcée also features in 'Croque-Mitaine' (see notes to 'Regret'). ET (pp. 164–72) suggests that both he and Alcée Arobin (*The Awakening*) were inspired by the handsome Creole planter, Albert Sampite, possibly KC's lover in Cloutierville.

184 *sailing about . . . in her white volante*: KC's use of French for Madame's billowing robe playfully preserves the pun on sailing. In *At Fault*, she glosses the term for readers from outside the region: 'She was dressed in a loosely hanging purple calico garment of the mother Hubbard type— known as a *volante* among Louisiana Creoles' (II. iv).

185 *cut into the rice like fine steel*: ET (p. 211) points out that in mid-June 1892, a terrible flood in Natchitoches Parish destroyed most of Albert Sampite's crops.

Natchitoches: a parish in northwest Louisiana, KC's home during the early 1880s: 'Pronounced Nack-e-tosh', *BF*, 4 (KC's note). Alphonse appears in 'In and Out of Old Natchitoches'.

"plumb in de night": dead in the middle of the night. (Also used in non-dialect contexts, e.g. of Arobin's cravat, p. 94.)

186 *"Ah Sainte Vierge! . . . va!"*: 'Oh Blessed Virgin, give me patience! oaf, get away!'

de quinine bottle: mixed with the whiskey, Alcée's massive 'hoss-dose' of quinine, the bitter bark of the cinchona tree, combines medicinal and popular preventative measures as a double insurance against fever, especially malaria, carried by the swarming 'skeeters.

He lows: (representation of dialect) an all-purpose verb: he allows, i.e. says.

John L. Sulvun: a topical allusion to John L. Sullivan (1855–1918), heavyweight boxer and hero of the South. As KC was writing, Sullivan had held the world's heavyweight title for the past decade (1882–92), but lost his championship to James J. Corbett in a twenty-one-round knock-out on 7 Sept. 1892, a month before the story was published.

187 *chicken gombo*: (or 'gumbo') a substantial soup, traditionally thickened with okra pods (gumbo), and flavoured variously with chicken, shrimp, etc. In 'A Night in Acadie' (1897), KC describes 'old black Douté' preparing a 'mammoth pot of gumbo' for the Saturday dance: 'into the pot

went the chickens and the pans-full of minced ham, and the fists-full of onion and sage and piment rouge and piment vert'.

le parc aux petits: the children's room, a traditional feature of an Acadian ball. The associated phrase, '*fais do-do*' (baby-talk: 'go to sleep'; from French, '*dormir*': to sleep) came to mean a country dance.

"Ces maudits gens du raiderode": those damned railroad people. As Rankin points out, the Acadians, who settled in Louisiana before the development of rail transport, evolved a distinct Americanized term, '*raiderode*', rather than the standard French '*chemin de fer*'.

grit: changed to '*nerve*' in *BF*. Either word places Alcée at the centre of a buzz of gossip, and emphasizes his stoicism, heightening the contrast with the bovine Bobinôt.

a brave homme . . . more panache than Boulanger: here, the French phrases all emphasize Alcée's courage, style, and class. The old gentleman presumably had in mind the charismatic career, and recent romantic death, of the celebrated French politician, General George Boulanger (1837–91). This popular leader had repeatedly overcome attempts by the opposition to repress him, but in the face of a trial for treason, he had gone into exile (1889), finally committing suicide on his mistress's grave (30 Sept. 1891).

188 *standin' planté là*: standing, stuck there, emphasizing his general inertia and awkwardness.

the younger generation, so preferred to speak English: alluding to the progressive assimilation of linguistically and culturally diverse Louisiana peoples into a more homogeneous, English-speaking, American populace. However, although this story participates in the movement to record a dying culture, even a century later the process was incomplete, and accounts of Acadian communities continued to remark on younger members' lack of interest in preserving French ways.

190 *"'Ah c'est vous . . .' '. . . mam' zelle?'"*: KC differentiates Clarisse's more refined French, 'Ah, is that you, Calixta? How are you, my child?', from Calixta's Acadian idiom and accent, 'I'm fine; and you, miss?' (in standard French, '*Ça va bien*'). In the Acadian dialect, according to Fortier, 'c' was a very pronounced 'tch' ('Acadians of Louisiana', 88).

192 *"le bal est fini"*: the traditional announcement that 'the ball is over'.

THE FATHER OF DÉSIRÉE'S BABY (DÉSIRÉE'S BABY)

Written 24 Nov. 1892. Accepted at once by the forthcoming new magazine, *Vogue*; pub. *Vogue*, 1 (14 Jan. 1893), 70–1, 74. (Paid $25.00. Text here.) Paired with 'A Visit to Avoyelles,' under general title, 'Character Studies', subtitled, 'The Father of Désirée's Baby — The Lover of Mentine'. Tenth story in *BF* with small revisions.

193 *L'Abri*: meaning 'The Shelter' or 'Cover'/'Shade'.

193   *a party of Texans*: a belief coloured by a prevailing stereotype of Texas and Texans as uncivilized and lawless. Compare 'In Sabine'.

corbeille: wedding gifts to the bride from the groom.

194   *yellow nurse woman*: racial classification, one of a set of conventional terms to designate the shade of skin colour, and indicate the relative degrees of 'white' and 'Negro' blood. There may be a further suggestion here of racial mixing in the Aubigny household, possibly during the 'old master's easy-going and indulgent lifetime'.

cochon de lait: endearment (literally, sucking piglet), also used as the refrain in a traditional Creole lullaby, '*Fais do do, Minette,* | *Chere piti cochon du laite*' ('Go to sleep, Minette, | Dear little baby').

finger-nails,—real finger-nails: Désirée innocently draws attention to the very feature which was said first to indicate 'black blood'. From early on, white ambitions to classify racial types led to confused lists of defining physical characteristics: Buffon thought genitals and cuticles of the nails were dark from birth, others maintained that babies were born light, with nails darkening first (or, indeed, last). Such pseudo-scientific notions passed into popular racist mythology.

195   *Négrillon*: (diminutive of *nègre*, Negro) a racially pejorative nickname, commonly used by white slaveholders: meaning 'pickaninny', a black child.

One of La Blanche's little quadroon boys: adding to the complex racial classifications of the story. 'La Blanche' meaning 'the White Woman' has a child with one-quarter 'black' ancestry and a 'white' father: one of several hints that the child may be Armand's son.

197   *After it was dealt he felt like a remorseless murderer*: in revision for *BF*, KC harshened the picture of Armand by removing this sentence.

CALINE

Written 2 Dec. 1892; pub. *Vogue*, 1 (20 May 1893), 324–5. (Paid $9.00. Text here.) Seventh story in *NA* with minor changes.

199   *the steel rails of the Texas and Pacific road*: linked Shreveport in northern Louisiana with New Orleans in the south, running along the Red River and the right bank of the Mississippi. It reached the Natchitoches area (1881–82) when KC was living there, dramatically slicing through the Chopin plantation. Its arrival in the Cane River country is a major disruption in *At Fault* (I. i), and its 'steel bands' again mark change in 'The Return of Alcibiade', written three days after 'Caline'. The whole journey from El Paso to New Orleans (Route 102 in Baedeker) took about fifty hours, for a fare of $33.40: a distance and sum of money unimaginable perhaps to many of the country people who lived within view of the track.

200   *loin la bas . . . "Djieu sait é ou"*: 'far away over there' . . 'God knows where'. KC sketches for her well-off *Vogue* readers in the North, the

'French patois', found so difficult by the similar class of ladies and gentlemen within the story. Her spelling of 'Dieu' (God) here accurately reflects accent: 'd — becomes dj: *Dieu* (Djeu)' (Fortier, 'Acadians of Louisiana', 88). In *NA*, standard accents were added: 'là' and 'où'.

flagman: on early railroads gave warning of the movement of trains.

the city in the south: New Orleans.

cotonade: also spelt 'cottonade' by KC. A coarse home-woven cotton fabric, particularly associated with Acadian women, but also worn by other country people (e.g. Jacqueline in 'Beyond the Bayou').

the French market: since the late eighteenth century, one of the most colourful scenes in the old French Quarter, mingling all the various linguistic and ethnic groups of the region. The market usually provoked rhapsodic descriptions in visitors' accounts. Caline visits the main New Orleans tourist sights (including the famous sugar and cotton landings) but her changing response is uncommon; many claimed their charms were inexhaustible.

handsome Gascon butchers: all guides commented on the monopoly of the meat market by handsome French butchers from Gascony.

lagniappe: (pronounced, 'lan-yapp') still a feature of New Orleans life today: a 'free gift', or 'small something extra', such as candies, fruits, little fancy cakes.

A MATTER OF PREJUDICE

Written 17–18 June 1893; pub. *Youth's Companion*, 68:3 (26 Sept. 1895), 450 (not 25 Sept., as usually given). (Paid $25.00. Text here.) Sixth story in *NA* with minor changes.

202 *levee bank*: the broad protective river embankment running along the left bank of the bend in the Mississippi, which gave New Orleans its title, the 'Crescent City'.

The house—an old Spanish one: built between 1763 and 1802, probably after the devastating fires of 1788 and 1794.

far down in the French quarter of New Orleans: Madame is entrenched in the old French-speaking Creole quarter, where 'French is the official language, and the manners and customs of "La Belle France" still prevail. The people keep to themselves, and many of the inhabitants have never crossed Canal street' (Zacharie, *New Orleans Guide*, 1893), 37.

white servants: blurred the boundaries of class and race, and thus seemed particularly dangerous to the self-definitions of the white Creoles, who wished to distance themselves from any suggestion (e.g. as in G. W. Cable's fiction) that some 'Creoles' might have African, or mixed-race, ancestry. KC's list of Madame's prejudices wittily encapsulates the sense of beleaguerment felt in the post-war years by Creole diehards such as KC's father-in-law.

202 *Germans*: in New Orleans by 1860, out of a white population of 155,000, 19,000 were German-born.

Anything not French . . . little right to existence: the Louisiana historian, Alcée Fortier, who came to master at least nine languages, emerged from a similar tradition: 'My grandfather, who was born during the Spanish domination, spoke French only, and did not allow English to be spoken in his family', *Louisiana Studies* (New Orleans, 1894), 6.

an American girl from Prytania street: Henri's marriage, like Mr Pontellier's, has taken him well beyond the Canal Street line, into the new, English-speaking suburbs created by affluent American businessmen. Prytania Street, running parallel with St Charles Avenue through the elegant Lower Garden and Garden Districts (constructed from the 1830s–1870s), was the site of many of the city's loveliest homes, set in beautiful grounds.

green tea . . . fleur de Laurier: Creoles were notable for their pride in drinking excellent coffee. Tea, like other infusions of non-French substances, seems as fatal to Madame as a poisonous brew of laurel flowers.

"Partant pour la Syrie": 'Leaving for the Holy Land', a traditional French patriotic song, composed by Hortense, Queen Consort of Louis, King of Holland: in English, better known under variants of 'Dunois, the Young and Debonair' (including a version by Walter Scott). Significantly, the song celebrates young love and valour, and ends in general blessings: 'The happy throng assembled there, | A joyous welcome gave, | And cried, "Love to the fairest Fair! | And Honor to the brave!"' trans. G. Linley (London: Schott & Co. [n.d.]).

203 *who did not understand French*: a topical observation, tapping into fears that American influences were rapidly erasing the Creole culture and the French language. The legislature's attempts to cancel divisions by eliminating French were hotly contested, but by the 1890s historians were certain that: 'The steady advance of the Anglo–Saxon race is gradually driving the French language out, so that in a few years, it will have died out entirely' (Zacharie, 46).

204 *unintelligible . . . negro patois*: a customary warning to outsiders that the version of French spoken by the black population of the Creole sections of Louisiana was 'difficult to understand' (Zacharie, 46): see Appendix, III, and notes to 'La Belle Zoraïde'.

orange-flower water . . . eau sédative: Louisiana was famous for various products derived from oranges, including a soothing water distilled from the flowers, and a syrup made by boiling the petals with sugar, a concoction, according to Zacharie, 'much prized by the Creoles' (p. 113).

205 *the Irish voice is distressing to the sick*: a typically derogatory remark about

Irish immigrants. However, Madame could not have gone far out of her stockade before hearing Irish voices in New Orleans, where, by the 1860s, the 23,000 Irish citizens had come to represent the largest segment of the foreign-born population.

the seed planted by . . . a little child: a stock motif, often associated with reconciliation of families divided by an unacceptable marriage. KC often used the figure of a child as a saviour, particularly in her stories for children (e.g. 'Beyond the Bayou'). As in *The Awakening*, she could also shock her readers by departing from the convention.

206 *the French Cathedral*: Madame's traditional place of worship would have been the Cathedral of St Louis in Jackson Square, founded in 1722, twice destroyed by hurricane and fire, rebuilt in 1794, and remodelled in 1845–51; still standing today.

"Plait-il, madame?": (expression of surprise) 'I beg your pardon, madame?' or 'What did you say, madam?'

St. Patrick's Church on Camp street: in a neatly ironical twist of the plot, François drives his mistress to the spiritual centre of the Irish in New Orleans. Opened in 1838, modelled on York Minster in England, the church was convenient for the area nearby, known popularly as the 'Irish Channel', home for many Irish Catholics working for the new American population. Guide-books highlighted, in particular, its inspiring patriotic painting of St Patrick baptizing the Queens of Ireland in the famed Halls of Tara.

207 *this new and splendid growth*: the journey along St Charles Avenue takes Madame to the prosperous Garden District (see note to p. 202, Prytania Street). Development here flourished, and, from the 1850s, stimulated the expansion of the city further and further upriver.

AZÉLIE

Written 22–23 July 1893; pub. *Century*, 49 (Dec. 1894), 282–87, illustrated by Eric Pape. (Paid $50.00. Text here.) Eleventh story in *NA* with a *Century* illustration as book's frontispiece: the hesitant Azélie of the opening paragraph is depicted as an assertive-looking woman, her head raised and bonnet flung back, determinedly holding her pail in readiness. KC's working titles suggest some uncertainty about the story's focus ('Polyte's Misfortune'), and about her heroine's name ('Amélite' and 'Amandine').

209 *calico*: a cheap, printed cotton fabric; the whole description introduces the theme of Azélie's sexual appeal to male eyes, in a manner acceptable to the genteel *Century* editors.

chinaberry-tree: ornamental tree, often planted in a position to be appreciated from the house: here, also marking the difference between the fields worked by Azélie and her family, and the leisure area around the house, enjoyed by the planter.

209 *le grand air*: the fresh or open air: for the landowner here, possibly with
something of the relish of 'the great outdoors'.

in no sense a store for the general public . . . Mr. Mathurin's 'hands': in an
ordinary local store, such as Oscar Chopin's in Cloutierville, credit might
be given, but transactions normally remained based on commercial prin-
ciples of cash exchange. The planter's store, in contrast, exists only to
furnish his tenants. Hiring 'hands' involved little direct payment of rental or wages; instead, tenancies operated on complex schemes of sharing
the yearly crop. Poor families seldom had cash to buy food, clothing, and
agricultural supplies outright, but were made dependent on the planter
for all necessities, a credit system which allowed landowners to exert
control over tenant farmers.

210 *Bonté! . . . eat up yo' crop befo' it's good out o' the groun'*: expressing the
stereotypical view of tenants as grasping and shiftless. His immediate
allusion here is to the credit system whereby families might amass a
running account throughout the season which would wipe out hope of
receiving any profit when the crops were harvested. These debts trapped
tenants either into accepting an unsatisfactory contract for a further year,
or facing the hazards of trying to find a new place, with no resources
behind them.

salt meat: usually pork preserved in salt: a crude form of bacon. Important to the diet of poor rural southerners, this was usually sliced thin,
fried, and eaten with flat griddle bread, made from corn meal and
water.

lazy-bone 'Cadians: extending 'Polyte's stereotypes to the Acadians,
popularly seen as idle and pleasure-loving; see Appendix, IV.

211 *She wanted tobacco*: whisky and tobacco were the only 'luxury' items
commonly ordered. Azélie's modest requests are in keeping with the
general range of the stock.

coal-oil: paraffin oil, kerosene, used mainly as lantern fuel.

212 *Li'le River*: the Little River, in central Louisiana, regarded by 'Polyte as
outlandish and alien.

but que voulez-vous?: (literally, what do you want?) what do you expect?;
what can you do?

Madeira vines: climbing plants with shiny leaves and white flowers, often
used to make a thick screen.

214 *to fetch a fine buckboa'd . . . an' he's on'y a nigga, après tout*: resentment
reflecting the complexities of status and race on the plantation, and
recalling older rivalries engendered between 'house' and 'field' hands in
the antebellum South. Although both parties here are in Mr Mathurin's
hire, that the black man, Ambroise, should be favoured with the use of a
light four-wheeled carriage offends the white Azélie, as, in her view, 'he's
only a nigger, after all'.

Baton Rouge: the capital of Louisiana, on the Mississippi River, a considerable distance to the south, and the centre for various state institutions, including a penitentiary.

A LADY OF BAYOU ST. JOHN

Written 24–25 Aug. 1893. Accepted at once; pub. *Vogue*, 2 (21 Sept. 1893), 154, 156–8. (Paid $15.00. Text here.) Final story in *BF*. *BF* is more heavily punctuated.

218 *in Virginia . . . with Beauregard*: setting the story during the early stages of the Civil War, after the transfer of the Southern Confederate capital from Montgomery, Alabama, to Richmond, Virginia, in May 1861. General Pierre B. T. Beauregard (b. 1818) was a Louisiana Creole, whose special battalion, the 'Old Creole Corps', was composed of the Creole élite. He led the Confederates to a famous victory in the first battle ('Bull Run') at Manassas Junction (July 1861). His death on 20 February 1893, a few months before KC wrote this story, prompted many Civil War memories.

Bayou St. John: one of the founding sites of New Orleans, this was an area of beautiful old houses and gardens along the attractive clear waters of the bayou linking the city with Lake Pontchartrain. Detached from the city, it attracted legends, ranging from traditions of the voodoo rites performed there by Marie Laveau II (d. 1890) on St John's Eve (23 June) to tales of disputes settled under the 'Dueling Oaks'.

Manna-Lulu: spelt by KC in various ways (e.g. 'Manna Loulou' and 'Manna-Loulou'): possibly also with a hint of 'Mamaloi', a voodoo priestess.

lonely: from *BF. Vogue*: 'lovely.'

this quarrel which was none of his: he felt detached from wars between American nationals. In antebellum New Orleans, European-born French represented the third largest immigrant section after the Irish and Germans, and were viewed as a distinctive group.

220 *the portrait of Gustave*: possibly recalling the legend of Chevalier d'Aubant who was said to have dwelt in solitude on Bayou St John, worshipping the full-length portrait of his lost love, Charlotte of Brunswick. Many contested the truth of the story but it continued to have a strong romantic appeal. KC herself found little satisfaction in shrines to the past.

LA BELLE ZORAÏDE

Written 21 Sept. 1893; pub. *Vogue*, 3 (4 Jan. 1894), 2, 4, 8–10. (Paid $23.00. Text here.) In her records, KC crossed out 'La Belle', 'Li Mouri', and 'One of Man Loulou's Stories' before settling on 'La Belle Zoraïde'. Twenty-first story in *BF*. *BF* more heavily punctuated, with small changes (and see notes below).

223 *across Bayou St. John*: written the same day that the previous story appeared in *Vogue* and using the same setting and characters, but narrated from Manna Loulou's perspective.

Lisett' to kité la plaine: song untraced in this exact version, but closest is that of Alcée Fortier who gives the first stanza of this 'celebrated San Domingo [Haiti] song', to exemplify a grammatical point, *PMLA* 3 (1897), 117. Through the song KC introduces a further viewpoint: that of a black man, the lover working in the fields. (See Appendix, III, for an English version.)

the soft Creole patois . . . no English words can convey: a very positive statement, through which KC sides herself firmly with those, like Fortier, who believed the language of black slaves was a rich one, worth preserving (see Appendix, III).

224 *skin . . . the color of café-au-lait*: indicating white ancestry, and conventionally intended as a sign of superiority: here, a reminder of the complex racial classifications in antebellum society, particularly as the speaker is a woman 'herself as black as the night', telling a story to please her white mistress. In *BF*, KC also removed any hint of criticism, changing 'so unfortunate as to gaze' to 'who gazed'.

la rue Royale: Royal Street, in the French Quarter of New Orleans.

the Cathedral: the Cathedral of St Louis (see note to p. 206). Even in favourable circumstances, Madame's promise would have been unconvincing. Slaves were permitted to marry other slaves with the consent of their masters (Article 182 of the 1835 Louisiana Civil Code), but these marriages had none of the usual civil effects, and were extremely rare.

corbeille: here, the bride's dress and gifts, provided by Madame.

dance the Bamboula in Congo Square: an allusion to the traditions of the old *Place des Nègres* in New Orleans (popularly 'Congo Square'): now Louis Armstrong Park. From the 1740s until the Civil War, it was famous for its Sunday afternoon African dancing, which would attract several hundred participants. White observers viewed the dance's slow rhythmical prelude, and its rising climax, as a pagan ritual, noting 'the vibratory motions of the by-standers . . . [and] the lascivious effect of the scene', Henry C. Castellanos, *New Orleans As It Was* (1895), 297. The Bamboula took its name from the accompanying drum (originally made from bamboo, covered with goat skin). The Protestant American authorities banned the dancing in 1856, and the square fell derelict. Its memory was revived in tourist publicity for the Cotton Centennial Exposition (1884–85) and in accounts such as G.W. Cable's 'The Dance in Place Congo', *Century*, 31 (Feb. 1886). KC's treatment is unusually free of moral disgust.

as proud looking as a king: drawing on the tradition that the leaders of the dance were of African royal descent, revived most notably in G. W. Cable's story of the gigantic black hero, Bras-Coupé, in *The Grandissimes* (1880). The legendary physical magnetism of such men as le beau (handsome) Mézor remained a compelling theme for white writers: 'There were among these Africans . . . several magnificent specimens, who were justly considered as models of physical development. . . . [C]ertain fellows pointed out in the Congo dances were distinguished by something of a royal bearing. They were of robust frame, broad shouldered and muscular. When attired in scant costume for the *bamboula* their almost herculean conformation was noticeable,' Castellanos, *New Orleans As It Was*, 296–7.

225 *hoeing sugar-cane*: recalling the lover in 'Lisett' above, and making the crucial social distinction between Mézor and M'sieur Ambroise, both slaves, as field- and house-worker.

Ma'zelle Titite: (*Mademoiselle Petite*) little Mistress, a pet-name and reminder of Madame's child-like character in her relationship with her old nurse (including the use of patois).

forgive me if you will: for *BF*, KC extended the sentence, to sanction Zoraïde's love with a formal declaration and a romantic excuse, not felt necessary for *Vogue*'s more sophisticated readers: 'but when I heard le beau Mézor say to me, "Zoraïde, mo l'aime toi," I could have died, but I could not have helped loving him' ('mo': black Creole patois for the standard French, 'je' ('I'); 'mo l'aime toi': 'I love you').

226 *sold away into Georgia*: reversing the geographical direction, but equivalent to the fate of being 'sold down the river': to an unknown master, perhaps yet more cruel than the old one.

dance Calinda: (sometimes 'Calenda') another favourite dance. 'Dance Calinda' was also the refrain of a well-known, and much adapted, song.

more precious than her own: as KC recalled of Jean's birth: 'the sensation with which I touched my lips and my finger tips to his soft flesh only comes once to a mother. It must be the pure animal sensation; nothing spiritual could be so real—so poignant', *Impressions*, 12.

227 *Zoraïde la folle*: crazy Zoraïde: compare Jacqueline in 'Beyond the Bayou'.

TONIE (AT CHÊNIÈRE CAMINADA)

Written 21–23 Oct. 1893. Six rejections; pub. *New Orleans Times-Democrat* (23 Dec. 1894). (Paid $5.00. Text here.) Fifteenth story in *NA*, as 'At Chênière Caminada'. For the Gulf setting and the Chênière, see *The Awakening* (notes: to pp. 3, 4, 18). The story suggests a precursor (or even stimulus) to *The Awakening*. KC made slight changes for *NA* (possibly in 1897 when starting on the novel), especially to the status of the Lebruns. The daughter becomes

Madame Lebrun, a widow, enabling KC to enrich her characters' history in *The Awakening*. There, she gives Madame two sons: Robert, 26, former admirer of Mlle Duvigné, and Victor, 19 (an age slightly inconsistent with his mother's twenty years of widowhood). KC also includes the scene at the Antoine cottage (where Tonie and Robert talk, their common background known only to readers), and gives Ma'am Antoine a major role as a story-teller. Changing the perspective, Edna's story mirrors Tonie's: one a wealthy American, the other a poor Acadian, both fall in love with the Creole world, and phrases used of one echo in the other's story.

229 *"Credo ... omnipotentem"*: (Latin) 'I believe in one God, the father almighty'.

230 *Mme. Lebrun and her daughter*: changed in *NA* to 'the widow Lebrun and her old mother'. Similar small changes throughout.

   "fiddler": a burrowing crab—possibly another smitten male (the large 'fiddling' anterior claws were used to attract females).

232 *English ... he hardly understood*: Tonie speaks the Acadian French dialect, rendered only briefly in the story.

235 *the Angelus bell*: here announcing the Roman Catholic devotions, the bell also has elegiac resonance. It was said that in the 1893 hurricane the bell tolled throughout the night; in the morning, the church was destroyed, the community laid waste, and the bell had vanished. (Found in a tomb in the cemetery in 1918, it can now be seen in the church on Grand Isle.)

   Our Lady of Lourdes: associates Claire with Bernadette's visions of the Virgin Mary (see note to p. 39); a note sustained in the allusion to the 'Holy Ghost' later.

A GENTLEMAN OF BAYOU TÊCHE

Written 5–7 Nov. 1893. Rejected by *Youth's Companion* and the *Atlantic*. First pub. in *BF*; twenty-second story. Text here: *BF*.

240 *Title*: Bayou Têche in southwest Louisiana ran through the area settled by the French Canadian exiles ('Acadians'; see Appendix, IV). It had been given lasting fame by Longfellow in *Evangeline: A Tale of Acadie* (1847), who used this landscape as a romantic background for the sufferings of the parted lovers, Evangeline and Gabriel. For many travellers, the region was 'the lost gate of Eden ... the promised land', Edward King, *The Great South* (1875), 85. KC's title plays on the pastoral image of an Acadian as one of nature's gentlemen, living in idyllic simplicity—a counter to the other stereotype of 'Cajuns' as unrefined swamp-dwellers. The story suggests the limits of these representations, even the most sympathetic.

   a picturesque subject ... bits of "local color" along the Têche: an ironically self-reflexive opening, within a collection entitled *Bayou Folk*. For 'local color', see Introduction, pp. xxxii–xxxvii.

one fine 'Mag'zine': in contrast with the local 'Suga Bowl', a national periodical, such as *Scribner's Monthly* which had commissioned Edward King's twelve articles on the South, printed in 1873–74 (collected as *The Great South*). *Harper's*, too, specifically sought writing with 'local color' focus (e.g. Charles Dudley Warner's 'The Acadian Land' (Feb. 1887)).

Carancro: (or 'carenco': meaning the 'black vulture, an Acadian version of 'Carrion Crow') a name made familiar by G. W. Cable's 'Acadian' story: 'Carancro' (*Century*, Jan.–Feb. 1887), collected in *Bonaventure: A Prose Pastoral of Acadian Louisiana* (1888).

Aunt Dicey's cabin: in the complex social divisions of this story, the African-American servant, Dicey, is given the title conventionally used of older black women working for white families. (Compare 'Old Aunt Peggy'.)

241 *one dem low-down 'Cajuns o' Bayeh Têche'*: a prediction reflecting 'local color' conventions. King's *Great South* included numerous vignettes of 'picturesque' Southern subjects with captions: 'One sees delicious types in these markets' (p. 48), 'A lazy negro, recumbent in a cart' (p. 29), 'The rude cabin built beneath the shadow of a huge rock' (p. 677).

242 *The silver dollars . . . the price of shame*: an allusion to the thirty pieces of silver paid to Judas Iscariot for his betrayal of Jesus: Matthew 26: 14–16.

Evariste winced: Acadians found the term 'Cajun' insulting. KC's treatment of the subject sets her apart from commentaries which asserted confidently that they were over-sensitive.

244 *It was with visible reluctance . . . that Wilkins served them*: an index of social divisions: the black house-servant despises the Acadians, but is forced to serve them at a white man's table, a privilege never accorded to African Americans. (Compare 'Azélie', note to p. 214.)

245 *he did not know how*: unlike many commentators, KC seems to regard illiteracy among the Acadians as a matter of circumstance, not innate incapacity. Like Alcée Fortier who viewed the Acadians as 'an intelligent race' ('Acadians of Louisiana', 80), she concentrates on Evariste's potential, allowing him to define his own identity and his own narrative.

IN SABINE

Written 20–22 Nov. 1893. Sent to *Atlantic*; but first pub. as third story in *BF*. (Text here.) Later syndicated: American Press Association (Jan. 1895), with 'In and Out of Old Natchitoches'. (Paid $42.10.)

246 *Grégoire*: one of the three Santien brothers who make various appearances in KC's fiction, including the first three stories in *BF*. Their grandfather, Lucien Santien, was a prosperous planter, mentioned in 'A No-Account Creole' (1891) as the owner of a hundred slaves and a

thousand-acre estate, now bankrupt and dismantled. The dashing Grégoire had a major role in *At Fault*.

246 *out of Natchitoches ... toward the Sabine River*: Grégoire's ride is taking him west from Natchitoches, his home parish (county), through neigbouring Sabine to the Texas border, a journey into younger and wilder country. Sabine Parish had been part of the 'Neutral Strip', a buffer zone dividing the United States from Spanish Territory after the Louisiana Purchase (1803). The Sabine River became notorious as the boundary line between civilization and wilderness, for outlaws and desperate men in flight to Texas and Mexico.

247 *Bayou Pierre, in Natchitoches parish*: running through the country to the north of the town of Natchitoches, west of the Red River.

Sanchuns: Aiken's crude rendering of 'Santiens'. He has similar difficulty below with the pronunciation of the French, 'Reine'. Aiken also features in 'Ti Frère' (1896); and one of 'Tite Reine's small brothers appears in 'Mamouche' (1893).

248 *truck*: an all-purpose word, including 'garden produce', 'stuff', 'odds and ends'; used here in the most general sense: 'rubbish'.

Grant ... Winn and Caddo: Aiken's failures have taken him on a circuitous route in every direction of the compass from Natchitoches. His resentful reference to Grant may be coloured by the parish's history as a former stronghold of Radical Republicans, where black citizens had briefly held control before being overthrown by white vigilantes in the bloody Colfax Riot of Easter Sunday, 13 April 1873. (Fifty-nine were killed; all but two of them black.)

Vernon: the next parish south from Sabine.

250 *the pain that a woman had inflicted upon him*: an allusion to Grégoire's romance with Melicent Hosmer, a high-spirited and stylish young St Louis woman who visits the Cane River country in *At Fault*. After Grégoire is involved in a murder, Melicent shuns him and returns to the city.

251 *He ... would hardly have considered it a crime*: a reminder of Grégoire's summary shooting of Joçint, the young man of mixed race who sets fire to the mill in *At Fault*.

a Texas drummer: a travelling salesman from Texas (originally, one who 'drums up' trade).

périque tobacco: a rare and costly tobacco grown on the uniquely suitable soil of St James Parish, one of the River Parishes on the Mississippi, north of New Orleans; supposedly named after the Acadian Pierre Chenet who first produced it. Grégoire has extravagant tastes.

252 *a pone of corn bread ... slices of salt pork*: corn mixed with water and fried in flat cakes on a hoe or griddle with thin slices of salt pork: a basic diet for poor tenant farmers.

worked the crop on shares: after the abolition of slavery, many former cotton plantations were divided into plots; tenants raised their own crop, but committed a fixed proportion of the future harvest to the farmer in lieu of rent (see notes to 'Azélie').

made a fool of himself in Cloutierville: Grégoire's wild last fling before departing for Texas, narrated at length in *At Fault* (II. viii). Here, KC substitutes Cloutierville, her Natchitoches home in the early 1880s, for *At Fault's* 'Centerville'.

gumbo-filé: the traditional stew (see note to p. 187), thickened with powdered dried sassafras leaves instead of okra.

254 *he done cross de Sabine befo' sun-up on Buckeye*: as readers of *At Fault* would know, riding to a violent death in a fight with a stranger in Cornstalk, Texas. (The news is reported to the novel's heroine—Grégoire's aunt, Thérèse Lafirme—in II. xii.)

A RESPECTABLE WOMAN

Written 20 Jan. 1894. Accepted at once; pub. *Vogue*, 3 (15 Feb. 1894), 68–9, 72. (Paid $15.00. Text here.) Nineteenth story in *NA*.

255 *Gouvernail*: an early appearance of this character, also in 'Athénaïse' and *The Awakening*.

big Corinthian pillars: the house is built in the American Classical-Revival style (most favoured by wealthy planters from about 1835–50) with ornately decorated columns. KC's description of the beauties of the plantation here is conventional, lulling expectation before she departs from tradition later in the story.

256 *grosbecs*: game-birds (see note to p. 78).

batture: the land by the river, formed by alluvial soils brought down by the waters and deposited against the embankment ('levee').

257 *'Night of south winds . . . | night—'*: from one of KC's favourite writers, Walt Whitman: 'Press close bare-bosom'd night—press close magnetic nourishing night! | Night of south winds—night of the large few stars! | Still nodding night—mad naked summer night' *Song of Myself* (1855; 'Deathbed Edition', 1891–2), 21: 436–7. While adroitly omitting the suggestive adjacent lines, KC alludes to the ardent sequence leading to: 'Prodigal, you have given me love—therefore I to you give love! | O unspeakable passionate love'. Whitman (1819–92) had himself once worked briefly as a journalist on the New Orleans *Crescent* (1848), where he was reputed to have fallen in love with an unidentified New Orleans woman [or man].

THE DREAM OF AN HOUR (THE STORY OF AN HOUR)

Written 19 April 1894. Four rejections: sold to *Vogue* at second attempt; pub. *Vogue*, 4 (6 Dec. 1894), 360. (Paid $10.00. Text here.) Planned as eighth story in *VV*. Title: 'The Dream of an Hour' in *Vogue* and in KC's lists of earnings and word-lengths; 'The Story of an Hour' written on clipping (Box 1 | Folder 19), and on KC's record of submissions.

259 *the railroad disaster*: recalling the death of KC's father, Thomas O'Flaherty, in the Gasconade Bridge disaster (1 November 1855).

261 *How fancy*: changed on the clipping to 'Her fancy', making a flatter statement out of an exclamation. (KC uses similar exclamations elsewhere: see, e.g., 'Lilacs', 'Regret'.)

   goddess of Victory: in Greek mythology, Nike. The marble 'Winged Victory' (*c*. third century BC), found on the island of Samothrace in 1863, inspired many statues of dynamic winged female figures, stepping forward in triumph.

LILACS

Written 14–16 May 1894. Eight rejections (including *The Chap Book*); pub. in 'Christmas Art Supplement', *New Orleans Times-Democrat*, 20 Dec. 1896. (Paid $10.00. Text here.) Planned as twentieth story in *VV*. In the *Times-Democrat*, the four sections were clearly distinguished ('III' and 'IV' by numbers). *Complete Works* omits the numbers, losing the dramatic division between sections one and two in a page break. Following KC's frequent practice, I use numbered headings throughout.

262 *Sacré-Coeur*: the image of Christ's Sacred Heart, a permitted object for devotion. Emily Toth's biographies show how far 'Lilacs' is coloured by KC's memories of her convent education, and of her close friendship with Kitty Garesché, who became a Sacred Heart nun. KC's religious devotion lapsed in later years. After finishing 'Lilacs', she recorded a visit to another friend who had spent her life in a convent, commenting on the limitations of such an existence (*Impressions*, 22 May 1894).

263 *Ste. Catherine de Sienne*: Saint Catherine of Siena (1347?–80). Stories of this attractive and energetic woman, famous for her social and political dynamism, as well as for her mysticism, would probably have appealed to the lively Adrienne.

   St. Joseph's mantle . . . embellished . . . the Blessed Virgin there neglected!: representations of the Holy Family. Again Adrienne comments that the female image is held in less regard.

265 *ma tante de Sierge*: my aunt from Sierge.

   St. Lazare: the madhouse.

266 *the angelus bell*: rung to mark the prayer commemorating the Incarnation, said at morning, noon, and sunset. *Angelus Domini*: Angel of the Lord (Latin), as repeated in the prayer below (see also Luke 1: 5–56).

267 *Jacob's dream*: of angels ascending and descending a ladder which reached from earth to heaven: Genesis 28: 12–15.

bénitiers: vessels for holy water (from French, 'bénit': consecrated).

268 *it was as far as she might go*: according to the rule that confined nuns to the limits of the convent grounds.

traînée of a café chantant: (French slang) a tart in a cabaret [literally, 'a singing café': where artistes provide evening musical entertainments].

269 *How can you ever expect Zozo to talk?*: according to KC, a vain hope at the best of times. See note to p. 3. 'Zozo' was also the Creole patois for 'oiseau' ('bird'), as in 'Lizette'.

Mons. Zola!: a warning in accord with KC's published opinions on the French Naturalist writer, Émile Zola (1840–1902). Avoiding conventional moral disapproval of Zola's supposed cynicism, atheism and obscenity, KC, like Adrienne, criticized his work on artistic grounds. Her review 'Emile Zola's "Lourdes"' (*St. Louis Life*, 17 Nov. 1894) acknowledges the 'masterly' style and 'suberb' descriptions, but laments Zola's sacrifice of his characters in the interests of remorseless didacticism.

270 *Château Yquem*: for Château d'Yquem, a superior French white wine from the hill region of Sauternes in Bordeaux. The discovery (*c*.1847) of a process using grapes affected by the *botrytis* mould (or 'noble rot') gave the wine a rich, honey-like sweetness which made it much sought after and supremely expensive: with the cigarettes, a useful index of Adrienne's generally decadent moral status.

273 *lilac blossoms*: linked by Helen Taylor with Walt Whitman, as connoting 'sexual desire and eroticism' (*Gender, Race and Region*, 154, n. 21), lilacs were also KC's favourite flower and were planted on her grave.

REGRET

Written 17 Sept. 1894. Sold at first submission; pub. *Century*, 50 (May 1895), 147–49. (Paid $30.00. Text here.) Fifth story in *NA*. In MS (in *Impressions*, 79–90), the main character is called 'Mamzelle Angéla'.

274 *an old blue army overcoat*: presumably, once the property of a Federal (Northern) soldier. How Mamzelle Aurélie has come to possess this man's coat is unexplained. Possibly, like Margaret Mitchell's Scarlett O'Hara (*Gone With the Wind*, 1936), she shot him.

Ponto: a common name for a gun-dog (a 'pointer'). Although the 'negroes' still come second to Ponto in this sentence, MS had 'darkies', a word more typical of cosy plantation fiction.

Ti Nomme: a pet-name, diminutive of '*Petit Homme*', little man.

alive encore: still alive.

276 *the story of Croque-Mitaine or Loup-garou*: traditional tales. *Loup-garou* (French) is a werewolf or, in children's stories, 'bogeyman'. In KC's own two-page story, '*Croque-Mitaine*' (written 27 Feb. 1892), a French

nursery-governess terrifies her charges with the tale of 'a hideous ogre, said to inhabit the strip of wood just beyond the children's playground'. Seeing Monsieur Alcée going to a masked ball, the little brothers and sisters believe they now know the comforting truth behind the story.

276 *it make 'em teeth hard to look in a lookin'-glass*: Louisiana proverb, noted by Alcée Fortier: 'If a child teething looks at himself in a mirror, his teething will be painful', *Louisiana Studies* (New Orleans, 1894), 132. The editorial gloss of 'bared [buried]' is KC's.

THE KISS

Written 19 Sept. 1894; pub. *Vogue*, 5 (17 June 1895), 37. (Paid $10.00. Text here.) Planned as fourteenth story in *VV*. In MS (in *Impressions*, 90–97), the words 'enormously rich' (p. 278) were followed by '—through no talent of his own': perhaps too pointed a remark for the well-to-do readers of *Vogue*.

HER LETTERS

Written 29 Nov. 1894. One rejection (*Century*); pub. in two parts, *Vogue*, 5 (11, 18 April 1895), 228–30; 248 (break after 'black boundless universe'). (Paid $25.00. Text here.) Planned as thirteenth story in *VV*.

282 *cast it into the roaring fire*: compare KC's translation of Maupassant's 'Suicide', which warns against disturbing old correspondence: 'if you are led by accident to do so, seize those letters by handsful and without a glance that might awaken remembrance, cast them into the flames' (trans. 18 Dec. 1895, pub. *St. Louis Republic* (5 June 1898)).

water in her veins to wine: an allusion to the miracle at the wedding in Cana in Galilee, when Jesus turned water into wine, John 2: 7–10. (Compare the language of sacrament six lines above. KC's word 'delirium' in this context anticipates Edna Pontellier (p. 63).

285 *He had once. . . . a dead woman's hand*: on the founding of the American Society of Psychical Research (1885), 'thought-transference' (telepathy) became a popular theme; KC used it in 'A Mental Suggestion' (Dec. 1896, unpub. but listed for *VV*). When pasting her clipping, she omitted this paragraph, perhaps to avoid repetition in *VV* or possibly in error. (As the story appears on both sides of a page, she cut her paragraphs from two copies, removing several inset drawings of fashionable accessories. The lines, at the foot of the last column (p. 229), might easily have been overlooked.)

the bridge that spanned the river: probably the Eads Bridge, spanning the Mississippi at St Louis; see Toth (ed.), *A Vocation and a Voice* (1991), 195. Built by the famous engineer James B. Eads (1820–87), whose motto was 'Drive On', the bridge embodied 'flashy civic optimism, entrepreneurial verve, technological audacity, and capitalist wheeling and dealing', Corbett and Miller, *Saint Louis in the Gilded Age* (1993), 88. KC attended its opening in 1874.

ATHÉNAÏSE

Written 10–28 April 1895. Rejected (*Century* and *The Chap Book*); pub. in two parts, *Atlantic Monthly*, 78 (Aug. and Sept. 1896), 232–41; 404–13 (break after section V). (Paid $75.00 and $80.00. Text here.) Second story in *NA*. In 'In and Out of Old Natchitoches' (1893), we hear: 'This isn't little Athénaïse Miché getting married! . . . it makes one old!' The subtitle, 'A Story of a Temperament' (often mistranscribed, without indefinite article) is generally held to be the *Atlantic's* editorial attempt to play down the story's doubts about marriage as an institution. (Compare, '*The Awakening* is a decidedly unpleasant study of a temperament', *The Outlook*, 3 (June 1899), 414.)

289 *rigolet du Bon Dieu*: in Natchitoches Parish, the setting for KC's 'Love on the Bon-Dieu' (1892). A rigolet, here, is a small stream off a bayou.

290 "*Ce n'est pas Chrétien, ténez!*": 'it's not Christian, see!' (translated indirectly below).

Juanita: [*c*.1850], words by the Hon. Caroline Norton; tune based on a traditional Spanish air. Norton (1808–77), a British beauty and aristocrat, was famous for her flight from her unhappy marriage and her public campaign to change the laws on marital rights and divorce. Her surprisingly sentimental words chime with the rosy visions that have fed Cazeau's dreams, and echo his crisis. Especially resonant are the refrain: 'Nita! Juanita! Ask thy soul if we should part! | Nita! Juanita! Lean thou on my heart' and the appeal, 'Wilt thou not relenting, for thine absent lover sigh?' The song ends: 'Be my own fair bride.'

291 *the old Gotrain place*: a former plantation: like several others in KC's fiction, run-down and unworkable without slave labour, after the Civil War.

gumbo filé at midnight: see 'At the 'Cadian Ball', and note to p. 252.

292 "*Cochon! . . . sacré cochon!*": Pig! . . . damned [or bloody] pig!': a variant of Cazeau's view earlier of 'those "lazy pigs," her brothers'. The explanatory paragraph is an indirect apology for the forceful swearword, 'Sacré', which Athénaïse herself calls 'disgusting'.

294 *Gordian knot*: a highly complex problem, solved by guile or force (cutting), rather than by slow effort (untying): from the Greek story of the intricate 'Gordian knot', designed to frustrate a prediction that whoever should unloose it would gain the empire of Asia. Alexander, supposedly, won the prize by cutting the knot with his sword.

295 "*La fille de son père*": her father's daughter.

alpaca: strong woollen fabric (genuine alpaca comes from a South American domestic animal, related to the llama).

295 *Cane River*: now Cane River Lake, a beautiful narrow stretch of water, which meanders for over thirty miles, through Natchitochēs and the Plantation Country. It was left stranded when the Red River changed course in the 1830s, moving its main channel some five miles East.

296 *The whole impression was . . . hideous*: although Cazeau remembers his father as a kind master, antebellum Louisiana had a notorious reputation as a particularly harsh slave-holding régime. Harriet Beecher Stowe (1811–96) chose the Red River country near Natchitoches for the harrowing scenes at Simon Legree's plantation, in *Uncle Tom's Cabin* (1851–2). Her reputed model, Robert McAlpin, lived on land later owned by the Chopin family. In *At Fault*, Grégoire (of 'In Sabine') takes Melicent to visit his grave ('McFarlane': the 'meanest w'ite man thet ever lived'). Swamps were the traditional hiding-place for runaway slaves.

299 *"Tiens! . . . Je ne veux plus de ce train là, moi"*: 'Here! you're going to look after them like you used to. I don't want anything more to do with this [house-keeping routine]'. (KC gives the general sense in the next paragraph.)

303 *Dauphine Street*: in the French Quarter; after the Dauphin of France, later Louis XV.

      "chambres garnies": furnished rooms, a familiar feature of this quarter: 'Here one can secure from the landlady (who is certain to prove either a very stout Creole, or, more likely a quadroon or octoroon) a furnished room, always kept in the neatest of order', *Coleman*, 83. In the 1890s, rooms cost from $10 per month upwards; Dauphine St was especially recommended.

304 *the back ell*: the back extension, projecting at right-angles from the main house, making an 'L'-shaped building.

      Sylvie believed . . . in maintaining the color-line: it was not the custom for white people to give black citizens courtesy titles (the issue of colour overrode other conventional hierarchies, such as the respect due to age or authority). Sylvie upholds this tradition, but at the same time recognizes her own importance as an efficient business woman in the community.

      quite [quiet]: KC explains her pronunciation for northern readers (compare p. 276).

305 *along the "coast"*: Montéclin devises an elaborate route, along the river side ('coast') to catch one steamer to Red River Landing on the Mississippi, and another to New Orleans.

      Athénaïse was to take her meals in . . . lodgers did: a dispensation probably on the grounds of gender. Guidebooks generally assumed that boarders were bachelors who would eat in local restaurants or be served by the many neighbourhood caterers.

      southern parishes: counties south of New Orleans.

307 *river-shrimps*: a seasonal delicacy, more subtly flavoured than the larger lake shrimps available all year round; usually simply boiled and served, as here, on a bed of ice.

308 *Corrupt Legislation*: a perennial topic in the New Orleans press throughout Reconstruction (1865–77) and its aftermath. Gouvernail's association with liberal thinkers in the American quarter suggests that his radicalism might be political as well as moral.

   des esprits forts: free-thinkers. Untraced, in this form, 'the traditional "sapeur" for whom "nothing is sacred"', but the term exploits a word-play: 'sapper', a military engineer who lays or disarms mines, and digs trenches, so 'undermining' authority.

310 *The Duchess . . . Mrs. Humphry Ward*: 'The Duchess' was the pen-name of the popular Irish writer, Mrs Margaret Wolfe Hungerford [Hamilton] (?1855–97), who had recently published *Neither Wife Nor Maid* (1892) and *Lady Verner's Flight* (1893), about an abused wife, titles suggestive in context. However, her novels were generally known as light-reading. They contrast here with the weightier, socially concerned, fiction of the English writer, Mrs Humphry Ward [Mary Augusta Arnold] (1851–1920), then commanding unprecedented sums in leading American magazines. KC respected Mrs Ward, but regarded her as 'a reformer, and such tendency in a novelist she considers a crime against good taste', William Schuyler, *The Writer*, vii (August 1894).

   A New England . . . Creole tale had offended her: contents typical of quality magazines of the time, such as the *Atlantic Monthly* (where 'Athénaïse' would appear) and *Century*, which, as KC wrote, was about to publish 'Regret,' and was her first choice for 'Athénaïse.' These regularly featured 'New England' stories by such writers as Mary E. Wilkins [Freeman] (1852–1930) and Sarah Orne Jewett (1849–1909), whom KC admired, but whose subdued landscapes and silent characters must have seemed remote to Athénaïse. Her response to the 'Creole tale' recalls that of Louisiana Creoles to the stories of G. W. Cable; but KC may also be making amused reference to her own publications.

311 *Remington's Cowboys*: Frederic Remington (1861–1909) was one of the most popular magazine artists. He illustrated numerous tales of the Wild West, including Theodore Roosevelt's accounts of ranch life for *Century* (1888), and was most famous for his images of manly cowboys, conflict on the frontier, and life in a legendary and romanticized West.

   the lake end: a favourite excursion to the resort on Lake Pontchartrain, about five miles to the north of the city, famous for its garden-restaurants, its Music Plaza, flowers, walks, and kiosks: Alcée Arobin drives Edna here in *The Awakening*.

312 *"Mo pa oua vou . . . Madame Sylvie?"*: (a transcription of patois) 'I didn't see you at table tonight; I thought you had already gone; truly! You won't complain about me to Madame Sylvie?' The following sentences effectively paraphrase this for northern readers.

313 *the French market*: see also 'Caline'. For 'a scene of the greatest picturesqueness and animation', Baedeker recommended a morning visit, 'best

about 6 or 7 a.m.; on Sun. 8 or 9 a.m.' (p. 369): early hours for Gouvernail after his midnight shift at the newspaper office.

316 *Harding & Offdean*: in 'A No-Account Creole' (*Century*, 1894), Messrs. Fitch Harding and Wallace Offdean are agents for 'the old Santien Place', and Offdean becomes involved in a romance, while visiting the Red River estate.

317 *"a set of pattern"*: presumably for baby clothes, such as Mme Ratignolle offers Edna.

318 *Eve after losing her ignorance*: in Genesis 3: 7–8.

reached her station: Athénaïse takes the most direct way possible back to Alexandria (196 miles from New Orleans): a contrast with the 'interminable and circuitous' route planned for her escape by Montéclin earlier.

319 *pauvre ti chou*: (in full, 'pauvre petit chou') expression of affection: poor little cabbage.

THE UNEXPECTED

Written 18 July 1895. One rejection; pub. *Vogue*, 6 (19 Sept. 1895), 180–81 [not 18 Sept. as usually given]. (Paid $10.00. Text here.) Planned as twelfth story in *VV* with slight changes on clipping.

322 *her "wheel"*: her bicycle: a touch of topical interest for *Vogue* readers. During the 1890s, *Vogue* regularly published bicycling numbers, which (like their equivalent sea-bathing and yachting issues) included articles on appropriate costumes, cartoons, club notes, and features on this fashionable pastime. As in this issue, wheel-wear (such as the 'Luey Cycle Habit') was widely advertised. However, in 1895, owning a 'wheel' still marks Dorothea as 'advanced'.

VAGABONDS

Written Dec. 1895. Rejected by *The Chap Book* and *Vogue*. First pub. in Daniel S. Rankin, *Kate Chopin and Her Creole Stories* (1932). (Text here: MS.) KC commented: 'Sometimes I've discovered a charming companion in a loafer . . . We never know what illusions are till we have lost them. They belong to youth, and they are poetry and philosophy, and vagabondage, and everything delightful', *Criterion* (St Louis, 13 Feb. 1897), 11.

326 *silence and mystery*: as Rankin first observed, at this point in the MS, KC emphatically crossed out the intriguing words: 'and sin'.

A PAIR OF SILK STOCKINGS

Written April 1896; pub. *Vogue*, 10 (16 Sept. 1897), 191–92. (Paid $5.00. Text here.) As KC wrote the story, the St Louis department stores were busy announcing their Easter Sales. Nugents strongly promoted their bargain kid gloves, and urged readers 'to take the road called Cash', *St. Louis Republic* (22 March 1896). Barr's offered 'SILKS, SILKS, SILKS' and an 'immense assortment of Ladies Fancy Hosiery', and Crawfords boasted 'Ladies' Imported Silk Plated Hose' at 50c., reg. price 75c. (*St. Louis Republic*, 5 April 1896).

327 *It seemed . . . a very large amount of money*: the story indicates how far the money in Mrs Sommers's 'porte-monnaie' (wallet) would go. (It is three times what KC was paid for this story.) Shirts for boys aged 8–15 were advertised in Nugents sale at 25c, and children's stockings from 12½–50 cents. Elsewhere in this issue, however, *Vogue* readers were recommended the latest in children's coats (silk, with lace trimming) at $26.50.

percale for new shirt waists: a strong cotton fabric to make blouses which will wear well.

328 *elevator . . . the ladies' waiting-rooms*: the luxurious giant department stores had tempting facilities. Wm. Barr. & Co in St. Louis (founded as a small business in 1849) became a vast establishment, known as 'a spot where feminine feet love to tread', *Pictorial St. Louis* (St Louis, 1875), 162. It promised 'every modern invention to facilitate the often fatiguing, but necessary occupation of "shopping," ' *Gould's* Directory (St Louis, 1892–93). D. H. Holmes of New Orleans was similarly famous for its sumptuous reception rooms and waiting parlours.

329 *two high-priced magazines*: *Vogue*, where the story was published, cost ten cents. (It does not appear to have had pages that needed cutting.)

330 *blue-points*: a small succulent oyster, with excellent flavour, found in the beds off Blue Point, and the southern shore of Long Island.

crème-frappée: a chilled creamy dessert.

AN EGYPTIAN CIGARETTE

Written April 1897. One submission lost, three rejected (including *The Chap Book*); pub. *Vogue*, 15 (19 April 1900), 252, 254. (Paid $6.25. Text here.) Planned as sixth story in *VV*. *Title*: suggests the Oriental theme which KC develops as a code for the exotic, in a manner often used in literature of the 1890s. Smoking was a popular motif in literature and art of the period, lending itself to decorative treatment in illustration, often with strong sexual associations. Images of women smoking usually signified some form of deviance. Although KC enjoyed cigarettes, in interviews she teased her public: 'Am I going to tell it out in meeting?' (*St. Louis Post-Dispatch*, 26 Nov. 1899).

332 *yellow paper*: with *fin-de-siècle* associations of decadent or illicit reading, as in Aubrey Beardsley's *Yellow Book* (1894–97), or Stone and Kimball's *The Chap Book* (1894–98), the aesthetic journals in which KC was keen to appear. Also used to refer to French novels, often with yellow covers— associations sustained in the metaphor of the 'sealed letter' below.

333 *inspiration*: a term for inhaling, again with connotations of writing and reading.

"*Ah! the sand has blistered my cheek!*": this section offers a version of the prose-poem, a popular *fin-de-siècle* genre: KC may have read translations of Stéphane Mallarmé in *The Chap-Book*, or even Lafcadio Hearn's dream-vision of the Gulf, 'Torn Letters', *New Orleans Times-Democrat* (14 Sept. 1884). There (section v), a much travelled friend gives the narrator a mysterious yellow sheet of paper, stimulating dreams (on a 'swift Camel of fancy . . . over the vast plain of Mitidja') and fantasies of a desert beauty.

ELIZABETH STOCK'S ONE STORY

Written March 1898. Four rejections. First pub. in Per Seyersted, 'Kate Chopin: an Important St. Louis Writer Reconsidered', *Missouri Historical Society Bulletin*, 19 (Jan. 1963), 89–114. Planned as second story for *VV*. (Text here: MS, Box 2/Folder 12). I have retained KC's (or Elizabeth's) form of 'aint' and 'Si [Shepard]', with no apostrophes.

336 *this here aint no story*: echoing KC's ironic vision of how Ruth McEnery Stuart was received in her Louisiana home parish: "Hit seems Ruth MicHenry's took to writin' books. But land! they ain't like no books I ever seen! Thes about common eve'y day talk an' people!" (*Criterion*, St Louis, 27 Feb. 1897).

that some one else had thought about: KC's own basic plot had been used before: (in lighter vein) in 'Our Post-Mistress; Or, Why She Was Turned Out' [n.a.], *Godey's Lady's Book* (Feb. 1850) [she has read a young Congressman's Valentine]; and, ET suggests (p. 315), in Bret Harte's 'Postmistress of Laurel Run' in *The First Family of Tasahara and Other Tales* (1896).

337 *Stonelift*: cancelled on MS, 'in south west Missouri.'

338 *Seaside Library novel*: this New York house purveyed by post, in journal format, a wide selection of world literature, classic and popular. The postmistress might have enjoyed a year's subscription (thirty-six dollars a year), or, more probably, ordered individual numbers. Its lists included among many others *Jane Eyre* (in small type for ten cents, or 'bold, handsome type' for twenty), and works by Jane Austen, Daudet, George Eliot, and Mary Elizabeth Braddon.

To a person that knew B. from bull's foot: 'to anyone with a grain of intelligence'. KC's handwriting often leaves room for doubt, but MS appears, in my view, to read 'bull's foot', rather than the more genteel 'hill's foot' as given in previous editions. In attempts to trace this lively country idiom, in either form, I have not found 'hill's foot', but Missouri and Western writers, including Mark Twain, have numerous variants of the alliterative 'Not to know a *B* from a bull's foot'; 'not an officer . . .

that knows a Bee from a Bull's foot'; or (more refined) 'Persons who . . .
had not sufficient discrimination to know the second letter of the alpha-
bet from a buffalo's foot'. See Bartlett Jere Whiting, *Early American
Proverbs and Proverbial Phrases* (Cambridge, Mass.: Belknap; Harvard
UP, 1977).

340 *Uncle Sam*: popular term for the United States government.

341 *it don't count*: MS (28–9) follows: 'Looks like I ought to have [more?]
[some?] with my position paying me so well for the past six years. But
putting Danny to the Academy and other things, and paying doctors
bills, here lately' (cancelled and altered by KC to text here).

THE STORM. A SEQUEL TO "THE 'CADIAN BALL"

Written 19 July 1898. No evidence that KC contemplated publication. First
pub. in Per Seyersted, *The Complete Works of Kate Chopin* (1969). KC's own
subtitle (MS: Box 2/19).

346 *"J'vous réponds"*: 'I promise you'.

GLOSSARY

In a complexly divided society, racial classifications designated the fraction of a person's African ancestry, labelling them legally and socially as non-white (Chopin uses only the most common terms): **griffe**: a person of three-quarters African descent (i.e. three black grand-parents; one white); 'griffe' women were particularly renowned as midwives; **mulatto, mulatresse**: a man or woman with one-half African ancestry (i.e. one black and one white parent), a term derived from the word for a mule, supposedly reflecting a belief in the sterility of half-breeds; **octoroon**: a person of one-eighth African descent (i.e. one black great-grand-parent); **quadroon**: a person of one-quarter African descent (i.e. one black grand-parent).

The following translations (from varieties of French, unless otherwise specified) gloss individual words and short phrases not explained in context in the notes, and the brief exclamations Chopin scatters liberally throughout her fiction.

accouchement(s) confinement(s), child-birth

à jeudi until Thursday

à point just right, done to a turn.

ami, amie friend (male and female); **en bon ami** just as a friend

armoire wardrobe, cabinet, with rows of shelves for keeping clothes

atelier artist's studio or workshop

au revoir good-bye

banquette pavement, sidewalk (from word for 'bench', so named because the wooden platforms were elevated above the mud of the streets)

(ma) belle (my) beauty (female)

bien (b'en) well (**bien!**) fine! good!

bonne house maid, servant

Bon Dieu! Good God!

bonjour (bonjou') good day

bonté! (or **bonté divine!**) goodness! gracious! good heavens!

bougie candle

buffet sideboard

cabriolet two-wheeled carriage, with a hood, light enough to be drawn by one horse

chambres garnies furnished rooms (see also note to p. 303)

cher, chéri, chérie dear, darling (form varies according to gender)

chiffonier a chest of drawers, or low cupboard

comme ça like that

comment! (all-purpose exclamation) really! what!

comment ça va? how are you?

les convenances the proprieties, expected social forms

couleur de rose rose-tinted

coup d'état sudden or violent seizure of power by force

coupé small closed carriage, for two people and a driver

court bouillon (also '**courtbouillon**') soup-like fish stew made with richly seasoned red stock

croquignoles small, crisp biscuits, cookies

désolé dreary and depressed, upset

Dieu sait! God knows!

donc (for emphasis) then

ennui emotional and spiritual weariness, deep boredom, a word with particular force in literature of the 1890s

enragée mad woman (with the further sense of 'rabid')

fanfaron (literally, 'boastful', 'showing off') swaggering, cutting a dash

faux-air a vague or faint resemblance

fiacre carriage, cab

(mon) fils (my) son

friandises luxurious little delicacies. Glossed by KC as 'luscious and toothsome bits' (p. 9)

(bon) garçon (good) boy, waiter. (Madame Ratignolle plays on the double meaning (p. 24))

hein? (all-purpose conversational interjection) yes? isn't it? won't you? doesn't he? eh? what?

hors de combat out of the running (literally, out of the contest)

jalousies traditional two-batten outdoor shutters, often painted in 'Paris Green'

layette the clothes and equipment needed for a new baby

ma, mon my (form varies according to gender)

ma foi! (literally 'My faith!') exclamation – 'For heaven's sake!', 'Oh, really!', 'Indeed!'

mais but

maître master (**cher maître**: dear master)

malheureuse! wretch!

marais marsh-lands, swampy ground

marron glacé preserved chestnut, glazed with sugar

maudit damned, cursed

(ma) mère (my) mother

merveille! excellent, wonderful (**in merveille**: excellently, wonderfully)

mets, entre-mets main dishes and side dishes

ménage household

nénaine/nainaine godmother (affectionate Creole diminutive of '**marraine**', godmother)

nom de guerre an assumed name

par exemple! (general expression of indignation, exasperation, or contempt). For goodness' sake! Really!

parbleu! good Lord! of course!

parterre formal flowerbed

pauvre poor (**pauvre chérie**: poor dear)

peignoir woman's loose negligee, dressing gown

pension boarding-house

picayune a trifling amount, insignificant, a small coin's worth (originally from the Spanish half-real, six and a quarter cents)

pied à terre a convenient and comfortable home from home, for occasional use

pirogue a small, shallow, canoe-like boat, originally from hollowed-out cypress trunks

poudre de riz rice powder

(ma) reine (my) queen

(grand) seigneur (great) lord; lord and master

(mais) si (but) yes

(bien) souffrante indisposed, not at all well

sacque a woman's loose, straight gown

svelte elegantly slender

tabouret a low stool, named for its drum-like shape

tamales (Mexican Spanish) Mexican dish of maize husks with a seasoned stuffing

terrassent overwhelming

tête montée an impetuous character, wilful, hot-headed

tiens! (all-purpose exclamation) well! look! look here!

tignon a traditional form of head-dress, made of a bright cotton handkerchief (a bandana), worn by women of colour

triste sad

va! go! go away!

vaurien good-for-nothing, n'er-do-well

vingt-et-un (literally 'twenty-one') card game introduced to New Orleans by the French aristocracy

viveur (or **bon viveur**) a man who indulges in good living

voyons! (literally, see) come now! look here!

WASHINGTON IRVING	The Sketch-Book of Geoffrey Crayon, Gent.
HENRY JAMES	The Ambassadors
	The Aspern Papers and Other Stories
	The Awkward Age
	The Bostonians
	Daisy Miller and Other Stories
	The Europeans
	The Golden Bowl
	The Portrait of a Lady
	Roderick Hudson
	The Spoils of Poynton
	The Turn of the Screw and Other Stories
	Washington Square
	What Maisie Knew
	The Wings of the Dove
SARAH ORNE JEWETT	The Country of the Pointed Firs and Other Fiction
JACK LONDON	The Call of the Wild
	White Fang and Other Stories
	John Barleycorn
	The Sea-Wolf
	The Son of the Wolf
HERMAN MELVILLE	Billy Budd, Sailor and Selected Tales
	The Confidence-Man
	Moby-Dick
	Typee
	White-Jacket
FRANK NORRIS	McTeague
FRANCIS PARKMAN	The Oregon Trail
EDGAR ALLAN POE	The Narrative of Arthur Gordon Pym of Nantucket and Related Tales
	Selected Tales
HARRIET BEECHER STOWE	Uncle Tom's Cabin

JANE AUSTEN	**Catharine and Other Writings**
	Emma
	Mansfield Park
	Northanger Abbey, Lady Susan, The Watsons, and Sanditon
	Persuasion
	Pride and Prejudice
	Sense and Sensibility
ANNE BRONTË	**Agnes Grey**
	The Tenant of Wildfell Hall
CHARLOTTE BRONTË	**Jane Eyre**
	The Professor
	Shirley
	Villette
EMILY BRONTË	**Wuthering Heights**
WILKIE COLLINS	**The Moonstone**
	No Name
	The Woman in White
CHARLES DARWIN	**The Origin of Species**
CHARLES DICKENS	**The Adventures of Oliver Twist**
	Bleak House
	David Copperfield
	Great Expectations
	Hard Times
	Little Dorrit
	Martin Chuzzlewit
	Nicholas Nickleby
	The Old Curiosity Shop
	Our Mutual Friend
	The Pickwick Papers
	A Tale of Two Cities

APOLLINAIRE, ALFRED JARRY, and MAURICE MAETERLINCK	**Three Pre-Surrealist Plays**
HONORÉ DE BALZAC	**Cousin Bette** **Eugénie Grandet** **Père Goriot**
CHARLES BAUDELAIRE	**The Flowers of Evil** **The Prose Poems and Fanfarlo**
DENIS DIDEROT	**This is Not a Story and Other Stories**
ALEXANDRE DUMAS (PÈRE)	**The Black Tulip** **The Count of Monte Cristo** **Louise de la Vallière** **The Man in the Iron Mask** **La Reine Margot** **The Three Musketeers** **Twenty Years After**
ALEXANDRE DUMAS (FILS)	**La Dame aux Camélias**
GUSTAVE FLAUBERT	**Madame Bovary** **A Sentimental Education** **Three Tales**
VICTOR HUGO	**The Last Day of a Condemned Man and Other Prison Writings** **Notre-Dame de Paris**
J.-K. HUYSMANS	**Against Nature**
JEAN DE LA FONTAINE	**Selected Fables**
PIERRE CHODERLOS DE LACLOS	**Les Liaisons dangereuses**
MME DE LAFAYETTE	**The Princesse de Clèves**
GUY DE MAUPASSANT	**A Day in the Country and Other Stories** **Mademoiselle Fifi**
PROSPER MÉRIMÉE	**Carmen and Other Stories**

The Oxford World's Classics Website

www.worldsclassics.co.uk

- Information about new titles
- Explore the full range of Oxford World's Classics
- Links to other literary sites and the main OUP webpage
- Imaginative competitions, with bookish prizes
- Peruse *Compass*, the Oxford World's Classics magazine
- Articles by editors
- Extracts from Introductions
- A forum for discussion and feedback on the series
- Special information for teachers and lecturers

www.worldsclassics.co.uk

American Literature

British and Irish Literature

Children's Literature

Classics and Ancient Literature

Colonial Literature

Eastern Literature

European Literature

History

Medieval Literature

Oxford English Drama

Poetry

Philosophy

Politics

Religion

The Oxford Shakespeare

A complete list of Oxford Paperbacks, including Oxford World's Classics, OPUS, Past Masters, Oxford Authors, Oxford Shakespeare, Oxford Drama, and Oxford Paperback Reference, is available in the UK from the Academic Division Publicity Department, Oxford University Press, Great Clarendon Street, Oxford OX2 6DP.

In the USA, complete lists are available from the Paperbacks Marketing Manager, Oxford University Press, 198 Madison Avenue, New York, NY 10016.

Oxford Paperbacks are available from all good bookshops. In case of difficulty, customers in the UK can order direct from Oxford University Press Bookshop, Freepost, 116 High Street, Oxford OX1 4BR, enclosing full payment. Please add 10 per cent of published price for postage and packing.